36

ELIZABETH WAITE OMNIBUS

Skinny Lizzie

Nippy

ELIZABETH WAITE OMNIBUS

Skinny Lizzie
Nippy

ELIZABETH WAITE

timewarner
paperbacks

A *Time Warner* Paperback

This omnibus edition first published in Great Britain by
Time Warner Paperbacks in 2002
Elizabeth Waite Omnibus Copyright © Elizabeth Waite 2002

Previously published separately:
Skinny Lizzie first published in Great Britain in 1993 by Warner Books
Reprinted in 1993, 1994 (twice), 1995, 1997, 1998, 2000
Copyright © Elizabeth Waite 1993

Nippy first published in Great Britain in 1997 by Little, Brown and Company
Published by Warner Books in 1998
Reprinted 2001
Copyright © Elizabeth Waite 1997

The moral right of the author has been asserted.

A CIP catalogue record for this book is available from the British Library.

ISBN 0 7515 3296 7

Printed and bound in Great Britain by Clays Ltd, St Ives plc

Time Warner Paperbacks
An imprint of
Time Warner Books UK
Brettenham House
Lancaster Place
London WC2E 7EN

www.TimeWarnerBooks.co.uk

Skinny Lizzie

For Doris, whom I
still miss every
day of my life

Chapter One

1932, London

'Aw, COME ON, Mum, if we don't get a move on we'll be late for the concert.'

'Oh, do shut up and stop fidgeting. It's no good us going out this early.'

Ten-year-old Lizzie Collins, thin as a whippet and just as quick, shook her long fair hair and accepted her mother's scolding with goodwill and cheerfulness. All the week she was able to take life as it came, but this was Saturday and Saturday evenings were different. They were the highlight of her life.

The Collins family lived in a typical back street in south-west London. Aunt Daisy took on the role of head of the family because each day her mother would be up early and off to her job at the Dawsons. Lizzie hated the Dawsons. They always seemed to come first with her mother. Half a crown a morning they paid her mum, and for that she did every menial task asked of her, even down to scrubbing the doorsteps.

Even Christmas morning was the same. Ever since Lizzie could remember, she and her younger brother Syd had walked to Balham with their mother. Down the back area steps they would troop

– into the kitchen, which was always a scene of great activity, women coming and going in all directions, calling Christmas greetings to their mother, not pausing long enough for an answer. Hanging her own and their coats on the hook behind the door and donning her flowered, wrap-around overall, their mother would hand tea cloths to Lizzie and Syd and then start work. Plates piled high, vegetable dishes and soup tureens, gravy boats and stands, platters so large that they needed two hands to lift them, glasses, cups and saucers.

She would fill the deep sink with hot water, adding soap flakes and a handful of common soda from the large brown earthenware jar which stood on the window sill, and then the washing-up would begin. With her arms in soapy water up to her elbows, her back and shoulders stooped low, she barely stopped to take a breath, let alone have a rest. She worked away until the stacks grew smaller, Lizzie and her brother hardly able to keep up with the drying.

The last stage was the worst. Every glass had to sparkle. Taking three dry glass cloths from a line strung beneath the shelf which was high above the kitchen range, Nellie Collins would help her two children. Each glass had to be held up to the light, checked that there were no smears or finger marks.

There was one thing in the Dawson's favour though. Mr Dawson always drove them home in his car, probably because he knew they were all too tired to walk.

Once home, Lizzie stopped envying the Dawson children their huge Christmas tree and toys and got ready to enjoy herself. All preparations for the Collinses' Christmas meal had been done days in advance and Aunt Daisy always had the cooking well under way. Lizzie loved Aunt Daisy, who was like a second mother to her. Daisy was her father's unmarried sister, and since he died Mum always said that if it hadn't been for Daisy they would have fared a lot worse.

Lizzie didn't miss her dad. He had hardly ever been at home anyway. Besides, there was always Leslie and Connie to turn to.

There were eleven years between her mother's first two children and Lizzie and only eighteen months between Lizzie and young Syd. Having Leslie for an older brother made up for the loss of her father. He adored Lizzie and she knew it, and Connie was the best of sisters. In fact, Lizzie felt so secure within the love of her mother, Aunt Daisy and her brothers and sister that it never entered her head that she should feel deprived.

Nellie Collins had been born within the sound of Bow Bells, making her a true cockney. Her actual place of birth had been The Cut or, to the uninformed, The Lambeth Walk, and she passionately loved London and its people. She had come to live in Tooting when she married Albert Collins, for better or worse as she had vowed – over the years it had turned out to be a bit of each. She was in her

early forties now, with a tiny face to match her stat-
ure. She was still a good-looking, slim woman after
having had four children and not exactly an easy life.
Early on in her days in service to the upper classes,
Nellie had formed a set of high principles. But, as
time passed and circumstances worsened, she had
tempered them with down-to-earth common sense.
She loved her children and lived for them, though
Lizzie worried her more than the other three put
together. Lizzie was skinny, far too skinny.

Not that she was undernourished, far from it.
Maybe they didn't always have the best of everything, but Daisy, who did all the cooking, was a
marvellous cook and no one in the house ever went
hungry. Daisy would say, 'Our Lizzie has hollow
legs.'

'Wiry, that's what our Lizzie is,' Nellie would
proudly tell folk. The truth was, she was never still
for two minutes at a time. She had reckless energy
and was brainy with it. Her teachers at school wrote
glowing reports of her work at the end of each term,
but still Nellie worried about her. She was far too
strong-willed for her own good. She wanted the
moon and the stars to go with it and God alone
knows what else.

An atmosphere of excitement always hung over the
house on Saturdays. The nearby Fairlight Hall,
which was run by the Shaftesbury Association, was
known far and wide. Church services, Sunday
school, prayer meetings, mothers' meetings, Girls'

Brigade, Boys' Brigade, magic lantern shows, all were weekly events at Fairlight Hall, but the Saturday concerts were the favourites. These were mixed entertainments with singers, dancers, comics and magicians. Short sketches always seemed to include a rich old gentleman with a heavily bandaged, gouty foot which the maid would accidentally trip over, and although this sketch in various forms would be performed each week, the feigned extreme pain on the face of the old man and his blasphemous curses never failed to bring roars of laughter and loud hooting from the audience. An entrance charge was made for these shows, sixpence for seats at the front of the hall and threepence for seats at the back. The Collins family couldn't always afford to go – until, that is, Mother got her job when Toc H decided to sell refreshments during the intervals.

Although Toc H was started as a club for soldiers during the 1914–18 war, it continued to do good works after the war, particularly in poor city areas. So, when a local member had approached Nellie Collins with the offer of an evening's work each week for the princely wage of three half-crowns, Nellie gasped in surprise and pleasure and accepted at once.

By this time Leslie had joined the Army, and Connie was 'walking out' with her boyfriend. So at about eight o'clock, Aunt Daisy, Mum, Syd and Lizzie would set off for Fairlight Hall. Their first job was to set out rows and rows of cups and saucers, for it was a very large hall, packed every week with eager audiences. Then, as the lights were dimmed and the opening musical number began, an official of Toc H would find them empty seats in the house. Often Syd and Lizzie ended up sitting on the floor between the gangways, but they didn't care; they got to see the concert for nothing. During the interval, it would be Aunt Daisy with her arms deep in soapy water at the sink doing the washing-up, while Syd and Lizzie dried. Nellie thought she had the easiest job, collecting the dirty crocks on large tin trays, making numerous trips from hall to kitchen and back again. All four of them were given a free drink, with iced or Chelsea buns for the two children. As a bonus, any refreshments which remained unsold were given to Nellie free of charge, plus those precious three silver half-crowns. Imagine! It took her three whole mornings to earn that amount at the Dawsons!

When saying her prayers on a Saturday night, Lizzie never forgot to say, 'God bless the Toc H.'

Between having their midday meal and getting ready to go to the concert, the shopping had to be done. It was always Lizzie who accompanied her mother on these expeditions to Tooting market. There were times when Lizzie found the bargaining that went on a great source of amusement, but on Saturdays she felt irritable and hoped her mother wouldn't take too long deciding just what she was going to buy.

It was a busy scene that confronted Nellie and her daughter on this particular evening, much as it was every Saturday evening. The open-fronted shops, the street traders and barrow boys, all plying their different trades, shouting their wares, each a keen competitor for customers. Shopping for food amongst the working class was undertaken on a daily basis, mainly because their income was earned and paid daily. The prosperity promised in 1918 at the signing of the Armistice had never come about. It was 1932 now and still men walked long distances in search of employment. One-day odd-jobs found eager takers; even one good day's work and pay made life look a little rosier.

'Are we going to the market first, Mum?' Lizzie wanted to know.

Her mother shook her head, 'We'll try the Mitcham Road first. Meat's the most important, we can get our vegetables on the way back.'

Late-night shopping at the butchers, of which there were at least four in the Mitcham Road, had become a battle of wits. Those well enough off to be choosy about their weekend joints would have shopped earlier in the day, but at this time of night it was a different matter. It was essential that the butcher sold off all his perishable items by the time he pulled down the shutters that night. Anything left would definitely not be in an edible state come Monday morning. Better to sell it off cheaply; a blessing in disguise for the poor.

Nellie had stopped at two butchers, hesitating while Lizzie impatiently scuffed her feet. She put a loving arm about her daughter as they walked on.

'Don't worry, love, they'll start auctioning the joints off soon, then we won't be long. We shan't be late for the concert, I promise.'

True enough, further along the road, a crowd of women had assembled on the pavement in front of the next butcher's shop. The proprietor was deliberately keeping them waiting, allowing the tension to build. The laid-out enamel trays were still full of meat, although the fresh parsley, arranged so neatly between the rows at the start of trading early that morning, was now visibly wilting. The men working at the blocks still wore their blue and white striped aprons, so clean and fresh at the day's start, now stained and bloody. The master butcher had donned a straw boater before coming out, setting it at a jaunty angle on his head. To his upper lip he had attached a false waxed moustache. This always made Lizzie laugh as it did all the other children in the crowd.

The November evening had turned bitterly cold, having rained heavily earlier on in the day. The pavement on which the women now stood was not only wet but had begun to harden into ice. Hardly any one amongst them was wearing boots or shoes that were weather-proof; their toes and fingers were stiff with cold; their winter coats far too thin to keep out the biting wind. Cold, tired, with hardly more than a few shillings in their purse each would be hoping for – no, praying for – the chance to pick up a bargain. In her mind's eye each woman was already seeing a joint roasting in the oven for tomorrow's dinner, big enough to feed the whole family and, with any luck, enough left over to be served up with bubble and squeak for Monday's meal.

That's the dream they had. It was often not the reality. Many a woman went home with her shopping-bag holding little more than odds and ends: a scrag of mutton, a piece of leg of beef (fit only for stewing), or a bit of belly of pork. Still, these working-class women were marvellous cooks, producing meals of great nourishment, roughened toil-worn hands making the lightest of pastry for a pie.

Finally, the master butcher came to the forefront, placed a large wooden crate dead centre to the waiting women, climbed up on to it and raised his megaphone to his mouth. The megaphone made his voice audible even at the back of the crowd where Lizzie stood with her mother. His patter started; a few bawdy jokes which were lost on those cold women, who were after food, not comedy: 'Git your money ready, ladies, I'm gonna give you all a treat tonight. Move in closer, there will be bargains for everyone.' Two assistants now took up their places on either side of the crate on which the butcher was perched, armed and ready with a stack of brown paper bags. When a price had been agreed and a buyer found, the meat would be tipped into a carrier bag, held up by one of the assistants. No effort was made to wrap each item separately, this being deemed an unnecessary luxury for the poor.

'Look 'ere me darlings, Sunday joint, sausages for the ol' man's breakfast and dripping to put hairs on yer chest.' Loud and rough, his voice droned on. Most in the crowd had heard it all before; it was the meat on offer that they were interested in, not his commentary. Still he kept trying to gain their good-will, working hard to induce amusement, even hoping for a laugh, but only provoking the odd half-suppressed giggle. He gave up. With an exaggerated sigh he shouted, 'Right, now to the serious business . . .'

He picked up an empty enamel dish. Silently he turned to the display of meat in front of which he was perched. Taking down a rib of beef, he held it aloft for a moment before placing it into the dish; two breasts of lamb were added with great cere-mony, a thin end of belly of pork, two long strings of sausages, and to top the lot a wax packet contain-ing beef dripping. Lowering the dish to the eye level of the women at the front of the crowd, brandishing the contents in front of them, he quietly said, 'Eight bob.' No response. Straightening himself upright, he yelled, 'First hand up gets the lot for seven and six.' Again no response. Everyone knew it didn't pay to rush. 'Six shillings,' his voice boomed out even without the use of his megaphone. No one in the crowd uttered a word. Leaning forward, the butcher focused his stare on a fat woman. 'Look luv, didn't you hear what I said?' Raising his voice even higher, 'Six bob the lot.' The woman shifted uncomfortably, saying nothing, averting her eyes away from his stare. 'Well, I'll to go hell and back. You lot can walk up and down this street till midnight, you won't find a better bargain.' He spoke quickly, 'Tell yer what I'll do. Do yer like offal? Yer should do, it's bloody good for yer.' Lowering the dish he scooped up a large handful of liver from a tin pail which stood on a bench to the left of him. Into the dish it went, slithering and slipping over the strings of sausages, now entwined amongst the red meat. 'Wait for it. I'm not finished yet.' A whole shoulder of lamb was quickly placed on top of the now overful dish. 'That's the lot.' This decided, there was a long pause before the butcher, his endurance now pushed to the limit, shouted, 'Now it's got to be worth three half-crowns of anybody's money.' Setting his feet more widely apart, he drew a deep breath. Again he threw out the challenge. 'Seven and sixpence.' Self-consciously, the women looked at each other. There wasn't one amongst them who wouldn't have dearly loved to call out, 'I'll have it,' but three to four shillings at most was their mark. Frustrated to the point of anger, the butcher lost his temper; as yet he had not made one sale since starting his auctioneering. 'Right, who'll take the bloody lot for nothing!'

'My Mum will. My Mum will.'

Lizzie's voice rang out sharp and clear. Nellie put her arm out to restrain this impetuous daughter of hers but Lizzie had gone through the crowd like lightning, not slowing down until she cleared the ring of pushing women. Then the audacity of what she had done dawned on her. Lizzie's heart was racing. 'Dear Jesus, let the ground open and swallow me up,' she prayed.

Nervously, she looked up at the great hulk of the butcher towering above her, still holding that dratted dish of meat between his hands. Hastily she dropped her eyes and hung her head. The silence which followed seemed to last forever.

Then the mumbling from the crowd began. 'Gawd bless the poor little mite,' one woman called out. Then the fat woman, who had been made to feel a fool earlier on, decided to put her twopenny worth in.

'Gawd bless her my arse. Cheeky little cow. Bloody good 'iding is what she needs.'

Normally Lizzie would have rounded on the woman, quick to repay in kind. Not now, though. She felt sick. Bending his knees but keeping his back perfectly straight, the butcher brought his face down almost level with Lizzie's. Her nostrils filled with the smell of dried blood coming from his stained apron and she felt even more sick.

Speaking gently, with a soft, quiet voice, the big man said, 'For your cheek, love, it's all yours.'

Straightening himself up, he turned to an assistant. 'Hold open a carrier,' he ordered. Slowly, deliberately, he tipped the whole contents of that enamel dish into the paper carrier-bag; liver clung to the sides of the dish, he removed it pushing with the flat of his hand. Now, for the first time, he stepped down from the crate, folding over the top of the brown paper bag. Not trusting the handles, he held it out towards Lizzie. Using both of her arms, she clutched it to her chest but found she couldn't move. She remained rooted to the spot, staring at the man.

'Off you go missy, you ain't as daft as you look,' and with that he laughed out loud.

This comical remark suddenly made Lizzie relax. She turned and walked back towards her mother. The women parted to make a path for her, and she stared insolently at the lot of them.

'You little bugger showing me up like that!' One of her mother's hands grabbed her, the other raised in anger to strike. Instinctively, Lizzie ducked. Still the blow caught the side of her head, leaving the ear stinging and the tears burning at the back of her eyes.

Rebellion seethed in her as her mother pushed and shoved her along the pavement. Hiccuping, trying to stifle her sobs, Lizzie asked herself angrily what had she done wrong? The butcher had offered the meat free and surely you had to be out of your mind not to accept an offer like that. Why was her mum so mad at her? She forced the tears back. She was not going to cry; she would not let her mother see how much she had hurt her. 'I'm never gonna come with her again to get the rotten shopping,' she vowed. Still holding the carrier-bag tightly to her chest but trying to think how she could get rid of it, they turned the corner of the street into the darkness of a side road.

'Lizzie, I'm sorry. I'm sorry,' Lizzie heard the sob

in her mother's voice and realized that she, too, was crying.

This sudden change of attitude not only baffled Lizzie but also set her off crying again.

'Can we go 'ome now,' she snivelled.

'Don't cry, don't cry,' her mother implored her. 'I didn't mean to hit you, truly I didn't.'

She relieved Lizzie of the dreaded carrier bag, totally ignoring the wet stain on the front of her coat caused by Lizzie having clutched it too closely, allowing the blood to soak through from its unwrapped contents, and dropped it whole into her large patchwork shopping-bag. Before moving, Nellie drew her young daughter into her arms and hugged her so tightly Lizzie rocked on her feet. Lizzie decided she would never understand adults, they seemed to have their emotions well and truly mixed up.

Walking quickly now, Lizzie's hand was clutching tightly to her mother's free one. Back in the brightly lit Mitcham Road, the gutter was packed with barrows. Barrows piled high with fruit; barrows offering vegetables, salad, flowers, even shell fish; the barrow boys had it all.

Nellie ignored them all, making a beeline for the cooked-meat shop. Pungent, delicious smells filled the air yards before they actually reached the shop. What a layout! Pigs' trotters, faggots in hot gravy, rissoles, shiny fat sausages, pease pudding, meat pies in all shapes and sizes, even pigs' heads split in half and roasted – the choice was endless. Lizzie's mouth was watering; suddenly she felt very, very hungry.

'What would you like, love?'

Lizzie couldn't believe her ears. Sometimes on a Saturday evening while shopping, her mum would buy a tuppenny pie and they'd have half each, eating it walking along. But it didn't often happen. Usually they passed this shop; her mother's finances didn't stretch to shop-bought cooked meats. Now she was being offered a choice. What a decision! Inside the shop nothing mattered at that moment but the fact that they were going to have something hot and tasty to eat.

Behind the counter an imposing lady with a fat red face smiled broadly at them as she asked, 'What's it to be, missus?'

Nellie had only a moment of indecision. 'Four meat pies, please.'

'Mince or steak and kidney?'

'Oh, steak and kidney, please.'

'Blimey,' the word came quietly from Lizzie's lips, they were the dearest and Mum was buying four!

Wrapping the hot pies in two large sheets of white paper the woman beamed as she handed the parcel to Nellie.

'They're nice. You'll enjoy them,' she said.

Nellie smiled and nodded as she bent to place the pies most carefully on the top of her shopping-bag. Then, opening her purse, she paused and impulsively said, 'And one hot saveloy for us to eat now, please. Oh, and would you mind cutting it in half?'

' 'Course, I will, luv.'

Taking a long, black-handled knife from the bench behind her, the woman easily sliced the large, red, spicy sausage into two equal parts, then, tearing off a strip of white paper, she wrapped each uncut end of the saveloy, leaving the hot, steaming end protruding.

Handing one half to Nellie and the other half to Lizzie, she asked, 'What 'ave you done my darling to deserve this treat?'

Lizzie smiled but didn't answer; she was impatient to get her teeth into the fleshy sausage.

'Well now, that'll be one and a penny, four pies at threepence each and one saveloy a penny.'

Nellie counted out the money and said, 'Thanks a lot.'

'You're welcome,' said the woman. 'Tat-ta lovey, 'ope to see you again.'

Lizzie, her mouth filled with hot sausage, grinned. Then, as chirpy as any sparrow, she called back over her shoulder, 'I hope so too. 'Bye for now.'

Nellie, having finished eating her half saveloy, hoisted her heavy shopping bag up into her arms and mother and daughter quickened their pace as they rounded the Broadway and made for the covered-in market.

Lizzie knew the routine off by heart. Passing Emanuel's and their beautiful layout of imported fruit and vegetables, 'Far too expensive,' her mother muttered.

'Hello, Jack,' she called as she propped her shopping-bag against the front of Smith's stall, where the sheet of imitation green grass hung down. 'Got an empty box for me?'

'Sure, Nellie, help yourself,' swarthy looking Jack Smith called in answer as he came towards them.

Nellie went behind the stall into the depths of the area at the back used for storing empty crates and unpacking them at the start of each day. She appeared a moment later, holding a light-weight wooden box; the bottom was firm but the sides were only slates of wood. Jack Smith bent low and lined the bottom with a thick wad of newspapers.

'Potatoes, Nellie?'

'Yes please, Jack, five pounds, and a pound of carrots and onions mixed.'

These items having been weighed and tipped into the box, Nellie added, 'One swede, two parsnips and a cabbage. That's the lot, thanks,' she said, opening her purse to pay.

'No fruit this week, Nellie?'

'I dunno,' she was slow to decide.

Reaching for a large orange as a specimen, Jack told her, 'These are as sweet as a nut. Penny each, but ter you, seven for a tanner.' Before Nellie even had time to agree, he crouched down and from beneath the stall produced a cardboard box. 'There's some specky apples here and a few loose bananas. Want the lot for tuppence?'

'Go on then, I'll have the oranges as well.' There was a wide grin on Lizzie's face as the fruit was added to the rapidly filling box.

'Right, that's one and ninepence the lot.'

Nellie took a florin from her purse and, as she passed it over to Jack, she exclaimed, 'Oh God, I've forgotten the celery.' Aunt Daisy would have been upset. Sunday tea was not complete without a stick of celery.

'Penny more to pay then, Nell. Fourpence a head it is,' he said as he totted it up.

Wrapped in newspaper, the great bunch of celery topped the vegetables and fruit, its green leaves, looking bright and fresh, sticking out from the rolled newspaper.

'Can we go home now, Mum?' Lizzie pleaded.

Opening her purse again, Nellie said, 'Just run up to Eggee's for me, there's a good girl. Get two pennyworth of pieces a bacon and that will be our lot.' Seeing the desperation in Lizzie's eyes, her mother added gently, 'It won't take you two minutes. We'll be home with plenty of time to eat our pies before we set off for the concert. Go on, love, I'll wait here with all the shopping.'

Lizzie took the threepenny piece from her mother's outstretched hand and ran off. She didn't mind going to Eggee's stall because it fascinated her. As the name implied, Eggee sold eggs. It was an extra large stall, divided into two halves. On the egg side was a grading machine, its many lights giving off warmth as brown, white and speckled eggs gently came down in a continuous line, to be sent off in different directions according to their weight and size. Mid-week her mother often sent her here with a basin to buy cracked eggs. She always came willingly, knowing that there would then be scrambled eggs for their tea. Besides she and Syd had great fun making the toast; kneeling in front of the bars of the grate, red hot from the range fire, they would use the long-handled, three-pronged toasting forks, daring each other to get closer all the time until the slices of bread ended up with burnt stripes. Making the toast was always a good laugh. No – it wasn't that she minded running the errand; she just didn't want to be late for the concert.

It was to the opposite side of the stall that Lizzie needed to go now. Every variety of cheese you could think of was sold here, plus bacon. Lizzie liked Mr Eggee. She was repeatedly scolded by her mother for not calling him by his proper name which was Mr Goldberg, but to her he was Mr Eggee and there was no disrespect in calling him that. He was a heavy-set Jewish man with black hair and bright dark eyes which now had a gleam of amusement in them behind his rimless spectacles as he watched Lizzie approach.

His voice was friendly as he called, 'Hallo, Skinny Lizzie.'

'Hallo, Mr Eggee,' she returned.

'Is it bacon you were wanting?'

'Yes, please. Mummy said, may she have twopennyworth of pieces?'

'Your mamma certainly may. Pieces, we have
plenty. 'Tis a good time you choose to come.' Turning, he tore down a large greaseproof paper bag
from a string of them hanging on a steel rail. Walking to the slicing machine, he began to fill the bag
from a white enamel tray which lay beneath the cut-
ters. Too small to be sold as rashers, he regularly
sold these pieces quite cheaply.

'There you are then, young Lizzie. Now be sure
my regards you give to your mother.'

Reaching up, she was given the bag of bacon
pieces plus one penny change from the threepenny
bit. 'I will, Mr Eggee. 'Bye, thank you.'

Her mother was right, Mr Goldberg was a kindly,
generous man, and Lizzie liked him because he was
always so friendly. There were not many she would
allow to call her Skinny Lizzie, not without giving
tit for tat. But with Mr Eggee Lizzie knew that it
was said affectionately.

Aunt Daisy always maintained that these pieces
of bacon were the best value to be found this side of
heaven. Firstly, she would sort out all the lean pieces
which provided a good breakfast for them all. Next,
the thick ends would have onions and sage added,
rolled in a suet crust and boiled in a pudding cloth
to create a good dinner. Lastly, the real fat lumps
were rendered down in the slow oven at the side of
the kitchen range to supply dripping for their toast.

Still waiting by Smith's greengrocery stall, Nellie
looked rather woebegone. 'What's the matter,
Mum?' asked Lizzie.

'Nothing, love, a bit weary, that's all.'

Making a space amongst the vegetables, Lizzie placed the bacon in the box. Now, how were they going to get this lot home?

'Come this side of me Lizzie.' Balancing the shopping-bag in the crook of her right arm, Nellie placed four fingers of her free hand underneath the first row of slats on the side of the wooden box, leaving her thumb on top. With a nod of her head she made a gesture for Lizzie to do likewise. 'Lift,' she instructed. Walking with the box between them required bodily effort. Nellie, although only five feet four inches tall, was a good deal taller than Lizzie. Unevenly balanced and looking peculiar to say the least, they made their way out of the market.

Outside, the weather had turned decidedly worse; the harsh wind was bitter, threatening a severe storm. They had to wait for their chance to cross the main road which was still busy with traffic. Trams rumbling, clanging and swaying, travelled in both directions. Lorries, cars, push-bikes, everyone seemed hell-bent on greater speed. At last there came a break in the traffic and they stepped forward, walking awkwardly, and, more by luck than judgment, they reached the far pavement in safety. They stopped a moment and drew a deep breath.

In Selkirk Road, the jellied eel shop was now open. Nellie called a halt.

'Put the box down, love.'

'We're not gonna have eels as well, are we?' Lizzie wanted to know.

'No, we're not.' Taking two pennies from the pocket of her coat, Nellie held them out to her daughter. 'Just go in and ask Beccy to put twopennyworth of mash in a bag.'

Of all the shops, the eel shop was Lizzie's favourite. Fish and chips was all right, even good sometimes, but pie and mash was better, and eels and mash with its green liquor was the best treat of all. The liquor (or gravy) was supposedly parsley sauce, but, as Aunt Daisy said, no parsley ever made her sauce as green. It was a well-guarded secret of the Harrington family who owned the business. On the rare occasions that Syd and Lizzie were given a penny each at suppertime, Syd would opt for a pennyworth of chips, while Lizzie would go for a penny basin every time. All the basin contained was mashed potato and the green liquor for a penny. Eels were three pence a portion. At the rear of the shop, there were many marble-topped tables with high-backed benches for seating; each table had its own huge tin pepper and salt pots and, best of all, chilli vinegar. Chilli vinegar was not like the vinegar they had at home; small red strips of cayenne pepper floated, clearly visible through the glass bottle. Seated at one such table, in the noisy, steamy atmosphere, greedily spooning the liquor, lavished with pepper and the hot, spicy vinegar, into her mouth, always hoping that an odd piece of eel had slipped in, was a treat indeed to Lizzie.

'Lizzie, come down here,' Beccy Harrington, the daughter of the shop owner, had spotted her in the crowded shop. Blousy, very fat, common even, but with a heart of gold was a good description of Rebecca. She and her parents lived directly opposite the Collins family. 'What-cha want, ducks?' Beccy asked as she bent low towards Lizzie.

'Would yer put twopennyworth of mash in a bag for me mum, please?'

'No bother, luv, wait there.'

Within two minutes, Beccy was back, handing Lizzie a parcel that was not only heavy, but very, very hot. Taking the two pennies, she bent and planted a smacking kiss on Lizzie's cheek.

'Off to the concert, are you?' Without waiting for a reply, Beccy pushed Lizzie in the direction of the shop doorway. 'Night, night Lizzie. See yer in the morning. God bless,' Beccy called affectionately.

'Night, Beccy. Thanks ever so much.'

Turning at last into Graveney Road where they lived, they found it deserted. Not teeming with children as was normal. No clanging of meat hooks against steel hoops, no girls skipping, chanting their timeless rhymes, no tops being slashed down the centre of the road by means of home-made whips. The cold weather brought a change of character to the street, giving it a desolate air. For once, the youngsters had obeyed their parents, staying indoors in the warmth of the family kitchen. Lizzie and her mother stooped and placed the wooden box on the pavement. Lizzie unlatched the front garden gate, took the shopping-bag from her mother's arm, and went ahead up the path to the front door. Using her knee to lever the box waist high, Nellie held it in front of her stomach, one hand on each side. Pushing with her hip and bottom, she got the front door open and called out, 'Daisy, come an' give us a hand, will you?'

The kitchen door opened, the lights from the gas mantles in the room beyond streamed out, lighting up the passage. Daisy's bulky frame filled the door-way. A few steps forward and Daisy stopped dead in her tracks.

'God above,' she exclaimed, 'whatcha do, rob a bank?' Nellie leaned against the wall, suddenly help-less with laughter, while tears streamed down her face. It took her a couple of minutes to collect herself and to be able to speak, during which time Daisy stood watching her dumbfoundedly.

'Help us get it all in,' Nellie managed to say, and then, speaking as if to herself, she added, 'you're never gonna believe it.'

Young Syd, hearing all the commotion, put down the comic he had been reading and came into the hallway. He was feeling irritable, his mum seemed to have been out for ages, and he was sure that Lizzie would goad him. 'I've had half a hot meat pie,' she would tease, 'it was ever so good.' Well, if she had, he hoped it choked her.

'I'm starving, Mum,' he whined.

'All right, son, give me a minute and we'll all eat.' Grudgingly, he helped his auntie drag the box down the passage and into the kitchen. Nellie worked as she talked. Four plates were placed in the oven at the side of the kitchen range. Daisy and she began to take the meat, piece by piece, from the sodden, bloody carrier-bag as Nellie told her tale, right down to the last detail. Lizzie, sitting on the fire box at the end of the fender warming her feet and holding her hands out to the red glowing coals, was tired of listening to them. Endless questions and answers.

'She never did,' said Aunt Daisy for the umpteenth time.

'She did, brazen as you like.'

'Mum. You've bin all through it a dozen times. Can we 'ave our pies?'

'Yeah, pie and mash,' Syd added, glinting at his sister as he sat up to the table. At last. No one was talking. The pies were good, much better than the twopenny minced meat ones, Lizzie decided. The pastry was fluffy, flaky, the inside piping hot, with a generous amount of meat and thick rich gravy. Definitely worth the extra penny if you could afford it.

Her plate now empty, Lizzie sat back and smiled to herself. It was because of her that her mum was able to buy those pies; it couldn't have been such a bad thing she'd done. No. 'I'd do it again an' all,' she promised herself, but she was level-headed enough to fathom that chances like that don't come twice in a lifetime.

*

Eventually they were ready. Aunt Daisy, as ever looking as neat as a pin, used her long hat-pin to secure her navy blue felt hat securely to her head. Mum had her best coat on, a hand-me-down from the Dawsons which secretly Lizzie admitted looked very nice, the fur collar framing her mother's lovely face and keeping her ears warm. Syd and Lizzie brought up the rear, each warmly clothed, long scarves wound around their necks. They all set off for Fairlight Hall and their Saturday concert.

Chapter Two

THE NEXT DAY was Sunday. Grandma's day. Grandma Collins was a small, weather-beaten woman only just turned sixty, but years in the open air selling flowers from her stall at the Broadway had dried up her skin so that she looked older than she was. Her shiny silver hair swept up on top of her head and her firm mouth reminded Lizzie of Queen Mary.

Harriet Collins had rarely, if ever, shown either of her two children the affection they deserved. Widowed while still young, she had become hard and bitter. Yet somehow Daisy had grown into a cheerful loving woman, despite the fact she had never married, and Albert had grown into a jolly, outgoing man, charming all the women with whom he came into contact. Half the time his affairs were no more than infatuation, but for Nellie, his wife, each new affair was disastrous. Disastrous because she truly loved him and suffered terrible rejection and humiliation.

Seeing Nellie's distress had brought anguish to her mother-in-law and she had often prayed that Nellie would come to terms with the inescapable facts of life about her son. When, however, Albert Collins was involved in a fatal accident, Harriet had

reflected bitterly that maybe she could be held somewhat responsible for her son's attitude to life. Yet,
even at the funeral, she had not felt able to voice her
feelings. Warmth and sentiment were lost to her.
Much as she admired her daughter-in-law, even
loved her, and longed to relieve her own pent-up
emotion, she could not get the words out. 'Perhaps,'
she told herself wearily, 'I've left it too late.'

Only Lizzie was the exception. 'Mischievous little
monkey,' her gran was often heard to mutter, but
those cold eyes would soften as she gazed at her
youngest granddaughter. Only Lizzie, with her
exasperating ways, was able to penetrate the invisible barrier and somehow manage to get her gran to
show her feelings.

Harriet Collins came in from the scullery, carrying
a scuttle of coal, as Lizzie opened the front door of
her grandma's cottage.

'Hallo, Gran. Mum says dinner will be on the
table for one o'clock and we've not ter be late.'

'She did, did she?' Harriet dumped three big
lumps of coal on to the glowing fire and then
upended the colander into the centre. The fire hissed
and steam rose as the wet vegetable peelings and
stale tealeaves banked down the heat. 'An' what 'ave
you been up to this week, Lizzie?' Gran asked as she
twisted round from the hearth and got to her feet.

Lizzie raised her eyebrows and put her hand over
her mouth. 'Eh, I don't think I better tell you. Wait

till you see what we've got for dinner today. Aunt Daisy said we can 'ave a choice.'

'A choice? What of – a stew or a pie, I suppose.'

'No, Gran, real roast. Honest. You'll see. Me, Mum and Aunt Daisy will tell you all about it. So come on, get yer hat and coat on.'

You bet they'll tell Gran the whole story and it'll take them for ever, Lizzie told herself. She was getting a bit sick and tired of her aunt's probing of every little detail and Syd's quizzing of the affair.

While Gran was getting herself ready, Lizzie had a good old poke around. To her, Gran's cottage appeared like something out of a story book. Silverdore Terrace has just five cottages, set beside Blunt's market and almost opposite the central hall in Mitcham Road. It was just a few minutes' walk from Tooting Broadway, and yet to anyone discovering these dwellings for the first time, it was as if time had passed by this tiny corner of South London. Outmoded, ignored, but loved by their elderly occupants, each cottage boasted a hundred-foot-long front garden. There was nothing at the back except a small yard, an outside lavatory and a cold-water tap. The front of the dwellings made up for this. A joy to behold at any season of the year, flower beds, flowering shrubs, and tall hollyhocks were tended with love and efficiency. In spring, flowers in abundance would nod their heads in the pale sunshine, while in summer, rose bushes bore blooms of every conceivable colour – pale pink, dark pink, white, yellow, peach, orange and every shade of red, all seemed to bloom for ever. There were lavender bushes and hydrangeas with flowers as big as dinner plates. Gran even had a holly bush in her garden and as Lizzie looked this cold Sunday morning at the bright red berries with which it was covered, she mulled over in her mind once again the difference between Silverdore Terrace and the street of back-to-back houses where she lived. It was only a two-up-and-two-down dwelling and the front door opened directly into the living room, but to Lizzie the garden alone made it a special place.

When they got to Graveney Road it was half-past twelve and Gran followed her usual procedure. She went upstairs and locked herself in the bathroom where she used the toilet and washed her hands, then went on up the extra five stairs into Nellie's big front bedroom and laid her hat and coat on the bed. This ritual took about ten minutes. Afterwards, she came downstairs and went straight through into the kitchen. Outside in the scullery, Daisy would grin at Nellie and under their breath, in unison, they would murmur, 'Inspection over.'

Connie had already laid the table for seven; Bill, her young man, having been invited to Sunday dinner this week.

'Sit up, all of you,' Nellie inclined her head towards Grandma and at the same time opened the kitchen door and called up the passage, 'Come on, Syd, and you, Lizzie, sit up at the table.'

As they took their places, Daisy brought the vegetable dishes in from the scullery, and set them down in the centre of the table. Nellie, her face red and wisps of hair escaping from her usually immaculate coiled plaits pinned each side of her face, entered, carrying a huge willow-patterned meat dish on which lay the now roasted rib of beef and the shoulder of lamb which she set down in front of Bill.

'Would you do the honours please, Bill?' Nellie quietly asked. 'I always feel a man carves meat much better than us women do.'

Bill Baldwin was grateful to Nellie; he had felt a bit out of place amongst all these ladies but she had set him at ease. 'I'd be honoured,' he told her as he picked up the carving knife and bone-handled steel which Nellie had set down beside the dish. With an exaggerated flourish he criss-crossed the blade of the knife back and forth against the hardened rolled steel, winking at young Syd as he did so. Satisfied that the knife was sharp enough, he asked, 'Now, Mrs Collins senior, what is it to be, beef or lamb?'

Nothing had been missed out today. Nellie had chopped the dried mint which hung in bags above the copper, adding a liberal amount of sugar before pouring on the hot vinegar; Daisy had dug up a root of horseradish from the backyard and had persevered with the grater, even though the strong herb had brought tears to her eyes. Daisy handed the plates around and soon there was a heaped plate set before each of them and they all began to eat.

The conversation was noisy until Aunt Daisy

pleaded, 'Let's eat up while it's all hot. You can all ask questions and get your answers,' she said, looking directly at her mother, 'when we get to pudding.'

The kitchen was warm, the fire burnt brightly as they continued to sit around the table. Apple pie and custard had been consumed by each of them, despite the huge first course, and now the tea tray with its large brown earthenware teapot stood centre of the table and a Sunday-best cup and saucer stood in front of each person. Daisy removed the woollen tea-cosy and began to fill the cups, having first poured in the milk. Explanations were over. Gran had gasped as Nellie had, for the hundredth time according to Lizzie, gone through the whole story. Connie and Bill thought it was hilarious.

Lizzie had had enough of being made to feel a fool. 'Well, Gran, what would you 'ave done?' she asked in a loud voice. 'There was this bloke propped up on a wooden box looking right comical an' all I can tell yer, what with his false moustache an' daft straw hat, doing his best to sell a load of meat. What 'appened? He got carried away. Nobody could afford all what he put in that dish and he ended up losing his temper. T'was his own daft fault. Showing off he were. "Who'll 'ave the bloody lot for nothing",' Lizzie mimicked. 'What yer supposed ter do? Stand there all posh an' quiet like, pretend you 'aven't heard him. Only a half-wit would do that. Anyway, I noticed you all enjoyed your dinner. Free or not, it never worried any of you.' Lizzie's tirade came to an end. It had to; she had run out of breath. Everyone glanced at each other.

Nellie finally broke the silence, 'Oh Lizzie love, we didn't mean to upset you.'

Then Daisy's voice held a note of pleading as she said, 'Of course we didn't, come on now, give us a smile.'

Lizzie's temper had burned itself out; slowly a smile came to her lips and quickly became a great grin as she felt Syd kick her leg beneath the table.

'Oh Lizzie! Lizzie!' Gran moved her face until it was touching Lizzie's and then pressed her lips against her granddaughter's cheek.

Dumbly Lizzie raised her hand and felt the place where her Gran had planted a kiss. Suddenly, everything was wonderful. Great. She began to laugh. The laughter was infectious, and soon everyone was laughing fit to bust. As Harriet Collins wiped her face, she cast her glance ceilingwards. It didn't do to have a favourite but how could she help it? One in a million was this harum-scarum granddaughter of hers. If she could hold on to that temper of hers she'd go far. Got a sensible head on her shoulders, our Lizzie has, if only life would give her a few breaks. One thing was for sure, no one could ever say that Lizzie was backward in coming forward. Harriet was surprised to find herself admitting that she loved her youngest granddaughter with all of her heart.

It was nearly dark when Lizzie got home from

school on Friday afternoon to find Syd sitting on the doorstep.

'What are you doing out here?' she asked.

He didn't answer and she tutted as she pushed by him. Opening the letterbox she slipped her hand in and pulled on the length of string which hung down with the key inside the door.

She unlocked the door and pushed it open with her knee. 'Come on Syd, you go first and light the gas mantle and as soon as I've got me coat off I'll make us a drink.'

Syd was on his feet now, but he hung back and hesitated. It dawned on Lizzie that Syd was afraid of the dark. Mum and Aunt Daisy were away at their mothers' meeting. They went every Friday afternoon to the Central Hall and didn't get home until about five-thirty. It was still only half-past four. If Lizzie hadn't come straight home, what would Syd have done? Stayed sitting on the cold flagstones? He knew the front door key was on the string. She wanted to hug him, but Syd wouldn't stand for being mollycoddled.

'I'll go first,' she said softly. 'What would you like, a cup of tea or Oxo?'

'I'd rather have Oxo, an' Lizzie, I'm starving. 'Ave we got to wait till Mum comes home before we get our tea?'

Lizzie laughed out loud. 'We'll find something,' she assured him.

Ten minutes later, after Lizzie had put the poker into the banked-down fire, the two of them sat on the hearth rug, each with a thick slice of bread and dripping, smothered with pepper and salt and a mug of scalding-hot Oxo.

'Wonder what we got for tea,' Syd said as he sniffed hungrily at the appetizing smell that was coming from the side oven.

'Smells like hot-pot,' Lizzie told him. They both liked that, plenty of vegetables, dumplings and gravy.

'Hope we've finished our tea before Tim and Joey come round,' Syd muttered to himself, while staring into the fire.

'Oh no!' Lizzie exclaimed, very annoyed. 'It's not bath night for the Hurleys tonight, is it?'

'So Tim said when I left him. "See you later for our bath", that's what he said.'

'I wonder why Polly never mentioned it,' Lizzie mulled this over in her mind.

The Hurleys lived in Selkirk Road, and their house stood back to back with number thirty Graveney Road which was where the Collins lived. John and Kate Hurley were warm, friendly people. John Hurley was a fortunate man in as much as he had a regular job; storeman up at the Co-op. Kate, his wife, was everyone's friend, a hard-working woman, whose hair had once been a lovely blonde colour, now turned grey. A lovely smile was always on her face, showing exceptionally good white teeth, and it lit up her merry blue eyes. There was a saying Kate Hurley was fond of: 'Never bother

trouble till trouble bothers you', and by that she
seemed to set great store. The Hurleys had three
children, two boys, Tim aged eleven, Joey just nine,
and Polly, who was older than Lizzie by just four
days. Lizzie couldn't remember, or even imagine,
life without Polly. They were best friends, always
had been.

The bath routine was a palaver Lizzie could have
done without tonight. She had wanted to go round
to Polly's house and discuss what Miss Roberts had
been talking about so earnestly before she dismissed
class – the dreaded scholarship exams. Still, never
mind, these bath occasions often turned out to be
quite jolly gatherings and she'd still get to see Polly.

There weren't many houses in the district that
could boast a bathroom. Indeed, Nellie would tell it
that when Albert Collins brought her from Lambeth
to Tooting as his bride, there were three things that
immediately made her take to the house. One, bay
windows upstairs and down. Two, Venetian blinds.
Three, a bathroom with an indoor lavatory. Once,
the great cast-iron bath had stood gleaming white
against the wall, now its under-belly and huge claw
feet had turned rusty. Dust had collected beneath it
in far unreachable corners. There was no running
hot water – there never had been. Just the solitary
brass tap which gave out only cold water. Two years
ago, the landlord had made life somewhat easier.
His workmen had removed the big old copper from
the scullery and filled the space with a gas cooker
and a gas copper. No longer did a fire have to be lit

beneath the grey hearthstoned beast in order to heat the water. All that was needed now was a supply of pennies to feed the slot-meter and just one match with which to light the jets, which were set underneath the bottom of the copper.

Having this new-fangled copper did not eliminate all problems. A water supply was not connected to it. Cold water still had to be drawn from the tap above the scullery sink which stood at least six feet away on the opposite wall. Bucket after bucket needed to be filled and carried across to the copper. When boiling, there was a tap placed low down from which the water could be drawn out. Then the fun would begin. From the scullery, through the kitchen, along the passageway, and up the stairs into the bathroom, buckets had to be lifted almost chest high in order to tip the boiling water into the bath.

At seven o'clock, Nellie was trying hard to get cleared up. The copper was nigh on boiling and condensation was running down the scullery walls. 'Move your books,' she said to Lizzie, as she threw the dark red chenille cloth over the scrubbed table top; she didn't want Kate to see the place in a mess.

Daisy was laying sheets of newspaper over the linoleum up the passage, which would soak up some of the water that would inevitably get slopped in the process of reaching the bathroom.

John Hurley preceded his family, taking off his coat as he came into the kitchen. He was a short, stocky man, with strong brawny arms. Kate followed, wearing her Sunday coat and hat. Tim, the eldest boy, had a sly look about him, in Aunt Daisy's opinion, while young Joey, with huge brown eyes and a mop of dark curly hair was everyone's favourite.

'Right, out the way kids,' John Hurley ordered, 'we'll soon have the bath filled.'

Lizzie looked at Polly and a nod of her head suggested that they made themselves scarce in the front room.

An hour later, John Hurley had taken himself off to Wimbledon dog track. Using the long, hooked poker, Daisy had removed the top plate of the hob, leaving the fire open. The flames, now exposed to all the draughts, were leaping and flickering, giving out extra warmth. Tim and Joey, wrapped now in towels, glowing and clean, their well-scrubbed faces a shiny red, sat giggling and laughing, playing marbles with Syd. Polly, who had bathed first, was dressed; her hair now straggled round her face in damp tendrils. Nellie came in from the scullery carrying a wooden tray; three cups and saucers holding strong, sweet tea were set down for the women and five tin mugs of cocoa were handed out to the children.

All eyes were turned to Daisy and dribble came from young Joey's lips as she asked, 'Who wants a lump of bread pudding?' Rich and dark, full of fruit and peel, the top heavily dredged with sugar, its spicy smell filled the kitchen.

'I do,' five voices called while heads nodded in eager agreement.

Time for bed. Lizzie and Polly clung together. 'See you in the morning,' Lizzie called after her friend.

'Yeah, night. God bless you,' Polly answered.

'Thanks, Nellie, you too, Daisy. It's bin a real treat,' Kate hugged them both.

'You're more than welcome any time,' they told her.

Closing the front door behind the Hurleys, Daisy grinned at Nellie as she gathered up the sodden newspaper. 'Only don't make it too often,' she muttered.

Pouring another cup of tea for themselves, Nellie and Daisy marvelled at the rigmarole they went through every time they or their neighbours wanted to use the bathroom.

'I'd just as soon sit in the old tin bath in front of the fire,' Daisy exclaimed.

Nellie gave her sister-in-law a lopsided grin and then both of them burst out laughing. Each was fully aware that that was exactly what Daisy did whenever she had the house to herself.

Christmas that year was marred for Lizzie by two things. Leslie was now stationed in Malta. Without Les, things couldn't be the same. Lizzie adored him, he was a father to her as well as a brother. The second thing really narked Lizzie. Her mother insisted she still had to go to work for the Dawsons on Christmas morning.

But there were some compensations. Snow was forecast and that meant great fun out in the street with all the other kids or even up on the common if Mum felt up to the walk, and Connie was getting engaged to Bill. Bill Baldwin was like one of the family already. He was a big husky lad with light brown hair, not a bit shy now he had got to know them all. Bill was devoted to Connie; he loved her with all his heart, and had known she was the one for him from the moment he'd set eyes on her. Since there was only him and his widowed mother, Nellie had invited them to join the family for Christmas dinner.

A week before Christmas, Bill came upon Syd arguing with Lizzie in the backyard. 'What's up, kids?' he wanted to know.

Syd confided in him, 'We've only got four bob in our money box and the present we want ter buy for Mum and Aunt Daisy costs five bob.'

Bill looked at them thoughtfully. 'That's a lot of money to spend on one present.'

'We know that,' said Lizzie, 'but it's what they want. We heard them talking.'

Bill worked in Billingsgate Fish Market. The hours were long and the work hard but he made good money working on commission. It was a problem how he could give these two nice children a shilling without hurting their pride. A penny from him every Saturday had become quite acceptable but a shilling was a lot of money. He was too wise to offer it outright.

'Tell yer what. I haven't got round to cleaning my bike for more than two weeks now. The front lamp is so dirty it's a wonder a policeman hasn't stopped me, and the rear light is not much better. Just 'aven't had the time.' He drew in a deep breath and pretended to be considering the matter. 'If I give you two sixpences each, you wouldn't clean me bike for me, would you?'

A great grin spread on Syd's face while a flash of hope lit up Lizzie's blue eyes. ' 'Course we will,' they chorused. Rags and a tin of Bluebell metal polish were produced and they set to with a will.

Once inside the china shop, Lizzie gazed fondly at the twenty-one-piece tea services set out on a stand behind the counter.

'Which one do you like best, Syd?' she said.

He pointed to a blue willow-patterned set. 'What d'you think of that one?'

'Oh, no. Gran's got that pattern, so has Mrs Hurley; let's buy Mum and Aunt Daisy something different.'

Twice the blonde assistant with the red-painted fingernails asked if she could help them.

'No, we won't be a minute,' they told her – but they were. At least twenty minutes had passed before they settled on a cream-coloured set with a honeysuckle design.

Handing over their shillings, sixpences and pennies, Syd nudged his sister, 'Go on Lizzie, ask her.'

The assistant smiled, 'Ask me what?'

'Please . . .' still Lizzie hesitated.

'. . . Deliver it to our house.' Syd got it out in a rush. 'It says goods costing five shillings or more will be delivered free of charge.'

'That's quite right, young man,' the assistant told him, as she reached for a pink form.

And so, on Christmas Eve, a puzzled Aunt Daisy signed for and accepted a large wooden box.

Lizzie and Syd clutched at each other's hands, squeezing every now and again as they watched their mother and their aunt discard the straw on to the kitchen floor and extract six cups, six saucers, six tea plates, a milk jug and sugar basin, and, lastly, the large bread and butter plates. Nellie's face was wet with tears, and Daisy, her eyes brimming, stared in amazement at the china and the straw now scattered widely.

'Come here, ducks, and give your old aunt a kiss,' Daisy said as she drew Lizzie to her.

Even Syd was smiling as he brushed at his cheek with his fist to remove the dampness where his mother has planted several kisses.

Christmas was good. Mrs Baldwin had proved to be a jolly sort, joining in games and giving a solo of 'Silent Night' whilst Nellie played for her on their upright piano. And on Boxing Day it did snow. Waking to a stillness that only comes with snow, Lizzie ran to look out of the window. A pure white, unblemished blanket covered everything except the tips of the chimney pots. The only sound was from a few sparrows visible in the yard, twittering away near the back door asking to be fed.

'Come on, Syd, wake up!' Lizzie shouted as she ran to the small box-room which Syd had as a bedroom all to himself. 'It's bin snowing.'

As she pulled the covers from his bed, Lizzie looked around the small space. Syd had a bookcase, which Leslie had made for him; it was full of comics and paperback books. He also had a small table and one chair, ideal for doing his homework, except that Syd never bothered to do any.

A thought came to Lizzie, as she tickled her brother's toes and he gave her a brutal kick. If, in the new year, Connie was to marry her Bill, she would then have a bedroom of her own. In her mind's eye, Lizzie was already seeing the room she now shared with her sister set out as she would like it, if only she could wheedle her mother round to her way of thinking. That should be easy, she told herself, and if her mum wasn't forthcoming, there was always Gran. Gran had some lovely pieces of furniture, much more than she needed. Yes, Lizzie was confident the new year would see her settled very nicely into a room of her own.

Chapter Three

As always, January was bleak, with short hours of daylight, and dark, bitter-cold evenings. One day, as Lizzie came through the school gates, she heard her younger brother yelling coarsely, 'Wait for me, Liz. You'll never guess what,' he panted as he drew near. 'Our teacher says we can 'ave all the tar blocks we want so long as we've got something to carry them 'ome in.'

'You're barmy,' Lizzie retorted. 'What would we want with a load of messy old tar blocks?'

'Bet Mum would be glad to 'ave some. Save her coal, wouldn't it?'

Lizzie pondered on this. Syd was a likeable little dare-devil with his friendly and carefree approach to life, and at times he could be very thoughtful, even loving.

'If I mend the wheel on me barrow, will you come up the High Street and 'elp me get some on Saturday? Will yer?' he pleaded. 'All the other boys are gonna get some.'

Lizzie nodded; her eyes were merry and her lips smiling as she took hold of his hand.

During the short walk home, Syd chatted away very excitedly, telling her what his teacher had told the class. The Ministry of Transport had commanded that all the tram tracks in the centre of main roads had to be renewed. Removal of the old tracks meant the discarding of wooden blocks embedded on either side.

As it turned out, the whole district was on to a good thing once work started. Men were taken on as labourers, digging out the existing rails, thrilled at the prospect of a few weeks' steady employment. There wasn't a kid who didn't enjoy the excitement of it all as they lined the gutter and stared in amazement. Pick-axes were vigorously swung, by tough, weather-beaten young men, in a repeated rhythm. The piles of old tar-sodden blocks grew larger as heap after heap was tossed aside. Great cauldrons of hot tar stood on the edge of the pavement, each with a fire glowing brightly beneath, and filled with thick jet-black steaming liquid with a pungent smell so strong it took one's breath away.

'Breathe deep,' mothers were admonishing their children. 'It'll do yer chest a power of good.'

If it didn't burst your lungs first, Lizzie thought, as she and Syd joined the scrambling, pushing, shoving mob to fill their barrow once more.

The whole show moved with great speed. All too soon the length of High Street from Trinity Road at Tooting Bec, right through to Tooting Broadway was completed. Four lanes of shiny steel rails were set centre to the road and the gangers moved on towards Colliers Wood and south Wimbledon.

Nellie went back and forth from the pavement, where Syd and Lizzie had tipped their load, to the backyard, transporting six to eight blocks at a time in her shopping bag. Daisy toiled away, stacking the rough, dirty blocks of wood as high as they would go in the garden shed.

'Don't sit on them chairs,' Nellie called out as Syd and Lizzie came in through the back door, 'and both of you get them dirty boots off.' She glanced across at Daisy, 'Look at them, right filthy the pair of them!'

In no time Nellie had stripped them of their outdoor clothes, made sure that they had washed their faces and that their hands were thoroughly clean. By now, Daisy had the table laid with a sumptuous feast of sausage and mash, with jam roly poly and custard to follow.

The tar blocks proved to be a godsend. The next few weeks were bitter. Snow lingered and turned into dirty, mushy heaps, ice formed in the gutters and no water came from the scullery tap. All the outside pipes were frozen.

Inside, the kitchen was warm and cosy. The fire roared away all day and was well banked down at night, never allowed to go out. It spurted and crackled dangerously as the children sat doing their homework while Nellie knitted and Aunt Daisy sewed. The tar blocks were pitted with gravel and as the tar melted the tiny stones were shot out, making sounds like pellets being shot through the air as they hit the hearth. Lizzie and Syd would laugh aloud and protest as their mother placed the fireguard in position.

'The only person not showing a profit from all of this is the local coalman,' commented Nellie.

'You can say that again,' Daisy retorted. 'Thanks to our two kids, those blocks will help eke out the coal for many a long day.'

Nellie nodded her agreement. 'And you know what, Daisy, there shouldn't be half the children bad with chest ailments this winter. You've only ter open the front door to realize that.' For there was hardly a family who hadn't amassed a store of tar blocks and everywhere the air was acrid with the fumes of burning tar.

As winter at last gave way, the pale early spring sunshine brought out the women to gossip over the back fences once more. Then there was another upheaval in the district – hard to believe, but true. Electricity was coming to Tooting. Arguments ranged back and forth as to the merits of this wonder. The municipality was undertaking to provide this service free of charge for a limited number of points in each house. Any additional sockets would have to be paid for.

Upheaval came to the back streets this time. Pathways and roadways were dug up and wide open trenches were laid bare during the laying of the cables. Boisterous kids harassed the workmen. Floorboards were taken up in downstairs passages and women fought a losing battle against the dust and dirt. When completion was almost reached, the inevitable official in his bowler hat appeared. Holding his clipboard firmly, pencil poised, he raised his eyes to the top of the front door.

'Ah, yes. Number thirty, Mrs Collins, right? How many extra points will you be wanting?' he enquired in his posh accent.

Daisy and Nellie answered in unison, 'None, thank you.'

'You do realize our free instalment offer only covers the ground floor?'

Nellie wrinkled her brow but said quietly, 'Never mind, we'll just have ter make do.'

'My dear lady,' he replied, 'you will have no light or power points in the upper regions of this house.'

Daisy scowled at the man, 'We've got by with gas all these years and it won't kill us now not to have electricity in the bedrooms.'

He smiled sardonically, turned away, then hesitantly said over his shoulder, 'If you change your mind over the next three days, the same offer will stand.'

They didn't change their minds, no more than many other occupants of the road did. In fact, it was a long time before the electric light which had been installed in the downstairs rooms was put to full use.

'Switch it off, switch it off,' Nellie screamed at Syd, who had demanded the honour of being the first to flick the brass switch.

Nellie was in a state of panic, 'It makes the place look so dirty,' she sadly remarked.

'Indeed, it does,' agreed Daisy.

The ceilings were smoke-blackened from the constantly burning kitchen range, and the gas jet fixed above the mantle shelf which gave out heat as well as providing light had left a filthy stain on the wall. The new light with just a bare bulb illuminated the room so brightly that it clearly showed the grime which had previously been ignored.

Lizzie was glad her bedroom still only boasted a gas bracket. At times, to save money, even this was not lit. She and Syd would be given a candle, placed in a saucer of water, to light up their rooms while they got into bed. Lizzie even liked to lie and watch the weird patterns on the walls and ceiling made by the flickering flame, but she hated the smell which lingered when her mother snuffed out the light between licked finger and thumb.

Tomorrow would be Good Friday and school had broken up at midday. There would be two whole weeks' holiday. Lizzie was spreading dripping on a slice of toast but her thoughts were elsewhere – on the fact that she had sat her scholarship exams.

After tea that evening, Lizzie walked round to Polly's house. She was longing to ask Polly what she had thought of the exam questions. The light was on in the kitchen and the fire glow showed clearly through the back window, so she knocked on the door and opened it, as she always did, and called out, 'It's all right, it's only me, Lizzie.'

The kitchen was deserted, but someone was moving about upstairs. Surprised to see neither Mr nor Mrs Hurley, she went to the bottom of the stairs and called up.

Polly answered, 'I'll be down in a minute.' She clattered down the linoleum-covered stairs, and came into the kitchen, grinning at Lizzie and pointing to a chair. 'Pull it up to the fire,' she ordered, and threw herself into another chair opposite.

Lizzie sat down and Tibbles, the Hurley's tabby cat, hugged against her legs. 'Where's your mum?'

'Gone to the pub with dad. Won't see them before closing time.'

Lizzie laughed, 'I'm glad they've gone out, I was going to ask you about the exam. How d'you think you got on?'

Polly frowned, 'Wouldn't like to say, really. How about you?'

Lizzie shook her head. 'Dunno. Glad it's over, though. Don't suppose I got many questions right.'

Polly protested, 'Oh, come on, Lizzie, they weren't that difficult, were they?'

Lizzie forced herself to agree. Now that she had found out what she wanted to know, she wished that they could just forget the whole matter. It would be weeks before they got the results. 'I hope we both pass,' she said listlessly.

'Well, worrying won't make it so. Will it?' Polly laughingly answered, as she suddenly stood up. 'Come on, let's go round to the Selkirk Pub. If we call through the door, me dad's sure to buy us a ginger beer and a Darby biscuit.'

Together they ran down the road, quickening

their steps as they neared the pub, taking the front steps two at a time. Polly saw her dad as soon as they opened the door, slumped in a chair near the dart board, a frothy pint in his hand.

'You've got a cheek, the pair of yer,' he told them, but his cheerful face was creased with laughter as he turned towards the bar.

Side by side, the two friends sat on the steps, glass in one hand, large round biscuit in the other. Easter would begin tomorrow. On Holiday Monday they would probably all go to Mitcham Fair. The scholarship suddenly didn't matter so much.

'Glad we came out, aren't you?' Polly asked.

'Yeah. Your dad's great,' said Lizzie. All the worry and agony of sitting the exam seemed remote and dim now. 'Want to come with me ter see me gran tomorrow?' she asked.

'Love to,' said Polly.

The lovely month of June came again. For the past weeks, there had been great excitement in the Collinses' house. Nellie had baked rich dark cakes which the local baker had promised to ice. Aunt Daisy had sewed a white silk dress for the bride and a pink dress for the only bridesmaid. Connie was to marry her Bill and Lizzie was to be her only attendant. Disregarding the cost, tradition was adhered to. Nearly all the neighbours were inside the church and everyone held their breath as Connie came down the aisle on John Hurley's arm.

Lizzie had always thought of her sister as plain,

even straitlaced, but nothing was further from the truth today. A crown of orange blossom with a froth of white veiling framed her face. She carried a small posy of pink roses and the colour matched her rosy cheeks. Lizzie stood shyly behind her sister and offered up a silent prayer that when the time came for her, too, to be married, she might look as beautiful as Connie did today.

Once outside, the crowd began throwing confetti and yelling good wishes. Syd was wearing his first pair of long trousers and Lizzie could scarcely believe that this clean, tidy, blond, curly-haired boy was her young brother.

The reception was a cold salad meal laid out in the function room of the Selkirk Pub. At six o'clock, when the public bars opened, spontaneous gaiety broke out and a good time was had by all.

Connie's departure from the house was not such a wrench. She and Bill had rented the top half of Dolly Whitlock's house, which stood at the far end of Graveney Road and meant that Connie would still be a daily visitor.

The wedding was over but excitement was still in the air. The summer horse-race meeting at Epsom was due and on the second day the most famous race of all would take place – the Derby. The Fountain Public House in Garratt Lane was running an outing, with four bus loads of people. The whole Collins family, with the exception of Gran, was going to Epsom for the day. Six-thirty in the morning and the pub was packed as folk filed through and out of the back door to board the buses.

'Can we go upstairs?' Polly yelled at her parents.

Mr Hurley set down the crate of booze he was helping his mates to load on board, wiped his sweaty forehead with his forearm and grinned at his only daughter, 'Yes, all right, but sit still. See the boys don't run about till yer mum and me get there.'

Five children made a dash for the stairs. Polly and Lizzie grabbed a seat together, while Syd, Tim and Joey squashed up on a double bench. Finally, to loud cheers, they were off! As they left London behind and entered the green Surrey countryside, they joined the already jam-packed main road to Epsom: open-top buses, hackney carriages, motor cycles with side cars, charabancs, all their seats filled to capacity.

Pearly kings and queens, regally seated in their horse-drawn carts, rubbed shoulders for the day with true royalty. Bumper-to-bumper with cars and commercial vans were Daimlers and Rolls Royce limousines, their occupants smiling and waving just as enthusiastically as everyone else.

They finally arrived at the course and were directed by policemen into a special parking area reserved for buses. Shopping bags and boxes were unpacked and food in plenty was set out on the grass. Serious drinking began for the adults. And the kids had all the pop they wanted. Spread out wide, away from the course, was the fairground. Coffee stalls, beer tents, tipsters, gypsies, fortune tellers and racketeers, all contrived and schemed to earn a few quid from the day's racing.

It was a brilliant day and the sun shone with a vengeance on the thousands who had turned up to chance their luck on the horses.

'They're off,' the cry went up as the first horses left the stalls.

'Quick,' Lizzie grabbed Polly's arm, causing her to drop the long iced bun she was munching. 'Let's get to the rails.'

They elbowed their way through the crowd, the shouting and cheering so loud it was enough to burst the eardrums. The two friends held on to each other tightly as the horses came into sight, their hooves pounding the track as they thundered past between the rails.

Later that afternoon the mums gathered the children together and took them over to the fair. Toffee apples, candy floss, humbugs and bags of hot chips combined with rides on the roundabouts and the big dipper.

All too soon it was time to go home, but the fun wasn't over by any means. Crowds lined the pavements, dozens of children to the forefront.

'Chuck out yer mouldies,' they bawled. By now ninety per cent of the racegoers were tipsy and they responded willingly. Handfuls of farthings, half-pennies and pennies were chucked over the sides of carts, out of the windows of cars, buses and the charabancs into the road. Dodging the traffic, evading the horses hooves, pushing, shoving, struggling with each other to reach the coins first, the children swarmed, unaware of the dangers, enjoying the rough and tumble and laughing gleefully as the toffs in the big cars raised their top hats to them.

Dirty and bedraggled they alighted from the buses in Garratt Lane. 'You go on 'ome with the kids,' John Hurley slurred as he and his mates tried to rouse one man who was paralytic with drink, unable to move from the pavement where he sat.

Wearily, the four women and five children set off for home. At the gate of number thirty, all good-nights having been said, Daisy almost as an after-thought asked, 'How much did you win, Kate?'

With a humorous grin on her face, Kate answered, 'Five pounds one shilling – not bad, eh? You and Nellie aren't out of pocket on the day, are you?'

Daisy looked at her sister-in-law and they both laughed. 'No,' they both answered, and Nellie added, 'We made a bob or two.'

Chapter Four

THE LETTER ARRIVED on a Saturday morning. Lizzie picked it up from the mat and stared at the envelope for a long time. Franked London County Council, she knew exactly what it contained and dallied with the idea of throwing it into the fire unopened. 'Oh, Jesus!' she whispered in an agony of frustration. 'What am I going to do?'

Lizzie lay in bed that evening and thought confusedly about her day and in particular about the examination for the scholarship. She had passed and that was something she had not really imagined would happen, although she had allowed herself to dream that it might.

Her delight was tinged with guilt. Why should she be privileged when her brothers and her sister hadn't been? To go to the High School would cost money. Maybe she would be entitled to a grant, but it certainly would not cover the cost of uniforms, books, travel to and from school and many more untold items.

Her mother's delight as she read the letter had been a joy to see. Tenderly she had hugged Lizzie to her, murmuring, 'Well done. Good girl.' Aunt Daisy's congratulations had been more hearty. She had grabbed Lizzie, sweeping her off her feet, and was triumphantly swinging her round and round when the kitchen door opened and Gran stood there.

'Our Lizzie's passed her scholarship,' Daisy quickly told her mother.

'I'm not a bit surprised; ever since she could toddle, she's had her nose stuck in a book,' the old lady retorted dryly.

'Oh, say you're pleased, Gran,' Lizzie pleaded.

'Of course I'm pleased,' she said quietly. And she was.

To Harriet, this little girl was everything. She wanted to pet and cuddle her but she was not used to showing affection. Silently, she vowed that nothing, if she had her way, would stand in the way of her favourite grandchild being granted the chance of a good education.

In the scullery, Lizzie was putting on the kettle when she heard her elders in the kitchen discussing finances. She wanted to put her hands over her ears as she heard her mother sadly say, 'I only hope we can afford it.' Whichever way she looked at it, Lizzie knew the cost would be far more than her mother could manage.

Double delight: Polly had also passed.

'How did your dad take the news?' Lizzie asked, as she cut two lumps from the cold bread pudding.

'He was very pleased,' Polly assured her, smiling at the memory. 'Mum said afterwards, it knocked him all of a heap. He wouldn't believe it at first, kept saying brains didn't run in the family. He said he is coming round to talk to yer mum about money, and how they are going to manage.'

During the whole of the summer, endless opinions were exchanged and ideas debated. Leslie wrote from Malta that his blonde whippet of a sister was a genius and for his mother to buy Lizzie a bicycle on the never-never and he would give her an extra sixpence a day to pay for the instalments.

John Hurley voted this a good idea for the pair of them. 'I'll see what Nick Shephard can do,' he told Nellie.

She grimaced. Nick was their insurance man whom Nellie never quite trusted. Black hair smarmed down with grease, blue eyes and a pencil-slim moustache and always smartly dressed in the up-to-date fashion, he was a hit with most women, though not with Nellie.

Every Saturday morning he called for the weekly payments on their Britannia insurance policies. 'Royal Britannia, two tanners make a bob, three make eighteen pence and four make two bob,' the kids in the street would chant as he did his rounds.

Nick Shephard had a sideline. He sold things on the weekly. Towels, sheets, boots, shoes, you name it, he would do his best to get it. Where from was a closely guarded secret.

'Two bicycles?' His brow puckered then suddenly he was grinning. 'Leave it ter me. I'll have them for you by next Saturday.'

He shook hands with John Hurley but Daisy

blocked his way as he made to leave their kitchen. 'These are for two young girls. We don't want no rubbish nor yer stolen bikes. Do you understand me?' She looked sternly into his eyes.

'Trust me, Miss Collins,' he entreated. 'As if I would do anything to jeopardize the good relationship I've had with this family for years now.'

But her next words were menacing. 'Just remember what I've said.'

The evening before school started found Polly and Lizzie in the big warm kitchen of the Collinses' house. Nellie and Aunt Daisy had taken themselves off to the Selkirk for a glass of stout and a singsong, and Syd had gone to his Boys' Brigade meeting. The two girls sat one each side of the kitchen table, labelling their books and sportswear.

'All finished,' Lizzie said as she put her plimsoles on top of her books and shut the lid of the small case.

John Hurley had bought Polly's uniform from Morley's, the official school outfitters, but Lizzie's had been lovingly and expertly made at home by Aunt Daisy. The regulation cloth and colours had been available from Smith's in the Mitcham Road. Both girls had been taken by their mothers to the Royal Co-operative Society. There, by means of mutuality cheques, navy-blue knickers, black stockings, shoes and plimsoles plus vests and blouses had been bought.

Mutuality cheques were a godsend and repay-

ments were strictly weekly. If you had a Co-op rep-
resentative call, one shilling in every pound had to
be paid extra as interest. However, if you took your
weekly payments to the Co-op bank (and this
entailed climbing a flight of forty steps) for twenty
consecutive weeks without fail, no interest was
charged. Come rain or hail, Nellie went to the bank
religiously each week. Using mutuality cheques, she
and Daisy could buy while prices were at their
lowest.

'So,' Polly concluded, 'tomorrow is the big day.'

Lizzie grinned, 'And about time too. Wonder
how we'll get on, it still seems too good to be true.
You and me going to the Elliott High School in
Southfields.' She nudged Polly and they both giggled. 'Hope the other girls in our class are not stuck
up.'

'Who cares if they are,' Polly looked lovingly at
her friend as she squeezed past the new Raleigh
bicycle which stood propped against the wall of the
passage. 'We'll have each other. We'll get by,' she
declared.

' 'Course we will,' agreed Lizzie.

Chapter Five

IT WAS NEARLY Christmas once more, the third since Lizzie had been at the Elliott School. Alone in the house, Lizzie, not yet dressed, sat in the old armchair by the fire. There was only one person outside her family who she had bought a present for, and that was Polly.

Lizzie disliked her classmates more than she dared to admit, and the very thought of Miss Dawlish, her headmistress, filled her with a forlorn air of defeat. Without the company of the happy-go-lucky Polly, she would really have hated school.

Miss Dawlish was a snob. There were no two ways about it. 'It is a privilege that should never be taken lightly,' she would intone from her high dais each morning as she gazed over her pupils at assembly. 'You are members of my school at the expense of the ratepayers,' she would insist. 'You owe it to them to prove that you are the cream of the cream.' Lizzie had never worked out the meaning of that statement.

Miss Dawlish failed to accept the fact that she had pupils from an impoverished background. A great charity worker, she would regularly urge her girls to bring donations for the relief of the poor.

Lizzie's contributions were small; more often than

not only what Gran gave her. She knew only too
well how her mother struggled to provide the
elementary necessities for her to attend the Elliott,
and so she rarely made a difficult situation worse by
asking.

'Old bitch,' Lizzie would mutter to herself when
Miss Dawlish smiled sweetly as better-off classmates ingratiated themselves.

'Boot-lickers,' Polly would mumble. She agreed
whole-heartedly with Lizzie about Miss Dawlish,
and certainly there was no love lost between her and
her condescending classmates.

However, she didn't fare as badly as Lizzie. She
had a father in full-time employment and was able
to acquire such things as her own sports equipment.
Although she willingly shared with Lizzie, it still
left Lizzie vulnerable to their sick jokes.

The highlight of the past year had been their street
party. Polly had let the cat out of the bag at school.
'A street party! How disgusting,' the tall, freckled-
faced teacher's pet Marion had mimicked.

All south London had street parties in 1935. King
George V and Queen Mary had been on the throne
for twenty-five years and their Silver Jubilee was a
grand excuse for a celebration. For weeks ahead,
men had collected pennies up and down both sides
of the street every Sunday morning. 'It's to give the
kids a good time. God bless yer,' they would say
at each house, as coppers were pushed into their
collecting tins.

The men were as good as their word. The great day had been declared a public holiday. From the pub, stacks of trestles were brought forth and set up in the centre of the road from one end to the other. Large planks of wood formed table tops, red, white and blue paper cloths were laid, and endless rows of benches provided the seating.

High above, lines stretched from upstairs windows were joined to their neighbours on the other side of the street. Banners and flags made out of old cloths dyed in tin baths to all shades of red, white and blue, showed how patriotic the Londoners could be.

Children were seated near to their own front doors and were waited on by the adults. There were jam, fish-paste and cheese sandwiches, lemonade and ginger beer, fancy cakes and chocolate biscuits, with jelly, blancmange and ice-cream to round it all off. 'Smashing,' was the unanimous verdict.

When darkness came, children sat along the kerb stones, watching the antics of the adults. Tunes were pounded out on old upright pianos, and accordions took over when the piano players had a rest for a few pints. 'Knees Up Mother Brown', 'The Lambeth Walk', 'Knock 'em in the Old Kent Road', 'My Old Man Said Follow the Van', 'My Young Man is Up in the Gallery' – these and many more well-loved songs were sung lustily, if not tunefully, as neighbours weaved their way back and forth across the street. In the morning, there were empty bottles by the dozen, beer bottles, pints and quarts, cider bottles, lemonade bottles all stacked up along the pavement.

'Wonder if we could nick a few, get the money back on the empties,' Syd considered as he went to call for the Hurley boys.

'Tell you what. It wasn't only the kids that had a good time,' Daisy declared as she swept the front path and Nellie retrieved more empty bottles from the front garden.

Lizzie found herself laughing at the memory as she told herself to get cracking and get dressed. Blow the Elliott, Miss Dawlish, and all those posh girls, who thought they were much better than anyone else.

The bells sang the arrival of 1936. Neighbours came out into the roadway to sing 'Auld Lang Syne' and to kiss and hug each other. Only one person was missing; that was Leslie. Lizzie missed her big brother. She wrote him a regular weekly letter, telling of her progress at school, which was surprisingly good, and skilfully she outlined her grievances. His replies never failed to make her laugh. 'Don't stand for no argy bargy from them. Give as good as you get, Lizzie,' was his advice.

The year had scarcely begun and the whole country was in mourning. King George V was dead. Connie said she didn't want to go to see the King's lying-in-state.

'I do,' Lizzie said. 'Please, Bill,' she implored her brother-in-law, 'will you take me?'

' 'Course I will, love, if your mum says it's all right.'

They came out of the underground tube station to find everyone else in London had decided to pay their respects; mounted police were controlling the crowds. They queued for well over an hour on a bleak January day made worse by a keen wind that was blowing off the River Thames. At last they entered Westminster Hall. It was difficult to see anything at first as they slowly shuffled forward in step with everyone else. Gradually their eyes became accustomed to the dusk interior.

A solitary wreath lay on the coffin and tall, beautiful floral tributes nearby made the air sweet and heavy with perfume. Women and children wept. Men looked solemn. Lizzie was afraid to look, attracted far more by the soldiers and their uniforms as they stood guarding the body – heads down, perfectly still like statues. As they passed out at the other end of the hall, Bill squeezed Lizzie's hand; she had never let go of his since entering the hall.

'There, Lizzie,' he said, 'you'll never forget the death of King George V, will you?'

'No, I won't,' Lizzie solemnly agreed.

Plans for the coronation of Edward VIII were going ahead, but all the time Mrs Simpson was on the scene. She became the main topic of conversation everywhere, discussed in shops, on buses, in the streets and pubs – not always discreetly. Boys and girls alike sang saucy songs about her, ridiculing her for having designs on England's future King. Opinion was divided. Many thought he would be a good King because he had shown a keen interest in social problems. Others were opposed to a marriage because she was a divorced woman and an American. Preparation for the ceremony of crowning the sovereign continued. Edward would be crowned King in Westminster Abbey, but would Mrs Simpson be his Queen Consort?

At last, in the following December, Edward VIII finally announced that he would abdicate. 'Good riddance to bad rubbish,' declared Harriet Collins. But the repercussions of his action were colossal. Souvenirs that had been made in their thousands for the coronation were now utterly worthless. There would be no coronation, and traders sustained great losses. No one escaped. From the largest stores down to fairground traders and barrow boys, all were left with coronation mugs, cups and saucers, wall plaques, bowls and teaspoons on their hands. Now they couldn't give them away, let alone sell them. Edward VIII's renunciation of the throne had been disastrous in more ways than one. Folk looked back over the past twelve months as 1936 drew to a close and shook their heads.

Lizzie wrote an essay as part of her English exam and for once won congratulations from Miss Dawlish. 'The past year has to be one of the most important years in the history of the Royal Family,' she wrote. 'Three different Kings had each sat on the throne of England in such a short space of time.'

The following year, 1937, was relatively uneventful in England, although there were disturbing rumblings from Germany, where Adolf Hitler was initiating a large re-armament programme.

'He won't stop till he dominates the world,' declared Fred Johnson, the milkman for the whole street.

'Rubbish,' declared Jackie Jordon, Nellie's next-door neighbour. 'We've sat on them once, you don't think we're daft enough to let 'im drag the Germans into another war?'

'We'll have to see, won't we?' Gran put her two pennyworth in, as she opened the front gate.

Actually, she wanted to get Nellie and her daughter inside, off the doorstep. She had more personal worries to discuss. She had lived through enough wars and wasn't about to get upset over something that might never happen. She'd bigger problems to worry about just now. Compulsory purchase of her house and the ground it stood on, that's what the letter had said. Well, she'd see about that!

''Allo, Gran, who's upset you?' Lizzie cheekily asked as her grandmother pushed past the knot of people on the doorstep and made her way down the passage and into the kitchen.

'Never you mind, just put the kettle on,' she snapped. Her eyes were blazing and her cheeks flamed as she savagely removed her hat-pin and hung her hat behind the door. It was not a bit like Gran to be so short-tempered, least of all with her beloved Lizzie.

By suppertime, the whole street knew that Silverdore Terrace was to be pulled down. The very thought of Gran's lovely home disappearing made Lizzie feel sick and she burst into tears and threw her arms about her Gran's neck.

'Stop it! Crying won't help. I'm going to the solicitors first thing tomorrow; I'm also going to make sure the newspapers hear about this.' Gran, pale and very angry, snatched her letter up from the table and shoved it into her bag. 'They'll 'ave ter do more than just send a letter if they want my house. Lived in Silverdore since I were married at seventeen – that's coming up for fifty-four years. Try chucking me out! Just let them try!' Gran yelled threateningly.

The young lady in the solicitor's office was brisk and efficient as she ushered Daisy and Harriet into the main office. Mr Martin came from behind his desk to shake their hands. Tall and neatly dressed in a navy-blue suit, striped shirt with a stiff white collar, he epitomized his profession.

Having read through the letter, he cleared his throat and with one finger eased the stiff collar about his Adam's apple. 'I'm afraid this is watertight,' he said. He was all sympathy. 'It's an odd business, I don't like it one bit,' he told them. 'Legally, though, there is not much I can do about it.'

With a melancholy nod of her head, Harriet Collins made to rise.

'Wait,' Mr Martin himself rose. 'Perhaps it would be better if you let me explain the situation fully,' he suggested. Harriet sat down again and nodded dumbly.

Mr Martin carefully weighed his words. 'Your ownership of the cottage is not in dispute. It is the land on which it was built. The freeholder, as he is known, owns the land for ever and he has fairly wide powers to do with the land as he wishes. These cottages were built in 1816 when a lease on the ground was granted for a fixed period only. Over the years, all owner-occupants, including yourself, Mrs Collins, have paid ground rent to the freeholder and observed the terms of the lease granted by the original freeholder. That fixed period came to an end twenty years ago. Clearly, then, the freeholder has been lenient and is now well within his rights to ask that the land be given back. There is nothing we can legally do to restrict the freeholder from having use of his land.'

Daisy felt utterly inadequate. Her mother sat still, eyes cast down, her body slumped; a sad sight indeed. Until two days ago, Harriet Collins had thought of herself as a house owner. Apparently she had been deluding herself. Ownership had been meaningless.

'No one will be harassed,' Mr Martin assured them as he saw them to the door. 'Indeed the company involved are being quite generous. They are offering compensation to all owners although the amounts will be relatively small.'

Harriet had a determined air about her in the days
that followed and everyone was careful not to ask
what her plans were come the day when she would
have to leave Silverdore.

'She'll tell us when she's ready,' Aunt Daisy told
Lizzie, but Lizzie still regarded her Gran with caution.

Then one day Lizzie called in unexpectedly and
found her Gran crying. It almost broke her heart.
'You must come and live with us, Gran. We'll take
care of you,' she said.

Gran nodded and held her arms out wide. Hugging Lizzie close, she pressed her lips to the top of
her granddaughter's head. 'Oh, I'm just a silly old
woman clinging to the past. I'm fine now that you
have come to see me.'

They had tea together and Harriet sat watching
Lizzie as she ate, with the light from the fire dancing
on her long, silky hair and her young, unlined face.

'I'll never see her grown into a woman,' Harriet
sadly told herself.

Sunday was a lovely spring day, really warm and
with just enough breeze to stir the leaves on the
trees. The sky was cloudless and the birds were singing as Lizzie set off to bring Gran back to spend the
day. Turning the Broadway, she broke into a trot.
Gran always had a treat ready for her every Sunday
morning: a brandy snap, a fairy cake hot from the
oven, or even treacle toffee.

'Your Gran's sleeping late, not like 'er,' old Mr

Thompson told Lizzie, his gnarled fingers clutching his walking stick as he leant heavily against his front gate.

'No. She'll be out the back,' Lizzie reassured him.

'I'm here, Gran,' she called as she opened the front door.

There was no answer. Lizzie didn't move for a long time, but stood looking at the cold ashes in the grate. No matter what time of the year, Gran always had a fire. A lump rose in her throat and tears stung the back of her eyes and she couldn't move.

She wanted the comfort and happiness of seeing her Gran. She wanted to be hugged and kissed. Intuition told her to be afraid. Her Gran had said no developer would get her out of this house alive. Lizzie's glance took in the orderly state of the room. The furniture shone, antimacassars on the chair backs were set dead straight and the brass firearms and fender gleamed. The room was perfect except for the dead ashes in the grate, and the total silence.

Slowly, Lizzie climbed the stairs.

Her grandmother lay still in her bed. She must be dead, Lizzie thought, trying to stay calm as she watched the sunlight playing on her grey hair. Around her Gran's lips, a slight sweet smile lingered such as there had never been in life. Such sadness swelled up inside Lizzie that she didn't know what to do, so she just stood there for an endless time beside the bed, her eyes never leaving the face of this grandmother she had loved so much. Then the tears came and she raged, 'You can't be dead, Gran. It's Sunday. I've come to take you to our house. I can't bear this. What will I do without you, Gran? Please, don't be dead.'

Lizzie only vaguely remembered walking home. First her mother, then Aunt Daisy held her and stroked her hair and wept with her.

The funeral was on Friday and Lizzie was surprised at the number of people who crowded into their front room. She was pleased, though, at the numerous funeral tributes which lay on the pavement outside their house. Going to the lavatory was the only excuse she could think of to escape when the black hearse, drawn by sleek grey horses, turned into the road.

She couldn't stay and watch the flowers being placed around the coffin which held her Gran's body. Relief was all that Lizzie felt when finally it was all over. Aunt Daisy was grey-looking and tired, and Nellie had cried so much she was unable to speak.

Lizzie did her best to console them and later it was she who coaxed her mother and her aunt to eat. When night came, Lizzie went wearily to bed, wondering if the terrible aching and longing for her Gran would ever ease. Saying her prayers, she still said, 'And please, God, bless Gran.'

Weeks had gone by when the letter from the solicitors arrived. No one, except Lizzie herself, was surprised to learn that Harriet Collins had left her house and all her worldly goods to her granddaughter, Elizabeth Louise Collins.

The special pieces of Gran's furniture John Hurley offered to store in his large shed. Wrapping the legs of chairs, tables and bureaux with sacking, he carefully stacked and covered it all. The rest was sold.

Once all the legal transactions of Lizzie's legacy were settled, there had been two hundred and forty-one pounds left to her, plus the settlement the developers had promised to pay when demolition of Silverdore took place. Her mother and her aunt persuaded Lizzie to put the whole amount into a Royal Arsenal Savings Account and forget about it until she was older.

By September, several things had happened in Tooting, all tied up together, changing the Broadway for ever.

A new market opened and Silverdore Terrace was destroyed completely. Once the clearance scheme started, it made great progress. The developers' intention was to build a cinema on the site. The surrounding ground would be a car park.

Lizzie went back only once more to see her little bit of countryside set back from the busy Mitcham Road. It'll be gone soon, she thought, and she felt angry at God for letting it happen and even more angry that He had seen fit to take her Gran. It was just a peaceful row of five white cottages, each with its own extremely long front garden full of flowers, but there simply wasn't anywhere else like this peaceful haven. Not in Tooting there wasn't.

Chapter Six

IT WAS BITTERLY cold out of doors and not much better within. The wind roared and found every nook and cranny. Windows rattled and curtains moved and the draught beneath the doors was enough to cut your feet off. Ice formed on the inside of the bedroom windows and still the snow didn't fall.

'Would be a damn sight warmer if it did snow,' Aunt Daisy said as if she were a weather expert.

The year of 1938 was only two weeks old and it had brought nothing but misery. Lizzie and Polly couldn't ride their bikes to school, not in this weather. The tram fare was a penny return but wherever they got off the tram, they still had a long walk. Southfields was such an awkward place to get to.

Polly stood with her hands spread to the kitchen range which, despite all Nellie's efforts this morning, was refusing to burn properly. A sudden gust of wind brought smoke swirling out into the kitchen. Usually, Lizzie was ready and waiting when Polly called for her, now she came into the room, flinging her woollen scarf twice around her neck.

'Oh, it's perishing upstairs,' she said, blowing on her fingers, putting on her gloves. ''Bye Mum, 'bye Aunt Daisy,' she called as the two of them went up the passage. It was a quarter to eight and it was still dark as they let themselves out into the street. It would be dark again by the time they reached home tonight.

Daisy wondered just how long her loving niece with the soft blue eyes and long fair hair would be able to stand the pace. She worked so hard, persevering at her homework every night, determined to be at least within the top ten girls in her class. As she had remarked to Nellie over the Christmas holidays, their Lizzie was far too thin. Her arms were so frail and her legs were like sticks, and just lately she had developed a dry cough.

Lizzie wasn't looking forward to going back to school. She had earned the respect of her teachers with her academic achievements and admiration from her classmates for the way in which she excelled on the sports field. Only Miss Dawlish remained a thorn in her flesh.

At first her mother had been reluctant to attend the school nativity play, in which Lizzie had been cast as an angel. On numerous previous such occasions, Nellie had been only too aware of the headmistress's condescending attitude and had been hurt by it. The audience had loved the show, jumping to their feet and applauding loudly as the whole cast took the last curtain call. It should have been such an enjoyable evening and Lizzie knew how proud her mother was feeling. She had, however, watched with dismay as Miss Dawlish approached her mother, manoeuvring her into a corner of the hall with great skill – expert that she was! Lizzie was fuming, knowing there was nothing she could do. By now, she was used to her headmistress's ruthlessness – but her mother was not.

Kind and compassionate herself, Nellie was nonplussed, not understanding this educated woman's self-assurance and worldly attitude.

'The old bitch,' Lizzie muttered aloud, 'she certainly picks her time.' But it was typical of the woman – the bigger the occasion, the more important Miss Dawlish felt. Lizzie was trembling as her headmistress turned away and her mother came towards her.

There was an uneasy look on Nellie's face, but she forced herself to smile and took hold of Lizzie's hand. No reference was made as to what had taken place, yet Lizzie could see that her mum was confused and had been thoroughly embarrassed by whatever Miss Dawlish had chosen to say. Unforgivable. That was Lizzie's reaction.

One day, she vowed. That woman will get her come-uppance – arrogant old cow!

All went smoothly that first day back at school. Lizzie hadn't been singled out at assembly by one of Miss Dawlish's barbs although she had fully expected to be. And her form mistress showed great kindness and concern about her.

At break time, Polly and Lizzie had decided to stay in the classroom. Lizzie shivered as she held her handkerchief over her mouth, trying to quell a fit of coughing. Miss Lemkuler looked into her pupil's face and felt pity and admiration. It was a shame that this girl came from such a poor home, but in spite of this she worked hard and was determined to make something of her life. To some extent she understood Miss Dawlish's attitude; so many girls from working-class families had been forced to leave the school without completing their education. Places in good schools should only be allocated to pupils whose parents could afford to keep them there until they were at least sixteen years old. Education, according to Miss Dawlish, was wasted on the poor of this world, and it was not in her nature to make an exception.

'You shouldn't have come to school this morning, Lizzie, if you are unwell,' said Miss Lemkuler, as she placed her hand on Lizzie's forehead.

'I'm all right,' said Lizzie abruptly. Then, involuntarily, she let out a cry as a pain shot through her side.

Miss Lemkuler calmed Lizzie down and sent Polly to the cloakroom to fetch her outdoor clothes. 'You are to go home and go straight to bed,' she said.

It was more than an hour later that Lizzie, dragging her feet, came down the front garden path. Aunt Daisy met her at the door, asking no questions. She flung her arms around Lizzie and led her into the kitchen. Within minutes, Lizzie had her face bent over a steaming bowl of boiling water to which Daisy had added Friar's Balsam, with a Turkish towel covering her head, and soon Lizzie was sweating profusely.

By the time Nellie arrived home from work, Lizzie was seated in a chair in front of a roaring fire. She was pale and silent, all her pains eased for the moment. A wad of thermogene wool had been placed on her chest by Aunt Daisy, kept in place by two strips of red flannel.

Two bricks, heated in the oven, and a stone hot-water bottle were carried upstairs and placed in Lizzie's bed. Nellie made her a cup of Oxo and told her to stay by the fire and give the bed a chance to get warm.

Three days later, and still Lizzie did not feel well.

'I think you should take her to see the doctor,' Daisy said as she and Nellie stood gazing at the sleeping Lizzie.

Nellie tucked the bedclothes tightly about Lizzie and sat beside her. 'If only she'd eat,' she whispered.

'Come on now, let's go to bed and make up your mind to get her to that doctor tomorrow. She'll be fine, you'll see,' but Daisy spoke without conviction.

The waiting-room was depressing. The lower half of the windows were crudely painted with dark green paint, keeping out almost all available daylight. A single gas bracket set on the wall to the left of the black iron fireplace struggled to burn brightly but only succeeded in casting gloomy shadows.

The buzzer sounded for the third time. 'Come on, dear, it's our turn,' said Nellie. Two old men moved their feet and one woman sneezed and shook her head as they walked by.

'Do we have to go in?' whispered Lizzie furtively. She was scared of doctors.

The surgery was more brightly lit and infinitely warmer. Doctor Pike did not bother to stand up, just raised his head from the book in which he was writing, and silently motioned Nellie to sit in the only available chair. It took only minutes for him to examine Lizzie. Blushing, feeling awkward, she stood before him in her vest, knickers and black woolly stockings.

'Deep breath . . . breathe out . . . say ninety-nine. All right, get dressed.' Turning to Nellie, he almost recited, 'Not enough sleep. Not the right diet. You might try her on cod-liver oil and malt; she needs building up.'

Washing his hands at the small sink in the corner of the room, Doctor Pike half turned and added, almost as an after-thought, 'Perhaps you should take her to St James's. I'll write a letter; it won't take me a minute.' Licking the flap, he sealed the envelope and passed it over to Nellie, saying, 'Outpatients, tomorrow morning, eleven o'clock.'

The consultation and advice cost two shillings.

Coal and food were expensive and money was short, so it fell to Daisy to take Lizzie to the hospital, whilst

Nellie was away doing her morning stint at the Dawsons.

That awful smell of carbolic! The long draughty corridors, loud footsteps ringing out on the stone-tiled floors, people in white coats hurrying in all directions. Shunted from one cubicle to another, Lizzie was weary. She had coughed so much, her chest was sore and her very bones ached. Lying now on a high metal couch, covered by a red blanket, she just wanted to sleep. Aunt Daisy pulled aside the curtain that divided one cubicle from the next, bent over and smiled lovingly at her niece. Lizzie stared at her with penetrating blue eyes, 'What's happening? Are we going home now?'

Daisy hesitated, her own eyes glistening with tears. 'They want to keep you in, Lizzie.'

'What?'

'Sh!' said Daisy. 'You mustn't get excited.'

Lizzie was shaking visibly and her big eyes looked at her aunt full of pleading, wanting to be taken home.

A sister-in-charge came. 'Now then,' she said, 'we'll put you into a chair and get you up to the ward.' Her voice was soft, but unwavering.

The kitchen was crowded. People seldom popped in and out of Nellie Collins's house. She didn't encourage them. Now Jackie Jordon and his wife Doreen stood by the fireplace, Mrs Beasley from number nineteen with her youngest baby cradled in her arms, Alfie Brown, the street bookmaker and his runner, Tommo, all were there. All had come to commiserate because young Lizzie had tuberculosis.

'Christ, that's infectious, that is,' wailed Nora Beasley, ''as it affected both her lungs?'

Neighbours and friends were all very well, but Nellie wished they'd go home. She appreciated their kindness but – but what? She hadn't really taken in what Daisy had so patiently explained.

All she knew, her Lizzie had been kept in hospital. Dare-devil, tomboy Lizzie had consumption. She'd seen it coming and shut her eyes to it.

'It's all my fault,' she reproached herself. 'I could see her getting thinner every day, and what did I do about it? Nothing! Oh, it's not fair, it's awful.' She backed away as Doreen Jordon tried to console her, took refuge in the scullery and gave way to a flood of tears.

Lizzie remained in St James's for six weeks. Her mother visited daily, and Aunt Daisy came with Kate Hurley when visiting times were allowed. John Hurley came up some evenings bringing Polly and young Syd with him, but they were only allowed to see Lizzie and wave to her through the window. No children were allowed in wards where patients had infectious diseases. Even adults had to don white masks which covered the lower half of their faces.

One day, two doctors endeavoured to explain to Lizzie why she couldn't go home. Instead, she was being transferred to a sanatorium.

Pinewood Sanatorium was at Wokingham in

Surrey, but as far as Lizzie was concerned it might just as well have been hundreds of miles from London. She had never seen anywhere remotely like it. She was settled into a room with just four beds, white walls and ceiling and white-and-black tiled floor. The curtains and bedspread and draw-around screens, all matching, were made from a flowery material so pretty as to delight the patients, and seeming to bring the garden into the room.

It was not a bit like the many-bedded ward she had just left. Through the wide-open windows, Lizzie could see a view that was unbelievable. As far as the eye could see there were trees; tall, stately, dark green pine trees. She had hidden her head beneath the bedclothes last night and cried herself to sleep. She didn't want to go to no rotten sanatorium, miles away from London, with no visitors – not even her mum.

A fresh-faced, smiling young lady gently placed a tray on the table which straddled Lizzie's legs and propped her up against a great mound of pillows. The smell of the cooked lunch was good and suddenly Lizzie realized she felt hungry.

It wasn't going to be so bad here after all, she told herself as she picked up her knife and fork.

Chapter Seven

AFTER WHAT, TO Lizzie, seemed endless examinations and tests, she was back in her bed. 'I feel sick,' she moaned. A nurse ran forward, grabbing a dish from the shelf; she held Lizzie's head whilst she vomited into the bowl. Then she wiped her mouth and laid her back on to the pillows.

Lizzie began to cry. She felt frightened and lonely. Had she been abandoned by her family, sent to this place out of the way? It wasn't fair. It wasn't her fault she'd got tuberculosis. Why, if she had to be ill, did it have to be something that was catching. In despair, she began to thrash about. The nurse came back over to her; gently she sat on the bed and drew Lizzie's head to her breast.

'There, there now, darling,' she said. 'Susan's here. I'll stay with you.' She rocked Lizzie to and fro and stayed with her until she sank into a natural sleep.

The next morning, after breakfast, the nurse Lizzie now knew as Susan draped Lizzie's dressing-gown around her shoulders. 'You look beautiful,' she told her, adding, 'and that's good, because Doctor Bennett is coming to see you.'

Lizzie looked startled. 'I haven't got to have more things done to me today, have I?' she asked.

Before Nurse Susan had time to reply, a jovial-looking young man approached the bed. He towered above Lizzie, smiling broadly, his hands in the pockets of his white coat, a blue striped shirt open at the neck.

Lizzie snuggled deep into her pillows, fear showing in her eyes. 'What are you going to do with me now?' she demanded to know.

'Tell you my name first,' he said, drawing a chair up close and taking hold of Lizzie's hand. 'You had a rotten day yesterday, didn't you?' Lizzie made no reply.

'Well, never mind. My name is Stephen Bennett. I know yours is Lizzie Collins and I am going to be looking after you.' Still Lizzie made no comment. She wasn't in a chatty mood this morning.

After a moment of tension, he nudged her with his elbow, leant forward and winked. 'Tell you a secret. I've only been here three days longer than you have. I don't know anyone and Nurse Susan doesn't cuddle me to sleep like she did with you.' Susan blushed scarlet and Lizzie stared at him in astonishment, dumbfounded as to how he knew about that.

'Come on, Lizzie,' he said casually, 'be my friend.'

'Well,' Lizzie appeared to be considering it, 'not till you tell me what else you're going to do ter me.'

The doctor stared at her and she stared back. Then he grinned. 'It's a deal,' he said, holding out his hand which Lizzie solemnly shook. 'Usually, when people are ill with tuberculosis, we have to give one of their lungs a rest. So, we do an operation which cuts the cord holding the lung up and it collapses. To keep the lung rested and to enable the patient to breathe, we pump air into it. Artificially we do the work the poor old lung would be doing if it wasn't so poorly.'

Lizzie's eyes had never left his face while he had been relating these details. Now she moved away warily. 'Well, you ain't gonna do that ter me,' she said.

'Let me finish, Lizzie,' he pleaded. 'All that business we put you through yesterday told us you don't need an operation.'

'Thank God for that,' Lizzie exclaimed defiantly. 'So can I go home now?'

Across her head, the nurse looked at the young doctor and they smiled at each other and he said, 'We've got ourselves a real bright spark here.' To Lizzie he begged, 'Be patient, there's a good girl.' Then, with a gentle expression on his face, he told her, 'You have fluid on your right lung and you need to stay with us for quite a while. Still, we shall get you into a healthy routine and you'll find out that those of us who work here are not such a bad lot. You might even come to like us.'

His lips were smiling as he finished and his eyes had a mischievous glint in them.

After several days had passed, Lizzie was well aware of the routine, though she was astounded to learn that she would still have to spend at least six more weeks lying in bed. At eleven o'clock each morning either Susan or Linda (Linda being the other nurse assigned to Lizzie's room) would stand over her as she swallowed a raw egg. Even beaten up in a glass with milk added, Lizzie found it revolting.

To follow was a section of a fresh orange on to which halibut liver oil had been dripped. Lunch was at one o'clock. By two o'clock, complete silence. 'Break it if you dare,' the red-headed freckled-faced Linda had warned Lizzie, though a smile had lingered about her lips as she spoke. Not a soul moved anywhere until four o'clock.

At bedtime, one of the nurses would command, 'Open wide', and two spoonfuls of Gee's Linctus would be poured into her mouth. Never did she have to settle down to sleep without a good-night kiss.

The two nurses liked her and Lizzie liked them. They giggled with her and made fun of Sister Cartwright, who bustled in and out of the ward, her eyes taking in everything, but who really was a nice old softie. They told her humorous stories about the doctors and they showed her affection. It didn't stop Lizzie missing her mum and Aunt Daisy or Polly, and as for her brother Syd, who was more often than not a little devil, she missed him like hell; but when Susan and Linda were around, she didn't feel quite so lonely.

Visitors were allowed once a fortnight on Sundays. When Nellie Collins had received the visitor's pass

she had sighed deeply and sought advice from
Daisy.

'I could just about scrape the coach fare together
but that would mean going empty 'anded,' she dolefully told her sister-in-law.

' 'Lotter good that would do our Lizzie,' said
Daisy, ever the practical one. 'No. Get together the
things we know she likes, some embroidery or knitting to keep her occupied and fer Christ's sake don't
forget her books. Toc H will let yer 'ave as many
books as yer want.'

'Then what will we do with them? Cost a fortune
to post a parcel like that,' Nellie's voice almost
broke. She was very upset.

'We'll take 'em up to the Elephant and Castle on
the tram. Stop worrying. It'll be all right. You'll
see.'

Come Sunday morning they were up and ready
early. Syd was sent to spend the day with Connie
and Bill.

'Wind's still cold,' Daisy warned, 'we'd both
better put a scarf on.' Then they were off to catch
the tram from the Broadway, each carrying a heavy
parcel.

An inspector at the bus station pointed out the
coach. 'Runs right into Pinewood grounds it does,
missus,' he told them. 'Fare's four and six each.'

Nellie couldn't bring herself to make the request,
but Daisy was not to be put off. 'That's what we
come 'ere for,' she muttered to herself as she

approached a group of drivers. 'Excuse me,' she
called, 'which one of you drives the coach going to
Wokingham?'

'I does, as it 'appens,' said one of them, separating
himself from his mates. 'What can I do fer yer, luv?'

Daisy hesitated. He was a big, red-faced man,
smartly dressed in his uniform overcoat, a white silk
scarf knotted at his throat.

'You wouldn't oblige me, would yer?' she got out
at last. 'Take a parcel for me niece? She's down there
in the Sanatorium.'

'Don't yer want ter make the trip, lady?' He could
have bitten off his tongue as soon as the question left
his lips. Nellie had come to stand alongside Daisy.

Two more forlorn-looking long faces, Ted Baker
told himself, he hadn't seen in many a long day. Yer
silly sod, he chastized himself, they ain't got the
money for the fare. God, he wished it was up to
him. He'd have them on that coach all right, and
bugger whether or not they could pay. 'I'll take it
fer yer with pleasure,' he said.

'There's two parcels,' Nellie spoke quietly.

'All the better, luv. What's the young lady's
name?'

'Lizzie Collins,' they answered in unison.

'Well, if yer Lizzie comes ter meet me coach, I'll
tell 'er you both send yer luv, shall I?'

'She's confined to bed,' Nellie said with a sob in
her voice.

'Well, never mind. This is me regular run. Nurses
are used ter me 'anging around fer two hours every

other Sunday, give me a cup of tea, regular as clock-work they do. They'll see your Lizzie gets her par-cels all right.'

'Mister, you're a good sport,' Daisy said.

'No trouble at all, darlings, and if yer want ter make it a regular thing, yer know every other Sunday I'd be more than happy ter oblige.'

'Please, have this for your trouble,' Nellie said, holding out a sixpence.

Ted Baker told his mates afterwards that a lump the size of a billiard ball filled his throat then. His big hand gently closed round Nellie's, curling her fingers inward over the coin. Kindly he whispered, 'Put it away, missus. I might need someone ter do me a good turn some day.'

They lingered long enough to watch the coach pull out from the bus station, a sad-looking pair. Daisy, a healthy buxom woman at least four inches taller than her sister-in-law, looked neat and tidy in a well-fitting brown costume with a lace-collared cream blouse. She worried about Nellie and wished that she had been able to afford to pay her coach fare.

'I miss Lizzie so much,' Nellie said, as she groped in her bag for a handkerchief for she was blinded by tears.

'I know yer do, luv, but she's in the best place. We'll have her home soon, you'll see.' And as she uttered the words, Daisy silently prayed that they were the truth.

Lizzie was thrilled. Fruit, boiled sweets, a new face flannel and lovely scented soap were in one parcel, and in the other were wool, knitting needles and a nice slip-over pattern, which had been cut out from *Woman's Own*, and there were lots of books as well!

'Look at all the letters you got,' cried Nurse Susan, as she tidied Lizzie's bed. 'Well, I'm off for my tea now, I won't be long. Don't go getting too excited.'

When she had gone, Lizzie began reading. One letter was from Mr and Mrs Hurley, who now signed themselves, Aunt Kate and Uncle John. That was nice. One was signed by several of the neighbours, and enclosed were four stamps. One was from Connie and Bill with a postal order for two shillings.

Tears trickled down her cheeks as she read the next one. 'Be good now, whippet. Eat all your food and take your medicine because I want to see you fat with rosy cheeks when I come home.' Oh Leslie, so far away in Malta.

She was slightly put out as she read one her mother had received from Miss Dawlish. 'We do wish Lizzie well, her classmates miss her, as does the entire staff. Such a bright pupil of whom I have great hopes.' Had she misjudged her headmistress all these years? Lizzie doubted it!

The longest letter was from Polly. 'Soppy old thing you, Lizzie, getting ill like that,' was how she started it. 'You'll never guess; I've got a boyfriend.

Fred Holt is his name.' Lizzie brightened up a bit as she scanned the pages. A good laugh was Polly, and a good friend. She read on, 'The Granada is open, you'll have to come when you get home. Expensive, though. Costs ninepence downstairs. Fred took me upstairs. You have to walk through a hall of mirrors. Costs one and threepence. Reginald Dixon was playing the organ in the interval. You know, we've heard him on the wireless. He plays in Blackpool Tower. Oh yeah, and everyone going into the pictures that week got a free stick of Blackpool rock. Want a lick? – HA, HA! Seemed funny though, Lizzie, going to the cinema built on the place where your Gran's house used to be.' Not funny, thought Lizzie, as she folded up the letter, real sad.

Lizzie had had a bad week. It started on Monday. Nurse Susan and Sister Cartwright had pulled the curtains around her bed, sat her up and removed her nightdress.

'Knees up my lovely,' said Sister Cartwright, 'lean forward, head down.' Her voice was kindly, but the determination was there.

Two older doctors talked *about* her, but not *to* her and Lizzie didn't like that. Doctor Bennett appeared, smiling broadly, his fair hair tousled, in need of combing; he winked at Lizzie as she raised her head. Tap, tap, the doctor's fingers beat along her ribs.

'Ah, there it is. Just a little prick, Lizzie,' he said casually. It wasn't. It hurt like hell and Lizzie cried out. Both Nurse and Sister held her hands.

'Be brave,' Susan whispered, 'it won't be long.'

It seemed to take hours and Lizzie got hot and flustered. One tall doctor loomed over her. 'All over, child,' he said. 'Look, we struck gold.' He held aloft a large syringe, the tube of which was filled with a murky yellow fluid. He patted her head and moved away with his colleague.

'Please, Nurse, may I have a drink?' Lizzie pleaded.

'Of course you may, pet,' said the motherly Sister Cartwright, pulling Lizzie's head towards her ample bosom. 'You've been a good, brave girl. You will get better now that the doctors have got that nasty fluid off your lung.'

Sister was right. Two weeks later and Lizzie was up and about. She was weak as a kitten at first, and the nurses laughed at her first attempt to stand. Her legs buckled beneath her. Dressed in a navy-blue skirt and neat white blouse, with shoes on her feet for the first time in weeks, Lizzie was ready to leave the main building. She was going to the camp.

Long rows of wooden huts, partitioned off to give each patient a single room, set in the heart of sweet-smelling green pine trees. All through the woods tracks had been cut and laid over with cinders. Each room had a large window in the outside wall, but no pane of glass. Whatever the weather, there were no shutters. If it rained too heavily, beds were covered by a tarpaulin.

Exercise, rest, and good food was now the order

of the day. Walking the cinder tracks between the tall pine trees was a morning routine. Each week the distance was extended. The afternoon two-hour bed rest was still obligatory. Twice a week, patients listened through headphones to a recorded message. 'Your illness probably started with a common cold,' the voice droned on, 'built up to bronchitis, developed into pleurisy, thus causing tuberculosis. The remedy is to eat fat. FAT builds up bodily resistance. It is good for you; you must eat it.' Lizzie vowed that she would.

The rooms on either side of Lizzie were occupied by young girls, for which Lizzie was grateful. In the main building, her room had held, besides herself, three older, very sick ladies. Nice enough, but not very companionable. Twenty-five-year-old Mary Gibson had a fresh, healthy face and didn't look at all ill. 'Blimey, she's young,' had been her first words when introduced to Lizzie. A proper cockney lass, was Mary. Do I speak like she does? Lizzie wondered after a day or two, and promised herself she'd try to do better.

Anne Caxton was almost twenty. Just the opposite from Mary, slightly frosty at first. Her eyes were deep brown and framed by long, stiff black lashes. Her expression was discouraging, as she eyed Lizzie up and down. Happily, she thawed as the days passed and Lizzie was pleased to have two friends.

Lizzie, arriving at the gate to pick up her weekly parcel from the coach driver, stopped to listen to what the older patients were saying.

'There is going to be a war,' said a tall, educated-sounding lady.

'Yes, you can bet on it now,' said another.

'We shall all be sent home,' a third patient told the group, as if she were privileged to prior information. Lizzie liked the sound of that. The thought of the country going to war didn't particulary worry her.

The coach turned in at the gates and came to a halt with a squeak of brakes. Ted Baker and Lizzie had become friends and, as the door of the coach opened, he grinned down at her and gave her the thumbs-up sign, nodding his head backwards. She looked in the direction he indicated and was flabbergasted. Her brother Syd was kneeling up on a seat, his nose pressed flat against the window. His eyes were wide and he was grinning like a Cheshire cat. In the gang-way, crushed with passengers, was her mum. Further down was Aunt Daisy. Lizzie was over-joyed. She jigged up and down on the spot. She couldn't believe it, she had visitors.

Nothing could spoil that day. They had a picnic in the woods, Lizzie showed them her room and took them to the main building to meet Nurse Susan and Nurse Linda. The time went all too quickly. Suddenly the bell went, summoning them back to the coach.

'Don't forget to say thank you to Ted Baker, will you Lizzie,' her mother said. 'Heart of gold that man's got, his mates too. It was them that helped us out with the fare.'

Ted Baker brushed aside Lizzie's thanks. 'See you in two weeks,' he called, as the coach door closed. Lizzie ran alongside waving until her arm ached.

'Crikey,' Mary said, 'you've got real nice folk, ain't yer?'

'Yes I have,' Lizzie agreed.

The patients didn't get sent home and England didn't go to war. Prime Minister Neville Chamberlain went to Germany to talk to Adolf Hitler. He was sincere in his efforts, and came back waving a piece of paper, saying, 'Peace in our time'.

At first Lizzie was disappointed not to be going home, but not for long. November came and Lizzie was much better. Now she could go home!

The ambulance came to a halt in Graveney Road, and when the doors had been opened it seemed to Lizzie that the whole street had turned out to welcome her home. Tears choked her. What a homecoming, what a surprise! The strong, tanned arms that lifted her down belonged to her eldest brother Leslie. His service of seven years in the Army was over. He had been given his discharge. Lizzie was happy, so happy! What a wonderful Christmas this will be, she told herself.

And it was.

Chapter Eight

ANOTHER NEW YEAR. 1939.

The papers were full of dire predictions and most people hoped they were exaggerating. Many others knew war was only a matter of time.

Leslie Collins was amongst those who were not lulled into a false sense of security by the words of Neville Chamberlain. Council offices were offering Anderson Air Raid Shelters free of charge and Leslie collected one. The erecting of this caused so much interest amongst the neighbours that the local paper sent a reporter to investigate. Come Friday, Leslie's picture was in the local paper. With Syd beside him, their shirt-sleeves rolled high above their elbows, they stood beside this ugly, weird monstrosity which now stood deep in the backyard. Both brothers had blond, almost white hair, masses of tight curls which hugged their heads and which they both hated. Their teeth were also alike. The top rows were white and even, the lower ones showing gaps.

'Lucky that is;' said Nellie, 'if you can put a sixpence between your teeth' (and both of her sons could) 'you were born lucky,' she insisted. They differed only in height. Syd, at fifteen years old, was already almost as tall as Leslie.

'Like his father,' Daisy remarked, 'gonna top six foot, you see if I'm not right.'

'Hope so,' said Syd. He badly wanted to get into the Army. If war did come and he was really tall, he could put his age up and get away with it, he told his mother. Nellie shuddered at the thought.

Lizzie didn't go back to school; she got a job.

Spring came and the trees on the Common were loaded with blossoms. On Whit Monday Leslie took them all to Hampstead Heath. Folk loved the Heath on a bank holiday because of the fair. Lizzie was breathless as she enthusiastically threw her last wooden ball at the elevated coconuts.

'Hopeless you are,' Syd told her, pushing her aside. Syd threw each ball with grim determination. He struck with his third attempt and Lizzie shrieked with delight as the coconut fell to the ground. Syd ran to retrieve his prize.

The stallholder put in a replacement. 'You're good you are, sonny,' he said, as he patted Syd's head.

'Yeah, bowl for England he might one day,' yelled an admiring onlooker.

Leslie and Bill treated them to rides and Lizzie found the swing-boats exciting. 'Pull harder,' Syd ordered, as the swing began to soar. Boys were hooting with laughter as they watched from the ground. Girls' dresses were billowing high, giving glimpses of petticoats and legs in silk stockings.

Mum and Aunt Daisy found them and said it was

time to eat. Families were flocking to the grass areas for picnics. Hard-boiled eggs, ripe tomatoes, cheese sandwiches, Swiss jam roll and fruit cake – everyone tucked in; Daisy poured tea from two vacuum flasks and there was lemonade for those who wanted it.

As they left the Heath, music still blared out from the merry-go-rounds. Shrieks and squeals still mingled with loud shouts of laughter. London families were still enjoying their bank holiday.

No gloom and doom talk of war. It had been a smashing day.

The sun had shone for weeks on end as if to defy the bad news. 'We definitely will have a war,' said John Hurley as he passed the official letter back to Leslie.

It was the beginning of August, only eight months since Leslie had been demobbed. He was to report to Aldershot. He was on the first-reserve register.

Seven days later, and again the local paper carried a photograph of Sergeant Collins who was receiving new recruits, known as militiamen, into Aldershot Barracks. Two weeks after that he was home again, this time on a forty-eight-hour pass.

'Remember, sleep in that shelter,' he repeatedly told Nellie, 'don't take chances.'

'Oh, they won't bomb London,' cried Aunt Daisy, wanting to evade the subject altogether.

When Leslie went back to barracks the goodbyes and hugs were emotional. Daisy had lost a fiancé in the last war and memories flooded back. Nellie's heart was full of fear as she held her first born. Syd made a joke, 'Have a uniform ready for me,' but Connie wiped away a tear and Lizzie locked herself in the bathroom. She didn't want Leslie to go away again and couldn't help herself. She had to cry.

Sunday morning, 3rd of September.

Folk were out on their doorsteps and all front doors were flung wide open. Those fortunate enough to own a wireless set had the volume turned full up, blaring out for all to hear. Big Ben chimed, then struck eleven o'clock. There was a silent air of expectancy throughout the whole street.

'It is with regret that I have to inform you a state of war now exists between ourselves and Germany.' Neville Chamberlain's voice came over the air with a feeling of finality.

The silence remained in the air for a full minute. Maurice Smith from the other side of the road broke it. 'What the 'ell did we go through the last bleeding lot for?' he stormed aloud. Everyone glanced at the pinned-up left sleeve of his jacket. It was twenty-two years ago that he had lost his arm in the First World War. His next-door neighbour let out a strangled yell of rage and then everyone began talking at once.

'Oh, the poor kids,' wailed Doreen Jordon, 'they'll all have to be evacuated.'

'I'll join up, soon as I can,' vowed Syd.

'Oh Christ, my Bill will 'ave to go,' Connie said, brushing away tears.

'What the 'ell is that?' The question came from several mouths as the air was rent by the wailing of the sirens.

'Bloody eerie, ain't it?' said one old woman.

Nellie gathered her family together and took them back inside the house. 'Let's hope it's only practice,' she said as she filled the kettle and got down the flask in readiness for the air-raid shelter.

But it was a false alarm, and soon the moaning, long drawn-out, all-clear sounded.

'We're all right now,' Daisy said calmly.

Nellie offered up a silent prayer and made the tea.

Children up and down the street were saying their goodbyes. Labels hung round their necks stating their names and addresses. Carrier bags held their sandwiches and gas masks in cardboard boxes hung over their shoulders. Women threw their aprons over their heads so that their tears wouldn't be noticed as teachers marshalled groups down the road. The street seemed different after that. Abandoned, clean and tidy, and far too quiet.

To top the lot, council workmen came with lorries to take down the iron railings which had adorned low garden walls, and dismantle the chains which had hung for years between posts. Wrought-iron ornamental gates were wrenched from their hinges and all were carted away.

'What the 'ell is going on?' residents wanted to know.

'It's to help the war effort,' was the only explanation the elderly council men could give.

Weeks turned into months and all the young men were getting called up. Connie's Bill went into the Navy and Leslie was back with his regiment in Malta. The new year came and wartime in London became a reality. Food was rationed, coal was short, fresh meat and fish were hard to get and corned beef was a handy substitute. Every single thing was rationed. The Ministry of Food dealt with the issuing of ration books. Fawn coloured books for adults, green coloured for children under five years of age.

Rationing made life hard for wives and mothers and rows brewed up in shops.

'Whatcha mean, I've had me tea ration?' they would shout.

'I dunno what the world's a coming to,' grumbled another. 'Not a bit of sugar in the 'ouse an' she says I can't 'ave any for another four weeks. A bloody month, mind you!'

Life was tedious. Stockings were hard to come by. Sally Silverman's stall in the market looked dull, dusty and empty.

'Only got lisle ones ter offer you gals,' Sally miserably told them.

'Not even fully fashioned, are they?' Polly asked.

'No, love, fully fashioned they ain't. Turn them inside out, cut the edges from round the heel why don't cher? That way they don't look so bad.'

'They don't look so good either,' grumbled Polly.

Silk stockings from Sally had cost one shilling a pair since God knows when, and they'd been fully fashioned. Now she wanted one and ninepence for lisle ones. They hated this boring old war; they hated the blackout and were already sick to death with shortages.

The last few days of May 1940 were like a nightmare. Rumours were unbelievable. France had fallen to Germany. British troops were stranded on the beaches of Dunkirk. German planes bombarded the helpless men. The sea lay in front of them, German troops behind them.

Old men stood in the Selkirk Pub and cried openly in frustration as they listened to the news on the wireless. The obscenities they yelled did little to relieve their anger.

Boats of all shapes and sizes were put to sea. Men who hadn't navigated a vessel for years volunteered. The Navy did their bit, under horrific conditions thousands of men, not only British soldiers, but French and Belgian also, were plucked from those beaches. Trip after trip was made and men still cried. Some were speechless with shock. A mass of dead bodies covered the beaches, with more floating gently in the sea. Yet it had been a miracle, the evacuation of Dunkirk.

Britain now stood alone.

Not long afterwards the bombing of London began. Night after night the sirens wailed the warning. Deep shelters in parks and on commons were filled with families. Hundreds more made for the Underground stations, sleeping on the platforms. Young and old alike endured the hardship, too nervous to be above ground where bombs were falling and the noise of anti-aircraft guns was deafening.

Lizzie got home later each evening. She had landed a good job as a ledger clerk with A. T. Hart, the quality butchers. With the outbreak of war, she, along with all the clerical staff, had had to leave the comfort of her office and come out into the shop, serving customers, wrapping meat, marking ration books and taking money. Because of a shortage of staff she sometimes had to work in different shops. For three weeks now she'd been in the Chapel Street shop. It was near the London docks, an area that was a prime target for the German bombers.

Sure enough, they came over early one evening. It was the roughest raid so far. Incendiary bombs rained down and flames shot high into the air; clouds of dust rose up and the acrid smell was choking. Lizzie walked over London Bridge, coughing and spluttering, her eyes were red and sore. Air-raid wardens and policemen were everywhere.

'Where yer making for?' someone asked her.

'Tooting,' Lizzie managed to mutter.

'Come along, this way,' a hand guided her.

'Buses are few and far between, but you might be lucky. Tube stations are all closed,' volunteered the warden.

'Thank you,' Lizzie blubbered, just wanting to get home.

The next morning, Lizzie awoke with a headache and sore throat. She staggered downstairs into the kitchen and gratefully sipped the tea that her mother had made for her.

'You'd better stay home today,' Nellie insisted.

'All right,' Lizzie croaked.

She pushed aside the plate of toast Aunt Daisy offered, but held out her hand as her aunt said, 'There's a letter for you.'

At that moment Polly pushed open the door and burst into the room, waving a buff-coloured envelope. 'Snap!' said Lizzie, waving her identical one. She tore open the envelope and a long whistle escaped from her lips.

'You too?' Polly asked. Their letters were the same. Call-up interview, Thursday, two p.m., in the Central Hall.

In just two weeks' time, they would both be eighteen.

Smiling slightly, the woman on the other side of the table agreed to interview them together. 'Stay calm,' Lizzie told herself. There was no way she was going to go into the Forces.

'How about munitions?' the posh voice asked.

'Oh no!' Polly looked at Lizzie and they both shuddered at the thought.

'Work in a factory?' was the next suggestion.

'Never!' they both agreed.

'How about the ATS? At a later date, of course,' the genteel lady offered.

'Me dad says it will be all over come Christmas,' said Polly defiantly. 'We ain't gonna go in no army.'

'We shall see,' the woman sighed. 'Meanwhile, these forms have to be completed.'

The interview wasn't going at all well. The lady took off her spectacles and rubbed the bridge of her nose. 'Land Army?'

They both gagged at the thought.

'The trams or the buses?' she put forward in desperation.

The two girls giggled. 'Don't fancy the trams,' said Lizzie, 'buses might be all right.'

'Yeah. Nice uniform they have on the buses,' said Polly.

Relief flooded through the interviewer. She was anxious to be on her way. London in the blackout was no place to be.

'So, I'll state your preference for war work with London Passenger Transport,' she said, writing on the forms, not waiting for an answer.

They contained themselves until they were at the bottom of the stairs, then the pair of them fell about laughing. Boisterously, they punched each other, 'We're gonna be clippies.' The very thought brought forth more laughter which echoed loudly against the tiled walls. Swiftly they ran out into the Mitcham Road. Who'd have believed it? They were

going to help the war effort, they were going to
work on the buses.

Chapter Nine

THREE WEEKS' TRAINING at Chiswick, on full pay, had gone remarkably well – except for one incident.

Alan Cooke, a retired driver, having served twenty-four years at Shepherd's Bush Garage, was in charge of the class. Twelve girls in all, Lizzie and Polly going to Merton Garage, the others to various depots.

What Alan Cooke didn't know about schedules wasn't worth knowing. Tall, good-looking in a rakish kind of way, he fancied he was God's gift to all women – even at his age. At break-time, Lizzie was unusually quiet.

'What's the matter?' Polly asked, as she set two large mugs of tea down.

'I can't stand that man. He's 'orrible,' said Lizzie.

'Why? What's he done now?'

'He pinched me nipple.'

'You're joking!' Polly couldn't help it, she laughed out loud.

'So you think it's funny, do yer? Well I 'ope he does it to you.'

'I'll bloody kill 'im if he tries,' said Polly, her temper rising.

During the afternoon session, Polly kept her eyes on Mr Cooke. He approached Lizzie, coming up from behind. Leaning forward, he placed his two arms over her shoulders, supposedly to check what she was writing. Quick as a flash, Polly was out of her seat. Between thumb and fingernail, she pinched a lump of his backside, giving it a good, hard nip.

He sprang backwards and let out a cry of pain. His instinct told him it was Lizzie's mate who had attacked him, but he couldn't prove it.

'He won't try his tricks on you again in a hurry,' Polly said with a satisfied smirk on her face as they walked to the bus stop.

'You're a bitch, Polly,' Lizzie laughed as she spoke. 'Did you notice he didn't sit down all the afternoon?'

They ran up the road, giggling as they went.

They left Chiswick the proud owners of a full uniform. A leather shoulder bag with two compartments, and a wooden ticket rack completed their issue. How neat they looked – Lizzie, small-boned, fair complexion, her long hair tucked into a snood; Polly, tall and slim, her dark hair cut to shoulder-length and worn with a fringe. Their only complaint was that the serge trousers were itchy.

Six weeks later, and they had taken to their war-time job like ducks to water. Both girls were on the same shift, but not the same route. Lizzie loved the job, she liked meeting people, but she did get tired.

The grimness of each day seemed to get worse. The air raids were becoming a habit, a fact of life accepted as an inconvenient annoyance but no more than that. Even the stories of bombed factories, direct hits on shelters and folk losing their homes didn't shock people as it had at the beginning of the war.

Lizzie, and many like her, began to think that it was safer to be in the open during a raid, rather than huddled up below ground. It was bad enough coming home by tube late at night. At Tooting Broadway, the whole platform seemed to be a tangled mass of humanity, huddled together, no room to turn, let alone move about. The stench of bodies was awful. Once clear of the arms and legs, Lizzie would run like a wild hare. At midnight, steel floodgates would slam shut and folk sheltering below were then entombed until the next morning. Lizzie couldn't bear the thought.

Finally, she decided she had had enough of their Anderson shelter. If she had to spend one more night sleeping against the damp wall, listening to Aunt Daisy snore, her mother sucking boiled sweets and old Mrs Ticehurst, whom Nellie had taken under her wing, cluck away at her loose false teeth, not to mention the lapping of water under the floorboarding and that horrid musty earthy smell, she'd go mad.

When she got home, she went straight upstairs to bed. Nellie objected, then pleaded. 'You'll be killed,' she wailed.

At least I'll die in comfort, thought Lizzie as she snuggled down in her clean, comfortable bed. She ignored the gunfire, the searchlights, which criss-crossed the sky and lit up her room, even the bombs, and had her first good night's sleep for months.

'About time we saw a bit of life. Never go anywhere now do we?' Polly sounded right fed up.

'Two toast and cheese,' Elsie called from behind the canteen counter. Lizzie rose and went to fetch her snack.

'You were a long time. What were yer talking to Elsie about?' Polly wanted to know.

'A night out for us, actually,' Lizzie said, wrapping up the large piece of cheese and putting it in the pocket of her overcoat. Her mum and Aunt Daisy looked forward to the bits and pieces she smuggled out from the canteen.

'A night out where? The last one didn't turn out so well,' grumbled Polly.

They had been on early shift, so one evening they had gone up to Rainbow Corner at Piccadilly. Talk about the League of Nations! Yanks, Canadians, Australians, Poles. The dancing was all right, they certainly didn't lack partners; it was the close clinches that bothered them.

'Elsie said troops are moving on to Garratt Green.'

'So?'

'Whatcha mean, so?'

'Well, what difference will it make ter us?' Polly grunted through a mouthful of rissole.

'Fairlight Hall is putting on a dance Saturday night, you know, to welcome them.'

'Only be a gramophone. Bet yer life they won't have a band.'

'Oh, for Christ's sake, what's the matter with yer, Polly?' Lizzie asked in desperation.

'Sorry, Lizzie,' Polly said apologetically. 'Don't mind me, I'm just having one of those days.'

On Saturday night, they fished out their high-heeled shoes and long skirts, made up their faces and curled the ends of their hair with hot tongs and went off to this sevenpenny hop at Fairlight Hall.

Lizzie looked across the hall at a dark-skinned, blue-eyed, wavy-haired lance corporal and fell head over heels in love. She felt good in her long black skirt and pretty pink chiffon blouse as she danced close to her new-found friend, whose name was Charlie Wilson.

Polly was getting on well with his tall, lanky friend, who was called Frank. So well, in fact, that when 'In The Mood' came blaring from the gramophone the two of them gave an exhibition.

Their bodies were as one as they matched their steps to everyone's favourite quick-step. Partners fell back, leaving Polly and Frank a clear floor. The record came to an end and they hugged each other, hot and sweaty as they were. A burst of clapping showed admiration and Polly blushed.

'Who's Taking You Home Tonight', was the last record to be played and couples dreamily danced the waltz with the lights dimmed. Charlie sang, his lips close to Lizzie's hair, "I'm pleading, please let it be me."

The four of them left the hall together Polly and Frank lingered in Garratt Lane, and Lizzie yelled back, 'We're going on, Polly. I'm on at a quarter-past five in the morning.'

'All right,' came Polly's reply, 'see you tomorrow'.

Charlie left her at the gate. He hadn't attempted to kiss her and Lizzie was disappointed.

'We'll be here for a while. I shall see you soon,' he promised, and Lizzie hoped it was a promise that he would keep.

On Wednesday when Lizzie finished her shift at one-forty-five at Tooting Bec, Charlie was there waiting for her. He bent down and gave her a swift kiss.

'Okay, Lizzie?' he asked as natural as you like, as if they had known each other for years.

His uniform was well pressed and you could see your face in the toe-caps of his boots. Lizzie gave him a lovely smile and he smiled back.

Catching her in his arms, he swung her in the air. 'Oh, I haven't been able to get you out of my mind, Lizzie. I want to spend every spare minute I get with you.'

Lizzie laughed; she liked his authoritative tone. He went back to the garage with her, waiting while she paid in her day's takings, then they walked all the way home to Tooting, talking non-stop.

Her mother and her aunt warned her to be careful. 'Take things slowly, please,' Nellie pleaded. 'Couples rush to get married in wartime and live to regret it,' she wisely told Lizzie. Their words were wasted.

Eight wonderful weeks and she had been with him wherever possible. Now, as the leaves on the trees began to turn beautiful shades of red and brown and the evenings drew in, Charlie came to say goodbye. His battalion of the Royal Artillery Corps was moving on. On the doorstep Lizzie snuggled close and Charlie covered her lips in a long kiss. It was wonderful. It was different from all the others kisses, long and passionate.

'You will write to me, won't you?' Charlie begged.

'Of course I will, darling,' Lizzie promised.

'If I get a long leave, will you marry me?' he asked.

'Yes, oh yes,' she answered, her eyes wet with tears.

''Allo, Lizzie. Long time no see.'

Lizzie's face broke into a smile as she punched the threea'penny ticket and handed it to Sadie Braffman. 'How's yer mum?' she asked.

'She's better. Misses me dad a lot though.'

'Yeah,' Lizzie muttered thoughtfully. 'A lot of people do.'

Bernie Braffman had been a great character and had had two stalls in the market for years. Lizzie had stood at the corner of Blackshaw Road and watched his funeral procession pass.

One bystander had uttered a statement that had struck in Lizzie's mind. 'In this life, you're as rich as the number of friends you got. Well, Bernie Braffman was a rich man.' What better epitaph could a man have?

'You finishing now?' Sadie asked as she watched Lizzie pick up her ticket box from underneath the stairs.

'Yep. Thank God. Not a bad duty, this one though. Six-three out of the garage in the morning, finished now at Tooting Bec twelve-forty-five. Two journeys to Shepherd's Bush, only one up to Crystal Palace.'

'Come and 'ave a cuppa coffee with me?' Sadie suggested hopefully.

' 'Course I will, can't stay long, though. Gotta pay in at the garage.'

They sat facing each other across the oil-cloth covered table in the steamy cafe, while Lizzie sipped her coffee and Sadie poured out her troubles.

'It's no joke 'aving to cope with two stalls,' she complained, staring fixedly at Lizzie, her stout body pushed tight into a grey costume which emphasized her ample bosom. Her jet black hair and olive skin were lovely, her best features really, thought Lizzie, who found herself feeling sorry for Sadie without really knowing why.

Lizzie listened attentively and made noises of encouragement. 'What's ter do, I don't know,' Sadie went on. 'Since my brother David got called up and me dad's gone, I 'aven't opened the bedding stall.

It's not worth it. Coupons for this, dockets for that, queues at the warehouses and what for? Nothing. You wouldn't believe it.'

Sadie paused for breath, 'I have to keep the grocery stall going, don't I? 'Asn't been too bad so far, but now, staff I can't get. Not a soul. I tell `yer, Lizzie, a man I wish I was. Off ter the war I'd be.' Then she shot a question at Lizzie out of the blue, 'Have you finished for the day?'

'Yes, I told you already.'

'Same time all the week?' asked Sadie.

'Till Friday,' Lizzie told her. 'Saturday and Sunday rosters are different.'

'Oh, Lizzie,' Sadie practically shrieked, 'you could help me out no end.'

'Me? How?' But already Lizzie suspected what was coming.

'Do a few afternoons on the stall with me, and what about when you're on late turns, a few mornings, eh? You'll do a few mornings maybe, then?' The worried look on Sadie's face tore at Lizzie's heart.

'Well, I'll give it a try. Nothing definite, you know. See how it goes.'

'Oh, d'yer mean it?' Sadie said and, to Lizzie's embarrassment, she flung her arms round Lizzie's neck and kissed her noisily.

So now Lizzie had two jobs.

It was pouring with rain when Lizzie came out of the garage. Wearing a long mac, with her hair covered by a scarf, she looked tired and dejected. All she really wanted to do was to go home and get into bed. Instead, she was doing a stint up at the market this afternoon.

She shouldn't grumble, she told herself. In the couple of months that she had worked for Sadie, she had done pretty well. Sadie was grateful, kind and generous, and what's more, they had a good laugh most of the time, especially when Polly was able to do a turn on the stall as well.

Lizzie was pleased to see her sister Connie in the scullery when she pushed open the back door. Short and sturdy, bursting with energy, she wore a smart, long dress. Being pregnant suited Connie.

'Hallo, love,' she smiled and greeted Lizzie warmly. 'Mum told me what time you'd be home. I've boiled some potatoes and I've got a tin of pilchards. You 'aven't eaten in the garage, 'ave you?'

'No,' Lizzie answered, 'I wasn't gonna bother.'

'I really wanted ter tell you about our Syd,' Connie said as she vigorously beat at the potatoes in the saucepan with a fork.

'Why? What's up with Syd?' Lizzie sounded angry.

'All right, all right,' said Connie, trying to calm her.

A few weeks before, the police had been round. Syd and his mates had stolen a bike. Since Bill had been called up, Syd had lived with Connie. It was better than being on her own, Nellie had decided.

''As he been a nuisance or 'as he been pinching again?'

'Nothing like that, 'onest Lizzie. Give me a chance. The fact is,' Connie hesitated, 'he's run off. Gone to join up.'

'What?' roared Lizzie. 'He's too bloody young.'

Connie plopped a spoonful of mash on to the plates, which each held two pilchards, then spooned the tomato sauce from the tin over the fish. Lizzie felt afraid; Syd could be a right little sod, but he was their young brother, the baby of the family. Trouble was, he looked so angelic. He could lie through his teeth, smiling all the time and folk believed him.

She ate her lunch without really enjoying it and was grateful when Connie cleared away their plates.

'Well now, what's Sadie got to sell that's special today?' Connie asked, as Lizzie pulled her trousers off and stepped into a brown tweed skirt.

'Dunno till I get there. Might be Camp coffee,' she suggested.

'Well, whatever, don't you go overdoing it, love,' Connie said kindly, 'and don't start worrying about Syd. What's done is done, and there is nothing we can do about it now.'

'Does mum know?' asked Lizzie.

'Yes, she does, and she didn't take it too bad.'

Lizzie wrinkled up her face. 'Poor old Syd,' she said. 'He's not so bad, you know; I hope he's got a guardian angel.'

There was a lively atmosphere in the market that

afternoon. Most of the stalls were open and each seemed to have something to offer because queues had formed everywhere.

'Marvellous, ain't it?' one woman remarked to Lizzie as she counted out her change. 'Now there's plenty of work about and we've gotta bit of money, the things ain't around to buy any more.'

Tommy Clarke's stall had oranges today and young women with babes in their arms, toddlers in push-chairs and prams waited patiently. Old Tommy served them from an open wooden crate only if they had green ration books. Oranges were only for the under fives. Probably the first time some kiddies had ever seen one.

Mrs Scott, seventy if she was a day, resolutely kept her son's hardware stall going. Today she had a few Axminster rugs but the supply would run out long before the queue had dwindled.

Sadie's voice was persuasive as she walked the length of the line of women who clutched their canvas and paper bags. 'Custard powder, matches, some bottled coffee, Daddie's Sauce, even a few Chivers' Jellies we've got today. So, spend some ration points with us, please.' It was only by taking coupons and bundles of points to the Ministry of Food that traders were able to obtain dockets which enabled them to replenish their stock from the warehouse.

Lizzie had just finished serving old Maggie Watson. She was a good customer, with a houseful of daughters and children, and she had at least a dozen ration books. Women gazed in envy as she packed jars of jam, packets of sugar and tea into her bag.

Sadie smiled sweetly and, turning to Lizzie, said, 'Let Mrs Watson 'ave another coupla jellies. A lot of children she's got to feed.'

'Fanks, Sadie, yer a sport,' said Maggie Watson, handing over the extra coppers to Lizzie.

'Next, please,' Lizzie called, after having paused to blow her nose. Her mum stood in front of her.

Nellie passed a dog-eared fawn-coloured ration book over to her daughter, saying, 'I'll 'ave all that's going and a tin of spam, please, don't think there's enough points left for anything else.'

Lizzie placed a packet of Foster Clarke's custard powder, a large bottle of Camp coffee, Scott's porridge oats, one jelly and one box of matches on the counter. 'Sorry, mum,' she said, 'all the Daddie's Sauce has gone. I want twelve points for the spam, please.'

With scissors in hand, Lizzie bent her knees and cut the strip of points marked C from the ration book and let them fall into the already overflowing tin, which was on a shelf beneath the counter. Flicking through the pages, Lizzie found what she already knew, no tea coupons, no sugar allowance, no soap docket. She hesitated. Then, with grim determination, she straightened her back and got up on to her feet. Boldly, she took two quarter-pound packets of tea down from the shelf, a two-pound bag of sugar, two tins of spam and a tablet of Lux toilet soap. Setting the lot down, Lizzie quickly totalled up the amount. 'Five and tenpence ha'penny, please, Mum,' she said, handing back the ration book, and reaching for her mum's shopping-bag in which to pack the goods.

'See yer later,' she said cheerfully to her mother, getting in return only a nod and a frosty stare. The queue moved up and Lizzie worked on.

Lizzie felt done in as she opened the front door. Hardly had she got inside the house when Nellie started.

'What d'yer think yer up to? Eh? You knew we didn't 'ave coupons for those things,' stormed Nellie.

'So I gave you a few extras, that's all.'

'That's all!' her mother yelled. 'Yer could go ter prison, so could I, so could Sadie!'

'She never meant no harm,' cried Aunt Daisy.

'Don't you side with 'er,' Nellie turned on her sister-in-law. 'You weren't there. Bloody awkward I felt.'

'You took it all though, didn't you?' Lizzie retaliated.

She regretted this remark immediately. Her mother went berserk.

Lizzie had had enough. 'Right,' she screamed, as she let her fist come down so hard on the table that the cups jumped. 'Put it all in a box and I'll take it back to Sadie in the morning. I'll tell 'er what I did. All right. That satisfy you?'

Silence. Silence so great you could cut it with a knife.

'Well?' Lizzie yelled so loudly that her mother and her aunt backed away. 'Well?' Lizzie repeated as she watched her mother shake her head and wring her hands.

'She can't,' Aunt Daisy said quietly.

'She can't what?' demanded Lizzie.

'Give it all back. Yer mum's given some of it away.'

Nellie put out a hand. 'Don't be cross, Lizzie,' she implored.

'Jesus Christ,' Lizzie muttered, gazing at her mother with perplexity. 'One minute you're gonna kill me, next yer tell me not to be cross. I don't believe this. So go on, tell me.'

'Well we didn't need the coffee. Not now we've got the tea. So I let Mrs Gregory have it.'

'And?' Lizzie asked loudly.

'Well, old Mrs Durrel's only got one ration book, living on 'er own. I gave her a tin of the spam.'

Lizzie looked across at her aunt. Daisy was having a helluva job controlling her amusement. She winked at Lizzie. That did it.

Lizzie suddenly saw how comical it all was. It was like a slapstick scene from the Saturday concert. Her hands flew to her mouth, but it was no good, laughter bubbled out and Aunt Daisy joined in.

The relief was apparent in Nellie's voice as she said, 'How about a nice hot cup of tea?' It was too much. The last straw. There hadn't been any tea in the house for the last three days, and wouldn't be now if it wasn't for this afternoon's do!

Chapter Ten

THE JUNGLE OF London's back streets now showed signs of being war-torn. Where once panes of glass had let the daylight into houses, now there was darkness. Windows shattered by bomb blasts weren't replaced, merely boarded over.

The raids tended to be lighter now and mostly on the coastal towns. People became complacent and none more so than Lizzie – until one night the droning of the incoming bombers throbbed menacingly once again. Bombs streamed down from the sky, one landing with a thud which shook the houses but did not explode.

Lizzie didn't realize just how near it had fallen until she left the house just after four o'clock the next morning. She found a scene of activity. In the darkness, torches flashed, voices came from all directions.

'Hoi! Don't go down there,' shouted an air-raid warden but his voice only panicked Lizzie into hurrying faster. Reaching the corner of the road, she came to an abrupt halt, trembling and unable to move she stood rooted to the spot.

The unexploded bomb had torn into the end wall of the first house. Its nose was embedded, its fin tail protruding at least two feet. Voices yelled at her from the darkness.

'Move. Come on, yer silly cow, move yerself,' a cockney voice boomed out.

'Cross over to the other pavement and walk towards me, slowly,' instructed a voice firm with authority.

Lizzie did move slowly, praying as she went, 'Please don't let it go off.'

Safely round the corner she wanted to be sick. Nothing had prepared her for this. Half of Selkirk Road had gone. Just a pile of rubble remained. Lizzie stared, speechless with shock, terrified for Polly and the Hurley family.

By some miracle, their side of the road had only caught the blast. 'Thank God,' she murmured; and again, 'thank you, God,' as Aunt Kate and Uncle John came towards her, dusty and battered, but otherwise unhurt. Now Lizzie began to cry, her legs were trembling. 'Where's Polly?' she whispered.

'It's all right,' Aunt Kate told her, 'she's been taken to hospital. She was cut a bit by the flying glass.'

Hardly had the mobile canteens moved off and the firemen rolled up their hoses, having hosed down the blackened framework and steaming bricks, than the sirens were wailing again.

At ten minutes to eight, the Bendon Valley Laundry suffered a direct bit. Only those who were late for work that morning escaped. Over seventy women, including Mrs Baldwin, Connie's mother-in-law, were killed in that raid.

Later the same day, the Bomb Disposal team safely defused the unexploded monster and carted it away on an army lorry. The gaping hole in the side wall of the house was crudely repaired.

A sad silence settled over the district for several days but life went on.

London became fairly quiet after that, as the air raids became far less frequent.

Connie gave birth to a seven pound boy, whom she named William after his father, and everyone was sad that Bill's mother had not lived to see her grandson.

Lizzie was doing very nicely financially. She drew her wages from Sadie and put them into her Post Office Savings Account. There were weeks when she was also able to save a substantial amount from her bus wages. This was because of spreadovers.

Crews took the buses out from the garage very early in the morning, carrying office cleaners and factory shift workers. The next couple of trips would be for the office workers. Then, to save petrol, the buses would be parked in the City, and the driver and conductors travelled home by tube train. They had four to five hours' free time before going back to collect their bus and doing the homeward runs. For these split duties, wages were paid from signing on to signing off – as much as thirteen hours for some duties. Lizzie was surprised at just how much she had managed to put away.

She was also surprised at the speed with which Polly decided to get married.

Polly had been badly shaken when Selkirk Road had been hit by bombs and had been allowed to leave her job on medical grounds. She had become good friends with Arthur Scott, who had lived in the same road all his life, and whom she knew quite well. It wasn't until Arthur was invalided out of the Army that Polly and he became interested in each other. He was a strongly built young man, aged about twenty-two, with broad shoulders and thick forearms. His reputation had always been tough and there was a rawness about him that made Lizzie feel apprehensive, but he and Polly seemed to suit each other well enough.

They had found a house to rent in Wilton Road, Colliers Wood, and had set the wedding date. The fact that Polly was pregnant probably brought the date forward.

The preparations for Polly's wedding made Lizzie feel quite envious. Charlie wrote regularly, but it wasn't the same.

There were sandbags piled up each side of the doorway at Wandsworth Town Hall, which slightly put the dampers on the wedding guests, but Polly looked lovely, her dark hair gleaming beneath the pale blue wisp of a hat she wore, and her bright eyes sparkling with happiness. The coupons for her cream-coloured two-piece had been begged and borrowed, but the outcome was worth it.

Arthur Scott looked quite presentable dressed in a suit, with white shirt and dark tie. He stood grinning as the registrar pronounced them man and wife. Suddenly Polly Hurley was Mrs Scott.

Wilton Road was only ten minutes' walk from Merton Bus Garage and Lizzie became a frequent visitor there. The house Arthur had found to rent was large and comfortably furnished. Lizzie loved it from the moment she walked through the door, even though most of its windows were boarded up. In the front room there was an open-ended sofa and two big armchairs, drawn up beside a blazing coal fire.

'Crikey,' said Lizzie, 'ain't you lucky? How long have you got it for?'

'Till the war ends, I suppose,' said Polly, shrugging her shoulders, 'but come on upstairs, I want to show you something.'

Polly flung a door open on the first landing, 'What about that then?' she cried.

Lizzie stared in amazement. 'A modern bathroom with a geyser an' all, oh, ain't you lucky!' she said again.

Seven months later, Polly gave birth to a tiny scrap of a girl. Strange how big, strapping Arthur was so gentle with the baby, and so proud of Polly. They named the baby Lucy, after his mother.

★

Lizzie picked her way carefully through the garage. She'd been on middle shift, having just paid in her takings. It was a quarter-past eight, no one was about and the great depot was eerie. Pitch dark. Because of the blackout, what few lights there were were covered by black tin shades with small slits to let through just a faint glimmer. Buses were shunted into position, ready for the morning, the concrete floor was smeared with petrol and diesel and the air smelt foul.

A man stepped forward, blocking her way, and for a moment Lizzie was petrified. The smell of the uniform told her it was a soldier. An arm stretched out and a familiar voice said, 'Hallo, Lizzie, my darling.'

'Charlie?' she asked with some apprehension.

'Who else meets yer from work and calls yer darling?' he answered and she knew he was smiling down at her.

'Oh Charlie,' she whispered, before his lips covered hers.

Holding her close, he said, 'I've got four days' leave before we take off again. I've been ter your 'ouse, yer mum said I can stay there.'

Four whole days, it seemed too good to be true. They clung to each other in silence until Lizzie said, 'Polly's is nearest, let's go and 'ave a cuppa with 'er and Arthur.'

Lizzie couldn't take her eyes off him as Polly busied herself making the tea. His mop of dark hair grew thick and curly at the nape of his neck and she longed to run her fingers through it.

Lizzie telephoned the garage and was granted leave. The next few days were bliss, every minute they spent together. At night, with Charlie lying so near in what was Syd's room, her longing for him grew. If only there had been enough time, they might have been married. If only . . .

Lizzie tried to take everything in her stride, but when Charlie left again, she felt very low. It seemed this war was lasting for ever.

They only got occasional letters from Leslie. The wireless told how the island of Malta was being bombed day and night. And young Syd was in Germany; they received a few airmail letters from him with many words crossed out by the censor.

Connie had left London, she and baby William were down in Plymouth. That way, whenever Bill got shore leave, he and Connie could be together. Like many other families, theirs was totally split up.

Lizzie's heart missed a beat when one lunchtime she got home and found not one letter from Charlie, but two. Aunt Daisy was away, doing her bit for the war effort (every afternoon she manned the mobile canteen on Balham Station), and her mum was busy ironing. Nellie took up another flat iron from the range, held it to her cheek, then spat on it, finally wiping it with a clean white cloth. 'Don't sit there musing over yer letters, Lizzie, open them, for Christ's sake!'

'I'll make us a cup of tea first,' Lizzie answered, playing for time.

Setting a cup down on the dresser, Lizzie said, 'Drink it while it's hot, Mum. I'm gonna take mine upstairs.'

Nellie sighed. Lizzie was such a good-hearted girl, a worker an' all. She proved that, but she didn't seem to have much luck. Life hadn't been that good to her so far, and Nellie hoped against hope that this Charlie was the right one.

Upstairs it was dark, chilly and drab in her bedroom. With the window boarded over for so long, she'd forgotten what it was like to be able to look out of the window, and with the wallpaper peeling from the walls it wasn't exactly the most pleasant of places to be. Lizzie lit the gas, lay on the bed and tucked the eiderdown tightly round herself.

The first letter was ordinary, saying how much he had enjoyed seeing her, thanking her mother and her aunt for putting him up. Only the last paragraph made Lizzie shiver with fear. 'God only knows when I'll see you again, Lizzie,' he wrote, 'we have been issued with tropical kit.'

The second letter was oh, so different. 'I love you, Lizzie,' was how it began. She could feel her heart thumping. The words were so sincere. A glorious feeling came over her; she closed her eyes and hugged her pillow.

They seemed to have had such a short while together and it was only from previous letters that Lizzie had heard about Charlie's earlier life. His mother had come to London from Scotland to be in service. She had died only days after he was born. No one had ever told him of his father and he had been brought up in a Shaftesbury Home for orphans near Blackfriars Bridge.

Now Charlie had opened up his heart to her and poured out his true feelings. He had been so moved by the sight of Polly and Arthur in their nice, clean, warm house and baby Lucy had been the icing on the cake for him. 'I've never had a family. Come to that, I've never had a home, not even a room of my own.' The words of his letter blurred as Lizzie's eyes filled with tears. 'Will it ever be our luck, Lizzie?' he asked. Sadness gushed through her. This rotten war, the loneliness, the longing, it seemed as if it was lasting a lifetime. 'Oh Charlie,' she cried, turning face down in her bed to muffle her sobs.

Later, she rinsed her face and hands under the cold tap in the bathroom and went downstairs to have her evening meal with her mother and Aunt Daisy. But her thoughts were miles away with Charlie. Come the end of the war, she'd have a home ready for him. A place that would be theirs, and they would have a family. She'd make it up to him for all those long lonely years.

By the time the day was over, she had made a firm decision.

She was going to buy a house.

Chapter Eleven

1943 CAME IN bitterly cold. Every single thing seemed to get worse, except for the fact that they no longer had to endure the Blitz.

All the STL registration buses disappeared from Merton Garage and were replaced by Daimlers. No longer were the passenger seats padded and upholstered. Rows of plain wooden benches had to suffice.

Lizzie, used to digging her knees into the sides of the seats in order to keep her balance when collecting fares, now found it much harder in more ways than one. After only one week, her shins were black and blue with bruises. 'Look on 'em as yer war wounds,' Polly laughingly told her.

Lizzie's bus route had also been changed as had her driver. She was now on the 118 which ran through Streatham Vale to Clapham Common. The route was mostly through nice suburban districts but in the Vale there were quite a few factories. Now her passengers were mostly young factory girls and women, her kind of folk and she liked the change a lot.

The Smith meters factory was on war work and the girls told Lizzie it was all very hush hush. And Payne's firework factory now made rockets and varicoloured lights for the Merchant and Royal Navy.

Pascall's sweet factory gave Lizzie the greatest laugh. 'God knows what their wartime turn out is,' she remarked to her mother one evening as she told of her day's work.

'But 'ow about this, Mum. One girl told me, if you go there on a Friday morning and take two pounds of sugar, yer can get a pound of boiled sweets or toffees in exchange.'

'Really!' Aunt Daisy butted in. 'But where does the sugar come from?'

'That's exactly what I asked her, Aunt Daisy. Who the hell's got two pound of sugar to spare? Seems some folk have, this girl told me. Big families mostly, I suppose. Still, she's promised ter bring me some off-cuts. Broken bits of sweets they are. They don't get many, but she said she'll try.'

'Cor, that would be nice,' said Nellie. The sweet ration was eight ounces every four weeks which didn't go far.

Also in Streatham Vale was the big cemetery and at its gates was a new double-fronted florist shop. Lizzie's new driver, Bill, jumped down from his cab and came round the bus to talk to Lizzie.

'I'm just gonna see if I can order any flowers from Mary. It's the wife's birthday next Monday. Ain't many flowers about anywhere, but old Mary seems to get hold of a good supply.'

Lizzie nodded and stood watching the queue of people board the bus and Bill walk over to the shop.

He was, or had been, a very tall man, but his shoulders now stooped and his uniform hung loosely on his lean frame. He should be enjoying his retirement really, Lizzie thought, even his eyesight wasn't all that good. Many a corner he turned with two wheels of the bus hitting the kerb.

Bill came out of the shop and Mary Chapman came with him, pausing only to lock the shop door.

''Allo Lizzie, my love,' Mary said as she heaved her great bulk up on to the platform. 'Christ,' she said, eyeing Lizzie from top to toe. 'This job ain't done you any 'arm 'as it gal. You look marvellous.' And she was right.

Despite the cold weather, Lizzie bloomed with health. Her skin glowed, her fine cheek bones had more flesh covering them and her long fair hair tucked into a lacy black snood shone through like golden corn.

'And rationing ain't made you any thinner, Mary,' Lizzie laughed as she pushed her towards a seat just inside the bus. Lizzie collected her fares and plonked herself down on the long seat next to Mary.

''Ere love, yer don't want a couple of days extra work, do yer?' Mary asked.

'Aw, gor blimey,' cried Lizzie, ''ow many more? I've got two jobs already.'

'Shame,' Mary muttered, 'I could do with someone like you. Knows hows ter keep her mouth shut.'

'I'm not with you,' Lizzie said, 'what's so secretive about your trade?'

'It's the shortages, ain't it? Funerals are like processions now. Sad, but a fact of life. Can't get any decent blooms and as fer the frames fer the wreaths, like bloody gold dust they are.'

'So, what can you do about that?' Lizzie wanted to know.

'Bribe the grave diggers of course,' Mary said. Lizzie looked startled. 'Don't hurt no one, you know. The dead can't see the wreaths, nor smell the flowers. They're only a comfort for the living. Soon as the relatives have gone, the old men pass the floral tributes through me kitchen window and I re-use the frames, even some of the flowers and most of the moss. God won't take umbrage over that, I'm sure.'

The look Mary gave Lizzie defied her to say otherwise. In spite of her misgivings Lizzie had to smile. Mary's sense of self-preservation was quite exceptional. Blame the war, she told herself yet again.

The bitter cold weather continued and the nightly black-outs made trips for pleasure almost impossible. It was weeks since Lizzie had heard from Charlie and she felt depressed. There didn't seem to be any bright spots left in her life.

She was awoken one morning by a piercing scream, a scream that she admitted afterwards she would remember for the rest of her life. She jumped out of bed and ran out to the landing.

Leaning over the banister, she took it all in at a glance and she felt her heart stop. The dreaded yellow telegram lay open on the linoleum. Her mother lay prone on the floor and Aunt Daisy was sitting on the stairs, silently rocking herself back and forth.

She didn't have to give a thought as to whom it was. Lizzie knew. She went bare-footed down the stairs, stepped over her aunt and picked up the flimsy paper. LESLIE COLLINS the words jumped forth. Killed in Sicily. What the bleeding hell was he doing in Sicily! Wasn't Malta bad enough? The lump was so large in her throat that Lizzie almost choked. Her chest felt as if an iron band encircled it, drawing tighter every minute. Her eyes and nose ran, and her ears ached.

Slowly, she went back upstairs, ignoring both her mother and her aunt. She couldn't console either one of them; her own pain was too severe. She loved Leslie so much and she would never see him again.

Then came one of the worst periods of the war. Hitler sent his doodle-bugs to England. Flying bombs without pilots – a mysterious danger droning their way through the sky, flames shooting out from their tails. Londoners raised their weary faces and stared in disbelief. Quite suddenly the engine would cut out, but it would not fall at once. On it would glide for breath-taking seconds before hitting the ground. Everyone held their breath, you could feel the unnatural silence. Lips moved and everyone prayed the same prayer, 'Please God, don't let it fall on us.' It fell elsewhere and people were safe – until the next time.

Aerial bombing had never been like this. The bomp-bomp, thud-thud of British anti-aircraft guns told people that their side was fighting back. Men and women had become defiant, cursed the Germans and got on with their wartime jobs. Now, with these buzz-bombs, they felt defenceless.

It was Sunday lunchtime and all three of them were at home. The sound of a single engine was suddenly immediately overhead. They froze. The heavy droning stopped. 'Down, quick, get down!' Nellie ordered, almost dragging Lizzie beneath the kitchen table. Seconds later, the kitchen door burst open, their last intact window blew in and dust and glass showered down into the passageway.

'Bloody Hitler,' yelled Daisy, forced out of her complacency for once.

They went out into the street. Black smoke and flames shot high above the rooftops of the houses opposite. The doodle-bug had dropped just two streets away. So near and yet, thank God, so far.

Lizzie would be twenty-one years old in August, and Nellie prayed that they would all live to see the day.

Summer came early. The lovely May days were really warm. Lizzie got compassionate leave from her job; she needed a break. *Gone With The Wind* was showing at the Mayfair Cinema and long queues formed to see it. Lizzie paid three and six each for three reserved seats and took her mother and her aunt.

Another evening Arthur's mother minded baby Lucy and he took Polly and Lizzie dancing at the Streatham Lyceum. Lizzie didn't really enjoy herself; she felt lonely. But returning home with these happy friends, she spied a 'For Sale' notice posted up on the front door of a house opposite. All her determination returned.

Wilton Road was a short cul-de-sac with a dozen semi-detached houses on the side where Polly now lived and only six large detached houses on the opposite side of the road. Colliers Wood was a very nice surburban district and Lizzie decided that she could do a lot worse.

The very next morning Lizzie took the tram to Wimbledon. William Fox & Sons estate agents obviously catered for opulent clients. The only sign of war was the scrim, glued tightly to the plate-glass windows and which obscured the comfortable office from the stares of passers-by. A portly, middle-aged man turned to greet her as she opened the door. A smile lit his face, a mass of fuzzy grey hair topped his head. 'Mr Brownlow,' he said, offering his hand.

Lizzie gave her name and explained that she was interested in the Wilton Road property.

'Ah!' he exclaimed. 'Come into my inner office, if you please, Miss Collins.'

Lizzie obeyed reluctantly, staring at him curiously as she walked slowly after him.

'Be seated, be seated,' he waved his arms towards

an armchair, then he turned his back on her and shuffled several papers from a cabinet. 'Are you in business, Miss Collins?' he unexpectedly asked.

'No,' she answered. Today, she wore an old, but still smart, pin-striped grey suit with a dusty pink tailored blouse. Her long hair hung loose, secured only on the side with two tortoiseshell combs. She wasn't about to tell this stranger that she was a clippie.

'Ah, ah,' he repeated in a low voice. 'Very wise decision,' he went on, 'to buy property at this point in time. Risky, but worth the gamble. Boys will be coming home. Whole streets of houses demolished. Thousands married in haste, nowhere to live.' He thumbed through the piles of leaflets now lying on his desk, his head bent low, his voice only a murmur. He might have been talking to himself. 'Terrible, terrible housing shortage come the end of this war,' he paused, raised his eyes to Lizzie, 'you mark my words.'

He sounded so kind, so reassuring, that Lizzie relaxed. 'Three properties in Wilton Road,' Mr Brownlow said as he held out the details. 'One, an executive sale. Number nineteen, owner in a nursing home, number twelve, family evacuated, decided to stay in Devonshire. Would you like an escort or shall I entrust you with the keys?'

When Lizzie felt she could get a word in edgeways and that Mr Brownlow was listening to her, she assured him she would be able to view the properties quite safely on her own. 'I'll bring the three sets of keys back to this office this afternoon,' she promised.

'How kind, how kind,' he repeated in his low voice as he handed Lizzie the labelled front door keys.

The first house, a few doors away from Polly, was nice and Lizzie was tempted. It was very similar to Polly and Arthur's but, being unoccupied, it looked dusty and wretched. The second one she dismissed straight away; there was too much structural damage.

The third one was on the opposite side of the road. Detached, with a large front garden and a circular drive, this looked like a rich man's house. Lizzie consulted her estate agent's list. Work had been started with the purpose of turning the building into flats, then abandoned.

She used the key and opened the front door. The hall was very long, with black and white ceramic floor tiles. The first room was enormous, with bay windows reaching from floor to ceiling and a huge fireplace with marble surroundings.

At the end of the hall, there was a wood-panelled dining room and, beyond that, a white-tiled kitchen. What she thought was a cupboard turned out to be a modern bathroom. That was wonderful!

The first floor had four rooms and an old-fashioned bathroom, complete with a copper geyser on the wall. The top of the house was a complete surprise. A door at the head of the stairs opened into a self-contained flat, just one large room, a small kitchenette and an alcove that held a toilet and a deep porcelain sink.

From up here, the windows looked down over a neglected garden where several shrubs still fought for survival. It also gave Lizzie a good view of the district and the River Wandle as it snaked its way through grassy banks. What couldn't I do with this place! I could make it pay, Lizzie told herself.

All the way back to Wimbledon, Lizzie was doing her sums. She found the offices of William Fox & Sons closed for the day. She slipped all three keys through the letterbox, glad to have time to ponder on things and make up her mind.

Indoors, Lizzie rushed upstairs and took off her coat. Excited now, she wanted to tell her mother all the news and sound her out over the ideas that were forming in her head.

Nellie was slumped in the chair, staring into space. A quiet 'Hallo' was all the greeting she gave Lizzie. In her lap lay a photograph of Leslie, and she sounded so depressed that Lizzie was alarmed for her.

'I'll tell you what,' she coaxed, 'come and sit nearer the fire while I make us a cup of tea, then I'll brush your hair for you. You always like that, don't you?'

Perched on a foot-stool behind her, Lizzie took out the many hair pins which held her mother's plaited hair in circles on each side of her face.

Then she unbraided it and began to brush her

mother's hair with long, firm strokes. Nellie sighed and closed her eyes and Lizzie's heart ached for her. Now was not the time to discuss buying a house with her mother. She would have to make her own decisions.

June came in wet and windy, a disappointment after the warm month of May. It was three days later when Lizzie, well wrapped up in her bus overcoat and with her hat pulled well down over her ears, braved the biting winds and went over to Wimbledon again. She shook hands with Mr Brownlow, who was obviously pleased to see her and made no reference to the fact that she was wearing the bus uniform.

By the time Lizzie had finished telling Mr Brownlow that if mortgages could be arranged she would like to buy number nineteen Wilton Road in her brother Sydney's name and number twelve in her own name, he was smiling at her with a drowsy, gloriously happy expression. Not much property was being bought. Not with this wretched war going on.

'Leave everything to me, Miss Collins,' Mr Brownlow said. 'First we should talk finances. Number twelve's asking price is £950. I don't think we can get the vendor to come down on that. Nineteen is a different matter.' He shuffled through his papers. 'Ah yes, ah yes,' he was repeating himself again, '£650. Too ambitious. We will make an offer of £500.

'Now, about deposits?' he asked.

Lizzie brought out her notebook and read from it, 'I could pay £250 on number twelve and £120 on nineteen.'

'Good, good,' he mumbled, as he wrote.

'Also,' Lizzie said, 'I would like to pay one year's mortgage on each property in advance.'

This statement did surprise Mr Brownlow, and he raised his eyebrows in question. 'I have quite enough money,' Lizzie assured him, 'and who knows, the war may well be over by then.'

'Indeed. Let us pray that it is, Miss Collins,' he answered, thinking to himself what an astute young lady he was dealing with.

Lizzie went to the same firm of solicitors that had dealt with her grandmother's affairs. They agreed she was perfectly entitled to use the amount the developers of Silverdore had paid over.

Within eight weeks she had signed contracts so that she and her brother Sydney were, in conjunction with the Abbey National Building Society, owners of two houses in Wilton Road, Colliers Wood.

Chapter Twelve

THERE WAS TO be more tragedy for the Collins family before the year of 1944 was out, for Hitler had one last surprise up his sleeve for the suffering Londoners. Deadly rockets, packed with explosives, were launched over the Channel. Because they were supersonic they gave their victims no warning whatsoever – no sound of engines, no rush of air, just the devastating explosions!

Lizzie was in Smith's the drapers in Mitcham Road when one landed on Tooting Bec Common. Luckily, she was only slightly hurt when falling masonry knocked her to the floor.

'What yer doing down there?' two air-raid wardens joked, as they shifted broken sandbags and helped Lizzie over the pile of debris.

'Well, me name wasn't on that one, was it?' she told them as she wiped the dust from her eyes.

But just a week later a rocket hit Balham Station. Aunt Daisy was killed outright.

Lizzie stood in the passage hugging her mother. Both of them were sobbing. 'Oh God!' Nellie cried. 'How much more can we take? I give up. I really do. I just want to die myself.'

Of course she didn't give up, but she raged in her

heart against the cruelty of this war, and her own suffering.

She and Lizzie, like everyone else, lived day by day, month by month, giving each what comfort they could.

The Allied troops had landed in France in June 1944, giving everyone hope that the war would soon be over. But the advance to Paris and beyond was painfully slow, with fierce fighting all the way. Many sons and husbands were lost and many tears were shed. Christmas came and went; it was 1945, and still the war dragged on.

One morning the alarm clock rang loudly and Lizzie, still muzzy with sleep, reached out and only managed to knock the clock to the floor.

'Damn and blast,' she said as she groped around in the darkness. 'Christ, it's only ten minutes past three.'

Still not fully awake she went downstairs and put the kettle on, lighting the gas beneath it. 'Damn,' she said again, as she held the empty tea tin. 'Oh well, if I sign on early enough, I can go into the cafe next door to sort out my ticket box and have a large tea and two slices of dripping toast at the same time.' She had a wash at the scullery sink and struggled into her uniform.

It was the first week in May 1945, still dark at that time in the morning, and still quite nippy, Lizzie decided, as she closed the front door behind her.

Rounding the corner she stood stock still. She was like a rabbit trapped in the headlights of a car.

She just could not move.

Not one, but two trams were standing at the Broadway. Both were ablaze with lights. From stem to stern, every window was unblacked. It could not be true. It had to be a vision.

'Run!' a voice yelled at her to get out of the way of the tram.

'Yeah, come on, run,' other voices chorused.

'The war's over', a deep-sounding response echoed again and again.

The war was over.

Germany had unconditionally surrendered to the western Allies, and the festivities began and continued for days. No one went to bed, street parties were the order of the day. Pianos were pushed out into the roads and were never short of a pianist.

Lizzie persuaded her driver to abandon their regular route and drive the bus to Graveney Road. He sat on an upturned wooden box outside number thirty, a glass of beer in his hand. Their bus, now parked by the kerb, was swarming with kids. They clambered over the wooden seats, they tore up and down the stairs, hung out of the windows and rang the bell non-stop.

And Lizzie did not give a damn.

Bonfires burnt all night; time had no meaning. For the first time in six years, folk felt free to laugh, sing, shout and to cry with relief. Many mourned their lost ones, others thanked God that their menfolk had been spared and would be coming home. For Nellie in particular, the deaths of Leslie and Aunt Daisy had left an unbearable sorrow and no amount of celebration could raise her spirits or comfort her heart.

Patching up the houses began. Boarding was taken down from the window frames and sandbags were removed. Holes in ceilings and walls had to be ignored for the time being. Some returned home, to sleep in their own beds for the first time in years.

But Japan still hadn't surrendered and the awful decision was made that brought about a swift and total end to the war. The first atomic bomb was dropped on Hiroshima on August 6th and, a few days later, a second bomb was dropped over Nagasaki.

'Jesus, Holy Mary,' whispered Nellie as she turned the knob to silence the wireless. 'It's beyond belief what man does to man in the name of war.' She turned ashen-faced to Lizzie, who was sitting silently, staring into the fire, tears running unheeded down her cheeks.

Charlie was coming home.

Lizzie flew about in a fever of anticipation. She had a bath and washed her hair and, wearing her favourite sage green dress, she paced the floor of the front room like a caged lion. She saw him through the window when he was halfway down the road – his cap on the back of his head, his kit-bag perched on one shoulder, his face deeply tanned. She opened the door and ran. The moment she reached him, he dropped his kit-bag and his strong muscular arms went around her.

'Oh, Lizzie, Lizzie,' he murmured.

Regardless of women on the doorsteps, children staring and the milkman in the middle of the road grinning broadly, they stood clinging to each other, lost in a world all of their own on the pavement of war-battered Graveney Road.

Clutching his arm tightly, they eventually went up the road and into the house. Once inside, they literally locked themselves together, their arms about each other, their bodies pressed close. 'Oh, God, I've prayed for this moment,' Charlie whispered.

When at last he released her, Lizzie was trembling violently. Nothing had changed. Charlie still had this extraordinary effect on her. 'I still can't believe it,' she cried as she put out a hand and touched the lean lines of his face and then ran her fingers through the dark hair which still clung in waves to the back of his neck. 'You really are home, Charlie!' she whispered.

Emotions ran away with them; they forgot about everyone except themselves. A discreet cough from Nellie brought them back down to earth.

'Welcome home, Charlie,' Nellie said with a sob in her voice. She was thinking of her eldest son who would never now come through that door.

Charlie walked forward and clasped her in a great bear hug. 'Thanks, Mum,' he said.

They were married five weeks later.

What a rush!

Sadly, Lizzie thought of Aunt Daisy, who undoubtedly would have made her wedding dress. Leslie, too, was uppermost in her mind, for it should have been him who walked her down the aisle.

In the end, it was Sadie Braffman who attained the unattainable – a wedding dress and veil for Lizzie, a cream linen suit for Nellie and a peach-coloured, floor-length dress for Polly who was to be matron of honour. Uncle John, gave her away. St Nicholas's Church was hushed as Lizzie at last became Charlie's wife. The guests were happy and Lizzie prayed that the dear ghosts whom she felt were truly present, were also happy.

Syd was coming home at last and, impossible as it seemed, he was already married! After days of waiting, the couple arrived.

Everyone stared open-mouthed at the slim, rather flashily dressed young lady with peroxide-blonde hair. She wore a bright red suit and a large black picture hat. A brilliant diamanté necklace hung at her throat.

Nellie's disappointment showed on her face as Syd introduced Doris as his wife. She was twenty-four years old, two years older than Syd, very shy and quiet despite her appearance and the fact that she had served five years in the R.A.F.

Lizzie liked Doris instantly. Syd had grown, now six foot two inches tall, but his gappy smile hadn't changed and his blond hair was even lighter. Syd had always been a bit of a devil; more than likely he had chosen Doris's outfit in order to shock. Lizzie understood him so well. Even now she could read him like a book and still she adored him. Doris's front teeth protruded slightly, but because of the frankness of her expression and the sparkle in her eyes, she exuded a bubbling attractiveness that Lizzie warmed to immediately.

Doris obviously liked Lizzie in return, for she said, 'It's nice to meet you; I've heard such a lot about you.'

Lizzie looked across at Syd. 'Don't believe all he tells you,' she said with a grin, 'we can be friends in spite of him.'

And they were.

Chapter Thirteen

AMIDST MANY PROBLEMS, they all moved into Wilton
Road and Lizzie carried on with her job on the buses
just the same.

Syd and Doris were fairly lucky. Number nineteen had had the carpets (such as they were) left
intact, together with several odd items of furniture,
so at least they had the basic necessities; and with
the dockets and coupons that they were allowed,
they set up a comfortable home.

Syd used his demob money to buy an open-
backed truck. He was down at the railway sidings
each morning before it was light, loading up with
hundredweight bags of coal. Touring the back
streets, he would sell the coal door to door, sometimes making two or three more trips when the weather was cold.

Polly and Arthur had now bought number seven
as sitting tenants, thus securing what had already
become a much-loved house with good furniture.
Arthur had been promoted and now had a good job
in the offices of a brewery firm at Morden.

Things were not so straightforward for Lizzie and
Charlie. The rooms at number twelve were vast,
the windows enormous. A utility bedroom suite,
obtained by docket, looked lost in the bedroom. It

was banished to the top flat, while Gran's lovely old pieces of furniture were brought out from Uncle John's shed and thoroughly cleaned. The elaborately carved side table looked well in the hall and two bedside cabinets went one in each of two bedrooms on the first floor. A hand-carved dresser fitted exactly into a corner of the top flat. Lizzie wished she'd saved more.

Beg, borrow, even steal if Charlie had his way, became the order of the day. Second-hand shops, junk yards and markets, everyone foraged for Lizzie. Syd threw thirty bobs' worth of lino off the back of the coal truck one morning. It was a god-send. Charlie cut and shaped it, fitting it into three ground floor rooms.

After a time spent cleaning and decorating number twelve, Charlie took a job on the buses at Merton Garage. He hated it. He hated the hours, the traffic, and most of all the uniform. But he loved the social side of bus life, especially the darts.

A buff-coloured envelope brought another set-back. Inside was a document stating that number twelve Wilton Road had to be registered under the Town and Country Planning Act. A visit to Somerset House was needed.

'No sweat,' said Charlie, 'a day up in town will be great. Go to a show, shall we, Lizzie?' he asked and she readily agreed.

Finding the registrar's department in Somerset House was something of a problem. Everyone in the building seemed hell-bent on rushing somewhere. At last, a kind, elderly gentleman with a thin face and rimless spectacles explained things. The Act had only come into being since the war and it only affected property costing more than seven hundred pounds.

Stamp duty now had to be paid according to a scale, which in the opinion of this legal-looking gentleman was not excessive.

A few moments later, he produced a seal with which he made an impression over wax on three sets of documents and indicated where Lizzie should sign. He looked up and said, 'The duty payable is ninety-six pounds exactly.' The bottom dropped out of Lizzie's world.

They didn't go to a show and Lizzie was very subdued all the way home. Her capital wasn't going anywhere near as far as she had hoped.

At least they had a double bed, which looked ridiculous standing in the centre of their enormous bedroom. All they had to hang their clothes on were nails knocked into the walls and Lizzie now felt these would have to suffice for some time to come.

She had let two bed-sitting rooms on the first floor. One to Paddy Betts, a tall, red-faced Irishman, and the other to a city-slicker type who travelled daily to Whitehall, a Mr Joseph by name.

The top flat had looked so homely and comfortable when finished that Lizzie had been tempted to move up there herself. Instead, she chose as tenants Hilda and Wally Saint, both of whom also worked on the buses out of Merton Garage.

'Oh, well,' Lizzie told herself, 'I will just have to keep our bedroom door locked so that the lodgers don't see we haven't got any furniture.'

Charlie didn't care two hoots either way. 'We have our bed,' he said with a wicked leer, 'what more can any man ask?'

What more indeed? Lizzie often asked herself.

She and Charlie had a relationship that was rewarding, full of warmth and certainly never dull. They had fun together, they argued and shouted at each other, they made love, and Lizzie counted her blessings.

One evening Nellie came in the back door, her face was red and her eyes excited.

'Hallo, Mum,' Lizzie called from the dining room, which only held a folding table and two wooden kitchen chairs, 'bring a cup through with you, I've only just made this pot of tea.'

Charlie stretched out on the hearth rug giving his chair to his mother-in-law. 'Had a win on the dogs, have yer, Mum?' he asked, winking at Nellie.

'No, I haven't,' she answered quickly. 'But I have found you a beautiful wardrobe for two pounds.'

'Two pounds! Crikey that's cheap,' exclaimed Lizzie.

'Well, that's what Mrs Dawson said you can 'ave it for.' Lizzie's hackles rose. The Dawsons again. Still her mother bowed and scraped to them.

'Must be rotten with woodworm if they're letting it go for two quid,' Lizzie said spitefully.

'Never mind her,' Charlie said, acting the peace-maker. He had heard all about the Dawsons and in a way he didn't blame Lizzie. Her mother did work hard for this family, had done for years, and Lizzie resented the fact.

They went to Balham in Syd's truck. Nellie and Lizzie squeezed into the cab with Syd. Charlie rode on the open back.

The Dawsons hadn't changed. They were just as Lizzie remembered them. Mrs Dawson, plump, big, towering over everyone, with hands that were podgy with gold rings on almost every finger. He, dressed in a dark suit, gold watch and chain stretched across his waistcoat, was as pompous as ever.

One glance at the wardrobe and Lizzie bit her tongue and kept quiet. She wanted it, very badly. Charlie paid the two pound notes and Mr Dawson helped Syd to dismantle this huge piece of furniture into three separate parts. Lizzie didn't believe what she was seeing and avoided looking at her mother who was smiling smugly.

Next morning, Lizzie had a rest day. She, Polly, Doris and Hilda Saint sat on the floor of Lizzie's bedroom. They were all seized with fits of the gig-gles. Each had taken a turn with a tin of Ronuck furniture polish and a yellow duster. The monster occupied the whole of one wall and was shining like a new dollar.

It was never meant for use in a modest home like Lizzie's. Each end section was a separate wardrobe with hanging space and footwear rails. The centre part had a full-length mirrored door, behind which lay glass-fronted drawers. Each drawer, and there were ten, held a slot-in label kept in place by brass fittings. Into the drawer marked 'Socks', Doris very solemnly placed four pairs belonging to Charlie. Polly then made a great ceremony of laying Lizzie's underwear into the space labelled 'Lingerie'. This set them off again, tears of laughter running down their cheeks.

'Well, you must admit,' Polly chortled to the others, 'it is a magnificent piece of furniture. Probably came from Harrods,' she added with a supposedly posh accent.

'One thing's for sure,' Lizzie piped in, 'I'll have ter work all me rest days if I ever hope to fill it.'

Within forty-eight hours Lizzie had added another great object to her room. She had swapped duties with another girl, just for the one day. Now on the 93 route there was a bus stop just outside a newly built parade of shops. A long queue of people moved slowly and Lizzie stepped down from the platform and idly looked at the window displays. A splendid sideboard caught her eye. 'Taken in part exchange', stated the Times Furnishing Company ticket.

Without regard for her passengers, Lizzie was in that shop before she could change her mind. 'How much?' she gasped to the astonished salesman. He must be dim-witted, Lizzie thought to herself, as he stared blankly at her.

She plucked at his sleeve and pointed at the side-board. 'How much?' she repeated.

'Er, five pounds,' he stammered.

Lizzie thrust a ten-shilling note at the now totally bewildered young man and fled, shouting back over her shoulder, 'Keep it for me, please. I'll be back about four.'

Lizzie's temporary driver wasn't too pleased with her, but she didn't care. They were late, the bus was overloaded with passengers and the one behind was half-empty. Lizzie collected fares, hummed to herself and pictured her new sideboard with its great ornate overmantle in her dining-room.

All she had to do now was to persuade Charlie to buy a couple of decent armchairs, or better still, a three-piece suite. Well, tonight would be the best time for that!

Time passed quickly and Lizzie wondered cautiously why she was so lucky. There wasn't a day that she didn't feel totally happy.

Doris and Syd were expecting their first baby. Polly's little Lucy had just started school. They spent evenings in each others' houses, playing cards or just talking.

Syd bought a television set. Well, he would! He would never alter – live for today was his motto, why bother to save, tomorrow could take care of itself. Doris was still a bit of a mystery to them all. Sometimes Lizzie thought she saw a scared expression in those lovely blue eyes.

'If Syd ever gets on ter yer, Doris, you let me know,' Lizzie repeatedly told her.

'No, I'm all right, really I am,' Doris would assure her. 'Syd is real good ter me.' That Doris loved Syd was only too obvious. In fact, what Lizzie feared was true, she was bewitched by him and even sometimes afraid of him.

Hilda and Wally Saint usually joined in their get-togethers and all eight of them would go off to other bus depots to watch two teams play darts. Charlie was the champion of Merton with Wally running a close second. When the game was over the fun began for the women, the home garage would supply food for a buffet, drinks would flow freely and, with any luck, the men could be persuaded to dance with them.

It was a good job that they went by a bus on loan to the darts team; the men were often too legless to walk to a bus stop.

Christmas was fantastic. All four families, friends and relations ate their Christmas dinner at Lizzie's. All, that is, except Doris. She was in hospital after having given birth to a bonny eight-pound boy. Lizzie went to the hospital on Christmas afternoon, armed with a bagful of soft cuddly toys for her new nephew, Raymond, and an expensive lacy night-dress for the sister-in-law that she had come to love so dearly.

The whole party had assembled in Polly's house by the time Lizzie got back and it was there that

Polly's parents and Lizzie's mum dropped their bombshell. They were going to Newquay in Cornwall to run an hotel.

At the end of the war, Connie and Bill had chosen to stay in Plymouth and they had only seen them and little William once since then. Lizzie felt like panicking. Was her whole family to be split up and scattered?

A distant cousin of John Hurley's had, before the war, bought a small hotel in Newquay, but she'd lost her husband in the war, had a bad stroke herself and was selling up. John and Kate had jumped at the opportunity and had talked Nellie into going with them.

'Don't worry, love,' said Nellie kindly, when all explanations had been given. 'I'm not giving up me house. I'm only going to help get the place ready, though I suppose I might stay for the first season.'

A smile crossed Lizzie's face, 'I can't see you, Mum, in a short black dress and frilly apron.'

'Don't be so cheeky. You want to save up and come down there for a holiday. Maybe next September, eh, Lizzie?'

'Yes, maybe,' Lizzie answered, 'but you haven't gone yet.'

Three weeks later, on a bitterly cold, frosty morning, Lizzie stood on the railway platform with Polly and waved until the train was out of sight.

'How d'you think they'll do?' asked Lizzie.

Polly screwed up her face, 'Dunno, bit old aren't they?'

Down the platform came a mobile canteen selling hot drinks and Lizzie immediately thought of her Aunt Daisy; she'd lost her, and now her mum had taken herself off to the back of beyond.

Still in a depressed mood, she suggested to Polly, 'Let's go and have a drink.'

Nearly an hour later they came out of the railway bar, Polly had drunk two gin and tonics and Lizzie had had two whiskys with dry ginger. Both girls were smiling now.

'Good luck to them,' Lizzie muttered.

'Yeah; that's it. If that's what they want, good on them for 'aving a go,' said Polly.

The next few weeks the weather didn't let up. Every day was bitterly cold. Already they had had snow, which hadn't cleared and the gutters were full of dirty brown slush. Nellie wrote each week, giving full details of how they were preparing Bay View Hotel for the coming season. She seemed determined that, come September, Lizzie and Charlie would be taking a holiday in Newquay.

At the end of February, Lizzie stood staring into their bathroom mirror, a satisfied grin spread over her face. A knock came on her kitchen door and she called out, 'Come in.'

'I thought I heard you being sick,' Hilda Saint said.

'I'm all right now,' said Lizzie in a clear, decisive voice, coming out of the bathroom.

'You haven't got the 'flu, have you?' Hilda asked.

Lizzie burst out laughing. 'Nothing could be further from the truth,' she protested. 'I'm on top of the world.'

Hilda stared at her and the truth dawned. 'You're pregnant!' she exclaimed.

'Yes, yes, yes,' cried Lizzie as she did a little jig around the kitchen, 'two months almost to the day'.

'How can you know that?' Hilda asked.

Lizzie smiled knowingly. That was a secret she was only going to share with Charlie.

In bed that night, Lizzie cuddled up to Charlie and reminded him. 'Charlie,' she whispered in the darkness, 'remember when you did a day's work on the 118s and we 'ad a row?'

Charlie had other things on his mind as he ran his hands up her smooth legs. 'We always have a row when we work together,' he said.

'Yeah, I know, but that was different. Oh, leave off, Charlie!' she protested as he tried to silence her by placing a hand over her mouth.

'Oh, all right then.' He gave in and half sat up, resting back on his elbows. 'Get to the point,' he insisted.

Lizzie switched the bedside table-lamp on, nestled close and kissed his rough, whiskery face. 'You need a shave.'

'For Christ's sake, Lizzie!' Charlie exploded.

'All right, all right,' she answered calmly and almost dreamily. She went on, 'We had stopped outside St Leonard's Church and among the people waiting to board the bus were a young couple with a young baby. I stowed their fold-up pram under the stairs for them.'

Charlie sighed and put his arms around Lizzie, pulling her head down on to his hairy chest. He hadn't a clue what she was talking about.

'I stood gazing at that baby, watching as the mother loosened the shawl. Next thing I heard was the cab door slam and seconds later you came around the back of the bus, jumped on to the platform and grabbed me.'

Recollection came back to Charlie. 'Hey,' he roared, 'I told you to stop day-dreaming and ring the bloody bell, and all you went on about was what a lovely baby it was.'

'That's right, go on, what else did yer say?'

'Nothing.'

'Not much you didn't, Charlie! You told the whole damn bus you were quite capable of making your own.'

'Get on,' he said through his wide grin.

'Yes, and that wasn't all,' Lizzie told him, disentangling herself from his grasp. 'You kissed me, and when I told you all the passengers were looking, you said, "Good, let 'em look." Everyone ended up laughing at me.'

'Ah, poor Lizzie,' he mocked, 'but what's made you bring all that up now, for God's sake?'

'Because I am going to leave the job.'

'What! After all this time you're gonna leave the job because I kissed you when passengers were looking?'

'No. Because that night you made me pregnant.'

Charlie sat bolt upright in the bed; he looked absolutely bowled over. Quietly he said, 'Why you sly old thing.'

'Not so much of the old,' she laughed.

'Oh Lizzie, Lizzie, Lizzie,' he murmured and there was deep affection in his voice.

Then suddenly he punched the bedclothes and let out a roar which must have woken up half the street. 'Now,' he said with a wicked gleam in his eye, 'if you've finished talking about the past, can we get back to the present?'

When spring eventually came round again, life seemed to Lizzie to be almost too good to be true. The girls worked hard in their houses during the morning, and then took themselves out for the rest of the day. They went to parks, up on to the Common, even took bus rides to Box Hill, where they lay on the grass, ate sandwiches, drank lemonade and watched Lucy play with Raymond. Weekends they walked to Tooting, bought their fruit and vegetables in the market and haggled with the butcher.

Charlie often said it was a wonder that the girls hadn't worn a triangular-shaped track in Wilton

Road as they went continuously from one house to the other.

Hilda was slightly the outsider, mainly because she still went out to work, but Lizzie knew she was happy enough. She never used make-up, her hair was always sleek and shiny but dead straight, and she adored her Wally. Lizzie thought it was a case of an attraction of opposites. Hilda was big-boned, fair and tended to be a bit overweight, while Wally was slender, dark-haired, dark-skinned, with a pencil slim moustache and eyes that were almost black. They were both good company, especially on the private outings.

These outings had become a regular thing, running every Sunday from each bus garage throughout the fleet to spend the day at the coast. Drivers were mainly volunteers. The cost was four shillings for adults return, and a half a crown for children. Lizzie, Polly and Doris would wash and set each others' hair, paint their fingernails and try on each others' dresses before Sunday came around. Polly was the tallest of the three, still slim, dark and with lovely soft skin that tanned easily. Doris and Lizzie could have easily passed for sisters. Same height, same slim build, same blue eyes and fair hair, though Doris still used peroxide which Lizzie thought was a pity. In all the time Lizzie had known her, she had never heard Doris raise her voice in anger. She seemed so demure and unobtrusive. Kind acts and deeds which she accomplished for elderly neighbours she did without thought of reward or recognition.

It was on one such outing to Bognor that they discovered what a truly lovely voice Doris had. The day had been grand; the girls had hardly left the sands. At lunch time, the men had taken themselves to the pub where they drank a considerable number of pints between them. They came back when the pub closed, sank down into deckchairs, put handkerchiefs over their faces and fell asleep.

The girls didn't mind; they were used to it, they told each other, as they played about at the edge of the sea, their dresses tucked into their knickers.

Everyone sat still and silent on the homeward coach until it was time again for the pubs to open.

'Pull up, driver, nice big coach park at the Wheatsheaf,' shouted Syd, whilst dozens of male voices backed him up.

Soon, Charlie was seated at the piano inside the bar, while Wally, Arthur and Syd belted out the words to the all-time favourites he was playing.

It began low-pitched. Lizzie and Polly turned and looked in amazement. Doris was singing. Gently the words of 'Charmayne' came from her lips; she looked utterly at peace. The whole busy bar became hushed, listening to Doris's soft crooning voice. There was a moment's complete silence as the last notes faded away, then thunderous applause came from everywhere.

Doris blushed and hung her head.

'You're gorgeous,' Lizzie whispered to Raymond,

who was asleep on her lap. She bent and kissed his warm forehead. 'And, young Raymond, there's a helluva lot for you to learn about your mum!'

It was late in August. Lizzie had been feeling rotten for two days when Doris resolutely took her by taxi to the Wilson Hospital.

'Her frame is very small,' the doctors stated, 'we shall transfer her to Hammersmith Hospital.'

Charlie was frantic when he came home and found Lizzie missing. But he was full of pride when, the very next day, she had the baby – a boy of almost eight pounds, with a shock of dark hair and those blue eyes so very much like his own.

Everyone had argued about the baby's name. If it was a boy, Nellie had said, call it Brian. Brian! Never in her life. That was the name of the eldest Dawson boy.

Phillip, Syd wanted. Or Frederick, suggested Polly.

Only hours after he was born, the registrar came around the ward. He peeped at the half-asleep Lizzie, and whispered, 'I won't bother you.'

'Please,' her hand stayed him, 'Robert Leslie Wilson,' she stated firmly, having sought no one's advice, not even Charlie's.

When Lizzie arrived home, they had acquired another addition to the family – an Old English sheepdog puppy. Charlie's conductor had been living in a Nissen hut and, when granted a council house, was told no pets.

'Couldn't let him be put down, could I, love?' asked Charlie.

'No, of course not, he is lovely,' Lizzie quickly assured him. 'What's his name?'

'Bob,' said Charlie.

'Yeah, Bob-Bob,' said Raymond, his big eyes pleading with his auntie to let the dog stay. Stay he did and became everyone's friend.

When the baby was just three weeks old, Polly came across the road waving a telegram from her parents. Doris had tagged in behind and they all laughed in disbelief as Polly read aloud, "Come on holiday now. All eight welcome. Don't forget the children. Love you. Mum and Dad."

They couldn't refuse. They didn't want to.

So it was all arranged. The train fare was very expensive but an overnight coach left Victoria at ten p.m. three evenings each week.

Their tickets cost four pounds return for each adult, two pounds each for Lucy and Raymond and the baby went free. Hilda and Wally Saint were thrilled to be included in the invitation and Arthur Scott assured them that Polly's parents were kind and generous folk and that the season was probably all over and the bedrooms would be empty. Paddy Betts and Joe Frost promised faithfully to take good care of Bob-Bob.

It was barely daylight when the coach driver pulled

into the Newquay terminal, but Nellie, Kate and John Hurley were there waiting.

Utter confusion followed; everyone wanted to hug everyone else, the two little ones were irritable after a long weary journey and wouldn't go to their grandmas, and Baby Robert started to cry.

Arthur took charge. The hotel was only a few yards from the harbour coach park and soon everyone was seated in the basement kitchen, around a huge circular table which had a well-scrubbed top.

Blue and white mugs filled with scalding tea were set in front of each of them. The two toddlers and the baby were already fast asleep and tucked up safely.

Quietly Lizzie took stock. Then she glanced at Polly and they each blinked to take away the tears.

Their parents looked awful! John Hurley had aged ten years in the past ten months; his hair had receded, leaving a shiny bald patch, his eyes looked sunk in their sockets and the amount of weight he had lost was considerable. Kate looked very pale and tired and Nellie was hobbling. She had tripped going up the uncarpeted stairs from the basement to the entrance hall, knocking her shin badly. A lump had formed, which the doctor now said was thrombosis.

Hotel life hadn't proved to be easy.

'Eighteen hours a day, seven days a week,' John Hurley told them quietly. 'We hadn't reckoned on being at the visitors' beck and call every minute, day and night.'

'Never mind,' Kate said, 'season's over and done with now and we'll see you all have a grand holiday. By Christ, we've missed you, ain't we, Nellie?'

'More than you know,' Nellie agreed as she gazed at the group of young friends, which included her son and daughter.

'Now, let's see about breakfast,' ordered Kate as she stood up and prepared to tie an apron around her waist.

'Oh no you don't!' Everyone turned to look at Doris as she spoke. 'We can get the breakfast.' She spoke quietly but with weight behind her words. 'Get your mum and your aunt and uncle upstairs to bed. Then you men can take all the suitcases to the rooms and by that time we'll be ready for you to lay the table.'

The men had been standing open-mouthed. No one had seen Doris in charge before, let alone heard her issue orders.

The gardens at the back of the hotel were beautiful. Lush lawns sloped directly down to Newquay's famous beach.

As a big family they did everything: took boat rides, swam and paddled in the sea, collected shells and picnicked on the golden sand. Everyone looked and felt better as the sun continued to shine down each and every day through that September.

Two days only were left of their fortnight's holiday and all was quiet and peaceful as they sat sipping coffee on the top lawn.

The bell in the reception hall sang, shattering the silence.

'Leave it, Polly,' her father said as she rose to go and answer it. Persistently it rang again, longer this time.

'I don't mind,' Polly said, 'I won't be a minute.'

She wasn't. Almost immediately she came across the grass, her long brown legs showing to advantage beneath her very short shorts. 'Eight people for bed and breakfast,' she called, 'they want four double bedrooms for two nights.'

'Tell them no. We're closed up for the winter,' John Hurley was emphatic in his refusal.

Polly didn't argue. Minutes later she rejoined the group, started to collect the cups and saucers on to a tray and said, 'Move yourselves, the beach is calling.' The matter was forgotten and everyone enjoyed another lovely day.

Except Charlie. It had turned eleven o'clock when they put the cards and the cribbage board away and everyone said a tired but happy good-night.

Lizzie reached over to put the light out when Charlie caught hold of her arm. 'Lizzie, how much does Uncle John charge for bed and breakfast?' he asked.

'Whatever are you on about?' Lizzie stifled a yawn. 'If you're worried about what he's gonna charge us, don't be. Mum has worked for next ter nothing. We won't have to pay him much.'

'No, it's not that. Listen, Lizzie, please. How much do you reckon he charges, have a guess?'

'Well,' Lizzie considered, 'twelve and six a night, maybe fifteen shillings.'

'Yeah, that's about what I thought. So even at twelve and sixpence, eight people for two nights comes to ten pounds.'

'Oh, I get it,' Lizzie cried, 'you're on about those people Uncle John turned away this morning, aren't you?'

'Well, yes I am,' he said thoughtfully. 'I push a bus around the streets of London for six days and all I get is five pounds eight shillings. Don't make sense, does it?'

'Oh forget it and let's get some sleep, Charlie,' she pleaded. 'It's our last day here tomorrow and we want to make the most of it.'

They did go to sleep, but Charlie didn't forget the matter at all.

Chapter Fourteen

BACK HOME IN London, Charlie promptly bought a copy of Daltons Weekly and eagerly scanned the pages which had hotels and guesthouses for sale. He wrote in answer to a few of the advertisements and received prompt replies.

Lizzie listened as Charlie read out the details, showing an interest she did not feel, never dreaming anything definite would come of this pipe-dream.

Two weeks later, a second letter arrived from the proprietor of a guesthouse at Woolacombe Bay in North Devon.

'As you have shown interest in my property, perhaps you would care to view, stay a couple of days,' the letter said. Enclosed were two return railway tickets to Ilfracombe.

'Well, he's keen,' Lizzie cried, as she and Charlie re-read the letter. 'You're not going, are you?'

'Why not?' Charlie asked. 'It's not going to cost us anything and I have got Tuesday and Wednesday rest days next week.'

During lunch, Charlie was very quiet and as Lizzie made a start on the washing-up he called out, 'I won't be long, I'm going to the phonebox.'

As he came back into the kitchen, grinning from

ear to ear, Charlie declared, 'All settled. That Frank Fleming seems a decent bloke.'

Lizzie had to smile; despite her misgivings she could see that Charlie already had a vision of himself as an hotelier.

Oh, what the hell, going to view a place didn't commit them to anything and it would keep Charlie happy. Woolacombe Bay, near Ilfracombe, she muttered to herself as she searched for the previous letter, which contained a brochure. She had never heard of either place.

At six o'clock on Tuesday morning, a taxi came to take them to Paddington. Robert had been left with Doris and Syd. A lot of persuasion had been needed to get Lizzie to agree to leave the baby behind, but in the end she saw the sense of it and it was only for two days.

For the first part of the journey, Lizzie slept and when she woke up the countryside had changed considerably. Through the carriage windows, she watched as the train rattled through tiny villages which had low-built farm houses, tall barns and green fields. Trees and hedges were decked out in all the glorious colours of autumn. She felt much more optimistic.

The train finally came to a halt. There were no tracks left. 'The back of beyond,' Lizzie said to herself, and all her doubts returned. It was raining, fine rain – half-rain and half-mist. Frank Fleming had no difficulty in identifying them for they were the only passengers to come through the barrier. Having shaken hands, he helped Lizzie into the back seat of his car while Charlie took the front seat beside him.

The journey to the hotel took about thirty minutes, during which time Lizzie clutched the seat as the car negotiated hills so steep that she wondered just what kind of a place they had come to. Mrs Fleming waited in the doorway to greet them, but as they climbed the front steps, the wind blew with gale force and the fine rain whipped their faces.

It was not a good beginning.

A hot meal was ready for them in the dining-room and as they ate Lizzie studied their hosts. Mr Fleming was not at all as she had imagined him. He was a good-looking gentleman in every sense. Nicely tanned, with a well-cut suit, a full head of bushy hair, dark but streaked with grey gave him a distinguished look, which was emphasized by thick horn-rimmed glasses. An egg-head type, Lizzie decided, not knowing herself exactly what she meant by that.

Lizzie settled in her mind that Mrs Fleming was about forty years old, tall and elegant. Wavy brown hair framed her oval face and when she smiled her mouth revealed lovely white teeth. Her manner was friendly enough.

They finished eating and went into the adjacent lounge. Mrs Fleming brought coffee for each of them, but made her excuses, saying she had to attend a meeting. Mr Fleming suggested that he and Charlie got down to brass tacks. 'Got a lot to accomplish in this short time,' he said.

Lizzie almost retorted, 'Don't mind me, I'm only here to make the numbers up,' as they began their tour of the guesthouse. There were two rooms they had not seen on the ground floor: one was a double bedroom and the other was the kitchen, which was spacious, clean and with more equipment than Lizzie had imagined.

The basement, a small, cosy sitting-room and just one bedroom, formed the Flemings' private quarters. There were three more floors above ground level, each having large landings and long corridors, four bedrooms and one bathroom on each floor.

All were nicely furnished.

Back downstairs, seated in deep armchairs, drinks were served and a fellow guesthouse owner from nearby joined the group. 'Bill Rush,' Mr Fleming said with a wave of his hand, 'meet Mr and Mrs Wilson.'

Bill Rush was a jovial, outgoing man with a big beer-belly and it was soon obvious, at least to Lizzie, that he was not impartial at this meeting.

Lizzie moved her seat backwards, letting the three men group themselves in a semi-circle. She had decided to be a listener to their conversation rather than a participant. Both Frank Fleming and Bill Rush extolled the virtues of the hotel trade. Besides the high profit on capital outlay, one enjoyed a marvellous way of life. According to them.

Mr Fleming was waging a battle he was determined to win, as he worked on Charlie and ignored Lizzie. He trotted out smooth, plausible reasons why Charlie should lose no time in going ahead with the purchase of this guesthouse.

'Do you mind if I go to bed,' Lizzie interrupted, 'it has been a long day.'

Much later, Lizzie feigned sleep as Charlie crept into the bedroom. She wanted no more discussion tonight. The mood she was in she might say something that she would be sorry for.

After breakfast next morning, they went for a walk. Just Lizzie and Charlie on their own. The beach was breathtakingly beautiful. Sheer golden sand stretched as far as the eye could see, banked by green cliffs and dunes. Hardly a word was spoken as they walked at the sea's edge, each deep in their own thoughts.

Mr and Mrs Fleming were ready to take them into Ilfracombe by the time they got back to the house. 'I've telephoned my bank manager. He will be more than pleased to see you,' Frank Fleming spoke directly to Charlie.

'Bank manager!' Lizzie hissed at Charlie as they went out to the car.

'Leave it out, will you, Lizzie?' he whispered aggressively. 'It's better to sort things out while we're on the spot.'

'What bloody things?' she demanded to know, her temper rising.

There was no time for Charlie to answer; Mr Fleming was holding open the door of the car for her. Perhaps it was just as well; Lizzie was getting a bit tired of being given the cold shoulder and was rapidly reaching the point where she would explode and a blazing row would be inevitable.

Charlie and Frank Fleming went off together; it had been half-heartedly suggested that Lizzie accompany them but she had refused. Mrs Fleming had business of her own to attend to, so Lizzie walked down Market Street to the seafront.

Horrible, was her first impression. Bleak, rugged and desolate. She had never encountered such a place before. Steep, steep hills, huge granite rocks at the base with the angry sea swirling and crashing over them, sending showers of spray high into the air.

'Oh, all I want is to go home,' she mumbled to herself. She missed Polly and Doris, but most of all she felt lost without her baby. This place felt lonely, not a soul was about. No, definitely not for me, she determined; I need folk around me. Give me good old London any time.

They were well on the way home when Charlie came over to where Lizzie was stretched out on the seat.

They had the carriage to themselves, just as they had on the journey down. He lifted her legs and sat down, letting her legs lie across his knees. 'Never seen you so angry, Lizzie, want to talk about it?' he asked.

'What's the point?' she argued. 'They've hooked you good and proper.'

'Oh, don't talk rubbish,' Charlie cried – but that was like a red rag to a bull.

'It's you that's been listening to all that rubbish. Rubbing his hands is Mr Fleming; thinks he's got a right bleedin' daft one in you.'

Charlie's hand flew up, but he stopped short. God, he thought, I almost whacked her one. He sighed deeply and went back and sat across from Lizzie.

'You don't believe it's a good business proposition, then?' he asked quietly. She didn't answer. 'Come on, Lizzie,' he urged, 'get it off yer chest; why are you so dead against the idea?'

Lizzie felt too upset to talk sensibly.

'They're taking you for a ride. I never heard no mention of any work. Do their guests take care of themselves? Who does the cleaning? Who makes the beds? Who prepares and cooks the meals? And, where do yer get the shopping from? I never saw no bloody shops.'

Charlie couldn't help it, he had to laugh.

'And no bloody market either,' Lizzie added for good measure, as she herself began to laugh.

The weeks raced towards Christmas, and although Lizzie was fully aware that Charlie was still negotiating with Frank Fleming she chose to ignore the fact.

An uneasy truce existed between her and Charlie. The parents all stayed down in Newquay but everyone crowded into a telephone box to talk to them on Christmas morning. Doris and Syd hosted the festivities at home and, with the children and an added baby, nothing was left to chance. Chocolate figures adorned the tree and dozens of gaily wrapped presents lay on the floor around its base.

Charlie did make one attempt to bring North Devon and the hotel trade into the conversation, but it was Doris who tactfully and quietly changed the subject. Lizzie had long since come to the conclusion that her sister-in-law was a rare person indeed.

With the coming of January, the pressure from Mr Fleming increased and Lizzie and Charlie rowed openly now. One very bitter argument ended by Charlie shouting, 'Do as yer like, I don't care, but I'm going to Woolacombe if I have to walk there.'

'Well, walk there then, damn you,' muttered Lizzie, but either Charlie never heard or he was past caring what she thought.

Every problem that arose, Frank Fleming found a way around it.

'He's got us an eighty per cent mortgage,' Charlie announced one morning as he read yet another letter. 'And we don't have to worry about the twenty per cent. He's willing to wait for that till we sell this house.'

'I bet he is,' Lizzie said over her shoulder as she left the room.

Lizzie thought she had heard it all until one day when Charlie came home jubilant.

'I've signed the contracts,' he cried. 'Completion day is 15th of February.'

Lizzie felt her heart miss a beat. Until this very moment she had never truly believed that Charlie would do this to her. Not go this far without really sitting down and discussing it with her.

Charlie watched as the tears filled Lizzie's eyes and ran unheeded down her cheeks, and the sight of her affected him so much that he almost cried himself.

'Please, Lizzie,' he began, 'it will be a wonderful life, truly it will. Think about our Robert, growing up down there by the sea, he'll be so healthy.'

'And London would kill him?' Lizzie asked sarcastically.

As usual it was Doris with her gentle, placid ways who became the arbitrator. 'You don't have much choice, do you?' she wisely pointed out to Lizzie. 'Not if you love Charlie and I know that you do. The only alternative is for you to stay here and then, as sure as eggs are eggs, you two will end up getting a divorce. Why don't you give it a try?' she beseeched Lizzie.

To Charlie she spoke outright. 'You've gotten away with murder, you have, Charlie Wilson! Just you remember this was all your idea and watch out for our Lizzie.'

Charlie at least had the good grace to look crestfallen and to keep his mouth shut.

An air of despondency settled over the house as it became obvious that Charlie was to have his way. Everyone made their own arrangements. Hilda and

Wally decided to leave London; a new bus garage was to be opened at Stevenage in Hertfordshire, and to every crew that volunteered, a brand new council house was on offer.

Joe Frost decided to marry a widow lady he had been seeing for the past ten years, and Paddy Betts was going home to his wife Oaife and his two children – he had found out that the streets of London were not paved with gold.

Moving day! Charlie had left with the removal van early in the morning and now it was time for Lizzie to depart. She had deliberately made herself look smart. She dressed in a well-cut suit and a pale blue blouse, her camel swagger coat on top, and her hair was tucked up in a cloche hat that would keep her ears warm.

It was a bright sunny morning and Doris told her that was a good omen. Doris got into the taxi that would take them to the station, while Lizzie gave Polly a final hug.

On the railway platform, the two girls clung to each other, oblivious to the hustle and bustle all around them, the shunting, hissing, steaming trains, the clanging of the wheel-tappers' hammers, the pigeons in their hundreds flying high up into the great glass roof. Taxis, porters, trolleys piled high with mailbags, people of all nationalities, the over-riding smell of soot, dirt and grime – this was the dear old City of London that Lizzie was leaving behind.

Reluctantly, Lizzie took her seat in the carriage, unhooked the lead from the dog and placed it in the bag that held napkins, baby food and sandwiches. Doris kissed the baby one last time and hesitantly held him out for Lizzie to take, then she stretched out her arm and patted Bob-Bob who lay on the floor between the two bench-seats.

'Bye, Bob-Bob,' she whispered and, as if in answer, he twitched his nose and gazed up at her with his soulful brown eyes.

'Stand back, mam,' a porter ordered as he slammed the door of the carriage. To Lizzie the sound had a ring of finality about it.

Hardly out of London, the sunshine disappeared and the weather turned horrible. High winds and sleet. Passing through the countryside, the sleet changed to snow, pure and white, the flakes splashing against the window panes of the fast-moving train. The scene was pretty; hills and fields lay as if beneath a huge white blanket.

Lizzie fed the baby and cuddled him tightly.

There was no one to meet her this time. Lizzie struggled to get everything out of the carriage and on to the platform. The solitary ticket collector offered to fetch the baby's pram from the guard's van. Suddenly a taxi driver appeared and took charge.

At least Charlie had remembered to send a taxi. The removal men had unloaded and gone and Charlie had been busy. The house was warm and the lounge and dining-room were set out, though Lizzie thought that their few bits and pieces looked ridiculous in such large rooms. The basement flat was cosy. The bedroom looked nice and Charlie had even made up the bed and placed Robert's cot close. The sitting-room had rugs on the floor, two armchairs, Gran's carved dresser and their wireless set.

'Welcome home,' Charlie said as he kissed Lizzie.

She didn't answer. A lot of water would flow under the bridge before she regarded this place as home.

They ate a good meal in the basement and Lizzie suggested that, before they settled down for the evening, they should have a walk around upstairs. Charlie seemed reluctant, but Lizzie went ahead.

She felt like screaming, but what good would that do, she asked herself as she slammed yet another bedroom door and ungraciously pushed past Charlie and went back downstairs.

Twelve rooms upstairs, and not a curtain at the windows, not a carpet on the floors and not a stick of furniture to be seen anywhere!

Passing the green baize-covered noticeboard in the hall, Lizzie tore down a handwritten account. Headed Mr and Mrs Wilson, it read: Items not paid for. Stair carpet £75.00, stair rods £10.00, television aerial £10.00, £95.00 to pay.

Now, she did scream.

'We haven't even got a bloody television,' she yelled.

There was worse to come! The kitchen had been

stripped. Only the gas cooker remained. Refrigerator, free-standing cupboards, kitchen utensils, even the china, all had gone!

'Calm down, please, Lizzie,' Charlie implored, as he pushed her down into an armchair and got down on his knees. He held her hands tightly as he explained, 'Frank Fleming is taking me to Bideford tomorrow morning where I will be able to order every single item needed to stock out this guest-house. He has promised me that no deposit will be necessary. It's the way they do things down here. Everyone makes the total payment at the end of the season.'

Lizzie only gazed silently at him. What she felt at that moment for Charlie was utter contempt. What had he done? That he had been conned was as plain as the nose on his face, but what were they going to do about it? She just did not know.

'Let's go to bed,' she said quietly, and Charlie sighed with relief.

Mr Fleming kept his word and took Charlie to Bideford. Lizzie kept out of his way.

That evening she and Charlie together looked through the order forms. Lizzie gasped as she entered each item into an exercise book. Twelve bedroom suites, ten double beds, six single beds, blankets, sheets, pillows and pillowcases, bed-spreads, towels, tablecloths and serviettes.

The total cost appalled her; they were getting deeper and deeper into debt.

She couldn't resist saying to Charlie, 'Let's hope we live long enough to pay it all off.'

Another thought struck her. 'What about chairs and tables for the dining-room?' she cried. 'And utensils for the kitchen, not to mention a bloody fridge!'

'Don't start again,' Charlie begged her. 'Frank said you can get most of those things at the auction sales.'

'Oh, it's Frank now, is it?' she said cynically. 'Well, you go with him and see how you get on.'

'I can't; I'm going home tomorrow.'

'Oh, you bastard,' she screamed, full of frustration, and tears welling in her eyes.

'We agreed, Lizzie,' he appealed, 'I'd stay on the buses at least until Easter. We need the money to live on.'

'Need the money, do we?' she said sarcastically. 'You're a bit late in the day to give that a thought, Charlie Wilson, and what's with this going home bit? You said welcome home when I got here – thought this was home now.'

'Oh, you know what I mean, Lizzie.'

She cut him short. 'Oh yes, I know what you mean only too well, Charlie. You go home, live with my brother and Doris, go to work, play your bloody darts and there's me stuck down here with the baby, no friends, no family, no money and no bleedin' furniture. Well, you want to tread carefully, Mr Bigshot, I might just decide to come home as well!'

Lizzie cried herself to sleep that night but she didn't resist when Charlie drew her into his arms and held her close.

'You needn't come to the station to see me off,' said Charlie. 'It only means more expense, bringing you back again.'

What you're afraid of, Charlie, me darling, Lizzie thought to herself, is that I might just get on the train with you. The taxi moved off and Lizzie closed the heavy front door. She paused a moment; the silence was deafening. She really was all on her own now, just her, the baby and the dog. No Doris and Polly just across the road. No Hilda upstairs. No trips to Tooting Market and a cuppa in the cafe. No dark-haired Lucy demanding a story, no chubby Raymond to throw his little arms around her neck. Slowly, she went to the basement and sat down. She was aware that her head ached and her throat felt so tight she could hardly breathe.

She buried her face in her hands and she began to cry as though her heart would break.

She hadn't felt so lonely before, not in the whole of her life.

Chapter Fifteen

THE BED WAS too large, the reading lamp too low, Lizzie missed Charlie and she hardly slept at all that first week.

The quiet, endless, lonely days stretched into even longer lonely nights.

'What in God's name am I doing here?' Lizzie asked herself a dozen times each day.

The weather did nothing to lift her spirits. It was raining really heavily; torrents of water slashing against the windows. She watched from the lounge windows, the sea showing signs of great turbulence, the high winds droning and whining, not a living soul in sight.

The front garden, which only the previous day had been so pretty, all the shrubs coated with fine snow, was now bare, flattened by the force of the gale.

She shuddered with dismay. There would be no going out today, not even for a walk. Bob-Bob would have to make do with the back garden.

Before leaving London, Lizzie had used the reference section of the local library, searching out which areas of the country had their wake weeks at different periods during the summer. She had placed small advertisements in local papers in such places as Manchester, Blackburn, Bolton, Liverpool, Derby and Birmingham, offering room and full-board for six guineas each person per week with big reductions for children.

One morning, she heard the letterbox click and was up the basement steps in a flash. Loads of letters were lying spread out on the mat.

Without waiting to get dressed, she read each one. For the first time in days her spirits lifted. She couldn't wait to get pen and paper and start to answer these enquiries.

'Dear Mr and Mrs Brown, with pleasure we can offer you a really nice room which looks out over the sea.' That was how she began each letter.

The trouble was, she had to run up and down the stairs, often with the baby in her arms, and always with Bob-Bob at her heels, trying to familiarize herself with the locality and number of each room and visualize whether just a double bed or maybe a double and a single bed for a child would fit into a particular room.

Not easy when every room was bare.

Lizzie was delighted as the deposits started to roll in, and she made a wallchart setting out the weeks from Saturday to Saturday, from Easter until October. As she filled in the definite bookings, it became apparent that she was only fully booked for the four peak weeks. Nothing at all for Easter and very little for May, June or September.

One morning, the post was all answered and Lizzie decided to give herself a break. It was a dry day, cold but bright. With the baby in the pram and the dog bounding along ahead, she took the winding path upwards away from the beach, climbing steadily.

Pushing the pram was no mean feat and Lizzie was thankful that she had worn flat-heeled shoes.

Finally, she reached the top of the cliffs. The view out over the Bristol Channel was glorious. She found a sheltered spot and sat down. Apart from the postman and the lady in the general stores, which served as the post office as well, Lizzie hadn't spoken to a living soul all week.

Not likely to find anyone to natter to up here, she told herself as she listened to the cry of the seagulls and the gentle noise from the sea far below.

It was much later when she set off in the direction of home, reaching the house just in time. As she put her key into the lock of the front door, there was a loud clap of thunder, the light seemed to fade, and an eerie greyness settled over everything, obliterating the cliffs.

'Good job we went out early,' she said to the baby, and to Bob-Bob. 'Do you think we're going to have a storm?' Neither one of them answered her.

At times, the only links she now had with reality were the Saturday night phone calls she received from Charlie. As she listened to him and longed to see him, she wondered why he was working in

London. Coin after coin she would hear drop into the telephone box as he prolonged those precious moments.

The new furniture arrived. Now Lizzie had plenty of jobs to do which would use up her pent-up energy.

She dusted furniture, unpacked bed linen and made up beds. She was a frequent visitor to auction sale rooms, and became quite good at catching the eye of the auctioneer, and soon crockery, cutlery, tables and chairs had all been purchased. Curtains remained a problem. Measurements had been sent to Doris, who purchased material as cheaply as possible from the markets. Charlie gave her the money, but his wages were being stretched to breaking point. He still had the mortgage on number twelve to pay and some weeks he had nothing left to send to Lizzie.

The stream of deposits was now drying up; the main four peak weeks being fully booked.

The day came when Lizzie had no money in the house. There was enough food in the cupboard to keep her going, but she had to have milk for young Robert.

With the baby in the pram, she walked to the clinic. After much hesitation, she swallowed her pride and entered.

The rosy cheeked, plumpish woman seemed nice enough.

'Please,' Lizzie began, 'would you allow me to

have a tin of dried milk and pay you next time I'm passing?'

'Of course we will, mi dear,' the kindly soul said cheerfully as she reached for the large tin. 'Is there anything else you'm be wanting?'

'No, thank you,' Lizzie said gratefully. The cost of the tin was one and tenpence-hapenny and Lizzie was almost in tears as she walked back to the guest-house. 'Jesus only knows how I came to be in this state,' she said to herself. 'One minute I had a big house, rents coming in regularly from three lots of tenants, and Charlie in a good job. Now I ain't even got two bob to me name. Fancy! Having to ask for milk on tick before I could make the baby his bottle!'

Aunt Daisy's old sewing machine came into its own. Evening after evening, when Robert was asleep, Lizzie slaved away on it until she had curtains, of a sort, ready for every room.

Saturday night came again and the telephone rang. 'Hallo, Charlie,' Lizzie said brightly after she picked up the receiver.

'That's where you're wrong, my love, it's me, not Charlie.' Nellie's voice was loud and clear, and Lizzie was so excited.

'Mum, how are you? Oh, it's so lovely to hear your voice. How's Aunt Kate and Uncle John? I'm sorry I haven't got round to answering your letters. Without your letters and those from Doris and Polly I think I would go off my rocker stuck down here.'

'Lizzie, Lizzie, stop it,' Nellie called down the

line, when at last Lizzie had paused to take a breath. 'We're all fine, stop worrying. How is baby Robert?'

'He's been a bit rough all day, wheezy-like, got a croaky cough an' all. What d'yer reckon, Mum, should I call a doctor in?'

'Without delay,' Nellie said and went on, 'I really rang to say I was coming to see you. Could you put up with me for a coupla weeks?'

'Oh, Mum, do you mean it? Really? When?'

'There you go again; like a bull in a china shop you are. It won't be for about ten days, when I've booked my ticket. I'll let you know. I'll be coming by coach.'

'All right, Mum. Make it soon as you can. I love you.'

'I love you too, Lizzie. Watch out fer the baby. Get the doctor to him. Night love. God bless you.' Nellie hung up and Lizzie replaced the receiver and hugged herself.

She hadn't seen her mum since last September and now she was coming to stay.

Lizzie spent the night tramping back and forth across the bedroom floor. Each time she looked into the cot the baby seemed worse, she had tried nursing him but he was so fretful. At last it was daylight and she telephoned the doctor.

'You must be very careful with him, Mrs Wilson,' the young doctor said when he arrived. 'Keep him in one room, constantly warm, no draughts and as much liquid as you can get him to take.'

'Is he going to die?' Lizzie asked with fear apparent in her voice.

'Oh, come now, Mrs Wilson,' the doctor protested. 'Your baby has bronchitis and he does need careful watching, but there is no need for such a pessimistic attitude.' Lizzie shuddered, and the doctor felt remorse. 'You look as if you could do with a rest, Mrs Wilson, have you anyone who will stay with the baby a while?'

'No, no one,' she answered sadly.

'Well, I'll get the prescription for you and you'll see, in a few days' time your baby will be well on the road to recovery.'

Charlie telephoned each night and Lizzie's first reaction was resentment. If she hadn't been stuck down here miles from everyone she knew and loved, in an unfurnished house, Robert never would have caught a cold in the first place.

The days were long and the nights even worse.

She listened to the wireless just to hear somebody's voice and on this particular morning she wasn't paying much attention to what the announcer was saying until the words 'Festival of Britain' made her sit up sharply.

Of course! It was 1951. Immediately all her longing for London returned. How many times had she been the conductor on a number 49 bus travelling from Shepherd's Bush to Crystal Palace! The bus would travel down Kensington High Street, turning right at the Albert Hall and into Gloucester Road, down Onslow Place on into Sydney Street, stopping outside the dear old Chelsea Palace. That had been a real treat that had, being taken by Mum and Aunt Daisy to see music hall at the Palace. On down Oakley Street and into Cheyne Walk. That was the lovely bit, a view of the Thames and, to the left, Albert Bridge. From here the bus turned right and continued on over Battersea Bridge . . . Battersea . . . Battersea Park – that's where it would all happen. For months and months plans had been under way in London ready for this Festival of Britain, and the main base of operations was to be on the South Bank of the Thames, overflowing into Battersea Park.

'Christ!' Lizzie muttered out loud. 'I've leant out from the back of the bus many a time and watched that entrance on the far side of Albert Bridge go up.'

She listened to the voice of the announcer forecasting how many visitors from all over the world were expected to visit Battersea when the Festival was opened by the King and Queen. Londoners in their thousands were certain to flock to the fairgrounds and exhibitions. 'Well here's one Londoner that won't be able to go,' said Lizzie who was now feeling very sorry for herself. It was bad enough being stuck down here in the back of beyond with a sick baby without having to be reminded of all that was going on back home in London.

She got up from her chair and went downstairs to her basement bedroom and tiptoed in to look at Robert. He was sleeping now, although his little face showed that he was still burning up. Quietly, she went back up the stairs and into the kitchen.

It wasn't fair, her being here. No family, friends, or even neighbours. The silence and the loneliness was driving her mad. What if Robert should get worse? What if he died? She couldn't wrap him in a blanket here and run with him through the park to The Nelson Hospital. She didn't even know where the nearest hospital was. There were buses, she knew that. About three a day. Maybe more on a Friday going to Barnstaple on market day. Market day! I miss the market every bloody day, she thought.

Here she didn't have a soul to say good morning to. For the umpteenth time she asked herself, 'How did I let it happen?'

It was Charlie who had thought himself the clever one but look who had ended up being conned rotten; it was her who has been turfed out of house and home to cope with this so-called gold-mine, with him still living in Wilton Road with her friends and family to see that he wants for nothing. If she stayed here much longer she'd forget what the sound of her own voice was like, never mind about other people's. 'I'll tell yer this, Charlie Wilson,' she said, 'if our marriage survives this, it'll be a bloody miracle. The way I feel right now I don't know whether to hit the bottle or cut me throat.'

On the third day, she bathed Robert for the second time that day, not immersing him in the water, merely sponging his hot little body and changing his damp night clothes. The doorbell rang just as she was laying the baby back down into his cot.

The doctor had shown compassion, calling in to see Robert each day, but he had already called at nine o'clock that morning and she wondered who her caller could be as she came up into the front hall.

She opened the door and then flung it wide as she stared in amazement. Doris and young Raymond were standing on the doorstep.

'I don't believe it!' Lizzie cried as she swept Raymond up into her arms and nuzzled her face into his hair. Doris flung her arms around Lizzie and they clung together for a long time.

Eventually Doris asked, 'May we come in?'

Lizzie laughed. 'Oh, sorry, come on in.'

'Well, I should hope so after all the miles we've travelled,' Doris said. 'And where is that nephew of mine?' Then, much more sombrely, she asked, 'Is he any better, Lizzie?'

Lizzie still couldn't take it in. She busied herself putting the kettle on, talking all the while, assuring Doris that she felt sure that the critical stage had passed.

'He's not nearly so fretful now. He's sleeping better, but his chest is still tight and that horrible cough seems to rack his little body.'

Lizzie couldn't put her finger on it but something was wrong. Doris seemed drained of energy. Surely the train journey couldn't have been that tiring. No, there was something else, Lizzie was sure of it. She settled Raymond with milk and chocolate biscuits and brought tea for Doris and herself to the table.

'Now,' she said, 'let's have it, Doris. Whatever it is that is wrong with you, you're gonna have to tell me.'

'I know,' Doris said, and she looked so sad that Lizzie felt her heart miss a beat as intuition warned her of trouble.

'Well?' Lizzie whispered.

'It's your mum, Lizzie. She died on Tuesday.'

For a long moment neither of them spoke, then Lizzie stood up and moved to the window.

'Tell me it isn't true,' she pleaded, but she expected no answer and Doris gave none.

'Peacefully. There was no warning. She had a heart attack.'

'I only spoke to her on Saturday. She said she was coming here to stay with me.' Her voice broke suddenly as tears spilled down her face, while Doris watched helplessly.

The funeral was to be in Newquay on the following Monday. Lizzie couldn't take the baby and she wouldn't go without him.

'That's why I'm here, love,' Doris said. 'No one expects you to go. Syd and Charlie are going with Polly and Arthur.'

'Oh,' was all Lizzie managed as an answer.

At two o'clock on Monday, when Nellie Collins was being buried in Newquay, Lizzie sat alone in a church in North Devon. She wasn't at all sure what she was doing there; she couldn't even bring herself to pray.

She did, however, talk to her mother.

'Sorry, Mum, that I am not there. You wouldn't want me to leave Robert would you? I love you, Mum, love you, love you,' she repeated over and over again.

Syd and Charlie arrived late on Monday night. It was not such a happy reunion as it should have been.

The two men did several jobs, such as stretching and laying carpet that Lizzie had acquired as a job lot.

Alone one morning, Syd told Lizzie all the details of the funeral. 'Aunt Kate and Uncle John were really upset,' he told her. 'It was such a shock. Polly and Arthur are staying on with them for a while. They're thinking of selling the hotel and moving back to London.'

'Wish some bugger would buy this place,' Lizzie muttered beneath her breath as Charlie came into the kitchen.

Saturday afternoon, and Lizzie stood forlornly watching the taxi disappear into the distance. They had all gone again, on their way home to London. 'Par for the course,' she said to the dog as she made a bottle for the baby.

Chapter Sixteen

SLEEP EVADED LIZZIE again that night, but rising next morning, looking and feeling like hell, she came to a decision. She was going to pull herself together. Charlie hadn't really forced her to come here. True, he had made it very difficult for her to say no, but all that was in the past and she could hardly back out now.

'So, stop wallowing in self-pity,' she said firmly to herself. 'Who knows, Charlie might just be on to a winner with this place.' If only she could be certain of that, she thought as she came up the stairs and opened the kitchen door.

Bob-Bob came leaping across the room to say good morning, licking her hand with his long pink tongue, his tail wagging furiously. Lizzie was all smiles as she patted him.

'You don't mind living in Devon, do you?' she laughingly asked as she unlocked the back door to let him out. She watched as he bounded off up the garden. 'He's happy enough,' she said aloud, and the thought crossed her mind that perhaps, if she stopped yearning for London, accepted the situation, maybe even started to count her blessings, then life for her would begin to look a lot rosier too.

'Right,' Lizzie decided, having bathed and fed the

baby, 'we'll put you in your pram and push it out into the garden this morning.'

She was wearing slacks, with a pale blue round-necked jumper, but as she looked in the mirror, she wrinkled her nose in disgust. Her hair was a mess. So, she spent a good ten minutes brushing it hard and then she tied it back from her face with a piece of black velvet ribbon. 'Now, how about some make-up?' Her expression was thoughtful as she did her eyes and eyebrows. For too long she had let herself go and she had to admit that she already felt much better for having made the effort. 'Definitely better,' she muttered after having applied lipstick.

Perched halfway up a pair of steps, Lizzie was happily humming to herself as she endeavoured to hang curtains at the lounge windows. She heard a sudden slight movement out in the hall and she almost toppled over, as Frank Fleming appeared in the doorway.

'Good morning, Mrs Wilson,' he said cheerfully as he removed his trilby hat.

'Good morning,' Lizzie replied, not feeling in the least bit pleased to see him. How dare he walk straight into the house without knocking! He must have come down the lane and in through the open back door. Daft old Bob-Bob hadn't even barked.

He came straight to the point. Looking up at Lizzie, for she hadn't bothered to step down, he asked, 'Has the sale of your London house been finalized?'

'Not that I've heard,' Lizzie said.

'Well,' Mr Fleming continued, 'there is the little matter of nine hundred pounds owing to me. Eight hundred to complete the sale of the house and one hundred for goods I left behind.'

Lizzie surveyed him in stony silence.

Mr Fleming's eyes narrowed. 'Time is going on, and I would like the matter settled. Your husband indicated to me that there would be no problem with him finding a purchaser. I, too, have commitments on the hotel that I am buying.'

Not wanting to lose her temper, Lizzie only said, 'I know that.'

'Well,' just the one word Mr Fleming uttered, but his voice had suddenly become much harder.

Lizzie's face went pale and she drew in her breath as she slowly came down the steps.

Now she was at a disadvantage for Mr Fleming was a good deal taller than her. Her temper was rising, but she held it in check as she said, 'You urged my husband to buy this property, you got him a mortgage, you said you'd wait for the balance. I don't recall any time being set for him to pay you the rest of the money.'

Mr Fleming's eyes blazed, 'Dammit, I did everything I could to help your husband. I understand the position you're in, but I have liabilities too. I need that money; I can't afford to wait for it.'

'Bit late now, isn't it? You should have thought about that when you were pushing my Charlie,' she fired back and watched the expression on his face turn to real anger.

Abruptly, Mr Fleming turned to go, then stopped dead in his tracks. 'One week today I'll be back, and let's hope we can sort things out more satisfactorily then than we have today.'

'I'll be here,' Lizzie said stubbornly.

Strangely, Lizzie didn't feel a bit nervous as she watched him storm off down the garden. At least she had stood her ground with Mr Bloody Fleming; she hadn't let him walk all over her.

After dinner that night, Lizzie didn't put Robert down in his cot; she sat nursing him. Bob-Bob settled himself in his usual place at her feet, his head raised to lie against her shins.

She was considering her options.

Suddenly she sat up very straight and Bob-Bob looked at her reproachfully with his doleful eyes, cross at having been disturbed.

Bank managers! That was what they were for, to give advice. She had opened an account at Barclays when the deposits had started to come in and had been given a cheque book. Well, now she was going to make an appointment to see the manager.

Next morning, Lizzie telephoned as soon as the bank was open. At two p.m. sharp she presented herself, together with the baby in the pram.

Graham Blackhurst, attired exactly as she had imagined in a charcoal grey suit, white shirt and striped tie, stood smiling in the doorway of his office.

Lizzie hesitated, her nervousness obvious.

'It's all right, Mrs Wilson, please bring the pram in with you,' he said reassuringly. Seated opposite him, Lizzie unbuttoned the jacket of her navy blue suit and decided that Mr Blackhurst was no more than forty years old, despite the fact that his fair hair was receding.

'Now, Mrs Wilson, how can I be of help to you?' he asked, and his voice was not only soft, but kind as well.

In a barely audible whisper, Lizzie said, 'I would like the bank to lend me nine hundred pounds.'

If Mr Blackhurst had burst out laughing, Lizzie would not have been at all surprised; her request spoken out loud sounded comical even to her. But he didn't laugh, he leant towards her and courteously said, 'Why don't you tell me what you need the money for.'

Lizzie sighed, wondering if she really did have to tell this stranger all the ins and outs as to how she came to be in such dire need.

'Take your time, Mrs Wilson,' he encouraged her.

Slowly, to begin with, Lizzie told the bank manager that she needed the money in order to pay Mr Fleming. Then her hesitation gave way to resolution. No longer were her words faltering; she held nothing back. It was as if she needed to talk. She had bottled things up inside her for so long, only able to speak out loud to herself or to the dog. Now she had the opportunity to unburden herself to another human being, someone who was a good, attentive listener.

She suddenly realized that she had been talking non-stop for a very long time. Not once had Mr Blackhurst interrupted her. Almost in mid-sentence, Lizzie paused and raised her head to meet the eyes of this quiet gentleman. The eyes she now looked into were an unusual shade of grey and Lizzie felt that they were smiling at her.

Very gently, Mr Blackhurst put a question to her, 'Do you have any collateral?'

Lizzie didn't even know the meaning of the word. He sensed her discomfort.

'Additional security?' Still Lizzie made no reply. 'Shares, jewellery or property? Anything of that nature, Mrs Wilson. I am not being inquisitive, I do need to know.'

Lizzie twisted her hands in her lap and bit her tongue, saying angrily beneath her breath, 'If I had all those things, I wouldn't be here asking you for money.'

'Sorry, Mrs Wilson, I didn't hear you.'

'No, nothing,' Lizzie said indignantly. Then, as an afterthought, she added, 'Only my London house.'

Graham Blackhurst straightened himself up in his chair. Already, he had a lot of respect for this young, slim woman who had come into his office, looking so very despondent. He had read her file, only a few pounds in a recently opened current account. It seemed that her resources were stretched to the limit and beyond. Then there was this matter of Mr Fleming. Everyone in the village knew Frank Fleming –

many to their cost. A good businessman, without a doubt, but God help anyone who crossed him.

'Tell me about your London house, Mrs Wilson, is it in both your husband's and your names?' He awaited her reply with interest.

'No, Mr Blackhurst.' Cautiously Lizzie considered the question before she continued. 'I bought number twelve and number nineteen Wilton Road in Colliers Wood during the war, or rather, I paid the deposits and got the rest of the asking price on mortgage.'

More and more, Graham Blackhurst was becoming convinced that this young lady from London had a great deal of common sense. He also suspected that, given half a chance, she could very well become a shrewd businesswoman.

'So, are both properties registered in your name?'

'Oh, no, I bought number nineteen for my brother.'

'And number twelve, is that jointly owned with your husband?' He was fully aware that he had asked this question previously but he wanted to be absolutely clear in his mind on this very important point.

'I wasn't even married then, Mr Blackhurst, my Charlie and I weren't married until the war was over.'

'I see,' he said, and his grey eyes twinkled at her. 'And you've never altered the registration?'

Lizzie was baffled again. Why the hell did he keep on and on about Wilton Road. 'I did have to go to

Somerset House once,' she shot at him. His hopes dropped drastically.

'Do you remember why?'

'Yes, the property had to be registered under the Town and Country Planning Act.' His hopes rose again.

'Did you have any legal papers to sign?' and he emphasized the word YOU.

Lizzie's thoughts went back and, without thinking where she was and to whom she was talking, she burst out, 'Yeah, and I had to pay bloody ninety-six pounds for stamp duty.'

The tension was gone. Graham Blackhurst threw his head back and burst out laughing. Would that all his customers were so straightforward!

Lizzie felt her cheeks flame and her hand flew up to cover her mouth.

She waited a few seconds and then she apologized.

'Not at all, Mrs Wilson,' he said, still grinning broadly, 'not at all.'

The baby, whom they had both apparently forgotten, began to whimper. Lizzie looked at Mr Blackhurst. She was still upset that she had sworn, and now Robert had to start.

He put her at ease straight away, 'Please lift him out of his pram. I only need to get a few details from you and then you can be on your way.'

Lizzie rose, loosened the pram covers, and took the baby up into her arms. Rocking him gently, she soon had him pacified. She liked this bank manager, she liked him very much, but was he going to lend her nine hundred pounds? And if not, why the hell didn't he get it over and done with and say so.

'Now then, Mrs Wilson,' Mr Blackhurst was all at once very businesslike, 'I need a few details from you. Firstly, the name and address of the firm of solicitors who acted for you when you bought number twelve Wilton Road.'

For the next five minutes, he fired questions. Lizzie answered to the best of her ability and he wrote notes on to a pad which lay in front of him.

Finally, he stood up, came around the desk, held the pram still while Lizzie put the baby down again, and then held out his hand.

Lizzle solemnly shook it.

Then Mr Blackhurst did surprise her. He put his arm across her shoulders and looked into her face. 'Now, I don't want you to worry. I am going to make some enquiries on your behalf and I want you to come and see me again on Friday.' He stopped speaking and pondered for a moment. 'If the weather is bad, or for any reason you cannot make the journey, please pick up the telephone. Let me know, and I shall come out to you.'

Jesus! Lizzie thought. Wonders would never cease; she had a bank manager as a friend.

Curiosity was killing Lizzie. She was relieved when Friday came. The bus was late and Lizzie felt flustered as a young fresh-faced boy held open the door of the bank for her.

Graham Blackhurst's greeting was cordial; he

even looked into the pram and asked how the baby was.

Once seated it was down to brass tacks immediately. Professionally, but with a good deal of patience, Mr Blackhurst explained the whole matter.

'It was Mr Wilson who had signed an agreement, undertaking to pay Mr Fleming the balance of twenty per cent of the purchase price of Sea View Guesthouse on the completion of the sale of property known as number twelve Wilton Road, Colliers Wood in Surrey.' Mr Blackhurst had read aloud this information from an official document which lay in front of him.

Now, he raised his head, his eyes met Lizzie's and the smile on his face deepened as he firmly stated, 'Mr Wilson owns no such property.'

What was he saying? Lizzie was no fool, but he would have to be a lot more explicit before she could actually take it in.

'That agreement between your husband and Mr Fleming isn't worth the paper it is written on.' Slowly, Lizzie smiled and Graham Blackhurst smiled with her. She would need a helluva lot of time to clear her thoughts but just at this moment she was cock-a-hoop. She wanted to yelp with joy, grab this bank manager and dance him around his office.

She restrained herself.

It wasn't Charlie she wanted to put one over on. No, never that. It was Mr Frank Fleming.

Graham Blackhurst sat back. Watching Lizzie's face, he saw disbelief turn to glee. He could read her thoughts. He had to chuckle to himself. What he wouldn't give to be a fly on the wall when the next meeting took place between this young woman who had been uprooted from London, and Mr Oh-so-clever Fleming.

'You could go back to London, Mrs Wilson, if you wish to. No one can force you to sell your house.'

'Thank you,' was all Lizzie managed to mutter.

Chapter Seventeen

LIZZIE PUT HER key into the lock, opened the door and let the dog out. 'Come on Bob-Bob, we're going down on the beach,' she declared. The afternoon was still bright since the evenings were drawing out and there were a few people, mainly with their dogs, down on the beach.

She took the zig-zag path down through the dunes and pushed the pram into a secluded recess between the rocks. Turning the baby on to his side, she propped the feeding bottle, half-filled with orange juice, close to his pillow. Baby Robert's chubby, dimpled hands clutched at it eagerly. His eyes began to droop, he blinked a few times, and then he was asleep.

Taking the now empty bottle away, Lizzie tucked the pram covers up around him, then she took off her shoes and stockings placing them into the end of the pram.

'Right, Bob-Bob,' she called out, 'let's go for a run.' The tide was well on the way out and her feet and the dog's paws left clear imprints in the wet sand as they ran. The water was freezing and Lizzie moved swiftly. Up and down at the edge of the sea she ran, kicking water into the air, splashing Bob-

Bob who thought it was a marvellous game in which he heartily joined in.

As she walked towards home, bare footed, for she hadn't brought a towel, Lizzie felt she could easily leap for joy. She had things well and truly in perspective now. But by the time she got home, washed, changed and fed the baby, her feeling of elation had dwindled quite a bit. Whichever choice she made, she knew she would have to bear the consequences.

Did she want to go home to London? All she knew was that she missed Doris pushing open the front door, calling, 'I'm going to the corner shop, Lizzie, is there anything you want?' She missed hearing Lucy's footsteps, as she ran down the side path, coming through the back door panting, 'Auntie Lizzie, Mummy says she's just put the kettle on, are you coming over?' She missed the bus outings, the dart matches and fish 'n' chip suppers in front of Syd's television set. Right now she wished that somebody would tell her what to do.

A sudden thought struck Lizzie – had Charlie known exactly what he was doing all along? Her thoughts flew around in her head. Londoners had a saying, 'Never con a conman'.

Had Charlie done just that? It was inconceivable, or was it?

All along, Lizzie had been thinking that Charlie was a pushover, easy game for Frank Fleming's persuasive tongue. What if she had been wrong?

She tried to see it from Charlie's side. He had

badly wanted a guesthouse and along had come Mr Fleming, doing every mortal thing within his power to get Charlie's signature on the contract.

Just what had it cost Charlie in terms of actual cash. Not one penny! Not even the railway fare to view the house in the first place. Lizzie vowed she wasn't going to think along those lines any further, and she certainly wasn't going to question Charlie.

Should she take the baby and go back to London? No, she told herself, though her decision was very half-hearted.

She thought about Charlie; there had never been anyone else for her from the moment she'd set eyes on him. Just what would it do to Charlie if she packed it all in and walked away? It just didn't bear thinking about.

There was still the mortgage – over three thousand pounds – to be paid. There was the matter of all that new furniture and bedding sitting in the rooms upstairs and not a penny paid on it yet. If she was honest with herself, and she was certainly trying to be, she didn't really have any choice.

Lizzie lowered the gas beneath the boiling kettle and her expression was thoughtful as she spooned tea into the pot. 'Well, Lizzie Wilson,' she said out loud, 'like it or not, I think you're stuck with this guesthouse,' then, as if to boost her morale, she quickly added, 'at least for this season'.

Lizzie looked much the same as she had on his last

visit. She had washed her hair the previous evening and had taken pains with her make-up this morning.

Mr Fleming advanced across the kitchen, hand outstretched, his mouth widening in a broad smile. All animosity apparently forgotten.

'Well, everything sorted out?'

'To the best of my ability,' Lizzie said seriously.

'Good, good. I knew your husband wouldn't let me down.'

'What I have to say hasn't anything to do with Charlie.'

'Carry on then,' Mr Fleming's voice was deceptively quiet.

'I'm afraid you are going to have to wait for the balance of your money.'

His mouth dropped open. With grim determination Lizzie continued, ignoring the fact that if looks could kill she would be dead.

'My husband had no right to sign an agreement stating that when our London house was sold he would pay you the balance.'

Reaching out, Mr Fleming roughly took hold of her arm. Lizzie stiffened instinctively. Her first impulse was to resist forcibly, instead she winced. 'You're hurting me,' she warned. He immediately let go of her arm and stepped backwards.

Leaning forward, Lizzie spoke.

'Our London house belongs to me; to me, Mr Fleming, do you understand? Mr Wilson doesn't own any property, he doesn't have a house to sell.'

Hysteria had made her raise her voice and by the time she had finished she was shouting.

The disbelief on Frank Fleming's face halted Lizzie, but she felt no remorse. 'What the hell are you on about?' he roared.

With a voice that was still shaking, Lizzie answered, 'You understood every word that I said. Now, if you'll excuse me . . .' and she waved a hand in the direction of the back door.

He left and Lizzie heaved a sigh of exhaustion, mingled with relief. She watched him walk the length of the back garden and she couldn't resist a sneer.

Two green-horns, that's what she and Charlie were.

Fancy even considering a twelve-bedroomed guesthouse that was totally devoid of furniture and working equipment, let alone going so far as to buy it. Well, perhaps now Mr Fleming didn't think they were quite as green as he had supposed.

Chapter Eighteen

CHARLIE GAVE UP his job and came to live in Devon two weeks before Easter.

Lizzie was on the station to meet him and spotted his laughing face as he hung out of the carriage window. They hugged each other for a long while and then Charlie lifted Robert from his pram and carried him in his arms.

'Christ, I've missed you,' he told Lizzie.

'Me too,' she agreed.

The house felt more of a home now, with Charlie around.

They only had one booking over Easter, a party of six – four adults and two children, who were due to arrive on Good Friday.

Alan Gregory was tall and thin and his wife, Winnie, was short and a little on the plump side. With them were their two children – a fair-haired girl called Darryl, who was six, and Neil who was four. The two grandmothers, Grandma Gregory and Winnie's mother, Grandma Eaton, completed the party.

No sooner were they inside the house than everyone was on first-name terms. It was more like having friends to stay than having paying guests, and Lizzie liked them all straight away.

Alan had hired a car for the holiday and on Saturday evening after dinner the two grandmothers pressed them to leave the children in their care, so that the two young couples could go out together.

For Lizzie it was a real treat, dressed up and sitting in a country pub, with Charlie sitting close to her side and these new Lancashire friends for company. The weekend was grand.

The following day, Woolacombe looked magnificent in the fine spring sunshine, with its lovely view across the bay and the high green hills stretching down to the vast expanse of golden sands. It was too early for many holidaymakers and the beach was not too crowded. The children threw bread and laughed as the great seagulls swooped low.

On Monday evening everyone was a little downcast, for tomorrow the Gregorys would be leaving. Even baby Robert would miss them, for they had all tended to spoil him.

'When have you got to have the car back?' Charlie asked Alan as he passed him his coffee.

'Oh, not until the end of the week. It wasn't much more money to hire it for the week, rather than just four days,' Alan explained. 'I've still got the rest of the week off from work, so I thought I would take the family on a few day-outings.'

'Why don't you stay here?' Charlie suggested.

'We would love to, but we can't afford it.' Everyone's face dropped.

'Please, be our guests,' Lizzie pleaded.

'Of course,' Charlie echoed. 'It would be our way of repaying you. You've mucked in with the washing-up, helped get picnics ready, taken us out and about in the car, oh, of course, you have to stay.'

'Please, Dad,' Darryl pleaded, and even quiet, shy little Neil added, 'I'd like to stop here.' Everyone laughed and it was decided.

Next morning they all piled on to the bus and went to Ilfracombe. They watched the fishing boats come into the harbour and they bought fish that smelt of the sea for their next day's dinner. It was a wonderful week and when Saturday morning came and the Gregorys finally did have to depart, they promised Lizzie and Charlie that they hadn't seen the last of them.

Several weeks passed before they had any more visitors. Lizzie longed for the season to begin and tried not to worry about their money problems.

During the day, she and Charlie would take the baby for long walks, and each day Charlie would sniff the air appreciatively and say, 'It's so fresh and clean. I love the smell of the sea.'

When summer finally arrived, they were rushed off their feet. Upstairs, doing the bedrooms, Lizzie would look out enviously as the holidaymakers packed the beach and romped in the sea.

Charlie surprised her. Not only was he marvellous at waiting at table, he prepared all the fresh vegetables in the evening, ready for the next day, would bone out a side of bacon, cut up steak and kidney, while she made the pastry for the pies.

In fact, there wasn't one job that he wouldn't tackle.

The height of summer passed all too quickly and then the visitors became far less frequent. Come September and only the odd few bed and breakfast couples came to their door. The situation had to be faced.

Carefully and methodically Lizzie and Charlie went through the accounts together. There was little enough money to pay the bills, let alone to keep them during the long winter months. The local traders, the wholesalers from whom they had bought their meat and dry goods, even the hire purchase on the refrigerator, which had been an essential item, would all have to be paid, declared Charlie as he wrote out the various cheques.

Laundry, rates, gas, electricity and telephone were totted up, and thankfully they agreed there was still enough in the bank to cover these items.

'Now, what about the Bideford Furniture Stores?' Charlie asked, not expecting any answer. 'I'll have to go and see Mr Channon,' he insisted.

'I'll come with you,' Lizzie said, and it was obviously what he had wanted her to say, because he gratefully accepted.

'Lizzie,' Charlie's voice was quiet with apprehension as he paused from packing away the account books.

'Yes?' Lizzie was at the door, about to go down-stairs and check on young Robert.

'I'll have to go back to London for the winter,' Charlie blurted the words out. 'I can probably get my job back on the buses.'

Lizzie had been expecting this. She knew it made sense. But in spite of all her resolution the tears came, hot and scalding, running down her cheeks.

'Oh Charlie!' She swayed and he was beside her in two strides. His arms about her, his lips pressed to her hair, he soothed, 'I know, I know, Lizzie. All that hard work, and for what?'

Mr Channon was in his early fifties. A shade shorter than Charlie, he had a mop of hair which was light brown and wavy and his eyes were set wide apart, which gave Lizzie the impression that he was a straightforward kind of man. There would be no pulling wool over his eyes.

Charlie must have had the same impression, for he laid their situation on the line as soon as they were seated in Mr Channon's office.

Silence hung heavily for a few minutes.

'So, you haven't made a fortune during your first season.' Mr Channon's voice was gruff as he continued, 'Too many liabilities. I thought that from the very beginning.'

Lizzie looked at Charlie and her heart ached for him. He was dressed so smartly today in his navy-blue suit, white shirt and paisley tie, now his face was red with embarrassment.

'Can you afford to pay anything now?' the question was shot at Charlie.

He swallowed deeply before answering, 'Only about twenty-five per cent of the total amount.'

Again, the office was quiet and just for a moment Lizzie was gripped by fear. Could they send Charlie to jail for not being able to pay his debts? She couldn't take her eyes off Mr Channon as she waited for him to speak.

'I'm a pretty good judge of character,' Mr Channon said at last. 'Yes, all right, Mr Wilson. I appreciate the fact that you and your wife have come to see me in person. You have been completely honest and that is another factor in your favour. I'll take your cheque for what you can afford and we'll leave the balance in abeyance.'

Despite Mr Channon's generosity, Lizzie couldn't help feeling humiliated as she watched Charlie write the cheque. There and then she made a promise to herself. Once they got out of all this debt she would never owe a penny to anyone, not if she could possibly help it.

A high wind was blowing and the sea was rolling in really rough, bringing with it a heavy rain which lashed against the windows of the house as Lizzie packed socks and underwear into Charlie's case.

'All finished,' she finally said as she straightened up. 'Plenty of time for lunch now before the taxi gets here.'

They sat opposite each other as they ate, each busy

with their own thoughts. Lizzie's blue eyes contemplated her husband thoughtfully. Was it right that they should be separated for weeks on end once again? Right or not, it was a necessary evil, she chided herself. They needed to have money coming in from some source and what other option was there?

'Come with me,' Charlie had urged and she had been sorely tempted. It would be heaven to stay with Doris and Syd, to be part of the family again. Number twelve still hadn't been sold and Lizzie knew that if she went she would never come back to Devon.

Charlie looked at his wife. The weeks of sun and wind had tinged her fair skin to a pale golden tan and brought out the hidden lights in her fair hair. How he hated to leave her, she had never looked more lovely and for the hundredth time he chastized himself. Why on earth had he been so pig-headed? What had made him even think he was capable of running a guesthouse and showing a profit?

The taxi came and Charlie went back to driving a bus around the streets of London while Lizzie faced a long lonely winter.

Chapter Nineteen

JANUARY 1952 HAD been bleak and cold, with snow flurries and bitter gusty winds, but Lizzie still went out whenever the weather allowed, walking miles with the baby in the pram and the dog tagging along by her side. Already it was February and it still hadn't turned much warmer. Lizzie shivered as she walked up the stairs and tugged her dressing-gown more tightly around herself. In the kitchen she filled the kettle and put it on to boil, patted Bob-Bob and let him out of the back door into the garden, then switched on the wireless. The King had died. Oh, how sad! He wasn't all that old.

For the rest of the morning the wireless gave out bulletins and played mournful music which did nothing to lift Lizzie's spirits. Like everyone else in Britain that day, Lizzie's thoughts were all of King George VI. It was a funny old world she said to herself; if his brother hadn't fallen in love with a woman who'd been divorced, an American woman at that, he would never have become the King at all. They said he'd died peacefully in his sleep and she was glad about that. She wondered if there would be a lying-in-state. She had to brush away a tear at that point as she remembered Bill taking her up to

London to see King George V's lying-in-state – all those years ago.

As she thought of the past, she remembered a day during the War when she'd been doing a turn on the 88s. As the driver had turned the bus round by the Tate Gallery he had been stopped by the police from driving down the Embankment. The whole of that area had been badly bombed the night before, and Lizzie had watched from the upstairs windows of the bus as the King and Queen had walked amongst the havoc of the demolished buildings talking to the air-raid wardens and consoling men and women who had lost members of their families in the air raids. From the little she knew of him, he had always seemed a quiet, kindly man.

Well, we won't have a King on the throne now, she thought, because King George only had two daughters. That makes Princess Elizabeth Queen of England. Fancy that! She'd been in the ATS during the war, done her bit for the war effort, so at least she knew how the other half lived.

'Oh well! Life has to go on,' Lizzie said to the dog. 'Seeing as how there's no one else here for me to talk to I have to make do with you. Come on, get yer lead, I'll get Robert ready and we'll go up over the cliffs. A good walk and we might all feel a bit better.'

It was the start of their second year at Sea View Guesthouse and Lizzie threw herself whole-heartedly into the preparations.

Bursting with energy, she worked from early morning until lunchtime. The afternoons she spent writing letters. She wrote to town halls, to Darby and Joan clubs, and to every organizer whose name she could glean from magazines in the local library, offering reduced terms for coach parties either at the beginning of the season or towards the end.

She was delighted by the response she received. But one evening, long after she had settled the baby down, she read through several of the letters again and sighed. Most of the groups that were making provisional enquiries had approximately forty to fifty members. Lizzie hadn't got that many bedrooms to offer. Eventually she went to bed still racking her brain as to what she could do.

She hadn't realized that, to make the long journey worthwhile from northern towns, the coaches would have to be either forty-two seaters or fifty-three.

In the post next morning there was a letter from Alan Gregory and, although she was pleased to hear from him, his news only added to her dilemma.

He had been promoted and was now transport manager for a large coach company in Blackburn. Would she like to send a quotation for four parties, two early- and two late-season, full-board?

'Wouldn't I just,' she said aloud, and Bob-Bob put his head on one side, peering at her, wondering what she was on about.

The doorbell rang and Lizzie picked up the baby and kissed him. 'Come and see the postman,' she said, fully expecting it to be the second delivery, maybe even a registered letter with a deposit on a booking.

Lizzie's face reflected her surprise as she stood in the open doorway holding Robert. The man at the door was Ted Armstrong, the manager of the Round House pub just four doors down the hill.

'Wasn't expecting me, was you, Mrs Wilson,' he said with a grin.

'Well, no,' Lizzie stuttered in bewilderment.

'It's just that the wife and me would like to have a talk to you, maybe put a bit of business your way. Would you like to come along to the pub later on, have a bit of lunch with us?'

'Oh, no, I couldn't,' Lizzie hastily told him, 'I couldn't leave the baby.'

'Of course you couldn't, we didn't mean for you to. Bring him along with you, we're not busy, not this time of the year. Push his pram into the saloon bar or into our sitting-room, whatever, we don't mind. Will you come?'

'Are you sure it will be all right?' Lizzie asked anxiously.

'The missus will be right pleased to see you – about half-twelve then?' He nodded his head and gave Lizzie a reassuring smile, 'Don't worry, love, I'll shut your door; you take the baby in the warm.'

There was an expression of doubt on Lizzie's face as she went back to the kitchen. She knew Ted Armstrong to nod to, even to say good morning, but no more than that.

At Christmas time, she and Charlie had popped into the Round House for a quick drink, but it was the only time, for Charlie had only been down for four days.

Visitors spoke very well about the pub, saying that they always got a good welcome there.

'Wonder what it's all about?' she asked herself.

Two hours later Lizzie sat on the wide window-seat and watched Ethel and Ted Armstrong working behind the bar. She was glad she had changed into her red dress, the long full skirt felt good around her legs, and so did the nylons and high-heeled shoes. It made a change to be dressed nicely.

The interior of the Round House was 'oldy-worldy', nice heavy oak tables and chairs, red velvet curtains and horse-brasses everywhere.

Ted Armstrong was a big-built man with a jovial laugh that was infectious: a typical publican, Lizzie thought, as she watched him squeeze past his wife giving her backside a hearty pat as he went.

Ethel Armstrong looked as if she most certainly did her share of the work. Like her husband, she was well into her fifties, her once auburn hair was streaked with grey, her face red and puffy. She served the drinks while Ted leant against the bar chatting to the customers.

Lizzie sipped her milk stout and wondered what she was doing here.

'I'm here. I'll be with you in a minute,' a female voice cried.

'That's Rosie,' Ethel called to Lizzie. 'She'll take over now; nice friendly girl she is, everyone likes our Rosie.'

Rosie appeared, tall and slim and dressed in a tight-fitting black dress.

'Right then, love, we'll go and eat. Bring your drink with you; it's all right, I've got the pram.' Ethel talked baby-talk to the wide-awake Robert as she led the way through to their private quarters.

The living-room was bright and cosy, the table set for three. Ethel nodded to Lizzie, 'Sit down, you don't mind a cold lunch, do you? I don't cook until the evening.'

'This is fine,' Lizzie answered. Before her was a platter on which lay a pork pie, a wedge of Cheddar cheese, plenty of salad and a baked potato.

As Ted Armstrong took a seat next to her, he blurted out, 'This is daft, I'm Ted and my wife's Ethel. What's your first name, love? Can't keep on calling you Mrs Wilson, can I?'

Lizzie laughed; both Ted and Ethel were regarding her with what could only be friendliness and now she felt very much more at ease. 'Please, call me Lizzie.'

'Right, Lizzie it is. Eat up lass, and then we'll talk.'

When they had finished eating, they moved from the table to sit in comfortable chairs by the window. Ethel lit a cigarette, having first offered one to Lizzie, who had declined, and slowly she blew out the match. 'Wish I could give it up,' she said in an undertone, 'but with this life and all the hours we put in I'd go crazy without my cigarettes.'

Still Lizzie was filled with curiosity, she liked these people very much, was actually thrilled at having been asked to lunch. Company was a rare thing to her these days.

Ted leaned forward and looked directly at Lizzie. 'What we want to ask you, lass, is would you like to rent our bedrooms? We've got nine upstairs.'

A few seconds passed before Lizzie had formed a reply. 'I'm not sure I understand what you mean.' She stared at them both in bewilderment.

'Of course, she's new at this lark, Ted. You go at things like a bull in a china shop,' Ethel rebuked her husband.

'It's quite common for folk to rent extra bedrooms, Lizzie,' Ethel explained. 'Visitors sleep out and come to the guesthouse for their meals.'

'Oh, I see,' Lizzie said very quietly.

'It's like this; I'm not having Ethel doing meals or even bed and breakfast this year. We've quite enough to do in the pub during the summer.' With a grim smile, Ted Armstrong got up and passed an ashtray to his wife.

'While she's showing visitors up to their bedrooms, especially on a Saturday night, the blasted part-time staff are giving the drinks away left, right and centre to their damn friends. We don't make a profit, all we do is end up well and truly out of pocket. So, now you've got the picture, Lizzie. Like it or lump it, my Ethel can rent you our rooms or they damn well stay empty!'

Ethel lowered her head, winked at Lizzie and stubbed out her cigarette. 'So now you know,' she said. 'But don't worry, love, his bark is worse than his bite.' Lizzie could hardly believe what she had heard. Maybe, just maybe, it could be the answer to her problem.

Ted smirked at them both, 'I'd best be getting back into the bar, I'll leave you two to sort out the details.' Then he stopped short, turned to Lizzie, and in a fatherly manner he told her, 'You take your time, young Lizzie, think it out well. There's the question of where would you seat these extra guests at meal-times, but there again I know a couple of my customers could sort that one out for you. Just come and see us, as often as you like, whether you say yes or no, don't make no difference. You know us now, so don't be a stranger. You'd be doing my Ethel a favour if you let her spoil that youngster of yours.'

He bent over and gave an affectionate tug to Lizzie's swept-back hair. 'Our two are grown up, both married, both settled in Wales, so no excuses – let's be seeing you, eh?'

'Yes, all right,' Lizzie promised in a voice that was husky with emotion.

The whole afternoon Lizzie just sat. She read through the notes that she had made dozens of times, and still all she felt was disbelief.

For the main ten weeks of the season Ethel Armstrong suggested that Lizzie paid her a set fee of £250 plus three shillings and sixpence per person for each night should she use any of the bedrooms at any time other than during those ten weeks.

Christ! Lizzie did her sums again.

Two pages of an exercise book were covered with figures. Whichever way she looked at it, she couldn't go wrong. There were seven double bedrooms and two singles all lovely and clean, nicely furnished and charmingly decorated. Accommodation for sixteen extra guests.

'They can use the lounge-bar, even drink after time, seeing as how they would be residents,' Ethel had cheerfully told Lizzie.

This arrangement, if it came off, would enable Lizzie to accept full coach parties. She scribbled away furiously; the one booking from Alan, for four weeks, fifty people at four guineas a week, would come to over eight hundred pounds.

She'd have to get some staff. A chambermaid for the Round House at least. It was only four doors away – would guests mind walking that far for their meals? Her head was beginning to ache. This pipe-dream was all very well, but could it become a reality?

That night, Lizzie wrote a long letter to Charlie.

His answer when it came was short and sweet. 'Grab them!'

It was all happening so quickly. Lizzie stood at the

sink, gently squeezing some woollies in the nice hot
soapy water. Four workmen were busy in the
garden plastering the new extension and in a couple
of days' time glass would be in the windows and
a large archway was to be knocked through their
existing dining-room wall.

Once again, Lizzie had gone cap-in-hand to see
Mr Blackhurst. He hadn't hesitated.

'A sound investment,' had been his verdict. 'It
could prove to be most profitable, Mrs Wilson, and
most certainly will add to the value of your property.' The bank would advance a loan.

As Lizzie thanked him, Graham Blackhurst had
pondered on her reasons for staying. He was aware
just how disastrous their first season had been in
Sea View Guesthouse and his good wishes for the
coming season were truly sincere.

The milk boiled over and Lizzie cursed herself for
day-dreaming as she mopped up the mess. She made
four mugs of coffee, set a plate of her home-made
fruit scones and a feeding bottle of warm milk on a
tray and walked down the garden path.

'Coffee up!' she called, and the men all grinned
and readily stopped what they were doing.

It was the least she could do, Lizzie told herself.
Three or four times a day she made hot drinks for
the men.

Robert had been as pleased as Punch ever since
they had started work. She had to laugh out loud
now as he stretched his little hands out for his
beaker. Sitting in a mucky wheelbarrow, dressed in

dark blue dungarees, a red high-necked jersey and a red woollen hat pulled down over his dark curly hair, he looked the picture of contentment. The bib of his dungarees was smeared with plaster and his face smudged with dirt as he chuckled away to himself. The workmen had been great; even when they had gone off in the van to get supplies, they had taken Robert with them.

He'll miss them when this job is completed, Lizzie said to herself.

Once more, Charlie had left his job and was back in Devon. Everything was ready as they waited for their first coach party to arrive. Unbelievably, Mr Channon had allowed them further credit. Four tables and sixteen chairs, all in a light oak, were set up in the new extension and in the main dining-room there were places laid for a further thirty-eight guests. They were now capable of accommodating fifty-four people in all.

It did not take long for them to get into a steady routine. They had two women who came in every day, plus two extra on Saturdays, all were very reliable and everywhere was kept clean and bright with vases of fresh flowers in the hall and the lounge.

Each meal-time, as the gong sounded, it seemed to Lizzie that people were coming from all directions, down the stairs, from the lounge and through the open front door. She and Charlie would grin at one another, still amazed at their own determination.

Saturdays were a bit hectic ('bloody chaotic' as Charlie put it) as women came from the bedrooms upstairs, arms full of dirty linen, demanding sheets, pillowcases and clean towels. Methodically, Lizzie made out lists and knew exactly what each room needed.

No sooner had the women gone about their tasks than through the front door came the chambermaids from the Round House. Charlie would stop what he was doing and carry the heavy, clean bedlinen down the hill for them.

And then, early in June, Syd got a very good offer for his house, which he accepted. This opened the way for an agreement between Lizzie and Syd which was to solve a great many problems and give Lizzie and Charlie the financial security that they longed for. For Syd and Doris decided to buy number twelve.

It meant that that lovely big old house, where Lizzie had been so happy, would remain in the family and, as Doris assured them, there would always be a bedroom for Lizzie, Charlie and Robert whenever they came 'home'.

When everything was finalized, Charlie went first to Bideford and paid Mr Channon in full.

He came back looking very pleased. 'Mr Channon said to give you his kind regards and to tell you that he hadn't been wrong. He was a good judge of character.'

Lizzie thought of Mr Channon as a compassionate

man. Then, Charlie paid a visit to Mr Fleming. What took place at his new big hotel was never mentioned.

'Did you have a drink while you were there?' Lizzie asked him very cautiously.

'Did I hell,' was all the reply she got.

Later she caught Charlie grinning to himself and she asked, 'What's amusing you?'

'Nothing, really,' he replied; then added, 'eighteen months Frank Fleming waited for his money.'

Lizzie's thoughts flew back; once again she had her doubts as to just who had conned whom. Wisely, she kept her thoughts to herself.

The golden weeks of summer slipped by and soon it was autumn. The early mornings were misty, the days were no longer so warm, and sharp breezes blew in across the sea.

Both Lizzie and Charlie heaved a sigh of relief as they stood on the front steps, waving goodbye to the last coachload of old-aged pensioners.

'I could sleep for a month,' Lizzie declared.

'Nothing to stop you,' Charlie answered.

'Oh, no, and whose gonna see to Robert and cook our meals?'

'Well, tonight no one's doing any cooking.' Charlie tenderly took her into his arms. The quietness was strange and the two of them stood in the entrance hall, locked in a close embrace for several minutes.

'We've made it, Lizzie,' Charlie said, his voice

now quite solemn. 'I shan't have to leave you this winter, and tonight I am taking my wife and my son out to dinner.'

A great tenderness filled Lizzie's heart as she realized that this man of hers was saying 'Thank you'.

Christmas came and Syd hired a minibus.

Lizzie was busy for days getting the rooms ready, taking the blankets out of the wardrobes, making up the beds. Charlie declared he would be the chef and wonderful appetizing smells rose up from the kitchen as he prepared many dishes in advance.

Lizzie could hardly contain herself, she was so looking forward to this holiday.

Syd, Doris and Raymond, Polly, Arthur and young Lucy, Aunt Kate and Uncle John, that would be eight from London.

Her sister Connie and Bill, with William, now wearing his first pair of long trousers, or so Connie had written, were coming from Plymouth. Who wouldn't be excited?

There would be fourteen of them in all over Christmas.

Log fires burnt in the lounge and dining-room and a ten-foot tree taken straight off Exmoor, now glittered with baubles and fairy lights in the hall.

The weather the previous week had been very bad, with gale-force winds and massive waves pounding the shoreline. Lizzie had pretended she didn't care, but when Christmas Eve dawned quiet and peaceful, she said a thank-you prayer.

On Christmas morning they all set off for church, Raymond holding Robert's hand, Lucy chatting away to William. They filled two pews and, as they sank to their knees, Doris reached out her hand to Lizzie and they both smiled – each knowing what the other was thinking.

How wonderful it was to all be together again!

Chapter Twenty

THE NEW YEAR got off to a wonderful start. Scores of letters came daily, many containing postal-orders and cheques. Some were from people from the previous year requesting the same dates, many stating a preference for bedrooms in the Round House. Lizzie made her wallcharts and looked forward to another season.

Forgotten were the days when nothing had gone right, when she had envied guests setting out for a day on the moors whilst she and Charlie had to cook lunch – and dinner again in the evening.

Forgotten were the nights when she had practically crawled downstairs to bed because her legs ached so much. When, just as she had snuggled up to Charlie, the front doorbell would ring at one o'clock in the morning and they would have to climb the stairs again to admit an inconsiderate visitor.

Charlie bought a car. 'Come and see,' he called from the front door, and while Lizzie stopped to dry her hands, Robert beat her up the hall.

Utter astonishment showed on Lizzie's face as she gazed at this immense blue car which stood in the street. Charlie laughed out loud as he swung Robert high in the air before opening the rear door and plonking him down on to the leather seat. Robert chuckled with glee as he bounced up and down and slid from side to side.

'It's a Morris Six,' Charlie told her with pride. 'They only made about fifty of them. Isn't she beautiful?' Lizzie had to agree. The interior was sheer luxury and smelled of real leather, and there were mahogany-faced picnic tables set into the back of each front seat. Oh yes, it was lovely.

Owning a car opened up new horizons for them as a family.

As spring came, they often took a day off from the spring-cleaning and set off with no particular destination in mind.

Exmoor was a favourite, with its wild and beautiful scenery, which Lizzie had read about in *Lorna Doone*, but had never in her wildest dreams imagined that she would see. Charlie played hearty, noisy games with Robert until they would both collapse thirsty and hungry on to the rugs where Lizzie had set out their picnic.

On one such day, Charlie stopped eating and his mouth hung open in amazement. Lizzie, too, stared in wonder and Robert let out a shriek of delight. There, not fifty yards away, stood several red deer. 'Majestic,' Charlie said, 'that's the only word I can think of to describe them.'

Friday became a day to look forward to, because it was market day in Barnstaple.

The produce was all fresh from the farms. There was Devonshire cream, thick as butter and as golden as the sun, plus every vegetable imaginable. Lettuce, cucumbers, radishes, tomatoes and mustard and cress, all had been freshly dug or picked that morning.

Home-made pickles and jams, cakes, sponges which were as light as a feather, home-made treacle toffee which was Lizzie's favourite, all were displayed on snow-white tablecloths and served by rosy, apple-faced women.

Large brown eggs lay on straw in huge china bowls, and plump chickens and fleshy ducks, all plucked ready for the oven.

Out in the street on one side of the road was a continuous line of butchers' shops, hence its name, Butchers' Row. No frozen or foreign meat would be seen here. With the abattoir only a few streets away, everything sold was fresh.

Lizzie never went home empty-handed.

Unlike the London markets, the pubs here stayed open all day. One Friday, while Charlie went off to have a pint, Lizzie did something she had been thinking of doing for a long time.

'Christ almighty, you look like an elf!' Charlie declared when they met up later. She had had her hair cut. Now barely shoulder length, it curled under in a page-boy style.

'It will be easier to manage in the summer,' Lizzie told him.

With the coming of May, the weather became more settled, with nice sunny days and long, light evenings. There still weren't that many visitors about, but Lizzie was hoping that they might pick up some more guests if the fine weather continued.

Hopefully, life for Lizzie and Charlie was not going to be quite so hectic this season and, as their debts were now paid off, Charlie had arranged for two local lads to come in every evening from the beginning of June to do the washing-up of the dinner things. It would make quite a difference – it would enable them to sit down and have their own dinner a lot earlier and enjoy longer evenings together.

But there were still times when Lizzie longed for her London life and her friends and family.

As the month ended and June was upon them Lizzie felt disappointed and angry. She knew she had no right to feel so annoyed but she couldn't help herself, for she would have given anything to have been in London this week. It was 1953 and on the 2nd of June the Queen was to be crowned in Westminster Abbey by the Archbishop of Canterbury.

'Thousands will line the route,' she said to Charlie. 'She's gonna ride in a gold coach. Oh, how I wish I could be there!'

'The newspapers will carry colour supplements every day this week, and you'll be able to read all about it and look at the pictures as well,' he said in that maddeningly tantalizing way of his.

'Get out,' she yelled as she threw a tea-cloth at him, 'we don't even have a television set to watch it on.'

The most galling thing of all to Lizzie was not that she wouldn't see the procession, though that was bad enough, but that she wouldn't be there for the street parties – and you could bet your last farthing that there'd be a party in Wilton Road. Syd, Doris, Polly and Arthur would be out there managing things, you could be sure of that. Christ! I'd better stop thinking about it, she thought to herself. For two pins I'd take Robert and get on that train!

Ah well, nobody gets everything in this life. Though that thought didn't make her feel any better.

One lunchtime, towards the end of the month, the phone rang as Lizzie and Charlie were frying fish and boiling new potatoes and peas.

'It's Ethel, wants a word with you.' Charlie came back down the length of the kitchen and took the bowl of creamy batter from Lizzie's hands.

'Hallo, Ethel.' Lizzie smiled into the receiver.

'Sorry to disturb you, won't keep you a minute. What are you doing this afternoon?'

'Taking Robert down on the beach, same as always. Why? Is something wrong?'

'I don't want to go into it over the phone, but I would like to see you.'

'Well, we've only got twenty-two in for lunch,

rest of them took a packed lunch, so we shouldn't be late finishing.'

Charlie had been listening and had got the gist of what Ethel had been saying. 'I'll take Robert down to the beach,' he volunteered. 'You put the deck-chairs out in the garden; have a cuppa with Ethel.'

'Did you hear that?' Lizzie mouthed her thanks to Charlie.

'Yes, so I'll see you about half-past two,' Ethel was saying, and Lizzie wondered why she couldn't have waited until she popped in to check the rooms, but she had sounded pretty flustered.

Ethel often looked tired to death, and no wonder with the hours she had to keep. Wouldn't have her job for the world, thought Lizzie, three hundred and sixty-five days every year; at least in this trade you get the winter to look forward to, though God knows there are enough jobs to do even then.

Charlie watched Lizzie replace the receiver and then smiled at her. 'Trouble?' he asked.

'I dunno. I hope not.' Yet she couldn't shake off the premonition that there might be.

Ethel looked all in, but when she smiled, her eyes still lit up warm and friendly.

'Sit down, luv,' Lizzie pointed to the two deck-chairs. 'I'll just go in and make the tea, I won't be a minute.'

Ethel's eyes were brimming with tears when Lizzie came back and set the tea tray down on the wicker table.

'Oh, love, don't cry. Nothing can be as bad as all

that. It's the season, gets us all, one way or another, bloody working seven days a week is no pushover.' She held out a cup of tea for Ethel to take. 'Come on, drink that up, a cuppa is everyone's answer when trouble is brewing.'

Ethel struggled not to blink but she couldn't help herself and the tears in her eyes brimmed over.

Lizzie settled herself in her own chair with her own cup of tea. 'A trouble shared is a troubled halved,' she ventured.

Ethel sniffed, 'We've got to go and I'm only sorry for how it's going to affect you and Charlie.'

Lizzie looked puzzled. 'I'm not with you. Where have you got to go to?'

'Anywhere, oh, I don't know. God alone knows, really.'

'Ethel,' Lizzie implored, 'start at the beginning and tell me what's happened.'

Ethel nodded her head. 'You're right Lizzie, there's no way of wrapping it up. My Ted's had an awful row with the brewery. Mind you, I can't really blame him, going to treble the rent. I ask you, treble it! They come down here in the summer, see the bar's packed and they think we're making a bloody fortune. Don't bother to think about the winter, do they? Oh no. Don't want to know about the nights when all we serve is a few pints to the local fishermen.'

Lizzie had an awful feeling that she knew exactly where this conversation was leading, but she did not want to believe it. For the moment she wouldn't let

herself think about it. She held out her hand for
Ethel's cup and poured each of them more tea.

Ethel was miles away, lost in thought. Lizzie
leaned forward and put a hand on her knee. 'So what
are you going to do?'

'What are we going to do? I wish I knew, Lizzie.
I wish I knew.' Ethel stared into space as if she had
almost forgotten where she was.

'Ted will sort something out, I'm sure he will,'
Lizzie's voice was full of compassion.

'That's just the trouble. My Ted blew his top,
told them what they could do with their so-and-so
pub.' Ethel's face was blood-red now, as she condemned the brewery. 'Took him at his word they
did. He couldn't keep his big mouth shut, could he?
Oh no, played right into their hands. Just what they
wanted. Get us out, new tenants in, agree a new
lease and charge what they like. One month is all
we've got. That's all we are entitled to. One month
either way, it's in our lease, can't get away from
that.'

The truth was out now and Lizzie had to face the
reality. Ethel's voice droned on. 'My Ted says he is
finished working for the brewery. Gonna see if he
can find a small place to buy, somewhere in Wales
probably; be nice to be near the children.'

She was rambling on, half to herself, saying anything that came into her head. Suddenly she seemed
to pull herself together and her eyes were alert again.

'Sorry to worry you, Lizzie, but I thought it best
to tell you myself. Mind you, nothing is definite

yet, no dates set. When Ted calms down, perhaps Charlie will come and have a chat with him; let's hope they can work something out for all our sakes.'

'I don't believe it!' Charlie sat forward in his chair and stared at Lizzie. She had waited until they had finished eating to tell him. 'Bloody hell! You realize what a mess this will leave us in.'

Lizzie took a book down from the shelf and rifled through the pages. She had known Charlie would go mad and who could blame him, it was a dicey situation to be in. There were the peak weeks of the season yet to come and they had accepted bookings on all nine of the bedrooms in the Round House. What if they couldn't fulfil that contract? If Ethel and Ted Armstrong went, who's to say that the new tenants would want to let out their bedrooms. They might have a family of their own and need some of the rooms for themselves. They may even want to take in visitors.

Dear God, the repercussions didn't bear thinking about.

Lizzie found the page she was looking for and pointed a finger to one of the paragraphs as she handed the book over to Charlie. Tension mounted in Lizzie as she watched him reading. 'Damn it, Lizzie, have you read this?' She nodded her head.

'So, if we can't keep our side of the bargain, guests are legally entitled to go to another guesthouse or even an hotel and claim the difference in cost from us!' Charlie's face was red with anger. 'Right bloody mess, ain't it?'

Lizzie wanted to calm him, she was just as worried as he was, but a screaming match wasn't going to help anyone. They were both tired, much better to leave things to quieten down and then sit down and talk about it.

She placed a bowl of fruit on the table. 'You haven't had any sweet yet,' she said eagerly; 'the grapes are nice and juicy, real sweet, or would you like some ice-cream?'

Charlie burst out laughing. 'If you don't take the cake, Lizzie, I'm damned if I know who does. You're talking in deadly earnest about us not having had any pudding, when all the time we're up to our ears in trouble. If it weren't so serious, you know, it would be downright funny.'

Even Lizzie grinned. 'Would it help if I burst into tears? Nothing's for certain yet, we may be jumping the gun.'

'And if we're not?' he asked.

'Well, we could wait until we know for certain before we blow our brains out, we don't have to meet trouble head on, do we?'

Charlie stood up and came to stand in front of her. 'You really do take the biscuit.' He was laughing now, fit to bust, his dark head thrown back, his mouth wide open showing his perfect white teeth. 'You're bloody marvellous,' he said as she stood laughing with him. 'Bloody marvellous!'

*

The following week was filled with anxiety, and though neither Charlie nor Lizzie broached the subject, each knew that it was uppermost in the other's mind.

'I've got the bloody jitters,' Lizzie muttered to herself as she picked up the broken pieces of a cup she had just dropped.

Ted had phoned and asked Charlie to pop down about eight o'clock. It was ten minutes past ten now – he had been gone over two hours.

One minute Lizzie had sunk into the depths of despair, and the next she'd been telling herself that Charlie wouldn't have stayed so long if the worst had happened.

She was baffled and worried, but just when she felt she would have to pick up the phone, she heard Charlie coming down the basement steps. The tilt of his head and the laughter in his bright blue eyes made Lizzie sigh with relief.

'Everything's all right, love. Put the kettle on; we've got a reprieve. The Armstrongs are going, but not until September, somewhere around the tenth.'

Almost all of their free time was now spent discussing their future. Charlie's ideas were well thought out and Lizzie listened attentively to all that he had to say.

'With just twelve letting bedrooms, we would be back to square one and our income would be greatly diminished,' he pointed out. 'But I don't care what happens, even if we sell up and go back to London, we are never again going to rent rooms from other people. It's far too precarious. God, we were lucky. I still break out in a sweat every time I think about what could have happened.'

It was a lovely afternoon, the sun shone down, the sky was cloudless and the beach was packed with holidaymakers.

'Let's go for a swim,' Charlie suggested.

'You know I can't swim,' Lizzie's voice was sullen, 'besides, I'm too tired and I look a right mess.'

'Poor old thing,' he teased, as he pushed towels and a beach ball into the bag. 'Come on, I'm not taking no for an answer, we'll pick Robert up on the way; he's only playing in the lane.'

Half an hour later and Lizzie felt a new woman. They had clambered over the dunes to a fairly deserted part of the beach, changed into their swimming costumes and romped in the warm sea. Now Lizzie lay back, resting on her elbows, and watched her son and his father as they swam quite a way from the shore.

Charlie was a fantastic swimmer and he had insisted on Robert being taught. 'I swear that kid could swim before he could walk,' she said to Bob-Bob as he came across the sand. 'Oh you horror,' she yelled as he vigorously shook himself and then lay down next to her, taking up more than half of the blanket she had spread out. 'Have they gone and left you too?' she said to him as she rubbed his wet sandy fur with his own doggy-towel. 'Well, they've both got webbed feet, you see, that's the difference between them and us.'

'I heard that,' Charlie sounded happy as he pushed the dog out of the way and lay down, all wet from the sea, beside Lizzie.

'I know what we're going to do,' he said grinning like a Cheshire cat, 'we're going to buy a big hotel.'

'Oh, no,' was Lizzie's first reaction, 'not again, not go through all that palaver all over again!'

Chapter Twenty-One

SEPTEMBER CAME, THE Armstrongs departed for Wales, new tenants with three children took over the Round House, and young Robert went to school.

Lizzie dubbed the school 'arsenic and old lace'. Not that she didn't like it, quite the reverse. It was called Adelaide College and it was owned and managed by two middle-aged sisters, both of whom were spinsters, with the help of just six dedicated staff.

The building itself was like a Southern plantation house straight out of a film. Wide wooden verandas, painted white, ran the length of the frontage; large, comfortable rocking-chairs placed at intervals gave one a view of the wonderful grounds. The whole place seemed unaffected by time.

There were only eight pupils to each class; it was an intimate friendly school and Robert loved it from day one.

It was Lizzie who shed a tear as she walked away and left him clutching Miss Warrell-Bowring's hand.

'He's only three years old,' she had reminded the stately lady with the black velvet ribbon encircling her throat.

'All the better, Mrs Wilson, and his classmates

will be of the same age,' she spoke flawlessly as she showed Lizzie to the door.

Just four weeks of coach parties and their third season in Sea View Guesthouse was over.

'Our final one an' all,' Charlie declared as he scanned estate agents' lists.

'Oh, for Christ's sake, let's have a rest before you start dragging me off to view hotels,' Lizzie pleaded.

They had a good rest. They stored all blankets away in mothballs, disinfected all toilets and bathrooms, cleaned the gas cooker, washed out the fridge and threw out all bits and pieces of perishable food. They bagged up piles of linen for the laundry and went back to bed every lunchtime and only got up again when it was time to fetch Robert from school.

Before they knew where they were it was October and Robert had a week's holiday from school for half-term.

Lizzie didn't ask Charlie, she told him. 'I'm going home.' She had all of her arguments ready in case he tried to stop her, but in the end she didn't need any of them. With a straight face Charlie said that he was going to suggest that they did just that. Lizzie wasn't quite sure that she believed him. But this time her face had shown such determination that he had known she really would have up-sticks and gone on her own if he had tried to stand in her way. Far better to go together and travel by car.

'Doris, Doris, Doris,' Lizzie called as they ran towards each other, arms spread wide ready to hug. It was Polly's turn next, as Lizzie broke free from Doris to put her arms around the girl who had been her friend for as long as she could remember. Lucy and Raymond were also claiming her attention and, as she bent and cuddled them both, Raymond whispered to her, 'Auntie Lizzie am I still your superman?' They were all still in a group, on the pavement outside number twelve, chattering away and laughing, when Syd came back out from the house.

'We've taken in all the gear, are you silly cows going to stand there all night?' he called out in a loud voice.

'Ssh, Syd, mind the neighbours,' Doris said in that little girl's voice of hers.

'Sod the neighbours. Charlie, Arthur and me want something to eat if you lot don't, so get in 'ere an' see about getting a meal; just because my daft sister's come 'ome it don't mean we've all got to starve.'

The three girls looked at each other and burst out laughing.

Doris had hold of Robert's hand, Polly had Raymond and Lizzie had Lucy up in her arms as they all went inside what had been Lizzie's first house.

'God, it's great to be home,' she said as her brother gave her a great bear-hug.'

It was after nine o'clock on the Saturday morning when Lizzie came down the wide staircase, through the tiled hall and into the living-room. They'd sat up half the night jabbering away, and when she'd got out of bed this morning she had stood for a long while gazing out of the big bay window at Wilton Road.

My, she'd done right to buy the two houses during the war, especially this one. It really was a beautiful house, so well built. It was all thanks to Gran though; without her legacy none of them would be so well off today.

I must ask Doris about the people that bought hers and Syd's house; being right opposite she must know all about them, Lizzie promised herself as she finally turned away from the window.

'You timed that right,' Doris called from the kitchen as Lizzie sat down. 'The kettle's just coming up ter boil.'

'Where is everyone? It's so quiet, what 'ave yer done with the boys?'

'They've only bin gone about ten minutes. Syd an' Charlie's taken them out; they didn't say where they were going an' I didn't ask.' Doris gave Lizzie one of her slow, mischievous grins before asking, 'Yer don't mind do yer? Got the whole morning ter ourselves.'

Lizzie laughed. 'Still scheming in yer own quiet way?'

'Got to ain't I? Don't do ter let Syd know what I'm doing half the time nor yet what I'm thinking come to that.'

Lizzie shook her head in disbelief as she drank her

tea and watched Doris cook bacon and eggs for each of them. Doris, so quiet, almost timid at times. I never thought she'd last, she thought to herself, not with my Syd and his ducking and diving I never. She's a proper little dark horse, but she seems to be holding her own all right.

They had finished eating their breakfast and the pair of them lapsed into silence, comfortable and happy to have each other's company, each absorbed with their own thoughts. The clock on the mantel-shelf ticked loudly, a cheerful fire glowed in the grate and Lizzie remembered when she had sat here in this same room and nursed and breast-fed her baby. Automatically she asked herself the question for which she had no answer. Why did I ever leave London? How did I come to be living in Devon? Working seven days a week when the sun was shining and not seeing a soul through the long winter months.

The door opened and Polly's voice broke the silence. 'So how are we this morning, an' what are we doing?'

'Has Arthur gone with the boys?' asked Doris. 'Yes, thank God. Lucy wasn't going to be left behind either.'

'We're all going ter get our hair done,' declared Doris.

'Oh, no,' Lizzie groaned. 'You don't want me ter bleach yer roots, do you?' she asked, remembering the times she had done them and what a messy job it was.

'No. I told yer we're all getting our hair done, fer free, at 'alf past eleven.' Seeing the glance that passed between Polly and Lizzie, Doris said, 'Do you remember Vi Dolby? Used ter do women's hair in 'er front room. Well, she bought a sa—lon.' They laughed at Doris's exaggerated use of the word salon. 'Right next door ter Colliers Wood tube station, but it ain't done any good and she wants ter sell it. I met her yesterday and she told me she'd got people coming ter view the place. She hopes they'll buy it. She wants ter make out that the place is always busy an' she said she'd do me hair for nothing if I'd come down there this morning, an' I told her I'd do better than that, I'd bring you two as well.'

'Are you serious?' Lizzie asked in amazement. 'Poor woman going to do all our hairs and not make a penny out of us?'

'We won't be the only ones; she's gonna fill the shop. Got two assistants coming in ter work there as well. It'll be a good laugh and the prospective buyers will think it is a good business, an' Vi will do all right out of it, so yer see it's us what is doing Vi the favour.'

Both Polly and Lizzie fell about laughing. The logic of Doris wanted some beating!

'We've got a good hour yet, so while Lizzie an' I make our faces up you make a fresh pot of tea Polly.'

'Yes, marm,' said Polly giving Doris a mock salute as she went into the kitchen.

They were sitting around the table drinking their

tea when Lizzie remembered she wanted to know about the folk who had bought Syd's house.

'Go on, tell her,' Polly urged Doris with a wide grin on her face.

'Don't laugh then or I won't.' They both agreed and did their best to keep a straight face.

'For a start there's Mr and Mrs Watkins an' they've got a son Tom, an' a daughter Mary. They let two rooms upstairs to an old lady on her own, her name's Thelma, or at least I think it is, though I got told off for calling her that. She said I didn't 'ave to be all lardy-dah with her. She calls herself Felma. Funny old girl, really nice but a bit queer, ain't got much. I took her over a cardigan and a warm dress, she put them on straight away, on top of what she was wearing.'

'Tell Lizzie about Felma's gas meter,' Polly insisted.

Doris shot a look of embarrassment at Polly, before turning to Lizzie and declaring very self-consciously, 'It isn't much. I started putting her money in the meter for her, that's all. Her hands are bad, crippled up with arthritis, and she couldn't get the coins in the slot.'

'That's not the end of it,' Polly took up the story. 'Felma was giving Doris a shilling an' moaning that the gas only lasted a couple of days; said Doris wasn't putting the shillings in right; so what does dozy Doris do now?'

Lizzie had no need to be told. 'She puts two or three of her own two-bob pieces in the meter.'

'You got it,' Polly said.

'Well it don't 'urt me, a couple of bob now an' again, does it?' Doris asked Lizzie with a pleading note in her voice.

'No, 'course it don't,' Lizzie assured her, at the same time thinking what a saint this sister-in-law of hers was turning out to be.

'You were going to tell me about the family them-selves,' Lizzie reminded her, and once again Doris looked across at Polly and was obviously embar-rassed.

'Don't tell me you're helping them out as well?' Lizzie couldn't help smiling as she spoke.

'I'll tell yer this story,' Polly volunteered. Doris half closed her eyes and gave Lizzie a saucy grin as Polly began.

'The father an' the mother 'ave a fruit stall outside Tooting Baths. Sell good stuff they do, always a queue ain't there, Doris?'

Doris was busy adding more boiling water to the pot so that they could all have another cup of tea, but she looked up and nodded her head in agreement.

Polly took up the tale again and Lizzie wondered when the pair of them were going to get to the point.

'The son an' the daughter work the streets, you know, pushing a barrow; well that Tom does the streets but in the fine weather his sister Mary has been selling from her barrow up on the Common.' Polly paused and giggled at her own thoughts and Doris nearly choked on her tea. 'Syd an' Doris,

Arthur an' me, we'd all been up to Streatham Lacarno for the evening. Well, as we came out it started to rain an' by the time we got to the bus stop it was coming down in torrents. As yer know the bus comes down by St Leonard's Church and runs right along side of the Common. There we were, minding our own business, when at one of the stops on the Common who should get on the bus but this Mary, looked like a drowned rat she did, water was dripping from her 'air and she was soaked ter the skin. Came an' sat on the seat right opposite to Doris an' me an' what do yer think our Doris said to that Mary?' Lizzie shook her head, speechless for once. 'She looked at Mary an' said, "You poor thing, you're soaked, get caught in the downpour did yer and run for it? What yer done with your fruit barrow? Left it under the trees?" I thought my Arthur was going to explode an' as for your Syd, you never heard anyone blow their nose so hard in all yer life. I didn't know where to put me face. I tell yer, Lizzie, we were all damn glad ter get off that bus an' I ain't bin able ter look that Mary in the face since then.'

'I'm not with you,' Lizzie said with a baffled look on her face.

'Oh, not you as well!' Polly screamed, while Doris almost fell off her chair because she was laughing so much.

'You silly cow, Lizzie, ain't yer fell in yet? That Mary's on the game. She weren't up on the Common that time of night selling no fruit!' Then the living-room was ringing with the boisterous laughter of all three of them as they clutched at each other for support.

When they'd wiped the tears from their eyes and settled down again, Doris, never one to mind others having a laugh at her expense, said, 'Here Lizzie I've just got time to tell yer about me taking a lodger, an' then we'll 'ave ter get going if we're gonna 'ave our hair done.'

'I don't know if I can take any more,' Lizzie gasped as she gave her eyes another wipe.

'Oh, you've got ter hear this,' Polly stated as she, too, struggled to stop laughing.

'Well,' (it seemed to Lizzie that all of Doris's stories began with 'Well') 'I thought I might try letting the top flat, like you did ter Wally an' Hilda. We weren't short of money but you know your brother, a millionaire this week, treats the world and his wife ter drinks in the pub, come the next week and he's selling anything he can lay his hands on. Not that me an' Raymond ever go short, far from it, but I thought a bob or two put away for a rainy day wouldn't come amiss. So I wrote out a postcard an' put it in the window of the corner shop. Same day I had a man come ter the door. He was lovely looking; tall and handsome . . .'

'Get on with the story,' Polly begged. 'We'll never get our free hair-do at the rate you're going.'

'He said he was a doctor at the Grove Hospital, went mad about how nice the flat was an' said fifty shillings rent was very fair. I let him move in the next morning. Syd said at the time that I was mad. Anyway, at the end of the first week I went up to clean his rooms an' to change his bed. Young Lucy was with me. No sooner had we got in the room than Lucy asked where the clock had gone to from off the mantelshelf. Then I stripped the eiderdown and the bedspread from off the bed an' I couldn't believe me eyes. My two big thick white blankets were missing an' a blooming old overcoat was lying on top of the sheet. I'll cut the story short. Syd nearly throttled the bloke. Made him turn his pockets out; he hadn't got any money but he had got two pawn-tickets. Syd put his toe up his arse an' kicked him out there an' then. It turned out I'd taken two weeks rent off him in advance, five pounds, an' it cost Syd a fiver ter get our stuff back out from the pawn-shop. I won't tell yer what your brother's threatened ter do ter me if I even think about taking any more lodgers.'

'Oh, my sides are killing me, I shall ache for a week,' Lizzie moaned as the tears of laughter were once more blinding her.

'You 'aven't heard the best bit yet.' Polly was ready with her two pennyworth.

'We were coming back from Tooting, Doris an' me, at the beginning of that week, the bloke had only been in the house for a couple of days. When we passed him, he said good morning ter us polite as yer like, but underneath his arm he had this dirty great big parcel; he even shifted it from one arm to the other as we watched him. What we didn't know at the time was that it was Doris's blankets and clock that the cheeky sod had got wrapped up in there.'

'Pack it in the pair of yer,' Lizzie pleaded with them as she held her arm to her side, which really was giving her gip and her laughter was in danger of becoming hysterical.

'Come on, then,' Doris said, 'get yer coats on an' I'll take yer ter get this free hair-do, and don't forget if the woman asks yer, we 'ave a job ter get booked up in this salon 'cos Vi is always so busy.'

All the way to Colliers Wood Lizzie was chuckling to herself. I knew I was missing a lot by living down in Devon, but not this much; it's worse than a Brian Rix farce.

Lizzie's hair had grown during the summer and was now just beyond shoulder-length. She had had it set on very large rollers, brushed out and clipped back with a wide orange hair-slide which Vi had sold her for one and tuppence. Polly still wore her dark hair fairly short, with a fringe and the ends curling upwards. Doris's hairstyle was the most elaborate; bleached almost white, back-combed until the front was piled high and sprayed with this new-fangled lacquer which Vi told her would keep the hair in place even in the rain, it felt as stiff as a board when Lizzie touched it. All three of them gave the two assistants a couple of bob each as a tip, called cheerio to Vi and walked about twenty yards up the road. There they fell against the wall and none of them could move for the next couple of minutes because they were laughing so much.

'I've never seen anything like it in me life,' gasped Polly.

'I told yer Vi was going ter do anything she could to sell that shop, didn't I?' Doris said as she fumbled in her bag for a handkerchief.

'Yes, you did right enough, but ter go to those lengths!' complained Lizzie as she tried hard to control her giggling. 'I don't know how those two girls kept a straight face. There was one of them kept opening the door to make the bell ring, then saying in a loud voice, "No sorry can't do anything for you today, we're fully booked." An' the other poor cow kept answering the phone that never stopped ringing, saying that they couldn't fit the customer in for at least a fortnight. The woman out in the back room with Vi must 'ave thought the place was a bloody gold-mine!'

Lizzie's description of events set them all off again and their uproarious laughing caused two old biddies who were passing to stop and stare at them. 'Painted molls,' one sniffed to her friend. 'Yeah, drunk this time in the day, should be bleedin' well ashamed of 'emselves,' said the other.

'Painted molls!' exclaimed Polly and this time they really were helpless with laughter.

It took some time for them to compose themselves and to start walking towards home.

'What will we give them to eat now?' asked Doris.

'I've got all the dinner ready for ternight but they'll want something now.'

'How about pie an' mash?' suggested Polly.

'No, can't be bothered ter walk all the way to Tooting now. 'Ere, Lizzie, d'yer, still like faggots an' pease-pudding?'

'Cor, yes, can't remember when I last 'ad them though.'

'Good, 'cos there's a cooked-meat shop opened up at the top of Marlborough Road, we can get some there.'

'What we going ter carry 'em home in?' Polly wanted to know. 'We ain't got a dish with us.'

'I'll buy one at the oil shop. I can do with a new one fer me rice puddings.'

The three of them trooped into the dark, smelly, oil shop and started sorting out the pile of baking tins and pie-dishes that were stacked on the floor.

'They must 'ave been here since the year dot,' Lizzie muttered under her breath as she spat on her handkerchief and rubbed at her fingers.

Doris walked towards the shopkeeper, a biggish man with a round red face, not a hair on his head and a beer-belly that overlapped the top of his trousers. 'Friar Tuck of Tooting,' Polly said in a stage whisper to Lizzie.

'Excuse me,' Doris said in a quiet voice, putting on her little-girl act once again, 'you wouldn't 'appen ter 'ave a kettle boiling out the back would you?'

'As a matter of fact I do, miss,' the bald-headed

man answered her, not in the least put out by Doris's question.

'If I buy one of those enamel pie-dishes, the big eightpenny ones, would you scald it out fer me 'cos we want ter take some faggots and pease-pudding 'ome with us; an' if we get them in paper bags we can't get no gravy, an' we all think the gravy is the best part, don't you?'

'Yes, I most certainly do. Without a load of gravy a faggot just don't taste the same. I'll scald a dish out an' dry it fer yer with pleasure, miss.'

Lizzie couldn't stay and listen to any more; she had to get out of the shop before she started to laugh again. Doris wasn't taking the mickey; she was deadly serious and the shopkeeper was treating her with the utmost respect. Only Doris could act like that and get away with it.

They walked three abreast down the street with their faggots and pease-pudding, Doris carried her pie-dish well out in front of her, very careful not to spill any of the rich thick gravy. As soon as one of them stopped chuckling another one started. 'What a morning,' Lizzie said to herself as she opened the gate and stood back to let Doris go in first.

With their midday meal over, Syd spread the pages of the *Sporting Life* out over the table and, with pencil and betting-slips at the ready, he said to Charlie, 'Come an' see what yer fancy fer the three o'clock. There's racing on the telly all the afternoon.'

Without saying a word, Doris got up from her chair and went to the dresser. From the drawer she took out a tin box that had a picture on the lid of the Changing of the Guard at Buckingham Palace. She spread the contents of the tin all over one end of the table – bottles of different coloured nail varnish, cotton wool, wooden tooth-picks, nail scissors, nail files, and a large bottle of nail-varnish remover.

'Oh blimey! We're not gonna 'ave ter put up with that bloody stink all the afternoon are we?' roared Syd as he got to his feet. With a swipe of his hand he swept the various bottles into a heap. From his pocket he pulled a roll of notes and, with a flash of anger, he pulled a fiver from the roll and threw it towards Doris. 'Here,' he yelled, 'take the kids round the park or something; buy yourselves all the ice-creams an' sweets you can eat but stay out of our way till the racing's finished.'

Doris still didn't say anything as she got the boys' coats out of the cupboard, but as she passed Lizzie a hint of a smile was playing round her lips and she dropped her left eye-lid and winked.

They had a marvellous afternoon, and when they got back Syd was in a really good mood so it was obvious that he had beaten the bookies for once. Polly and Arthur brought Lucy over to number twelve about half-past seven, and Mrs Thompson's daughter from the corner shop came at a quarter to eight to stay with the children while the grown-ups all trooped along to the Horse and Groom.

The pub had a piano and a pianist was always

hired for Saturday nights. As the evening wore on, and the drinks had taken effect, the pub became very lively with all the customers joining in singing the ever-popular old songs. This was Lizzie's idea of a good night out.

All too soon, though, it was time to go back to Devon. But there was one thing that Lizzie vowed and declared to Charlie as he packed their cases away in the boot of his car. 'I don't care what yer do or say; it's not gonna be three years this time before I come home again.'

Chapter Twenty-Two

THE WEATHER HAD stayed pretty good. There was not much warmth in the sunshine now, and the dark nights were cold, but for October it wasn't at all bad. At least there was no sign of rain.

They had had breakfast with Doris and Syd on the Monday morning and set off from Wilton Road just after ten o'clock. Charlie had made good time, stopping only once in Taunton for them to have some lunch and go to the toilet. He had pulled into their own garage just as the village church clock was striking four. By the time Lizzie had unpacked the cases, put the dirty washing in the sink to soak, cooked the dinner and seen Robert to bed she was whacked. Slouched down now in an armchair in front of the fire, which Charlie had lit in the lounge, she was half-asleep, her mind miles away, when suddenly she was brought up with a jerk as Charlie said, 'I think we'll keep Robert off from school for another week.'

'What the hell for?' she muttered as she struggled to sit up and gather her wits about her.

'Because I want this thing settled one way or the other,' he snapped back.

'Well, there's no need ter be so crabby; just say what's on yer mind an' we'll talk about it.'

Charlie had been in a funny mood from the moment they had arrived back and now Lizzie decided that her best bet would be to tread warily. She knew he had discussed the matter with Syd and she understood why he would like the sale of this guesthouse to go through. If the local agent was to be believed, there wouldn't be any problem finding a purchaser, but what was the point if they had nowhere to go?

Yet to stay on here now would be ridiculous. Without the extra rooms at the pub, there wasn't enough income to give them a good living, unless they had another string to their bow. Lizzie knew exactly what she would like to do – sell up and go back to London. But at this point it wouldn't be fair, she told herself, even to suggest it to Charlie. What would he do for a job? He'd been really good all the time they'd been staying with Syd and Doris. Lizzie chided herself; Charlie deserved a chance to see if he could find an hotel that would be for sale at a price that they could afford.

'I'd like to take a look at Bournemouth,' Charlie's statement broke into her thoughts again. 'What d'yer think? We could take Robert, set out early in the morning, stay a few days in an hotel an' check out the estate agents. By all accounts, Bournemouth has become one of the most popular pleasure resorts in the country.'

Lizzie just stopped herself in time from making an ugly grimace; Bournemouth! Still, if that's what he wanted to do she'd do well to go along with him.

'All right,' she agreed in a happy tone of voice which was far from what she was really feeling. 'Why not? A few days being waited on in someone else's hotel will be a nice change.'

They were in Bournemouth by lunchtime and Charlie booked them into the Royal Exeter Hotel. The large bedroom they were assigned had one double bed and one single bed and looked right out over the sea. By the time Lizzie had freshened up she was feeling much more relaxed, determined to enjoy this unexpected holiday. After they had had lunch, Charlie declared that he was going to visit some of the local estate agents and if possible obtain details of any hotels that might be for sale in the vicinity. Lizzie breathed a sigh of relief when, instead of asking her to accompany him, Charlie suggested that she took Robert on the pier.

Later that night, when Robert was in bed and fast asleep, Charlie persuaded Lizzie to come downstairs into the lounge-bar and have a drink. Settled comfortably at a table near the window, their drinks in front of them, Charlie began to read through the particulars of properties that he had managed to collect.

'Interested in buying an hotel, are you?' A tall, middle-aged man in a well-cut suit held out his hand. 'Martin Fenwick,' he said and, with a grin, added, 'joint owner of this place with the bank.'

Charlie laughed as he got to his feet and shook the fellow's hand. 'Charlie Wilson, and this is my wife. She won't mind you calling her Lizzie, everyone does.'

Martin Fenwick shook hands with Lizzie. 'How do you like Bournemouth? Bit quiet here at this time of the year.' Without giving Lizzie time to reply he went on, 'You're staying a few days, aren't you? You must meet my wife and my two sons. Stephen is just four, the other one, John, has turned six.'

He was a likeable man, Lizzie decided as she went upstairs, leaving Charlie to have one for the road. He hadn't put on any airs and graces, even though he owned this large hotel. Quite the opposite, he had made her feel very welcome and he might turn out to be very useful to Charlie. At that thought Lizzie smiled to herself; she certainly didn't want Charlie getting himself involved in any more complicated deals. The buying of Sea View Guesthouse had proved to be enough of a headache for one lifetime.

Sunday was a lovely autumn day, not in the least bit cold. There was bright sunshine and the few clouds that there were in the sky were the white fluffy kind like cotton wool.

Lizzie felt a great deal more relaxed as they walked along the seafront in the direction of the hotel they were about to view.

It was Mr Fenwick who, having made several phone calls on their behalf, had finally arranged this appointment.

'Seems a bit odd viewing on a Sunday,' Lizzie had ventured.

'Not at all, quietest day of the week,' he had assured her, 'and, by the way, no need to drag your son along with you. Leave him with us; he'll be happy enough with my two.'

When Robert had been shown the electric train set, he had made no fuss about being left.

Charlie wore a new overcoat, which wasn't really necessary on a day like this, but it made him appear even more broad in the shoulder. His beige cavalry twill trousers were sharply creased and his feet were shod in the very finest brown brogue shoes, for if there was one thing Charlie was particular about it was footwear. Only leather would do, nothing imitation.

Lizzie looked up into his face as they came to a halt outside the hotel. You wouldn't think he had just finished a season; his face glowed with health and his hair was still thick and glossy.

Lizzie herself had lost over a stone in weight since last Easter, and although the brown skirt she wore fitted well, the jacket hung a little loosely.

As if reading her thoughts Charlie said, 'Come on, my Skinny Lizzie, let's go in.' Lizzie was taken aback. No one had called her that for years!

The outside of the building hadn't impressed either of them. Dingy, they thought. The brick-work was dirty and colourless. The entrance hall wasn't much better, gloomy and shabby with arm-chairs that were frayed and faded. No one came, in spite of the fact that they had rung the bell twice. Sounds of music and laughter were coming from below, and they trod the wide staircase that led downwards. A game of bingo was being played in a colossal basement lounge that was crowded with elderly folk.

It was mainly the ribald remarks of the gentleman seated on the raised platform calling the numbers that accounted for the amusement of the players. 'Bit near the knuckle!' Charlie said beneath his breath as the caller's jokes became more and more indelicate.

They wandered off to one side of the hall and found themselves in what could only be described as a casino. Every conceivable type of gambling was there, plus machines which dispensed hot and cold drinks, bars of chocolate, packets of sweets and nuts, even packets of aspirin.

Lizzie thought of the endless hours that she and Charlie had spent in the evenings making pots of tea or coffee and boiling milk for Ovaltine or Horlicks.

They retraced their steps and each of them was embarrassed as a pot-bellied man with a high-coloured complexion stared angrily at them.

'Are you Mr Petrock?' Charlie asked in a composed voice.

'Yes, you must be Mr and Mrs Wilson; didn't expect you this early.' He ignored Charlie's outstretched hand, and merely said, 'I'm the warden.'

'Warden?' Lizzie spoke without thinking.

'Yes,' he replied, giving no further information.

'We'll start with the bedrooms.' He stalked off, leaving Charlie and Lizzie to follow.

'I don't like him,' Lizzie thought, 'miserable old beggar.'

The corridors were forbidding, very narrow, with no windows and badly lit. The decor and colour scheme consisted mainly of fawn paint. At first, Lizzie couldn't grasp the layout at all, as Mr Petrock opened door after door without saying a word.

Suddenly Charlie clutched at Lizzie's arm and held her back for a moment. His voice a harsh whisper, he said, 'I've just fell in. I've got it now. Apart from the main building, this place is a series of terraced houses with connecting doorways.'

There wasn't time for Lizzie to answer. Mr Petrock flung wide yet another door and stood back, though why he is bothering himself, I don't know, Lizzie thought, every room is exactly the same.

Each contained the maximum number of beds it was possible to squeeze in, and the vacant floor space was hardly enough to enable the occupants to walk around the beds. No chairs, no wardrobes, just a hanging space on the back of the door, covered by a dingy curtain.

The rooms were barren even of necessities, let alone any items of comfort. Door handles were broken, dripping taps over wash-basins needed new washers, carpets were frayed, rucked up in some places, light bulbs were burnt out, leaving sections of the corridors in complete darkness.

'Do you have a maintenance man on the staff?' Charlie asked.

'This is not The Ritz,' was Mr Petrock's ill-tempered reply.

Lizzie was about to say that they had seen enough when she saw that the room she had just entered was occupied. 'I'm so sorry,' she murmured, as she backed away towards the door. She suddenly felt frightened, although she could not have said what of. All she knew was that something was very wrong.

She turned, seeking Charlie, who, seeing the fear showing in her eyes, hastily pushed Mr Petrock to one side. Lizzie had to stifle the scream that rose up in her throat as her glance fell upon a seagull. The huge, fat, grey and white bird was perched on the window sill, not outside but *inside* the room.

As she watched, it took off in flight around the room, its great wings beating and thrashing in frustration. It appeared incredibly menacing at such close quarters, as it swooped low, squawking and shrieking, heading straight for Lizzie.

She screamed and covered her face with her arms, but Charlie shoved her aside. With long strides he was across the room to where an elderly man lay wedged between two beds. Kneeling, Charlie raised the man's head by placing his arm under his neck. Softly he murmured over and over again, 'It's all right, old chap, it's all right; you're safe now.' But the man was in such a state of agitation, rocking himself frantically from side to side, that he finally collapsed heavily against Charlie.

Quickly enough, Mr Petrock caught the gull and put it out through the window. 'Rough high-tide last night. Must have got in through the window and couldn't find its way out,' he complained – though there was a slight hint of an apology in the tone of his voice.

'Get some brandy, man, don't just stand there,' Charlie was fast losing his temper. Mr Petrock didn't bother to reply, he just went.

Judging from the shocking state of the room, the gull had been imprisoned for some length of time. Its droppings had soiled everything – the counterpanes on the bed and the carpet were liberally spattered, even the curtains were covered.

Charlie wouldn't leave until the man was obviously a lot calmer, and as Lizzie waited in the dingy hallway she asked herself what would have happened if they hadn't gone into that particular room.

The estate agent's list had detailed that this hotel was not an orthodox hotel in the accepted sense, rather a balance between a holiday home and a rest home for elderly people. The owners had contracts with various city councils and civic homes to take old-age pensioners, some on a long-term plan, others for shorter periods of approximately a month.

What had attracted Charlie was the hint that all-the-year-round trade was possible, rather than just a seasonal period.

That was all very well, but elderly people needed constant surveillance. If you took on the responsibility, you should damn well carry it through, Lizzie thought angrily. Like Charlie, she had been appalled at the conditions in which these old folk were roaming about. The whole place was fraught with danger.

'I've made you some tea,' Mr Petrock called from the top of the stairs.

'Have you now,' Lizzie said in a mocking voice, just as Charlie emerged from the bedroom.

'Leave it out, Lizzie,' he ordered. 'Christ, I can do with a cup of tea, the stronger the better, then we'll get out of here.'

A few minutes later they were seated in a private sitting-room. No penny pinching here. There were deep armchairs with plump cushions, thick pile carpet on the floor and full-length velvet curtains hung at the windows. They drank their tea in silence, then, reading each other's thoughts, Charlie and Lizzie stood up.

'Just one question, Mr Petrock,' Charlie said, 'where are the owners of this hotel, is it their day off?'

Mr Petrock was in a cold sweat, the incident upstairs had frightened him. The old man might have died. His hands dropped limply to his sides and he moistened his thick lips before he answered, 'No. They're abroad on holiday.'

'So, you're in sole charge?'

'In a manner of speaking.'

'Oh no, there's no two ways about it. Either you are in charge or someone else is,' Charlie's manner was furious by now. 'For God's sake, man, aren't you at all worried about what happened?'

Mr Petrock looked about him vaguely, then, turning to Lizzie, he murmured, 'I'll show you out through the kitchen, save you going upstairs again.'

The kitchen was the last straw! Both Lizzie and Charlie were horrified. Lizzie couldn't move, she just stood and gawped. Everything was so disorganized, and the smell was dreadful!

The flagstone floor was thick with grease. A complete wall of shelves held vast numbers of cups, saucers, plates and dishes, and even a quick glance showed that the china was far from clean.

Two beautiful, expensive commercial cookers made Lizzie feel sick just to look at them. They were not just messy or mucky, they were plain filthy – absolutely soiled with grease. Unwashed saucepans cluttered the top of each stove.

Neither of them could wait to get out into the fresh air.

Having related the whole experience to Mr Fenwick they sat together quietly, deep in thought until Martin Fenwick made a profound observation. 'You know, Mr Wilson, someone will come along and buy that hotel. They'll have a lucrative business for a few years, then they'll sell it and end up just as rich as the present owners no doubt are.'

Under his breath, Charlie muttered, 'Well, it

won't be us.' Aloud he said, 'I don't understand how they get away with it. Aren't there regular checks on establishments that take elderly folk on a permanent basis? Surely, the local authorities should be involved.'

'I shall certainly raise the matter at the next meeting of the local hoteliers' association,' Mr Fenwick said and Charlie knew that his concern was genuine.

Chapter Twenty-Three

CHARLIE HAD TAKEN Robert to school and Lizzie was not yet dressed when the telephone rang.

'Phillips and Ashfield here, Mrs Wilson,' a smooth voice stated as soon as Lizzie picked up the receiver. 'We have a property on our books which may interest you, would you like me to mail you the details?'

'Well, we shall be coming down to the village later on. We'll call in and pick them up.'

'Thank you, Mrs Wilson, goodbye for now.'

Lizzie and Charlie were in Mr Phillips' office by ten-thirty.

'My, you're keen,' John Phillips said as he shook hands with Charlie. 'I've never had the pleasure of meeting you before, Mrs Wilson, though I have downed the odd pint with your husband before now.' Actually, he was quite surprised – Mrs Wilson wasn't at all what he had expected: small-boned, slim, sleek fair hair, a woollen two-piece with shoes, gloves and handbag which all toned in extremely well.

She was no Devon dumpling.

'How does the Manor House Hotel at Milton grab you, Charlie?'

Lizzie watched closely as Charlie scanned the typed sheets of paper. First name terms, these two. Well, well.

This John Phillips was big, and handsome with it, and to be fair, he was the type who would be popular with men as well as women. He turned now and smiled broadly at Lizzie. Yes, he could be a useful friend, she thought approvingly.

That evening, Charlie looked through the motoring guidebooks.

'Yes, here it is,' he pointed out to Lizzie enthusiastically. 'Manor House Hotel, well established, popular with tourists and near a famous beauty spot.'

They were on their way before ten o'clock the next morning. The countryside, though not at its best, still looked fresh and good. The hills were green, the cattle in the fields looked well fed and contented, and the agricultural land was tilled ready for the winter frosts.

Even from the outskirts of the village, the hotel was visible. Perched on a hilltop site, it was very prominent. Clearly sign-posted, Charlie soon drew the car to a halt. Ahead lay a surprisingly lengthy driveway.

Lizzie held her breath for a long time before letting it out in a loud gasp. Formal gardens with low hedges lay each side, and groups of trees and flowering shrubs were still vivid with colour.

They sat in silence as Charlie drove up to the hotel.

Four wide marble steps led up to a huge oak door. 'What do you think of it?' Charlie asked.

'Beautiful,' Lizzie said, 'but we could never afford anything like this.'

The big door opened before they had got out of the car and a slim young woman in a flowered dress walked down the steps to meet them. Lizzie thought her to be about thirty-five. She had a country look about her, rosy cheeks and her cotton dress was stained with earth as if she had been working in the garden.

She came towards them eagerly. 'I'm Phyllis Martin, my parents are expecting you. I'm their youngest daughter. Come in, you're staying for lunch, aren't you?'

Lizzie was amazed at such a welcome.

Mr and Mrs Jeffries were waiting in the entrance hall. Both Charlie and Lizzie soon surmised that Jeffries was not the original surname of this nice couple.

Charlie found holding a conversation with Mr Jeffries heavy going. His birthplace had been Poland and, although he had lived in England for a good many years, his English was not that good. Approaching seventy, he was pleasantly fat, but he had a further handicap, a gammy leg. When seated, it stuck out straight in front of him and, even with the aid of a stick, he couldn't walk without difficulty.

Mrs Jeffries was a homely type of woman; an older version of her daughter, uncomplicated and easy to be with. She ushered them through into a very large kitchen, sympathizing about their long journey, exclaiming over the rawness of the day despite protests from Lizzie that it wasn't at all cold outside. Moving quickly, she drew chairs near to a roaring fire. 'Take your coats off, come along, make yourselves comfortable. Phyllis is just making the coffee. Do you know this area?'

Charlie and Lizzie smiled at each other, Mrs Jeffries didn't seem to expect any answers.

Phyllis came through from what looked like a smaller kitchen, pushing a loaded trolley. The cups and saucers were attractive, white patterned with bold blue stripes, almost matching the gingham curtains which hung at the kitchen windows. The aroma of the coffee was good as Phyllis poured and handed the cups around. Mrs Jeffries handed out matching plates, insisting that everyone must eat a scone, piping hot and served with thick yellow clotted cream and strawberry jam.

While they were eating, Mr Jeffries told them that he had another older daughter. 'Karie . . .' the old man actually stopped smiling as he spoke her name. He took a deep breath and continued, 'Karie, she is on holiday in Jersey with her husband,' and Lizzie felt sure that his expression indicated his relief.

'If you're all set, shall we start the inspection? Are you coming with us, David?'

'Yes, yes, my dear, I'll tag along behind you all. Slowly it might be, but I'll make it.'

Mr Jeffries smiled apologetically at Lizzie and Charlie, then nodded gently to his wife and daughter. 'Go ahead, go along,' he shooed them.

The main staircase swept up to a semi-circular gallery which led to the bedrooms.

On this floor, the rooms were large, light and airy, not at all like the usual hotel bedroom. Lizzie's first thought was that they were typical of a country manor house, then she laughed at herself. How would she know? She'd never seen the inside of any manor house. Each room had an enormous, high, double bed, massive sized furniture and deep, comfortable armchairs which were drawn invitingly into the bow-shaped window recess so that any resident could view the grounds through the windows while relaxing.

The hotel had twenty-five bedrooms and, as they proceeded, Charlie and Lizzie exchanged glances. They were able to read each other's thoughts.

To each of them, it was obvious that Mr and Mrs Jeffries not only had a deep affection for each other, but also treasured their hotel and were proud of what they had achieved. Lizzie even felt a little guilty; the whole place had such a warm atmosphere, much more like a home than an hotel. She felt that she and Charlie were intruding and even began to ask herself why this dear couple had decided to sell up when, without a doubt, they loved this place.

On the second floor, the rooms were not so spacious but were equally charming. A lot of thought had been given to the furnishing of the bedrooms, although Lizzie got the feeling that most of the furniture had been installed there since the place was built many years ago.

It was the little final touches which added to the attractiveness of this floor. The windows were much smaller, yet the curtains were exactly right; each set was made to be in keeping with the surroundings. Rich, heavy, fully lined fabrics had been hung at the windows of the rooms on the floor below, with bedspreads and chair coverings all co-ordinated, but here the accessories were totally different in style and manner. Bright floral, cotton chintz had been the main choice. In parts, the carpets were old, even showing signs of being threadbare, but bright soft rugs had been scattered to compensate for this.

At the far end of this top landing were three rooms set apart up a further short flight of stairs, each so in keeping with the character of the house that Lizzie exclaimed, 'Oh, aren't they marvellous!'

'Not when it comes to working them, they're not,' was Phyllis's quick retort. 'They're very popular with the foreign tourists though.' Everyone laughed. Americans would term them 'quaint'. There was no running water here, only hefty marble-topped wash-stands on top of which stood ornate china jugs and bowls, each elaborately decorated with gilt.

At the base of the staircase, a panel of wood was

fixed to the wall from which hung two rows of brass bells, each suspended loosely by means of a hook-shaped spring. Above each bell, a plaque bore a number which presumably corresponded with a bedroom.

Lizzie's imagination ran riot. Supposing several rang at once, noisy, jangling, ear-splitting sounds – and how many staff would you need to keep running up and down the stairs in answer to their summons?

'It's all right, my dear,' Mr Jeffries chuckled, 'they don't work. The bell push-buttons are still in each bedroom, but they are all disconnected. I fear the days when such service was given are long gone.'

Lizzie and Phyllis exchanged conspiratorial glances.

'Thank God for that,' was their silent answer.

Charlie declared the dining-room to be his favourite.

All the tables were made of oak, and the high-backed chairs had upholstered seats. There was no carpet but the parquet flooring was so highly polished that one could have used it as a mirror.

'We cheat; we use an electric floor polisher,' Mrs Jeffries said proudly.

Next came the lounge. Lizzie unintentionally let out a shriek of amazement. Stepping further into the room, she felt that she had gone back in time – a high, moulded ceiling, an enormous white marble fireplace, bright wood panelling on the walls and a view of the sea in the distance from the windows.

Armchairs and settees were arranged into groups, even a chaise-longue, all covered in uncut moquette of a deep, rich red colour. The floor-length curtains were velvet with a deep valance which was decorated with heavy silk tassels. Small side tables and reading lamps had been placed at strategic points around the room.

By now, Mr Jeffries was visibly tired and limping badly.

'Do you mind if we ask to be excused? Phyllis will finish showing you around; lunch will be ready soon. David come, rest your leg; leave the youngsters to it.' Mrs Jefferies ushered her husband gently out of the room.

'You'd better come and see my quarters,' Phyllis frowned as she spoke.

'You've been marvellous, Phyllis,' Charlie patted her shoulder, 'we don't want to bother you if you'd rather not.'

'No, it's all right, really it is.'

Two minutes later, Lizzie understood the reason for Phyllis's reluctance.

Coming out into a courtyard, Phyllis led them down a ramp and opened a heavy door which was set into the brickwork, revealing a flight of steps leading downwards.

As they hesitated, two bonny little girls, aged about seven and eight, came running up the steps.

'Mummy, you've been a long time, may we go

over to Grandma's now?' the taller of the two pleaded.

'Just a minute. Say hallo to Mr and Mrs Wilson, and then we are all going to have lunch with Grandma.'

'Hallo,' they chorused, now happily hopping back down the steps. Lizzie chuckled as she watched them; they both looked so pretty, shining and spotless in identical blue dresses and hand-knitted white cardigans. Even Charlie was struck by their open smiling faces.

Phyllis's home was a basement apartment; nothing would disguise that fact. Clean and comfortable, but Lizzie concluded that not much daylight ever penetrated down here.

Soon they were back up in the yard, the two little girls, now running and skipping ahead of them. 'We've got plenty of garage space,' Phyllis said, pointing to what could have been a stable block in years past.

'Are these more sleeping quarters?' Charlie asked, stopping and raising his eyes to what appeared to be a recently built apartment over and above the whole block.

'No, that's where my sister Karie and her husband Ray live. It was built for them three years ago.' Then she added, with abruptness, 'They don't have any children.'

With a sigh, Phyllis led the way up the outside staircase. 'I don't have a key, you'll have to peer through the windows.'

It was very modern in appearance, with wide, clear windows, but this one-storey apartment was totally out of keeping with the main building. Noses pressed to the glass, hands cupped around their eyes, they could see that white was the predominant colour – the walls, the furniture, even the carpets were all white.

Lizzie thought it gave a clinical effect, you could tell at a glance no children lived in there. They almost tip-toed back down the iron stairway, acting as if they had been trespassing.

Charlie hung back and, taking hold of Lizzie's arm, he nodded towards Phyllis's back and murmured, 'A sight different to where she has to live.'

Lizzie was still curious and, as she entered the main door held open for her by Phyllis, she asked, 'Where do your mother and father sleep?'

'In one of the main bedrooms during the winter months, but they use a bed-settee in the preparation room when we're busy in the summer.'

At their age! Lizzie almost answered back, for there was something terribly unfair about this set-up.

Charlie quietly asked, 'Why do your parents want to sell this lovely place?'

Phyllis shuddered and, for a moment, Lizzie thought she was about to cry; instead, she changed direction, moving back towards the dining-room.

'Sit down, it's better if we talk in here; I don't want my dad to get upset.'

Slowly, almost reluctantly, she told them, 'When

my father reached the age of sixty-five, which was almost five years ago, in order to be eligible to draw his old-age pension he officially resigned from the business. Legally he made Mum, Karie and me a three-way partnership. We each, from then on, owned one-third of the hotel and all its assets. The trouble started from that very moment, and it was all Karie's fault.' Phyllis sat forward in her chair; her dark eyes were blazing.

'We came close to getting a divorce, my Ron and me. Sorry, Ron is my husband. He's a skilled engineer with a good job in Exeter. That's almost seventy miles and he does the journey every night and morning. Mind you, I freely admit, Ron does his fair share of moaning; he doesn't like living where we do, calls it an underground rat-hole.'

Who could blame him? Lizzie thought. An apt description in her opinion.

Charlie smiled and shook his head. 'I doubt you're any different to any other family, everyone has their squabbles.'

'Um, well,' Phyllis sighed, 'he doesn't like me to be working when he gets home, says the girls are left too long on their own.'

'What about staff?' Charlie stuck his neck out and asked, 'Couldn't you take on more?'

'There's no bus service that comes up here. Besides, the year before last Karie sacked two girls on the spot – caught them putting tinned stuff into their bags on the way out. She should have turned a blind eye, but no, that's not Karie's way. The people down in the village are a tight-knit community, they only heard those girls' side of the story. Anyway, they have never trusted us. Foreigners we are to them in every sense of the word; you'd think we'd all just got off the boat from Poland only yesterday. My mother and father have been in this country for forty-two years.' Her last sentence was said with bitterness in her voice.

Pulling herself together, Phyllis stood up, 'We'd better go and find Mum and Dad.'

Mrs Jeffries had food ready in the lounge and, in answer to Lizzie's protests, she insisted, 'It is only a light lunch to hold you over until you get home.'

They were each given a tray on their laps in order to eat the crisp cheese salad and hot rolls with butter. Rosie and Linda, Phyllis's two little girls, threw themselves down on to the floor and their grandma lovingly placed a tray in front of each of them. It seemed to Lizzie like a cosy family party.

Later, Phyllis left the room and returned with a glass of milk for each of her daughters and a cup of tea for everyone else.

Soon, Charlie stood up. 'We mustn't intrude any longer,' he said, but Mr Jeffries waved him back into his seat and leaned forward himself.

He was agitated, a fact that did not improve his speech. Mrs Jeffries did her best to calm him down, while Phyllis asked, 'Father wants to know, are you interested in buying our hotel?'

'Yes, we are,' Charlie said without any hesitation. 'Naturally, there's a lot to sort out. We have to sell

our own place and we'll need a loan from the bank.
Depends a lot on the bank, really.'

Mr Jeffries, calmer now, spoke slowly. 'If
additional finance is a problem, I myself would be
prepared to give a second mortgage.'

'Well!' the one word burst from Charlie's mouth.
'I don't know what to say,' he stammered, 'only,
thank you.'

As Charlie drove away, Lizzie felt that their day had
been spent in a completely different world. She sat
day-dreaming, picturing herself cooking in that
pleasant kitchen and reading in the long winter evenings, snug and warm in that wonderful lounge.

Turning his eyes away from the road for a
moment, Charlie looked hard at Lizzie and considered his words carefully. 'Don't build your hopes
too high,' he said, 'there's something wrong with
the set-up there.'

'Oh Charlie, don't put the dampers on it. It was
a lovely day, wasn't it?'

'Yes, it was,' he readily agreed, 'and nicer people
you couldn't wish to meet. I'm just saying . . .'

What he was just saying Lizzie would never
know, and she had the good sense not to ask, yet
for one awful moment she had doubts. She shook
her head hard; she wasn't going to let anything inter-
fere with her dream of living at the Manor House
Hotel.

That same evening, Charlie was on the phone to
John Phillips for quite a long time. 'He feels sure

he's got a cash buyer for this place,' Charlie said, smiling as he sat down, and that was all that was said on the matter that evening.

The following morning, Phyllis Martin rang. 'Would it be asking too much for you to come back again tomorrow?' her voice sounded strained.

'We'd love to,' Lizzie assured her, then her inquisitiveness got the better of her. 'What's happened, are your parents all right?'

Phyllis ignored the latter part of the question. 'Karie's home,' she said, and Lizzie heard her make a cynical sound. 'Father said it's best if we all meet. Mother said lunch would be ready at one o'clock, so we'll see you then, Mrs Wilson,' and the phone line went dead.

'Bit quick, isn't it?' was Charlie's only comment.

He was ready first next morning, wearing a suit, collar and tie, looking every inch a businessman. He scowled as he looked at his watch. Lizzie came through the door, her thin silk dress rustled as she walked.

'Do you think I shall be warm enough in this dress?' she asked and she smiled at him with eyes filled with excitement.

'How the hell should I know? You're taking a big coat, aren't you?'

'Yes,' she said, 'I'm ready.'

'About time, too,' he retorted, still scowling a little.

Lizzie came near and kissed him on the cheek. 'Something worrying you?' she asked.

'I don't know,' he moved quickly towards the door. 'I'll feel a lot better when I find out why the Jeffries have invited us back so soon. At least I hope I shall.'

'Why? Do you think they've changed their minds?'

'Just let's stop supposing things and get going, shall we?' Charlie said abruptly as he opened the door of the car.

When they arrived, it was Phyllis who came down the steps to greet them.

'Come inside first. Mother said we'll have a drink together.' Seeing their puzzled expressions, she quickly explained, 'We're having lunch at Karie's.'

The sherry was good, and the Jeffries seemed exceedingly pleased to see them both again. Phyllis's husband Ron was there, an ordinary, everyday type of fellow, rugged in appearance as if he spent a great deal of his time out of doors. Charlie and Ron Martin hit it off from the moment they shook hands.

Lizzie wasn't prepared for meeting Karie. She gaped almost open-mouthed until Charlie nudged her.

Inches taller than either her sister or her mother, Karie had a fantastic figure. The cream silk dress she was wearing didn't just fit well, it looked as if it had been moulded around her. Most lovely of all was her thick, shiny, auburn hair. Most probably the colour comes out of a bottle, Lizzie thought enviously. Everything about Karie was immaculate, her sheer stockings, elegant court shoes, even her long red fingernails. She was most certainly different to any other member of this family and Lizzie felt sure that this was no accident. One could tell that Karie strove hard to be different. Her husband introduced himself first to Charlie and then to Lizzie.

'Ray Daniels, pleased to meet you,' he spoke quietly.

He was a tall young man in silver-grey trousers and a well-cut black velvet jacket. His eyes were brilliantly blue and shiny, and his smile was warm and friendly. In fact, his whole air was open and boyish, even if his dress was a bit showy.

The lunch was excellent, down to the last detail, but what surprised both Lizzie and Charlie the most was that a dark-haired and dark-skinned young lady in uniform waited on them as they all sat around a glass-topped dining-table.

The mood while they were eating was very different to that of their previous meeting. There were long silences, especially between courses.

Finally, when the last dishes had been removed by the maid, Karie said brightly, 'Shall we have our coffee in the lounge?'

Mrs Jeffries's eyes never left her husband's face as they sat drinking their cups of coffee. The atmosphere felt decidedly strange and Lizzie was beginning to feel uncomfortable. As she repeatedly said to Charlie afterwards, 'I'll never know in God's name what sparked that lot off.'

Until that moment the whole family had been tolerant of each other, then suddenly it was as if a bubble had been burst. Everyone began to talk at once and in seconds the place was in an uproar.

Karie dominated the scene. Staring directly at Charlie, she left him in no doubt as to the frame of mind she was in. 'You are here under false pretences. I don't know why my father contacted an estate agent.'

'Now, dear,' Mrs Jeffries said, seeing her daughter's temper getting out of hand, 'there's no need to be rude to our guests.'

'Well, it can't go on. I won't stand for it. All he thinks about is selling the hotel. An hotel in which he has no legal part.'

'Oh, how can you be so cruel,' Mrs Jeffries uttered a groan while Mr Jeffries took out his handkerchief and wiped the sweat from his face and hands.

Lizzie had never felt so uncomfortable in all her life.

Charlie looked hot under the collar, and, but for the fact that he had just eaten a meal at Karie's table plus the kindness of the old couple, he would have stormed out there and then.

The argument continued in earnest now.

Ron Martin taunted Ray Daniels with the fact that he had no job. 'You live off your wife you do,' he spat out, his face only inches away from his brother-in-law's.

Karie turned on Phyllis. 'You only want money. Sell, sell, sell, is all I hear from you, just so that you can get your hands on a third of the money.'

'Christ! You're the right one to talk about money. You spend it quicker than we can make it. Yes, and I do mean *we*. Mum and Dad and me, we're the general dogs-bodies around her. It's us that does every job imaginable while you swan around playing the lady.'

Mrs Jeffries, her complexion quite flushed by then, placed herself between her two daughters.

And only just in time, thought Lizzie, she'd seen women row, even fight, in London, and this little do was fast getting out of hand.

'Do as your father wants,' Mrs Jeffries pleaded. 'If we sell this place, you can each buy a nice house, and your father and I can have a nice little bungalow; why not be reasonable?'

'It's nothing to do with our father; how many more times do I have to tell you?' Karie shouted.

Mr Jeffries, struggling to stand on his feet, implored his eldest daughter, 'All I ask is that you sign the contract.'

'No. I've told you and I mean it, no.' With a defiant look in Charlie's direction, Karie turned her back and walked out of the room.

Lizzie found that her thoughts were all mixed up. No way did she condone Karie's attitude towards her parents nor yet tolerate the fact that she was ashamed of them, for it was obvious that she was. In spite of all that, Lizzie found a part of herself admiring Karie. Who could blame her for being so stubborn? The business here provided her with a lifestyle she enjoyed, she was well set-up in a home of her own choosing, and she wasn't about to give it all up without a struggle.

She was utterly selfish, of course she was, but Lizzie couldn't help wondering how she might have reacted, given the same set of circumstances. Twice she asked herself the same question and still she honestly didn't know the answer.

To be fair, Ray Daniels did try to ease the situation. He went into the kitchen and made fresh coffee, offering brandy with it as he handed it round. The silence in the room hung heavy and both Lizzie and Charlie were relieved when at last they could say their goodbyes and make their escape.

It was a relief to be out in the fresh air.

Mr Jeffries had been visibly upset and had tried to apologize to Charlie. The women had kissed each other goodbye and all three of them had been close to tears. The journey home promised to be a solemn one indeed. For they now realized that owning the Manor House Hotel had been nothing more than a pipe-dream.

Chapter Twenty-Four

IT WAS GETTING towards the end of October now, and neither Lizzie nor Charlie had much enthusiasm left in them to go searching for another property. And yet the prospect of only having twelve bedrooms to let for the next season was not very encouraging.

John Phillips had twice shown the same couple around the guesthouse, a Mr and Mrs Sadler from Birmingham. They had both expressed an interest in the property. Lizzie had liked them well enough and on each occasion she had cut sandwiches and made coffee for them, but when it came to answering Mrs Sadler's questions as to the running of the guesthouse, Lizzie couldn't be bothered, and even Charlie refused to discuss business details with Mr Sadler.

'What's the point?' Lizzie overheard Charlie saying to John Phillips. 'We can't sell this place until we find an hotel for ourselves, and if we don't do that before Christmas, we might as well forget it.'

That's true, Lizzie agreed with Charlie. Once Christmas was over, there was never much time to spare. The mail had to be the number one priority. Every morning, letters had to be answered and replies back in the post by noon whenever possible.

After all, one could get the place looking like Buckingham Palace, but without any subsequent bookings, you'd be wasting your time.

Lizzie felt sorry for the Sadlers, they wanted an answer; their future was in the balance just as much as Charlie's and hers.

Two weeks slipped by during which nothing of importance took place and Lizzie was quite glad when Friday came round again and they could have their day out in Barnstaple. Having finished the weekly shopping, Charlie asked, 'Where would you like to have lunch?'

'Anywhere that suits you, I'm easy,' Lizzie replied.

'Right, let's make it the Imperial.'

They had almost finished eating when Mr and Mrs Farrant stopped by their table. Mr Farrant was a local solicitor with his own firm in a nearby village. On two occasions, Charlie had taken Lizzie to his office, once when needing advice, and a second time when Mr Farrant had taken care of the legalities when Lizzie's mother had died. Lizzie had also formed a friendship with Margaret Farrant while doing voluntary work for the WVS.

'When are you moving?' Mr Farrant asked.

Charlie's face must have had a blank look, because Mr Farrant immediately said, 'Didn't John Phillips put you in touch with the Jeffries out at Milton, the Manor House? I understood you were going ahead with that.'

Charlie laughed, 'I only wish we were. It all fell through.'

'Oh, I'm sorry to hear that. Well, finish your meal and come through to the bar, I may have some interesting news for you.'

Fifteen minutes later the two couples were settled with their drinks, on a window-seat in the lounge. After the usual small-talk, Mr Farrant said, 'Well, now to business.'

Taking a card from his wallet, he wrote a few words on the back of it, and then, passing it to Charlie, he spoke quietly.

'Take that to Freddie Clarke and he will arrange for you to view an hotel. It's a bit hush-hush, not yet officially on the market, but ideal for you two, I should think. Anyway, Freddie will fill you in on the details.'

Today, Charlie thought, it is not *what* you know but *who* you know that makes the difference.

Freddie Clarke was a well-known local character. His main occupation was as estate agent but by no means was it his only method of earning a living. He had earned the reputation of being a Mr Fix-It.

Not much was said over the telephone when Charlie rang him, except that he would be in to see them that same evening.

It was a little after seven o'clock when he arrived and the first thing Charlie did was offer him a drink, which he readily accepted. When they were all settled comfortably in the lounge, the two men with whisky and soda, Lizzie with whisky and dry ginger, Freddie opened his case and took out some papers and, nodding grimly, he said, 'These are the only details I have got. This hotel will be going up for sale but with certain drawbacks.'

'Oh, no, here we go again,' Lizzie said beneath her breath.

'Why all the mystery?' Charlie questioned.

'Because the owners don't want to sell,' said the up-to-now serious Freddie Clarke, then he leant forward, picked up his glass and drained it quickly.

'Mind if I smoke my pipe?' he asked, and Lizzie was surprised at just how old this man looked as she waited while he filled the bowl of his briar with tobacco and Charlie refilled his glass. Without his trilby hat, which he always wore when he was out, she could see that he was almost bald and he appeared tired and sluggish. He once more turned his attention to the papers which lay in front of him.

'It's not an unfamiliar story,' Freddie began, 'especially in this trade. Four proprietors, two couples, own one hotel, living in each others' pockets seven days a week, and you end up with friction. Plus the fact this lot has no business sense. Spent more than they earned. It has reached the stage where they have no option. The bank is about to foreclose.'

'Oh, no!' Lizzie muttered to herself. 'Does every family fall out if they work together in an hotel?'

'We can't do anything over the weekend, I'll make an appointment for you for Monday, shall I?'

Charlie agreed and they all got to their feet and shook hands.

'Remember now, just look over the property, don't discuss any business while you're there. It's a Mr and Mrs Fletcher and a Mr and Mrs Kirkland you'll be seeing. Good-night, Mrs Wilson, sorry to hurry off, but I've had a helluva day. Good luck.' He placed his hat on his head, shrugged himself into his raincoat and went with Charlie to the front door.

On Monday morning, if the weather was anything to go by, it was not a good omen.

'As filthy a morning as I ever remember,' Charlie said as he came in from having taken Robert to school; he shook his raincoat before hanging it up and Bob-Bob gave a low growl.

'Who's upset you, old boy?' He patted Bob-Bob on the head.

'You just shook all the rain off your coat on to him,' Lizzie said.

'Has he been out yet?'

'No, not yet,' Lizzie answered.

'Well, it's about time he did. Come on, Bob-Bob.'

Lizzie watched as Charlie opened the back door. The rain was simply lashing down and the high winds blew at gale force.

Bob-Bob took one look, turned tail and went back to lie on his bed in the corner. Charlie stood, and hesitated.

'Leave him be,' Lizzie laughed, 'he'll go out when he's good and ready.'

'Yeah, he's got more sense than we give him credit for,' and Charlie laughed with her as Bob-Bob barked at them both.

They started off on their journey, but with less enthusiasm than before.

Highland Heights was the name of the hotel, situated close to a small harbour just the other side of Ilfracombe, which meant that they hadn't too far to travel.

After about forty minutes they found the place and they looked at each other as they took stock of their bearings. Winding down the window, Charlie exclaimed, 'Look, it's only built about nine foot from the sea!'

The sound of the sea was deafening as great waves rolled in to crash on to the rocks far below.

'Cor blimey,' Lizzie cried, reverting back to her cockney dialect. 'Ain't it rugged here? Look at those cliffs, they look like masses of great boulders.'

Straining her neck, she saw that the building was at least five storeys high. 'The texture and colour of the outside makes it look as if it's built of granite,' Charlie observed. 'Really intimidating on a day like this!'

They both ran from the car to the side entrance, where a man signalled for them to come in.

'Do take those wet coats off,' said a woman standing inside.

They introduced themselves, which wasn't necessary as obviously they had been expected. In turn, the gentleman said, 'We are Mr and Mrs Kirkland. Come through to the kitchen, I have the kettle boiling.'

By now, Lizzie was feeling cold and Charlie reached for her hand as he said, 'a hot cuppa wouldn't come amiss, will it, love.'

Their footsteps echoed with a hollow ring as they crossed a large tiled hall and went into what seemed to be a small kitchen. Mr Kirkland made the tea and set the pot down on to a tray that was already laid out with cups and saucers. Then he excused himself, saying, 'I'll be back shortly.'

His wife had disappeared already. Gratefully, they drank their tea and Lizzie poured a second cup for each of them. Still, no one came. Restlessly, they began to wander.

There were three kitchens, each one leading through from the other. It was amazing the amount of equipment there was, mainly of stainless steel, each item scrupulously clean. Catering-sized saucepans and steamers, machines for peeling potatoes, a washing-up machine, three trade-sized washing machines; 'Perhaps they don't send the linen out to a laundry,' Lizzie whispered. There were two double-bowled sinks, each with double drainers, an electric slicing machine which Charlie switched on and, as it burred into life, quickly switched off again.

There were two commercial cookers, each with six burners and a vast oven, beside which stood a massive cast-iron grill. 'This lot must have cost a fortune,' Charlie said in a hushed tone. 'It's certainly a very professional working area. You could cook for an army with this lot.'

Mr Kirkland reappeared. 'If you're ready, I'll take you up to meet Mr and Mrs Fletcher.'

Going up a narrow flight of carpeted stairs, they found themselves in the main entrance hall, one wall of which was taken up by the reception desk and glass-fronted office. They both now realized that the side door through which they had first entered led only to the kitchens. The hotel was built on steeply sloping ground so that the kitchens, though on basement level at the front of the building, had large windows at the back overlooking the sea.

They were ushered into a small, but comfortably furnished sitting-room where Mrs Kirkland was sitting in an armchair close to a bright log fire. Again Mr Kirkland said, 'I'll be back shortly,' as he closed the door behind Lizzie and Charlie.

Without being asked, they both sat down and in silence Lizzie looked at Mrs Kirkland. She seemed a fragile, timid lady and Lizzie noticed that her thin, fair hair was streaked with white which added to her general appearance of delicacy. Lizzie thought that the poor woman must have been very ill. By comparison, her husband had appeared an active, vigorous man, bursting with good health.

A log moved in the fire, sending sparks up the chimney and at the same moment the door opened;

Mr Kirkland was back and with him were Mr and Mrs Fletcher.

'How d'you do?' said the short man with bloated features. He spoke gruffly as he took Charlie's outstretched hand and merely nodded in Lizzie's direction.

Funny how opposites attract, Lizzie thought, as she said good morning to Mrs Fletcher. She was a striking-looking woman; her shiny brown hair was brushed into a French pleat at the back, leaving a few curls on the top of her head, but it was the deep suntan, set off by the white jumper she was wearing, that gave the greatest effect.

After the polite greetings were over, Mr Kirkland said, 'I'll show you around.'

The back of the hotel faced the sea. The layout had been so well designed that in the majority of the bedrooms, which were spaced out on three floors, one could lie in bed and watch the sea.

There were twenty-seven bedrooms, not lavishly furnished but adequate. All had wash-basins and hot and cold running water. Landings were spacious. On each floor there were two bathrooms and three separate toilets.

The staircase was grand. 'A work of art,' Charlie remarked as he walked down the wide treads and Lizzie ran her hand over the dark grained wood of the banister rail, noticing how elegantly it curved at each floor.

The public lounge was on the first floor. A plaque over the doorway stated, 'To stay here is to be on

board a luxury liner'. Hardly inside the room and
Charlie and Lizzie knew that was no exaggeration.
An uninterrupted view of the Bristol Channel
stretched before them. The size of the room threw
Lizzie off balance for a moment.

There were five sets of windows!

Curtain material alone must have cost a fortune,
she thought. The windows were gigantic, reaching
from the floor almost to the exceptionally high
ceiling.

The many deep armchairs all matched, having
floral, chintz loose covers, but the dominating feature had to be that view of the sea directly outside.

Lizzie and Charlie held hands as they looked out
of one of the bay windows and they were speechless.
The huge panes were being lashed by the rain, and
the turbulent sea beyond rolled in and crashed on to
the huge jagged rocks, sending mighty plumes of
foaming spray high into the air.

Reluctantly, Charlie and Lizzie turned away.
Reaching the ground floor once more, Lizzie this
time noticed port-holes set into the walls of the
entrance hall and a board above the reception desk
which read, 'The Captain's Cabin'.

On into the dining-room, almost an exact replica
in size and shape of the lounge. Here, the nautical
look had been maintained. A large anchor entwined
with ropes was fixed to an end wall with more port-
holes in evidence around the room. Here also, the
grey angry sea, with huge waves topped with what

looked like galloping white horses, swept over the rocks immediately beyond the windows.

Mr Kirkland had hardly spoken a word while they had been doing the rounds. He had merely opened doors and stood back.

Returning to the sitting-room, Mr and Mrs Kirkland said a cordial goodbye to Lizzie and Charlie and left them alone with the Fletchers. There was a curious hesitation to all of Mr Fletcher's movements. Eventually he asked, 'Would you like to look over this lot?' and he pointed to a table which was placed beneath the window.

'Incredible!' Charlie said without thinking. The whole table was covered with stationery: menu cards, account forms, booking forms, memo pads, wage slips, writing paper that looked almost regal it was so heavily embossed. There were small envelopes and large envelopes all of which were overprinted on the outside in royal blue with the name and location of the hotel. Not just a few of each, but boxes and boxes of them.

Again, Charlie spoke aloud, 'God! The printing bill for this lot must have been colossal.'

Behind them Mrs Fletcher coughed and her husband said indignantly, 'The brochures are in those boxes on the floor by your feet.'

The brochures were coloured. Views of the interior and exterior of the hotel were on every page. The write-up had been done by experts. The coloured plates and blocks were also there and this time, as he examined them, Charlie kept his thoughts to himself, for this also must have been a very expensive operation.

Mr Fletcher was pouring himself a stiff drink as his wife led them back downstairs and struggled against the wind to open the side door for them.

'Well, that was over quick enough,' Charlie said as they reached the safety of the car.

Lizzie gave him a sudden quick smile, 'We do get around, don't we? At least we're seeing how the other half live.'

Then, to her astonishment and delight, Charlie leaned across his seat, put his arms around her and very tenderly kissed her. He held her close for a long moment and when he did release her, he said with all seriousness, 'We're going to have that hotel, Lizzie.'

Chapter Twenty-Five

During the days that followed, Charlie walked about the house singing to himself and occasionally grinned from ear to ear.

He had numerous telephone conversations with Freddie Clarke and twice Lizzie got the impression that he was speaking to Mr Farrant. Lizzie had attempted to ask questions, but all she got from Charlie was an instruction to be patient.

Then, one Friday morning, as Lizzie took care with her make-up and hair while deciding what to wear (for she was never quite sure where Charlie would end up taking her for lunch) she heard the telephone ring yet again.

A few minutes later and Charlie almost bounded into their bedroom wearing an open-necked, short-sleeved shirt and still looking very tanned.

'Mr Farrant is sorry for the short notice, but he wants us to be at his office two-thirty this afternoon.'

'What for?' Lizzie asked, squinting into the mirror as she softly pencilled-in her eyebrows.

'How the hell do I know? I'm going to get changed.'

'You don't have to be so irritable,' she muttered and then thought to herself, of course he knows what it's all about, it has to be concerning Highland Heights.

Beyond that she would not let herself think, but if they got a bank loan . . . If – Oh stop it, she told herself angrily, don't build your hopes up again.

Mr Farrant's office was one of several sited above the bank, all were occupied by professional men.

A clerk looked up from his work. 'Mr and Mrs Wilson?' he enquired, then led them through from the outer office and opened a door on which gold lettering spelt out 'Farrant, Day and Dalston'.

Mr Farrant himself welcomed them, giving Lizzie a charming smile which immediately put her at her ease.

Two other men were sitting comfortably in chairs placed behind the huge desk. 'Mr Harding you already know,' Mr Farrant said, as indeed they both did, for he had acted as their accountant for the past two years, preparing Sea View's books for the Inland Revenue, 'and this is Mr Sims. He is here to take notes. We are only waiting now for Mr Parker.'

Only recently, Graham Blackhurst had been promoted, moved on to a much larger branch of the bank, and this had made Lizzie sad. He had been a good friend to both her and Charlie, always available for a chat, ever ready with good, sound advice. She wondered what this new man, Mr Parker, would be like.

She didn't have long to wonder.

A sharp tap at the door and he entered, earnestly

shaking hands with Charlie first and then Lizzie, before taking a seat. He was very tall. The tallest of all the men present. At least six foot three inches, he looked every inch a successful bank manager, if a trifle flashily dressed.

An informal meeting began, though Lizzie was conscious of the fact that both she and Charlie were being scrutinized. Weighed up and judged, she thought to herself.

Mr Harding read out facts and figures on their progress since taking over Sea View Guesthouse. Mr Parker had a bulky file in front of him, which he flicked through, pausing now and again to scribble columns of figures on to a pad.

Mr Farrant caught Lizzie's eye, and again he smiled at her, this time in an encouraging way. She thought, not for the first time, how handsome he was.

Mr Parker took off his heavy-rimmed glasses and looked directly at Charlie. 'I understand that, in principle, the bank has agreed to grant you a loan. Well, on your past record and on the recommendations of Mr Blackhurst, you can go ahead now with your purchase of Highland Heights. That is, if you are willing to comply with certain conditions.'

His pause then was so long that Lizzie felt everyone in the room could hear her heart thumping and she saw that tiny beads of perspiration had formed on Charlie's forehead.

'The main condition being that a company be formed, thus allowing the bank to take a debenture on the hotel.' Maybe Mr Parker sensed Lizzie's confusion. He explained more fully. 'A debenture would acknowledge the debt to the bank, repayable with guaranteed interest.'

Mr Farrant and Mr Parker, now with heads close together, had a quiet exchange of words.

'All right? Are you happy about everything?' Mr Farrant, with pleasure showing on his own face, directed this to Charlie.

Apparently, Charlie was more than happy, for he leaned forward and gravely shook hands, first with the new bank manager and then with Roger Farrant.

'Providing all the searches and paperwork can be got through, all loose ends tied up, shall we suggest January 11th for completion date?'

Charlie's mood could only be described as exuberant as he drove to Adelaide College to pick up their son, while all Lizzie felt was utter bewilderment.

Forces behind the scenes must have been working on their behalf, she told herself, but why did they warrant such help? They were going to buy Highland Heights. Even a completion date had been set and yet they had only had a brief look over the hotel.

They had had no real meeting with the owners. Sadly, Lizzie reflected that if the bank was foreclosing because it was owed money that must effectively make the bank the owner.

What misery and anguish those two couples must be going through, the very thought of them having to leave that lovely place made her feel wretched. I hope to God it never happens to us, she mused.

Minutes later, a smile spread over Lizzie's face as she watched Robert raise his cap to Miss Warrell-Bowring and set off at a trot down the drive.

The run-up to Christmas was spent in cleaning rooms, washing blankets and generally making the place look nice. Charlie did all the repairs that were necessary, including replacing tap washers. They were selling Sea View Guesthouse to Mr and Mrs Sadler, fully furnished as a going concern, goodwill included. Lizzie was more than pleased that she had already taken quite a few bookings for the next season and had quite a tidy sum of money taken as deposits to turn over to the young couple.

The Christmas period was spent very quietly, just Lizzie, Charlie and young Robert alone in the guest-house.

There were several reasons for this, the main one being that they were short of money. The cash left over from the previous season had been used to place a deposit on their new hotel. The guesthouse deal was not to be completed until 10th of January and even then the profit from the sale would have to go towards the purchase of Highland Heights.

Once again they were getting into very deep waters. Lizzie had worried herself sick when all these negotiations had begun, but now she kept telling herself that Charlie knew exactly what he was doing and that this time he wasn't on his own. He seemed to have professional men not only acting for him but decidedly on his side.

She hoped with all her heart that her assumptions would prove to be right. God help them if they didn't!

Lizzie kept telling herself that she was enjoying Christmas and she was to a certain degree. When she thought back over the years of the war, with their austerity and danger, she realized just how lucky she and her family were – a roaring log fire, plenty of good food to eat and presents and toys spread out beneath a glittering tree. But it was the sight of the Christmas cards standing on the furniture and strung around the walls that brought on the wistful thoughts.

Doris and Syd wouldn't have ordered their turkey from the butcher. They would have waited till it was dark on Christmas Eve before they'd have gone down to Tooting Market and along the Mitcham Road in search of their bargains. She could imagine Syd and Arthur, with a few pints of beer inside them, playing Father Christmas, filling Lucy's and Raymond's stockings, letting the kids put a carrot out for the reindeer, which Syd would probably have a good old gnaw at to show that the reindeer appreciated their kindness.

Boxing day made Lizzie really homesick. The Horse and Groom always put on a party for the kiddies during the afternoon. What wouldn't she give to be there. Whistles, drums, cymbals, trumpets, anything that made a noise would be used; hats, funny masks, streamers and indoor fireworks – the place would be like bedlam!

The men would be making utter fools of themselves, crawling about on all fours. It was the one day of the year when that pub was geared to nothing more than ensuring that every child in the neighbourhood had a good time and received at least one Christmas present. Jack and Dolly Hawkins were publicans of the old type and their customers loved them.

Lizzie didn't voice her thoughts aloud, but she vowed silently to herself that never again would she willingly spend a Christmas away from dear old London – unless, that is, her family came to Devon again for the holiday. For Christmas was a time to be with one's family and to have those that loved you and whom you loved around you.

The Sadlers came and stayed with them as their guests from the 6th of January.

Having their company eased the strain of the last few days. At last, it was the 11th, and Lizzie, Charlie and Robert had breakfast with Mr and Mrs Sadler at seven-thirty in what, legally, was now the Sadler's house.

In the basement bedroom, Lizzie viewed herself in the familiar mirror for the last time. Was she dressed suitably? She had spent ages pressing the grey suit and white blouse she was now wearing. Oh well, she sighed, too bad if she wasn't.

All her other clothes were packed, and already the cases were in the boot of the car. Charlie stood in the doorway, looking spruce and smart. Robert clutched tight at Bob-Bob's lead. Margaret Farrant had offered to have both Robert and the dog for the day, since two of her boys were Robert's school chums.

They kissed the Sadlers goodbye; everyone called out their good wishes. Charlie started the engine and then, with a final wave, moved off.

Assembled in the chambers were five men, Roger Farrant, Gordon Parker, Mr Harding, Mr Sims and one rather young-looking clerk, and now, Charlie made six.

This meeting was vastly different from the previous one, nothing informal about these proceedings. A small table had been positioned against a far wall at which Mr Sims and the young clerk now sat, one on each side. Mr Parker and Mr Farrant sat in their usual position behind the vast leather-topped desk.

Mr Harding sat next to Charlie, facing them, with Lizzie on his right. He agreed to be the company accountant. Mr Farrant used a very authoritative tone of voice to say, 'Charles James Wilson and Elizabeth Louise Wilson as sole directors. Elizabeth as company secretary, Charles to be treasurer. The company to be known henceforth as Highland Heights Hotel Ltd.'

At this point, Mr Harding bent forward and, from

a case which lay at his feet, he took what to Lizzie looked like a heavy press.

'The company seal,' he said, and very formally got up and placed it on the desk. Returning to his seat, he again reached into his case and took out a cheque book which was at least twice the size of an ordinary one. On each cheque, the name of the company was embossed, together with both sets of initials and the surname Wilson. Mr Harding passed the book over to Mr Parker, who immediately began to write out cheques, stating aloud each amount and giving a clarification of the purpose for which it was needed, pushing each one towards Charlie for his signature.

The amounts seemed enormous to Lizzie. She felt queasy. It was all much too complicated. She screwed her eyes up tight and bent her head forward. The next thing that she was aware of was Mr Farrant standing near, a shadow of a smile on his lips.

'All right, Mrs Wilson? I've opened the window, we'll take a break, have some coffee.'

When a young lady, dressed in a severe dark outfit, came into the office bearing a tray on which were several cups and saucers plus a large coffee pot, Lizzie's only thought was, thank God I haven't got to stand up and pour it out, for she felt that her legs would buckle beneath her.

While they were drinking their coffee and Charlie was deep in conversation with Mr Harding, Roger Farrant did his best to put Lizzie at her ease. 'It's not every day one becomes a company director.' His lovely grey eyes sparkled as he teased her.

The cups were cleared away and it was back to business. Try as she might, Lizzie couldn't keep her hands from trembling as first Charlie was asked to sign several legal documents and then herself. During the whole of this time, Mr Sims and his clerk had been busily writing and entering figures into a ledger.

Mr Sims looked up, coughed discreetly and drew the attention of Mr Farrant who left his seat and joined him at the table. The two men had a quiet conversation during which a lot of head nodding and hand gestures took place, resulting in Roger Farrant returning to his desk and turning towards Mr Parker.

'Gordon, how about granting Mr and Mrs Wilson an extra five hundred pounds on their loan? They are on a very tight budget and an extra five hundred would see them in with a lot more ease. In fact, from their point of view, it is almost a necessity.'

It seemed to Lizzie that whole minutes elapsed before the silence was broken. She glanced furtively at Mr Parker; his face was stony, his lips set in a firm line. Lizzie wished she was anywhere but in that room.

Finally, shaking his head, Gordon Parker said, 'No. From bus personnel to company directors in three years is not bad going. As from today, they are on their own.'

Lizzie felt the colour drain from her face. Quickly

she turned to look at Charlie; she was choked. She wanted to put her arms around him, there and then, to tell him to ignore that bank manager. What did he know about them? He'd only just come to the village. Her anger was now getting the better of her. If Mr Parker said just one more word, I'll tell him to shut up, she vowed.

Poor Charlie, he looked so embarrassed; his cheeks were red and his hands clutched together so tightly that the knuckles showed white through the skin. Even Roger Farrant seemed speechless; you could have heard a pin drop, the silence was so great. No answer, not a comment from anyone was made in reply to Mr Parker's judgement.

Finally, it was all over. Everyone in the room, including Mr Parker, shook hands with Charlie and Lizzie and congratulations were offered.

'The keys to the hotel are in the outer office,' Roger Farrant said, insisting that he escort them to the car park.

Although he did not show it, Mr Farrant felt responsible for Lizzie and Charlie. It was he who had set them on this road. From what he had heard, Mr Wilson was a conscientious man, a hard worker, and as to Mrs Wilson, well, Graham Blackhurst had had great admiration for what he had described as a gutsy woman.

He hoped they hadn't gone too deeply into debt.

When they reached the car, Mr Farrant turned to Charlie, saying, 'I'd like you both to listen to what

I have to say. I am convinced that you two, working together, will make a success of Highland Heights. You'll be all right, you're going in at the right time, deposits should be coming in.'

He stopped speaking, looked at them both as if considering something, then, slowly, he continued, 'The forming of the company and preparing of the documents, plus the registration fee has been calculated in your accounts at five hundred and five pounds. That amount is what is owed to my firm. What I am trying to say is that we won't be sending you our statement for at least one year. That will give you a little more time to get on your feet.'

Charlie held out his hand and in silence the two men shook hands.

Lizzie was stunned – such generosity! She swallowed deeply before she was able to say, 'Thank you, Mr Farrant.'

She couldn't get over it. Roger Farrant was everything a woman likes in a man, naturally sophisticated, with a nice sense of humour, but it had always been his jaunty, almost flirtatious manner that had made Lizzie like him. Not a bit stuffy like the usual run-of-the-mill solicitors. Now she was overwhelmed.

Not only was his offer very generous, it was also a face-saving gesture towards Charlie.

It was eleven-thirty when Charlie drove up to Highland Heights. He unlocked the side door, and they smiled at each other, held hands and went in.

Relief! All the waiting, the tension and anxieties were over. They were in their own hotel.

They spent the rest of the morning exploring, in and out of bedrooms, gazing over the banisters from what seemed a great height, staring out of the windows of the lounge, still utterly amazed at the sea that was so close. They lingered in the dining-room watching the seagulls swoop and listening to them screeching. Finally, they went to the kitchens downstairs.

'What's through there, Charlie?' Lizzie called as she watched him disappear.

'My God!' she heard him exclaim.

'It looks like a ballroom. Never been used for years, I shouldn't think.'

'There's three more small bedrooms down here,' Lizzie cried, 'I think they must be staff rooms. Come on, let's put the kettle on. You did put that box with the tea in it in the car, didn't you?'

There was no need for Charlie to go to the car and fetch the box. On one side of the cooker there was a caddy filled with tea, a bowl of sugar, two pints of fresh milk, and further back was a crusty new loaf, a half-pound packet of butter and a wedge of Cheddar cheese.

A hand-written note lay on the cabinet. 'Good luck', was all it said, but it had been signed by M. and T. Fletcher, and H. and D. Kirkland.

'Isn't that kind?' Lizzie murmured.

'Certainly makes a nice beginning,' Charlie answered.

*

The telephone rang, and from then on it never seemed to stop all afternoon. Good wishes from all sides; a florist's van arrived with two bouquets, one from Syd and Doris and one from Arthur and Polly, the postman brought 'Welcome to your new home' cards from Connie and Bill and Aunt Kate and Uncle John.

By the evening they had two adjoining bedrooms on the first floor made up, plus the private sitting-room, now bright with vases of flowers, and their own china ornaments and photographs set out. Though they were thoroughly exhausted, they were both very pleased with the results.

During the rest of the week, apart from taking Robert to school and meeting him, they only went out once. Charlie remarked, 'You'd better come out for a walk, get some fresh air into your lungs.'

It was a very raw, cold morning and, though the sun was shining, there was a keen January wind blowing in from the sea. The surrounding hills were extremely steep and the coves very rugged. Bob-Bob was in his element as he bounded on ahead. Having walked as far as the harbour, they were both glad to turn back. Nevertheless, Lizzie admitted that she felt better for having been out in the open air and their faces were glowing by the time they got back indoors.

At the weekend, the question of insurance arose. Up until now, Charlie had only obtained temporary coverage. Now a more clearly defined policy had to be considered, on this the bank was most insistent.

'Ten o'clock Monday morning, they are all meeting here,' Charlie said as he replaced the telephone receiver.

Promptly on time, Mr Hutchinson, an inspector from the insurance company, arrived. Mr Parker and a colleague from the bank were late.

'Better open the main entrance doors before the bank officials arrive,' Mr Hutchinson whispered to Lizzie. She ignored his advice.

Mr Parker and the official from Head Office came in through the side door. He introduced himself as Mr Thompson, and Lizzie took to him straight away. 'How does it feel to own one's own company?' he asked Lizzie in a friendly, almost jovial kind of way.

'First, we have to assess the building and the contents,' Mr Hutchinson said and Charlie led the way.

Mr Parker hung back. 'I would have appreciated it if you had opened up the main entrance for Mr Thompson,' he said, and his manner was aggressive.

'Why? The side door is good enough for us,' Lizzie answered, and her tone of voice was insolent.

'Careful!' he spat the word out sharply, but before he could say more Lizzie stopped him. Tall as he was, she wasn't about to be intimidated by him, not this time.

'Mr Parker, you have made my husband and myself company directors and this hotel is now the registered office of that company, but it is also our home.' Without pausing for breath, because her courage might have failed her, Lizzie pressed on. 'Please, don't think we're not grateful for all the help and advice the bank has given us, but as I understand it, we shall be paying a large amount of money in interest on the loan and, as you so aptly pointed out the other day, from here on we are on our own. We don't have to kow-tow to anyone.'

To Lizzie's utter astonishment, Mr Parker threw his head back and laughed, a vigorous, strong sound which had Lizzie staring at him open-mouthed.

He took a step towards her and, placing a hand across her shoulders, he said, 'You'll do. You'll make it, Mrs Wilson, without a doubt you'll make it.'

As he turned away to join the other men, Lizzie could still hear him chuckling to himself as he walked down the corridor. Thankfully, she sank down on to a chair. She had made her first impression as a company director.

Talk about being thrown in at the deep end!

Life in an hotel, especially one where the trade was seasonal, was vastly different to living and working in a guesthouse.

They needed staff. Waiters, chambermaids, kitchen boys to prepare the vegetables, work the dishwashers and clean the ovens, girls for the still-room to make endless pots of tea and coffee and wash the silverware, Saturday boys to carry luggage and show guests where the garages were.

They decided not to employ a chef. Charlie boned his own sides of bacon, roasted numerous legs of pork and lamb and huge, succulent pieces of beef. He spent hours preparing chickens, turkeys and cutting up pounds of steak and kidney for pies. Ham cooked on the bone was his speciality. Lizzie made all the pastry, she also made the soups, gravy and sauces and prepared large quantities of fresh fish and side salads.

The sweet trolley, cheese trays, plus the hors d'oeuvres were tasks that they shared. They prided themselves that they could make sixty cold decorative sweets in individual sundae glasses in just fifteen minutes.

All did not go smoothly. Not all the time.

Staff failed to turn up. Guests arrived late, sometimes past midnight. Laundries failed to return the linen on time. The poultry man's van was not the most reliable of vehicles and Lizzie would hold her breath some mornings as she cracked eggs into an oval pan that cooked ten at a time and prayed that some guests would prefer kippers or smoked haddock, because their stock of eggs was running low.

It was no exaggeration when Charlie spoke of an eighteen-hour day, seven days a week. Six in the morning until midnight at least.

From two p.m. until four p.m. was their free time. Maybe! Except on Saturdays, when folk were leaving and arriving all day long. Not Thursdays either because guests' accounts were made up then. Lizzie would write while Charlie would call out names, room numbers and whatever extras, such as early morning tea, had to be added to the bill.

On Fridays Charlie would sit at the reception desk while visitors paid their accounts. The money had to be sorted, staff wages made up and then Charlie would dash into town to bank the remaining money, while Lizzie counted the clean laundry, hoping it had all been returned safely.

There was a bright side. Charlie applied for and was granted a licence. Women dressed in their pretty summer dresses, men in flannels and open-necked shirts would sit, making friends, chatting and laughing in the bar at the end of warm, sunny days.

All were exceedingly sociable to Lizzie, whenever she decided to join Charlie for a drink. Everyone complimented her on how well the hotel was run, insisting that she look at the photographs they had taken and would not take no for an answer when requesting Lizzie and Charlie pose for a photograph together.

We shall have enough snaps to fill a dozen albums by the time we retire from here,' was the thought that struck Lizzie.

The first week in July 1954 turned out to be a week that Lizzie would remember for a very long time. The hotel guests were mostly from London, which was unusual, since the majority of bookings, Lizzie had found, came from northerners, and during the wakes weeks every guest in the hotel would be from Lancashire or Yorkshire.

The newspapers had been full of the fact that America had sent two of her special sons to England. One was Billy Graham, a Southern Baptist minister, who had, in May, held a mass meeting in Wembley Stadium. The papers had reported that thousands of people had attended and that hundreds had surged forward pleading to be converted.

The other American to cross the Atlantic was an entirely different kettle of fish. Bill Haley and his Comets were to introduce a new rock beat to country music, an exciting combination which immediately achieved immense popularity. Their first recording, 'Shake, Rattle and Roll' sold thousands of records up and down the whole country.

It was on a warm sunny night in June, that Charlie played this record and, although space in the bar was limited, a couple in their early thirties got to their feet and started to dance to the music. Lizzie had just walked into the bar with a plate of sandwiches and she stood stock-still staring in amazement. 'You couldn't call it dancing,' she remarked to Charlie, as she set the plate down behind the counter. It was all arms and legs as the fellow swung his partner from side to side, twirling her like a top to the beat of the music, finishing by sliding her through his wide-apart legs.

As the record came to an end a spontaneous burst of applause came from almost every guest in the bar.

Whenever Lizzie was to tell this story in the future she always emphasized that not everyone approved. A dear old couple, well turned seventy, rose to their feet and the man, speaking in a very loud voice, said, 'Barbaric! Like a pair of savages. You'd do better to listen to Billy Graham and turn to the Lord.' You could have heard a pin drop as the old folk, quietly and with dignity, made their way through the tables and left the bar. Lizzie hadn't dared to look at Charlie as she beat a hasty retreat muttering as she went, 'Oh well. It takes all sorts to make a world.'

Chapter Twenty-Six

EARLY IN THE new year of 1955, the weather-men on the wireless had forecast that the country was in for a bad winter. That had been putting it mildly! January wasn't even halfway through yet and already the weather was absolutely terrible.

During the last seventy-two hours it had never stopped snowing. Heavy falls meant that most villages in north Devon were already cut off. There was ice everywhere and the roads were treacherous. Lizzie moaned to Charlie that despite all the extra woollens she was wearing she just couldn't seem to keep warm.

'Yer don't wonder at it do yer,' said Charlie, lowering the scarf that he had wrapped round his neck and face so that he could be heard. 'The bloody temperature dropped well below freezing last night and it hasn't risen at all this morning yet. Not likely to either, by the look of that sky.'

The week wore on and they felt like prisoners in the hotel as the weather worsened. The hotel gardens jutted out to the sea, and were reached only by climbing several stone steps. To Lizzie it was madness even to think about climbing up there. Nevertheless that was exactly what Robert and his father insisted on doing every morning. Lizzie watched anxiously from the dining-room windows as the two of them, muffled to the eyeballs, did the precarious climb. Robert had both hands free and was able to clutch at the rocks for support. Charlie had only one free hand, because in the other he carried a shopping-bag filled with soaked bread, dried fruit and dishes of fat. It was the only way that they could think of to keep at least some of the birds alive.

It wasn't too bad for Charlie, his feet were much bigger and he had strong sturdy boots. All Robert had on his feet, other than two pairs of thick socks, was a pair of wellingtons. More than once Lizzie's heart came up into her mouth as she watched Charlie put out his free hand to steady Robert.

Face flushed and excited, Robert would come bursting in again through the back door calling, 'Mum, Mum, you ought to see them all, they were waiting for us to feed them.' But it was a sad little boy who came back a few days later. There had been no let up in the great freeze, in fact the winds had whipped up the snow into drifts, making matters very much worse. Charlie had picked up five dead birds, all frozen stiff.

By the end of the week Charlie declared he had had enough of being indoors. 'Come on, muffle up well an' we'll go for a walk. See how far we get. We can always turn back if the going gets too tough.'

It was slow going as they turned towards the hills, their feet leaving deep imprints in the snow. Already the dog was racing ahead of them. 'He seems to like it even if we don't,' Lizzie said, her voice muffled by her thick scarf.

On the way back, the noise from the sea was deafening, the wind was almost up to gale force and as they no longer had the wind at their backs it was a job for them to get along. Charlie stopped and, much to Robert's delight, swung him up on to his shoulders. As they got near to the hotel Lizzie exclaimed, 'What a welcome sight.' Before they had left, Charlie had switched on every light in the porches and around the building.

Their private sitting-room on the ground floor was cosy and warm, but going up to their bedrooms on the first floor where the wind howled and rattled the huge bay windows was another matter. The kitchens being downstairs didn't help either. The entrance hall became known to them all as No Man's Land.

One night, as Lizzie came up from downstairs carrying a loaded tray, she plonked the tray down, shivered and hugged herself, then held out her hands to the blazing fire.

'I wish we had a smaller cooker,' she said half to herself, 'it takes ages for one of those huge ovens to heat up, and those great big burners are ridiculous when I only need to heat a small saucepan of milk.'

'You're always wishing for something,' Charlie murmured, not really paying any attention to what Lizzie had been saying.

Busy putting the hot pies on to three plates, Lizzie

suddenly exclaimed, 'OK, clever clogs. I've forgotten the teapot. I've only brought the hot-water jug. You cross No Man's Land, go down the stairs and through to the second kitchen and fetch it for me.'

Rather sheepishly, Charlie got to his feet, but had to laugh as Lizzie added, 'If you run quick enough, you won't freeze.'

They were grouped round the fire tucking into their meat pies and jacket potatoes, which Lizzie had split open and lavishly spread with butter, when Charlie asked, 'How about a separate house, or even a bungalow?'

'What?'

'We could live in it in the winter. Be less expensive than to heat this hotel. You and Robert could even live in it during the summer. I could sleep in this room on a divan, and we could then let our two bedrooms.'

Lizzie put her hand behind her back, drew out a small cushion and chucked it at Charlie's head. It missed. Robert and his father both chuckled. 'You never could bowl, Mum,' Robert said.

'What's the matter?' Charlie wanted to know. 'Don't you like the idea? I thought you'd be all for it.'

'Oh, I like it all right,' she leant forward and nudged Charlie with her elbow, 'it's you. You've got our bedrooms let to guests before we've even moved out. Besides, talking about another house and buying one is an entirely different matter, and by the way, if, and I said if, this comes about, do you think I might have a choice?'

'Lizzie, my darling,' Charlie bowed his head in mock adoration, 'the choice shall be entirely yours.'

The weather gradually improved and, armed once again with details from estate agents, they were out and about looking at small properties. Nothing suited.

Charlie's arguments were, one, they had to live close enough to the hotel to keep an eye on the place and, two, from Christmas onwards, they would have to pick the mail up every morning. It was essential that all enquiries were answered on the same day, otherwise they would start to lose bookings.

The agents had given details of every property on their books, but Lizzie hadn't seen one that she wanted as a home.

Charlie grew bad tempered. 'You're too critical,' he flung at her.

'Waste of time to look further,' Lizzie decided. The subject wasn't mentioned again for at least a week.

They were sitting in the car outside the gates of Adelaide College waiting for Robert, when Charlie came out with another suggestion. 'How about having a place built?'

'How? Where? How much would it cost?' the questions poured from Lizzie.

'Hold your horses, for Christ's sake, I dunno any

of those answers yet, do I? It was only a thought I had.'

But early next morning, Charlie was off. Curiosity was killing Lizzie as she made the beds and washed her hair to pass away the time.

It was three o'clock in the afternoon before Charlie drove his car up the drive and behind it came the conspicuous car of Freddie Clarke – Mr Fix-It had come to call.

To see Freddie was a tonic, bright and breezy, with his trilby tilted jauntily to the back of his head. The way in which he greeted Lizzie, arm around her shoulders, kiss on both cheeks, made her feel that all was well with his world.

'I've bought a field of Christmas trees,' Charlie blurted out.

Now what? Lizzie had visions of Charlie going to London in December and selling Christmas trees on street corners. Before she could tell him that this time he had gone too far, that he ought to be certified as mentally insane, Freddie calmed her down.

'It's a plot of land. Residential building permits have already been granted. I've got three adjoining plots to sell. I never gave it a thought before. Be just right for you, Lizzie, I promise you'll love it.'

'Where it is?' Lizzie got a question in at last.

'About two miles out on the old road. Get your coat, we've just got time to show you the plot before it gets dark.'

They all piled into Freddie's car.

The surroundings where the plots were situated was truly lovely.

'Makes a change from being right on the sea's edge,' Lizzie said as she stood on the sloping hillside and sniffed deeply at the smell of the pine trees and noticed that there was still a good view of the sea, shimmering away in the distance.

She understood why Charlie hadn't let the grass grow under his feet.

Locally there was only one builder, whose name was Ron Geering, and he was honest enough to admit to Charlie that the job of building a house was too big for him to handle. He admitted he would very much like to be considered for sub-contracted work on the project, but as to being the main builder, definitely no.

Meanwhile, he was prepared to give as much help as he could and Charlie gratefully accepted the benefit of his advice. Discussions began.

'Talk a lot,' he advised, 'before approaching an architect. They charge a helluva lot of money for their time. What type of dwelling do you prefer – house or bungalow? What type of heating – electric or gas?'

No sooner had they settled one thing, than Ron Geering would suggest another point to bear in mind . . . it went on and on. Reluctantly, Lizzie agreed she didn't have the technical knowledge needed for her to join in these discussions. Even Charlie began to wonder whether this time he had bitten off more than he could chew.

Ron advised them to leave it a while. 'The ground won't lose any value,' he assured them. 'You both want to give a great deal of thought to all the matters that I've raised. Don't make any decision in a hurry.'

Charlie thanked him and promised to keep him informed of whatever conclusion they came to.

Lizzie felt defeated.

About ten days had passed during which Charlie had twice driven Lizzie out to visit their plot. Sold notices were now on the two adjoining lots.

It was a quarter-past eleven at night when the shrill ringing of the telephone made Lizzie jump; she had her book in one hand and a hot drink in the other and was on her way up to bed. She left Charlie speaking into the receiver.

'Who was on the phone?' Lizzie raised herself up on one elbow as she spoke.

'Freddie Clarke. He's bringing a chap called Michael Gale to see us in the morning.'

'Who's Michael Gale?'

'I can't rightly say, Freddie said he's known him for years.'

Promptly, at ten o'clock next morning, Freddie was in the hotel introducing Mr Gale, who was a tall, athletic-looking man in his early forties, with blond, almost white hair.

Lizzie made coffee and soon everyone was on friendly terms. Mr Gale certainly had a way with women. While he was speaking to Charlie and Freddie he had Lizzie feeling that she was included, that nothing would be decided without her knowledge or participation. Lizzie liked that.

Having established the fact that Charlie had bought a plot of land and that, yes, it was his intention to have a private dwelling of some kind built there, Mike, as Charlie was by now calling him, stated that he was a member of the Federation of Master Builders.

'How would you feel about a package deal, involving all three owners of those plots?' he tentatively asked.

Charlie looked dubious.

'Have you approached any firms?'

'Only a local builder,' Charlie told him.

'Right,' the self-assured Michael Gale began. 'On such a project as this, insurance is absolutely vital. You must make sure that you don't sign any contract which makes you legally liable for accidents to contractors or workmen. Don't make yourself liable for theft or damage to materials and equipment whilst on your site. Some insurance companies will arrange special temporary cover for building materials and machinery, but would probably charge very heavily for materials that were being left out in the open on your site . . .'

Charlie sighed heavily and Lizzie suggested more coffee.

Freddie Clarke winked at her as she took away his cup to refill it.

'You must also insist on setting a completion date . . .'

Mike Gale was off again with his dire warnings as he spooned sugar into his cup from the bowl that Lizzie held. 'Equipment doesn't always arrive on time. At various stages during the building, inspectors have to attend. Inspectors lead very busy lives, probably have a long way to travel each time to your site, Charlie. You'd have to make appointments to fit in with their schedules, not yours. My firm could save you all those headaches . . .'

Lizzie could see that Charlie was almost ready to surrender. She found her courage and spoke up. 'When you say a package deal, exactly what do you mean? Do we end up with what you want us to have? Have the other two owners agreed yet? Or haven't you spoken to them?'

'Whoa, whoa, you're going too fast for me, Mrs Wilson, let's take your questions one at a time. Package deal first. You allow us to tender for a prototype external house or bungalow, to be decided at a later date. All three properties to all extents and purposes would be very similar, though not exactly the same from the outside. All your personal preferences and ideas could and would be incorporated inside. It could work out very much cheaper, save all three plot owners a great deal of money. Secondly . . .' and on, and on.

At last Charlie was able to chip in. 'You still haven't said whether the other two owners have agreed.'

Very reluctantly, Michael Gale said, 'No, they have not. They are still considering the matter.'

Then he played his ace card.

'Come to Bristol. The other two couples have agreed to that. An architect and several members of my firm will be there. We'll show you plans, a film and several colour slides to help you make a final decision as to the type of building you would all choose and decide on. Nothing definite, you don't have to sign anything, just come as our guests. Nice hotel . . .'

'OK, Mike,' Charlie said as they shook hands, 'we'll come to Bristol. Make a nice change for Lizzie if nothing else. Beyond that, I'm promising nothing.'

Turning to Freddie, he grinned, 'Probably cost me a bloody fortune, if I let Lizzie loose in Bristol.'

Freddie hung back and his face became quite serious. 'I didn't pull Michael out of any old hat, you know, Charlie. He *is* trustworthy. His firm is bona fide, honestly.'

'I know,' Charlie told him, equally serious, 'it's just that I need time to think and talk things over with Lizzie.'

When the two men had left, Charlie turned to Lizzie, saying, 'We'll go to the bank in the morning, together. I'll ask Mr Harding to meet us there.'

The meeting at the bank didn't take long. Mr Harding produced copies of the company's returns. Mr Parker approved the idea of a private house as a sound investment and put forward the suggestion that the purchase should be a private one. Outside the company.

'Repayments on the loan can be made from your own income,' Gordon Parker smiled at Lizzie, 'just in case.'

He laughed now, and Lizzie turned to Charlie, 'Just in case of what?'

'Just in case the company should flounder,' Charlie told her. 'No creditors would be able to claim on our home.'

'Oh,' was all she said, but inwardly, Lizzie liked the sound of that.

'Make a detour, Charlie, please, let's go and look at the site again,' Lizzie pleaded as they drove home from the bank.

Charlie just nodded, and before long they were there. They held hands like a couple of teenagers and climbed right to the top of the hill. Out of breath and trying to breathe deeply, Lizzie stood still while Charlie wandered off on his own.

The view was fantastic. The winter sunshine was streaming through the green trees and suddenly she felt a surge of excitement. This spot was going to be their home. Not the company's property. Not to be used in any way for business purposes, every room would be theirs. All of it would be theirs.

All this surrounding natural beauty, it was breathtaking. She wished she could wave a magic wand, have the house built now. She hoped that if and when building did start, as few trees as possible would be disturbed.

From that vantage-point, so high up, she could

see right across the Channel and, way below, the surf was still booming on to the rocks. Here, please God, they would eventually have stability, an environment of normality, a home where their son could bring his friends.

Charlie made Lizzie jump as he came up behind her and nuzzled his face into her neck. 'You were day-dreaming, miles away, do you know we've been up here for over an hour?'

By lunchtime, a week later, Charlie and Lizzie were in Bristol. Robert was safely away on a school trip, and Mr Gale had arranged everything perfectly.

The Hydro was a nice hotel. Charlie registered at the reception desk, and booked them in for a stay of at least four nights.

They freshened up and then went downstairs into the bar. Michael Gale bought a drink for each of them and introductions were made.

The other two purchasers were a Mr and Mrs Courtney and a Mr and Mrs Marshall. Not local people, in fact, one couple had travelled from Birmingham.

After a very nice informal lunch, during which everyone seemed friendly and at ease, they moved off into a large room which was obviously used for business meetings, and here everyone gathered around a circular table as drawings and plans were laid out. There was talk amongst the men of ground-floor plans, upper-floor plans, south elevation, north elevation. Lizzie heaved a sigh and withdrew to the back a little and so did Mrs Marshall.

'Do you understand the drawings?' Mrs Marshall asked in a quiet voice. Lizzie shook her head and whispered, 'No, I don't.'

'If you will all take a seat now,' Michael Gale gestured to where chairs had been set out in a row, 'we will show photographs of suitable dwellings designed with your situation in mind. If any of you spot anything with which you feel you would be happy, both in size and type, please stop me and I'll be happy to discuss such a property at length and in much greater detail.'

Blinds were drawn down over the windows, the projector started to make a purring sound and the first colour slide appeared on the screen.

The second slide came up, much the same as the first, a dull, long, low type of bungalow.

It was when the third slide came up that Lizzie let out an exclamation of surprise without stopping to think. It wasn't that the house being shown was large or even very impressive. It was different.

'This is a split-level bungalow,' Mr Roberts, the architect, was saying. Lizzie glanced quickly at the other two ladies; both smiled and were very clearly impressed.

Now, having everyone's full attention, Mr Roberts showed more slides of this bungalow from various angles, the interior, lower floor, entrance hall, bedrooms, shower room, bathroom and separate toilet.

'Why bedrooms downstairs?' Mrs Courtney asked.

Mr Roberts grinned, 'I'm coming to that.'

Technical drawings came up on the screen. 'Split-level means that by building the second half high up on and into the hill, one will gain all the benefits of the views. The upper-ground floor, as it is known, would house the kitchen, dining-room and lounge. The lounge would be thirty-five foot long, one wall of which would be mainly glass.'

Suddenly, another slide appeared and even the men gasped. It showed the exterior of the lounge. The glass doors in the photograph were opened on to a huge veranda fenced in by ranch-style white slats and the solid floor was two-toned concrete slabs.

The decision was unanimous, at least amongst the ladies it was. Was all of this real? Lizzie asked herself.

She was bursting with excitement. Had they found the ideal bungalow? Would it eventually be built? Would it look exactly like those colour slides or would it all turn out to be an unachievable dream?

She wanted to laugh, yet she also felt like weeping.

She wanted to throw her arms around Charlie, hug him, kiss him, share all this excitement, but there were too many people around. He must have been having similar feelings, as he tucked his arm through Lizzie's and squeezed so hard it hurt.

That was a very intimate moment.

No one else in the room mattered, just each other.

Chapter Twenty-Seven

THE SECOND SEASON hadn't proved too difficult, the weather had been good most weeks, which must play a great part in any holiday. The guests could get out and about and there were less moans to contend with.

However, with the coming of their third season in Highland Heights, Lizzie felt she was a lot wiser and certainly not so starry-eyed about the job.

They were well into July 1956 when Charlie put the fear of God into her. The pair of them were in the court-yard, which was outside the main kitchen, slumped in deckchairs, having a quiet hour before lighting up all the ovens and getting the evening dinner on the go. Suddenly Charlie lowered the newspaper he was reading, leant forward and touched her knee. 'Do you realize Lizzie, it's quite possible I might get called up?'

Lizzie's heart missed a beat. 'You shouldn't joke about a thing like that,' she quickly rebuked him.

'Who's joking?' he retorted. 'I know you don't get much time to read the papers but even you must be aware of all the trouble there is with Egypt over the Suez Canal.'

Lizzie didn't answer. Of course she had heard rumours, but she took the attitude that she had quite enough of her own problems to contend with without trying to solve matters that were going wrong on the other side of the world.

Charlie continued to read his paper, now and again making a comment out loud. 'Sir Anthony Eden's not very popular with the Americans. Both Eden and France want to send troops in. There's talk of it going to the United Nations.'

'Well, wasn't that why the United Nations was formed? To act as peacemaker?' she asked.

Charlie only mumbled something about her having her head buried in the sand.

Lizzie got up, folded her chair and leant it against the wall. 'Let's 'ope to God that all these men in power see a bit of sense for once,' she flung back over her shoulder at Charlie; 'surely one war in anyone's lifetime is more than enough. Come ter that there's many a person still alive that is still suffering from the First World War.'

The days and weeks of August and September seemed to drag. Life became monotonous, the same old routine day after day, sweltering in the hot kitchens while the guests lay on the beach or swam in the sea, the scorching sun shining down on them.

By the time the season was over once again Lizzie was thoroughly disillusioned. Despite all the promises that she'd made to herself, she had not been back to London since 1953. Doris phoned regularly and she herself would often telephone Doris or Polly. But these conversations only made her feel worse.

Her thoughts would be back in London and it didn't take much for her to conjure up pictures in her mind of what her friends and relations were up to.

This particular Friday seemed endless to Lizzie as she wandered about the hotel. She found herself doing the same job over and over and the silence was becoming eerie; her footsteps sounded loudly each time she crossed the tiled entrance hall and she prayed that the telephone might ring. It could be anyone on the other end, she didn't care who it was as long as it was someone to talk to.

Charlie had gone to Cardiff for the weekend, to see a football match. It was a long-standing arrangement, an outing for the local darts club that Charlie played for. The men had caught The Cardiff Queen at eight o'clock that morning, the last paddle-steamer to leave Ilfracombe harbour this season. Lizzie didn't begrudge Charlie his weekend with his mates but it had coincided with the weekend that Robert was away, staying with a school friend named Stephen Banks, whose father and mother owned holiday flats and a caravan park out at Heale, a very picturesque village on the way to Combe Martin.

Lizzie had found it hard to make friends down here in Devon; she fell between two stools. The largest of the hotels in the vicinity were company owned and run by managers put in for the season only. During the winter months such hotels would be closed up. No one there to get friendly with. She liked some of the women who worked for her and

Charlie, especially the real Devonians and she had tried hard to get one or two of them to go into Barnstaple with her for a day's outing or even into one of the local pubs for a drink. She'd had no luck. They regarded Lizzie as a foreigner from London, their boss and not someone with whom they could socialize.

As the short October day drew to a close and the daylight began to fade, Lizzie could hear the wind howling and the waves crashing on to the rocks. It would probably be a very high-tide tonight and she was thankful that Charlie wasn't making the return crossing until Sunday.

What could she possibly do with herself during the long evening that stretched ahead? 'I know what I would do if it weren't fer you,' she said crossly as she opened the door at the foot of the stairs and let Bob-Bob bound up to the sitting-room. 'I'd be on that first train up ter London. What the 'ell 'ave I got ter keep me 'ere.'

With that thought came the action. None of them had to stay here. Not for another long dreary winter. 'Jesus Christ!' she exclaimed and the sound of her own voice seemed to mock her. People were fond of saying that seasonal hoteliers only worked six months of the year. Well, she now knew for a fact that you did a year's work in that six months. Then what did you get? Maybe October, November and December off, but you had to be here every day from the beginning of January to answer the mail each day and to do all the running repairs that were necessary.

Lizzie dialled the number of her brother's house, but when the phone rang and rang with no one there to answer it Lizzie could have cried with temper. It seemed that everyone else in the world had somewhere to go and more than likely someone they could go with.

It was only after the third attempt that Doris finally answered the phone.

'I can't stay in this bloody place a minute longer. Charlie's took 'imself off to Cardiff, Robert's staying the weekend with his school friend, an I'm stuck in this blasted hotel on me own with no one to talk to but the bloody dog.'

Doris listened to Lizzie's outburst and now in her own placid way she calmly said, 'Why don't yer come up? We've got stew for dinner.'

That was exactly what Lizzie needed. The logic of Doris. She threw back her head and laughed so hard she almost dropped the phone. Stew for dinner!

'Doris, much as I would love a plateful of your stew I don't own an airplane. What I want you ter do for me is ter go to the estate agent's at Wimbledon first thing in the morning, see if they've got a furnished house to rent for three months, tell them it's for me, maybe someone there might remember me.'

'Who's the house for?' Doris's sing-song voice

came down the line and Lizzie was sure she was taking the mick.

'You know damned well it's fer me and Charlie. If we don't get away from 'ere, at least for a while, I shall end up killing him.'

'Anyway, why d'yer want a house, you can all stay 'ere.'

'Doris, if I were near you at this moment I would strangle you!'

Lizzie heard Doris's soft tinkle of a laugh and she relaxed.

'Seriously Doris, it would be better if we rent a house, that way we won't get under one anothers' feet and Charlie won't be able to moan so much if he's in a place of our own.'

Suddenly Doris's voice sounded very serious as she said, 'OK, Lizzie, I'll be round at Wimbledon nine o'clock in the morning. I'll phone you as soon as I've found you something, and Lizzie . . .' Doris hesitated.

'Yes, love?' Lizzie queried.

'Take it easy tonight. Have a drink and go to bed early. I'll ring you before ten in the morning. Night Lizzie. God bless.'

'Good-night Doris. God bless you.'

Lizzie felt a whole lot happier as she replaced the receiver, though she was a little apprehensive when she thought about how she would tell Charlie of her decision.

'Sod him,' she said aloud in an attempt at bravado, 'if he don't want ter come 'ome he can bloody well stay down 'ere in Devon an' see how he likes talking to himself.'

Lizzie spent an awful night, tossing and turning, punching her pillow and moving from side to side in the big double bed. When she did finally fall into a light sleep it was almost day-break and it wasn't long before the noise of the sea and the screech of the gulls had her awake again. She gave it up as a bad job, got out of bed, pulled her dressing-gown tightly around her and made the cold trek down to the kitchens.

'Talk about madness,' she mumbled to herself as she waited for the kettle to come to the boil, 'all in all there must be more than thirty rooms in this hotel an' there's me rolling around the damn place like a bloody pea in a colander.'

It was twenty minutes past ten when the phone rang and Lizzie snatched it up with a sigh of relief.

'I've found you somewhere, Lizzie, only five minutes' walk from us.' Doris sounded excited as she poured her news down the line. 'No houses I'm afraid, but I've put a deposit on a maisonette. Do you remember the big 'ouse on the corner of Longley Road, we used to call it the two-faced 'ouse cos it 'ad windows side and front.'

'But that place is enormous,' protested Lizzie.

'Wait, just let me tell yer, it's bin turned into flats an' they're all being let furnished. Only the bottom one is still vacant and the old boy at the estate agent's said they'd only take a six-month let, nothing less. Well, I told 'im all about you. He said he remembered yer, but I don't know if he did. Anyway, I said you only wanted somewhere ter stay while you were looking for another house ter buy, 'cos you were coming back ter live in London and you 'oped he'd be able ter find you something nice.'

'And?' Lizzie asked but she knew what was coming and there was laughter in her voice.

'You got the garden flat, as the old boy called it, for three months as from a week terday. Next Monday yer can move in, that's if Charlie don't kill yer first.'

'Oh Doris, trust you!'

They talked for another few minutes till Doris said, ''Ere this is early morning rate an' if I don't soon put this phone down Syd will kill ME when he gets the bill.'

Charlie's reaction surprised Lizzie. He put up no resistance to the idea, not even any argument. She had fully expected that they would have a right old barney, and had been prepared to tell him exactly what he could do if he didn't want to go with her to London. Instead, he had smiled in such a way that would normally have aggravated her, and from then on had been thoroughly cooperative, going so far as to offer to go to Adelaide College and make it right for Robert to be absent until the new year.

It was the end house in a row of terraced houses with a bay window in the front which looked out at the houses opposite, and another bay window at the side of the house which looked out on to the High Street. Situated on the opposite corner was a small shop which seemed to sell every imaginable thing.

The furniture in all the rooms was adequate, but nothing at all to get excited about. Mostly it was 'utility' – furniture that had been available during the war, and then only on dockets issued to newly-weds or people who had been bombed out.

The first thing they set about doing was finding a local school that would take Robert. They were lucky. The headmistress of Colliers Wood Junior School was most understanding and said they would be happy to offer a place to Robert for as long as his parents deemed it necessary.

Their first week in London was progressing nicely. Syd had started his own business, hiring out cars for weddings and such like and had taken a lease on premises in Totterdown Street at the back of Tooting Market. It was Thursday morning, Charlie had gone off with Syd, and Doris and Lizzie had just arrived back at Doris's house from taking Raymond and Robert to school. Raymond was in the junior section, while Robert had settled into the infant department.

'We'll wash up these breakfast things, 'ave a cuppa an' then go down Tooting, shall we?' Doris asked as she put the bung in the sink and poured a kettle of boiling water over the dirty plates.

'Yeah,' Lizzie said, picking up a tea-cloth ready to dry up. 'We can give Polly a knock as we go.'

Doris laughed, 'Polly'll be over 'ere before we're ready ter go. We always go down Tooting on Thursdays.'

At a quarter to eleven the three of them were just going out of the front door when the phone rang. 'I've a good mind ter let it ring,' Doris moaned. 'It's more than likely only Syd wanting me ter do something or other.' The ringing persisted as Doris closed the door, and then something made her change her mind. Putting her key into the lock, she opened the door and ran down the hall. Two minutes later she was back and the colour had drained from her face.

'It's Robert! He's missing! They've rung the bell after playtime an' no one can find 'im.'

'Oh my God!' Lizzie's heart was already beating like a drum inside her chest as she threw down her shopping bag and purse and ran back inside the house. 'I'm gonna phone the police,' she called back to Doris.

'Lizzie! Lizzie! He's 'ere.' Polly was out at the front gate and was pointing a finger up the street.

Lizzie spun round on her heels and was up and out in the road in a few strides, then she stopped, staring in disbelief. Her young son was a few feet away from her, looking very bedraggled, his cap was on crooked, his plimsoles, tied together, were strung round his neck and he was dragging his satchel along the pavement. 'I'm never going to go to school ever again,' he declared as Lizzie swept him up in her arms.

'How did you get home? How did you manage to cross the main road? How did you know to come ter Auntie Doris's house?'

'Lizzie leave him be for now,' Polly put out a restraining hand on to Lizzie's shoulder. 'Come on, let's get him back inside the 'ouse. Doris has gone ter phone the school ter tell them that he is all right.'

'All the boys keep calling me a Devon dumpling,' was the only explanation that they could get from Robert.

They phoned Syd and within twenty minutes Charlie was home. Having found that his son was safe and sound Charlie laughed, which was a great relief to Lizzie. She had fully expected to get the blame.

At one-thirty Charlie took Robert back to the school and once again the headmistress was most kind, promising that she would sort the matter out. Both Lizzie and Charlie were outside the school gates at a quarter to four when Robert came running towards them with three other bigger boys in tow. 'Dad, Dad,' he yelled, 'will you take Jimmy, Sam and Freddie home in our car because they're my friends now, Miss Thompson said they're to look after me.'

From then on Charlie gave all three boys a ride home every afternoon, because, as he said, 'What choice have I got. I've got to look after my son's minders!'

The third weekend that they were 'home' Syd got

tickets for the six of them to go to Chelsea Palace on the Saturday evening. He couldn't have picked a worse night.

They got off the tram outside The Weatsheaf at Trinity Road and walked to the bus stop. It was almost impossible to see a hand in front of your face because the damp thin fog, which had swirled round during most of the day, had now become much denser. How glad they were when they at last saw the headlights of the bus penetrating the blackness. The journey took longer than usual but they were grateful to the driver of the bus when it pulled up safely outside the theatre.

'Don't fink we'll be going much ferver, it's turning out ter be a right pea-souper,' the driver called down to his conductor who had come off the bus and was standing on the pavement looking up at his mate in his cab.

'Did yer 'ear that?' Polly called to the men who had walked on in front of them. 'If the buses stop running 'ow the 'ell are we gonna get 'ome?'

Arthur, usually the one with the least to say, turned his head and called, 'You can start walking now if yer like. Yer silly cow, we've only just got 'ere an' you're worrying about 'ow we're gonna get 'ome. Fer Christ's sake, let's git ourselves inside an' maybe we'll 'ave time to 'ave a drink before the show starts.'

''Ark at 'im getting out of his pram,' Polly said in a whisper to Lizzie, and they were all laughing as they went inside the warm foyer and made for the bar.

The applause was thunderous as Winifred Atwell seated herself at her Honky-Tonk Piano. 'Ma, she's making eyes at me', 'Bye, Bye, Blackbird', 'California here I come', 'Who were you with last night?', 'Fall in an' follow me', all these great songs were belted out as the audience sang at the tops of their voices and the rafters of the old Chelsea Palace rang as they hadn't done for many a long day. The audience was loath to let her go and for an encore she played a quiet tune, 'Who's sorry now?', which was sung by men and women alike with a great deal of feeling.

When they came out Syd suggested that they walk over Battersea Bridge. A wind had got up and the fog had lifted a little, but as they crossed the bridge the dampness from the river Thames below seemed to Lizzie to spread right over her and she was glad when Syd broke into a run flagging a taxi down.

'I'm on me way 'ome mate, I live at Wimbledon an' I ain't about ter make a detour fer nobody ter-night.'

'That's all right. Can yer drop us anywhere between Tooting Broadway and Colliers Wood?' asked Syd, adding ruefully, 'But there's six of us.'

'Must be your lucky night,' the old cabbie said as he put his arm backwards and unlocked the door of his cab. 'Me son's just drawn in behind me, he'll take a coupla yer.'

On the short walk to the house Lizzie huddled up

close to Charlie; the wind might be a good thing, getting rid of that acrid smell of fog, but it was bitterly cold. There was one thing, though, that they were both agreed on; it had been a smashing night out.

Doris and Lizzie were making their way home from the shops, their coat collars turned up against the cold. 'Doris, Doris!' a voice called out as they reached the front gate. ''Ang on a minute, I've got somefink I wanna show yer.'

'Oh hell! Aggie Baggie!' Doris told Lizzie as she put the key in the lock. Half turning she said to the scruffy-looking woman who was by now right on their heels, 'I suppose you'd better come in.'

Lizzie started to take the shopping from the bags while Doris took a poker to the fire. Lifting the banked-down coal, letting a draught through, she soon had bright flames darting up the chimney. Getting up from her knees, Doris spoke to the woman, 'Aggie make it quick, I gotta get the dinner and yer know what my Syd's like.'

Aggie sniffed and, lifting the large patchwork bag from her arm, she emptied the contents on to the table. Lizzie's eyes lit up. There were four or five skirts, real quality, expensively tailored skirts.

'I like the grey one,' Lizzie murmured as she picked it up and fingered the cloth.

As if on cue, the door opened and Syd came into the room. He took everything in at a glance. Thumping his fist down on to the table he shouted at his sister, 'Lizzie, you must be out of yer bleedin' mind, they're Braffman's skirts.' Taking a step towards Aggie, he spoke with menace in his voice, 'You bin up ter yer tricks again? You nicked them, an' all right it ain't nothing ter do with me what you get up to, but I've told yer before keep out of my 'ouse and don't try flogging yer stuff ter my family, 'cos if we get the coppers round 'ere so 'elp me God I'll see you pay for it. As fer you, Lizzie, you might 'ave known she was a tea-leaf. An' you, Doris, what the bloody 'ell did yer let 'er in 'ere for?'

Lizzie put the skirt down on the table and, as she looked up, she saw Charlie was leaning back against the door; she hadn't heard him come in.

Syd wasn't finished by a long chalk. He grabbed the bag from Aggie and shoved the skirts inside it. Charlie moved and Syd shoved Aggie through the door and up the hallway. When he came back he spoke, taking in both Doris and Lizzie, 'If either of you 'ad worn one of those skirts down the market, Wally Braffman would 'ave recognized it an' he'd 'ave the coppers on ter yer as soon as yer put yer foot in the place. Yer pair of silly cows! Ain't yer learnt? Yer never make a mess on yer own door-step.'

The pair of them decided it was safest to keep their mouths shut as they bustled about making a pot of tea and setting the cups out.

'Shall we not bother to cook tonight?' Doris suddenly said as they all sat near to the fire drinking their tea. 'We gotta go over the road ter get the boys from Polly's and we could pop up the road an' get fish 'n' chips fer us all. You might as well stay 'ere for yer dinner, eh Lizzie?'

Lizzie looked across at Charlie and he nodded his agreement.

'It's lovely fish up there, cheap an' all,' Doris said; 'anything yer like as long as yer don't mind waiting while old 'Arry cooks it. Even get a Dover sole if yer fancy it.'

Charlie brought his head up with a jerk, looked at Syd and asked, 'Is she joking?'

'No. 'Arry's brother works at Billingsgate Market; he keeps his brother well supplied with fish that's how come he can do it so reasonable.'

'Gawd blimey! Every bugger up 'ere seems ter be on the fiddle!' Charlie muttered and then, looking at Doris, he spoke in a voice that was very quiet, 'Mind you I could really go a nice thick Dover sole.'

It had become a regular thing for the six of them to go out together on Saturday evenings and the word had got around that the King's Head in Merton was putting on a live show at weekends.

'Come on, we'll give it a go,' said Syd, as he pushed open the swing door and held it back for the girls to go in first.

They had a job to find a free table and were about to walk back and stand against the wall when a thick-set fellow, who was obviously acting as a bouncer, called out, 'Syd, 'ere Syd, over 'ere.' He then spoke to a couple who were sitting alone at a round table and they immediately got to their feet and moved over to join another group where there were two free seats.

'Thanks Mike,' Syd said. 'Ain't much good though, mate, there's six of us.'

''Old yer 'orses, will yer, Syd? Let the girls park their backsides an' I'll git yer another table from out the back an' we'll push 'em together.'

When they were all settled, the men with pints in front of them and the girls with shorts, Doris leant across the table and touched Syd's arm. 'Why did that bloke do that fer us? Do yer know 'im?'

''Course I bloody know 'im, yer daft cow! 'Ow else would he 'ave known me name. I'm doing 'is daughter's wedding next Saturday; booked all three of me cars he 'as. Nice little earner that'll be.'

Part of the show was this new craze for mime. The master of ceremonies stepped to the front of the stage and, with the mike close to his mouth, bawled, 'Ladies an' gentlemen, I give you, JOHNNY RAY.'

Behind the curtains a record was placed on the record-player. A slim, blond young man in his early thirties, flashily dressed in a checked suit and wearing a spotted bow-tie, crossed the stage and took the mike. The music blared out.

The young man's impersonation of Johnny Ray was fantastic; he imitated every action of the well-known singer as he mimed – 'Let your hair down 'n' go on 'n' CR – Y – Y'.

The applause was deafening and as the customers stamped their feet and yelled 'More', Arthur remarked, 'He wouldn't 'ave done 'alf so well if he 'adn't 'ave been 'alf cut.'

'Yeah!' Syd agreed. 'A right piss artist!'

Lizzie fell about laughing. Saturday nights in Devon were nothing like this!

Lizzie loved the trips they made to Tooting Market. There were still some of the old traders left who remembered her from when she had worked there during the war. No matter how many times she went there, they would still call out to her, 'Watcher, Lizzie, 'ow are yer, me old darling?'

There was old Annie, still running her salad stall, lively as ever. She had gazed in wonder at Lizzie when Lizzie had first gone to say hallo to her.

'Cor blimey, you've put some meat on yer bones,' she had cried as she flung her arms around Lizzie. 'I remember you as a skinny bloody urchin; I used ter fink that was why yer mum sent you on the errands, 'cos every bugger felt sorry fer yer, fought yer needed a damn good meal so they always gave yer a good whack fer yer money. Yer mum was a good'n', God rest 'er soul; she was an' all. There's many a one still around 'ere what yer mum helped out of 'n 'ole.'

That had brought a lump to Lizzie's throat and made her smile at the same time as she remembered how, in this very market, she had given her mum rations which they hadn't been entitled too.

And what a fuss there'd been over that!

*

One morning Lizzie was feeling particularly happy. Christmas was only weeks away and, although she was suffering from sheer exhaustion because Doris and Polly had dragged her round so many shops looking for presents to buy for the men and the children, she was really looking forward to the holiday. 'At last!' Lizzie breathed a sigh of relief as they reached the cafe in the centre of the market and they dumped their shopping-bags down and lowered themselves onto chairs.

'Must admit I'm dying for a cuppa,' Polly said as she got straight back up on her feet again. 'I'll go an' get us three large teas while yer make up yer minds what yer want to eat.'

It was about twenty minutes later, as the girls were tucking into hot meat pies and a second steaming mug of tea, when a gruff voice boomed at them, 'Ah! Just the three luvverly girls I was 'oping ter see this morning!'

'Watch out!' Doris said in a stage-whisper. 'When Fred 'Arris pays anyone a compliment it only means one thing. He's after something.'

'Yer right, Dorris me ol' luv,' he said as he took a chair from another table, swung it round and placed it back to front next to Polly. Then he straddled his legs across the seat and rested his arms over the back and faced them all.

'Next Saturday week, ten days before Christmas, we're giving a party in the Central 'All fer the widows, widowers and pensioners. Could do wiv yer 'elp all day if yer ain't got nuffin' better ter do.'

The three looked at each other and all nodded but it was Polly who said, 'We don't mind, glad ter 'elp, but we can't make it all day; what would we do with our kids?'

'That's just it.' There was a beaming smile now on the face of Fred Harris as he licked a stub of pencil and wrote the girls' names down on a long grubby sheet of paper. 'We've told all the 'elpers ter bring their kids along wiv them. Brighten up the place they will an' the old folk'll enjoy watching the antics some of the little sods get up to.'

'Why do yer need us all day? Isn't it just a tea that you're giving them?' questioned Lizzie.

'No it ain't!' declared Fred. 'It's gonna be a proper Christmas dinner wiv all the trimmings. Hemmingway's the bakers are gonna cook the turkeys fer us an' boil the puddings an' all. There's still the soup ter get on early in the morning, all the veg ter do, the tables ter be laid and before yer can do that we 'ave to set up the trestles an' see ter them blasted folding chairs. The bloody china will probably need a good wash, we'll need gallons of custard – there's about an 'undred coming. An then there's the carrier-bags ter fill 'cos every one of 'em is going 'ome wiv a load of goodies, all given free by the stall-'olders of this market.'

The tears of mirth were by now running down their faces as Doris tried to stop laughing and pleaded, 'OK, OK.'

＊

The talk now was of nothing else. Arthur, Charlie and Syd were all for giving their services. Syd offered his cars to transport any of the old folk who would have difficulty in getting to and from Central Hall, Charlie put his own car at the organizers' disposal and also said he would come to the hall with the girls early in the morning and help with any of the more heavy type of jobs.

When the day arrived, Charlie made two trips before nine o'clock in the morning, taking first the girls down to the hall, where they were pleasantly surprised to see about twenty other women already there, about the same number of children and six men, mostly retired costers. On the second trip, Charlie brought Lucy, Raymond and Robert with him, and everyone, kids and grown-ups alike, got stuck in.

It was a long, hard day for all the helpers; many more would have gladly been there to give a hand but being so near to Christmas, trade was brisk in the market and they had to be on their stalls. Placards had been displayed for days stating that the market would be closing at six o'clock that night but would make up for it by remaining open every other night until nine o'clock right up to the holiday. Every man and woman who owned a stall would be coming straight round to the hall as soon after six as possible to help with the entertaining of the old folk.

The hall looked marvellous, hung with chains and

bunches of balloons, and holly and mistletoe adorned with tinsel hung in bunches from the walls.

At last dinner was over! Nobody quite knew how they had coped. It had fallen to Charlie to carve the large turkeys and to plate up the meat, while the women strained pots and pots of vegetables into dishes and did their best to keep everything piping hot while the guests had their oxtail soup.

Roars of approval had gone up as the male helpers carried in ten big, round puddings, all ablaze from a liberal soaking of brandy.

It was now seven o'clock and the women all breathed a sigh of relief as they stacked away the washed china and put the saucepans back in the cupboards. The men would take over completely now and they could have a well-earned drink, sit back and watch the fun.

Even the kerb-side barrow boys, who had their pitches outside the rear entrance to the market, had turned up to do their bit. While the band was being set up, two of these young lads came on to the stage with accordions strapped around their chests. They started the ball rolling by playing 'Maybe it's because I'm a Londoner' and there wasn't a silent voice in the hall. As the last notes died away someone shouted, 'It's old Lil's birthday.'

Instantly the men ran, forming a line in front of the raised stage, and with a nod from Fred Harris the music started to play and the men sang at the top of their voices: 'It's 'er blooming birthday, so wake up all the town, Oh, knees up, knees up, knees up, knees up, knees up, Muvver Brown'.

Suddenly all the chairs were vacant. Everyone was on their feet. Kids were in the middle as the old women lifted their skirts and bounced up and down to the music, urged on by the men who were clapping like mad. Not to be out-done, the band took over and within minutes the crowd was shouting 'Oi!' and stabbing the air with their raised thumbs as they sang and danced 'The Lambeth Walk'.

'Take a breather,' Fred told them as he announced that Maureen, who had the flower pitch, would now sing to them. You could have heard a pin drop in that vast hall as she sang 'I'll take you home again Kathleen, to where your heart will feel no pain'.

This was quickly followed by one of the young lads who gave them his version of 'I wanna girl, just like the girl that married dear old Dad'. Lizzie felt a great surge of tenderness fill her heart as she watched Charlie raise a white-haired lady to her feet and stand there, holding her hand. Oblivious of everyone, he sang, in a voice that tugged at every mother's heart, 'To that old-fashioned mother of mine' and as he finished he raised the lady's hand to his lips and gently planted a kiss on her fingers. It became too much for Lizzie, she burst into tears which only made Doris and Polly burst out laughing.

'Come on Syd!' Fred Harris called across the room as he watched Syd toss his head back and drain his pint glass. 'Yer turn ter give us a song.'

'This one's fer the kids,' Syd said into the mike, then, after wiping the back of his hand across his lips, he took a deep breath and began, 'There'll be pennies from heaven fer you an' me'. As he sang the words he tossed handfuls of pennies up into the air and of course the kids were running everywhere, dashing here and there, scrambling to see who could pick up the most. Minutes later, Robert held his hand out and said, 'I got seven, Uncle Syd.' 'I got twelve,' Raymond proudly told them.

'I only got three,' Lucy sadly announced. Doris bent her head and whispered into Raymond's ear. After a moment's hesitation he held out four pennies to Lucy and said, 'You have these, Lucy, then we've all got nearly the same.'

The lights were now turned down low; lanterns were lit, the band quietly played all the old Christmas carols and, as the old folk sang, imitation snow fell gently down on them from the rafters. It was a perfect end to the day.

It took a long while to help the old folks on with their coats and to organize which car or coach was taking them home. As they filed past the table behind which all the women helpers were lined up, each person was given a carrier-bag which contained a gift from every stall-holder in Tooting Market. There was everything from fruit, nuts, oranges and dates, right down to a packet of cocoa, a quarter of tea and packets of dried peas and haricot beans. A bar of chocolate hadn't been forgotten nor had bags of boiled sweets. There was even a two-bob voucher for each of them to change at the butchers.

'Won't buy 'em a turkey but it will buy the sausage-meat for the stuffing,' Fred Harris had joked as the women had spent more than an hour packing those bags.

'Gawd bless yer,' was said over an over again as the folk accepted their gift and many leant across the table to give a hug and a kiss to the women who had helped to give them all such a happy day.

When Doris turned to Lizzie there were tears in her eyes. 'Did yer see the look on those old folk's faces as they peered into those carrier-bags?'

'Yeah,' said Lizzie.

For Lizzie, Christmas was a time of sheer enjoyment and high hopes. She wasn't lonely, she was surrounded by her family, friends and neighbours and to her that meant more than anything.

On Boxing Day they took the children to the pantomime, and the biggest thrill for the three sets of parents was to watch the expressions on their children's faces as they cheered the good fairy and booed and hissed the wicked uncle. Muffled up against the cold wind in brightly coloured woollen scarves and gloves, the kiddies faces shone with excitement as they waited at Wimbledon Broadway for the train that would take them home.

Next morning when Lizzie came out into the kitchen she couldn't find Charlie or Robert. She hadn't slept that late, it was only ten minutes to nine;

surely they hadn't gone up to the Common this time of the morning. But even before the kettle had come to the boil she heard the front door being opened and, poking her head out into the hallway, she saw Charlie coming in.

'Where's Robert?' she shot at him as he stood wiping his feet on the doormat. 'He's all right. Give us a chance ter get inside the door an I'll tell yer.'

When Charlie had taken his overcoat off and hung it on a peg in the hall, Lizzie was ready for him. 'Well where is he?' she demanded.

'I've told yer, he's all right. He's round at Syd and Doris's; I've asked them to 'ave him fer a while 'cos I want ter take you out somewhere.'

'Oh yeah? Well, you had me worried,' Lizzie grumbled. 'Why didn't yer wake me?'

'You were sleeping so peacefully. Anyway it's all settled now and I thought we might 'ave a run out ter Epsom, 'ave a bit of lunch out, 'cos I want the two of us ter 'ave a good talk.'

'On our own!' Lizzie laughed. 'What 'ave you got ter say ter me that is so important that you're going to wine an' dine me?'

'Who said anything about wine?' Charlie cut in loudly, putting his arm around her shoulder. 'Look, Lizzie, it's almost time for us ter go back ter Devon an' I don't want us two ter end up 'aving a screaming match. Far better if we clear off this morning, away from everyone, an' discuss our problems sensibly. Then it should be easy fer us ter work things out.'

'Easy!' Lizzie said sarcastically.

*

By the time Charlie had got the car out and they were on their way, they had both calmed down. The weather wasn't at all promising; it was bitterly cold and the dark grey clouds that filled the sky looked full of snow.

When they had left Sutton behind and were approaching Banstead Downs, the scenery was much more interesting. Although most of the trees had shed their leaves and just the long bare branches reached up to the sky, there were still several shrubs wrapped in glory, their foliage shining with rich dark colours made all the more beautiful against the stark background of winter.

At a quarter to one, Charlie drove the car into the forecourt of a hotel at Tattenham Corner. Lizzie excused herself to go to the toilet while Charlie went to the reception desk to request a table for two for lunch. Having combed her hair and refreshed her lipstick, Lizzie came out of the ladies' room to see Charlie standing waiting for her at the entrance to the bar. 'About twenty minutes before they'll 'ave a free table,' he told her, as he put his hand under her elbow and propelled her towards the bar. 'Might as well 'ave a drink while we're waiting.'

Lizzie walked to the other side of the room and stood staring out of the immense plate-glass windows. Even on a dull day like today the view was stunning. Epsom Race Course! Where great horse races such as the Derby and the Oaks were run.

'What yer standing up for?' Charlie's question

broke in on her thoughts. She smiled at him and he smiled back as they both chose a seat near the window. Charlie had finished his pint and Lizzie was just draining the last of her schooner of Bristol Cream when a waiter came to tell Charlie that their table was ready.

The dining-room was elegant, the food superb and they lingered so long over their meal that it was turned half-past two by the time they went into the lounge and found two empty chairs near the enormous fire-place in which a bright log fire was burning.

It was impossible to raise one's voice in such surroundings and in that respect Charlie had the advantage as he put his points to Lizzie.

'Spending three months in London is all very well,' he said softly, 'but coming back to live for good – is that what you really want, Lizzie?'

Lizzie made no answer as she picked up her cup and saucer and sipped her coffee. It seemed that Charlie expected none, for he went straight on talking in low tones. 'Have you given a thought ter Robert's schooling? There's his future to take into consideration. At the moment he's 'aving all the advantages you or I never 'ad.' Charlie paused and picked up his cup of coffee and the silence hung heavy between them for some while.

When, finally, Charlie spoke again he sounded even more serious, if that was possible. 'The prospects of me finding a job in London that will enable me ter provide you and Robert with all the things you've both become used to are pretty slim, wouldn't yer say? I 'aven't got a trade to fall back on.'

'Oh, Charlie,' Lizzie sighed. Her heart ached for him! And at that moment she felt she had been thoroughly selfish.

Again, the silence was long and Lizzie refilled their cups from the silver coffee-pot.

'By the way, it's about time you learned to drive.'

'What?' Lizzie had raised her voice and Charlie laughed at the expression on her face.

'It makes sense yer know. Why don't we give Devon a few more years, at least until Robert is older, see him off to college. As hoteliers we're not doing so bad are we? And if we get you driving you won't feel so isolated; you'll be able ter get out an' about a bit more. Even pop up ter yer brother's on yer own now an' again.' The last statement Charlie had said with a saucy grin on his face.

'Oh, I see! A sprat ter catch a mackerel, is it?' Lizzie asked and there was no smile on her face. 'Don't tempt me too much,' she said beneath her breath. To be honest she did see the benefits of all his arguments. To stay in Devon, at least for the time being, was certainly the wisest choice. Reluctantly, she admitted to herself she didn't have any alternative. They had put up with all the hardships and the rough times of being up to their ears in debt. Charlie was right, damn him, when wasn't he? They would have to be mad to walk away just when all their problems were being ironed out and they were becoming successful.

'All right,' she said grudgingly, 'but it's still the back of beyond and the seasons are bloody 'ard work.'

'Lizzie, if they cut your head off you'd still 'ave the last word!'

Chapter Twenty-Eight

NOW IT WAS time to start thinking seriously about yet another season.

Easter wasn't too far away and the hotel was fully booked for that long weekend. Charlie's time was taken up with repairs and decorating; he reckoned to paint and re-paper between six and eight bedrooms each winter. Lizzie's mornings were spent entirely in the office answering on average forty letters at a time.

Many were from previous guests with cheques enclosed to reserve a particular bedroom for their holiday. These, Lizzie would set aside. They could be answered and receipts sent later in the day; they were definite bookings. Any new mail, either enquiries from the Town Guide or recommendations, she answered straight away and had them back in the post by midday.

They had come to know only too well that hotel life was a highly competitive business. Only by working on the enquiries received, giving each one full personal attention, were they going to achieve the maximum amount of bookings.

To Lizzie, it now seemed a very long time since they had been to Bristol. All the legal formalities had been taken care of, but still she was barely able to contain her impatience.

Week followed week, and nothing seemed to be happening.

'You just have to be patient,' Charlie told her time and time again. 'They can't dig the footings while the ground is still freezing.'

Patience was not Lizzie's strong point.

When the thaw finally did set in and Michael Gale telephoned to say that work could now begin in earnest, Lizzie was up there on the site to see the machinery close in to start on the footings.

With the improvement on the roads, Lizzie was able to take her driving test. The whole village must have known she had passed! Driving back from Barnstaple in the green Austin 1100 that Charlie had bought for her and which Robert had immediately nick-named 'Brussel Sprout', the examiner's words were still loud in her head.

'Congratulations. I wish you many happy years of safe motoring.'

Approaching the hotel, she put her finger on the horn and kept it there until she reached the main entrance.

'Cocky, aren't we!' Charlie said, grinning from ear to ear.

With the season, came the usual problems. One morning, while doing her rounds, Lizzie heard the Hoover going but couldn't see where.

She opened a bedroom door. There, sitting on the bed, reading a magazine, was the young chambermaid who had only recently come to work at Highland Heights. The Hoover was plugged in and switched on, but stood there quite stationary.

'What are you doing?' Lizzie asked firmly.

No answer.

Lizzie looked around the room. Under the washbasin there was sand, the dressing-table was dusty and the towels needed to be changed.

The girl got to her feet and turned on Lizzie, practically screaming, 'The trouble with you is you think this hotel is a ruddy palace!'

Lizzie held her temper in check, but her big blue eyes flashed. In low-pitched, precise tones, she said, 'If it is, then I'm the queen that reigns here and your services are no longer required.'

The older, more conscientious chambermaids, who had worked for Lizzie since she had first taken over, were huddled together on the landing; they hadn't missed a word.

Lizzie heard what they said as she swept by. 'Missus must be in a good mood. Wonder she didn't grab that one by the scruff of the neck.'

Lizzie had to laugh to herself. They didn't know just how near she had come to doing just that.

In what free time they did get, Charlie usually opted to go for a swim, mainly in the sea, using the swimming baths in Ilfracombe only as a last resort if the weather was too foul.

Lizzie would drive out to the site. She was a bit disappointed in the early stages, the area of the footings looked so small.

'Not to worry, mi-dear,' the workmen told her, 'that be everyone's first impression.'

To get up there over the weekends was an impossibility. So, four or even five days might pass without Lizzie being able to pay a visit. Then the progress would be noticeable.

The framework developed at an amazing rate and the buildings began to develop character. At each stage, they were consulted by both Michael Gale and Mr Roberts, who wanted to know their preference for the interior work and design, even down to the smallest detail, such as door design for the garage.

Charlie and Lizzie thought it was great to be actively involved in the building of their house and each trip that Lizzie made out to the site could be guaranteed to bring her back to work in a very happy frame of mind.

Miraculously, by mid-August the house was completed.

Strangely, Lizzie lost the urge to visit it so often. The season was at its peak. Days for them both still had to start very early in the morning and finish very late at night, so, not surprisingly, their energy began to flag and they were often very tired by the end of the day.

But at last another season was over; it was the

second week in October and they were standing in the grounds seeing the last coach party of guests off on their homeward journey.

During the next few days, with the help of all the staff, the hotel was shut down. Bedrooms were closed up, silver cleaned and packed away, all kitchen equipment scalded and thoroughly cleaned and dust sheets thrown over furniture in the first-floor lounge. The place took on an air of despondency.

Charlie paid off the staff, adding a bonus for each of them and everyone was well satisfied.

The next few days were grim. Charlie wisely said, 'Don't rush things, breathe out. No one is so resilient that they can spring back to a normal way of life after working seven days a week since last Easter.'

So they were lazy, sleeping a lot, eating when they felt hungry, not watching the clock at all. Ten days later, with batteries recharged, they were both raring to go.

'Furniture for the house or a holiday?' Charlie queried.

'What d'you think?' Lizzie asked, giving him a smug look.

That evening they talked and talked, made lists and wrote out suggestions as to what they would like to buy for their new home, and the next morning they set off for Bideford to see Mr Channon. This time they didn't need credit, they would pay cash for whatever they purchased.

The memory had never dimmed for either Charlie or Lizzie. Mr Channon had not only treated them fairly, he had been an absolute brick. When all the odds had seemed stacked against the pair of them ever making a go of Sea View Guesthouse, he had shown faith and understanding. Neither of them would have dreamt of going to any other furniture store.

Lizzie had a whale of a time. She quickly chose a bedroom suite and a smaller, slightly more masculine suite for Robert's room. Upstairs in the showrooms, she bounced on beds and divans. Brass headboards? Wooden headboards? She couldn't make up her mind. In the end, she settled on newly imported continental ones, woodgrained to match the suites. One was nine feet wide with bedside tables attached and individual reading lights. Robert's was similar, but half the size.

The dining-room suite was also a relatively easy choice. Charlie liked good wood and traditional styles. Lizzie, in her imagination, was already seeing the oval table with its claw feet, set up and laid. Candles lit, a bowl of flowers set in the centre, she couldn't wait for them to eat their first dinner in their own dining-room.

There was still the question of what to put in that gigantic lounge. They sat on comfortable sofas and easychairs; nothing seemed right. Even with the addition of occasional tables and various lamps the room needed more than an ordinary three-piece suite.

'How about these?' Mr Channon asked, producing three glossy brochures.

This furniture was unique. Expensive for sure, but even Charlie exclaimed that he'd never seen anything like it before.

'It is going on show in London from next week. I've got swatches of colour and fabrics I can show you,' Mr Channon said.

Charlie made a snap decision. 'No, we'll go to London. I'd like to see the actual furniture, wouldn't you, Lizzie?'

'Not half I wouldn't,' she answered, thinking at the same time, a weekend in London, great!

Friday afternoon, with the car well packed, they were outside Adelaide College to meet Robert. Charlie broke their journey in Taunton where they all had a meal in a steak house. Soon they were on their way again and Robert was asleep. Lizzie, lulled by the steady motion of Charlie's driving, also began to doze.

Doris and Syd had the front door open before the car had stopped. Raymond practically dragged Robert out, and there were hugs and kisses for everyone.

At nine o'clock next morning, Charlie and Lizzie set off for the West End. Although it was Saturday, traffic seemed horrific and Charlie had great difficulty in finding somewhere to park.

The three gentlemen in the showrooms, most would say, looked the perfect image of success. To

Lizzie, they looked like tailors' dummies with their pin-striped trousers, cut-away dark grey jackets and starched white shirts.

One man stepped forward and introduced himself, 'Mr Westland, how may I help you?' He shook hands, but his fingers hardly touched Lizzie's. Yet, as he showed them around these expensive show-rooms, Lizzie found herself liking this Mr Westland. He wasn't the cold fish she had first taken him for and neither was he stupid. He knew his job; he was intelligent and interesting to listen to.

See! She chided herself, you shouldn't be so quick to form an impression.

The furniture was upholstered in leather. Leather so soft and supple it felt like velvet. The design just as exciting as the brochure had promised. They chose an enormous settee, five-seater open-ended. It had a wide armrest at one end, the other end curved and rounded off to a half circular shape. Also a traditional three-seater settee together with two large, well-cushioned, deep armchairs.

Mr Westland was a little persuasive when it came to pouffes. 'One cannot imagine you would ignore them,' his rather grand voice beseeched as he ran his hand through his mop of blond curls. 'These are the *pièce de résistance*.'

They ordered two. Each three foot square; the top cushion, when removed, revealed a well-polished grained wood table top. 'Great for playing cards on,' Charlie commented.

'You'd have to sit on the floor to do so,' Lizzie retorted.

Import licences and delivery dates were discussed. The actual retailer would be Mr Channon of Bideford. Charlie asked several questions all of which Mr Westland answered with ease. Lizzie, in the end, felt that neither fire nor flood would ruffle that young gentleman's composure.

Saturday afternoon, Syd and Charlie took the two boys to watch Chelsea play an at-home football match, while Doris and Lizzie set off for Croydon and the shops.

At seven-thirty, a taxi came. They were off to the Selkirk Pub for a drink, taking the boys with them. 'Do they still have a children's room?' Lizzie asked Syd.

''Course they do.' Brother and sister grinned at each other, recalling the old days when they themselves had been kids.

Pushing through the swing doors at barely eight o'clock, the place was jam-packed. The band struck up; 'For he's a jolly good fellow' was sung with gusto. Everyone rushed towards Lizzie and Charlie. It was a party in their honour!

All their friends, and what few relatives that were left, were gathered there. Half the street where Lizzie had been born had turned out. Neighbours Lizzie only half remembered. She had forgotten what a cockney welcome could be like.

Lizzie was choked; fancy wanting to cry on such a happy occasion. What an evening! Drink flowed like water. The band never seemed to stop playing and Lizzie told herself over and over again how lucky she was.

On Sunday evening, Polly and Arthur had the two boys while Doris, Syd, Charlie and Lizzie went to Kensington. Flanagan's Restaurant had sawdust on the floor, and a menu chalked on an old blackboard. A pianist sitting at an upright piano belted out all the old songs non-stop.

Lizzie ordered skate and chips.

Charlie was astounded. 'You've never come all the way from Devon to the Royal Borough to eat fish 'n' chips?' he cried.

'It's not fish 'n' chips, it's skate 'n' chips,' Lizzie hurled back, smacking her lips in anticipation.

From Flanagan's, they took a taxi to the Victoria Palace. Tonight's performance was in aid of Jewish Benevolent funds. All the stars were giving their services free. For Lizzie, it was Ann Shelton who stole the show as she sang 'My Yiddisher Mamma' and there wasn't a dry eye in the house.

Monday came and it was back to north Devon.

'That was some weekend!' Charlie said as he shook hands with Syd.

'Yeah, wasn't it?' Doris whispered to Lizzie, as once more they hugged and said, 'See you soon.'

It took nearly a month for the carpets to be delivered and laid. Furniture arrived and was set out in appropriate rooms. A local lady had made the curtains, and Charlie put up curtain tracks and poles and saw to the hanging of them.

Lizzie became a constant visitor to the nearest garden centre. Vans drew up delivering shrubs, small trees, earthenware urns, tubs of all shapes and sizes, colourful hanging baskets, and bag upon bag of peat and John Innes' mixtures.

'Might as well bury money in the earth, the amount you spend,' Charlie grumbled, but Lizzie only smiled sweetly.

The actual day dawned; they were moving their personal belongings from the hotel into their own home.

By evening, the bungalow was filled with familiar, well-loved things and had really begun to feel like home.

Robert's bedroom looked lovely, with his belongings already scattered about and his books all set out on the shelves. The bathroom was a dream, everything co-ordinated, beautiful soft towels – none here with Highland Heights printed in red running through the middle.

Upstairs, the dining-room was to the right, perfect in every detail. Beyond was the kitchen, the only room in the whole house that did not give a view of the sea. It was, however, a cheerful, bright kitchen with large windows looking out over the steep sloping garden where several Christmas trees and other shrubs had been left intact and which Lizzie now thought of as their rural area.

The lounge was open and spacious, the end wall, apart from two foot on either side, was entirely glass, the centre being an enormous set of sliding doors which led on to the upper terrace. Running the whole width of the house, the terrace was so big that Lizzie remarked, 'You could hold a dance out there.'

The concrete paved slabs forming the base were alternately green and white and with the white ranch-style railings all around it looked splendid.

Charlie and Lizzie were very pleased.

Chapter Twenty-Nine

THE NEW YEAR of 1958 was only a few weeks old and every morning Lizzie's first job was to sort and answer the mail.

'Has the postman been yet?' Lizzie called up the stairs to Charlie.

'I haven't heard him but I'm just gonna pick the paper up, I'll bring the mail down if he has.'

Two minutes later Lizzie heard Charlie shout, 'Oh no!' The tone of his voice was so distressed that Lizzie ran to the foot of the basement stairs. 'Charlie,' she called loudly, 'are you all right?'

'Yes, Yes, I'm coming down. I won't be a minute.'

Lizzie was halfway up the stairs before she could see him walking very slowly across the entrance hall with the newspaper opened wide and his head bent low as he read. Lizzie hurried to see the headlines. There had been an air crash in West Germany. The whole of the Manchester United football team had been on board.

They sat facing each other at the kitchen table and listened to the news being relayed over the wireless net-work. The crash had happened because the plane had failed to clear a fence on take-off; the weather was foul and the rescue workers were being hampered by driving snow. Charlie looked thoroughly dejected, eight members of the team were among the twenty-one dead. Lizzie got up and went to the gas-stove. 'I'll make us a coffee,' she said as she filled a saucepan with milk and put it on to heat.

'Poor old Matt Busby,' Charlie said half to himself. 'He's a damn good manager, he's become so popular that the team has been nick-named the "Busby Babes". Eight of the boys dead! It's not fair!'

All day Charlie couldn't get it out of his mind and Lizzie let him rattle on about football because it seemed to make him feel better to talk about it. On the six o'clock evening news they heard that Matt Busby had been seriously injured in the crash. 'It's not bloody fair,' was all that Charlie could mutter.

Life went on and Lizzie concentrated on getting as many bookings as possible for what would be their fifth season in Highland Heights Hotel. With the coming of the very busy weeks of July and August the weather was as good as it had been bad at the beginning of the year, which was fine for the visitors but not so good for the hotel workers. A veritable heatwave had the beaches and the surrounding little coves packed with holidaymakers. The hotel kitchens became unbearable as the scorching sun beat down relentlessly.

Lizzie sighed with relief one Monday evening about nine o'clock when Charlie switched off both ovens and the hot plate.

'I think I'll come home with you, love, for an

hour or so, there's plenty of staff on duty.' Charlie sounded really done in.

They walked in silence to the garage. Lizzie backed her car out first, then Charlie did the same, taking to the road first while Lizzie drove home behind him.

Dawn had hardly come and Lizzie was up again, after a hot, restless night.

On the upper terrace they kept a set of wrought-iron garden furniture, four chairs, table with centre umbrella and two sun-beds. She carried out the green and white striped mattresses, returning indoors to fetch the matching seat-cushions for the chairs.

A breakfast of toast, marmalade and orange juice, eaten out on the veranda, and Lizzie felt much better.

The sky was a clear blue; the heat was still there and it seemed certain to be another hot day. In the silence all she could hear was the gentle whirring of a lawnmower and even that seemed miles away.

It was almost ten o'clock and Lizzie stood by the railings looking down the hill and beyond to the sea. She saw Doctor Whittaker's car coming along the lower road; there was no mistaking it – a dark green MG sports car, roof down. He slowed, tooted his horn and waved. Lizzie raised her cupped hand to her mouth and mimed, drink. He tooted his horn again and gave a thumbs-up sign.

Lizzie had first met Jeffrey Whittaker while

delivering meals on wheels with the WVS. He wasn't their family doctor, he belonged to a panel of three doctors.

The WVS covered a wide area, including many outlying villages. The volunteer women often saved the doctors a journey by delivering a package or even reporting to them how the elderly folk were getting along.

Although quite young in comparison to the other doctors, Jeffrey Whittaker was conscientious about his work. Unmarried, scrupulously clean yet never formally dressed, he mainly wore slacks with sporty-type shirts and, when necessary, a zip-up jacket. He would come bounding into the building where the WVS ladies cooked and packed the dinners, and so invigorating was his attitude that Lizzie always half expected him to call out, 'Anyone for tennis?'

Everyone was on first-name terms with this young doctor. But only being able to do voluntary work during the winter months, it was weeks since Lizzie had had a chance to talk to him.

She heard his car park below, in front of their garage. He used the outside staircase which brought him directly up on to the terrace without going into the house.

'Gee! This is absolutely marvellous, Lizzie,' he exclaimed as he threw himself down on to one of the sun-beds.

'Yeah, fantastic,' Lizzie called back as she went inside to make the coffee.

He must have noticed the weariness in her voice

because, as she came out and put the tray with the coffee cups and saucers on to the table, he gently asked, 'Everything not right with your world?'

'Oh, don't mind me, Jeff, I didn't sleep that well last night, that's all.'

He sat up straight and proceeded to pour out the coffee. 'Milk and sugar? Help yourself,' he stated as he handed a cup to Lizzie.

She had to laugh. Talk about making yourself at home. He certainly was an easy person to be with.

She glanced at her wristwatch, 'What are you doing out so early, Jeff? No surgery this morning?'

'I've been out to Combe Martin. The church camping site. You know thè big hut come hall; the scouts use it and the girl guides. Well, they've got a party of young boys staying in there this week. Managing well really, mattresses on the floors. Hotels, guesthouses, cafes all mucking in, helping to give the little lads a free holiday.'

He stopped talking, took out his handkerchief and wiped his forehead. 'It's hot again, isn't it? I can't remember it being as hot as this. When this weather does break we'll have such a storm.'

'Jeff,' Lizzie grasped his arm, 'go on, tell me more about those boys.'

'Well, they probably come from your part of the world or near enough. East End of London, some home, not Doctor Barnardo's, but similar, can't recall the name. You'd have laughed, Lizzie, climbing about the rocks wearing thick, knee-length socks, heavy laced-up shoes, most likely they've never seen the sea before.'

Lizzie winced, 'Thick socks on a day like this? Who's in charge of them?'

'Four men.'

'I might have guessed that.'

'Now hold on, Lizzie, I doubt even you could have got those youngsters to part with their clothing. You should have heard them; they were in their element but still highly suspicious of change or anyone that wanted to do things for them.'

Lizzie's mind took her back in time. Charlie had spent his childhood in an orphanage. When she had first met him, he had been starved of love, yearning for a home to call his own. Look what they had now. She thought of the advantages her son had and then she got cross with herself. Seeing the anger appear on Lizzie's face, Doctor Whittaker wondered whether he had gone too far.

'Have I upset you, Lizzie?'

'Hell, no. There's me wallowing in self-pity all night, worried sick because Charlie was so tired, and there's those unfortunate kids out there glad of a free holiday.'

Jeffrey Whittaker smiled to himself, he had achieved what he wanted to; it had helped to snap Mrs Wilson out of what could have been a nasty spell of depression, had it gone on too long.

Aloud he said, 'You mustn't blame yourself, Lizzie. You and Charlie are both hard workers. You put the maximum effort into every job you tackle.

Now you're both strung up like overwound clock-springs. It'll be September come next Monday, season will soon be over. Book yourselves a holiday; best tonic in the world having something to look forward to.'

Later, when Jeffrey Whittaker left, he tooted the horn of his car and Lizzie stood leaning over the balcony until he was out of sight.

What a kind, caring person he is, she said to herself as she went indoors and picked up the telephone.

'Please, Charlie,' Lizzie pleaded, 'I'll come down to the hotel when we get back. Help get the dinners through. I don't need the evening off.'

'All right. I'll organize it,' his reply came quiet and firm over the line, 'be at the foot of the hill; I'll make it by a quarter to two.'

She had told Charlie everything that Jeffrey Whittaker had told her and really he hadn't hesitated for a second.

The couple of hours that she and Charlie spent out at Combe Martin would remain vivid to Lizzie for a very long time. Charlie had met the organizer of the party, established the name of the children's home and offered a week's holiday to a party of children for the following year at Highland Heights. He had also been to the local haberdashery shop.

'You're too late,' a beaming shop assistant told him. 'Local people have already bought up our entire stock of swimming trunks for the boys. My guvernor has gone to Barnstaple to get some more.'

Lizzie had to smother her sobs as she watched Charlie romp with a couple of five year olds and her heart almost burst with love as she watched him quietly hand some notes over to one of the men in charge.

'See they have a few ice-creams and what nots,' he said in a voice that was barely audible.

Chapter Thirty

'COMING WITH ME tonight?' Charlie asked enthusiastically.

Lizzie was doubtful. Darts matches in Devon were sombre affairs compared with those in London. No food provided, no dancing afterwards, in fact, few wives bothered to accompany their husbands.

On the other hand, this match was being held at The Foxhunter's Inn, a rather lovely road house well out in the country. Young Robert was going to play water polo, they could pick him up on the way back.

'Yes, all right,' she agreed, having weighed up all the pros and cons.

Just as she thought, she was the only woman.

'You don't want to stay in this public bar,' Charlie whispered rather sheepishly. 'Go through to the lounge, I'll bring you a drink.'

She had finished her drink and was sitting, idly looking through the evening paper, when she heard a loud cheer go up in the public bar.

'Is that the first leg over?' Lizzie asked as Charlie came through the archway carrying a fresh drink for her. With him was the captain of the team Charlie played for, Harry Baldwin, well known to Lizzie because it was he who delivered fresh fruit, salad stuff and vegetables to their hotel during the season.

'Harry's been telling me there's to be an auction at Rillage View,' Charlie said as he placed the glass and a fresh bottle of dry ginger down on to the brass-topped table.

'Coming up soon it be, Mrs Wilson. Several properties, contents an' all. Make a nice day out it will. Shall us be seeing 'ee there?'

'More than likely,' Lizzie smiled as she answered. She liked Harry, no side with him. A good-natured, down-to-earth sort of bloke.

Rillage View was a local landmark, a very old type of hotel standing high up on what was known as Harbour View Terrace. Difficult to gain access to, the road being narrow and steeply winding, but once there, as its address implied, you had a commanding view of the harbour.

On the morning of the sale they laughed at each other, both had opted to wear what they described as their country outfits. Charlie had on cavalry twill trousers, a suede-fronted jerkin and a Harris tweed sports coat.

'You look every inch a squire,' Lizzie scoffed at him.

'You'd pass at a horse show,' he retaliated.

'Thanks a bunch,' Lizzie said as she half turned to check herself in the hall mirror. She wasn't too happy with the low-heeled shoes she was wearing, but she liked the heather-coloured woven costume.

The pale lavender cashmere jumper with its high neck toned in extremely well, 'At least I think it does,' she muttered, determined not to let Charlie put her off.

'Well,' Charlie made a mocking bow, 'Rillage View, here we come.'

Within minutes of their arrival Lizzie had lost Charlie. She wandered off into the hall and up the staircase. Every item of furniture she passed was marked with a lot number. Looking in through the doorway of each room, Lizzie found it all unbelievable. Everything looked as if it had come out of the Ark.

Having got to the top floor and been really nosey, peeking in all the corners and opening cupboard doors, Lizzie began making her way downstairs. She had to be very careful since the staircase was not only very narrow, it twisted and turned quite sharply at every landing. She reached the first floor and was frightened for a moment; not only was the landing crowded with people, but, looking over the banister rail, she saw that the staircase was also jam-packed.

The auction had started. Lots were being sold from exactly where the various items were situated. Presumably the ground-floor contents had all been disposed of and the auctioneer was moving upstairs to start on the sale of bedroom furniture.

It was like a stampede. Lizzie panicked. There was no way she could possibly get through that crowd. She felt herself being half pushed, half carried into a bedroom. Packed like a sardine, she couldn't move. The auctioneer climbed up on to a wide window sill and the sale carried on. Small objects were held high in the air by men in brown overalls, while large items were pointed to with the aid of a long cane. The auctioneer's gavel fell with monotonous regularity as each article went to the highest bidder.

Lizzie looked around; the room was very large. One double bed, two single beds, each having old-fashioned brass rails at the head and foot. Large cumbersome furniture. A marble-topped wash-stand complete with an ornamental china jug and bowl. God help the chambermaids who had to work in this hotel, Lizzie thought to herself.

Suddenly, Lizzie felt a tug at the hem of her skirt. Moving her feet and knees as much as was possible, she looked down. Charlie's face was peering up at her.

'What the hell are you doing?' she uttered almost under her breath.

He was on his haunches almost underneath the double bed. 'Bid, bid!' he ordered in an undertone.

'What?'

'Don't ask questions, just bid for this carpet,' he hissed.

She glanced at her programme. The carpet was lot number 315. Now she paid attention. 'Lot three one three, a unique pair of vases . . . ' the auctioneer's voice droned on.

Only two lots to go.

'Three one five, ladies and gentlemen, the carpet

on three one three which you are standing.' There was a general shuffling of feet as folk attempted to look down.

'Who will start me off with a fiver?'

Lizzie was too nervous to do anything; three bids had been taken, her skirt was being yanked at again.

She didn't bother to look down, just raised her programme high in the air. Two counterbids were made, each time Lizzie waved her programme.

'Going, going, gone,' the gavel fell. 'Name?'

'Mrs Wilson,' Lizzie said in a voice that didn't sound a bit like her own.

Lot number 315 was hers, whether she wanted it or not.

The crowds moved on and Lizzie made her escape – down the winding stairs and out into the fresh air. Within ten minutes, Charlie had joined her.

'Dirty old carpet,' she shot at him straight away, 'what in the world do we want it for?'

'That's a *real* carpet. One hundred per cent pure wool Wilton. Cost a fortune to buy one that size today. All it needs is cleaning, you'll see. Got ourselves a great bargain there.'

Lizzie gave up. No use arguing about it now, was there!

'Come on, we'll have lunch. Nothing I'm interested in now, not until this afternoon.'

The brightness in Charlie's eyes and the colour in his cheeks as he grinned at her told Lizzie that he was more than pleased with his purchase.

Charlie drove the car down to what was the only

public house on the harbour. Lizzie sat outside on the quayside while Charlie went into the pub. The fishing boats were in, unloading basketfuls of shining herrings and pots which held struggling crabs and lobsters. Huge gulls were screeching overhead, swooping in low for scraps, and yet the whole harbour had a peaceful air.

They had crusty bread, local cheese and big pickled onions to eat, washed down by cool, sparkling lager, and were back at Rillage View by a quarter to two.

The afternoon's sale was to be conducted in the original dining-room. A makeshift platform had been set up at one end, with rows of chairs placed in front, most of which were already taken. Charlie led Lizzie to where there was a single empty seat on the end of a row by the middle aisle.

'What about you?' she asked.

'I'll be all right,' Charlie answered, 'I'm just going to have a word with the auctioneers.'

There were more than a dozen men clustered in front of the platform. Charlie was soon in their midst, having quite an animated conversation with two of them.

'Wonder what he is up to now?' Lizzie asked herself.

To one side of the room, two men were seated at a table with lots of legal-looking papers spread out in front of them. One man was quite old, the other, barely thirty, was writing with his head bent low, intent upon what he was doing.

'Solicitor and his clerk,' the woman sitting next to Lizzie obligingly said, nodding her head in the direction of the two men.

What are they here for? Lizzie wanted to ask, but merely murmured, 'Thank you.'

Groups of men were standing around the sides of the room, some talking so loudly that Lizzie thought they were having an argument.

Suddenly, the auctioneer rapped loudly with his gavel, and all the men made a general movement to the back of the hall. Lizzie couldn't see where Charlie had got to.

Now there was complete silence in the large room.

'Before the commencement of this sale, I must impress upon you all the legality of these proceedings.' The gentleman conducting this part of the sale was totally different from the previous auctioneer.

His voice was that of a well-educated gentleman, although to look at him, he seemed a typical north Devon farmer. A real open-air type of man, his tweed jacket had leather patches at the elbows, his shirt was open at the neck and he wasn't wearing a tie.

'The highest bidder to whom each property will be sold must be prepared to sign contracts this afternoon and pay to the vendor a deposit of ten per cent of the selling price which will be irretrievable.'

He paused, consulted his programme and went on, 'Mr Button, the gentleman on my right, is acting for each and all of the vendors. We have five properties to be disposed of this afternoon, so if you are all clear in your minds as to the legal points, we will make a start.'

There was a shuffling of feet, a clearing of throats, and the auction began.

'Lot number one. Agricultural land known as Dene's End.'

Lizzie lost interest. She looked around the room. All the furniture had been pushed aside leaving the floor space free. It was all heavy-framed dark wood pieces now bearing 'Sold' labels.

There was an extremely large glass-fronted bookcase filled with books which were so dusty they looked as if they hadn't been taken down from the shelves for years, never mind opened and read.

The auctioneer startled Lizzie, his voice got louder, his movements more rapid. 'T'be done, t'be done, t'be done. Sold to Mr Hutchinson,' his gavel fell loud and final.

'Look at your programmes, ladies and gentlemen, lot number two, Hampton Cross Farm.'

Only two serious bidders, same procedure, it was all over.

'Lot number three, known as Ivy Cottage, Larks Lane, and number one, Leigh Lane.' Murmurings came from the audience.

'That's perfectly correct,' the auctioneer said. 'This cottage does in actual fact have two postal addresses. Dilapidated, needs renovating, will take low bid to start.'

Very quiet now, no takers. Lizzie was reading her

programme. The two addresses had intrigued her. She heard the auctioneer plead for someone to start the bidding, but it was slow and she wasn't taking much notice.

'The bidding is against you, Mr Wilson.'

Wilson, did he say Wilson? There was no mistaking this time as she heard the auctioneer say, 'Thank you, Mr Wilson.'

Lizzie jerked her head round so quickly her neck snapped and it hurt. She still couldn't see Charlie. She twisted the other way, still no sign of him. Too many men crushed together at the back of the room.

The gavel fell again with a firm, loud bang.

'Sold to Mr Wilson of Highland Heights.'

Lizzie sat through the rest of the sale in a daze. Charlie had done some daft things in his time, but this beat the lot. Lovely new split-level bungalow built especially for them and he goes and buys a run-down ramshackle old cottage.

The sale was finished and refreshments were being offered. Lizzie pushed her way through and made for the car. She couldn't really analyze her feelings.

She saw Charlie coming and wrenched open the car door. Even before he reached her, she yelled, 'You've just bought a cottage!'

'I know.'

'I know you know. What I want to know is what you are intending to do with it?'

People were looking. She knew she was being stupid.

'Don't be so emotional,' Charlie rebuked her.

Well! That was like showing a red rag to a bull. 'We haven't even seen the place. Come to that, I don't even know where it is, don't suppose you do either. It's got to be derelict, nobody else wanted it. Did you have it surveyed? No, 'course you didn't. You're the great man, Charlie Wilson.'

'Calm down,' Charlie said very quietly, 'trust me. I'll tell you all about it later. Come back inside and countersign the contract.'

'What?' Lizzie was off again. '*You* bought the bloody cottage; *you* sign the bloody contract.'

'God give me patience!' In exasperation, Charlie grabbed her arm and his words to her now were hissed through teeth that were almost clenched. 'This property has been bought by the company. It is an investment. I should have discussed it with you, but I didn't. I'm sorry. None the more for that, it's done. The company has purchased it, and that means you, Lizzie, as well as me. Joint company directors. You and me. Now, will you please sign the contract?'

Lizzie jerked her arm away from his hold; he had said sorry, probably for the first time in his life. Still, that didn't alter things much. He was still an impulsive know-all.

'You haven't left me much option,' Lizzie said, still showing ill-feeling as she walked away.

They each signed the contract, Lizzie wrote out a

cheque for the ten per cent deposit and Charlie signed it.

'You've made a good buy today,' Mr Button said as he took hold of Lizzie's hand. 'I've known Ivy Cottage since I was a lad. Sadly neglected, very sad, but its structure is sound.' Wistfully he turned away to shake Charlie's hand.

'Wise decision, young man, so near to your own hotel. It would have been a mistake to let it go to others.' For the first time, Charlie smiled.

'Thanks, Mr Button, thanks for your help.'

Lizzie watched and waited while Charlie took his leave of several men. 'What now?' she asked as they walked to the car.

It was a foolish question, she knew. Mr Button's comments had aroused her curiosity but her pride would not let her question Charlie outright.

He didn't answer her, but as he held the car door open for her, he said, 'I'm sorry, Lizzie.'

Two apologies in one afternoon, she smiled briefly. 'I am too.'

Before starting up the engine, Charlie placed his hand on Lizzie's knee. She dropped her head a little and clenched her hands together in her lap. She was fed up. Charlie was headstrong and her own temperament wasn't all it should be. That was the whole damn trouble, they clashed.

'Lizzie, look at me.'

She raised her eyes and Charlie chuckled, 'Perhaps you would like to see this cottage?'

They had almost reached the hotel when Lizzie exclaimed, 'I thought you were going to show me this cottage.'

'I am. We'll leave the car in the hotel drive.'

Lizzie was even more confused now.

When the car stopped, Charlie was out and off down the hill like an excited ten year old, his dark hair fluffed up high by the breeze as he ran.

'Come on, run!' he yelled back over his shoulder, and Lizzie found herself doing just that.

She stood there panting, her chest still heaving as she gasped for breath.

Minutes passed and still she could hardly believe it.

Finally, she turned to Charlie, amazement uppermost in her voice. 'I must have passed Leigh Lane hundreds of times. I had no idea that there was a cottage here.'

'Well, you know now,' Charlie said, grinning broadly, 'and what's more, it belongs to us.'

Lizzie stepped back and scrutinized the cottage. It looked as if it hadn't been occupied for years. The windows had odd pieces of wood nailed together covering them. Even the roof was covered with what looked like boards and a waterproof sheet.

Suddenly, she couldn't help herself, she burst out laughing. It was hilarious, it had to be a joke; she laughed so much she had a stitch in her side. Her laughter was infectious.

'You can scoff,' Charlie said as he, too, let out a great belly laugh, 'this place will make us a fortune.'

For once in her life Lizzie kept her mouth shut and listened with deep interest to what Charlie was saying as he sat opposite her at the dinner-table.

'I knew I could buy it for next to nothing and, as Mr Button said, I would have been mad to let it go to somebody else. Staff quarters!'

The sharp and sudden explanation had Lizzie wanting to bombard him with a dozen questions, but no, she still kept silent. Charlie waited for her outburst and grinned when none was forthcoming.

He continued, 'We're losing money in the hotel. Since we've had our bungalow built our private rooms hardly get used. Then there are the three rooms downstairs taken up by staff living in. That's why it is money well spent, that cottage will pay for itself over and over again.'

I must be thick as two planks, Lizzie thought to herself. She couldn't keep quiet any longer.

'So you do that cottage up. Probably cost us a bomb just to make it habitable. Then, you use it as sleeping quarters for the staff? Have I got things right so far?'

'Yes,' Charlie confirmed.

Lizzie smiled at him brightly, then, with a sigh, asked, 'How will the cottage ever make money if we are only going to use it to sleep staff in?' Lizzie put down her knife and fork. 'You are deliberately trying to rile me, Charlie, you know I haven't got the foggiest what you're on about. You just keep throwing out scraps of information, and you sit there watching me get more and more confused.'

'OK, OK,' Charlie threw his hands up in mock surrender. 'Pour me a cup of coffee and I promise I will explain everything, down to the last detail. The huge ground floor dining-room could easily be divided into five bedrooms. All would have sea views and, being on the ground floor, they would be easy to let during the summer and absolutely invaluable for the coach parties of old folk. Do you agree?'

'Yes, of course I do,' Lizzie said but she couldn't keep a hint of sarcasm from her voice as she asked, 'then, just what do we use as a dining-room?'

Charlie thrust out his chest as he delivered his masterpiece. 'All the lower ground-floor rooms beyond the kitchens we turn into a complete new dining-room.'

Excitement now showing on his face, Charlie got up and came round the table, drew Lizzie to her feet and hugged her.

Speechless, absolutely stunned, that's how Lizzie felt. The very idea staggered her. Finally, she did manage to mutter, 'Charlie, you're forever conniving some new scheme.'

Now Charlie held her closer, eagerly as if he would never let her go. 'It will all work out fine, you'll see,' he assured her, and as Lizzie broke free from his arms, she believed him. His eyes were brilliant, he was smiling his loving smile, his whole mood was frank, even boyish, and he was certainly very pleased with himself.

Next morning, Lizzie was awake early. She got out of bed quietly and went upstairs.

The kitchen clock said five minutes to five. She made a pot of tea, drank several cups and was bathed and dressed by the time Charlie came upstairs.

'Seldom seen you ready to go so early in the day,' was Charlie's greeting as he kissed her cheek. 'Can't you wait to get cracking?'

Breakfast was all ready and as they sat eating Charlie seemed so calm and self-assured that Lizzie kept trying to smother her giggles.

They say nothing ventured, nothing gained, but boy, this was some venture even for Charlie!

The kitchen was bright and cheery, the windows were open and, although the breeze was fresh, there was a bite in the air – a sure sign winter was coming again.

Lizzie thought of the hard winter they had experienced the year that they had had this split-level bungalow built, and silently she prayed that this new venture they were about to embark on would turn out just as successfully.

Glancing at his watch, Charlie said, 'Come on, get your coats on, time to go.'

At the first stop they dropped Robert off at school, and at the second stop, the offices of Roger Farrant their now long-term solicitor and friend.

'Success breeds success, eh Mrs Wilson?' Mr Farrant said warmly as he shook hands with them both and offered his congratulations. Lizzie's smile deepened, she liked coming to this office. She sniffed the smell of good leather upholstery as she sat down on a high-backed chair and listened to what the men were saying.

'Mr Harding will present the company accounts to the bank, no problem there,' Roger Farrant confirmed.

Lizzie's thoughts again went back over the past. The bank had been marvellous, helping them at every turn. Without their help, they could never have achieved so much. In the early years, though, it hadn't exactly been easy or without anxiety trying to borrow money. Yet now, it seemed, Charlie had only to ask and further loans would be granted.

Roger Farrant was right, success must breed success.

As always, Lizzie felt the urge to kiss Mr Farrant as they said goodbye.

He still had that flirtatious manner about him as he held her hand longer than was necessary and said in that soft drawl, 'We'll meet again soon.'

Charlie swung the bunch of very odd-looking keys.

'What will it be, coffee or a drink to celebrate?'

'Celebrate what? Our personal disaster?' Lizzie asked, but she smiled as she spoke.

'Pessimist,' Charlie taunted.

They settled for a quick cup of coffee in a nearby restaurant. Lizzie wanted to get to Ivy Cottage as quickly as possible. She fervently hoped it would look better in broad daylight, but her hopes were not fulfilled. If anything, it looked worse!

There was a short rise of steps leading to the front door. Charlie went up these and tried several keys from the bunch, all to no avail. One large key he was able to turn, but even with his shoulder to the door it wouldn't budge.

Looking down over the steps, they saw what they thought was a basement, but which had been detailed in their programme of sale as the ground floor with an address of Ivy Cottage, Larks Lane.

'This door must be bolted from the inside,' Charlie said. 'Now all we have to do is find Larks Lane.'

They walked further down the hill, turned a sharp corner and eventually discovered Larks Lane. Neither of them had been aware of its existence before.

Originally, the pathway must have been coarse cobbles. Now it was covered with a thick growth of moss. The surface was wet and slimy and Lizzie was afraid of slipping. Quite clearly, they heard the sound of water gurgling and bubbling. On one side of the lane, overgrown bushes were forming a fence, even a barrier, and into these Charlie thrust his arm, making a parting. He had discovered a brook. Rushing along, crystal clear, the water flashed and sparkled.

'Oh, it's lovely to watch,' Lizzie declared as Charlie let go of the branches and they fell together again.

It was quite a walk further on before they reached the cottage. Lizzie stood and looked silently at this old dwelling.

'Gran,' she whispered to herself, and then she had to moisten her lips with her tongue. She couldn't have explained her feelings at that moment, not for all the tea in China! It was nothing like Gran's immaculate cottage in Silverdore, and yet it brought memories flooding back. It had the same air of tranquility. Lizzie began to feel optimistic.

It had a front garden, albeit in an extremely overgrown state. They had virtually to fight their way through masses of green foliage and numerous tangled shrubs and bushes.

The front door was almost completely concealed by foliage and Charlie had to clear many branches away before he was able, this time, to turn the key and open the door.

It appeared that this door opened directly into the kitchen. Cobwebs were everywhere.

'It's so gloomy and dusty; put the light on,' Lizzie called to Charlie.

'There isn't electricity in the house, nor gas,' came his answer. 'No water either.'

Dear God! Lizzie didn't believe him.

Taking candles and a box of matches out of his coat pocket, he laughed as he said, 'See? I've come prepared.'

Lizzie was at a loss for words.

Charlie lit several candles. It didn't make much improvement. The guttering sounds from them seemed weird and they sent shadows flickering around the walls. But soon their eyes became accustomed to the gloom.

All the walls appeared to have been painted but

had become so dirty that whatever paint had been used was now an indistinguishable grey.

There was a fair-sized kitchen with an old-fashioned, coal cooking range, on which still stood a large soot-blackened kettle.

Above the range, a high overmantel took up one wall and each side of the range was flanked by two deep cupboards.

'Have them out and you could have two lovely inglenook seats,' Charlie said.

Lizzie wrinkled her nose in disgust and didn't bother to answer.

The centre of the kitchen was taken up by a table. It was a mystery to Lizzie how it had ever got to be in that room. Certainly not through that low, narrow doorway. It must have been there forever. It was thick with dust but she could see that over the years it had been well scrubbed.

Under the small window, which they couldn't see out of because the panes were so dirty, was an old brown china sink, badly cracked and very chipped. Two built-in cupboards underneath the sink didn't look much better.

From the kitchen, a stone-floored corridor led to the only other room on this level, a preparation room of sorts which housed two enormous walk-in larders.

A short flight of steps led up to the ground floor. Charlie's assumption had been right; the front door was bolted and barred from the inside. There were two rooms on this floor, both dirty and bare.

Another short flight of stairs and they came to two bedrooms. These rooms seemed brighter with windows front and back.

'It's because they are on a higher level,' Charlie said, 'they get more daylight.'

One thing Lizzie did like about these two rooms was that each had a small outside balcony, skirted by a wrought-iron trellis, well in keeping with what she was by now thinking of as their rustic cottage.

Coming out into the garden again, having finished their tour of inspection, the daylight was so bright after the gloom inside that, for a few moments, Lizzie had to shield her eyes. Charlie was busy pulling brambles and other prickly hedge plants away from an old garden shed.

Lizzie picked her way cautiously through weeds and stinging nettles to join him as he cleared the door to the shed and, with a tug, opened it.

Inside was a lavatory pan. Spread across the top were wooden planks forming a seat, in the middle of which was a circular hole. They looked at each other and fell about laughing.

A few feet away stood another creeper-covered shed. Charlie hesitated a second before lifting the rusty latch.

Surprise, surprise. It was a wash-house. It had a sink and one tap, which Lizzie couldn't turn but Charlie did. It spluttered into life spitting out filthy rust-coloured water.

'Marvellous,' Lizzie said, 'I had visions of having to draw water up from an underground well.'

'You might have to yet,' Charlie said with a grin. There was a large copper and across the far wall, wooden slats were fitted, like rungs of a ladder.

'Marvellous,' Lizzie said again. 'We could do the hotel washing in here. Hang it all up there to dry and air.'

Charlie swiftly came to where she was standing and grabbed her. 'Any more bright ideas like that and I'll put you in that copper and put the lid on.'

Lizzie tried to wriggle away from his grasp but he held on to her tightly. 'Two kisses before I let you go,' he said.

'I knew you were mad,' she retorted.

It didn't matter one jot that Charlie's suit was covered in dust, that his hair looked as if birds had nested in it and that one of Lizzie's stockings now had a long ladder in it. They had each other and that was enough.

Chapter Thirty-One

WORK COMMENCED ON the cottage first. This would enable the furniture from the staff rooms to be transferred, leaving the entire area clear for the dining-room.

Top two priorities were the roof and electricity. The roofers did a grand job. Two days and they were finished.

It turned out that the roof was structurally quite sound. The steeper upper part needed no attention; the lower part had several slates which had worked loose and quite a few that needed replacing.

The gas company declined to run a supply to such a remote area unless Charlie agreed to bear the whole of the cost. He came to the conclusion it would be far cheaper to rely solely on electricity.

The electricians were very efficient. Lizzie constantly took them hot drinks and certainly didn't envy those men their job. Just taking up all those old floorboards seemed hazardous and dangerous to her. When they had finished the job, Charlie said he was well pleased, although Lizzie thought that the new white power-points looked out of place on the ancient skirting boards.

Next came the plumber – just one local man who had previously done work for Charlie.

As well as running a water supply into the cottage, installing an inside toilet, and turning one of the walk-in larders into a shower cubicle, he also replaced the old cracked sink with a gleaming stainless-steel unit above which the electricians positioned an electric water heater.

Now the job of cleaning the whole place right through could begin.

Three of their regular chambermaids said they were only too willing to help, even though Lizzie stressed how dirty the work would be. So at nine o'clock on a Monday morning, the three of them set off from the hotel with Lizzie.

'A right bunch you look,' Charlie joked and he had to duck to avoid being hit by a brush which Lizzie threw at him.

He was right though, they did look peculiar! All four women had their hair tied up in turbans, and they all wore old slacks. Armed with buckets, scrubbing brushes, numerous cloths and old rags, they made their way down the hill. It was an unanimous decision for each of them to tackle a separate room rather than the four of them working together in a restricted area.

By midday, all the windows of the cottage were flung wide open and the women had worked really hard. Charlie came and was warmly welcomed, for he had brought with him ham and cheese rolls and two large flasks of coffee.

They ate, sitting on upturned boxes in the garden. The weather was kind – a good drying day with a stiff wind and pale sunshine. They didn't feel cold, for the overgrown hedges gave great protection from the wind, and they all agreed that it had been a satisfying day.

'It being so dirty, us is bound to see an improvement,' said Mary with her down-to-earth Devonshire logic.

Over the next few days, they stumbled upon some interesting discoveries.

They came to learn just how good most of the woodwork was beneath the layers of old paint. By continuous use of sugarsoap and Brillo pads, they ended up with lovely surfaces which Charlie decided to varnish, thereby showing the natural grain of the wood.

In the kitchen, they decided to leave the coal fire cooking range intact. Not that there was ever any likelihood of its being used, but it did make a good focal feature.

Lizzie had great difficulty in finding a shop which sold old-fashioned black-lead, finally tracking one down in Barnstaple. After the use of much energy and elbow grease on her part, she declared the end result well worth the effort.

By the end of the second week, the whole place looked different. With the windows open to the morning breeze, the panes now sparkling and clear, the whole place smelt fresh and nice. No more dirt or cobwebs.

Cupboards had been scrubbed out and lined with

fresh paper. Cups and saucers, plates, a milk jug, together with a matching sugarbowl and teapot had been brought over from the hotel.

On the draining board beneath one of the new powerpoints stood an electric kettle. Little things such as these would make their seasonal staff more independent.

Here, during their time off, they would be able to unwind and relax in pleasant surroundings.

Downstairs, there was now a gleaming kitchen, one shining chrome shower unit with sparkling white tiles on the wall and one modern toilet. As they walked through, viewing all that had been accomplished, Charlie leaned forward and pressed the flush lever of the toilet – it was almost a cere-monial act!

Of the other rooms they had made one on the ground floor into a sitting-room, while all the others were now twin-bedded rooms.

The windows were so small that Lizzie had been able to make all the curtains herself. She had chosen cotton material in bright colours. And at last the furniture had been transferred over from the hotel and installed into Ivy Cottage. It was ready for occu-pation!

Chapter Thirty-Two

To CONVERT THE existing hotel dining-room into five extra bedrooms presented no problems. Mr Roberts, the same architect who had done such a superb job on the bungalow, agreed to draw up and submit the plans to the council, but where on earth could they store all the furniture?

Only one solution. It had to go into various bed-rooms up on the first floor. Tradesmen and friends all offered their help. Numerous trips were made up and down the elegant staircase. Soon, all bedrooms were packed with tables, chairs, china and glass-ware. Cutlery and silverware were packed away in boxes. The overspill of trolleys and two sideboards had to be left on the landing and covered with dustsheets which gave the place a dismal, abandoned look.

Just shut your eyes to the muddle, Lizzie repeat-edly told herself, hoping that the end would justify the means.

When drawing his plans, Mr Roberts had been able to utilize all the existing windows, including the two large bays which almost jutted out to sea. They would eventually have three additional double bedrooms and two single bedrooms on what would now be an entirely new corridor.

It was surprising, indeed, how quickly these rooms took shape, and very luxurious they were, too, with coloured hand wash basins, backed by tiled vanity units which housed strip-lighting and shaving points. Because of their size, they were able to make the end of each bedroom into a lounge-type area, thus creating bed-sitting rooms rather than just functional bedrooms. And there were bathrooms and toilets where the old still room had once been.

The construction of the new dining-room on the lower-ground floor, was entirely different. It was a much more arduous and lengthy job.

The workmen had erected sheets of hardboard which sealed off the area and at least partially diminished the amount of dust and dirt which must inevitably rise when the walls were demolished and the floors dug up – for every single interior wall at the rear of the hotel had to come down.

Charlie was totally involved in the project, while Lizzie did her best to keep out of the way. When work was nearing completion, Charlie coaxed her to take a look. She was amazed at how spacious the new dining-room was. The windows, with their immense panes of glass, were truly colossal. In future, when the guests were seated, they would no longer have to look down on the sea, they would henceforth be almost at the same level as the waves.

As much cleaning as possible having been done, the carpet layers arrived. Rolls and rolls of dark red

Wilton, patterned with gold scrolls, had to be laid. The finished effect was rich, bold and regal.

Everyone pitched in to help carry the chairs and tables down the stairs. Every person who was working that day seemed caught up in the excitement of having a dining-room in a completely new setting.

Early spring had arrived once more, and in a few days from now, their first coach party of the season would be arriving.

Lizzie decided to take a tour of the hotel by herself, beginning on the very top floor. Every bedroom was well co-ordinated; bedspreads and cushions matched the curtains; even wastepaper bins Lizzie had covered with remnants of material.

Reaching the first floor, she opened the glass doors of the lounge; they were bright and clear, no finger marks. She stood a while on the threshold. The whole room looked fantastic. The sun was shining through the huge bay windows, a bit weak perhaps, but bringing a promise of summer days to come.

Outside, the sea was calm and way over in the harbour a few gaily painted boats were already bobbing about at their moorings.

Everywhere smelt fresh and clean and the green foliage plants banked up in front of the fireplace looked bright and healthy.

Back then to the ground floor. The reception desk was ready for business, with plenty of writing paper in the pad, pens at the ready in their holders, a vase of fresh spring flowers standing on a ledge.

The new bedrooms still gave Lizzie great pleasure as she checked them once again.

On now to the kitchens, all three were clean and bright, all was shining. The boys had done a good job here.

Last of all she went into the new dining-room. Standing there surveying this magnificent room, Lizzie found it hard to believe that Charlie had brought everything to such a successful end. Had they really accomplished so much that winter? The tablecloths were snowy white, serviettes were folded neatly and everywhere silver was glistening, glasses were sparkling, all in all a picture of elegance.

The following morning Lizzie decided on a visit to Ivy Cottage. Living-in staff would be moving in the next day.

She walked slowly down the hill, approaching the cottage from Larks Lane, which she thought was by far the most attractive entrance. The front garden was neat and tidy by now. It would be a good place to take a deckchair, relax in the sun, read a book or have a snooze.

Going from room to room, the beds had already been made up; Lizzie decided that everything was fine. It felt like a quaint old-fashioned cottage. As she locked the door and walked back down the cobbled path, she looked back at the shining windows and she felt proud of a job well done.

So, they were all set for yet another season.

On her walk back to the hotel, Lizzie began to deliberate in her mind about all the past events. They had achieved so much – their beautiful hotel, a staff cottage and their own lovely bungalow out in the country – it was all a far cry from what they had started out with when leaving London to purchase that first guesthouse.

How lonely she had been in the beginning. God alone knew how much she had missed London. But would she go back now, given the chance?

She wasn't quite sure. She thought back to the years of the war, the humdrum existence, the air raids and the rationing. What of her friends, and Doris and Syd? They still lived there.

She thought of the crowds, so much traffic, travelling perhaps on the stuffy Underground trains. Having to go to the same job day after day. And then she thought of her life here, never far away from the sea.

Lizzie knew better than most that life offers no guarantees, but as far as she could tell Charlie's, hers and their son's future was secure so long as they continued to run an hotel. It was a good living, they had everything they could wish for, and more, but material things weren't everything. People mattered too! At least they did to Lizzie.

She considered, taking everything into account, that she had done very well over the years. She had coped with being dumped in an unfurnished guesthouse in a strange village where she hadn't known a soul, with a young baby to look after, a mountain of debts and a business, which she had known nothing at all about, to get off the ground. If you looked at it that way it had been like taking a small London sparrow, bringing it to north Devon and setting it down amongst the seagulls. And clipping its wings so there was no way it could fly back, she mused with a wry smile on her lips.

If she lived to be a hundred she would never forget the loneliness of those first few months.

Dear daft Charlie! Never happy unless he was thinking up some scheme or other. Well he wasn't the only one who could be a bit foxy. She would let this season get well under way, pick the right moment, and then put her proposition to him, she solemnly vowed. If he could acquire all these properties in north Devon, what was to stop her buying a place in London? Lizzie grinned to herself at the thought, but why not? She was a director of this company, she earned half the money.

Not a big place, she mused wistfully, a flat would do. Just so that she would always have somewhere to go to, even if it were only for weekends and holidays. Charlie loved London just as much as she did, but it was actually getting him there that was so difficult. Perhaps if they had their own place he wouldn't always be so reluctant. A sudden thought came to Lizzie and she stopped in her tracks and laughed out loud. The bugger would more than likely want to let it when they weren't using it them-selves.

'Ready?' Charlie's voice called to her, bringing her back from her day-dreaming. 'I've done enough fer today,' he said as she drew level with him.

Lizzie nodded and looked up into his eyes with love and affection, then, reaching up, she softly kissed his cheek.

'What brought that on?' he asked as he put his arm around her waist.

'I just felt you deserved it,' she answered. She was thinking of that day, long ago, when she had first glanced across the hall at the sevenpenny dance and found Charlie, a blue-eyed, wavy-haired young cor-poral. There had never been anyone else for her. Just him.

Nippy

Acknowledgements

I would like to say thank you to a few people who helped and encouraged me to write this book. Firstly to Alan Samson, from Little, Brown and Darley Anderson, my agent. I hope I have justified their faith in me.

Mr Y.A. Walker, Information Manager for J. Lyons & Company for his information and references about Nippies.

Peter Bird, who so generously sent me copies of articles he had written for *Choice* magazine, entitled 'The Tea Shop Story'.

Elsie Pickering, and her daughter Molly, who took the time and trouble to do some research for me even though they had only met me briefly.

My Yorkshire friends, Peter and Norma Cooke, who never fail to be there when I need them.

My dear friend Audrey Bolton, who shared her nostalgic memories with me. And last but by no means least, Pat Pizzie, Sales Manager for Mills & Boon, who started the ball rolling and gave me a 'crazy' day out in London.

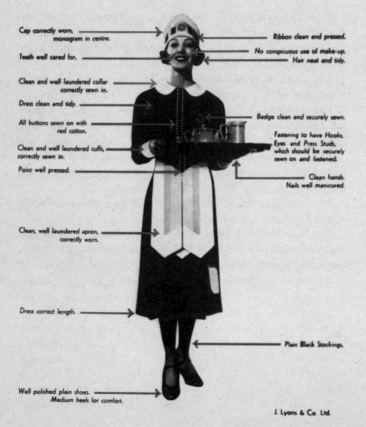

The PERFECT NIPPY

Cap correctly worn, monogram in centre.

Ribbon clean and pressed.

Teeth well cared for.

No conspicuous use of make-up.

Hair neat and tidy.

Clean and well laundered collar correctly sewn in.

Dress clean and tidy.

Badge clean and securely sewn.

All buttons sewn on with red cotton.

Fastening to have Hooks, Eyes and Press Studs, which should be securely sewn on and fastened.

Clean and well laundered cuffs, correctly sewn in.

Point well pressed.

Clean hands. Nails well manicured.

Clean, well laundered apron, correctly worn.

Dress correct length.

Plain Black Stockings.

Well polished plain shoes. Medium heels for comfort.

J. Lyons & Co. Ltd.

Chapter One

The Summer of 1920

MISS MACFARLANE, HEADMISTRESS of Malden East girls' school, stood in the playground with the hot tarmac burning her feet as she watched her girls disperse for the long summer holiday.

Her eyes were focused on two girls in particular and there was one thought uppermost in her mind. 'The good ones should always be rewarded, the bad ones get their just deserts.'

If life were really like that then Rebecca Russell and Eleanor James should have a long and happy life.

Miss MacFarlane smiled to herself. Those two were a perfect foil for each other. Rebecca so dark yet with pale, creamy skin, her eyes a rich, deep brown. Eleanor fair with rosy cheeks and deep blue eyes that twinkled in a strong-featured face, her skin turned golden by the sun.

They walked slowly hand in hand which was as it should be, for this was the day that they were leaving school, fourteen years old and about to face the big outside world. As headmistress scores of girls had passed through her school but few had left such a lasting impression on her mind. They were both intelligent quick-witted lasses and their education should not be cut short. If only they had been born in different circumstances they would never have been going to start work. And at the Wellington Laundry of all places! What would their pay be? Seven shillings a week, if they were lucky.

Suddenly Miss MacFarlane laughed out loud, for Rebecca
had pulled the two ribbons from her hair and shook her head
hard. It was a gesture of defiance. Her dark hair, which
had been tied back tightly in two neat bunches, now fell
unrestrained, a vibrant mass of thick ringlets reaching well
past her shoulders.

'Bye.' Eleanor had turned and seen that Miss MacFarlane
was still watching them. Both girls waved and their headmistress returned the wave. They were of the same height
but Miss MacFarlane guessed that Eleanor would love to have
the same figure as that of Rebecca. Such a slim dainty girl
was Rebecca and her oval face had a gentle look, as though
nothing would ever upset her.

Poor Eleanor looked totally different. She was buxom, and
that was putting it kindly, although perhaps it was just puppy
fat and she would lose it soon enough when she started work
in the laundry. It was to be hoped so. Her hair was as fair as
ripe corn and today, probably for the last time, it was neatly
braided into two long plaits.

Although so unalike in both appearance and temperament
they were inseparable. Throughout the infant school and
right on up until this important day they had been together.
Oh, there had been times when they had squabbled, but
such was their friendship that they became known as the
daring double.

At this point Miss MacFarlane sighed, turned and went
back into her school building. She wished nothing but the
best for those two happy, spirited, intelligent girls. Would
life give them chances? Treat them kindly? Only time would
tell.

Outside the school gates the two friends turned and looked
back at the building where they had spent much of their lives
for the last ten years. Ella's eyes twinkled. 'Well, Becky, we're
finished with all that.'

Becky gazed at her friend, her eyes thoughtful. 'You were

the one who couldn't wait to leave school and get a job. Are you having second thoughts now?'

'No, of course not. Just think of all the things we'll be able to do,' Ella quickly retaliated.

Becky laughed. 'Beside working five and a half days a week, name two.' They were now standing on the kerb waiting to cross busy Burlington Road. An open-topped tram rattled by followed by a delivery boy on his bike whistling 'It's A Long Way To Tipperary'. Further along a group of boys was also waiting to cross the road and one of them yelled out to the delivery boy, 'Oi, don't yer know the War's all over?'

On the opposite pavement two boys were running, bowling huge iron hoops in front of them, and yelling their heads off.

It seemed as if everyone was happy today because the long summer holiday was about to start.

'Well,' said Ella, as if considering the matter, 'we could doll ourselves up and go to the dance that's going to be held in the church hall this Saturday, what d'you think about that for a start?'

Becky giggled. 'Doll ourselves up? Fat chance. Where are we supposed to get dance frocks from?'

'You daft ha'perth,' Ella playfully punched Becky's shoulder. 'It won't be that kind of a dance, it's only being run by the youth club. Here, hold my hand and let's run, now, while there's nothing coming.'

Mrs Turner, who ran the Cosy Café, which was on the corner of George Road, the road in which Eleanor James had been born and bred, heard the girls' lively laughter and came to stand at the open door of the café. Both girls smiled at Mrs Turner, an elderly lady with grey hair swept back into a tidy bun. It was rumoured that Ma Turner had been serving large cups of tea, big breakfasts and even bigger hot dinners in that café since before she was big enough to see over the counter.

'I bet I know why you two are so chirpy. School broken

up for the summer holidays, has it? Have to have eyes out
me backside now, won't I? What with all the little horrors
roaming the streets and the pair of you living only a stone's
throw from me front door.' She laughed loudly, her plump
bosom heaving with the effort, and nodded her head towards
the now-empty playground on the other side of the road.
'That school ain't ever going to be the same now that you
two won't be pupils there any more.'

'We're going to have a week off, then we are both starting
work down at the laundry.' Becky made this statement
quite flippantly. Her dark ringlets now hanging free and
her cheeks flushed with excitement, she explained further,
'And on Saturday we're thinking of going to the local church
hall dance.'

Ella, who always did things on impulse, burst out, 'Yes, we
really are. Not that there will be a band or anything big like
that, just records on a wind-up gramophone, but we'll have
a smashing time, won't we Becky?'

'We will if we can sort out what we're going to wear,'
Becky answered.

Ma Turner grinned broadly. 'I don't suppose the young
lads will give two hoots to what you're wearing. In any
case if your mothers are to be believed the pair of you are
both very good with yer needles and it is only Wednesday
so you've got plenty of time to add a few touches to some
of those pretty dresses I've seen you wear.'

'We've got t' go now, bye,' their laughing voices called
back to the old lady who raised her eyes expressively and
said out loud, 'What's going to happen to those two girls is
anybody's guess.'

Ella made to turn down into George Road, saying, 'Call
over the fence when you've had yer dinner and we'll decide
what we're going to do this afternoon.'

'I will,' Becky said, 'but don't forget we ought to look
through what dresses we've got if we are going to go to the
church hall on Saturday.'

For answer Ella waved her hand and broke into a run.

Becky had only a few yards to walk on her own for she lived in the very next road at number twenty-four Albert Road, the garden of which backed directly on to the garden of number twenty-four George Road which was where Ella lived.

Her imagination was running away with her as she walked. They hadn't got to go back to school this afternoon, in fact they never had to go back again. A whole new life was opening up for her and her best friend. Together they would be starting work, earning wages, having money of their own. She smiled secretly to herself; suddenly she couldn't wait to tell her mother that she and Ella would like to go to a dance this coming Saturday. What an adventure! Oh, life was going to be so good from now on, she was convinced of that.

Turning into Albert Road, Rebecca decided that living here was like living in another world. Unlike George Road that had a long stretch of terraced houses on both sides of the road, there were only twelve houses on the right-hand side of the road, just the even numbers, and nothing but open fields on the opposite side. The Russell family lived in the last house. Beyond was Harry Horsecroft's farm. The very thought of Harry Horsecroft brought a grin to Becky's face. Her dad said Harry was more of a character than he was a farmer. On the farm he kept chicken, geese and pigs, but added to his living by being a part-time carrier with his horse and cart. Most nights Harry drank in the Tavern which was in Malden Road. Come closing time he just about managed to climb up on to the box seat of the cart and the horse would bring him home. His antics when trying to climb down from the cart provided a great source of amusement to his neighbours.

'Cor, lovely,' Becky exclaimed as she opened the front door and sniffed the smell of their dinner. Then, seeing her dad seated on the bottom of the stairs tugging to get his boots off, she darted forward. 'Here, let me,' she said, dropping down on to her knees.

At the age of forty, Joe Russell was a contented man who had worked for the railways since he was fourteen and had lived all his life in New Malden, Surrey.

At eighteen he had met and married Joyce Wilson, and they had set up home here in Albert Road. Married life had suited them both fine. Jack was born in 1900, Tom in 1901, Fred in 1902 and Rebecca in 1906. Joe hadn't minded a bit that their first three children were all boys but when the last one had been a girl his cup had run over. She was the apple of his eye and he spoiled her as much as he could on his limited wages.

In return Becky adored this big man. He had a ruddy complexion from being out in all weathers and although streaked with grey, his hair was still thick and curly. Her dad was forever laughing, as though inside himself he was always happy. He thrived in company, and had a keen sense of humour. He enjoyed a pint and a game of darts at the local pub with his mates. Her mum had a totally different personality. She was always so serious, preferring to stay close to the house. Whereas her lovely dad was instantly likeable and made friends easily, Mum appeared offhand to strangers.

Boots now off, Becky made to rise. 'Oh, so you ain't got a kiss for your poor old dad that has been at work since four o'clock this morning? Don't matter though, I know plenty of young ladies that will be only too willing to hug an' kiss me.'

Becky stared at him, letting him know she didn't approve of that kind of teasing. He smiled, and put his arms around his daughter's shoulders and squeezed. Becky returned the hug and planted kisses on his cheeks and on his forehead.

'You're an angel, that's what you are, my own very special angel, put on this earth just to make my life a happy one,' her dad was telling her, using a loud and cheery tone of voice.

'Yeah, well, angels still need feeding, you know,' her mother called from the open kitchen door, and Becky thought how tired her mum looked despite the fact that she was smiling.

Going down the passage with her dad she asked, 'Did you know I finished school today, Dad?'

'Of course I did my luv, and already I feel ten years older having me lass going out to work.'

'I'm not starting for a week yet.'

'You'll not be starting at all if you don't sit up and eat this dinner before it gets all spoiled,' her mother retorted.

Becky did as she was told, thinking to herself how lucky she was to have such a loving family. Her big jolly father, her quiet but warm-hearted mother who kept this house as spick and span as a new pin, using what she called good old-fashioned elbow-grease to polish the furniture until you could see your face in it. Then there were her three big brothers so noisy and full of life. She also appreciated the good and plentiful food that was served in this house.

Her best friend Ella wasn't so lucky. Ella's father had been killed in the War, leaving her mother short of money and facing a hard struggle to provide for Ella and her two brothers.

Joyce Russell was thinking along the very same lines as she watched her husband carve the pot-roast. God had certainly been good to them and their four children. She felt a milestone had been reached today. Her baby, Rebecca, named after her own dear mother, was now fourteen years old. Ready to face the world. She couldn't put her feelings into words; she certainly had hoped for better than Becky taking a job in the Wellington Laundry.

She stifled a sigh. There were so many disabled soldiers unable to find employment of any kind. She should count her blessings and be grateful that at least all her boys were working and Becky had at least found a job.

She passed the dish of vegetables down the table and, watching Becky, she grinned. It might not be much of a job but once her daughter got her teeth into something, she wasn't going to give up easily.

They would all have to wait and see how things turned out.

Chapter Two

PUSHING ASIDE HER doubts about starting work in the laundry on Monday, Becky set off to meet Ella, determined to enjoy herself at this youth club dance.

She had accepted her mother's offer to wash and arrange her hair into a neater style. Joyce had brushed the mass of unruly thick ringlets into shining waves tying them back with two lengths of royal blue velvet, allowing soft curls to remain free about her cheeks, thus softening the severity of the style.

Both Becky and Ella had made a peasant-type skirt by cutting the bodice from an old dress and adding strips of velvet at different lengths starting from the hem of the skirt and working upwards. Each skirt was made from different coloured and textured material so there was no question of them wearing identical outfits. Ella was to wear a beige, high-necked blouse given to her by an aunt. Becky's blouse was of fine cotton, embroidered down the front by herself.

Ella's mother Margaret, more often referred to as Peggy, was generous with her praise, coming out to greet Becky with outstretched hands and welcoming smiles. 'My, how lovely you both look, the lads won't be able to take their eyes off you. I hope you both have a good time,' she said, her gaze resting on Becky.

About to say, 'So do we,' Becky remembered her manners and changed the words to, 'Thank you, Mrs James, I'm sure we shall.'

Holding hands the girls walked quickly up the road. What a picture the pair of them made. On this warm summer's evening there was no need for coats, so each girl had a white shawl draped over her arm in case they might need to put them around their shoulders when they were walking home. The church had given out that the social dance would end at ten o'clock and Joe Russell had said that he would be outside the hall to meet them. That made Peggy feel grateful, but it also made her feel sad. Bad enough that she had been widowed at the age of thirty-two.

She would freely admit that despite having three children she still often felt lonely and longed for someone in her life to love her. How much worse for her young daughter. Best of friends with Becky, there must be times her Ella felt envious of the way Becky was loved and protected by her father. They say what you've never had you never missed. It wasn't true. Ella had been just ten years old when the news came through that her Bert had been killed in France, old enough to miss the father that she had barely got to know.

Peggy, a faded ash-blonde who was still slim and quite beautiful, gazed after her plump daughter. The only things that Eleanor seems to have inherited from me are my hair and colouring, she mused. Maybe Ella would slim down a bit as she grew older; meanwhile her mop of gorgeous golden hair was something to appreciate. Tonight she had helped her daughter to pile a few curls on top of her head, leaving tresses to flow freely down past her shoulders. The curls would give her added height and so make her look less chubby.

Margaret James turned to go indoors just as her two sons came through the front door. Jimmy was the next one up to Ella, at fifteen, and thanks to Joe Russell he had a job on the railway. Ronald, her eldest at sixteen, hadn't been so lucky and was threatening to join the Army. Three children in three years. She found herself smiling as she watched them grinning at each other.

'And where are you two off to then?' she asked.

'Just out an' about, Mother, we won't be late,' Ronnie assured her.

'See you're not then,' she called out after them as they swaggered away up the road.

What it is to be young, especially on a Saturday night! She was thinking she'd give a lot to be dressed up and going to a dance herself, but no such luck.

The church hall was ablaze with light and decorated with fresh flowers. Lemonade and orange squash flowed freely for it was included in the entrance price of fourpence.

'Boys, take your partners, please,' Mr Barrett, the local Scout master, instructed, and the boys who'd been lining one wall moved towards the girls lining the wall opposite, most of whom were sniggering and giggling.

Suddenly there was two boys standing in front of Ella and Becky, mumbling the words, 'Would you like to dance?' Both lads' faces were flushed. They clearly found asking a girl to dance acutely embarrassing, which amused them both.

'Thank you,' they replied in unison, each thinking that they had never seen either of these lads before.

'A waltz,' Mr Barrett announced, before bending to the old gramophone on which a record had already been placed. The girls glanced at each other, raising their eyebrows questioningly as they went into the boys' arms, and then they were off, one, two, three, one, two, three, trying to keep in time to the somewhat scratchy music.

Ella was doing well. Her partner was a good dancer, easy to follow, and she relaxed as they circled the floor.

Becky was not so lucky. Her lad was a terrible dancer, stumbling over his own feet and hers. During their last year at school they had been taught ballroom dancing by Miss Patterson and Miss Brown. Learning had come easily because both teachers demonstrated the steps so well. That didn't help if your partner hadn't a clue as to how to keep in time with the music. Halfway through the dance he stepped heavily right on to her foot.

'Sorry,' he muttered.

'Don't worry about it, I shall only be crippled for life,' she answered testily, but immediately wished she hadn't when she saw how her reply had upset him. 'You just need to practise more. We all have to learn. It might help if they hold a few more of these get-togethers,' she added, giving him a smile.

For a brief second he looked into her eyes, then he quickly glanced away, his entire face turning red.

This lad really is shy, Becky thought, which she didn't find unattractive. Most of the boys around where she lived were far too big for their boots, and cocky with it half the time. Someone as shy as this lad was made a pleasant change.

When the record came to the end Mr Barrett told them all to separate into their lines again, then proceeded to describe the Paul Jones. 'This dance will enable each of you to dance with several different partners,' he declared.

Two circles were formed in the centre of the hall, girls on the outside, boys on the inside and to the music they trotted round holding hands. When the music stopped Becky found herself facing Ted Berry who always looked as if a good wash would do him good. She had no choice. Whoever was facing you was your partner. Reluctantly, she went into his arms, praying that before the night was much older her luck might change. After a break and a welcome drink she wondered if the shy lad would ask her to dance again, but he didn't, he asked Ella instead.

Suddenly out of the mass of boys a dark-haired young man appeared and muttered, 'Would you like to dance?'

'Yes please,' she replied, and followed him out on to the floor. God must have heard her prayer!

This boy was tall and he could dance. In fact he was an excellent dancer. Rebecca relaxed; this was more like it. Her wide full skirt swirled as he swung her round, using his elbow to make more room for them on the floor.

'Thank you for the best dance I've had yet,' he said, as the record came to an end, then with what seemed to Becky like reluctance he left her. When later on he asked her if he could fetch her a drink she was more than pleased.

Ella gave a knowing grin in Becky's direction as they watched this dark-haired lad approach them, bringing a mate with him, as the last waltz was announced. As they circled the floor both girls were happy, wondering if and when another dance would be held in this church hall.

Perhaps it was as well that Becky's father was going to be outside waiting to escort them both home.

Their week of freedom had passed all too quickly. The weather had stayed exceptionally warm and the girls had made the most of it by taking themselves off to the river, running through the long grass and scrubby bushes enjoying each sun-filled day.

Soon it was time to start work.

It was just a quarter to eight on the Monday morning when Ella and Becky ran up the outside steps of the Wellington Laundry and pushed open the door that had OFFICE painted on its glass panel in black and gold lettering. Two older girls were working busily at a long table set back against the far wall. One seemed to be adding up columns of figures in a very large book while the other girl was typing on a large upright machine, her fingers flying over the noisy keys. As Ella and Becky entered they both looked up and regarded the pair of them kindly.

'I'm Rebecca Russell and this is Eleanor James, we're supposed to start work here today,' Becky said. 'I think we're a bit early, eight o'clock the manager said.'

The dark-haired girl smiled. 'That's only because you're new. Everyone here, laundry workers and office staff alike, all start work at seven thirty.'

'Oh,' was all that Becky managed to say.

Ten minutes later Ella and Becky stood on the concrete floor inside the main laundry building and they looked at each other in dismay. The rough overall, mobcap and sacking apron they were being asked to put on weren't at all what they had expected, nor were the surroundings.

The heat and the rising steam was frightening, coppers full of boiling water stood everywhere. Becky felt ill as she stared at the women bent over scrubbing boards, their aprons sopping wet. The whole place looked mucky and damp. She offered up a silent prayer that they might not have to work in this department.

'One of you come over here,' called out a deep male voice, 'the other one wait and I'll have someone take you down to the pressing room.'

'Oh hell, suppose it's best if I stay here,' Ella said, doing her best to raise a smile as she crossed the wet floor.

'The pressing is done down the corridor,' a young lad was saying to Becky. She turned to face him and found she was looking into the eyes of the shy lad who had stepped on her feet a week ago at the youth club dance. 'Hello,' she said.

He gave her a startled look, not having been aware of whom he was talking to. 'Oh, hello.'

'Are you going to show me the way?'

'Yes, it's quite a walk, though it is all under cover.'

Becky thought that was a shame. Outside the sun was shining. As she and Ella had walked to the village of New Malden the sun had been bright and warm, giving out a promise of another lovely day and yet here she was shut up in this dreary steamy building with the prospect of spending her working life doing other people's dirty washing.

Oh NO! This wasn't at all what she had in mind when seeking her first job. The likelihood of finding something better might be slim but that would not deter her from trying. Give it a chance, she chided herself. Well of course she would have to do that because at the moment she had no choice.

As they walked, and talked, Becky discovered that he'd only been working in the laundry for a few weeks. He lived in Kingston.

'Whereabouts in Kingston? I've got an aunt an' uncle that live there.'

He hesitated slightly before answering, 'Mill Street.'

She knew Mill Street was in a rough area, quite different from the nice quiet Albert Road where she lived. Mill Street was lower-class, the houses weren't up to much and the lavatory was outside in the back garden. There weren't many men who lived in that area could say they had a decent job and quite a few that wouldn't have a job at all.

'Do you like working here?' she asked.

He shrugged his shoulders. 'It's not that bad once you get used to it. Suppose it takes time.'

Becky felt someone should take this boy under their wing, and suddenly realized that she didn't know his name yet. 'I'm Rebecca Russell, but everyone calls me Becky. What's your name?' she asked.

He gawped at her. 'I've never met a girl called Rebecca before. I'm Tommy Ferguson,' he said, and grinned.

They came to the end of the long corridor. 'Through there is where you've got to go,' he told her, nodding his head towards a large metal door.

She was about to thank him and say goodbye when an idea came to her. 'Do you ever go to the picture show that the Salvation Army put on?' she asked.

He shook his head.

'It's every other Friday night in the congregational hall. I know for a fact they've got two great pictures for this week, *Rin-Tin-Tin* and *Elsie Dies For Love*. We get there about quarter to seven, and it starts at seven. Why don't you come along? You could sit with us, we don't bite, in fact all my friends are very friendly.'

'I don't fancy it. It's not real pictures like you see at the cinema, is it? More like a magic lantern show. No thanks.'

'What do you want for a penny, my lad?' she answered. 'Pity you feel like that. I certainly enjoy my nights there, we even get given free refreshments in the interval. Still, if you've got such a good social life elsewhere good luck to you.'

'Could I bring me mate?' he answered, sounding wary.

''Course you could,' she replied, eyes twinkling mischievously. 'More the merrier, you'll see if you come along and find out.' Moving abruptly, she pushed open the door and let it clang behind her leaving him staring perplexedly after her.

'I'm Mrs Bradford. You are?' It was a short, stout, middle-aged woman who faced Becky. She had a kindly smiling face and her fair hair was set in deep rigid lines of waves very close to her head.

'Becky Russell,' Becky answered in a quiet voice.

'Well Becky, did you choose to be a presser?'

'Not exactly, madam.'

Mrs Bradford studied this new employee; they seemed to get younger every month. 'You don't have to call me madam; Mrs Bradford will do nicely. Have you ever used a flat iron before?'

'Only a small one at home, nothing like the size of the irons those girls are using,' Becky said woefully.

'Or a steam press?'

'Sorry. I've never even seen one of those.'

'Don't worry, you'll get used to them. The size always seems off-putting to new girls. Come along and meet the girls you will be working with.'

Becky followed her down the length of the room, feeling the heat hit her face as she passed young women, all ironing away busily. The steam presses were frightening. At one point they stopped to watch as one girl with bare arms flexed her muscles, rose up on to her toes and with what seemed to Becky a great effort used both hands to grasp the wide handle and bring down the great white pad on to folded articles of linen. The hissing and the burst of steam had Becky jumping backwards out of the way.

The room itself was certainly better than the wash house

where she had left Ella. The light came in from two high windows and the walls were painted yellow. In all Becky decided it was a bright room.

'One moment, girls,' called Mrs Bradford, 'this is Becky Russell.' She introduced all the workers to Becky who quickly became confused, finding it impossible to remember any of the names which were rattled off so quickly.

A table was allocated to Becky and she was instructed on how to heat the gas iron and to use the sleeve boards.

'Try her out on flats first off with just a flat iron,' Mrs Bradford said to the girl working at the next table. 'I'll leave her in your charge for now and I'll be back as soon as I can.'

'Hello Becky, I'm Rose,' the girl said, her smile as merry as her bright blue eyes. She had short brown hair, and looked quite smart in her white overall. At least in this room the employees were not wearing the awful sacking aprons. Becky smiled back, guessing that she was a good few years older than herself.

'Is Becky your real name?'

'No, it's Rebecca, but everybody shortens it to Becky.'

'Well, let's see how you get on. Don't be afraid to ask if you can't manage something, and by the way the girl working opposite to you is Mary.'

They all sounded friendly enough, but Becky was feeling terrified at the thought of having to pick up one of the three huge flat irons that she felt by now must be red-hot. Dear God I wish I was anywhere but here, she sighed to herself.

She and Ella hadn't given much thought to the work that went on in a laundry. All they had been concerned about was the fact that they had been lucky enough to get a job and that they would be earning a regular weekly wage.

Seeing the pile of what seemed to be damask tablecloths that Rose was setting out on her allocated table, Becky groaned.

'These are usually done in the press. Mrs Bradford is being kind to you, starting you off lightly,' declared Rose.

Becky supposed that she should feel grateful, but she didn't and seeing the expression on her face Rose burst out laughing. That made Becky see the funny side of the situation and she also began laughing. But what if she should burn a hole in one of the items? She banished the thought from her head as quickly as it had come.

It was the longest morning of her young life. When at one o'clock the hooter sounded Becky Russell breathed a heavy sigh of relief, spat on to her fingers and gently rubbed two red patches on her forearm which showed signs of having been burnt. At one o'clock the laundry closed down for one hour. Quickly the women turned everything off, snatched up their bags and hurried away in all directions.

Ella looked a sorry sight as she came towards Becky. From head to toe she looked damp. Her lovely fair hair clung to her head as if she had been in a steam bath.

'Come on, luv,' Ella hissed in Becky's ear. 'Shift yerself and let's get out of here.'

The two girls walked through the now-deserted building and down the outside staircase. The warm sun hit them as they reached the street and both girls thankfully turned their faces upwards. They weren't used to spending so long indoors, let alone in a place like that. They ran down Burlington Road until they parted at George Road.

'See you here at a quarter to two,' Ella yelled back over her shoulder.

Hearing Becky enter the house by the back door her mother called out, 'How'd it go, luv?'

Becky forced herself to smile as she opened the kitchen door to greet her mother. Joyce Russell's heart sank as she gazed at her lovely young daughter. Five hours in the Wellington Laundry and already she looked washed out. 'Come and sit up, I've got a full jug of lemonade ready, I made it earlier and when I was squeezing the lemons I knew I wouldn't be wasting my time. You are ready for a cold drink, aren't you?'

'Mum, you're wonderful. I'm parched.'

'Well, it's only salad with a nice bit of cold boiled bacon to go with it, I didn't think you'd fancy anything hot.'

An hour for lunch wasn't long enough by any means.

Ella and Becky were very subdued as they joined the other girls hurrying up the stairs and when they reached the wash house and Ella turned to go in she heard Becky sigh heavily.

Ella stopped in her tracks, turned and patted Becky's arm. 'Stick it out luv, won't be forever.'

Becky nodded her head but as she walked the corridor tears pricked the back of her eyes. 'It certainly won't be,' she promised herself in an agonized whisper and her heart felt lighter as she decided that she was going to make sure that her working life would not be spent in this laundry.

On Friday night at seven o'clock on the dot Tommy Ferguson and his mate Stan Rogers appeared at the door of the congregational hall and handed over their pennies to the smiling lady who was wearing her Salvation Army uniform complete with black and red straw bonnet. Up until the moment they entered, Becky hadn't believed that they would come.

Seeing Tommy look uncertain, Becky dragged Ella over to be introduced. Both lads were well-built with fair hair. Tommy's mate obviously did not work indoors as Tommy did because he had a freckled, weather-beaten look about him and a rugged face which looked as though it had been carved out of granite. Both lads had made an effort; they had polished their shoes and were wearing dark trousers and very clean short-sleeved shirts.

'This is my friend Ella,' Becky told them. 'She knows who you are Tom, from the dance, but we don't know your friend.'

Tommy was too surprised to answer. He simply stared

straight at Becky, thinking how pretty she looked in her pale pink floral dress and her dark ringlets framing her face.

'Come on then,' Ella said, grabbing the other boy's arm. 'You tell me your name.'

Taken aback, but more than willing, he muttered, 'Stan, Stan Rogers.'

'Well, Stan Rogers, the films are gonna start any minute now so we'd better find ourselves a seat.'

Actually, neither Tommy or Stan could have cared less about the films. What had brought Stan along was Tom's description of the girls who had been at the youth club dance.

Becky suddenly realized that Tommy was grinning at her, and she grinned in return. She was ever so pleased he'd come, but it didn't occur to her to ask herself why.

The first film was over. Elsie, the heroine, had been tied to the railway tracks by the wicked villain. The train was fast approaching. Elsie was struggling. Would she die?

The caption came up on the screen: TO BE CONTINUED NEXT WEEK. Becky and Ella rose to their feet, making a beeline for the kitchen. Refreshments were served and when Ella came back to her seat without Becky, Tommy was afraid she had gone home.

Minutes later his face was wreathed in smiles. 'Where have you been?'

Becky laughed, 'Finishing the washing-up.'

Suddenly Tommy was shy again, completely lost for words. Silence fell between them as the lights were dimmed and the next picture began.

'Nine o'clock, time to go home,' Ella was saying to Stan as the film finished.

'Yeah, suppose that's it. We'd better be on our way,' he said, reluctance sounding in his voice.

Ella hadn't minded sitting with Stan. He was quite nice-looking in a rugged thickset sort of way, much more brainy than that clod Tommy, who seemed to have set his cap at Becky. 'Listen,' she said, 'we usually go to Kingston market on a Saturday morning, maybe we'll see you there tomorrow.'

Both Stan and Tommy looked disappointed. 'Couldn't we take you to a café, have a cup of tea and a bit of a natter, get t' know you better like?' Stan boldly suggested.

'No you couldn't!' Becky was first in with her reply. 'Nine o'clock this show finishes an' if we aren't home by twenty past my dad will be up here to know the reason why.'

'I have t' work every other Saturday morning, on the delivery vans,' Tommy quietly whispered to Becky, 'I'm working tomorrow.'

She touched him lightly on the shoulder, sending a shiver through him. 'Well I'm glad you came tonight. Good night then.'

'Good night.'

Becky took Ella's arm as they left the hall. 'Is that Tom tied to his mother's apron strings?' were the first words that Ella came out with as soon as they were out of earshot of the boys.

Becky was more than surprised. 'What on earth made you ask me that? I don't know any more about him than you do.'

'Just curious.'

Becky found this hard to believe. There was more to Ella's question than she was letting on. 'I know he's a bit nervous, didn't you like him?'

'His mate Stan seems all right . . .' Ella dithered, 'but Tommy is a bit simple, isn't he?'

'Ella! You've no right t' talk about the lad that way. We don't really know anything about him.'

'You want to be careful is all I'm saying. I tried to put it nicely, I mean, he's all right, nice really, but no one in their right mind could say he's bright, now could they?'

'What's that got to do with me being kind to him?' Becky asked impatiently.

Ella looked at her friend, her eyes wide with amazement. 'Haven't you cottoned on to the fact that Tom is crazy about you? He doesn't want you t' be kind to him. There's a lot more on that lad's mind than kindness.'

'Oh, Ella! Don't be so daft. We've only just left school, we don't want serious boyfriends for ages yet, do we?'

'We aren't talking about what we want. I'm sorry if you can't see it, but please Becky, luv, be careful, don't lead him on.'

Becky took hold of Ella's hand and squeezed it. 'All right, Ella, I'll treat him with kid gloves when I see him again, but I still think you've got it wrong.'

Joe Russell was waiting at the corner of George Road and he greeted the girls by hugging them both. 'Had a good time, did you?' Releasing Ella but still holding his daughter close to his side, he said, 'We'll stand here till we see you turn into your gate, Ella.'

'Thanks, Mr Russell, I won't be a tick. See you tomorrow, Becky.'

Ella ran, turning at her gateway to give them both a wave. Her face was sad, her thoughts serious. Becky might only be a few weeks younger than she was but she wasn't very worldly. She was such a nice kind girl, someone she was proud to have as her best friend but she had to be mad to see that Tommy Ferguson wasn't the type of boy she should be taking up with. And it wasn't going to happen. Not if she could help it.

Chapter Three

1924

SUNDAY AFTERNOON AND Becky was spending it in the way she loved best. She was sitting on the river wall at Kingston. She loved to watch dear old Father Thames flowing relentlessly on. What a lovely sight, she thought to herself as a saloon steamer came into sight on its way to Henley. Life on the river was never dull, always varied, and today with the sun shining on the old buildings everything seemed to glow.

It wouldn't be like that for much longer. Being the third week in September the pleasure boats would soon be laid up for the winter. Already the trees were beginning to display their bright autumn colours and she found herself wondering where the time had gone. It wasn't only the summer months that passed so quickly; the years themselves were speeding by.

It seemed only recently that she and Ella had been thrilled to be given employment at the Wellington Laundry. She pondered on that thought for a moment then shook her head in disbelief. In actual fact they had been working there now for four years.

'Becky, Becky!'

She looked up and saw that Ella was running along the towpath towards her. 'Hello! What are you doing?' Ella called out and without waiting for a reply she rushed on, 'I must look like a drowned rat.'

Becky reluctantly climbed down from the wall and really looked at her. 'Whatever happened to you?'

Ella's hair clung to her head and her dress was covered in mud splashes. 'It's like always, that daft Tommy tagged on and he's in a right mood because you aren't with me.'

'I didn't know Tom was here. You went off with that new van driver, what's his name? I didn't want to play gooseberry. I knew you'd be back in time to go for some tea.'

Ella held out her hand to her. 'His name is Pete, Pete Tomson, and he's old enough to be our father, but he's ever so nice and I think he's lonely cos he's only moved here when he got the job at the Wellington. You didn't have to stay behind, we were only going for a walk.'

Becky was grinning broadly. 'Ella, you do exaggerate! Pete Tomson can't be much more than thirty years old and that makes him just twelve years older than us. But never mind him, how did you meet up with Tom?'

'Hmm!' Ella sniffed and shrugged her shoulders. 'How do we ever meet up with Tommy Ferguson? He pops up like a bad penny wherever we decide to go at weekends. I told you years ago when you first started to take him under your wing that you were storing up trouble for yourself, but you wouldn't listen, would you?'

'Oh, Ella, he's not that bad.'

'Maybe not. But let's face the truth for once. Tommy is besotted with you. He gets really aggressive if he thinks any man is paying you too much attention. One day he may go over the top and then there'll be trouble.'

'I know,' Becky sighed, 'I can't help feeling sorry for him but I certainly don't encourage him.'

'You may not be responsible,' Ella pointed out, 'but that's not going to stop him feeling the way he does about you.'

'Well, what do you imagine he's going to do about it?'

'I don't know.'

'In that case, Ella, let me tell you. Nothing. Because unless I let him there is nothing he can do even if he wanted to. No, Tommy won't overstep the mark.'

'How do you know?'

'Because I know Tommy.'

'I know him too. In fact I think right from the beginning I've been able to read him like a book. Becky, you're too nice by far. You only see the good in everyone. Well not everyone is as good and kind as you are but I hope in this case you don't live to find that out.'

'What's that supposed to mean?'

Ella sighed. 'Oh nothing. It's just that sometimes Tommy gives me the creeps. Anyway, I'm going to the toilets, see if I can clean myself up a bit and then we'll make our way over the bridge an' have our tea, shall we?'

'Yes, that's fine by me, I'll wait here. By the way, you haven't said how you got yourself into such a state.'

Ella laughed now. 'I started to slip down the bank and daft Tommy, instead of helping, splashed handfuls of water over me.'

'What had you done to upset him?'

'As if you need to ask! I told him I didn't know where you were.'

Becky watched as Ella half ran towards the public toilets. She had grown into a sharp-witted, shrewd young lady with a really nice figure. Becky smiled to herself. She loved Ella dearly, even though she knew her own mind and wasn't afraid to voice her thoughts. That didn't deter her or anyone else from liking her. Oh no! Everyone made an exception for fair-haired blue-eyed Ella, because in the main what she said turned out to be right. A smile returned to Becky's face as Ella came towards her accompanied by Peter Tomson and Tom Ferguson.

Ella rolled her eyes. 'Tommy insists he wants to buy you tea, he said you paid for his drink twice last week in the work-break, so I've invited Pete to join us as well. All right?'

'Of course,' Becky said, falling into step beside Peter. He had been taken on by the Wellington four weeks ago to drive the van.

'How are you getting on?' Becky asked as they walked, more out of politeness than because she was interested.

'Not bad at all,' he smiled, adding quickly, 'but I miss my family.'

'Oh, where did you live before?'

'In the Midlands. I had a nervous breakdown when my mother was killed in a train accident. This job came up and my father thought a change of scenery would be good for me. He's gone to live with my married sister.'

'Uprooting yourself like that was a brave thing to do,' said Becky in amazement.

'Needs must when the devil drives,' he smiled and in that moment Becky decided he was a nice man.

They had their tea and Tommy was all smiles when Becky said he could go home with her on the tram because she had some sewing she wanted to do that evening. Ella shot Becky a grateful smile. It was what she had been longing for, a little while on her own with this new man in her life.

Tommy held on tightly to Becky's hand while the tram took them on the journey home and she was relieved when they came to New Malden village. Tugging to free her hand, she said, 'Ah, next stop's mine. See you at work in the morning, Tom, ta-ta.'

Tommy took a deep breath and said in a rush, 'I'll get off with you. I want to ask you something.'

Becky turned to him in surprise. The look on his face made her realize that their friendship did indeed mean something totally different to him than it did to her. How stupid she had been! She should have been aware of what was happening a long time ago. You've been a right silly fool, Becky Russell! she chided herself. You've had your head buried in the sand.

'I'm sorry Tom, I can't stop and talk tonight,' she replied lamely.

'Why not?'

She knew she had to be honest with him for once, what

else could she do? 'I don't want to, I've a whole lot of things I have to do this evening.'

'Oh!' Tom was fighting to keep himself under control, but if she wasn't careful he was going to let his temper get the better of him.

'I will see you at work in the morning,' she said gently as he moved his knees to allow her to push past him.

She breathed out as soon as her feet touched the pavement and she watched with relief as the tram pulled away from the stop. She could kick herself for having let things get to this pitch. Why hadn't she been aware of it before? She must have been blind. And daft not to have listened to Ella's warnings.

Back home she was relieved to find that her parents and her brothers were all out. With the whole house to herself she could sit down in peace and quiet and sort out her thoughts. Once she had washed her hands and face, she sat down, picked up her sewing and went over the day's events in her head. She knew now that what Ella was saying about Tommy was true. Today's events had proved her right. Why, he had even taken to waylaying her during their tea breaks at work. In fact he got right ruffled if she sat with the girls instead of with him. She was worried, even if she wouldn't admit it to Ella.

Something had to change and if she had her way it would be her job.

Four years earlier she had been delighted to be given a job. Any job would have done just so long as it was honest employment. How quickly she had changed her mind when she had first stepped into that wash house. She had been horrified when faced with the conditions in which they were expected to work.

Eleanor, being the strong-willed tomboy that she was, even at the age of fourteen, had taken the harsh conditions in her stride. If she were to ask her today if she were happy working in the laundry, Becky felt sure that Ella's reply would be, ''Course I am.'

It wasn't like that for herself. From that very first moment she had vowed that she would stay there no longer than was absolutely necessary. So what had gone wrong?

She was eighteen years old, which meant that she had been working at the Wellington for four years now. True, Mrs Bradford had taken pity on her and after just one year had seen that she was transferred to the packing department. Perhaps that was the reason that she hadn't put herself out to find other employment. No it wasn't, not if she was being honest with herself. Truth was she hadn't got the confidence any more. Well, she would jolly well have to find it again. And quick too, before things with Tommy Ferguson got out of hand.

I'll talk to me dad. Yes, that's what I'll do. He'll know the right way for me to go about getting a different kind of work. Her dad was a lovely man. Look how he treated her mum. Like she was his queen.

Sighing softly she packed her sewing away, climbed the stairs and began to lay out her clothes ready for work the next day.

When she finally got into bed, Becky realized that she was mentally exhausted and her last thought before she went to sleep was that she hoped one day she might be lucky enough to find a young man who would love her in the nice kind way that her dad loved her mother.

It wasn't natural, the way Tommy wanted to monopolize her.

Chapter Four

HARDLY HAD HER father stepped inside the house than Becky ran to his side, saying urgently, 'Please Dad, I want to talk to you.'

'All right, my love,' he smiled, 'don't look so worried. What's it about?'

'Can we go out into the garden?'

'No, I need to get this uniform off, else your mother will wonder what's wrong. Come on, we'll go upstairs.' And without waiting for Becky to reply, her father set off up the narrow stairs, his long legs taking the steps two at a time.

Becky followed him quickly, before her mother should start to wonder what was going on. Her mum and dad had the big bedroom with the bay windows that faced the fields opposite and to the side looked out over Harry Horsecroft's farm.

Her dad told her to sit down, then he shut the door and opened the window. The curtains started to flap gently for there was quite a breeze on this autumn evening. Then he seated himself in the other chintz-covered chair, that she had always thought looked so pretty because her mother had also made a frilled skirt for the dressing table out of the same chintz material, and began to unbutton his jacket.

Becky watched and waited.

When her father had hung his railway jacket on a coat hanger and rolled his shirtsleeves up to his elbows, he bent his head until his face was level with Becky's and kissed her soundly before saying, 'Well, my lovely girl? Nothing's ever so bad that we can't get it sorted.'

Suddenly Becky felt tongue-tied. It was going to be so difficult to explain to her father all the reasons why she wanted to leave the Wellington Laundry. 'Dad, I wish I could have a different job.'

'About time you did, if you want my opinion.'

'Dad!' She couldn't believe what she had heard him say. Oh, he was such a wise man. A good man. He understood before she had even said two words. Then it all came pouring out. The laundry was a hateful place. Nothing ever altered there. Monotonous tasks, day after day. Everything stayed the same, nothing to look forward to. Was that all there was to life? Did she have to stick at it? She hated it.

Her dad very nearly laughed but managed to keep a straight face. 'Rebecca,' he said softly, using her full name, 'of course you don't have to work there. You've been trudging backwards and forwards to that place for four years now so no one can say that you haven't given it a good go. Not that it would matter if they did. All your mother and I ever wanted is for you to be happy. Everyone has to work, but seeing as such a great deal of our lives is spent in employment I don't think it is asking too much that we should be happy there.'

Becky's face lit up. 'Oh Dad, I knew you'd understand.'

'Yeah well, one thing is for sure, it won't be that easy to find a different kind of work. Jobs aren't two a penny. Who you know goes a long way rather than what you know.'

He had dashed her hopes and he saw her bottom lip tremble. Quickly he added, 'I'll keep my ear to the ground and now you have actually made the decision to change your job, you'll see, something will turn up.'

Becky felt as if a load had been lifted from her shoulders. She was so lucky to have such wonderful parents; even her brothers were special. And her home was such a happy one. Fresh flowers in earthenware jugs were in evidence most times of the year as were fresh vegetables and salad, all thanks to the hours that her dad spent on his allotment. They were a team, her mum and dad. She couldn't imagine life without either of them, or without her brothers. Jack, her eldest brother, was happily married to Ada. They had a little boy, Ronnie, aged two. He was already a lovable little tinker, into everything but still the apple of his parents' eyes. Tom, the brother that Becky thought took after their father both in looks and personality, was also married. His wife, Joan, had only recently given birth to a baby boy. He was to be christened Joseph, after his grandfather. That left only Fred living at home. Both Jack and Tom had rented flats in Kingston, which made sense because they both worked at Kingston Tannery, but it didn't stop them bringing their families to Sunday afternoon tea, every week without fail.

Fred had a good job with the Co-op bakery. He was tall and quite good-looking, a fact that he took advantage of when it came to the girls. Fred wasn't going to settle down, not yet anyway, he's like me, Becky thought, appreciates his home too much to want to leave it for pastures new.

Joe Russell stared at Becky, wondering what had brought things to a head and a little afraid now to break the silence that had settled between them. With three sons and now two grandsons his only daughter was very special to him, as he knew full well he was to her.

'Rebecca's a Daddy's girl if ever there was one,' his wife was fond of telling folk and he wouldn't argue with that.

Joe didn't want Rebecca to be any different, but there were times when he couldn't help wishing that his darling girl wasn't quite so sensitive. Even as a child, however, Becky had shown signs of individuality, always so impressionable where others were concerned. From an early age, she had always been quite creative, especially when it came to clothes. Her mother raved about what Becky could do with a length of material or indeed with a second-hand frock. Pity she couldn't have found work in that line. But not in the London sweatshops that he'd heard so much about. Oh no! He liked his daughter nearby where he could keep an eye on her. But if she wasn't happy, well, that was a different story.

He smiled at his daughter and she smiled back, but she wasn't surprised when he gently took hold of her hand and said, 'You've only told me half the reason why you want to leave the Wellington. Go on, let's hear the rest of it.'

'Oh Dad! I think you already know, it's Tom Ferguson. He seems to know exactly where I'll be. I keep thinking I'm eighteen and I don't meet anybody else. I don't want to spend my life with someone like him. I think of all the places I read about, places I've never even seen and never shall if I stay in this rut. I scarcely ever remember even going to London.'

'Then go. Go soon.'

'Dad! You know it's not as simple as that.'

'It could be. If you put your mind to it.'

'Perhaps, but I just don't know where to start. Maybe I'm all talk and when it comes to it I won't have the courage.'

'Nonsense. I'll tell you what you're going to do. You are going to have a trip up to London for a start. Yes. I mean it. Next Saturday evening we'll leave our Fred to fend for himself and your mother and I will take you up to sample the bright lights of the city. After that we'll decide what you're gonna do about Tom Ferguson.'

'Do you really mean it, Dad?'

'You bet your life I do,' he said, holding out his hand to her. 'I'm already looking forward to it myself. Come on, let's go down and tell your mother.'

Becky didn't walk down the stairs, she ran. She was going to London with her parents. Not just to see the sights, but to sort things out in her head. She couldn't make up her mind whether she dreaded the day when she might start a new job or whether she was looking forward to it. Then, as she entered the kitchen, came a sobering thought. First she had to find another employer who would look kindly on her.

Her mother stared perplexedly at Becky as she took her seat at the table. One moment her face had been wreathed in smiles and now, seconds later, she was frowning. Now what on earth's got into her? she wondered.

'Youngsters!' she muttered to herself.

You never knew where you were with them.

Her father had kept his word.

Becky still couldn't quite believe that she was standing on the pavement in Oxford Circus. Her eyes were wide with amazement, as were her mother's. Come to think of it her mother looked an entirely different person tonight. She looked beautiful!

She had made her navy-blue outfit herself, its narrow skirt reaching only to her calves. She wore a jade-green cloche hat with her dark hair tucked up tight out of sight. She hadn't had her hair shingled as so many women had recently, her face was powdered, and her lips showed a trace of lipstick.

Becky felt she herself looked a fashionable young woman. She had thought of buying herself a new hat but the only millinery shop in the village of New Malden charged such outrageous prices she had changed her mind. Instead she had retrimmed her straw hat with multi-coloured ribbons to match the floral high-necked blouse she was wearing above her long grey skirt.

Becky now glanced at her father. The word to describe this big man was hard to find. Neat he most certainly was, but not very much in fashion. Quickly she suppressed a giggle. Younger men were wearing wide-legged trousers, navy-blue blazers and straw hats known as boaters. Her dad's plain dark suit, white shirt and modest tie topped by his hard bowler hat suited him well. Wonder of wonders, he had discarded his boots for a pair of well-polished, black laced-up shoes.

'Well, have the pair of you finished yer star gazing? Cos if you have perhaps we could move along.' Joe Russell was feeling really pleased with himself. It had been a bit of a battle, getting his Joyce to dress herself up, but the effort had been well worthwhile and he felt quite proud as they strode off, his wife on one arm and his daughter on the other.

It was grand to see all the different shops, each window-display a show in itself, gleaming with clothes they'd never seen the likes of.

'Oh, Lord,' Joyce muttered. 'Look at that poor man stood in the gutter.' A tray hung round his neck, loaded with boxes of matches. One empty sleeve of his jacket was pinned up, showing that his arm had been amputated. They stopped and Joe put three pennies into his cap which lay on the pavement.

The young man had a card propped against the kerb, on which he had written, I SERVED MY COUNTRY, NOW I NEED HELP TO SUPPORT MY WIFE AND TWO CHILDREN.

'Thank you,' he said as Joe straightened up.

Joe's face reddened and he turned to Joyce. 'There are still so many disabled servicemen, why can't the Government recognize their worth and do something to help the poor blighters?'

Their mood lightened as they looked into some windows which were displaying corsets. Becky looked at her mother and they both had to smother their giggles. The models were male: the corsets were for men!

Now they were in Regent Street. Dickins & Jones, Robinson & Cleaver and then the windows of Liberty's loomed ahead.

'Becky,' her mother said, tugging at her sleeve. 'We'll have to come up to town another time during the day when this shop is open. You'll never believe all the things they sell for people who are interested in sewing.' Becky took two steps backwards and tilted her head in order to read the nameplate above this shop that her mother was drooling over – the Needlewoman.

It was a dream of a shop. 'I've heard it called by several different names,' said Joyce, the nostalgia evident in her voice as she explained further. 'For all brides-to-be a visit to this establishment was a must. Young girls and their intended bridesmaids would be busy sewing for months ahead of the wedding. As indeed would the bride's elderly female relations. A girl was judged on what she had in her bottom drawer.'

Becky laughed, and her mother rebuked her. 'You can laugh young lady, but it is to be hoped that you'll be doing similar work before long.'

'Mum, I didn't mean to laugh but a bottom drawer sounds so funny.'

'Funny it never was,' Joyce snapped. 'A very serious business, believe you me. Tablecloths, napkins, huckerback hand towels, guest towels and pillowcases all had to be hand-embroidered.' She paused as if deep in thought. Smiling softly, she pointed to the skeins of silk laid out so decoratively in wicker baskets. 'I'd like a guinea for every one of those I used when I was filling my bottom drawer. Those extra fine ones my mother used to stitch lazy daisies on the top and bottom of my nightdresses.'

Joe Russell placed his hand on his wife's shoulder. 'And very fetching you looked when you wore them,' he quietly told her.

Becky had to tear herself away from the Needlewoman. What she wouldn't give to be let loose in that store with an unlimited amount of money to spend.

They walked past Hamley's. 'That 'appens to be the most famous toy shop in the world,' her father told her with pride.

A little further on they reached Mappin & Webb. 'THE jewellers and silversmiths to the nobility,' Joe informed them.

'Mine of information tonight, aren't you,' Joyce teased her husband, but there was fondness in her voice.

Down into Piccadilly Circus they went. 'Oh, look!' Becky cried out in sheer amazement.

Her father laughed as he watched the different expressions flit across his daughter's face. For one so young who had rarely in her life visited London, Piccadilly Circus, with its brilliant flashing lights and cascading advertisements, had to be a wonderful sight.

'Mum, all this electricity!'

The babble of conversation that was now taking place between mother and daughter had Joe Russell laughing fit to bust.

'Why do we only have gaslight? Why are our streets still so dim of a night-time cos we've only got those funny old lampposts? Will we ever get lights like these? Why should London be so different from everywhere else?'

'Put a sock in it,' Joe pleaded. 'To answer your last question first, young lady, London is the capital city of England. The powers that be will get around to seeing that the whole country has the benefit of electricity one day. Won't be for a while yet though.' Turning to his wife Joyce, he lowered his voice. ''T'was worth bringing her, wasn't it?'

'Most certainly was. For me an' all. I never knew it was lit up like this.'

'Funny really, with me being in the parcel office most of the time I 'ardly ever put a foot outside of Waterloo Station. True, the platforms have had electric light for some time now though the waiting rooms still have their gaslights an' coal fires. You know, luv, I was talking to one electrician only the other day an' he told me that at the last count two an' a 'alf million light bulbs were being used in London. That's something to think about, eh?'

'Dad,' Becky was tugging at the sleeve of her father's jacket. 'Are we near Trafalgar Square?'

'About a stone's throw away, why? Do you want to go an' see Nelson's Column?'

'Yeah, but mostly I'd like to see all the pigeons and the fountains. May we feed the pigeons?'

Joe shook his head in disbelief. Nelson's Column against pigeons and the pigeons win! Ah well, as long as she's happy. 'Anything you want, my luv. But first I'm gonna buy my two ladies a little present. No gent worth his salt comes to Piccadilly Circus without doing so. Wait there,' Joe ordered as he stepped briskly towards the statue of Eros. The well-known flower seller – an old lady, dressed in black, a heavy shawl around her shoulders and a wide-brimmed hat on her head – sat at the foot of the statue and watched him approach.

'Gonna buy a button 'ole for yer ladies?' she called out.

'Wouldn't miss the chance for the world,' Joe answered as he fished in his pocket for some loose change.

''Ere,' she grinned broadly, showing several of her front teeth were missing. 'A rose for yer missus, an' a sweet bunch of violets for yer young gal.'

Joe handed over a silver shilling and was rewarded by the old lady's jolly remark of: 'Gawd bless yer. You're a gent an' no mistake.'

'Next time we come up we'll tackle the window-shopping from another direction,' her father promised. 'We'll have a look at all the theatres, especially the London Hippodrome, maybe 'ave supper somewhere.'

'That's as maybe,' Joyce quickly butted in, 'but promises are like pie-crust, made to be broken and I'm hungry now. How about you, Becky?'

'Me an' all. I'm starving.'

'Tell me,' Joe said grinning, 'how does fish an' chips sound t' the pair of you?'

'Scrumptious,' Becky cried before her mother had time to answer.

'Well, me money won't run to these London prices, so we'll make Trafalgar Square our last port of call for this trip. Then as soon as we get home you two go indoors, light the oven and put the plates in to warm and I'll trot off for three of the biggest portions of cod an' chips you've ever seen.'

On the homeward journey a tired but happy Rebecca was reminding herself that it was as she had always known, her parents were smashing. The memory of this London excursion would remain with her for a very long time.

During the following weeks a number of things happened which made the future seem a whole lot more rosy to both Becky and to Ella. There was to be a Harvest Supper, followed by a social, in the local church hall and notices were being sent out from the organizers pleading for volunteers to come forward and lend a helping hand.

One afternoon, Becky and Ella were sitting on the outside steps of the laundry during their tea break, discussing this coming event when Ella suddenly said, 'Pete's going to see t' the music.' She glanced quickly at Becky to see what Becky's reaction was, for she knew that Becky wasn't aware of just how often she and Peter had been out together.

Becky smiled to herself before answering. So that was the way the wind was blowing. 'For the Harvest Supper you mean?'

'Yes, and for the entertainment during the evening.'

'That's good, let's hope he comes up with something a bit more lively than the usual rubbish we have to put up with when the village has a do.'

'He will. And by the way, Pete's going to do you a big favour.'

'Me?'

'Yes, you. We were talking about you and Tom Ferguson one evening and I told Pete that you were sick an' tired of the way Tommy always dogged your footsteps.'

'Did you now? And what did your Peter have to say to that?'

Ella's cheeks flushed a bright red. 'Don't be like that, Becky, please. He's not my Peter, it's just that he's lonely an' we seem to get on with each other.'

'Well, well,' murmured Becky, then she relented and stopped her teasing, turned to Ella and said, 'I'm pleased for you both. Honestly I am. I could see from the moment he started at the Wellington that you two suited each other.'

'Aw, thanks, Becky. I've been wanting to tell you. I really do like him and he's not as old as we thought. He's twenty-six. He was in the Army during the War. Saw a bit of service in France, that's probably what aged him. But we're getting away from what I was gonna tell you.'

'Something about him doing me a favour, wasn't it?'

'Yes,' Ella said, a triumphant tone in her voice. 'You remember the Saturday you went up to London with your mum an' dad? Well Pete an' I went to the pictures and Tommy asked if he could tag along. Having said yes, Pete had a brain wave, he invited his landlady's daughter to come as well.'

'And?' Becky asked, her eyes bright with curiosity.

'Her name's Mary, Mary Marsden.'

'Oh, for goodness sake stop yer tantalizing and tell me what happened.'

'Nothing happened. Mary's not the brightest person on God's earth. Seems she's been in service for some time but she was so unhappy her mum persuaded her dad to let her come home. She's not got a job at the moment. She an' Tommy seemed to like each other. Anyway Pete's been busy scheming and singing Tom's praises and the long and short of it is Tom's been asked to Sunday tea at the Marsdens' and Mary's coming to this Harvest do.'

'Are you sure about this?' Becky asked.

'Oh yes, I'm quite sure of it.'

Becky reached out for Ella. She put her arms around her friend's neck and they were laughing loudly. Suddenly Ella, her eyes twinkling, enquired, 'You're not in any way jealous?'

'Jealous! Oh you, Ella, you're mad.'

'Well, I just wondered, he's been your Tommy from the day we started at the laundry. No. I've just remembered from the day he stepped on your foot at that first dance we went to. Own up an' shame the devil, you'll be really annoyed if Tom transfers his attentions to Mary.'

Becky gently slapped Ella's shoulder. She was shaking her head from side to side and still laughing fit to burst.

When their merriment had settled down, Becky muttered, 'Thank God for small mercies. Maybe I'll be able to enjoy the evening without Tommy glaring at me all the time if I so much as speak to another fellow.'

The whistle went, signalling that tea break was over, but Ella couldn't resist having one more jibe at Becky. 'You'd better not start feeling fancy free, thinking you're gonna be the belle of the ball an' have the pick of the field at this barn dance. After all, you weren't there when we went to the pictures. Tommy might have cottoned on to Mary, thinking any port in a storm. When he sees you, arrayed in all your finery, he might just decide there's no one in the world like you, that he can't live without you, you're the love of his life. Then what will you do?'

'I know what I'll do to you right now if . . .' Becky didn't have to finish what she was saying. Ella had fled, her laughter echoing back down the corridor.

Chapter Five

WHAT A WEEK! Everything that could go wrong at the Wellington Laundry had gone wrong. One of the main boilers had packed up, so all the others had to be shut down while plumbers did their best to find the trouble. There had been a fire in the pressing room, albeit only a small fire, but it was a wonder that it hadn't spread. An extra van had been needed to cope with getting the backlog of deliveries out on time. No motor van had been available for hire and as a last resort Harry Horsecroft had been offered the chance of a few days' work.

It had taken more than an hour to load the neat parcels and boxes of freshly-laundered linen on to his cart, because each batch required full details of the route he must take and what roads came first regarding delivery.

'No, there is no need for you to ask for payment from any of the customers,' Mrs Bradford assured a flustered Harry, 'these are all account customers.'

'I doubt whether half of what we've said has got through to that man,' Mrs Bradford whispered to Becky. 'Do you think he's been drinking? Surely not, not this time in the morning, but he is giving me that impression.'

Becky busied herself with the ledger, ticking off each item that had been entrusted to Harry. She made no answer to Mrs Bradford, who had answered her own questions. Probably he's not yet sobered up from last night's session, Becky was thinking to herself.

Why did everybody presume that Harry Horsecroft was dim? Quite the opposite was Becky's opinion. He led a good life doing just what he wanted to. Neither he nor his wife seemed to bother what they looked like or what anybody thought of them come to that. It was as her dad said, 'There's none so daft as those that don't want to know.'

Harry took a reasonably clean handkerchief from his pocket and wiped his sweating brow, tugged his flat cap further down over his forehead and managed to manoeuvre his horse and cart safely out of the yard.

When he pulled his horse to a stop outside the butcher's shop and got down from his seat the horse had bolted before he had time to walk to the back of the cart and take off the box containing the butcher's clean aprons. It seemed that the whole village got to know that Harry Horsecroft's horse and cart were on a runaway expedition and for a while it provided quite a commotion and a great deal of amusement as men and boys tried to grab the reins of the horse.

Such was the situation in the laundry that most of the pressers and packers, including Becky, had been sent to lend a hand in the boiler room once things were on the way to being normal again.

Her back ached, her arms ached, her legs ached, in fact there wasn't a bone in her whole body that didn't ache. The only good thing was, Becky kept reminding herself, today was Friday and at least she had the weekend to look forward to.

She had asked herself a number of times this week how Ella had managed to stand the work in the wash house all these years, and not only stand it but to have got so used to the hard work that she actually liked it. Becky sighed. Why was it that she couldn't be contented? She had never liked her job and never would.

Since her talk with her father she had applied for two new jobs. One was in the local dry-cleaners; she wasn't sorry when she wasn't offered the post because the work hardly differed from what she was doing now. The other position, advertised in the local paper, had been at the cigarette kiosk down on the railway station but it had gone to an older woman. She sometimes despaired that she would ever be able to break away from this place.

'You might feel better if you put a smile on that face of yours.' Ella had come up behind Becky without her hearing.

'Must be looking the way I feel,' Becky answered, and tried to smile. The smile came out as a grimace, and made Ella feel so sorry for her. Becky was different, always wanting the moon, never that which was within her grasp.

'Cheer up for God's sake,' Ella implored, 'there's a heck of a lot t' look forward to in the next couple of weeks. Hope you haven't forgotten the jumble sale tomorrow afternoon. You haven't, have you?'

'No.' Now Becky did smile. 'Ma Turner in the café told my mum that it was gonna be worth going to. Said she'd heard that most of the stuff had come from the big houses.'

'Well, there you are then. Might even find ourselves a decent dress seeing as how the Harvest Supper is the Saturday after.'

'Decent dress! You've got some hopes. Anyway it's supposed to be a sit-down meal with entertainment afterwards. My brother Fred said he's thinking about coming and if he does he's going to offer to do a turn.'

'A turn? What kind of a turn? I would have thought your Fred would make a good comedian, he's always telling jokes.'

'Funny you should say that, Ella. My dad told him the same thing but to remember it would be a family show and not to tell near-the-knuckle jokes nor any about the vicar.'

'Bet that's put him right off coming.'

'Don't suppose he ever had any intentions of coming in the first place. How about your Jimmy? Will he come?'

'Don't know, depends on what shift he's on. He's a damn sight more sociable since our Ronald joined the Army. Ronnie was always jealous because Jimmy had a job and he couldn't get one. Can't say I blamed him, he was the eldest and it must have been awful for him, never having a penny in his pocket except what me mum or Jimmy gave him.'

'Yeah, can't have been easy,' Becky agreed. 'Still your mum told my mum that Ronald was doing well. Said that by all accounts Army life was suiting him.'

'When you've quite finished your little meeting, there is quite a bit of clearing up to be done before the whistle will be sounding.'

Both girls stopped talking and turned to face Mrs Bradford in surprise. 'Sorry,' Ella mumbled, walking hurriedly away.

Once again Becky thanked God it was Friday as she returned to the arduous task of transferring wet linen from one vat to another.

'Gosh, someone important, or at least well-off, must have died.' Becky's voice was quiet and soft, filled with emotion.

Ella, standing next to her, nodded her head. 'I'm sure you're right.'

The two friends grinned and Becky put out her hand and squeezed Ella's arm, saying, 'We've hit the jackpot coming to this jumble sale today, it was worth coming early and queuing outside, wasn't it?'

Ella again nodded her head. 'It certainly was. I've never seen such an array of clothes and most of them are really good quality.'

Rebecca's lovely face lit up with a lop-sided grin as the lady standing behind the long trestle table handed her the black dress, now neatly wrapped in brown paper, that she had just paid ninepence for.

'You'll be able to turn that into something quite dazzling,' Ella beamed at her.

'I'll try,' Becky answered.

'You won't just try, you'll do it.'

'Bully,' Becky teased, pushing the parcel into her almost full shopping bag.

Ella frowned. 'I didn't make you buy it against your will, did I? You do like it?'

'Don't be silly, Ella, I think it's probably the nicest dress I've ever owned, it's . . . well . . . kind of graceful. The material is lovely and I don't want to spoil it. I just think it might be difficult to alter.'

Ella relaxed and laughed. 'Honestly, Becky, you really are an old fusspot. Look at the amount of sewing you do. Loads more than me an' I do my fair share. 'Course it won't be difficult. Not if you put your mind to it. Now, come on, let's see what else we can find, I wouldn't mind a skirt an' a top if we can find one that's halfway decent.'

'Look over there.' Becky's finger was pointing, her eyes twinkling with delight.

'Oh yeah, it's our mums. Did you know they were manning a stall together?'

'No, I never,' Becky protested. 'Wonder why they never said. Let's see if they've got any bargains left.'

Peggy James and Joyce Russell watched, pride evident on their faces, as their daughters came across the hall. Both girls had grown into young ladies worthy of a second glance.

Peggy was asking herself why had she worried for years because her Eleanor was plump. It had only been puppy fat. Today, at eighteen, she still had plenty of flesh on her bones but looked really quite fit and healthy. A real picture. She hadn't lost that country look despite having worked in that laundry for four years. She was still too much of a tomboy but nobody was going to be able to change her. To live for the day seemed to be Eleanor's code of behaviour.

Joyce was also reflecting on how grown-up her Rebecca was – still small-boned and slender, with dark hair that had a sheen all of its own, clear, flawless skin and cheeks that reminded one of a ripe peach. A dainty little miss was how her eldest son Jack had described his sister and today, looking at Rebecca, Joyce had to admit that he hadn't been far wrong.

'They've both hung on to their long hair,' Peggy observed to Joyce.

'Yeah, can't say I'm sorry, can you?'

'Well, in a way I suppose not, though Ella did tell me that they were both considering having it cut in that new style, you know, a short, swinging bob, I think is what it's called.'

Joyce thought for a moment before answering her friend. 'Don't seem only yesterday they each cut their first tooth and we took them down the village for their first trim. Bet it would cost a fortune to have their hair cut now if they wanted that new style. Have to go to an expert, I expect.'

'Wouldn't want to be there, would you? See all that lovely hair falling to the floor. My Ella's so fair an' your Becky, all those gorgeous curls that you used t' do in ringlets, all being chopped off. Don't bear thinking about.'

'Doing your good deed for the church fund, are you?' Ella's loud voice put a stop to all their reminiscences.

'Yes,' Ella's mother smiled, 'and we've got just the thing for two young ladies who are thinking of going out on the town.' With this remark she placed an assortment of beaded handbags on top of the table. 'A lot of work has gone into them but no one seems to want to buy them.'

Becky handled a bag, and murmured, 'They're lovely for evenings, but not much use to us.'

Ella wrinkled her nose. 'You'd have t' be really dressed up to use one of those.'

'What about these?' Joyce Russell was holding aloft two waistcoats, one plain black, the other in pale pastel colours on a grey background. 'We'll let you have these for a couple of coppers each.'

'What would we do with them?' queried Ella. 'They're gents' waistcoats.'

Becky raised her eyes to meet those of her mother and they both smiled. 'I know what you're thinking, Mum. Embroidery down the front of the plain one and it would look gorgeous with a plain black skirt, yes?'

'Exactly,' her mother agreed. 'Set a new fashion. Something out of the ordinary. You can have it for threepence.'

'Done.' A grinning Becky was already fishing in her bag to find the pennies.

'Now, Ella,' Joyce turned to Eleanor, 'you'd knock spots off any other girl if you wore something like this. Better than all the new skinny fashions, especially for the Harvest Supper. Wear something long and flimsy, match up a blouse to one of these colours in this waistcoat, you wouldn't even have to alter it.'

'Better still,' Ella's mother chipped in, 'wear this. I jumped the queue and bought you this long grey skirt, hope you like it.'

Ella gasped as her mother fanned the skirt, displaying the fact that it was very full, the material soft chiffon, fully lined with dark grey silk. Ella took the skirt and held it up against herself. It was calf-length, just right. 'Oh it's gorgeous!' she breathed, letting the chiffon trickle through her fingers.

'Well, any white blouse would go well with the skirt and waistcoat.'

'Yes, I'm sure it would,' Ella said.

Her mother heard doubt in her voice. 'But what?'

'It buttons up on the wrong side.'

Becky looked at her mother, Joyce looked at Peggy and they all three burst out laughing. 'Who's going to notice that?' Becky said, doing her best to control her merriment. 'You can always leave it undone.'

Now it was Ella's turn to laugh. 'Oh, all right. As you say, at least wherever we go nobody else will be wearing the same outfit.'

'True. True,' Becky added. 'You could change the buttons, whatever, we'll look tip-top, you'll see.'

There was no going out for Becky or Ella for the next week.

'You'll have blunted every needle in the house so you will,'

Joyce laughed, using her hip to push open Becky's bedroom door. 'I've brought you each a mug of cocoa, it's time you packed up all this sewing for tonight and you, Ella, ought to be thinking of getting home.' She set the tray holding the mugs down on to the bedside table and stooped to lift some pieces of material from the floor. 'You two certainly got yourselves some good bargains at the church's jumble sale.'

'We sure did,' Ella replied in a frivolous mood. 'We've spent the last half-hour making these velvet bows to tie up our bonny brown hair. Well, Becky's bonny brown hair and in my case, bonny fair hair.'

Joyce grinned. 'There'll be no stopping the pair of you when you step out in all your finery on Saturday, will there?'

'Not unless the fellows are all stone blind,' Ella joked.

Joyce looked at her daughter. 'What's making you so quiet, Becky? Aren't you going to show me what you've done to your dress?'

'No, not tonight, Mum. When I've finished it I'll try it on, see what you think then before I press it.'

'All right, luv, but start clearing up now and don't let your cocoa go cold.' She turned and went out of the room and down the narrow flight of stairs. They're both good girls, she told herself. It said a lot for each of them that the clothes they wore were always nice. It wasn't as if either of them had a lot of money to spend. Come to think of it, hardly ever did they have any new outer garments. Underwear and shoes were about all that they ever bought new. Most of their dresses, yes, and even coats were second-hand, came from the gentry a lot of what they picked up, so I suppose you could say they were lucky. By persevering they managed alterations. If it were a plain dress or skirt often all they did was add a belt, different buttons, or a lace collar. That's where I come in. She smiled to herself and thought, crocheting is the one thing I do well, I can turn out a piece of decorative lace with the best of them. Suppose we've all been gifted in different ways and when it comes to Becky and her friend Ella, well, they are undeniably gifted with their needles.

Harvest Festival time was lovely. It did mean that summer was almost over but there were still the golden evenings. Everyone was out to enjoy themselves, get together, have fun before the dark evenings and short days came to lower their spirits. Although Kingston was in Surrey it did have many large factories and streets of small two-up and two-down houses and the poverty was about equal to that of any South London area. However this time of the year belonged to the country folk. With the harvest safely gathered in, the surrounding fields were yellow with stubble. The river boats were still operating, the dark blue skies still reflected in the dear old Thames and Hampton Court Palace was still attracting lots of visitors.

It was Saturday night and the whole village of New Malden would be socializing, before the long winter closed in on them all. Old and young alike would gather in the congregational hall for this Harvest Supper. Quite a few older members of the community would leave once the supper was over, though others would stay to enjoy the music and to watch the brave ones climb the platform to do a turn.

It had been raining earlier in the afternoon but now Ella and Becky could scarcely believe their good fortune. They couldn't have asked for a more pleasant evening as they set off to walk down to the village, their parents having gone on ahead some time ago.

When the girls arrived at the hall on Saturday evening Peter Tomson was already there waiting for them. As they headed for the cloakroom, with Peter chatting to Ella, Becky thought about how much Ella had mellowed in the past couple of years. This quietly spoken, nicely made-up and elegantly dressed young lady was completely different from the tomboy Ella used to be.

But then she herself was also totally different to what she had been when they had first started to work at the Wellington Laundry. Long-forgotten memories came flooding back to Becky. She recalled the horror she had felt when she saw the sack aprons and the coarse overalls they had been given to wear. She remembered saying to herself, I won't be working here for long.

Whatever had happened to that resolution? The truth was she hadn't made much of an effort. Lately she had fantasized about working in London, maybe in one of the big stores around Regent Street. Talk about going from the ridiculous to the sublime!

Once inside the ladies' room Becky watched as Ella made straight for the mirror. 'It's going to be a marvellous night, I know it is,' Ella was saying, bubbling with excitement. 'And you look smashing in that dress,' she said, admiring Becky from a few feet away. 'It really does suit you.'

Becky smiled. She had worked hard on this dress but it had been worth it. She hadn't altered the length, just the sleeves, which had been too fussy for her liking. Around the bust she had put in quite a few tucks and she had done away with the collar altogether. 'You look a proper treat yourself,' Becky said, 'suppose we had better sally forth before your Peter starts to worry that you've gone off somewhere without him.'

A great deal of time and effort had gone into making the hall look as nice as possible for this Harvest Supper. The backdrop to the stage had a country theme. Sheaves of barley and wheat together with various bunches of tall grass had been woven together and strung from corner to corner and side to side.

Gramophone records were now being played but after the meal there was to be a live band as part of the show.

Becky and Ella's eyes were everywhere, taking it all in, the music, the decorations, the smiling older folk, the young girls in their pretty dresses, the lads decked out in best bib and tucker. Ella spotted Peter and Becky sighed as she saw a smiling Tommy was with him. A few seconds later Peter excused himself, saying he wanted to introduce Ella to some of his mates. Becky was left alone with Tom.

She was speechless. This was the last thing that she had wanted to happen right at the start of the evening. If Tommy was going to monopolize her she would never get to meet anyone else. Then suddenly it came to her that Tommy wasn't the lad she was so used to. Looking directly at him, she was amazed, he looked so different, better than she had ever seen him look before. He'd had his hair cut, he was wearing a navy-blue suit with a white shirt that was open at the neck and for once he didn't have that hangdog look about him.

'Hello, Becky,' he said, smiling broadly. ''Aven't 'ad a chance t' talk to you for a long time. At work I think you've been avoiding me.'

She couldn't have felt worse if he had knocked her for six. 'Don't be silly, Tom, you're just imagining that.'

What had happened to him? Becky asked herself the question, but couldn't answer it. Tommy Ferguson not only looked different, he sounded different.

'Can I get you a drink? There is just about time before we have to sit down.'

'Yes please, that would be nice.'

'Then, Becky, will you do me a favour? Later on in the evening will do.'

'Of course, if I can.'

'I want you t' come and say hello to my friend Mary, I've taken her to see your mum and dad. They liked her. Look, there she is, talking to Ella.' Tommy called out, 'Won't be long, Mary.'

Across the room, Becky saw a plumpish young lady stand up and give a friendly wave. Her round face had a smile on it that spread from ear to ear, but that old-fashioned dress! It was meant for someone years older and as for her hair, shiny and clean but cut short close to her head with a fringe which lay long on her forehead, it was the hairstyle of a young schoolgirl.

Becky thought with satisfaction of the lovely frock she was wearing, and the time that she and Ella had spent in arranging their hair then immediately she chided herself not to be so spiteful.

Tommy was waving back and Becky realized how happy he looked. And that wasn't all. He no longer looked shy or out of place. Without saying a word he went to the bar and returned with a glass of orange squash, which Becky took, murmuring, 'Thank you.'

He answered, 'See you later,' turned on his heel and left her. Before, he had always been all fingers and thumbs. He held himself more upright as he walked, she decided as her eyes followed him across the floor. More than that, he radiated confidence.

That Mary Marsden had done wonders for him concluded Becky as she went to find her parents.

Several women had contributed to the baking of the food and everyone said the pies and the boiled ham were surprisingly good. The meal was complemented with traditional flagons of home-made cider, with fruit juice for the children. Speeches were made, the vicar said how pleased he was to see so many folk there and he gave thanks to God for the bountiful harvest. Then the tables had to be cleared and the hall set up ready for the entertainment to begin.

Becky couldn't believe just how well in with the organizers Peter Tomson seemed to be. It almost looked as if Peter was in charge. It was Peter who asked the band to set up, and who suggested the best place on the stage for them to do so. It was also Peter who organized the acts that had volunteered to be part of the evening's entertainment, and jollied Tommy into helping to line up the chairs for those who'd be watching.

'Marvellous how well Peter has settled in, isn't it?' Ella smiled at Becky. 'I just hope that everything goes off well.'

Becky gave an answering smile and held up crossed fingers for luck. Peter seemed to have become a very important part of Ella's life. Standing next to her friend now, Becky felt a bit neglected. If she sat with her parents it wouldn't seem right; if she sat with Ella and Peter during the concert it might look as if she were playing gooseberry, yet she could hardly sit on her own.

'Becky.' Tommy's eyes met Becky's. 'Will you come and say 'allo t' Mary like you said you would?'

Tom didn't sound quite so sure of himself now, so she gave him a nod of encouragement and said, 'Right now, you lead the way.'

Becky offered up a silent prayer that she might say all the right things to this new friend of Tommy's. It was obviously so important to him. Mary was a short dumpy girl, very intense-looking, and Becky felt hard pushed to guess her age. One thing in her favour was her eyes, big, wide and the deepest blue she had ever seen, Becky decided as she held out her hand. 'Hello, Mary, it's nice to meet you and really nice to know that you and Tom have become friends.'

Mary laughed into her hand.

Becky racked her brain for something else to say.

'D'you like Tommy?' Mary asked abruptly.

'Yes, I do. We've been friends for a long time.'

Mary made a face. 'I've never made many friends because I've been away in domestic service.'

'You'll make a lot now, Mary,' Tom quickly assured her, 'won't she, Becky? You'll help her, won't you?'

Mary laughed and Becky laughed with her. 'Of course I will.'

'D'you mean that?' Mary asked, excitedly raising her voice so that it was overheard by those standing nearby.

Becky took hold of Mary's hand, saying, 'I think it's a smashing idea. Come on, no time like the present, come and meet some of the girls I work with, you'll like them, I know you will.' Still holding hands Becky urged Mary forward.

They took a few steps and then Mary paused, turned and gave Tom a wave of her hand, and he waved back.

Becky took Mary around the hall introducing her to different groups of girls that she knew, all the time smiling and talking, but there was a lump in her throat and a blur before her eyes. She hoped against hope that Mary and Tommy would be good for each other, that life would be kind to them. They seemed well-suited. Two more genuine young folk it would be hard to find.

'The evening has been a great success, and on behalf of us all here I would like to thank the committee for all the hard work that they have put into making it so, and ask that they give some thought as to when the village might next enjoy such a lovely get-together.' Applause instantly broke out and amid great cheering Joe Russell left the platform and rejoined his wife and daughter.

Earlier the vicar had whispered to Joe that Peter Tomson was supposed to be making the closing speech but he couldn't be found and would Joe kindly step into the breach?

'Did you see Ella leaving?' Becky's mother asked as they were helping to pack the chairs away.

Becky shrugged. 'No, I had a drink with her and Peter during the interval, but I haven't seen her since.' They must have cleared off then, Becky told herself, feeling a little put out that they hadn't said they were leaving. Still, it's none of my business what they choose to do.

Chapter Six

MONDAY MORNING. EIGHT weeks since the Harvest Supper and less than a month to go until Christmas.

Peggy James had been downstairs before five o'clock this morning to cook breakfast for her son, Jim, and see him off to work. Slowly she had gone about her daily tasks. Lit the fire, sorted the washing out, putting the whites in to soak. Spread damp tea leaves on to the big rug in the front room to lay the dust before getting down on her knees to sweep it with a stiff hand broom. Through the open window she could see and hear George Road coming to life. Smoke was rising from chimneypots, the lampposts were still alight, relieving the foggy gloom of this November day. The clatter of the horse's hooves drawing the milk cart told her it was half-past six. She listened to the sound of milk bottles clinking on stone doorsteps. Next came the tuneless whistle of the paperboy.

Peggy made another pot of tea, sat and drank a cup, thought about what she was going to say to her daughter and wondered what the hell the outcome would be. 'I'd better go and wake her up, take her up a cup of tea.'

Upstairs she set the cup down and gently shook Ella's shoulder. 'Wake up luv, time t' get up or else you're going to be late for work.'

Ella sat up in bed, smiled at her mother and drank her early morning tea. Peggy gazed at her. Silly, silly girl! She probably hadn't given a thought to the consequences of what she and Peter had been up to. Her head ached, the inside of her mouth was dry, she couldn't put it off any longer. Something had to be said to bring it out into the open. 'You're pregnant,' Peggy stated bluntly.

Ella could only stare at her mother. She hadn't wanted her mum to know, didn't want to talk about it, hoping against all the odds that her period would suddenly appear.

'I'm not sure,' she whispered at last, only because she knew she had to make some answer.

'You've missed two periods,' her mother blurted out. 'I consider that pretty conclusive. Or are you waiting for further proof? Have you been to the doctor's? Told anyone?'

Ella shook her head.

'Well?' asked Peggy. 'Say something, for God's sake. When an' where did it happen?'

'Oh Mum . . . It was the night of the Harvest Supper. Peter an' I came back here early. It was warm an' cosy down in the front room, so we . . . kind of . . . just let ourselves go.'

'God give me strength!' her mother snapped. As she stared down at Ella, her feelings were a combination of love and regret. Such a lovely girl, a good daughter, so kind, outgoing, outgoing was right! It had been her downfall. Where would she go from here?

'Does Peter know?' she asked more gently.

Ella nodded. 'He said when I was absolutely sure we'd get married.'

'Sure! What does he want, the baby to be put into his arms?'

'Don't shout, Mum, they'll hear you next door.'

'Bit late for that luv, people will talk an' you won't be able to stop them, but that can't be helped.'

Ella looked terrified.

A surge of relief went through Peggy. She'd had her doubts about what Peter's reaction would be, but as long as he'd promised they'd be wed, well, the sooner they got it sorted out and a date set the better. She picked up the now-empty teacup and made for the door.

'Get yourself up now and ready for work, we'll talk about

what's going to happen tonight. You'd better get word to Peter to be round here by seven.'

If only she hadn't hidden her head in the sand, she chided herself as she filled the kettle once again. She and Ella must both have been mad. If they'd faced the problem earlier instead of waiting so long they might have been able to explain the baby's early arrival to the neighbours as being premature. Time they got her married now she'd be well on the way. Nobody would need any telling, they'd all be able to see for themselves that her Ella had been well and truly caught.

The local gossips would have a field day, she thought bitterly.

Peter felt really cold as he trudged towards Albert Road. As ye sow so shall ye reap, he was thinking to himself. Ella had been frightened when she had told him she thought she was pregnant and he had made up his mind there and then that he would stand by her. Nevertheless, it hadn't stopped him from berating himself for having been so stupid. When he had left home and come South to look for work he had reckoned on bettering himself. The van driver's job at the laundry was only supposed to be a stop-gap until something better turned up. Wasn't much chance of that now.

Married? He couldn't take it in. He hadn't a penny behind him, only a few bob he'd put away for the railway fare so that he could go to his sister's one weekend, see his father, find out how he was getting on. Right mess he'd made of it all.

The road where Ella lived with her mother was nice enough but the houses seemed to him to have a mournful look. There was nothing about them that spelt prosperity. Two rooms, a scullery and an outside toilet downstairs, a box room at the top of the stairs, five more steps up to another two bedrooms. The few times he had been inside the house he had thought how well-worn everything looked. No carpets, only linoleum and a few rugs, and the furniture and the curtains all seemed fairly shabby. Back home his mother had kept their house like a new pin. Perhaps he shouldn't be too hard on Mrs James, since losing her husband in the War and being left with two sons and Ella to bring up couldn't have been easy. It was different for my mum, he mused, Dad was always in work. As a boy he'd served his apprenticeship as a shoemaker, well, being born in Northampton, a place famous for the manufacturing of shoes, it had been inevitable.

Pity he hadn't followed in his father's footsteps. Right from a lad his dad had taught him how to repair his own boots and given the tools and the right type of leather he could still make a jolly good job of it. Time was I thought I might be lucky enough to get a job with a large firm of shoe repairers, but no such luck. Damn sight better prospects if I had! Never going to get anywhere if I stay as a van driver for the Wellington. He sighed heavily as he turned the corner into George Road.

I'm twenty-six years old, like a good many more men my age the years we served in France during the War took their toll and since then life hasn't been easy. Jobs are scarce and that's a fact. Still, if I'm to be married and become a father I'd better start looking around and fast.

Ella opened the door in answer to Peter's knock. He wrapped his arms about her and drew her close. To him she felt incredibly small, and he knew she was scared. He made a vow to do whatever he could to put matters right. He would take good care of her. As his lips came down gently on to hers Ella was telling herself that things could have been a darn sight worse. Peter might have cleared off, leaving her in the lurch.

When Peter released his hold on her, Ella gave him a tight smile. 'Come on through,' she said, 'Mum's waiting and my brother Jim has stayed in.' She stood aside while he closed the door behind them. He squeezed her arm, a gesture of encouragement, trying not to let on how apprehensive he felt.

The warmth of the kitchen hit Peter and he felt he wanted to turn about and run. Jim fixed Peter with an unblinking stare, nodded his head but didn't speak.

Peter said, 'Hello, Jim,' before turning to face Ella's mother. He wasn't given a chance to say a greeting before her first words came out like a shot from a gun.

'Have you set a date for the wedding?'

Peter looked at her in disbelief. 'There hasn't been time,' he answered frantically.

Peggy rose from her chair, drew herself up to her full height. 'Let me tell you this, Peter, before we go any further. Time is what you and Ella have not got. She is by my reckoning about eight weeks' pregnant. You do admit you're the father, don't you?'

Peter took a step backwards. He hadn't expected to be treated this way.

'Mum!' Ella cried, shocked.

'Ella, just be quiet a minute, let Peter speak for himself,' Peggy commanded.

Ella glanced over at Peter, doing her best to smile. Her mum shouldn't be so nasty to him. 'Jim, you say something,' she wailed.

'Get us all a drink,' Jim instructed his sister, 'and you Peter, sit yerself down, my mother is upset which is only natural but we'll all feel better with a glass of something in our hand and then perhaps we can talk calmly, get things settled.'

Peter breathed a sigh of relief as he took the chair indicated.

Peggy stared at her young son in amazement. It seemed there was a lot more to Jimmy than she'd ever given him credit for.

Ella hurried to get the glasses, 'There's only sherry or whisky,' she told her brother.

'Pour a sherry for Mum an' yerself, I'll see to Peter.'

The whisky bottle was less than half full. It had probably been standing in the cupboard since last Christmas. He poured a good measure into two glasses, holding one out to Peter.

Peter took the drink from Jim and tossed a drop down, paused to catch his breath, then more slowly took another sip. 'Thanks,' he murmured.

Poor sod, Jim was thinking, watching the colour rise in Peter's cheeks. What on earth had he been thinking about? Bad enough to take a girl down but no need to put her in the family way. You'd think a man like him, been in the Army an' all, would have had more sense. There was only one answer of course, Ella had led him on. She's my sister and a damned good girl most of the time but from what he'd heard and seen for himself she'd been no angel. According to his mum, it had happened here in this house.

When Ella had brought him back she must have known the house was empty and if that wasn't asking for it . . . I'd say our Ella set her cap at him good an' proper. Well, one thing was certain, Jim said to himself, our mum is never going to let him get away without marrying our Ella. He'll be a married man before he knows what's hit him.

He looked across to where his mother was now seated, sipping at her sherry, and he found he was grinning to himself. She was scheming. There was no other word for it. She was wearing that look, a look he knew so well. Mind you, he reflected, she's a damn good mother and no one could say any different. Her life hadn't been a bed of roses but she'd done her best for us children. More so when we were kids, gone out cleaning, even scrubbing doorsteps so that we never went short.

He knew roughly what she was about to suggest. It was all that she'd been able to come up with but her plans were hardly likely to please Peter. That's if he agreed to them!

'Any ideas as to where you're going t' live, the pair of you?' Peggy jumped in, once more on the offensive.

Peter blinked, completely taken unawares. 'Sorry, Mrs James, I hadn't thought that far ahead.'

'Then it's about time you did. Don't suppose you've got much cash to throw around, you wouldn't be living in lodgings if you had.'

Peter fancied that he'd heard a softening creep into Peggy's voice, so he took a deep breath and rushed in. 'Mrs James, I'm here to tell you that I want to ask Ella to come with me tomorrow to see the local vicar, make arrangements for us to be married as soon as possible, before Christmas I hope, if I can get a special licence.'

Peggy smiled for the first time since Peter had entered the room. 'I'm glad to hear it. Very glad.'

Jim grinned, raised his glass and winked at Peter. So far, so good.

Peter drained his glass, then said, 'As to funds, I can't promise what I haven't got. The church fees, the wedding ring, and a couple of weeks' rent in advance, if we can find a flat which we can afford that is, and I'll be cleared out. I am sorry. I was unemployed for months before I came South, with no chance to save. My Dad will help out a bit, I'm sure he will, if I ask him.'

'We can do better than that,' Peggy told him, her tone now much quieter. 'You can both live here.'

'Here, Mum?' Ella cried, her eyes wide in disbelief.

'Seems best t' me,' her mother said, 'for the time being anyway, give you both a chance t' get on yer feet.'

'But where, Mum? There's no room,' Ella whispered in embarrassment.

Peggy ignored her and turned to Peter. 'I've talked it over with Jim, he's been pretty good about everything. Reckons he'll give up his bedroom, move into the boxroom and I'll get a bed-settee for the downstairs front room which will do for me. We can fold it up during the day. That will leave the top two rooms all on their own for you two. We could get on t' the gas company, get them t' fix a gas stove out on the landing, and that way you'll have a little flat all on yer own an' neither me nor Jim will bother you.'

Game set and match, thought Jim, as he watched Peter doing his best to take it all in.

Ella was all smiles. 'Oh, Mum! Jim, would you really squeeze into that little room at the top of the stairs?'

Jim rose from his chair, held up the whisky bottle and grinned at Peter. 'Might as well see this drop off,' he said as he poured them both another drink.

Could have been a lot worse, Peter was telling himself. Ella looked as if she was ready to jump for joy as she threw her arms around his neck and smothered his cheeks with kisses. Disentangling himself, Peter crossed the room to stand in front of Peggy. 'Thank you,' he said, his voice tight with emotion. 'I'll do my best for Ella and the baby.'

Peggy opened her arms and they hugged one another, 'I know you will, lad,' she whispered. 'Everything will work out fine, you'll see.'

Later, as Peter walked back to his lodgings, he felt as though he'd been punched in the stomach. Again he was trying to convince himself that things could have been worse. He smiled, but it was a cynical smile. They could have been better an' all. A damn sight better if only he hadn't been such an idiot.

Rebecca was looking forward to Ella's wedding, and the fact that she was to be the only bridesmaid. Shame that it had to be such a rushed affair. After all the girls' talk and plans that she and Ella had made over the years there was to be no white wedding. Such a pity. Between them, with their mums lending a hand, they could have turned out a couple of beautiful dresses in no time at all. Peggy James wouldn't hear of it.

'White weddings are for virgin brides,' she declared. 'How can you possibly think of entering the church decked out in white? The vicar wouldn't know where t' put his face. He knows well enough you'll be along there soon after the wedding making plans for the christening. You, my girl, want to be thankful that the Reverend Davis is such a good man.'

The wedding was to be the day before Christmas Eve. Then would come Christmas and then . . . Rebecca hugged her arms around her chest and squeezed hard. She couldn't wait. It was going to be the best Christmas present her dad could possibly give her.

He kept telling her not to build her hopes up. She couldn't help it. The chances of her getting this new job might be slight but she was going to go for it, give it everything she'd got. The prospects, if she landed it, would be endless.

When Ella had come out with the fact that she was pregnant and that she and Peter were to be married, she had been down in the dumps. More than that, she had been jealous. Not of the fact that Ella was going to have a baby. Oh no, not for that reason. It was that lads, men if you like, looked twice at Ella and asked her out. It had always been that way. True, lads looked at her, but nothing ever seemed to come of it. It was as if in some way she scared them off.

She'd love to get married, one day. Even have a baby, one day. But not yet. Life was suddenly offering her more. Much more, she hoped. When she was ready to settle down and start a family she wanted it all planned out. Where they would live? Somewhere in a big house. In a nice neighbourhood. In the meantime her dad had come up trumps.

She could recite word for word how it had come about. It had been a dirty dark night and her dad had seemed really relieved to be home safely and the first thing he wanted was to get his boots off. Becky had watched as he'd started to unlace them.

'Here, Becky, pull,' he'd said, holding up his foot, and Becky had pulled off the boot. Her dad had groaned with relief, then wriggled his toes. Together they had repeated the process with the other boot.

'Listen pet, how would you feel about being a waitress?' he had asked. Hardly daring to believe that she had heard him right, Becky had raised her head and looked up into his face. Wonderful, her dad was grinning like the Cheshire Cat.

She laughed and gave him a playful punch before saying, 'You pulling my leg, Dad? Where would I get a job as a waitress?'

Her father wiggled his toes and again sighed with relief. 'Oh, it's heaven t' get me boots off.'

'Dad! Stop mucking about. Are you just teasing me?'

Her father grinned. 'You haven't answered my question.'

'Dad, of course I'd like to be a waitress, I'd like to try my hand at anything so long as it meant I could get away from that laundry.'

'Well, you might just get the chance.'

The look she gave him showed how doubtful she was about that.

'Honest, Becky, I'm doing me best for you. One of my regular travellers, a right city gent, was telling me about J. Lyons & Company. You know, they've got teashops all over the place. There's one at Wimbledon Broadway an' another at Tooting Broadway.'

'I know about them, Dad, but knowing doesn't get me a job with the company. It's not as if I have any experience of waiting on table.'

'Becky, luv, don't try jumping fences till you come t' them. Just listen. I told this gent about you and he's written down the address of Lyons' head office, Cadby Hall it's called, you've to write to them with all particulars and maybe you'll get an appointment to go for an interview.'

'You really mean it, don't you, Dad?' Becky's eyes were now gleaming with excitement.

'Yes,' he nodded, feeling pleased with himself. He hoped it would go well for his Rebecca. She was so full of dreams, so full of spirit. He didn't want a lad coming along and spoiling her future. It was bad enough that it had happened to young Ella. Starting married life in two rooms with a baby on the way, with no money and no prospects was no joke. In his experience poverty soon made short work of love. For his daughter he wanted more.

'You won't hear anything until after the Christmas holidays are all over,' he warned.

'I don't care, Dad. I'll write the letter and then we'll see. Oh, you're a dad in a million,' she'd told him as she flung her arms around his neck.

She'd written the letter, time had passed, five days, each one marked off on the calendar. Then it had come. A buff-coloured envelope, franked on the outside with the one word in block capital letters, LYONS. To her disappointment, the large envelope held only a slip of paper. 'Thank you for your enquiry, we shall be in touch at a later date.'

Nothing to do but wait and hope.

She'd drifted ever since she had left school, kidding herself that life would be so different when she got another job. Had she really tried to change her way of life? She'd applied for two jobs. Two, and then only after having stuck at the Wellington for four years. Now, J. Lyons! It was like dangling a carrot in front of a donkey. For goodness sake stop thinking about it. Daydreaming won't make it any more of a possibility. Please God, let the New Year come quickly. Let's get rid of 1924 and see what 1925 has to offer.

First though, she reminded herself, there was Ella's wedding to be got through and then the Christmas festivities.

Becky was ready to go round to George Road. 'I think I've got everything, Mum, you bring the buttonholes, will you?'

'Yes, luv. Stop fussing, get yerself away and help Ella get ready. Dad an' I will follow when it's about time for the carriages to arrive.' Joyce Russell opened the front door and stood aside to let Rebecca out. 'My God, it's cold,' she said, and shivered. 'Wrap that shawl round your shoulders and wear it to the church an' all. You can take it off and leave it in the porch. I shouldn't wonder if there's no heating on in the church today an' we'll all be left standing there freezing.'

Becky pulled up the collar of her coat and stepped out gingerly. The pavement was slippery with a dusting of snow and the dark sky looked full of more to come. She hoped this was going to be a happy day both for Ella and Peter. The whole of George Road would be on the lookout, watching what was going on. Of course the truth had got out. Ella had to get married. Most of the neighbours were kind and generous with their approval, taking the line that it takes two. As always there were the odd few, discontented bitchy women, who whispered that Ella was no better than she should be. Becky kept telling herself that she wished the wedding could have been under different circumstances but Ella seemed happy enough to start off her married life in a couple of rooms in her mother's house. It wouldn't do for me, she muttered to herself. Unlike Ella, she couldn't see herself settling for so little. The man she'd marry would have to provide her with a lot more. A whole lot more, she decided as she knocked on the front door of the James house.

Two hours of confusion, bickering and reminiscences later, bride and bridesmaid were ready.

'Look at you!' Becky cried. 'You look absolutely wonderful! Being pregnant must suit you.'

Ella was wearing a blue two-piece, a spray of tiny white rosebuds pinned to her shoulder. During the night her long fair hair had been twisted tightly up into strips of wet rag. Freed, the hair had been springy enough to wind upwards into a nest of wide curls. The hat she wore, if it could be called a hat, was a tiny cream-coloured straw shrouded with fine veiling.

'You don't look so bad yerself,' Ella retorted. 'In fact you look so grand the men will only have eyes for you,' she joked, her voice crackling with nervous laughter.

Becky's dress was long-sleeved and simple, a deep blue like the colour of Christmas hyacinths thus complementing the paler shade that the bride was wearing. She held out her arms and clasped Ella close, hugging her gently. 'Get away with you, it's your day today,' she grinned, straightening up and slipping her arm through Ella's. Then she glanced fondly around the bedroom. 'Be strange coming round here after today, this will be yours an' Peter's living room.'

The snow was falling softly and gently and the two grey horses whinnied as Ella's eldest brother handed her up into the carriage. Ronald was home on leave from the Army in order to give his sister away.

The village was bright with Christmas decorations and the lights from the church glimmered through the snowflakes. Ella gasped to see so many people. It was bitterly cold as she stepped down and Ronald hurried her towards the protection of the church porch.

A pretty young woman in a shabby coat called out, 'Good luck, luv.'

An older woman tugged her shawl tighter around her shoulders and muttered, 'She'll need it.'

'There's a good omen!' the cry went up from several different voices and Ella turned to stare. She looked at her brother and they both laughed. Near the churchyard, leaning on the lychgate, was a sweep, his long-handled brushes perched on his shoulder. Two grubby, ragged little boys stood by his side. They wore neither coat nor hats, snow clung to their hair, the whiteness emphasizing their dirty faces. Their jerseys and short trousers were in need of repair and the socks they wore had slipped down to the top of their scuffed boots, thus revealing little legs and knobbly knees that were well smeared with soot.

'Chuck us a tanner for luck, guvernor,' the tallest of the two lads yelled. Ronald grinned widely as he fished in his pocket and a great cheer went up as the lad caught the coin.

Peter waited at the altar, his eyes bright with admiration

as Ella came towards him. Ella had never thought to see Peter looking so handsome; dressed in a dark grey suit, white carnation in his buttonhole, he looked inches taller than usual.

When the ceremony was over they came out to be smothered in confetti and roaring cheers from friends and neighbours. As bridesmaid, Becky stood with the bride and groom to have her photograph taken. Snow still swirled mixed with confetti and Becky thought what a lovely scene it all made.

Ma Turner from the Cosy Café had saved the day by offering to not only hold the reception on her premises but to see to all the catering as well. Invitations to the reception had been restricted to family, near friends and just a few neighbours. Peggy had sent an invitation to Peter's father and his sister and her family and was so pleased that they had all accepted.

The food was great. The party that followed went marvellously.

It was getting on for nine o'clock when Peter said he and Ella were about to leave. There had been no question of a honeymoon, but Peter's father had booked them a room at the Fountain public house for the night. Once inside the room, Ella kicked off her shoes and sat down on the side of the big double bed.

'I'll go down to the bar and get us both a drink, shall I?' Peter asked.

'Oh, luv, I don't want any more alcohol, see if they'd let you have a pot of tea for me.'

'Frightened of getting drunk are you?' he teased, then relenting he pulled her up and put his arms around her. 'We'll have a proper honeymoon one day,' he promised.

'Oh, Peter, what does it matter? It's been a lovely day. I didn't know we had so many friends. I couldn't have asked for better.'

Peter sighed. 'Do you really mean it?'

'Yes, I do. Everything has been lovely,' she declared.

'Well,' he smiled broadly now, 'tell me, how does it feel to be Mrs Peter Tomson?'

'Wonderful,' she told him, throwing herself into his arms again.

'We'll get by,' he assured her softly, running his hand through her hair, letting loose the tight curls. 'I'll get another job, we'll find a place of our own before the baby is born.'

And at that moment he meant every word.

'I love you, Peter,' Ella murmured, cuddling him.

'I love you too and that's all that really matters,' he answered softly.

Chapter Seven

THE FOLLOWING SPRING provided a sharp contrast to the bad winter. Although it was now only May the fields and surrounding gardens looked very dry. Up on the allotments, beyond the fields that belonged to Harry Horsecroft, men toiled, the young ones stripped to the waist, the older ones in shirtsleeves, their braces dangling loose, planting young lettuces and the first of the runner beans. On a browning patch of grass, Becky sat watching her father work. Beside her lay Ella, stretched out in an ancient cane chair.

'Sunday afternoon is supposed to be a time to rest,' Becky murmured, 'still I suppose weekends and evenings are the only chance a lot of the men get to come up here.'

Ella didn't open her eyes, just turned her head to the side. 'Yeah, but it's not work t' most of them though, is it? I know my Peter can't wait to come here. We can never thank your dad enough for speaking up for him an' getting him that plot.'

'It wasn't nothing, he was only too pleased to help, an' Dad says Pete's doing marvellous.'

'Becky, even my mum said these plots are like gold dust. Pete's made up with having this patch of allotment. Money's short as you well know and the veg and stuff he brings down from here make a world of difference. It helps me mum out an' all. Besides, coming here an' laying out like this is a treat for me, won't I be glad when this baby is born. I'm sick t' the teeth of waddling along like a deformed duck.'

Becky threw back her head and laughed loudly. 'Bit overweight for a duck, aren't you?'

'Thanks a bunch!' Ella cried. 'You're great for a girl's morale.'

'Sorry, luv, didn't mean it. Anyway, you've only about another month to go and then you'll have your figure back an' as my mum says, all your troubles will be in your arms.'

'Can't wait. It seems as if I've been this huge size forever,' Ella said as she clutched her swollen stomach and pulled a face.

They fell silent. It was very warm, even under the shade of the umbrella that Peter had fixed up for them. Becky closed her eyes. She hoped for Ella's sake the baby would be born on time. She really was huge. Ella and Peter had coped well these past months. It couldn't have been easy. Ella had worked hard on their two rooms. She'd made the big room into a bed-sitting room and it was ever so pretty. Once again, being handy with her needle had helped a great deal. Remnants of chintz had been used to transform second-hand furniture and besides making all those loose covers, Ella had stitched some really beautiful baby clothes. I don't think I would have settled down so well and accepted the little that Peter had been able to provide, Becky was saying to herself when Ella broke into her thoughts. 'You've never heard from Lyons, have you?'

There was a pause. Becky still kept her eyes closed; she would rather Ella hadn't raised that subject. The fact that she hadn't heard any more was a sore point. The hopes she had built up no longer seemed a possibility. The whole episode rankled. 'No I never did,' she eventually answered.

'Shame,' Ella sympathized. 'The reason I brought the subject up was because of something I read in the paper. Our Jim brought the paper home. He often does. People read them and leave them behind in the railway carriages all the time.'

'So what was it you read? Something about Lyons?'

'Yes, it was. When we go back I'll get you the paper, I said to Pete that I'd save it for you t' see.'

'Just tell me what it said,' Becky pleaded.

'Well, it started off by saying that J. Lyons and Company were transferring their tea, coffee and confectionery production out of London, to a site in Greenford, though their main food supplies will still be distributed to their teashops from Cadby Hall.'

'That's where I wrote to, Cadby Hall.'

'Listen to the rest of it,' Ella chided softly. 'Because the company are so pleased with the way the teashops have been doing, not only in London but up and down the whole country, they have hit on the idea to have more posh places in the West End. They will be ever so grand an' they'll be known as Corner Houses. What d'yer think of that?'

'Sounds great, but not much help to me. Did it say anything about staff?' Becky queried.

Ella raised her head and prodded Becky, 'Yes, I'm coming t' that. There was a picture of a waitress, dressed in . . . well you know, the usual black dress and white apron only somehow the girl looked different and above the illustration it said, "The perfect Nippy".'

'Why Nippy?'

'I dunno, do I. It also said it was going to advertise on hoardings an' buses in the city with messages like, "Let Nippy take care of you", and "Lunch at Lyons".'

'Nothing about staff?'

'Why don't you shut up an' listen t' what I'm telling you?'

'Cos you're taking yer time over it, I'm beginning to think you're writing a book.'

'Right.' Ella raised herself up on her elbows, her face suddenly bright with enthusiasm. 'Now I'll tell you the best bit, Becky, it said the company was about to start a recruiting campaign to find suitable young ladies who are willing to go on a training course.'

Becky let out a cry of triumph, 'Please God, let that mean

they'll be in touch with me. Please, please,' she yelled. Then glancing at Ella she felt her conscience prick her. 'Oh, Ella! I'm so sorry. Did I make you jump? I'm right selfish, aren't I?'

''Course you didn't, don't be so daft,' Ella protested gallantly. 'I hope just as much as you do that they write an' offer you a job, you've been at that crummy laundry quite long enough.'

'Oh, bless you Ella. You really have made my day. I'll be up bright an' early every day now, waiting for the postman. Tell you what, you're such a lovely pal, I'm gonna treat you. What d'yer fancy, I'll get us both an ice cream an' one each for me dad and Peter, and shall it be a bottle of cream soda or would you rather have plain lemonade?'

'Just get the ice cream,' Ella said, lumbering to her feet. 'Yer dad brought two flasks of boiling water with him and I've got some tea, milk and a few biscuits. I'm sure we'd all rather have a cuppa, so I'll make it while you've gone over to the shop.'

Becky hesitated, watching Ella walk towards the wooden hut where her father kept all his gardening tools. From the back Ella looked like an old woman and as she reached the doorway she had to clutch at the frame to heave her bulk over the step. Poor Ella. The sooner this pregnancy was over the better.

A whole week went by without any letter arriving for Becky. She was so tensed up that her mother remarked that were she a clock her spring would have busted by now.

'There's always tomorrow,' Becky kept saying as she watched the postman walk by the house each morning. She was no longer sure whether she longed for the day she might hear from Lyons or no longer expected to. There was so much at stake. She had accepted that Lyons were not going to keep their promise and contact her, then Ella had told her about the newspaper article. Hope had been rekindled. The waiting and wondering were driving her mad. Lyons had said they were going to get in touch at a later date. Surely big firms such as Lyons kept their word?

It was Tuesday of the following week when Becky woke early, at seven, to the sound of the postman's rat-a-tat-tat. A crack in the curtains showed the sky was blue and the sun already bright. There was no wind. It was going to be a very warm day.

It felt as if her heart was in her mouth as she shoved her feet into her slippers, pulled on her cotton housecoat and went downstairs. Her mother was in the kitchen and sounds of her preparing breakfast could be clearly heard. If the truth be told Joyce had already been out into the passage, picked up the letter, seen it was from Lyons and addressed to Rebecca Russell and very furtively had laid it back down on the mat.

Becky gasped as she now picked up the letter, hugged it close to her chest and hoped with all her heart that it contained the news she had been longing for. Should she wait until later to open it? Should Mum be there when she did? Supposing it didn't say what she wanted to hear?

Oh for God's sake, she chided herself. Then, not hesitating any longer, she tore at the flap and withdrew the single sheet of paper.

Joyce Russell had been holding her breath for ages, or so it seemed, as she waited in the kitchen, ears alert to every sound. A great whoop of joy, loud enough to wake the dead, split the silence of the house.

'Oh . . .' Joyce let her breath out in one big gasp. 'Thank Heaven for that,' she cried out loud as Becky burst into the kitchen with a smile on her face that spread from one ear to the other.

'Mum, I'm t' go for an interview in London. I can't believe it.'

'When?' her mother laughed.

'Next Monday, oh Mum, how am I ever going t' get by till Monday?'

Joyce set a cup of tea down on to the table and then went back over to the gas cooker to see to the bacon she had in the frying pan. 'You'll live. Besides, these next few days will give you time to think about what you're going to say and also what you'll wear.'

'Mum, I don't even know how to get to Cadby Hall, the address is in Kensington.'

'Never mind about that now, luv, drink yer tea and go and get yerself washed, breakfast is nearly ready. You can talk t' yer dad tonight, he'll know how to get there. Might even go with you if you ask him nicely.'

'Cor, d'yer think he would? I'd dread the journey on my own. Not too much breakfast, Mum, I'm going to leave early, call at Ella's on me way to work. I've just got to tell her that I've heard at last and that I've got an interview.'

As always the main road was busy at this time in the morning. Everyone rushing to get to work on time, Becky thought, as she hurried along Burlington Road and half-ran down George Road. Using the key on the latch string, Becky opened the door and immediately Peggy James popped her head out from the kitchen and yelled a greeting at her. 'By the look on your face you've had some good news,' Peggy said as she came up the passage wiping her wet hands on her apron.

'I have an' all,' Becky grinned.

'Must be the day for it. Ella's up, she'll tell you.'

Becky flew up the stairs and found Ella sitting reading what looked like an official form.

'Hi yer,' Becky greeted her.

'Crumbs, don't need any telling that you've had good tidings.'

Becky nodded, raised her eyebrows and with a big smile said, 'Guess what, it's been a long time coming but I've got my appointment for an interview with Lyons.'

'Oh, Becky, that's great. I'm really pleased for you,' Ella said, with a catch in her voice. Then she stood up, opened her arms wide and with a twinkle in her eyes, she said, 'Come here an' let me give you a hug.'

It was a few minutes before they drew apart. Rebecca was thinking that Ella was someone special, a good friend, the salt of the earth, when suddenly she remembered what Mrs James had said. 'Your mum said you'd had some good news this morning. Sorry, luv, I was so taken up with my own affairs, come on, tell me.'

Now there was a wide grin on her face and a gleam in her eyes, as Ella told her, 'Peter and I have been offered a house to rent. I'm not sure how it's come about. Peter had already left for work when the post came.' Ella giggled. 'It's not in the best of districts, but at least we'll have room to move about and we won't have to keep telling each other to be quiet, you know . . . when we're in bed together,' she giggled again.

Becky joined in her laughter. 'Marvellous, what a day of surprises, eh? I'm going to be late for work if I don't run, I'll come round tonight and we'll have a good natter then.'

'Yeah, if you're late you might get the sack and you don't want to lose yer job.' It took a minute for the fact that Ella was making a joke to register. They grinned at each other.

'D'you know I am late already so I might as well be hung for a sheep as a lamb. I'll think of some excuse. It will be the first time. How about putting the kettle on and making a pot of tea and you can tell me more about this new place you'll be moving to?'

'Peter hasn't seen the forms yet. He won't like the area.' There was something in Ella's tone that made Becky look up.

'Are you saying there's the possibility he may not want to take the house?'

Ella was on her feet, bending over with difficulty, filling the kettle from a jug of water that stood in the corner. 'He will if I have anything to do with it,' she answered with determination. 'I'm sick an' tired of lugging water up the stairs all the time.'

When the tea was made and they were seated opposite each other at the table, Ella asked, 'Are you looking forward to Monday, Becky?'

To tell the truth Becky felt lighthearted with joy, but she played it down by nodding, 'Of course I am but I won't deny that I'm a little bit frightened.'

'Frightened,' Ella repeated.

'Yes, or maybe apprehensive is a better word, but I'm also excited, excited beyond belief if you really want to know. Just think, this time on Monday I shall be on my way to London.'

Ella gave an amused laugh. 'And when you come home you'll know that you're gonna be a Nippy.'

'Bless you, Ella. Wish I was as sure of it as you are. What's worrying me is the fact that they are not looking for girls to work in South London, in their teashops. This is the West End of London we're talking about. The real city of London. Who knows whether my face will fit?'

Ella leant across the table and laid her hand on Becky's arm. 'Don't put yourself down. You'll take it in your stride. Nothing daunts you. I learnt that when we were kids at school.'

Ella's words cheered her on but they also made her feel that she was getting the best of the bargain. Today both she and Ella had been offered a chance that might open up a new chapter in each of their lives. If she were to get this job with J. Lyons it could be a better chapter than any that had gone before. Would it be such a wonderful opportunity for Eleanor? Only time would tell.

Chapter Eight

PETER TOMSON WAS over the moon. Getting this house was a godsend. Never mind that Mill Street was in a rough area of Kingston, it was a house of their own with a front door that they could close on the world and live their lives as it suited them. God knows he'd been almost at the end of his tether, living in those two rooms. As the only water supply was in the downstairs scullery and the lavatory stood out in the back garden it had been a misery. Bad enough for him, creeping down in the middle of the night to have a pee, doing his best not to wake the house up. Poor old Ella, they had resorted to having a pot under the bed for her.

His mother-in-law, Peggy, had come out on top, one of the best, and Jim, his brother-in-law, had turned out to be an absolute diamond. This didn't alter the fact, though, that he felt he was under everyone's feet all the time and when the baby arrived God knows how they would have managed. Still, that worry was behind them now.

He knew who he had to thank for getting him this place to rent. Tommy Ferguson's mother and father had spoken up for him and Ella and he certainly wasn't going to look a gift-horse in the mouth.

He hadn't let the grass grow under his feet. He had hurried round to see the rent collector the same night the form had arrived and he and Ella had viewed the place the next morning. As they had entered the empty house Ella had sighed heavily. There was so much that needed doing. He hadn't been able to get any time off work but Peggy, neighbours and friends had all pitched in and lent a hand.

Now it was Saturday morning, the sun was shining and Harry Horsecroft's largest horse and cart was outside Peggy James's house. So were half the inhabitants of George Road. Harry had done them proud. The cart was clean, and loads of old blankets and sheets had been provided to cover what few bits and pieces they were taking with them.

A nice oak sideboard and a three-piece suite had been discovered in a second-hand shop and for a shilling extra the owner of the shop had been persuaded to deliver these items direct to Mill Street.

'She can't ride up front with me, it'll be too bumpy, she might get hurt,' Harry said quickly, as Ella made for the front of the cart.

'Well, what am I going to do?' Ella moaned.

Peter gave Jim a sideways glance, and they grinned and nodded at each other. 'Ups-a-daisy,' Ella's brother cried as he and Peter lifted her feet up off the ground. Several men rushed forward to help and Ella found herself suddenly sitting in an armchair high above the pavement in the back of the cart, surrounded by her belongings.

Peter held a clean cloth high and shook it open. 'I'll wrap you in tightly with this, don't want you falling out do we?' Peter smiled at her.

'We won't be too long getting there,' Harry assured her, 'but I've got some canvas strips I could tie you in with if you don't feel safe.'

Ella shook her head. 'I'll be fine,' she said bravely.

'Well, if that's the lot then we're ready to go,' Peter called to Harry.

'Thank Gawd for that,' Harry muttered as he climbed up and took the reins.

Jim looked up at his sister and winked knowingly. 'Mum and I will more than likely be there before you, and Becky and her mum must be there by now so between us we'll soon have that place ship-shape.'

'Thanks, Jim,' Becky murmured, her hands gripping the

arms of the chair tightly as Harry indicated he was ready to move off.

Peggy James smiled happily at her son-in-law. She was glad he had been given the offer of this house. Pity it wasn't a little bit nearer, but then you can't have everything in this life. 'You hold on tight to her now, Peter,' she commanded. 'I don't want nothing happening to my first grandchild.'

Peter grinned as he jumped up to sit beside Ella. 'I'll carry the coal in from now on an' I'll chop the wood but she's going t' have to do all the heavy work like scrubbing the floors,' he told her.

Peggy tossed her head in feigned disgust. 'If I thought you meant it, my lad, I'd have your guts for garters.'

Harry flicked the whip and amid cheers from all the onlookers the horse took its first steps.

Ella bit her lip hard to keep back the tears. This wasn't how her life was meant to be. It was wrong, so wrong. Everything had happened so fast. One minute she was young and fancy-free. Then one night of passion, if you could call it that, and she was married with a home made up of odds and ends and a baby due any time now. The constant fear that the baby might not be perfect never left her. Oh, she would be so glad when it was born. Peter was good and kind but this wasn't what he had wanted any more than she had. It was a good thing he was the strong one. He'd certainly paid the price for letting his feelings get the better of him but he never moaned, and was always ready to comfort her. It was silly to keep dwelling on the past; both she and Peter had acted like a pair of idiots, but it was over and done with. There was no going back.

Perhaps now that they had their own place things would be different, though with rent to pay money would be a darn sight tighter.

You know you might be able to find yourself a job, even if it's only a part-time one, once the baby has been born, she comforted herself.

'We'll be there in a few minutes,' Harry said as he turned his head to look back at them. 'Hope one or the other of your 'elpers has got the kettle on.'

That's if they've got a kettle with them, Ella laughed to herself.

As he pulled the horse to a halt, Harry pushed his cap back, scratched his forehead, and gazed down in amazement. 'Gawd 'elp us, the whole bloody street has turned out t' help you. I can see I ain't gonna be wanted here,' he grumbled to Peter. 'I might just as well clear off up to one of the pubs, quench me thirst an' leave you lot to it.'

Peter looked at the folk gathered outside the empty house and wondered what he had done to deserve such good friends. On the pavement was Becky, her mother, and two young women he knew to be the wives of Becky's brothers. One had a little boy holding on to her skirts, the other one had a youngster in her arms. They each called out a greeting, smiling up at them. The large bulky figure of Tommy's mother, Mrs Ferguson, filled the gateway, and through the open door he saw Becky's two elder brothers, Jack and Tom, leaning against the wall. He suddenly remembered that those two not only lived nearby but they worked in the local tannery. Damn good of them to give up their Saturday to come and help, after all they weren't relations but the two families having grown up in houses that backed on to each other he supposed made a difference.

A shuffling of feet could be heard as the women were edged aside and Becky's two brothers went into action lifting Ella down on to the pavement as if she weighed no more than a bag of feathers.

Ella's mum and Jim arrived and between them the men seemed to make light work of bringing in all Ella's and Peter's belongings. Very soon a motor van drew up outside and their sideboard, settee and two armchairs were carried into what was to be the parlour.

Ella stood looking around for a few minutes before saying,

'I just don't know how to say thanks to all of you. This place was so dirty, thick with dust when Peter an' I viewed it.' Looking across at Joyce Russell she added, 'You and Becky must have been here at the crack of dawn to have got this place looking as it does now. Even the windows are sparkling.'

Peter spoke up. 'I'd like to add my thanks to Ella's. It really has been very good of you.'

Joyce smiled at them. 'Becky and my two daughters-in-law here, Ada and Joan, did most of the cleaning.'

'It weren't nothing,' Ada told them.

''Course it wasn't, our pleasure,' Joan added.

Joyce Russell, always a warm-hearted woman who believed that actions spoke louder than words, felt her heart go out to Ella. She was so grateful that it wasn't her Rebecca who had got herself into trouble. Eleanor, so young, talented, so much to look forward to and now what? Landed here in this two-up, two-down little house and a baby due almost any day. Some prospect when you knew that poor Peter barely earned enough to keep himself, let alone three of them.

So far in all their married life, she and Joe had been lucky. Their two eldest boys were both married with wives that she thought the world of, each had given them a lovely grandson and thank God both sons were in work and had a decent home around them. Fred and Becky were both still at home but they were no problem.

She took a deep breath and quietly said, 'If some of us could unpack one of those tea-chests we might find a kettle and then we can see about making a pot of tea.'

'No need for that,' a voice called and a woman came through the front door which was still propped wide open. She was carrying a heavily-loaded tray. Tall and thin, this young woman had a mass of copper-coloured hair hanging down around her shoulders, but the hair on top of her head was rolled up in two lines of curlers. ''Allo, everyone,' she called, 'thought I'd come and introduce meself, I live next door, I'm Martha Tubman. Bet you can all do with a cuppa, it's me big pot I've brought and there's a bag of doughnuts there, fresh this morning they are.'

'Gawd above, save us, another woman!' Tom Russell muttered to Peter. 'What say we men leave 'em to it, clear off and get something a bit stronger than bloody tea?'

'I'm with you,' came the general answer from the blokes, as mob-handed they made for the street door.

'Won't be long, luv,' Peter said as he bent and kissed Ella's cheek. He was the only one who had the grace to tell the women that they were leaving.

Martha Tubman pulled a face. 'Well, they'll be spoilt for choice,' she commented.

'How's that then?' Joyce Russell asked as she took the heavy tray from Martha.

'Didn't ye know, luv, this street alone can boast two pubs, besides 'alf a dozen round about.' Martha was laughing fit to burst as she set the tea things out on to the table. ''Alfway down we've got the Coconut, got a jolly good darts team 'as the Coconut, but if that don't take yer fancy there's always the Swan at the bottom by the little bridge which looks out over the fields. Mind you, the locals don't call it the Swan, the Gobbling Duck is 'ow they see it.'

'Whatever you care t' call it, that's a right nice 'ouse is the Swan,' Dolly Ferguson declared as she pushed her big bosom up higher and glared at Martha. 'Annie Smith runs that place practically on her own and she don't stand fer no nonsense. Fair with it an' all. We always send our Tommy up to her jug an' bottle bar of a Sunday dinnertime, great drop of mild she sells.'

'I was only saying,' Martha smiled at Dolly. She didn't want to fall out with Dolly Ferguson — she had too much sway in the street to make an enemy of her.

'Yeah well,' Dolly was still glaring, 'ole man Smith has too many irons in the fire t' be of much 'elp in the pub. All the veg an' flower stalls on the market are 'is. Up an' away to

Covent Garden before the streets are aired he is. I like 'is missus, I think she gets a raw deal from 'er old man.'

'Don't we all,' Martha muttered under her breath.

Joyce Russell slipped quietly out into the tiny scullery, having unearthed a kettle from amongst Ella's pots and pans. She filled it at the sink, lit a gas jet and placed it on to boil. They were sure to need some more hot water.

Peggy slipped out behind her, wrinkling her nose as she asked her friend, 'Well, Joyce, what d'yer think? Will my Ella take t' these neighbours? Won't be like we've been over the years, will it? We've had our ups an' downs, good times an' bad an' still we're the best of pals. But then we've always known when t' keep ourselves to ourselves. Seems like this lot round here are in an' out of each other's houses as the mood takes them.'

Joyce swilled the sink round and hung a new dishcloth over the tap, and being the peacemaker that she'd always been, she said, 'Maybe that's to the good. Ella's going to need all the help she can get. With us over at New Malden it must be a weight off your mind, Peggy, to know that Ella's got neighbours she can call on.'

'Yeah, suppose you're right . . . it's just . . . well you know, curlers in their hair this time of a day?'

Joyce grinned. 'Perhaps she's going to play darts at the Coconut tonight.'

Suddenly they were both laughing. 'Come on,' Peggy said. 'It's a long time since I had a doughnut.'

The women sat sipping their tea and Becky was feeling comfortable and relaxed, pleased that from now on things might work in Ella's favour. The house, now that they'd all helped to clean it, wasn't half as bad as she'd expected and Ella seemed much more contented. Although she was huge and heavy, Ella's face had a bloom to it that only happy pregnant women seem to acquire. Her blue eyes were clear and bright and her fair hair had lost none of its lovely sheen. Becky couldn't help thinking to herself that if Ella should give birth to a little girl it would be nice if the baby took after Ella in looks. A fair-haired, fresh-complexioned little mite toddling around the place would do wonders for the morale of both Ella and Peter, not to mention everyone else.

Becky finished her tea and stood up. 'If you're ready, Mum, I'd best get going. I've loads I need to be doing. I'll see you,' she called across to Ada and Joan. Then getting down on to her hands and knees to where her two little nephews were playing on the floor she cuddled them each in turn. ''Bye Ronnie,' she said, and tickled baby Joey. 'I'll see you both on Sunday when you come for yer tea with yer Gran. Be good boys.'

Ella got slowly to her feet, 'I'll come to the door with you. Thanks ever so much, both of you, for all your help.' Then, leaning towards Becky, she put her arms around her and it was then that she broke down. 'I'll miss you so much,' she whispered, the tears trickling down her cheeks.

'And I'll miss you, too.'

They hugged one another, each squeezing the other tight. 'Don't be a stranger, will you?' Ella pleaded.

'Don't be daft. Of course I won't be,' Becky hastened to assure her. Then, disentangling herself, she brushed quickly at her own eyes and added, 'The way we're carrying on anyone would think you'd moved a million miles away. I'll be over more often than you think, after all you have promised I can be godmother to your baby.'

'Who else but you? See you soon.' Ella gave her a slight push. ''Bye for now.'

Becky hurried to join her mother, only turning once to wave to Ella who was still standing out on the pavement.

Chapter Nine

THE OPEN-TOP BUS jerked its way through the morning traffic and the crowded, summery streets of London.

Inside Becky sat next to her father. During the train journey up from Raynes Park she had been anxious and unsure of herself. It would be all too easy for her to fluff this interview. She wanted this job with Lyons so badly, she would make every effort to answer questions correctly. But what if she didn't make it? What if the outcome was rejection? To be told that she was unsuitable to be a waitress would be too embarrassing for her to bear.

All the same, as the bus turned into Kensington High Street her spirits lifted. It was a lovely June day, sunny and warm with only puffy cotton-wool clouds in the bright blue sky.

'Nearly there,' her father said, squeezing her hand tightly.

Joe Russell felt a proud man as he saw the look of admiration a fellow passenger was giving his daughter. She deserved it. She was a lovely young nineteen-year-old lass, still small, slim and dainty and today she was dressed up to the nines. Rebecca's shining hair was coiled up at the back of her head, and she wore a dark grey suit with a crisp white cotton blouse. Black shoes and black stockings completed the outfit which made her look sensational: smart, businesslike and intelligent.

'This is our stop,' Joe said, leaping to his feet and holding out his hand to Becky.

The bus ground to a halt, and they stepped down on to the pavement.

Afterwards, Rebecca could never remember which direction they took or how suddenly they were outside, looking up at Cadby Hall. Confronted by such a great building, she began to wonder what she had let herself in for.

'I'll take meself off, have a bit of a look around,' her father said softly as he bent his head and placed a kiss on the side of her face. 'Remember, we're all rooting for you, stay calm an' you'll be fine. Come through with flying colours, I know you will. I'll be around, waiting, when you come out.'

'Thanks, Dad.' Becky hugged him, then quickly turned and climbed the stone steps which led up to the main entrance.

A burly looking man in a braided uniform stepped forward. 'Morning, Miss,' he said, touching the peak of his cap with a forefinger. 'Here for an interview, are you?' he asked. Rebecca nodded and smiled.

'Top of the stairs, can't miss the room, several young ladies waiting,' he told her.

Rebecca wasn't too happy about the several other girls. I only hope there are a good many vacancies to be filled, she was muttering to herself, feeling the relief of actually having made it this far.

The room was crowded, or so it seemed, as she pushed open the door. Heavy leather furniture and wonderful draped curtains hung from the tall windows. Every inch of wall space was taken up by chairs on which were seated young women. 'There's room for you 'ere beside me,' a quiet voice called to Becky.

'Thank you,' she answered as the young lass slid further along the sofa and she squeezed in to sit beside her.

Ten minutes ticked by, but nothing happened. Most of the girls had begun to fidget and Becky was thinking that were they to be seen one at a time she would be here all day. Then the door clicked open and the sound of stiff skirts could be heard as a formidable lady walked to the centre of the room. She clapped her hands together and then such silence settled over the room that one could have heard a pin drop. This was a lady with authority and obviously someone to be obeyed. She wore a wide-skirted black dress so long that it barely showed her ankles. A heavy white lace collar was the only decoration. From beneath the hem of the dress protruded dainty black shoes with three straps, brilliantly polished, and to Becky's way of thinking her feet looked far too small for such a tall lady. But it was the face above the lace collar that stopped Becky's heart from thumping. It was the sweetest, kindest face with a short nose and pale pink cheeks. Her eyes were unusual, soft grey, and although looking into them Becky felt their owner would brook no nonsense, at the same time they gave her the feeling that if you played fair by her then you would be all right. Her thick dark hair had been expertly cut into a fashionable style.

'Good morning, ladies,' the lady said. Without waiting for a reply she went on, 'You will be split into three groups; that way we shall get through the interviews more quickly. Your names will be called in alphabetical order.' She had a musical voice, soft and gentle, and to the surprise of all the girls she smiled and wished them all good luck before leaving the room.

Becky settled herself for what she thought would be a long wait. Clasping her handbag on her lap with both hands she rested her head back against the top of the sofa and closed her eyes. She felt a nudge in her side.

'Shouldn't think we'll 'ave to wait that long.'

Becky opened her eyes and turned to face the girl who had moved along to give her a seat. 'I hope not,' she answered.

'I'm May, May Stevens. What's your name?'

'Rebecca Russell, though most folk an' all my friends call me Becky.'

'Well I'm pleased t' meet you Becky, an' I 'ope you do well.'

'Likewise.' Becky grinned, instantly deciding that she liked this friendly person who had thick straight reddish hair and green eyes.

'Where d'you come from, Becky?'

'You mean where do I live?'

'Yes, not round 'ere that's for sure. Not even in London I'd take a bet.'

'Well, you would be right,' Becky agreed. 'I was born in New Malden, which is near Kingston-upon-Thames, lived there all my life.'

'No wonder you talk so nicely,' May murmured. 'Me, I come from the East End of London. Born and bred on the other side of the river. 'Ere, what did you think of that woman? She seems a bit stuck-up t' me, though I suppose we shouldn't judge a sausage by its skin, wait an' see, eh? Might turn out t' be all right.'

'I shouldn't worry too much,' Becky tried to reassure her new-found friend. 'By the way, not everyone speaks nicely where I come from, a good many originate from London, and as for that woman seeming to be a bit offhand, we'll both think she's the cat's whiskers if she gives us a job.'

May put her hand over her mouth to smother her giggles. 'You're dead right there, Becky.'

The girls had been called three at a time, and from what Becky had been able to gather, outside in the corridor they were sent in three different directions. Not one had returned to this waiting room. She sighed deeply, wishing that her turn would come soon. She longed to get it over and done with, whatever the outcome.

For the umpteenth time the door opened, and this time a young man stood in the open doorway. Tall, slim, fair-haired, dressed in a dark suit, waistcoat buttoned over an immaculate striped shirt, he smiled and called, 'Miss Russell, Miss Smithson and Miss Stevens.'

'That's us,' May muttered. 'Best of luck, Becky.'

'You too, May,' Becky whispered as they followed Miss Smithson out of the room.

May and the other young lady were sent off, while Becky was requested to accompany the slim man who had summoned them. Becky's heart was pounding and, as if he sensed this, the man turned, and looked down at her, smiling.

'I'm Robert Matthews. There's nothing to be afraid of,' he said, 'this interview is all very informal. It serves to sort the wheat from the chaff.'

Well, that statement did nothing to reassure her!

Walking down a corridor, Becky decided this Robert Matthews was not much older than herself. There was something about him that gave her the impression that he was shy. His movements were gentle, his voice soft and kindly as he opened a door and bid her enter.

The first lady they had seen sat behind a square table, flanked on one side by a gentleman whose face had more whiskers than Becky had ever seen and now Robert Matthews, having guided Becky to an armchair, went behind the table and took the empty seat on her other side.

Looking up from a sheaf of papers that lay in front of her, the lady smiled. 'How d'you do, Miss Russell, my name is Florence Nicholls, the gentleman on my left,' she indicated Mr Whiskers, 'is Mr Fairbrother and Mr Matthews, I'm sure, has already introduced himself.'

Becky relaxed. It was going to be all right. She wasn't so sure about 'Whiskers', he frowned a lot, but the other two were friendly.

By the time the clock on the wall had moved on twenty minutes, Rebecca, as they had chosen to call her, had been closely questioned by this extraordinary trio. And finally they seemed satisfied.

'Very well, Rebecca,' Florence Nicholls spoke kindly, 'if you wouldn't mind waiting just a little longer.'

Robert Matthews was on his feet. 'I'll show you where to go, refreshments are being served.'

Becky's skin was crawling with excitement. At least they hadn't rejected her out of hand. They were even going to give her refreshments. The quiet Robert Matthews was holding another door open for her and ushering her into a light and sunny room and then he was gone.

This smaller room was crowded with about a dozen young ladies and bustling with activity. It smelled of mouth-watering food and fresh coffee. May Stevens spied Becky at once, rose to her feet, and came across the room saying, 'Oh Becky, you made it as well, I'm so glad.'

Becky gawped at her. 'Being in here, does that mean we have been given a job?'

'Well I would think so, wouldn't you? I saw some of the girls leaving the building, not everyone got shown into this room. Anyway, let's go and get somethink to eat, it's all free, come on.'

'Cor,' Becky exclaimed as they each took a plate and cast their eyes over the refreshments that were being offered. 'Isn't all this grand?'

Two very young men were serving the coffee. 'Find yourselves a seat at one of the tables and we'll bring your drinks over,' they told the girls. The sandwiches and the hot coffee were delicious. Soon Becky leant back in her chair and glanced around the room. All the girls there were what she would call willowy. In the waiting room earlier there had been a couple of dumpy lasses, even one who could only be described as fat. It didn't look as though they had been selected.

The tables were being cleared and Becky was beginning to wish that someone would come and tell them exactly what was happening. From the snatches of conversation she had heard going on around her most of the young ladies seemed confident that they were going to be waitresses for Lyons. Becky wished that she felt as cocksure.

Finally the door opened and much to Becky's surprise, Mr Fairbrother, or Mr Whiskers, as she had fixed him firmly in her mind, was standing in the centre of the floor.

'Ladies,' he said loudly, and Becky thought how much younger he looked standing up. He was tall and broad with it. 'I am very pleased to be able to announce that each of you has been selected to take part in a training scheme.'

May Stevens leant forward in her chair and winked at Becky while sounds of relief and delight were coming from all corners of the room.

Unhurried, Mr Fairbrother outlined what the course of training would entail and told them it would last for a period of three weeks.

'It will take place here in London and for that period you will stay as guests of Lyons. Your board and lodging will be free. Does that present a problem for any of you?'

There was much shaking of heads.

'Good. At the end of your training, if you all measure up to our expectations, as I feel sure you will, you will be measured for your uniforms. Now, have you any questions you would like to ask me?'

Becky felt there was a hundred and one things she would have liked to ask but like all the other applicants she kept her lips tightly together.

'Very well,' Mr Whiskers' deep voice now sounded a whole lot more kindly. 'You will each receive a letter within the next couple of days which will set out accurately the conditions of employment, when and where you are to report to and for what period of time you will be given this training. At the end of the course a decision will be made as to which Corner House you will be assigned to. So, it only remains for me to wish you every success in your newly-chosen profession and I look forward to meeting you all again in the very near future.'

Becky was finding it hard to believe. She was going on a training course which hopefully would end with her working at a Lyons Corner House in the West End of London.

'Yippee,' May Stevens whispered in Becky ear, 'I'll be looking forward t' seeing you. Can't wait. D' you feel the same?'

'Of course I do,' Becky smiled. 'But right now I'm busting, I need to spend a penny.'

'Gawd luv yer,' May exclaimed. 'Ain't you got eyes in

your head? The ladies is right over there in that corner. It was the first place most of us made for when we got put in 'ere. It was that or pee our knickers.'

Becky was on her feet and making a beeline for the toilet, thinking as she went, there won't be a dull moment on this course if May is around. She certainly calls a spade a spade.

'That's better,' Becky said aloud as she came out of the cubicle. She washed her hands, inspected her face in the mirror above the washbasin, dabbed her powder puff over her nose, faintly outlined her lips with her new pale lipstick and went back to find her new friend.

Outside in the corridor Robert Matthews was talking to Mr Fairbrother. Both men nodded and smiled their goodbyes. Becky was thoughtful as she smiled back. That Robert Matthews was a nice young man, she decided. With his thick mop of fair hair and light blue eyes there was something appealing about his manner and his smile was certainly attractive, though somehow she still had the feeling that he was very shy.

Leaving the building together, May kept up a constant flow of chat. It was just as if she and Becky had known each other for years.

'There's my dad,' Becky called brightly and Joe Russell immediately sent up a prayer of thanks. Just looking at her he knew his little girl had done it and he was so pleased for her. 'Dad, this is May, May Stevens, we are going on a training course together.'

Joe returned the broad grin that May was giving him and surveyed the pair of them. 'So, you've been living it up in there while I've been wearing me boot leather out worrying over you.'

The laughter of the two girls was spontaneous.

'Can I buy you a drink of some kind?' Joe asked May.

'No thanks, Mr Russell, kind of you t' ask but we've been well fed an' watered by Joey Lyons, ain't we Becky? In any case I want to get home, tell me mum all about it. I'll see you soon then,' she said to Becky, 'I'm ever so glad we met up. Nice t' think we'll be training together, ain't it?'

'It certainly is,' Becky quickly agreed, 'I was thrilled to see your friendly face. See you soon.'

Becky and her father watched May depart and then Joe opened his arms. 'Who's a clever girl then?' he teased as he pulled his daughter close to his chest, and disregarding the passers-by he held on to her, tears of joy dimming his vision.

The train snaked its way out of the station, past all the blackened smoke-stained factories and warehouses and over the bridge, giving Becky a delightful view of the dear old Thames. Much busier up here than it is in Kingston, she mused, just look at all the boats. Seems funny that it is the same river, such a distance away, Becky was thinking to herself as she watched her father stand up and place his bowler hat up in the rack above his seat, unfurl his newspaper and settle down to read it in comfort. Soon she would be coming back to London. Learning how to wait on table, leaving home, her parents and her brothers. Suddenly her hopes had become reality.

Would she be happy? You'll be barmy if you're not, she chided herself drowsily as her eyelids closed and the wheels of the train seemed to be saying, soon be home, soon be home.

She wanted to see the smile on her mother's face when she told her all the news.

Chapter Ten

BECKY ARRIVED IN Kingston at just after six on Tuesday evening. She was tired out. She had given a week's notice at the Wellington Laundry first thing yesterday morning. It hadn't been accepted gracefully. It seemed for the short time she was to remain there as an employee she was to be given every hard task that was going. Mrs Bradford had tried to ease the situation, to no avail. With four more days to go she was fed up. Turning into Mill Street she saw that Peter was standing in the small front garden watching her approach.

Becky didn't like Mill Street. It reeked of poverty. Even the men who did have jobs only earned a pittance from the factories hereabout. Jobs on the building sites and on the river were few and far between and the women seemed to be everlastingly pregnant. What future was there for these children? Some lovely countryside lay within easy distance yet the kiddies were always in the street. It was gone six and still ragged snotty-nosed boys played marbles in the gutter while little girls skipped, their ropes stretched across the middle of the road.

The main aim of their fathers appeared to be get home, eat their meal and spend the evening in the pub.

Becky quickened her footsteps and tried not to think too much about what would happen to Ella if she had to live here for any length of time.

'Hello, Becky, you look all in. Come on inside an' see what a lovely surprise we've got for you,' Peter said as he led the way indoors.

Though the outside of the terraced house was nothing

to write home about, it was meticulously neat inside. The curtains were bright and fresh, the fire-range had been recently black-leaded and polished until you could see your face in it. But the furniture was shabby and the rugs showed very much that they weren't new.

Becky had to stifle a sigh. How she wished that things could be so much better, both for Ella and for Peter. They hadn't got off to a very good start in their married life.

She turned to face Peter. He was smiling broadly, looking all bright-eyed and bushy-tailed.

'Something's happened!' Becky exclaimed, her tiredness forgotten.

'It sure has! Ella's had the baby. I'm a father.' His voice brimmed with excitement.

'When? How is Ella? Is the baby all right?' Becky's questions came out in a rush, all jumbled up.

Peter laughed out loud, but his expression changed as he told her, 'Ella's fine now, she's sleeping, she had quite a rough time of it.'

Becky shook her head in dismay. 'Poor Ella. You still haven't told me about the baby, boy or girl?'

Peter smiled, remembering. 'A little girl, so tiny, I held her soon after she was born.'

Becky took hold of his hand and squeezed it tightly. 'Tiny, you say? She is all right, isn't she?'

'Yes, yes, she's perfect. Ella's mum was here, she's only just gone. She said Eleanor was only small when she was born. Shall I make us a cup of tea? You look as if you could do with one, or would you rather go straight up to see Ella?'

'You said she was sleeping, let's leave her for a while. I certainly could use a cuppa, I came straight from work. I'll make it.'

'You certainly won't. I've been home all day, pacing the floor mostly, you set yer bones down in that chair and I won't be a jiffy.'

Becky did as she was told, thinking about all the years that she and Ella had spent growing up together. When they were small they had the whooping cough at the same time. Then the measles, later the mumps. When it was freezing cold they had run like wild deer to school and during the hot summers the riverbank had been their playground. With their frocks tucked in their knickers they had paddled and splashed in the muddy water. Somedays they walked out to the park taking a bottle of homemade lemonade and bread and jam with them. As soon as they got there they rode on the swings. Now Ella was married. Nineteen and a mother already. Don't get maudlin, she chided herself, just remember how great it was to have such a good friend to grow up with.

Peter came in with the tray of tea and Becky poured them each a cup. She drank her own tea scalding hot, gulping it as if she had been dying for a drink.

Putting down her empty cup she grinned, and the sight made Peter ask, 'What's tickling you?'

'The fact that the baby is a girl. Suppose you'd have preferred a boy but a girl is what I was hoping for.'

'No,' Peter was quick to protest. 'I didn't mind boy or girl just so long as Ella was all right.'

'That's good. Me, I've already got two little nephews, it will be great having a little girl around. Can't wait to see her.'

'No sooner were the words out of Becky's mouth than there came a wailing from upstairs.

'There you are, yer see, the baby is demanding that we go up and pay her some attention.' Peter grinned.

This time Becky led the way as they tiptoed up the stairs to Ella's bedroom. Opening the door, Becky smiled in wonder as she said, 'Ella, we thought you were sleeping. How come your sitting up?'

Ella shrugged. 'I have been asleep for ages, now I feel fine.'

Becky crossed the room, sat down on a chair that had been drawn up beside the bed and took Ella's hand in hers.

'You clever old thing, Peter tells me things didn't go so well to start off with though.'

'Well, the midwife took her time getting here, and me mum did most of the delivering. About all old Marie Wilson had to do was clean me an' the bed up.'

Becky felt an absurd lump in her throat hearing Ella tell how she had given birth. A great rush of affection for her friend washed over her.

'Well, where is this little miracle?'

At that point Peter straightened up from bending over the wicker basket and began doing a little dance. 'She smiled at me,' he declared.

'Get on with you,' Ella grinned, 'she's too tiny to smile, it's probably just wind.'

'You, my darling wife, may believe what you like but I know our daughter just smiled and told me she is happy to have us for her parents. So there!'

Ella laughed with delight; her relief at the birth being over and the fact that Peter was acting like a dog with two tails made her feel really happy. She nodded at her husband and he, reading her message, gently lifted the baby out of the basket and placed her in Becky's arms. 'Say hello to your Aunt Rebecca,' he crooned.

Becky looked down into that tiny pink little face and smiled. 'My, look at her tiny fingers, she's beautiful.' Her voice was thick with emotion.

'We're going to call her Margaret after my mum. And we won't let it get shortened to Peggy.' Ella lay back, her face showing exhaustion. 'You promised you would be her godmother, Becky, does that still stand?'

'You bet your sweet life it does,' Becky answered, snuggling the tiny baby up close to her chest.

'I'll go an' get us some fresh tea,' Peter said, feeling he ought to leave the two girls alone for a while.

'Becky? While Peter's not here can I ask you something?'
Becky nodded. 'Of course, anything.'

'If anything ever happens to me, will you watch out for my baby?'

'Ella! Again the answer is yes, of course, but what the hell do you imagine is going to happen to you? You've done so well. Mother and baby doing fine, what more could you ask for?'

'I know all that,' Ella pleaded, 'it's just that Peter isn't in the best of health and, well, times are difficult and I don't want my baby to have to go short of too many things just because we had to get married before we'd even saved a penny.'

'Becky, we've been friends from the day we were born and I promise that if ever the time should come I will see to it that baby Margaret has everything that's in my power to give her, but nothing is going to happen to you. So, stop nattering and start thinking about something more cheerful. Now, sit up again, I can hear Peter coming with your tea.'

The frown vanished from Ella's face and in its place came the sweetest smile. 'Becky, I knew I could rely on you.'

Holding the door open wide for Peter to come in with the tea tray, Becky was hoping she might never live to regret the promise she had just made.

Every day for the past week Becky had come to Kingston. Now she and Ella sat side by side on the windowsill out front in the small front garden staring down at baby Margaret lying in her pram. She was asleep on her stomach, tiny hands balled into fists. As the two girls looked at her, each was filled with love. She was awfully small, which made her mother and her 'Aunt' Becky feel very protective.

Becky put out a finger and stroked the downy head. She had the same fair hair as her mother and the same deep-set blue eyes. To be honest, though she wouldn't admit it aloud, Becky could see nothing of Peter in her. She couldn't wait for her to get just a little bit bigger. She wanted to buy her a pretty dress and maybe a lacy jacket as well. She was thrilled to have a goddaughter.

'Don't look now,' Ella turned her head and whispered, 'but Tommy Ferguson's mother is making a beeline for us.'

Dolly Ferguson heaved her great bosom up with one forearm and with the other hand she patted her thick greying hair, doing her best to fix a flyaway strand behind her ear. Then opening the iron front gate she pushed it so hard it clanged as it hit the low fence.

''Allo you two, enjoying the fine weather? An' how's the baby?' she panted, her breath laboured as if she had walked miles rather than a few yards up the street.

'We're all fine, Mrs Ferguson', Ella answered.

'Well shove up a bit so's I can put me bum on yer windowsill, take the weight off me feet, they're playing merry 'ell wiv me this morning.'

Becky nodded sympathetically and immediately got to her feet, knowing full well it would be a tight squeeze for the three of them to perch side by side.

'Come on Mrs Ferguson, settle yourself alongside Ella and I'll lift baby Margaret out of the pram so's you can have a good look at her.'

'Apart from your feet are you keeping fairly well, Mrs Ferguson?' Ella enquired.

'Yeah, me legs play me up an' all but ain't much good moaning is it? All that apart, it's about time you two girls started calling me Dolly, all this Mrs Ferguson gets on me nerves, so let's 'ave less of it. All right?'

''Course it is, Dolly,' they said in agreement, grinning at each other.

'How's Tom?' Becky asked, thinking it was up to them to make conversation.

''E seems all right an' I've got quite a bit of news t' tell yer. First off 'e's got anuvver job an' that seems to 'ave brought 'im round to getting things settled in 'is mind.'

'Oh, I am pleased,' Becky said, patting Dolly's arm.

'Me too,' Ella agreed, smiling. 'Tell us all about it. Where's he working now then?'

'E's got in at the tannery, I think one of your brothers spoke up fer 'im Becky,' Dolly answered as she took a handkerchief from the pocket of her flowered overall and wiped her nose. 'I'm ever so grateful, wait till I see your brothers, buy 'em a pint I will, that's fer sure. 'Course, I don't know yet what 'e'll be doing there,' Dolly sighed. 'My Tommy's got a good 'ead on 'is shoulders an' 'e's not afraid of 'ard work, though I've got t' admit he's not always quick on the uptake. 'E worked 'ard at the Wellington though. Earned every penny they ever paid 'im. Trouble was, they never appreciated 'im, put on 'im day in day out, an' when this offer came along I sez t' him, you take it lad, about time you got a break in this life.'

Both girls murmured their approval and Becky said, 'I'm sure my brothers were only too pleased to help. Everyone likes your Tommy.' She stopped rocking the pram and added, 'Would you like to hold the baby? Ella won't mind, will you, Ella?'

'Leave the baby be a minute cos there's something that's worrying me a bit an' I'd like you two youngsters t' tell me what yer think about that Mary Marsden.' This last request had been said in a quiet voice, which was most unusual for Dolly.

Ella turned and laid her arm across Dolly's broad shoulders. 'Don't you like Mary? We all thought she and Tom were kinda made for each other.'

Dolly heaved a great sigh. 'Yer right, they are good fer each other but marriage! Well, I don't know about that, an' I'm worried. She's got 'erself a job in the canteen of the tannery an' now it's like they are living in each other's pockets. All I 'ear when my Tommy gets in of an evening is Mary this an' Mary that, can't do no wrong she can't.'

'What's this about marriage?' Ella asked, curiosity getting the better of her.

'Ain't 'e mentioned it t' yer?'

Ella shook her head. 'I only see Tom as he walks past and

then only if I'm in the front room. Baby keeps me busy now. Sorry.'

'What about you, Becky? There was a time when your name was on my Tommy's lips all the time.'

Becky thought hard before answering. 'That's true Dolly. Tom an' I have always been great friends. He helped me out a lot when I first started in the laundry. But your Tom left the Wellington about three weeks ago and I no longer work there now so I don't get t' see him so much and I don't hear all the gossip.'

'What d'yer mean, you left the Wellington an' all?'

'That's right Dolly, I gave a week's notice and I finished there last week.'

'But what yer gonna do, gal? Jobs don't grow on trees.'

'I'll tell you what our Rebecca is going to do,' Ella said, smiling at Dolly. 'She's going to work for Joey Lyons!'

'What, yer mean in the tearooms?' Dolly's eyes were wide with wonder.

'Not exactly,' Becky said in a quiet voice, 'I hope I'm going to be a waitress in one of the Lyons Corner Houses.'

'Gawd above gal, what d'yer mean you 'ope? You ain't given up a good job before yer got another one, 'ave yer?'

Strictly speaking I suppose that is what I have done, Becky was saying to herself. Aloud she said, 'It's like this, Dolly, I've been accepted to go on a three-week training course. It starts in about ten days' time and hopefully at the end of the training I shall be told that I am capable of being a fully fledged waitress.'

'Oh, you will, you will, of course you will,' Ella burst out. 'She went to London for the interview, Dolly, an' they told her ever so much about what she'll be doing.'

'Good luck ter yer, Becky,' Dolly exclaimed, amazement in her voice. ''T'ain't everyone that gets a chance like that.'

'Thanks, Dolly. To get back to Tom and the question of him an' Mary getting married, has he told you that they are seriously considering it?'

Dolly wriggled her bottom and untied the tapes that held her pinafore, then loosening it she let out a big breath. 'That's a bit better. Not in so many words he ain't said so, she's either round my place or he's round her 'ouse every day of the week an' I 'ear bits and pieces of news that they let drop. My Tommy's certainly taken with 'er and I 'eard her telling 'im they'd 'ave t' go to church soon. T' see the vicar an' put up the banns is the only thing I could think of.'

'I shouldn't worry too much,' Becky tried to reassure her. 'Tommy's old enough to take care of himself an' one thing's for sure, he knows his own mind.'

'If that's the case,' Dolly said, sighing, 'why don't he come out in the open an' tell me t' me face that 'e's leaving 'ome an' getting wed? Surely I should be the first t' know.'

Ella was thinking to herself that it was nearly time for her to feed the baby and if she didn't make a move Dolly would have them wasting the whole morning.

'Well, I for one don't think it would be a bad thing if Mary and Tom do decide to get married. After all Dolly, he's been so well looked after by you all his life he must think he's found a good one in Mary or he wouldn't even be considering it. Would he?'

'I agree,' Becky said, 'Mary might well turn out to be the making of Tom. I hope we both get an invite to the wedding.'

Dolly Ferguson slid her backside off the windowsill, flinched as her swollen feet touched the ground, bent low over the pram and made clucking noises at the baby. Then, sighing heavily, she made her way out of Ella's front garden. It was all right for those two lasses to talk about getting married and living happily ever after. She would be left on her own but what would anyone care about that? Mary Marsden would be the one that was getting the best of the bargain. I only hope she doesn't get too possessive towards Tom otherwise I will have to tell her where she gets off. Don't want no uppity miss for me daughter-in-law.

Ella put the finishing touches to the pram, checked that baby Margaret was lying safely on her side and she and Becky were ready to set off on their stroll. As they walked out into the sunshine they were both grinning. Dolly's words were still ringing in their ears.

'You know what it is that's getting Dolly's goat, don't you?' Ella asked, grinning. 'It's the fact that poor Tommy is standing on his own two feet for a change. That mother of his would still be taking him to the lav an' wiping his backside if she had her way.'

Becky gave her a broad smile. 'Don't need no telling, do I? But I like Mary, I was thrilled to bits when your Peter told me about her and Tom getting together, and when I met her I thought how well-suited the pair of them were.'

'Not to mention the fact that she was doing you a favour,' Ella answered, giving Becky a sly lopsided look.

'Yeah, well, there was that,' Becky admitted, 'got him off my back. Still, honestly, you have to agree those two were made for each other.'

Ella raised her eyebrows. 'I'm not disputing that for a moment. As a matter of fact I think that girl is the best thing that could have happened to Tom but I wasn't going spell it out for his mother. You're all right, but I've got to live in the same street as her an' believe you me Dolly Ferguson can make her presence felt.'

This set the pair of them off giggling, much to the amusement of passers-by as they turned into the High Street. Suddenly Becky reached out and covered Ella's hand on the handle of the pram. 'Mary Marsden is coming across the road,' she said softly.

Ella put her other hand on Becky's shoulder and whispered, 'Let's be nice to her.'

'Oh I am so glad to meet up with you two,' Mary said as she smiled shyly and looked into the pram. 'Ain't she tiny, I wish she was awake so's I could see her properly.'

Ella bent and pulled the loose covering back a little, 'She

won't sleep much longer, have you got time for a cup of tea? We were just going to treat ourselves, weren't we Becky?'

'You mean I can come with you? Oh, that would be ever so nice. I'll buy you both a cake if yer like.'

The three of them sat in the café, sipping their tea and nibbling Chelsea buns which Mary had insisted upon. Suddenly the baby yawned and her little fists beat the air.

Ella bent and lifted her from the pram. 'So, you're awake are you, my little precious,' she crooned as she rocked her baby tenderly in her arms. 'Would you like to hold her, Mary?'

Mary's eyes widened. 'Would you trust me? I would be ever so careful.'

'Here.' Ella placed the baby gently into Mary's outstretched arms. 'She won't break,' she assured her.

Ella and Becky exchanged glances as they watched the expression on Mary's face. 'Oh, she's the most beautiful little baby I've ever seen. You want to know something? One day I hope Tom and I will have a baby.' Having made that statement she smiled wanly before quietly adding, 'That's if Tom's mother will ever let him marry me.'

Becky reached out and took Mary's hand in hers. 'If you and Tom love each other I'm sure nothing will stop you from getting married,' she said softly.

'Me and Tom do love each other. We want to be together all the time.' Mary's eyes brimmed with tears.

Becky handed her a handkerchief and Ella said, 'Here, let me take the baby, you can hold her again later.'

Becky patted Mary's shoulder. 'Don't get upset. Have your parents been to see Mrs Ferguson?'

'No. Me mum's a bit afraid of her an' me dad says he wants no rows with her.'

'Maybe if they asked her to your house for tea one day when Tom is coming to see you, that might do the trick. At least that way they'd get to know each other,' Ella spoke up, playing peacemaker.

'Now that is a good idea,' Becky laughed. 'Look at it this way, Tom's mum might be a big woman but even she can get frightened and lonely. She may be thinking that if Tom marries you she'll be all on her own. Never seeing either of you.'

'Crikey, it wouldn't be like that. Honest it wouldn't. I wouldn't expect Tom t' neglect his mum. I'd see he didn't.' Mary sniffed and rubbed her eyes.

Becky winked at Ella before saying. 'Mary, you're a good girl. Why don't you go an' see Tom's mum on your own, tell her what you've just told us and then when the date is set, just make sure you invite us to the wedding.'

Mary put her head to one side and stared at them with a funny look on her face. 'Are you 'aving me on?'

'Of course we're not,' Becky hastened to soothe her. 'Ella and I have both said we've seen the change in Tommy since you an' him have been going out together, everybody has. We think you make a lovely couple, an' if you can't win Mrs Ferguson round to that way of thinking then she must be blind.'

Mary stared at Becky in disbelief. 'I wish I could believe you. I told you the first time I met you, I ain't never made many friends an' now, well . . .'

'Now you've got us,' Ella butted in. 'You do as Becky says, have a talk with Tom's mum and get your parents to do the same, you'll see, you won't have nothing to worry about.'

'Except getting yourself to the church on time,' Becky said quickly.

Mary looked at them each in turn and then she chuckled, 'You're a grand pair an' no mistake. I can't see it happening though . . . Tom's mum ain't 'alf got a paddy on 'er.'

'Aw, come on, Mary, cheer up,' Ella pleaded, 'Mrs Ferguson ain't going to eat you alive. When she gets to know you well she'll probably wonder how her Tommy ever got along without you. You'll see, you'll have her purring like a pussy cat.'

The thought of big buxom Dolly Ferguson purring like a cat was too much. All at once the three of them burst out laughing and it was a minute or two before they settled down again.

Mary took a ten shilling note from her purse, then, as Ella and Becky watched in surprise she walked quickly to the counter and paid for all their teas. Smiling broadly she came back to the table. 'You've been like a dose of salts for me, today. Meeting yer like this. I'm coming round to your house, Ella, the minute Tom an' I get things settled. Will that be all right?'

'More than all right,' Ella grinned, 'I'll come looking for you if you don't.'

'And yer mean it? You'll come to me wedding?'

'We'll be in the front pew,' they promised.

Mary seemed a different girl as she practically skipped away, pausing a few yards up the pavement to stop, turn and shout back at them, 'It's unlucky to break a promise.'

'Gosh I hope things go well for her,' Ella sighed

'Me too,' Becky cried. 'If Dolly Ferguson doesn't take to that lass then she wants her brains seen too.'

'I'm with you there,' Ella said, 'that's one wedding that we'll make sure we go to, eh?'

'Wouldn't miss it for the world.' And Becky knew from the feeling in the pit of her stomach that each of them had done Mary a good turn today and that they ought to make sure they looked her up again, and soon. There was a lot more to Mary Marsden than met the eye and she deserved to have friends that were loyal to her.

Chapter Eleven

BECKY FELT LIKE a schoolgirl as she looked around the room. There were eighteen other girls there beside herself and this morning was to be the first day of their training with J. Lyons.

The weather continued hot. Florence Nicholls climbed up on to the platform fanning herself with a sheaf of papers she carried. Her face was flushed and there were beads of perspiration on her upper lip. Looking down, she counted the heads and looked doubtful.

At that moment the door opened and a flustered-looking May Stevens burst in.

'I'm sorry I'm late.' May directed her apology to Mrs Nicholls who merely nodded and indicated that May should find herself a seat.

'I thought you weren't coming,' Becky chided softly as May sank down on to the chair next to her own.

'I almost didn't, my mum's been taken bad.'

There was no more time for chatter. Suddenly everyone was called to order by a slim lady who had joined Mrs Nicholls. She had brown hair piled neatly on top of her head, a delicate fine-boned face and a body to match. Unlike Mrs Nicholls, who was still dressed in black, she wore a pale coffee-coloured dress, trimmed with narrow lace. The sleeves were full to the elbow then narrowed with rows of pearl buttons down to the cuffs.

'Lovely dress. Very becoming,' Becky whispered to May.

'Cost money!' May answered drily.

Greetings were exchanged and the girls learnt that Miss

Timson, the lady in the beige dress, was to be in charge of their training course.

'The group will work as a whole most of the time, the exception being when you are actually waiting on tables, then you will be split into five groups of four.' Miss Timson had an oval face with pale blue eyes, and her voice, as she continued to instruct the group, was clear and steady, her movements quick and easy.

'There are tables at the back of the room, laid out with exercise books and pencils, if you would like to settle your-selves four to each table, please,' Mrs Nicholls requested, as she came to the fore again. 'I will leave you in the capable hands of Miss Timson.'

Swiftly the girls rose and did as they were bid. Some felt hesitant and unsure as to where they could choose to sit. May was the first to hold out her hand and make the introductions as she and Becky were joined by Joyce Johnson and Maisie Roberts.

After two hours of lectures and taking notes from what was being written on a huge blackboard by several different women and men who came into the room at intervals, each furnishing the group with more information, Becky was dismayed. At one point she felt her throat tighten, and for a moment tears stung behind her eyes. What had she done? Would she ever be able to take in everything that was being said? What if at the end of this course she was told she had failed? She had no job to go back to. She fought back the tears, telling herself sternly that she was not going to be beaten, she would pay attention and she would make herself learn and do well.

Then came the moment when Miss Timson announced that they would take a break. 'I have ordered refreshments,' she said, smiling.

Sighs of relief came from all corners of the room.

They were brought to them by four young men so slim and smart that both May and Becky caught their breath in surprise. They looked every inch top-class waiters dressed in black trousers, short neat black jackets, snowy white shirts with stiff high collars, narrow black ties and a long white apron to finish the outfit.

The young men deftly transferred the cups and saucers and the silver tea and coffeepots and sugar bowls and milk jugs from the heavy silver trays to the snowy white tablecloth that had been spread over the trestle table on the platform. Then they hurried away to return with trays filled with dainty sandwiches and tiered plate-stands laden with small savoury pastries.

'Everything looks delicious,' Becky murmured to May, who was busy filling a plate which had been handed to her by a good-looking lad with sleek black hair.

'Don't it just! I could stand this treatment any day of the week,' May grinned in answer.

During the break May and Becky learnt that Joyce and Maisie knew each other before coming here. They lived near to each other. 'In Chestnut Grove,' Joyce volunteered, 'that's quite near to Balham Station.'

'Oh, that's south London isn't it?' Becky queried.

'That's right, not too far from you. I've been to Kingston once or twice – that's near to New Malden where you live, isn't it?'

Becky agreed it was and the four girls relaxed.

Every one of these girls seem to be Londoners, Becky was thinking to herself. I must be the odd one out. Yet each and every one is friendly, she decided, as they freely chatted and exchanged views on what they had learnt so far. Both Joyce and Maisie seemed to be of the same age as May and herself, all of us coming up to nineteen or twenty, she calculated. These two new friends had short brown hair cut in the same style as May's reddish hair was and she fell to wondering if at some time she would be asked to have her own long hair shortened.

'Girls, I would like to point one thing out to you.' Miss

Timson's voice rose above the chatter and silence fell. 'You may have been too taken up with talking to each other to notice that between each item of china a small doily had been placed. As you proceed with your training this will become second nature to you. It is a practice that Lyons is very proud of and is adhered to at all times, whether you be serving a single cup of tea, a bowl of soup, a cucumber sandwich or a five-course meal. A doily must go between a cup and its saucer, between a soup bowl and the plate it stands on the same applies and food such as sandwiches and pastries must always be laid on a doily, never directly on china.

'That is the first and most important thing for you to learn. One never leaves the still room, kitchen or breakfast bar without first checking that the doilies are in place. It is partly for presentation and partly for practical reasons which you will learn as you go along. Now if you will finish your tea or coffee and return to your places we will proceed.'

'What's wrong with your mum?' Becky asked May as they retook their places.

'She has funny turns sometimes. She'll be all right, her sister is spending the day with her.'

'Quiet, please, I want you to pay attention.' Miss Timson was an easy-going teacher, with the knack of holding her pupils' interest. From that very first day Becky liked her very much and was keen to learn as much as possible. After a few days she began to relax and it seemed to her that she had truly chosen well when she had applied to work for Lyons.

Most days there was little time to think of anything else other than how to wait on table.

During the training period the twenty girls lived in a hostel located behind Cadby Hall and Becky spent what little off-duty time they were given with May Stevens and her mother, a jolly happy-go-lucky woman who, whenever they arrived to visit her, usually had her flat filled with neighbours.

Mrs Stevens certainly made her very welcome though at

times Becky felt she asked so many questions she wanted to know the inside-out of a donkey's hind leg. Another thing was, she was missing her own family and the countryside. The first visit to the district where May's mother lived had been quite an eye-opener for her. The grimy cobbled streets, the tenements so small and cramped without even a small garden, just a concrete back yard that was criss-crossed with washing lines. The dirty industrial buildings which made everywhere look dark and damp. Then there were the pedlars and barrow boys shouting their wares in loud voices, so different from the pleasant village where she had been born and until now lived all her life. When she thought about how she and Ella had everlastingly moaned about the permanent steamy fog in the Wellington Laundry she told herself they hadn't known just how lucky they were.

Near to Cadby Hall she was thrilled by the sight of many fancy carriages as they rattled by; some of the women occupants wore breathtakingly beautiful clothes. To Becky, men and women alike mostly looked as if they had stepped out of a bandbox. And the ladies' hats! Well, never in her life had she seen such creations.

It wasn't like that in the East End of London!

May warned her to be aware of pickpockets and not to upset the painted, gaudily clad women who stood around the street corners near to the tenements that housed her mother. These strange women baffled Becky.

'They're on the game, poor cows,' May told her.

Becky looked mystified.

'Prostitutes, dummy,' May whispered out the side of her mouth. 'Someone's got to earn the money t' put food on the table. Half the men round here haven't worked since the Armistice was declared and the Army slung them out. 'T' ain't their fault.'

Becky sighed. London certainly had many different faces. She was doing her best but there were times when she wondered if she would ever fit in.

*   *   *

The three weeks flew by. Each girl on the course agreed that their feet never stopped aching and others said that their arms had developed muscles due to the heavy trays they had learnt to load and carry. A written examination had been set and now the hour of truth had arrived.

'Young ladies, I am most pleased to tell you that all of you have passed and are being offered employment.' Mrs Nicholls had to pause because the sighs of relief followed by squeals of delight which greeted this statement were extremely noisy.

Some minutes later, Mrs Nicholls looked at their upturned faces and smiled. 'Now, I will read out to what Corner Houses you are to be sent and then we'll go into details of when and where you will receive your uniforms.' May and Becky stood as close together as they could get, fingers crossed behind their backs as the names were read out by Miss Timson.

'Miss Russell and Miss Stevens, to Coventry Street Corner House.' Becky's fingers flew to cover her mouth. Oh, she wasn't to be parted from May. The two of them could remain friends and become workmates, things couldn't have worked out better.

'Cor, I didn't reckon that was on the cards, did you?' May exclaimed happily.

'No, aren't we lucky,' Becky chuckled with glee. 'We're actually going to get our uniforms.'

'No one would ever believe it,' Becky declared in a shocked voice to May as they went through the business of what was what for the umpteenth time that morning.

'Right.' Mrs Morgan, a short thin little body of a woman, and her three seamstresses straightened their pincushions, which they wore on their wrists secured by a velvet strap. 'Let's go through it all once more and remember this.' She stared at the six girls whose uniforms she had been ordered to see to. 'Each morning before you venture out into the hall you will be inspected. From the top of your head to the tip of your toes and that inspection will take into account not only your dress and cap but whether your hands are clean, your nails well manicured and also whether the seams of your plain black stockings are straight.'

'What a palaver!' May grinned. 'Only hope it's all going to be worth it.'

'It will be,' Becky assured her as she looked into the mirror checking that the monogram of JL was in the centre of her cap.

'Take note,' Mrs Morgan said as she bustled to Becky's side, 'that ribbon running through the white part of the cap has to be cleaned and pressed daily, so don't go forgetting it.'

After at least ten attempts May and Becky decided they now knew exactly how the cap should be worn, and Mrs Morgan was able to announce they had got it correct.

Now came the fitting of the dress.

'Jesus wept!' The five other girls, including Becky, roared with laughter as May started to count the two rows of pearl buttons that adorned the front of the neat black dress.

Even Mrs Morgan found herself smiling. 'There are thirty of them,' she enlightened the group of girls, 'and each one has to be sewn on with red cotton.'

'Gawd luv a duck!' Molly, a decent sort of girl who had been on the course, puckered her brow and glared at her friend Elsie. 'I've never been any good at sewing,' she moaned.

Her mate laughed, 'Well, you'll have to learn to cope, won't you.'

'Honest t' God, we'll need to get up at the crack of dawn to get ourselves ready,' May said, looking worried. 'You any good at sewing, Becky?'

Before Becky had a chance to answer Mrs Morgan was droning on about all the other things they would regularly have to check.

'Your white collars will have to be well-laundered and sewn in neatly, and that goes for your cuffs as well; as for the aprons, you will be given three each. They are of the utmost importance, especially the points, pay a lot of attention to the pressing of those points.'

Suddenly Becky laughed out loud. 'At least the years I spent in the laundry won't be wasted,' she said to May.

'Yeah, well, in that case you can lend a hand with mine.'

Becky made no answer to that, thinking it was as well that she had kept the fact that she could sew to herself.

Considering the endless number of things that would be needed to keep her own uniform in good order she'd be kept busy enough without taking on the responsibility of anyone else's.

By the time the correct length of the dress had been decided for each girl and a leaflet passed around informing them to provide their own plain black stockings and black shoes with only medium heels for comfort, the group as a whole felt worn out.

Florence Nicholls followed Miss Timson into the room and saw the girls flopped back in their chairs. They got to their feet quickly, looking embarrassed.

'Don't worry,' Mrs Nicholls smiled, motioning the girls to sit down, 'I come bearing good news. This being Wednesday, you have four days in which to relax, go home and see your families, before you report for duty at ten o'clock on Monday morning.'

The girls, all smiles, now sat up straight as Mrs Nicholls continued. 'To start off with you will be on duty from ten in the morning until six o'clock at night, with a meal break in between. That will enable each of you to travel to and from work at a reasonable hour. Then, shift work will have to be taken into consideration. Will it be too far for some of you to travel back and forth? Especially when a shift is late at night or early in the morning. Discuss this with your parents, heed their advice. The company does have an arrangement with a long-stay hostel here in London, or Miss Timson has names and addresses of homely landladies who have been

thoroughly vetted and approved. Some of you may prefer
to seek lodgings with one of them.'

Becky's heart sank into her boots. She hadn't given a
thought to shift work, although she had learnt that Coventry
Street Corner House had opened an all-night café back in
1923. What would she do? Why hadn't she thought about
the travelling part before now? She comforted herself with
a fact she had gleaned from one of the waiters. Only lads
were expected to be on duty during the night, but that didn't
alter the fact that the Corner Houses catered a lot for the
late evening theatre trade and surely she would eventually
be asked to do late turns.

May Stevens leant forward. 'What's up, Becky? Don't you
want to go home and see yer folks?'

''Course I do,' Becky said as she smiled briefly. 'It's just
that I hadn't given a thought to how I'm going to get to
work when we get put on to shifts.'

'Well, you will live out in the sticks,' May grinned at her.
'Didn't you tell me your dad works on the railway?'

'Yes, that's right an' he does different shifts but I can't see
how that's going to be of any help.'

'Well, you got all the weekend to think about it and then
we're only doing ten till six for a while so why start thinking
about 'ow you're going to cross yer bridges before you've
even come t' them?'

'What a friend you are,' Becky declared.

'And just what d' you mean by that?' May asked, eyebrows raised.

'Down to earth and very sensible, you've given me good
advice,' Becky said, placing her hand on her friend's shoulder.
'I shall miss you, but isn't it great to have these free days before
we start work?'

'Sure is,' May agreed. 'Shan't see you now till next
Monday.' Then grinning and doing her best to speak really
nicely, she added, 'Ten o'clock at Lyons Coventry Street
Corner House.'

They stood up and their arms went round each other, hugging tightly.

'I never thought I'd really make it,' May whispered to Becky. 'You, yes, but me, I had me doubts.'

Becky clutched May's hand as they broke away. 'Thank God we both did. Enjoy your break and I'll be looking forward to seeing you on Monday.'

'Me too,' May answered with emphasis. 'Having found you as a friend is a bonus.'

Later, Becky stood on the pavement and watched May as she took big strides towards her bus stop. From the beginning I decided that lass had a good head on her shoulders and I was right, she told herself, and what's more she's got a good heart as well. I couldn't have asked for a better friend to work with. All the same as she rode the short distance to the railway station her heart was still full of misgivings as to just how her future with Lyons would work out.

Chapter Twelve

It was past four when Becky climbed down off the local tram and took a moment to look around. In the warm late summer sunshine New Malden looked a picture. Not much traffic, no big dirty warehouses, not even the posh department stores, just lovely green grass on the verges. Beyond the few houses in Albert Road lay Harry Horsecroft's farm and further over the allotments where her dad spent much of his spare time.

She stopped in her tracks and took a really deep breath. Oh, it was good to be home, so good, it seemed that she had been away for ages. Her footsteps quickened and as she neared her house, the front door was thrown open.

'Mum!' Small, plump, warm, smiling, her mother stood there. Becky threw herself into her mother's outstretched arms. 'Oh, Mum, I've missed you. It's so good to see you.'

'Not half as much as I've missed you, lass.' Joyce Russell sniffed away her happy tears. 'There's only been me against all the males.'

A jumble of excited voices came up the hallway. Then she was surrounded by her three brothers, Jack, Tom and Fred. 'Who's been gadding about up in the Smoke then, leaving me to cope with a miserable mother?' young Fred asked, playfully punching her shoulder.

Then there were her two sisters-in-law, each kissing her with a great deal of enthusiasm. 'Hey, hang on, Ada, and you, Joan,' Becky pleaded, laughing, 'give me a chance to get a kiss from my nephews.'

Bending her knees, she put her arms round the two little

boys, Ronnie and Joey. 'I've brought you each a stick of rock from the Tower of London,' she whispered.

'Don't believe you,' Ronnie retorted as he made a funny face at her. He seemed to have grown a few inches in the short time she'd been away.

'It's true,' she told him, delving into her handbag and fetching out the pink peppermint sticks. 'You'll see when you suck it, it says Tower of London all the way through the rock.'

Suddenly the whole family was pestering her with questions.

'Give her a chance, let her get inside the house, will you?' Her father had, until now, hung back wanting her all to himself.

'Aw Dad!' A lump had come into Becky's throat, threatening to choke her. 'Dad,' she said again, and without so much as a word, Joe Russell, big man that he was, found himself grabbing his slim daughter and holding her close to his chest.

'Didn't reckon on the house being so empty,' he spoke half to himself. 'Are you well, pet?' Holding her now at arm's length, he said, 'God above you've grown up! Quite the sophisticated miss, aren't you? An' you've only been away three weeks.'

At last Joyce managed to get them all seated in the front room. 'I'll away and make the tea,' she said.

Joan put young Joey down on the hearth rug and followed her mother-in-law out to the kitchen. Becky watched the two boys struggle to undo the paper from their stick of rock and she realized just how much she had missed her family. Her two eldest brothers were big and strong, just like her dad, and they were nice with it. She felt a twinge of envy. Her sisters-in-law were lucky. They were happily married with children of their own. A depressing thought came to her. It might be years before I ever get married, let alone have children. You're never satisfied, she chided herself, you wanted a career and now even before you've started out on it you're having regrets.

'Becky, you didn't say how long you're home for,' her mother said, pushing the door open with her hip and guiding in the tea trolley.

'I haven't got to go to work until next Monday and after that I shall be home every night for quite a while.'

Her mother raised her head from the task of pouring out the tea, a question showing in her eyes. 'Quite a while, what's that supposed to mean?'

Becky glanced at her father for help and saw him shake his head at her mother in stealthy reproach. 'Give the girl time to have her tea,' he reprimanded her, 'there'll be plenty of time for us to hear all the news later on.'

'Oh all right,' her mother smiled, 'dinner won't be too long. It's special, Harry Horsecroft let me have two lovely chickens so there's plenty for everyone.'

Their evening meal was jolly. A real family affair with Joyce Russell constantly urging everyone to eat up. 'Especially you, Becky. You're far too thin,' she sternly told her daughter.

All too soon dinner was over; Joan and Ada began to gather together the paraphernalia that was part of travelling with young children.

'Come on Jack, tomorrow's still a work day,' Ada said as she picked up Ronnie's toys. 'You won't be so chirpy when the alarm goes off at five-thirty.'

'Joey, will you stand still an' let me wipe your sticky fingers?' Joan scolded. 'Trust your Aunt Becky to buy you sweets,' she smiled as she took the stick of rock and endeavoured to wrap the paper back around it.

'You eat enough sweets,' Tom told his wife, 'and you don't look so bad on it.'

Joan looked up at her husband, grinning. 'Don't stand there paying me compliments, it won't get you anywhere. You've also got to be up at the crack of dawn, remember.'

When Jack, Tom and their wives and children had left,

Joyce told Becky that Ella was expecting to see her tomorrow. 'I met her down the market, baby's doing ever so well though I thought Ella looked a bit washed out. Still, she was thrilled when I told her you were coming home.'

'Right,' Becky answered thoughtfully. 'First thing after breakfast I'll go round and see her mum, then I'll go to Kingston later.'

It was good to be home, Becky thought, while she listened to her parents fill her in on the lives of her brothers, uncles and aunts, neighbours and friends.

'Joe, come an' have some cocoa and cake before we go to bed. You too Becky, it will help you to sleep well,' her mother called from the kitchen.

'Your room's all ready, Becky, you go on up, I'll pop in and see you're all right in a few minutes,' Joyce said to her daughter, as she cleared the empty cocoa mugs off the table before kissing Becky on her cheek and patting her shoulder.

Then it was her dad's turn. He walked with her to the foot of the stairs and all at once she felt like a little girl again.

'Going to offer to give me a piggyback, Dad?'

'None of yer cheek, young lady,' he grinned, 'it's not so long since I used to run up these stairs with you on my back.'

'Couldn't do it now,' she teased.

He swatted her behind and they walked up the stairs side by side. When they came to her bedroom, he bent to kiss her.

'Good night, Becky, it's great to have you home.'

'Good night, Dad, I do love you.' The words just slipped out naturally. She looked up at him, her eyes bright, and with that he gently put his arms about her again, and she felt safe and loved.

'Good night, pet,' he whispered, gave her a little push and turned to go back downstairs.

Becky opened the door of her old bedroom and gasped. The gas had been lit, casting a shadowy glow around the walls that looked so different. 'Of course they're different,' she exclaimed, 'they've been freshly papered!' What a lovely surprise! The furniture had been rearranged. Even the bed had been moved so that it now faced the window, and her chest of drawers was on the other side of the room. The curtains and the bedspread matched and were all new, a soft floral pattern on a dusty pink background. The material must have cost a lot of money and her mother must have spent hours making them. I must go back downstairs and say thank you to them, she decided.

Her hand was on the door knob, about to turn it, when she heard her parents talking in hushed tones; then her father chuckled. She threw open the door.

'You two are marvellous, even if you are devious with it,' she declared.

'Just so long as you are pleased with it, you are aren't you? Fred did the decorating.'

'Mum, it's lovely, truly lovely!'

'That's all right then.'

More hugs and kisses followed.

She undressed, turned the gaslight out, and climbed into bed, thinking she must be the luckiest girl alive to have such wonderful parents and brothers. Then as she lay in bed she took to wondering how Ella was doing. Had things worked out well between her and Peter? Had baby Margaret brought them closer together or had the added expense of a baby proved a big burden?

Stop worrying, go to sleep, she rebuked herself. You'll see Ella tomorrow and be able to judge for yourself.

Becky was awake before it was light and she lay listening to the rain beat against the windowpane. Gosh, the wind sounds terrific, it hasn't rained for ages but it's certainly making up for it now, she told herself as she got out of bed, pulled her dressing gown on and went downstairs to be thoroughly spoiled by her doting mother.

They say rain before seven will clear before eleven, and

that was exactly what happened, though the gutters were still running with water and the pavements were wet and slippery as Becky left Peggy James's house. At the corner of George Road she turned to give a final wave to Peggy. Her visit had set her thinking again. Peggy's version of Ella's married life hadn't described a bed of roses. Like her own mother, Peggy was of the opinion that Ella was looking tired, not at all well. 'Too much to cope with and not enough money coming in,' was how Ella's mother saw it.

Ella beamed when she opened the door to find Becky on the doorstep.

'Becky! Cor, it's marvellous to see you.' Ella came forward with hands outstretched. 'My, I can't believe how different you look, you're wearing make-up! An' you look so well.'

'Are you going to keep me standing here on the doorstep all day? I'm dying to see baby Margaret,' Becky said, stepping in to the narrow passage. 'Where is she?'

Ella's smile faded and she sighed a little despondently as she led the way through to the kitchen. 'I haven't had time to bath her yet, she had a fretful night and then after her early feed she went off to sleep so I let her lie.'

'That's good,' Becky said eagerly, taking off her jacket as she walked, 'I'd love to help bath her.'

One glance around the room and Becky was appalled.

'I've been trying to earn a few extra shillings,' Ella said quietly, sensing that Becky was embarrassed by the state of the place.

Ella's living room smelt of damp washing and ironing and three string lines had been placed, stretching from wall to wall, each covered with damp articles of linen.

'I'm a bit behind with the ironing,' Ella apologized, 'I was hoping to get it all finished before you arrived. I have to return it all this afternoon.'

'That's no problem,' Becky answered, doing her best to hide her real feelings, 'let me just have a few minutes with the baby. It seems so long since I've seen her. Then we'll both get cracking – be like working together in the laundry again.'

'Hardly that, here it's all slog on me own. It was hard work at the Wellington, right enough, but everyone was pally and we did have mates to have a good laugh with. There's days here when I don't see a soul.'

'Ah, but today you've got me. We'll skip through all the jobs, bath and dress Margaret up fit to kill and then we'll go into Kingston and have a bite to eat out. How does that sound?'

'Wonderful, but I still have to make my deliveries.'

'If we pack it all up after we've done the ironing can't we put it in the pram and deliver it on our way?'

'Yeah, suppose we could.'

'Well, there you are then! Come on, where are you hiding the baby?'

'She's still in her cot, upstairs.'

'All right if I go and fetch her down?' Becky asked, not waiting for an answer but thinking to herself as she climbed the stairs that all these signs of poverty were making her tense. Four years and more she and Ella had put up with the drudgery of working in a laundry and all Ella had swapped it for was this.

Well, it isn't going to happen to me, she vowed. I'll make it to the top, I don't know just how I'll do it but do it I will. I'm never going to live like this.

Margaret, bathed, fed, powdered and dressed had been put in her pram while Ella and Becky together, rotating three flat irons, made short work of the ironing.

Ella seemed much more relaxed, the baby was cooing happily and Becky was sighing inwardly with relief as she pushed the pram towards Kingston.

The next three hours flew by. Laundry was delivered and cash collected. People leant over the pram admiringly with remarks such as, 'What a beautiful baby.' They ate a meat pie and two veg in the market café, and now both girls, feeling a whole lot more contented, made their way towards home.

'What on earth is happening?' Ella cried as they turned the corner into Mill Street.

Women were crowded out on the pavement all up and down the street. Others were leaning out of their upstairs windows.

Just as they drew level with Martha Tubman's gate, her front door flew open and she came running down the path.

'The police are down outside the Swan,' she yelled, 'it's that poor blighter Tommy Ferguson, they think he's interfered with a little girl.'

'What the hell are you saying?' Becky sounded furious. 'There's no harm in Tommy, no harm at all, he wouldn't hurt a fly.'

Martha looked sheepish. 'Well that's what they reckon, come down the road and see for yerself.'

Ella had never liked her next-door neighbour and she avoided her as much as possible, but as she looked at her now she could cheerfully have killed her. 'Tommy's just a bit different, quiet like, but I agree with Becky, he wouldn't harm a child.' Feeling sick to her stomach she took hold of the pram and told Becky, 'I'll take the baby inside and feed her, you pop down and see if there's anything you can do.'

Normally Becky wouldn't have gone within a mile of a noisy crowd but she had to find out what was happening to Tom. It sounded so terrible, this awful accusation, his poor mother must be going out of her mind with worry.

'I'll be back as soon as I know what's going on,' Becky assured Ella, before turning and running after Martha Tubman, all the while telling herself, Tommy might not be the brightest of lads but there was nothing wrong with his heart. Go out of his way to help folk, Tom would. And since he'd been courting Mary Marsden there'd been a marked difference in him. Meeting Mary had been the best thing that ever

happened to Tom. No one is ever going to convince me
that Tom Ferguson hurt a child.

Becky stood at the edge of the crowd, mainly women, that
had gathered outside the Swan public house and clutched her
side, giving herself a minute to get her breath back.

'You can't take my boy off just like that, he never did
nuffin to no kid, I'd bet me life on that,' Dolly Ferguson
implored, her voice an anguished wail as she tried to push
past the policeman.

Becky couldn't believe her eyes! By the look of it Tom
had been manhandled to the ground and another policeman
was standing guard over him.

'Oh, it's you, Becky.' Dolly turned her head and gasped
as Becky put her arm around her shoulders. At the same
moment Tom looked up, tears were glistening in his eyes
and at the sight of her his cheeks turned red with shame.

'Please, Becky, believe me. I've done nothing wrong. I
was helping the little girl, truly I was, please believe me,' he
begged.

'Come on. On your feet,' the policeman said. 'The van
will be here shortly.'

'Let me go,' Tom pleaded as he struggled.

'You ain't going anywhere, me lad, except to the station
where you'll be locked up while this matter is sorted out.'

'I don't think so,' a woman's voice yelled from the back
of the crowd.

Women began to take sides. 'He's a good lad, do anything
for anybody,' was the general cry. Only Martha Tubman
and a few of her skinny cronies seemed to want the show
to go on.

'Ain't no smoke without fire,' one young mother screamed,
hoisting her infant higher on her hip and shoving a dummy
into its mouth, 'an' I saw the girl, frightened out of her wits
an' covered in mud she was.'

'You'll be asked to make a statement later, Madam,' the
policeman said calmly.

'Yeah, well, I'll do that all right,' the woman replied, 'I know what I saw.'

Tom had risen to his feet shakily and was brushing himself down.

'You stay still,' the policeman ordered him as his mother made to take his arm and lead him away.

'I've told you he ain't going nowhere, should be ashamed of yourselves, the bloody lot of yer.' Annie Smith, landlady of the Swan, used her elbows to edge her way to the front of the crowd. 'I saw it all, a damn sight more than that skinny cow reckons she saw, an' I'd 'ave been down 'ere a lot quicker except I was in the bathroom starkers when it 'appened. Good job the bathroom steamed up and I opened the window when I did. Been wedged shut for years an' it weren't easy t' open but I'll say again, damn good job I persevered because that lad's a good 'un, he's no more a child molester than you are, Constable.'

'Gawd luv yer, Annie, I'll be in yer debt for the rest of me life.' A tearful Dolly Ferguson used the corner of her flowered overall to wipe the corner of her eye. 'There's always someone ready to put my Tommy down but they're knocking on my door quick enough when they want some rough work done. Two-faced bloody lot some of 'em are, an' as for these coppers, only too ready to condemn, ain't yer, wouldn't listen to my son's side of the story, oh no, but you'd take 'er word,' Dolly thumbed her hand towards the young mother who reckoned she had seen the child, giving her a look that boded no good. 'Be a damn sight better if she stayed in 'er own 'ome and took care of 'er kids instead of spending 'alf the day on the doorstep gossiping and picking other people to pieces.'

The constable had the grace to look sheepish. 'Only doing me job, Mam.' Then, turning to Annie Smith, he added, 'You'll need to come to the station an' all, give your statement. The little girl in question and her friend have gone ahead in the doctor's car . . .'

He was interrupted by the arrival of the black police van.

'All right, all right, what's going on here?' The voice of authority made himself heard and the women drew back as Sergeant Burton looked suspiciously at everyone.

Annie Smith stepped forward, her face dark with anger. 'You, Sergeant, had better listen to me, never mind none of the others. See that little window up there, the one that's wide open?' She paused and pointed a finger upwards. 'That's where I had me head stuck out when the biggest of the two kids pushed the other one.'

'Madam . . .'

The sergeant didn't get any further. Annie took a step forward.

'Don't "madam" me, Sergeant Burton. A wrong's been done 'ere and I'm the one that can set the record right so the sooner you listen the sooner we can all go about our business.'

'You must come to the station to make a statement,' the police sergeant insisted.

'I'm going nowhere till I've had me say. Not you, Sergeant, nor a team of wild 'orses is going to drag me away. Let these scandalmongers that ain't got nothing better t' do than spread rumours 'ear the truth.'

'Gawd bless yer, Annie,' Dolly put her spoke in yet again.

The sergeant sighed heavily. 'Well, we all know how obstinate you can be, Mrs Smith, so get on with it, if you must,' he pleaded.

'Like I said, the two girls were on the bridge and the older one was kind of daring the little 'un to jump the brook. They got to the edge of the water and the youngster drew back, she was afraid, I could tell that much. They argued for a few seconds then the dark-'aired one, she lost her temper and shoved the little 'un in her back, pushing her forward. What with all the rain we 'ad this morning the bank was slippery like and the kiddie slid down, landing flat on her face in the mud.

'The other little bitch starts screaming at the top of her voice. Tommy was coming across the field, God knows what might 'ave 'appened if he 'adn't been there. Anyways, he broke into a run, waded in an' grabbed the toddler out and was doing his best to clean the mud off her face an' the front of her dress when the crowd gathered and the oldest girl told them it was Tommy that pushed the kid in. Wants her backside whacked if you ask me.'

'Right then you lot, let's see you move off to your own homes,' the sergeant said, stern-faced, 'unless any of you want to contradict this lady's version of what happened.'

Most of the women gave a noncommittal shrug of the shoulders. Annie was not finished, however.

'This matter is over and done with. Tom Ferguson has shown what he's made of today an' anyone that wants t' say different will not only 'ave t' answer to me but to me ole man as well an' you all know how nasty he can get.'

Becky patted Dolly's shoulder, 'I'm off back to Ella's,' she said in a soft voice. 'She'll be wanting to know what's happened and I'm sure Tom will be all right now.'

'Yeah, all right, lass, thanks for your concern,' Dolly answered as she heaved her bosoms higher and watched her son climb into the police van. 'Looks like they're still going to take Tom down the station so I'm going as well. I'll see yer later.'

Becky was smiling to herself as she walked back up Mill Street. She wouldn't mind being a fly on the wall at Kingston police station. What with both Annie Smith and Dolly Ferguson being there stating their case, the next hour should be quite lively.

Over a cup of tea Becky related all the details to Ella.

'Just shows you what mischief kids get up to when they're allowed to run wild in the streets. Could have been real nasty for Tommy,' Ella said thoughtfully. 'I hope Peter has found us somewhere better to live before Margaret is old enough to go to school.'

Becky, too, was having sobering thoughts. That older child must be a right little terror; she knew what trouble she was causing when she accused Tom of having done the pushing. Would baby Margaret grow up to be like that? The responsibility of raising children could weigh heavily, she was thinking to herself, as she pondered on how Peter and Ella were ever going to better themselves when their income was so little.

Peter came in just as Becky was ready to leave.

'Aw, Becky, it's great to see you, don't go on my account,' Peter said, having given her a peck on the cheek.

'No, I'm not,' Becky smiled, 'it's just that me mum will have tea ready and I said I'd be home. Still, I'm glad I caught you. How's things at the laundry?'

'Could be better. A darn sight better if you want the truth. With all this lovely weather we've been having even the big houses don't put out so much laundry. Still, autumn's nearly here and winter won't be far behind, so things will pick up, I'm sure.'

He didn't sound as if he were sure. Neither did he look well, any more than Ella did. They both looked as if they hadn't had a good night's sleep for ages. Becky felt really sorry for them both. But me being sorry for them isn't going to help, she was quietly saying to herself, at the same time feeling irritated because she just couldn't think of any way in which she might be able to help.

Leaving the baby with Peter, Ella saw Becky to the tram.

'I told your mum I'd come over with her on Sunday afternoon,' Becky said, doing her best to keep the conversation cheerful while they waited for the tram. 'I'll get my mum to bake us a cake, come to think of it me mum might come as well.'

'Your mum has all yer family to tea on Sundays, they'll want you to be there,' Ella reminded her.

'Oh yeah, well, never mind I'll make it Saturday afternoon, how's that?'

'Fine,' Ella said, but she didn't sound too keen.

I'll bring plenty of things with me to make a spread, Becky vowed to herself, as she kissed her dear friend goodbye.

Going home, Ella walked faster. It would be so easy for her to be jealous of Becky but come what may she mustn't let that happen. She had made her own mistakes and now she had to live by them. But what a difference there was between Becky and herself now! Look at the skirt Becky was wearing: it was a wool suiting. She'd been ashamed of her own skirt, which had certainly seen better days. Well, things would pick up soon. Peter had promised they would. Meanwhile they had baby Margaret and there wasn't anything in this world that could make her regret having had her. She was a sweet little darling and Peter was good and kind, always doing his best. So what more could she ask for?

Reaching her front gate she didn't bother to search her mind for an answer.

Chapter Thirteen

THE DAY HAD dawned.

If I live to be a hundred I'll never forget the excitement of this first morning, Becky was saying to herself as she listened to the soft but firm voice of Robert Matthews wishing them luck as they prepared to step out and offer their services as waitresses for J. Lyons & Company.

'One last thing you may like to know,' Robert's voice held a hint of amusement as the four new girls turned their heads towards him, 'most of you have probably heard our waitresses referred to as Nippies.' There was a murmur of agreement. 'That came about at one of the big Masonic events attended by female staff for the very first time. An enthusiastic newspaper reporter wrote in his article that the young ladies could not be alluded to as waitresses because they nipped about so quickly. The name, Nippy, was quickly adopted and as such has remained.'

'Don't think we'll be doing much nipping about this lunchtime,' May Stevens commented out of the side of her mouth. 'Don't know about you, Becky, but all that carry-on as to whether or not our uniform was perfect got me down a bit. Talk about grooming a horse! If we don't look the part by now we never will. Surely we won't have to go through all that palaver every blinking morning.'

Becky's only answer was a smile. She thought they looked a treat. A real transformation, she assured herself as she took a last glimpse in the long mirror. Her cap was correct, the badge on her dress securely sewn on. Those cuffs had been a job to sew in and she'd spent a long time pressing the points of her white apron. One last job: fix her order-pad and pencil, which were secured by a bulldog clip and fastened with a fine chain on to the waistband of her dress.

Heart hammering, she threw her shoulders back, took a deep breath and stepped out through the swing doors into the real world.

Today they only had to work the lunch shift. She couldn't believe it! Even in the middle of the day the customers were so glamorous, their clothes so beautiful and as for their scents, men and women alike smelt lovely as she bent over to place the dishes of their choice in front of them.

It was nearly seven o'clock by the time Becky climbed into the railway carriage and thankfully sank into a corner seat. My legs are killing me, and my poor feet are on fire, she moaned softly as she leant back and closed her eyes. What a day!

She, Rebecca Russell, had spent eight hours in the very heart of London's West End. Waiting table at Coventry Street Corner House. God knows how many trips I made to the kitchen and back, she mused. It wasn't only Londoners that ate there – provincial and overseas visitors had helped to keep her busy. In some cases it had been a little difficult to understand their accent. She had constantly reminded herself of a saying that Miss Timson had frequently used during their period of training.

No matter who it is, or where they come from, at Lyons Corner Houses, everyone is served with equal courtesy and consideration.

For everything good in this life there is a price to be paid.

Becky felt that she had got through the first eight weeks of her employment with Lyons reasonably well. The good things, of course, had far outweighed the bad. Now her probation time was over, she needed to make some decisions.

The terms of her employment now meant that she would have to do shift work and travelling home to New Malden in the early hours of the morning was out of the question. It would also prove very difficult, were she to remain living at home with her parents, for her to get into the West End in time to start the early morning shift.

During the test period, all four of the girls had been offered the chance, once the shifts started, to stay at the hostel for a further three months. After that they were on their own. This meant that she had to start searching for somewhere to live without delay. Somewhere she could afford and that would be within easy distance of Coventry Street.

Part of their training had been carried out at Orchard House, Orchard Street, W1, only a stone's throw from the great departmental stores like Selfridges. Becky adored window-shopping in that area but to find accommodation anywhere near that she could afford was out of the question. She had never had to think about money before. Not seriously. There had always been her parents to provide food, warmth and shelter. She had given part of what she earned at the Wellington Laundry to her mother each week and had been allowed to keep the remainder as pocket money. Most of her clothes had been made by her mother until she grew old enough to learn how to make her own. Leaving home meant being responsible for herself. Would she be able to cope? She'd have to, there didn't seem to be much choice.

'Don't be too nervous,' Mr Gower, the short, stocky head waiter, told Becky and May before they started their first late night shift. 'I won't tell either of you not to be nervous at all, because you're bound to be. Serving dinner, especially to the theatre-going customers, is vastly different to serving morning coffees and lunches.'

'I'm too terrified to be nervous,' Becky answered.

'There's really no need,' Mr Gower assured them both. 'I've never had two newly-trained girls in whom I place so much confidence. Each of you is very good at your job, and I'll be on hand should you get into any difficulties.'

Mr Gower was right. Everything was vastly different. The small restaurant to which Mr Gower had assigned them was small and intimate, distinguished by its red plush chairs and sections divided off into convenient corners.

'Talk about a carry-on!' May muttered as she and Becky waited while the commis brought their orders for the hors d'oeuvres.

One of the lads winked at May. 'Seeing how the other half live tonight, aren't you? Plenty of tête-à-têtes going on in those cosy corners, eh?'

'It's what is known as the cosmopolitan atmosphere,' a blond-headed lad said, grinning cheekily. 'You ain't seen nothing yet. Wait till the theatres turn out and the toffs 'ave downed a load of bubbly, that's when things start to get serious.'

'Cosmopolitan ain't what we call it where I come from,' May said, her eyes filled with laughter.

One of the chefs flicked a cloth around the lad's head, gave him a wicked look and said, 'Things will be very serious in this kitchen if you don't move yourself a bit quicker an' allow these young ladies to get on with their job.'

Even the front of the house, as it was referred to, changed its style by night. Colourful window displays encouraged the men to buy presents for their lady companions. Spotlights illuminated exquisite boxes of chocolates of all shapes and sizes resting on carefully ruched satin. Just inside the door orchids and carnations made up as a corsage were displayed on a black velvet board ready for the male escort to purchase and to pin on to the fur coat of his beloved before setting off for the theatre.

The whole building was very much alive, even more so than it was during the day. Customers were shown to a table by black-coated male floor-walkers, always under the stern eye of Mr Gower.

The first sight of the hors d'oeuvres trolley had Becky gasping in admiration. There was a choice of at least eighteen dishes: eggs stuffed with anchovies; tomatoes scalloped and filled with delicious mysteries; sardines, rollmops, Russian salad, red cabbage, asparagus, diced beetroot, fancy-cut colourful radishes, not to mention the various cooked meats, and all offered merely as a start to the main meal!

'God rest their stomachs,' grinned May as they each trundled a trolley through the swing doors.

Becky spent a few seconds thinking how wonderful the friendship with May had turned out. She really liked May and she knew that May felt the same way about her. Some changes had taken place in each of them since they had first met. Becky felt she was less uneasy about things in general and May had settled down very well. She had taken to being a Nippy like a duck to water. She had even altered her speech somewhat. Becky knew without asking what an effort that must have been for May. Nevertheless she had succeeded. She no longer dropped quite so many aitches and she checked herself if the word 'ain't' came out. Becky made sure that she never laughed at May's efforts.

Whatever the diners chose as their main meal it was either served in an individual dish or from a silver salver. Grilled fish served with a creamy rich sauce was Becky's favourite and the Knickerbocker Glory served with a long-handled spoon had her in raptures on the odd occasion when the staff were allowed one for themselves. At such times, May would go off into fits of laughter, watching Becky stand up in order to eat the very last morsel of fruit and ice cream that remained in the glass.

Halfway through the second week of their late shift the police came to the Corner House to inform May that her mother had been taken ill and had been admitted to hospital.

'Of course you must go straight away,' insisted Mr Gower, reaching into his pocket and withdrawing a half-crown. 'Take a taxi, go on, don't bother to change, take off your apron and put your coat on, nobody will notice your uniform.'

'Thanks ever so much, Mr Gower,' May mumbled, the colour slowly draining from her cheeks.

'I hope you find your mother feeling better,' Becky called out as May practically ran from the still room.

It was a long night after that. The compliments the toffs often paid Becky fell on deaf ears and she was truly grateful when Mr Gower signalled that she might leave the floor.

Her room at the hostel felt cold and lonely when she opened the door half an hour after midnight. It was only a short walk from Coventry Street to the hostel and Becky had been glad of the sharp fresh air. May had been in her thoughts the whole evening. May worshipped her old mum. They only had each other. Apparently her father had been killed in the dockyards when May was quite young and her mother had never married again.

Becky was talking to herself as she prepared herself for bed. If it weren't so late and I didn't feel so dog-tired I'd go over to her mum's flat and see if May was back from the hospital yet. At times like these one needed friends or family. For a moment she wished she was at home. Able to open her bedroom door and call down to her mum and dad. They'd come running, I know they would but they aren't here now, are they? She told herself to stop being silly, but it wasn't easy.

It was three days before she saw May again. She turned up at the hostel at nine o'clock one morning. Becky wasn't dressed. She heard May's voice, rough and familiar. Still in her dressing gown she got up and opened the door and held out her arms to her friend. May was trembling, she looked strange, drained of all feeling and Becky didn't need to be told that her mother had died.

'Becky, she wasn't there. I never got to say goodbye. A heart attack they said. She never came home again and that flat is bloody terrible without my mum being there.'

'I know, I know,' Becky soothed. She wanted to cuddle her

again, but didn't dare touch her. May wasn't one for showing emotion.

'Want a cup of coffee?' she asked softly.

'That all you've got? No tea?'

Becky shook her head.

'That'll do.'

They drank their coffee in silence until May gave a deep sigh.

'Want to talk about it?' Becky asked her quietly.

'Nothing I say will bring me mum back, will it? I'm just grateful that I've got a job that will help take my mind off things.'

'Shouldn't you ask for more time off?' Becky suggested.

'I can't stand the flat now, it's so empty, every single sound is like an echo. The neighbours have been wonderful but it's not the same. Time seems to hang so long. And at night I can't get to sleep.' With the words hardly out, May burst into tears.

The next moment Becky was hugging her and murmuring soft words that were meant to be comforting.

'It's funny,' May said as she struggled to pull herself together, 'through all that's happened I've hardly shed a tear and here I am babbling like a baby.'

'And a jolly good job too. That's what friends are for, a shoulder to cry on when it's most needed. As for time on your hands, wait till you get back to work and every moment is occupied with fulfilling other people's needs. You'll be rushed off your feet again with no time to brood and come night-time you'll sleep all right cos you'll be dead exhausted.'

May rubbed her eyes and managed to smile and Becky smiled back at her.

'I just feel so guilty cos I wasn't there when she died.'

'I know,' Becky did her best to console her. 'Let me tell you something, May. One of your mum's neighbours came in to see Mr Fairbrother, to tell him your mum was dying, and I had a word with her. She told me that your mum thought you were the best thing that ever happened to her. She thought the sun and the moon shone out of you. You told me she was always a good mother to you, well, she thought you were a good daughter to her. You haven't got anything to reproach yourself for and there's not many can say that when they lose someone.'

'Thanks, Becky,' May whispered as fresh tears rolled down her cheeks.

Becky waited a few minutes, while May searched in her bag for a clean handkerchief, then she suggested, 'Shall I get dressed and we go to a Lyons for a cup of tea?'

May looked at her in surprise and then laughed. 'Why not. Might as well give ourselves a busman's holiday.'

The laughter reassured Becky. She couldn't begin to imagine what it must have been like for May to lose her mother so suddenly.

At the same time May was deciding that she was very lucky to have made a friend such as Becky.

Before that week was out Becky was given cause to say to herself, It's an ill wind that blows nobody any good.

It was the following Monday week before May returned to work.

'Thanks, Becky, for sending flowers,' May said as they stood ready for inspection, before starting work. 'The funeral went off quite well, I was surprised at how many neighbours turned up.'

'All your mum's neighbours were her friends,' Becky told her. 'It was natural they wanted to pay their respects.'

'Yeah. Becky . . . will you do me a favour?'

'You know I will if I can.'

'Come back with me to the flat when we knock off. Stay the night, will you? Please.'

'Yes . . . of course.' Becky stumbled over the words, wondering what on earth May wanted her to stay the night in that tenement flat for.

'Thanks, I'll explain it all tonight.'

With that, Becky had to be satisfied. Still troubled as to what was on May's mind, she had a word with Mr Gower.

'Don't fret yourself, lass. Miss Timson is going to have a chat with May, during your break. The firm will do all it can to help at a time like this.' Mr Gower patted Becky on the arm. 'You young girls need never fear that just because you have left home you are on your own. Lyons prides itself on being one large family. All employees are treated fairly and with kindness, unless of course they should prove themselves unfit to receive such good treatment. Run along now Rebecca, and just remember there is always a member of staff only to willing to listen, at any time, should you feel the need of help or advice.'

'Thank you Mr Gower,' Becky said, wondering to herself whether he was married and had any children. He'd be a nice kind dad, she smiled to herself, almost as nice as her own father.

It was pitch dark as May and Becky felt their way up the flight of stone stairs to the first-floor flat. May already had the key in her hand and set about opening the front door. At the same moment the door to the kitchen opened, letting out rays from the gaslight. Becky gasped. The faded wallpaper showed clean patches where, until recently, pictures had hung.

'Mind yer shins on the boxes,' May urged as they walked down the short passage. Cardboard boxes were piled high up on one side of the drab lino. What on earth had May found to put into these boxes? Becky wondered.

'Aunt Lil, what are you doing still here? You said you were off home when I left for work.'

Becky took stock of the tiny grey-haired woman who was peering out at them. She looked so neat and tidy in a dark dress more than half covered by a white bibbed apron. Stepping back to let the girls into the kitchen, May's Aunt Lil shrugged.

'Couldn't leave the place, not the state it's in. Better t' get it all over an' done with. Besides I wanted t' know what yer friend said. You must be Becky,' she added, peering hard into Becky's face.

'Move yer body, Aunt Lil, let Becky sit down. You're a crafty old devil, you had no intention of going back to your place.'

Aunt Lil smiled, showing a remarkably good set of teeth for an old lady. 'Like I said, luv, didn't want t' leave you with all this mess to sort out. I've got you a nice bit of supper in the oven. You can wait on yerselves. I'm off t' bed. Good night, May.'

May had to bend her knees to kiss her aunt on the cheek. 'Goodnight, Aunt, thanks for staying,' she said softly. 'See you in the morning.'

'Good night, Becky, afraid there is only the one double bed, I've put a bottle in to warm it up like, you won't mind sharing with May, will you?'

'Of course not,' Becky answered quickly, thinking she was glad she wouldn't be in a room on her own. This place felt strange, perhaps because she had never stayed in a flat before. 'Goodnight . . .' she said hesitantly, not sure how she should address this tiny lady.

Lily Maynard smiled. This young lady was very different to the usual run-of-the-mill girls that May had grown up with. You'll do my sister's girl a power of good, she was thinking to herself, knock the rough edges off our May and maybe she'll end up talking the way you do and that wouldn't be a bad thing. Not bad at all, she decided as she smiled at Becky, saying, 'Lass, I'm Aunt Lil, to any number of young folk, though I was never lucky enough to be blessed with kids of me own, but seeing as 'ow me sister 'as been taken, God rest her soul, I reckon it's a blessing that May's got me. And now, we can't 'ave you feeling left out of things, so 'ow about you calling me Aunt Lil?'

Becky chuckled. What a character! 'Aunt Lil, it would be an honour, thank you.'

'Yeah, well, good night again.' Lily Maynard was well pleased. Reaching the door she turned and added another caution, 'Don't stay up all night chewing the fat,' then giggling to herself she muttered, ''alf the night's gone anyway. Soon be daylight.'

In a short while Becky and May were seated at the table and despite it being the early hours of the morning they enjoyed a tasty supper and felt all the better for it.

May pushed her plate to the side, leant back in her chair and with a smile on her lips, she turned to face Becky. 'How do you fancy renting a room in my Aunt Lil's house? She's offered to have both of us an' she'll be in her element if she has the pair of us under her roof.'

'I'm not sure I know what it is you're suggesting,' Becky said, a puzzled frown wrinkling her forehead.

May sighed. 'About time I told you why I asked you to stay here tonight, Becky. The truth is I've got to get out of 'ere. Council won't transfer the tenancy to me. Rotten lot! They'd let a son take it over, but not an unmarried daughter. They want me out.'

'Good job too, if you ask me,' Aunt Lily cried out scornfully as she poked her head round the door. 'These tenements should 'ave been pulled down years ago.'

'Well nobody's asking you, an' I thought you'd gone up t' bed,' May said sternly.

'I 'ad. I've come down cos I forgot me drink of water. I'll need it in the night.'

'Yeah, I believe you, thousands wouldn't,' May grinned. 'Now you are 'ere, will you tell Becky or shall I?'

'You do yer own telling, and clear that table. Put the plates in the sink, leave 'em for me t' do in the morning.'

'Aunt! Go to bed! Before I do something to you that I'll be sorry for.'

'I'm going,' she said as she turned towards Becky. 'Yer see

what a moody temper our May's got, always wants 'er own way. Yer wanna watch 'er Becky, see 'er bad habits don't rub off on to you,' Lily advised, giving Becky a sly wink as once again she made for the door.

The two girls looked at each other and burst out laughing.

'Aunt Lil loves to know what's going on,' May said with a grin. 'She's got ears as sharp as a bat's, especially when it comes to other folk's conversations. Still, her heart's in the right place. The long an' short of what she's suggesting is that you and I both go and lodge with her. Said we can each have a room of our own.'

'Well,' Becky said, delight and surprise expressed in her wide smile, 'that would solve your and my problem. I can only stay at the hostel for a few weeks more and I am getting desperate, but you haven't told me where your aunt lives. Has she got a big house? Would it be easy for us to get to and from work?'

'Yes, she's got a big house. On three floors it is and it's in South Lambeth Road, only a stone's throw from the Tate Library.'

'I'm not even sure where the Tate Library is,' Becky answered, feeling naïve.

'It's easy to get to, over Vauxhall Bridge and you're practically there. Buses now run through and they stop almost outside Aunt Lil's front door. Besides if we take up her offer, there's a couple of the other waitresses on our shift who live at Stockwell an' we could always share a cab with them when we're on late turn.'

'Sounds too good to be true,' Becky said, doing her best to stifle a yawn. 'Sorry, May', she added quickly, trying to hide her sudden embarrassment.

'It's me that should be saying sorry, keeping you up like this, you must be dead on yer feet. Come on, let's go up to bed. If you like we can take Aunt Lil home in the morning, that way you'll get to see her place and then you can think about it and make your mind up later.'

Becky smiled, colouring up slightly. 'I won't be sorry to get my head down.'

The great big feather mattress was a joy to wriggle into and the stone hot-water bottle was still just hot enough for Becky to put her feet on.

'If things work out as my aunt plans it won't seem so bad, me losing me mum,' May said, snuggling into her pillow. 'Hardest part is getting rid of all Mum's bits an' pieces. Not that any of it is worth much but to Mum an' me it was our home. Aunt Lil reckons the best thing is to give it all to the Salvation Army, we'd only get coppers if we did call the second-hand totters in.'

'You'd know for certain the Sally Army would see it went to a needy family,' Becky replied, her voice sounding very sleepy.

'Yeah, you're right, not a lot else I can do, is there?'

'Except be grateful to your aunt. I expect if you go to live with her you'll be able to take most of your own bits and pieces.'

'Trust you to give out sensible advice,' May said, pulling the bedclothes up higher over her shoulders.

She got no reply this time from Becky. She was fast asleep.

'What's the hurry? Can't I even 'ave another cup of tea?' May asked her aunt, using a tone of voice that was more a wail.

'No you can't. Move yourself, I wanna get 'ome while there's still some daylight left.'

Becky was smiling to herself as she helped to clear away the breakfast things. The relationship between May and her Aunt Lil had to be seen to be believed. There was a bond of understanding, and that it was a bond formed out of love for each other, Becky was in no doubt. They were rough and ready, both of them, but Becky knew that she'd have to go a long way to find better friends.

The sky had darkened, the rain was now falling heavily and Lily Maynard opened up her umbrella as she stepped off the bus on to the pavement. May took hold of Becky's arm, holding her close as they hurried along the few yards from the bus stop to the row of tall terraced houses that had steps leading up to the front doors. 'Number five,' May said, as they practically ran up the steps into the shelter of the wide porch.

When Aunt Lil opened the big front door and Becky stepped into the passageway she breathed a sigh of pleasure. The ceilings were high, the wallpaper bright and the cream-coloured paintwork shone. A half-moon shaped oak table was set against the wall; on it rested a huge copper bowl filled with evergreen plants.

Aunt Lil gave Becky a smile and May put her arm around her shoulders as they went through to the big old-fashioned kitchen.

'The fire's out,' Aunt Lil told them matter-of-factly, as she picked up the poker and rattled the bars of the gleaming black-leaded range. 'Won't take me long to get it going.'

'Aunt Lil,' May began, 'Becky and I have to go to work tonight and we have our uniforms to see to yet. May we just have a look round and then we'll 'ave a cuppa with you before we go?'

Lily smiled. 'I ask yer ter come as me lodgers but what I really wanted to say ter both of yer is, you'd be doing me a favour, I rattle around this place like a pea in a colander. There was a time when I looked after young kiddies while their mothers went out cleaning offices but now they reckon I'm too old ter be trusted with their kids.'

Both girls made sympathetic noises but Lily put her hand up. 'Let me finish. If you do decide to come 'ere, it will be yer home. In every sense of the word, an' I mean that, Becky. May 'as 'ad the run of this place since she could walk an' it would be the same for you. Yer own room. Bring anything yer like with yer and although I know yer get well fed at

Joey Lyons there'll always be a bit of something ready for yer when you finish work an' on yer days off I'll do a roast an' all the trimmings.'

May was shaking her head. 'I don't believe you! Why don't you just let me show Becky around upstairs and then she will be better able to see if she likes the look of the place. Though 'ow she's gonna cope with you an' the way you carry on, Gawd knows.'

'Don't be so cheeky, May! And as it 'appens I ain't finished with Becky yet.'

Becky was laughing. 'I'm listening, Aunt Lil, don't pay her any attention.'

'First thing you got t' do, Becky, luv, is 'ave a talk with your parents. They don't know me from Adam an' they ain't about ter let you move in 'ere without first giving me and the 'ouse the once-over. I wouldn't think much of them if they did.'

May realized she was wasting her time trying to argue with her aunt and she raised her hands in a token of surrender and burst out laughing. 'All right, 'ave you finished what you wanted to say now? Cos if you've no more objections Becky and I will take ourselves upstairs and begin our tour of inspection.'

'And I will light the gas and put the kettle on to boil,' her aunt said, mimicking the posh accent May had just used.

Somebody had been hard at work.

The whole house was spick and span and every room smelt of lavender. On the first floor there were three bedrooms, one large one in the front, two slightly smaller at the back and, heaven-sent, a lavatory on the same landing. The top floor consisted of one huge long room, which ran the width of the house, had three small windows and was charmingly set out.

There was a small gate-legged table folded down in front of one window and an armchair placed on either side. A tall single oak wardrobe stood against one wall with a chest of drawers further along. The walls themselves were wood-panelled halfway up from the floor, the top half decorated with a pretty tiny flower-patterned paper, and the ceiling looked freshly painted. The single bed was covered with a white counterpane the fringe of which reached to the floor and on top of that there lay a patchwork eiderdown.

Wonders would never cease; there was a bathroom. Set at the centre of the wall, the huge white monster of a bath stood on cast-iron claw feet. It had a single brass tap and above it gleamed a copper geyser.

'However much do you have to put in the gas meter to get enough hot water to fill that?' Becky asked May, sheer amazement visible on her face.

'God knows. Whenever I've stayed here I've aways had me bath in a tin bath in front of the kitchen fire,' May laughed.

Becky laughed with her, thinking of her home in New Malden.

'Can I go back into the long room, have another look?' Becky asked.

''Course you can,' May agreed.

Becky crossed the polished linoleum, noticing it was well-worn in places but two pretty rugs had been placed one each side of the bed. She stood looking out of the window.

'What a view, you can see half of London from up here. I bet it would be smashing to lie in bed in this room when the wind is really blustering.'

'You can't hardly see a thing,' May retorted, 'the rain's still lashing down.'

'Use your imagination,' Becky said dreamily.

'Use what you like. I'm going downstairs to have a cup of tea before we think about setting off and getting ready for work. Are you coming?'

'Yes,' Becky answered quickly, her head buzzing with thoughts, 'but tell me, how come your aunt lives in a big house like this all on her own?'

'Well, in a nutshell, she got served the dirty.'

'That's no answer, what happened?'

'If you must know she married a widower, sixteen years

older than she was at the time. He was living in this house with his three young boys and he knew he was on a good thing when he moved my Aunt Lil in.

'She slogged her guts out doing her best to bring those boys up. When Tom died the boys wanted to turn her out of house and home. Nearly succeeded an' all. The landlord was a gentleman, he said the rightful tenant was my aunt. The boys cleared off an' left her, she's not seen hide nor hair of them from that day to this. Been a bit of a struggle for her to pay the rent over the years but one way an' another she's got by. Bless her.'

Becky reached out and patted the back of May's hand. 'What a sad story,' she exclaimed softly as side by side the two girls went back downstairs.

'Yeah, well, that's the way it goes sometimes,' May sighed.

'Well?' Aunt Lil demanded as they sat down at her table, now covered with a snowy white cloth.

'Got the best china out, I see, all in Becky's honour is it?' May chivvied her aunt.

'Good job you're not staying long today my girl, cos if you were I'd end up boxing your ears. Now cut a piece of that gingerbread and pass it to Becky.'

'Gingerbread an' all,' May said as she grinned at Becky. 'You are getting the royal treatment.'

Becky smothered a giggle. 'I love that long room at the top of the house,' she boldly said.

'You mean what I think you mean?' Lily asked softly. 'Cos, if you do, why don't you ask yer mum an' dad to come and see me, then if they think it's all right you can 'ave that room.'

'I'd like that, and I'd be ever so grateful,' Becky replied.

'Good, but you don't 'ave t' go on about being grateful cos the favour will work both ways. So, if your parents agree, that's settled then.'

May touched Becky's arm, gave her a big smile. 'It'll be smashing, you'll see. We'll have a great time.'

'Hang on a minute, Miss.' Lily raised her eyebrows, pretending to glare at her niece. 'I'm not 'aving you out all hours of the day an' night so you can put all those kind of thoughts out of yer 'ead.'

May winked at Becky, ignoring her aunt. 'She won't know whether we're working or not. Get ourselves a coupla those toffs an' we'll be away up West every night.'

'I've got news for you, young lady,' Lily sniffed at May, 'I shall make it my business to find out what shifts you're doing, make no mistake.'

'Aunt Lil, you couldn't be a dragon no matter how hard you tried.' May got to her feet and flung her arms around her aunt's neck, rubbing her face against Lily's cheek. 'I love you,' she whispered in her ear.

'Get off!' Lily wriggled free, winked at Becky and said, 'You'd better get going if you've both so much t' do.'

'Well, it's not bad, is it Becky?' May asked, shivering as they huddled together under an umbrella while they waited for the bus. 'What d'you think?'

'I think I must have landed on my feet the day I met you, May Stevens. Your Aunt Lily's house is beautiful. An absolute credit to her. I thought I'd had my share of good luck when I landed a job with Lyons. The hostel hasn't been so bad but you've no idea how homesick I've been at times. I know my mum an' dad will be over the moon to think that I'll be with you and we'll both have someone to keep an eye on us.'

'Yeah, I'm glad you feel that way. I'll still miss my mum but at least I won't be lost for company.'

'And you'll be able to keep up your running battle of wits against your aunt,' Becky chuckled.

'It's only a game between us,' May said, laughing at her. 'She loves a bit of a skirmish. I've got a feeling this is all going to work out well for all three of us.'

I'm sure it will,' Becky answered, and there was a note of strong conviction in her voice.

Chapter Fourteen

As the weeks went by Becky couldn't believe how well everything had worked out. She and May were well settled in at Aunt Lil's. Her mother and father had approved wholeheartedly of both the accommodation and Aunt Lil herself. In fact it would be true to say that a good friendship had sprung up between the three of them. Having been made so welcome on the day that they had come up to London in order to see over the house in South Lambeth Road, Joyce and Joe Russell had insisted that Lily must respond with a visit to New Malden.

'Salt of the earth, your parents are, Becky, and that's no exaggeration,' Lily never tired of telling her.

By now Becky had also got to know some of her customers quite well. Morning coffee time had its regulars. The old lady in the hat adorned with glistening cherries probably had more money than she knew what to do with. Time and time again she tried to press a coin into Becky's hand, sometimes as much as a florin. Becky would gently curl the old lady's fingers back over the money, pat her hand, smile softly and point to the large sign which said 'No Gratuities'. Tipping was greatly discouraged by Lyons. Loneliness was that lady's problem.

Then there was a tall striking man, who had probably spent his life in the forces, who barked his order at her, stayed about half an hour then moved into the smoking room to read the paper and enjoy his pipe. At the end of the first month of serving this gentleman he had left a small box, prettily wrapped and tied on top with a tiny bow of ribbon, on the table as he made to depart. Becky was reminding him of the no-tipping policy when Miss Timson had appeared from nowhere.

'In this gentleman's case we waive the rule,' she said so softly that Becky had to strain to hear her.

Aunt Lil had blushed with pleasure when Becky had presented her with the box containing Fuller's handmade chocolates.

'Pity they don't let us take the money instead,' May complained on one occasion when a gent had given her a bottle of lavender water. 'We could end up being real rich if they did.'

Trust May to see the logic in it all.

Lunchtime crowds were the ones Becky liked the best. Young people mostly, always in a hurry, they were sparkling and jolly, living life to the full.

One woman Becky did not take to.

'She frightens the hell out of me,' Becky whispered to May, as she made sure the china and coffeepot were set out right on her tray.

May bent her head towards Becky, her voice a low whisper. 'Word has it that her husband left her for some flighty young girl and she sits out there planning her revenge.'

'Get on with you,' Becky grinned, 'if we believed half the rumours that fly around this place we might well come to the conclusion that every man in London has a mistress on the side.'

'Stick around, Becky,' May called after her, 'you never know, your day may come.'

'Well yours won't if you don't get a move on and do some work for a change.' May's face flushed up as she turned to see Robert Matthews grinning at Becky over the top of her head.

Becky was laughing fit to burst as she made her way back out on to the floor.

Only one thing was bothering her. Miss Timson was forever telling her at morning inspection that her cap did not sit properly on her head.

'And no wonder,' Miss Timson remarked, time and time again, 'it's all that hair you are trying to poke under it.'

Having given in to Miss Timson's insistence and egged on by her workmates Becky had made an appointment for her day off, at a hairdresser's in Stockwell, to have her hair bobbed.

She wasn't looking forward to it a bit.

'Come on,' May urged, staring at Becky. 'By the look on your face anyone one would think you were going to the dentist instead of to the hairdresser's.'

'I half wish I were,' Becky mumbled. 'We're both dressed up, surely we could find something better to do on our half day off.'

May was dressed in a navy-blue suit with a long straight skirt and a kick pleat back and front. Beneath the boxy jacket she wore a high-necked white blouse, the front adorned with a small cameo brooch.

Becky was wearing a pale pink crepe-de-Chine blouse with a soft bow at the throat beneath a loose grey jacket and grey skirt that fitted extremely well over her slender hips, the hem flaring out to reach her ankles. They each wore buttoned black boots.

May was able to wear a stylish close-fitting cloche hat over her short thick reddish hair while Becky, with her long dark thick hair, still clung to the larger boater-shaped felts which she spent a great deal of time retrimming.

The salon was somewhat more elegant than Becky had imagined but the reception she received was most friendly.

Minutes ticked by as the hairdresser, quite obviously a lady of fashion herself, ran Becky's long ringlets through her fingers, lifting the tresses high in the air and letting them fall loosely over the colourful cape that had been draped around her shoulders.

Finally she seemed satisfied. 'Beautiful hair,' she murmured, 'I know exactly what style will suit you to perfection.'

Becky screwed her eyes up in fright as she listened to the snip-snip of the scissors. Parts of her hair were tightly drawn back and dampened, other bunches were piled on top of her head, as a different style started to take shape.

'There you are then,' the stylist said when she finally stepped back and held a mirror at several different angles for Becky to see her whole head. All members of the staff gathered round the chair, assuring her that the new style suited her so well. Reluctantly Becky turned her head this way and that as she gazed into the mirror in front of her. She felt unsure. A different person altogether.

Her hair, still thick and glossy, although tons of it seemed to be lying on the floor around her feet, was now neat, framing her cheeks softly with a soft swirl. She put her hand up to touch the back. It felt good, bouncy, but her neck felt so bare.

May, standing behind her, nodded enthusiastically. 'It's fabulous, you look marvellous.'

'I look so different,' Becky said, voicing her fears.

'Not before time!' May responded with a grin.

At inspection next morning, Miss Timson was on duty.

'Excellent, my dear,' Miss Timson remarked as she gazed at Becky's new look. 'I'm sure you will find it a great deal easier to keep your cap on straight now. And believe me the style certainly suits you. Yes, most flattering.'

Becky flushed with pleasure.

Unseen, standing in the background, Robert Matthews wasn't so sure. From the first moment of setting eyes on Rebecca Russell his imagination had run away with him whenever he had gazed at her oval face framed by those gorgeous thick dark ringlets. No matter how hard she had tried to push her mop of hair beneath her cap some wisps had always escaped. The image of all that hair allowed to hang freely, blow in the breeze, while the slim dainty owner ran through green fields, had been a picture in his mind for some time.

As he made his way to the basement to examine the perishables left from the previous day, all of which would have been listed by the manageress, Robert Matthews was a very thoughtful young man.

Chapter Fifteen

'HOW MUCH HAVE we got to spend?'

'Quite a bit what with us getting paid a bonus as well,' Becky answered May.

They were sitting side by side on the top deck of a bus on their way to Oxford Street to do their Christmas shopping. It was the first week in December and bitterly cold and both girls laughed as they tugged their fur collars more tightly against their cheeks.

Becky hadn't been a bit surprised when her mother had turned up in South Lambeth Road bearing a gift of fur for both herself and for May. Parading up and down in Aunt Lil's warm kitchen the girls had thrown the long strips of fur carelessly over their shoulders, pretending casualness, secretly thrilled.

'How come?' May had been anxious to know.

Becky had already guessed.

'A village jumble sale,' Joyce Russell said triumphantly. 'I asked how much the vicar wanted for the manky old fox fur and he said he'd take half-a-crown. I ended up giving him one an' sixpence.'

'Mum!'

'Well it wasn't worth any more, not the state it was in. Took me ages to clean it and I paid fourpence for a long silk underslip which I used to reline the two parts of the fur which ended up as neck trimmings for you two.'

'Cor, you've shaped them beautifully, we can use them on jackets or on our winter coats,' May enthused as she kissed Mrs Russell on the cheek.

'I got this for you, Lily,' Joyce said, handing over a heavy cardigan knitted in fawn and brown with a cable stitch running up each side of the front.

'Why, it's really lovely,' Lily exclaimed loudly, her face wreathed in smiles. 'Don't tell me you got that at the jumble sale as well.'

'Kind of, but not exactly,' Joyce admitted.

Lily looked at Becky, her face showing bewilderment.

'What my mum means is, yes, she did buy the original at the jumble sale but then she unpicks the garment, washes the wool and reknits the whole thing.'

'Gawd luv us, Joyce, you're a bloody marvel an' no mistake. I ain't got the patience to do anything like that. I promise yer I shall wear this lovely warm cardy till it falls off me back. Thanks ever so much.'

Joyce had beamed with pleasure, her efforts well rewarded by the fact that the receivers of the gifts were so pleased.

Oxford Street was jam-packed.

May laughed and grimaced as they pushed their way to the kerb. 'Let's cross the road and go straight into Selfridges,' she said cheerfully as she tucked her hand through the crook of Becky's arm.

The beauty and cosmetic counter was just inside the door and Becky decided that it was here she would best get a present for her sisters-in-law and also probably something for Ella.

'Ponds cold cream for night care, and vanishing cream as a powder base,' stated the placard above the prettily gift-wrapped boxes.

'I think I'll get one each for Ada and Joan, but I'm not sure that Ella would want that,' Becky said.

'Does she use perfume?' May queried.

'She probably would but I don't think her money would run to it. I'll leave Ella till last, see if I've got enough to buy her something to wear.'

May was having the time of her life. She had pounced on a box of Potter and Moore's soap and lavender powder cream for Aunt Lil.

'Decide for me, Becky please. Shall I buy Evening in Paris, don't you just love the dark blue and silver bottle? Or shall it be Californian Poppy?'

'Depends on the person you're buying it for,' Becky sensibly remarked.

'Don't be daft,' May grinned, 'the perfume is for me.'

'In that case I'm half-inclined to treat myself too,' Becky said, returning the grin. 'What do you think of these tiny pots of solid perfume? Smell that,' she ordered, holding out her arm to May. The very refined lady assistant had just placed a tiny dab of the wax on to Becky's wrist.

'Works wonders for a girl's morale,' intoned the chief saleslady.

May sniffed, raised her head and rolled her eyes heavenward, before saying, 'Go on, be a devil, with a dab of that behind your ears you'll have half the men in London swarming round you.'

'Perhaps you ought to settle for this then,' Becky retorted, her eyes full of devilment, 'between us we'll bewitch all the men '

Their mood was very lighthearted.

With their packages bought and paid for the two girls moved along.

'Cor, look at that advertisement. "Tangee", funny name for a lipstick,' May remarked, her eyes wide with wonder.

'Strange name and a strange colour,' murmured Becky. 'Whoever would want to use an orange lipstick?'

The actual lipstick was set on a velvet base within a glass box. As Becky made to replace it back down on the counter the smooth box almost slipped from her fingers. Both she and a man standing nearby tried to catch it, and as they grappled their fingers met. Becky looked up into the light blue eyes of Robert Matthews.

The apology she had been about to make died in her throat. She felt her cheeks turn crimson and her hands trembled. He took the box from her, made some comment and replaced it on the counter. She mumbled her thanks, keeping her head down so that he wouldn't see how embarrassed she was. It was a relief when he turned towards May, saying, 'Doing all your Christmas shopping?'

'Trying our best, sir,' May answered with a laugh, not in the least bit daunted by having met one of their bosses on their day off.

'Happy hunting,' he said, smiling at them both, and a moment later he had disappeared into the throng of shoppers.

'Don't know quite what t' make of that bloke,' May said as they stood undecided as to where to make for next. 'He always seems so kind of distant, as if he was lonely all the time. One of the older waitresses told me he's a relation of the Lyons family. Went to public school by all accounts and then Oxford and straight from there into the service of Joey Lyons.'

'What about his parents, or doesn't he have any family?' Becky asked.

'How the hell would I know?' May cried. 'Let's get on with our shopping an' make up our minds that this coming Christmas will be one of the best ever. Agreed?'

'Agreed,' Becky smiled her answer. 'Let's make for the toy department. I've two nephews to buy for not to mention my six-month-old goddaughter, Margaret.'

'How can she be your goddaughter when she hasn't been christened yet?' May was curious to know as they elbowed their way though the shoppers towards the great winding staircase.

'Ah! I've been meaning to tell you. I've had a word with Mr Gower and he sent me to see Miss Nicholls, remember she's over Miss Timson. The long an' short of it is, I'll do extra hours over the run-up to Christmas and then get a few days' leave all together in the New Year.'

'What do you want New Year off for? You're not Scottish.'

'Nobody said I was, dummy. I'm going home for a double celebration. Ella and Peter are having baby Margaret christened, and Tom Ferguson and Mary Marsden are getting married.'

'Is that the Tom you told me nearly got himself locked up when he saved that young kiddy from drowning?'

'Yes, that's the one. I reckon the whole of Kingston will turn out to see those two tie the knot.'

'Ah, that'll be nice,' May said as they joined everyone else hellbent on buying toys for Christmas presents.

Almost unnoticed the weeks slipped by, filled with long hours of hard work and growing proficiency for both May and Becky as Christmas came and went.

May had been able to cope right from the beginning. For Becky it had taken longer. With her slight frame, her huge brown eyes and deceptively gentle voice Becky seemed very vulnerable and many a gentleman tried it on. They had flowers delivered to the Corner House for her with cards offering to take her out to dinner. The bolder ones suggested she might like to visit London's night spots.

Always in the background Mr Gower hovered, ready to protect her should the need ever arise. So far Becky felt she had coped very well. A big factor in helping her to settle into a steady routine was living with Aunt Lil and May in that lovely old house in South Lambeth Road.

Whether it was late at night or during the day when she and May arrived back from a shift she repeatedly told herself how lucky she was to have found such a haven in the heart of London and as for Aunt Lil, that tiny lady never ceased to amaze her.

On the go from morning to night, she never seemed to

tire herself out. Either of the girls had only to leave a soiled blouse or an article of underwear hanging over the back of a chair in their rooms and by the time they returned it would be laid out on their bed freshly washed and ironed.

The only problem was Aunt Lil fed them too well. Appetizing smells met them the minute they set foot in the hall, no matter what the time was. Irresistible puddings were offered and both girls complained that they would end up looking like real ten-ton Tessies.

Pub nights were hilarious. The first time they took Aunt Lil for a drink Becky found it almost unbelievable. Two glasses of port wine and Aunt Lil was standing on a chair singing her heart out to the delight of all the customers. Whether she sang slow sentimental songs or a bawdy ballad her voice held listeners spellbound. Trouble was, all the customers then wanted to treat Aunt Lil to another drink. Once, she had suddenly slipped to the floor and lain full length. So still was she that May and Becky ran to crouch at her side, only to find that she was faking.

'Are you sure you're all right?' May asked.

Aunt Lil merely winked her eye and told them brightly, 'You ain't seen nothing tonight. One day I might surprise you and have a skinful.'

'God forbid,' both girls had cried out.

Ah well, Becky was saying to herself as they led Aunt Lil home that night, there is never a dull moment when this little lady is about.

Christmas wasn't all hard work.

Becky went home for Christmas and Boxing Day. On Christmas Day the whole family gathered in Albert Road and Joyce Russell was in her element with her whole brood to cook for. Two more guests swelled the numbers on Boxing Day when Aunt Lil and May came down from London.

With the midday meal over Aunt Lil sat back in an armchair

and looked at the huge Christmas tree which had already started to shed its needles.

'Well, Joyce and Joe, I never expected anything like this welcome we've had today,' she said quietly. 'All your lads and daughters-in-law pitching in to help, talk about a real family do, it's smashing. Thanks ever so much for inviting us.'

'We're glad you decided to come,' Joyce replied. 'It kind of makes up for the way you look after our Becky. And it's nice the way she and May get on, isn't it?'

Lil nodded and jumped as one of the logs dropped lower in the grate, sending out a shower of sparks, and she was silent as Joe took two more logs from the basket and made up the fire. When he had settled back in his chair Lil spoke again.

'D'yer know what really did me heart good t' see today, Joyce? It were your grandsons' faces when May gave them those little presents. Ronnie's eyes nearly popped out of his head, an' young Joey looked really pleased. We ain't used t' aving young kiddies around, it's a real pleasure just to sit an' watch them.'

Joyce laughed. 'They weren't expecting more presents today. They were thrilled, that motor and the fire engine you an' May bought them are lovely. You ought to be here sometimes, hear the racket they make.'

The afternoon was full of excitement as grown-ups joined in silly games such as pass the parcel, postman's knock and spin the bottle. The kiddies were giggling and uttering shrieks of delight when it was Grandad's turn to kiss their nanna.

Christmas cake and mince pies with cups of tea and fizzy lemonade for the children was followed by trifle well laced with sherry.

All too soon the light faded. Joe put on his overcoat and bowler hat in readiness to escort Lil and May to the railway station. All the women and the men lined up to put their arms around Aunt Lil and plant a kiss on her cheek, while Becky and May stood in the doorway smiling at how popular she had become in such a short time.

Becky watched with her mother as they set off down the road and she heard her father say, 'One each side of me, c'mon, take hold of me arm, pavement's a bit frosty, don't want either of you slipping an' breaking yer neck.'

'Dad likes them, doesn't he, Mum?'

''Course he does, pet, so do all the family. We'll have to make sure that we ask them more often. Perhaps even have Lily down here for a holiday next summer.'

'Thanks, Mum.'

'For what?'

'Oh, you know. For such a lovely Christmas, for making May and her aunt so welcome, for having all me brothers here, the kids as well, for everything, mostly for being my mum.'

Joyce took hold of her hand and said, smiling, 'You're making me feel old. Let's go in, it's getting real cold.'

It was back to work next day for Becky but she left with the sure and certain knowledge that within a week she would be back home to take part in two very different ceremonies, both of which would be very dear to her heart.

Chapter Sixteen

THE FIRST SATURDAY of 1926 dawned bright and clear with a weak sun showing up the heavy frost that had formed during the night. Becky had arrived at Mill Street before nine that morning and was immediately given the task of hemming up the bottom of the pretty dress Ella had made for baby Margaret.

'We won't dress her till the last moment,' Ella said cheerfully to Becky as she stitched. 'With my luck she's sure to be sick.'

'I wish t' God I'd gone to work,' Peter moaned with mock seriousness. 'It seems as if half the blooming street has popped in here this morning on one pretext or another. You'd think it was us getting married instead of just going as guests to Tom's wedding.'

Ella looked a bit guilty as Becky raised her eyebrows in query. 'I made a two-piece for Annie Smith, you know she's landlady of the Swan, well she had this lovely length of material an' she paid me well. She came to collect it.'

'That's only one,' Peter said, laughing loudly. 'You'd have been better off opening a millinery shop the number of ruddy hats you've trimmed.' Turning to Becky he grinned and said, 'Yer know she's always going on about how much she dislikes Martha Tubman, well, she practically remade an old hat for her.'

'Oh, leave it out, Peter, she lives next door and it's far better to hold the candle to the devil, anyway she's been ever so appreciative. But what about you? You've been more hindrance than help this morning. Standing about like a lemon. You're never going to be ready on time. You'd better get down to the cleaners an' pick up your suit,' Ella ordered.

'Are you sure you two can manage without me?' he asked sarcastically.

Ella ruffled his thick hair and kissed him on the cheek. 'Of course we can,' she told him fondly, then quickly added, 'Don't bang the front door as you go out. I'm still hoping the baby won't wake up till we're nearly ready to leave for the church.'

'Are you and Peter coping all right?' Becky gently asked as soon as she and Ella were alone.

'Yes, but . . .' It was difficult to explain, even to herself. 'Peter doesn't talk to me much and some evenings he goes off on his own and I don't see him for hours.'

'Does it matter? He always was a bit on the quiet side.'

'Sometimes it matters. When I'm feeling a bit down. I'm not sure if he's all that well, not that he ever complains. It's just a feeling I get, more so when he has a bad night.'

'What do you mean by a bad night?'

'He cries out, quite loudly, though he doesn't wake up, but he twists and turns and his pyjamas are wringing wet because he sweats so much.'

'Have you suggested he goes to see a doctor?'

Ella turned from the sink, laid down her tea towel and looked Becky full in the face. 'Of course I have,' she said irritably. 'He doesn't want to know. Tells me I imagine it half the time.'

Suddenly the clock on the mantelpiece chimed the hour and both girls were amazed to see it was already eleven o'clock.

'We'll talk later,' Becky said her voice sharp with concern. 'Right now we'd better go upstairs and get our glad rags on and then see to baby Margaret.'

The church looked beautiful; a lot of work had gone into the floral decorations and the sides of the front pews were decked with bows of white ribbon. Most all of the pews were full and people were beginning to fidget and then the bells pealed and the organist began to play 'Here Comes the Bride'.

All heads turned to see Mary walking down the aisle on her father's arm.

Ella nudged Becky. 'What a transformation!' she whispered.

Nobody ever spoke a truer word, Becky thought to herself.

The high-necked white satin dress Mary wore fell to the floor in soft loose folds beneath the gathered bust. It made her look slim and taller. On her straight shiny hair she had a circlet of orange blossom entwined with seed pearls. A long veil was secured by the headdress and hung in folds, framing Mary's chubby face with its lace edging.

As the bride and groom joined hands at the altar half the congregation gave a sigh of joy and Dolly Ferguson, dressed today in a grey silk dress with long loose jacket and wearing a hat that would have done Queen Mary proud, was heard trying to sniff back the tears.

When the ceremony was over, Tom walked, holding himself erect, with his bride on his arm, smiling selfconsciously at all the well-wishers. The photographer continued to gesticulate excitedly until he was sure that no one had been left out of such a momentous occasion. Then everyone went back into the cars and off to the hall for the reception, where great quantities of food were consumed, toasts were drunk and finally glasses were raised to Mr and Mrs Ferguson.

It was Peter who summed up the day. He rose to his feet and in a loud clear voice declared, 'Anyone with half an eye can see that Tom and Mary were made for each other.'

Besides friends and relatives the entire street had turned out for Tom's wedding and they showed their agreement with Tom's statement by much foot-stamping, clapping of hands and very loud cheering.

The dancing started, the first waltz led off by the bride

and groom. Dolly Ferguson, though clearly worried at the thought of losing her son, had borne herself well throughout the proceedings. Then Tom came up to her and asked, 'Mum, will you dance with me?'

Dolly's eyes were watery as she got to her feet and murmured, 'Thanks, son.'

Tom took his mother by the arm and slowly led her on to the floor. 'Everything will turn out all right, you'll see, Mum.' Tom's voice was soft but steady as he did his best to reassure his mother. 'Mary's a good girl and you'll love her when you get t' know her better.'

Dolly took her hand off her son's arm and rubbed her eyes. 'I know, son, I know. An' I promise yer, lad, it won't be for the want of trying on my part.'

The dance ended and Dolly had two fingers crossed as Tom escorted her back to sit with all the other ladies. She was vowing to herself that she wouldn't be so sharp off the mark to voice an opinion in future. I'll keep me thoughts t' meself an' with a bit of luck an' the blessing of God Almighty me daughter-in-law and me might get along quite well. Slowly she unwound her fingers from behind her back. She'd done enough praying for one day. Time I had a few drinks, she mumbled to herself, as she made her way to the bar that had been set up at the back of the hall.

By mid-afternoon the next day the hall, front room and the living room of Ella and Peter's house were crammed with people. The christening of baby Margaret had taken place in the same church as Tom and Mary's wedding and a great number of the people packed into this small house today had been guests at both events.

A group of women was perched on the stairs while kiddies, including Becky's two nephews, were dashing here, there and everywhere, flushed with the excitement of attending two grown-up parties in two days.

The baby looked beautiful in a long christening dress of white lace trimmed with tiny rosebuds. She lay in her grandmother's arms, cooing contentedly, getting lots of ooos and ahhhs as everyone admired her creamy complexion and downy covering of fair hair.

Peggy James sighed as her old friend Joyce Russell planted herself down next to her on the settee. 'What's the matter, luv?' Joyce asked with growing concern. 'I'd have thought you'd be over the moon today.'

Peggy wasn't able to form a reply because Dolly Ferguson pushed her bulky figure through the crowd with a tray of small sandwiches. Handing a plate to Peggy and one to Joyce, she said, ''Ere, take a couple t' be going on with, there's egg an' cress or salmon an' cucumber. Living it up, ain't we? Two days running. Annie Smith's doing the tea an' your Ella's going to cut the cake next. Can't get over 'ow good that baby 'as been. Lawd luv 'er, she's a right precious little mite.'

Joyce watched with amusement as Dolly moved on with her tray. 'Don't she ever pause for breath?' she said to Peggy grinning.

'Don't sound like it, does it?'

Then Joyce raised her eyebrows as she caught sight of a man across the room. 'Who's that, Peg?'

Peggy followed her gaze. 'That's Peter's father. You've met him before, when my Ella got married.'

'Really? I never recognized him. I don't remember he looked so well turned out before.'

'Somehow I don't think he was. Spruced up all right today though, ain't he?'

'Yes, he is an' all. Perhaps he's got a new woman in his life.'

'Wouldn't blame the man if he had,' Peggy said, lifting the baby from the crook of her arm and resting her up against her shoulder. 'Peter told me his dad went to pieces when his mother died so tragically.'

'Has he come all this way just for the christening?' Joyce asked.

'No, I think he's going to stay a couple of nights.'

'Oh, that's all right then. You were about to tell me why you were sighing so heavily when Dolly barged in. Is there anything wrong?'

'No. Not so's you'd notice. It's just that I get this feeling that my Ella's not really happy. She adores the baby, no getting away from that but . . . money's tight . . . it could be that.'

'We still worry about our kids no matter that they're grown-up, don't we? We'll have to talk later, maybe I'll make time an' come round to you tomorrow.' Joyce had to cut the conversation short because a growing number of people were crowding into the room.

'Cake time,' Ella called, adding sweetly. 'Thank you all for the lovely presents you've given us for the baby. Now Becky, her godmother, is going to do the honours and cut her christening cake.'

When the time came to leave Peter gently kissed Becky's cheek, then Ella hugged her.

'I'll see you tomorrow,' Becky said, 'I haven't got to go back to work until Tuesday.'

'Great, I'll have the house a bit more straight by the time you get here. I hope,' Ella ended on a laugh.

'Don't worry about it,' Becky told her, then over Ella's shoulder as she returned the hug, Becky caught sight of Peter's father standing alone at the foot of the stairs, his hands in his pockets, his face frowning. Something was worrying him.

Walking with her mother and her father to where they would catch the tram back to New Malden, Becky felt that she would give a great deal to know just what it was that was worrying Peter's father so much.

Her parents and she were glad when at last the tram rumbled into view. They were all feeling tired and no wonder, it had been a hectic two days. A lot of hard work and preparation had gone into both events. But it had been well worth it.

Oh yes, Becky decided. It had been good to see so many happy people gathered together.

Chapter Seventeen

'GOD ALONE KNOWS what's going on in there this morning,' Martha Tubman called out, tossing her head in the direction of the house next door as Becky came within yards of Ella's house.

'Sorry?' Becky paused, a frown creasing her forehead.

'I've never 'eard the likes of it before, not from in there I ain't.' Martha came down her front path and out on to the pavement to meet Becky. 'After everyone having such a good time over the weekend I can't make it out. The baby's been screaming her head off for the last half-hour and Ella's been yelling at the top of her voice. I've banged on the wall but it ain't made the slightest difference.'

Becky's heart turned a somersault. 'Is Peter in there?' she asked.

'No, he's gone t' work. I know cos I saw him set off when I was getting the milk in just before seven.'

'All right, thanks, Martha,' Becky said.

There certainly was a right hullabaloo coming from inside the house. The front door was ajar and as she pushed her way in Becky felt alarm bells start to ring in her head. The pram was wedged across the foot of the stairs. The baby looked to be in a terrible state and she smelt horrible. Her napkin, into which she had emptied her bowels, had slid down over her little legs leaving her dirty bottom bare. Red in the face, still crying, her tiny fists frantically beating the air, she looked awful.

'There, there my pet,' Becky crooned. 'Whatever have they done t' you? Ssh, ssh, Auntie Becky's here now.'

Wrinkling her nose, Becky coupled the baby's feet together and with one hand lifted her up by her ankles while with her other she removed the soiled napkin to the bottom of the pram. Sliding the undersheet free she used it to wipe the baby's dirty bottom as best she could. Freeing the underblanket from the pram she wrapped it closely around Margaret and took her up into her arms.

'There, there, my little darling,' she hummed, walking up and down all the while rubbing the baby's back with circular movements. 'That's better, isn't it?' The baby's crying grew quieter but as Becky walked down the passage there was sadness in her heart. Whatever had happened that would make Ella leave the baby so long in such an agitated state?

Not knowing what to expect, for she could still hear voices being raised in anger, Becky tapped on the kitchen door and turned the handle. On the table stood the remains of what must have been breakfast and dirty crocks were piled up at one end. No fire burnt in the grate.

Ella jumped to her feet saying, 'Oh, it's you, Becky.'

All Becky could think of was what a sorry sight she looked. She wore a thick skirt and a well-darned jumper. Her long fair hair was parted in the centre, dragged back and tied with a piece of tape. Slumped in a chair, still drawn up to the table, sat Peter's father.

He looked up. 'Hello, Becky,' he mumbled in greeting.

He looked as if he'd spent some time washing and shaving and he wore the same clothes as he had done yesterday even down to the smart jacket, as if he were ready to set off on a journey.

'The baby needs a clean napkin.' Becky spoke the words softly, afraid that the rowing might break out again at any moment.

'Give her to me,' Ella said, making an obvious effort to pull herself together. Taking the baby from Ella, she looked across at her father-in-law. 'I can't believe it,' she said sadly in a voice that was no more than a whisper.

'What can't you believe?' Becky put her arm around Ella, drawing her close.

'That I'm not really married because my Peter is a bigamist.'

'What?' Becky had sensed something was wrong but nothing like this. 'Whoever told you that?'

'His own father.'

Becky saw the tears swimming in Ella's eyes and at that moment she felt she could cheerfully kill the man sitting at the table.

Ella carried on talking, more to herself than to Becky. 'All this time and he's never said a word. Great sense of timing, don't you think?'

'I've tried to explain.' Mr Tomson got up from his chair and came towards Becky. 'I couldn't leave without telling her. Not this time.'

'Why not?' Ella asked.

'I just couldn't,' he said loudly, trying hard to make his voice sound normal.

'I want to know why you've kept silent about this for so long,' Ella insisted.

Peter's dad had the grace to look sheepish. 'My conscience has been troubling me ever since I signed your marriage lines as a witness in the church vestry. That's when I noticed Peter had described himself as a bachelor.'

'Took yer time, didn't you?' Ella accused. Then, shoving the baby back in to Becky's arms, her voice rose to a scream. 'Why tell me now? I have another baby on the way. You've kept quiet all this time, why suddenly tell me now? What I didn't know wasn't hurting me.'

'Stop it,' Becky said firmly. She could see that Ella was exhausted and the baby had begun to cry again. 'Calm down luv, come on, this isn't doing you any good and it's upsetting Margaret. Go and put the kettle on, I'll nurse her while you make her a bottle and then I'll make a fresh pot of tea.'

Slowly Ella shuffled towards the scullery and Becky turned

to Mr Tomson. 'Well? Hadn't you better explain to me just what is going on?'

He pulled a chair up to the table for Becky and when she was settled with the baby on her lap, he seated himself next to her.

'It's true,' he told her and gave a noncommittal shrug of his shoulders.

Becky didn't want to get into a lengthy argument. She couldn't force this man whom she hardly knew to tell her anything because strictly speaking it wasn't anything to do with her, but she couldn't let it go just like that. Besides, who else was here to help Ella?

'Why didn't you say something yesterday? When everyone was here. Surely it would have been better for Ella if you'd spoken up when her mother was here to listen to what you had to say.'

'I thought about it but it didn't seem the right time.'

Becky's eyes flashed. 'No, the right time would have been before Ella and Peter were married.' Suddenly Becky was angry. If it weren't for the fact that she was nursing the baby she would have lashed out at this man who was sitting there so calmly. 'Didn't you even think it would have been better to say what you felt you had to say when your son was present?'

'How can I make you understand?' He shifted uncomfortably in his chair, refusing to look at Becky. 'Anyway all the talking in the world won't alter the facts and I'm going to get ready, it's best if I go home today.'

'God, I don't believe you!' Becky looked astounded. 'Aren't you even going to wait until Peter gets home?'

'No, it's best if I don't. I'll call in and see him at the laundry, I will tell him that I've told Ella.'

Becky sighed heavily, wishing her father was here to deal with all of this. 'At least tell me the truth, has Peter got another wife tucked away somewhere?'

'I don't really know. At least not for sure.'

'What!' Becky hadn't meant to shout at him. Anger was making her reckless and she had made the baby jump.

'It's kind of complicated. Peter did get married in 1916. He met this Vera Brady just before he went off to war. They never really lived together, never had a place of their own like. Though he did come home on leave twice and as far as I can tell you they spent the time at her father's house. He was a widower. By the time the Armistice was declared both she and her father had disappeared.'

'And Peter never tried to trace her?'

'Not to my knowledge he didn't. What you've got to remember is he was only eighteen when he went to France.' Mr Tomson sighed and ran his hand through his hair. 'Came home a sick man, just twenty, but you never would have believed it to look at him. Those lads must have gone through hell in those trenches.'

That's all very well, Becky moaned to herself, everyone had heard the shocking stories of what went on in France during those awful years of the War. That didn't excuse what Peter had done to Ella and certainly his father had a lot to answer for in not speaking up before now.

Ella kicked the scullery door open with her foot. 'I've made the tea and brought clean cups. I'll see to that lot later on,' she apologized, looking at the dirty things which still lay on the table. 'You pour, Becky, and I'll give this bottle to Margaret.'

Peter's father got to his feet. 'If you don't mind, Ella, I'm going to be on my way. I have packed what few things I brought with me and I'm sure there will be a train about lunchtime.'

'Don't you want a cup of tea first?' Ella asked, her expression still downcast.

'No, I won't if you don't mind.'

Becky put baby Margaret on to Ella's lap and looked on as she coped with putting a clean napkin on her in a competent way; it wasn't until the baby was settled in the crook of her arm and contentedly sucking at her bottle that Ella broke the silence.

'So you're not going to wait and see Peter? I think you've acted in a very cowardly way,' Ella said honestly. 'But you know your own business best.'

Her father-in-law, about to leave the room, stopped in his tracks. 'I more than likely would have told you when I first met you, Ella, but just you remember one thing, you were pregnant at the time and my son must have thought he was doing the decent thing by offering to marry you.'

Ella raised her eyes to meet those of her father-in-law and he staggered at the sadness he now saw.

'I'm sorry, truly I am,' he said emotionally looking at Ella so anxiously that for a moment she felt sorry for him, but then she quickly glanced away. She couldn't bring herself to say another word to him.

Becky headed for the door with Mr Tomson close behind her. Stopping in the hallway to pick up his case and put on his macintosh, he put out a hand to Becky, saying, 'She will be all right won't she? I really think I've acted for the best.'

'Ella will cope, Mr Tomson. She'll have to, won't she?' Becky said in a dull voice.

No other words passed between them but Becky stood on the doorstep watching his back until he was out of sight.

When she returned to the room she felt a lump as big as a golf ball rise up in her throat and her heart simply ached at the sight of her dearest friend. The baby was snug in her mother's arms, still contentedly sucking away at her bottle, one tiny fist curled round Ella's forefinger, holding on so tightly. Ella's head was lowered yet Becky had no difficulty in seeing the tears that were trickling down her cheeks.

Becky was plagued with terrible thoughts on her journey home to New Malden. She was only inside the house a few minutes before, very near to tears, she was telling the whole terrible story to her parents.

'Dad, Ella was all on her own when I came home. She looked awful. It was such a shock. What will happen to her now?'

'Don't get yourself worked up so,' Joyce Russell pleaded with her daughter. 'Give yer father a few minutes for it to sink in an' then maybe he'll know what to do.'

'To sort this lot out will need a lot more than a few minutes I'm thinking,' Joe said sternly, doing his best to hide his anger. 'What a man, eh? Opening up that can of worms to a young lass when she's in the house on her own. Good job you went there today, Becky, wish t' God I'd been with you.'

'I've just had a thought,' Joyce cried out in alarm. 'One of us ought to go round and see Peggy.'

''Course you're right,' Joe agreed with his wife. 'There's no man there to deal with this an' the last thing we want is Peggy hearing it second-hand. God knows what it will do to her. I'll put me boots on and go straight away.'

'Peggy is going to feel very bad,' Joyce said thoughtfully.

'And what's that supposed to mean?' Joe asked as he saw the distress clearly showing in Joyce's eyes.

'Well, it was Peggy that practically forced Peter to marry Ella. Oh, it was the right thing to do at the time. Nobody is going to dispute that, not seeing as Ella was already pregnant, but I'd bet my bottom dollar she'll blame herself now.'

'Dad, shall I come with you?' Becky asked.

'No, pet, you stay here with yer mother. I'll bring Peggy back here for the night if she wants to come.'

It was two hours later when Joe Russell came back from George Road. Becky and her mother were sitting close up to a blazing fire, drinking cocoa, each staring into the flames deep in thought.

'Peggy didn't come back with you then?' Joyce asked as her husband sat down and with a sigh started to unlace his boots.

'No, luv. Said she'll be all right, her Jimmy will be home soon.'

'How did she take it, Dad?' Becky asked.

'Stunned at first. Like us she couldn't believe what I was telling her. Anyways I've told her I'll do me best to help. First thing I reckon is for me to have a word with our union bloke, he'll put me on to the legal section, see how we go about tracing missing persons. That's after I've been over and got the facts straight from Peter.'

'You are good, Dad,' Becky exclaimed, jumping to her feet and planting a kiss on his forehead.

'What do you want to know about missing persons for?' Joyce queried.

'Peter's so-called wife. From what Becky's told us nobody has seen hide nor hair of her since 1916 so in my book that makes her a missing person.'

'Oh, I see,' Joyce muttered.

Becky hid a smile. She was not at all sure that her mother did see.

For the first time Becky felt slightly reluctant as she got herself ready to catch the train next morning. It wasn't that she minded going back to work but she did feel awful having to leave without seeing Ella again. It had been such a lovely happy weekend until Peter's father had dropped his bombshell.

She remembered how carefree she and Ella had been when they were growing up. What a pity Peter had come along when he did. If things had turned out differently she and Ella could both have been working for Lyons in the West End of London. As it was she and Ella were treading very different paths.

'You promise to look after Ella, don't you Dad?' Becky needed to be reassured before she stepped on to the train.

'Becky my luv, I've told you, I will do everything I possibly can for Ella, and before you ask me yet again, yes, I will be in touch with you the minute there is anything to tell you.'

Becky went into her father's arms. He hugged her tight

and patted her back as if she were a small child. 'Go on,' he said, giving her a push, 'get yourself back to London and the glamorous life you lead up there.'

Becky laughed. 'You wouldn't say that if you knew how my feet ached some nights when I finish work.'

'Get on with you, lass, you love every minute of that job, you know you do.'

True, she was saying to herself as the train pulled out of the station and she waved a last goodbye to her dad. Even so, for once she wished she had an extra day off to go back to Kingston and see how Ella was.

Chapter Eighteen

IT WAS NINE o'clock in the morning and still there was no sign of Peter. He hadn't been home all night.

Once more Ella opened the front door and stood outside on the doorstep looking up and down the street. Then her whole body sagged and she sighed heavily. She hadn't been to bed. She had found jobs to do, keeping herself busy so as not to brood on the future. Since she and Peter had been married, though of course that was an absolute sham now, she reminded herself, money had been desperately short but they had managed and been reasonably happy. The baby had made all the difference. Even Peter's face would light up whenever he leant over the pram.

'You'll come home, Peter, I know you will,' she whispered, staring down at the corner, willing him to come into view.

Becky had told her that her father-in-law was going to the laundry to see Peter. What on earth had he said that would stop Peter from coming home? She looked up at the grey skies. It was such a miserable cold day for him to be trudging the streets. Perhaps he wasn't, perhaps he had gone into work. But where had he spent the night?

'There's no use standing about out here,' Ella said aloud, pulling her long cardigan tightly round her body. Hearing the baby whimper made her mind up for her. I'll get Margaret ready, put her in the pram and go see for myself if Peter is at the laundry.

Moving quickly now she wrapped a blanket firmly round the baby, settled her in the pram making sure that her bonnet was covering both her ears and laid another thicker cover on top.

'Go to sleep, my pet,' she told her softly.

Twenty minutes later, Ella had washed and changed her clothes. In her long dark grey coat, wide-brimmed felt hat, laced-up boots and woolly gloves she looked neat and tidy.

'What's the hurry, Ella?' Martha Tubman called cheekily as Ella bumped the pram out on to the pavement. 'I didn't see your Peter go off this morning, ain't he well?'

A hot flush came to Ella's face and she wished the earth would open up and swallow her. Either that or Martha Tubman should drop down dead. Nosy cow, she muttered. What she said aloud was, 'Peter left early, he forgot his sandwiches so I'm just taking them to him.'

'Best hurry then, it's gonna pour before long,' Martha said briskly, thinking to herself, there's more going on in that house than meets the eye.

Once again Ella's big blue eyes glittered with tears as she hurried along the main road. Walking alongside Kingston market set her thoughts flying back to the lovely happy Saturday and Sunday she had just spent. Inside that market was the second-hand clothes stall where she had bought a dress three weeks ago. A light navy crepe it was, calf-length, with long sleeves and a V neck that had plunged far too daringly for her to wear it as it was.

I worked hard on that dress, she was thinking to herself. I washed and ironed it so carefully. Sewed a lace inset to the front. All the time I was sewing I dreamed of surprising Peter when I wore it to our first baby's christening.

Well, she had surprised him. And herself more so. Hours she had spent. Not only altering the dress but washing her long hair, curling the ends with the tongs so that it hung softly on her shoulders.

Peter had gasped in admiration when she turned round and faced him in their bedroom. She hadn't meant to tell him about the baby, not yet anyway. It was as he held her close and her tummy was pressed against him that she had blurted it out. 'I'm pregnant again.'

'Good gracious!' he had said, and beamed. 'Let's hope it's a boy.'

Relief had flooded over her. 'I didn't for a moment think you would be pleased. I worry as to how we will manage,' she had confessed.

He had declared that he would move heaven and earth to find himself a better-paid job.

She had hated the next few minutes because she sensed that he was feeling guilty because he had made her pregnant for the second time so soon.

Then Tom's wedding had been a lovely affair and the next day had astonished both Peter and herself. They were filled with gratitude at the way their friends had lavished gifts and small sums of money on the baby. It had all been so unexpected.

As they had climbed the stairs that night it had been Peter who had more or less summed up the day. 'We may have had to penny-pinch since we got married,' he said, 'but I am not the least bit envious of what other people have. I'm just grateful that our baby daughter is so beautiful and healthy and all I really want for the future is the chance to be able to provide for you, and her.'

'And?' She had smiled, patting her stomach.

'Him an' all,' Peter had laughed out loud.

'Don't be so cocksure,' she had chided him. And that night Peter had made love to her so expertly that she felt from that day on everything must go well for them as a family. Had all that happened only two days ago?

At that moment she hated her father-in-law. Why oh why couldn't he have kept his mouth shut? Why travel down for the christening knowing that he was going to spoil everything for them as a family?

As she had told him then, she would have preferred never to know. Together Peter and she were coping fairly well, as well if not better than most folk were in these hard times.

'Ella!'

'Wotcher, luv.'

Several voices called out as she pushed the pram into the Wellington's yard. High in the cab of his van Peter sat, lost in thoughts of his home and family. Hearing the excited voices as women ran to see the baby he opened the cab door and quickly closed it again. Oh no! he wasn't ready to face Ella yet.

He wished she had waited until he got home. It was his own fault, Ella turning up here. He hadn't been home all night. He shivered, he couldn't just sit here, he had to get down and face her. His throat almost closed and he found it hard to breathe.

The cab door was opened from the outside.

'You'd better take a bit of time off,' Bill Yates, the other van driver, insisted. 'Your missus is here and she looks all done in.'

But when Peter made to move, Bill laid the palm of his hand on his knee and gently pressed him down again as he said, 'Take yer time, lad, and if I can be of any help you know you only have to say the word.'

'Thanks, mate,' Peter said. 'You saw my dad come here yesterday, didn't you?'

'Yeah, an' a blind man could have seen he wasn't the bearer of good news.'

'You're not wrong,' Peter told him sadly, the frown in his forehead deepening.

'All the same Peter, I'm not prying. Go on, I'll see to your load, take yer missus over t' the market caff an' get her something hot t' drink.'

Ella watched as Peter crossed the yard. He looked utterly wretched. By the time he stood in front of her all her anger had drained away, and nothing but fear and depression remained.

Walking the short distance to the café they barely spoke a word to each other. Peter settled Ella at a table well away from the door and she bent over the pram, loosened the wrappings from around the baby and propped her higher on the pillow. Peter stretched out a hand to stroke baby Margaret's face and was rewarded by a dribbling smile.

'Tea?' he asked Ella. 'Anything to eat?'

Ella shook her head.

'I'll get us a plate of toast,' he muttered, turning and walking to the counter. Minutes later he set two steaming mugs of tea on the table and went back to the counter for two plates and the dish of thickly buttered toast.

'Do you feel really bad?' Peter asked carefully.

'That's a daft question,' Ella retorted quickly.

'I suppose we have to talk about it.' Peter lowered his gaze until it rested on Ella's face, and it hurt him to see her lovely blue eyes were sad and serious.

'I can't see what good it will do. All you have to tell me is whether it is true or not.'

'Don't you want me to try and explain?'

'Not really. It wouldn't do any good. All I need to know is are we married or not?'

Peter smiled. A thin, sad smile that went straight to Ella's heart. 'Condemned without a hearing?' he dared to ask.

The colour had drained from Peter's cheeks and the sorry look he had about him made Ella relent as she said, 'I wish you had told me.'

'You were pregnant. I couldn't bring myself to,' he said regretfully.

'The weekend was so lovely,' Ella said wistfully.

At that moment the baby cried. Peter watched with pride as Ella lifted Margaret out of the pram, pressing her close as she sat down again. Loosening her shawl and taking her bonnet off she fussed over her for a while. There was no doubt that the baby was very special to both of them and it would be her and the coming infant who would hold them together.

'Where did you spend the night?' Ella shot the question without looking up.

'Well, when I first left work I went to see your mum. I felt I owed her that much.'

'Go on,' Ella instructed, thinking to herself, what about me?

'Becky's dad was there.'

'And?'

Peter sighed heavily. 'And that seemed to make it worse. Him telling me that Becky walked in when my dad was telling you. I guessed you wouldn't have liked that.'

'Oh, Peter! For God's sake! What I didn't like was being told that you had another wife tucked away somewhere. Finding out that our baby daughter was actually illegitimate. The fact that my best friend was there to hear the sordid details doesn't seem to me t' matter a tinker's cuss one way or the other.'

Peter was taken back by Ella's sudden burst of outrage and he hurriedly said, 'Mr Russell was ever so understanding. He promised to have a talk with a legal fellow who is attached to the railway union. Said he'd know how to go about finding the records on missing persons.'

'Peter,' Ella cried out in exasperation, 'get to the point. Did you stay all night at my mum's? I can't believe she would have let you without letting me know.'

'No,' he said sheepishly. 'She told me to go home. I couldn't face you. I walked for ages. Spent some time on the railway station. Got meself a wash an' brush up and went to work. I've not been able to stop thinking about you. I just can't find the words to tell you how sorry I am, Ella.'

Silence hung heavy between them for several minutes, until Peter reached across, touched the baby's face with one finger and then took hold of Ella's hand. 'I know it's no excuse but after the War was over I never considered myself a married man. It was wartime. Young folk were rushing to get wed before the fellows went over to France. I hardly knew Vera really.'

Ella decided now was as good a time as any to ask questions. At least here in this warm café they weren't likely to raise their voices and get into a slanging match.

'Your dad said you spent two lots of leave with her.'

'No. Only one. I wrote several letters but she never answered and what made it seem more final, she never registered the marriage with the Army.'

'I don't understand. Should she have done?'

'Oh yes. I filled in forms for her to have the wife's allowance, can't remember how much it was, only a small amount and the Army would have made it up to about thirty-two shillings, seeing as I was only a private. She never put in for it. Never claimed a penny.' He paused, took a deep breath and Ella felt frightened because his face was the colour of chalk.

It was only after he had taken a few sips of tea that he was able to go on. 'I was ill when I was first demobbed, but my mum was alive then and she made enquiries at the Town Hall and every Post Office in Northampton. There were no records of Vera anywhere.'

Ella tried her hardest to smile and transferred the baby from her lap up on to her shoulder. Cautiously, she asked, 'And you've never heard from her from that day to this?'

Peter shook his head. 'Not a word. I promise you, Ella. I took it that she'd gone off with another bloke.'

Ella's face showed signs of relief. 'I'm glad,' she admitted. 'We'll just have to wait an' see what Mr Russell comes up with, won't we?'

The café was beginning to fill up with customers.

'Would you like to have a lunch here?' Peter made the suggestion half-heartedly.

Ella appreciated the offer and any other time might have said yes, but now she thought they had done enough talking and it would be better if they made a move. It would soon be time for the baby to have a bottle and she had come out in such a rush that she hadn't given a thought to that.

'I'd better get home, I didn't make a bottle for the baby,' she told him as she got to her feet and gently lowered Margaret down into the warmth of her pram.

'I'm coming with you,' Peter declared. 'Bill will have put someone else on my round by now. I'll take the rest of the day off.'

It was Peter who pushed the pram.

There was a moment when Ella, walking beside him, almost laughed. Not because of what she had found out but because of the cowardly way her father-in-law had chosen to tell her. And on the very day after they had stood side by side in church and watched as their baby daughter had been sprinkled with holy water and christened in the name of God. The very same church in which she and Peter had made their wedding vows! Laughter turned to tears which she struggled hard to keep back.

'Oh, Peter,' she moaned, taking hold of his arm and hugging him close. 'If we can survive this we'll survive anything.'

Chapter Nineteen

ATHOUGH BECKY AND May worked hard they also played hard. Big Ben had often long since chimed midnight when they let themselves into Aunt Lil's house. The young men who so often escorted them were renowned for their generosity and the majority for their splendid manners.

Becky especially had been excited when she and May had first accepted an offer to join a group that were going to the theatre. That first evening out on the town had opened up for her a world far removed from the world in which she had grown up.

After only a few visits to the theatre Becky managed to square her conscience as to the amount of money these young gentlemen were spending in one night. They were sons of rich people who, if the unions were to be believed, didn't give a damn how they made their money even if it meant grinding the workers down, especially if they happened to be miners.

Nineteen twenty-six was proving to be a very disturbing year for the likes of the poor. The newspapers were full of stories.

'Almost unbelievable,' Mr Gower had declared when reading an article in his morning paper during their mid-morning break.

'What is?' May had saucily enquired.

'Why, the fact that the Samuel Commission has proposed that all employers should lower the wages they pay to the coal-miners.'

Shaking his head and with sadness in his voice he had told

all the staff that were present that his sister's husband worked down the mines.

'Lives in Durham, they have four childen and although my brother-in-law spends two-thirds of his life grovelling in the bowels of the earth he doesn't bring home enough in wages to keep body and soul together. None of them do. And none of those miners will make old bones, their lungs will be shot to pieces before they're forty. Take a cut in their wages? There'll be trouble. Mark my words there will be. They can't live on what they get paid now, never mind accept less.' His voice broke, and sensing that he had let his feelings run away with him he had added lamely, 'We don't always appreciate how lucky we are to work for Lyons.'

Rumours dominated every conversation.

It was the evening of May the first and both May and Becky were run off their feet as they sought to satisfy the customers who on this May Day evening were mostly males. They were working in one of the small upstairs restaurants distinguished by its red plush chairs, Viennese chandeliers and lace curtains.

Five toffs, seated at a circular table, all seemed to be pacified. Becky had served three of them with mutton pie, the traditional London delicacy; the other two had chosen ribs of beef.

'Another chair, if you please, Miss.' Becky frowned in annoyance. A gentleman had stepped in front of her, barring her way. 'I shall join these gentlemen and I too shall have mutton pie.'

She raised her eyebrows at his arrogance and saw a man so tall that she had to tilt her head back to look at him. He had to be well over six feet. He was in evening dress and looked so handsome she gasped. He had thick dark hair and enormous eyes, different to any she had ever seen. They weren't blue, more grey and at that moment they seemed to be laughing at her.

'I'm sorry,' he apologized, 'I wasn't thinking. I'll fetch my own chair.'

'I'll bring your order, sir,' she told him with as much dignity as she could muster, turning away she walked slowly around the table.

'The miners have come out on strike,' she heard the newcomer announce as he drew up a chair and seated himself amongst his friends.

His statement, important as it was, didn't register with Becky for the moment. God, that man was attractive! She was still pondering his good looks as she wrote his order on her pad, admitting to herself that she was fascinated by him and at the same time alarmed. But why him? What was so different about him?

She had no answer to that.

The less she thought about him the better. Determinedly she concentrated on her work, intent on forgetting him. After all he was a customer and at best he would see her as a friendly waitress.

Two days later the Trades Unions Council brought havoc to London, and Mr Gower was proved right.

They called a general strike in support of Britain's coal-miners, two-thirds of whom had been locked out by their employers for refusing to accept the lower wages. The next nine days were a nightmare for everyone and that included the entire staff at each of the Lyons Corner Houses. There were no trains, trams or buses. No newspapers were printed. Iron and steel industries shut down and the docks lay idle.

Many society figures took on the jobs of driving buses and lorries. Listening to the young gentlemen when they came into Coventry Street Lyons for refreshment the Nippies were appalled to hear them laugh and joke about the situation.

It took a while for things to get back to normal, more so because the nine-day general strike had achieved nothing. The miners were still out on strike.

May had taken up with a young gentleman by the name of

Roger Macclesfield and it was Roger who finally introduced Becky to the man that May had teasingly started to refer to as Becky's heart-throb.

Roger had broad shoulders and a real masculine appearance which had attracted May to him in the first place. She had sent Becky off into a fit of giggles when they'd first met.

'He's a joy to behold,' May declared. 'So many men we come across these days are ruddy dandies.'

'You'll like him,' Roger whispered just before he introduced Gerald Palmer to Rebecca Russell.

She did too.

From the moment she had set eyes on him he'd set her heart fluttering. Now his handshake was so strong that it made her wince.

'Will you come to the theatre with me on your first free evening?' Gerald Palmer's voice flowed, so smooth it rolled off his tongue.

I'd go to hell and back just to be near you, is what she was thinking as he held on to her hand, letting his thumb caress her palm.

'I really want you to,' he said huskily, those grey eyes looking down at her twinkling merrily.

'I'd like that very much,' she said, realizing that she was trembling.

He smiled with pleasure. 'I shall count every minute.'

As she walked away, Becky half expected him to reach out and pull her back. But as she took each step away from Gerald Palmer she began to breathe normally again though she had a hard job resisting the impulse to turn and look back at him just to see if he was still watching her.

May was waiting for her as she entered the still room.

'Well, has he asked you out?' May asked, shifting about with impatience.

'Yes,' Becky breathed. 'God that man is . . . well, he just is.'

'Unusual?' May ventured.

'He's that all right,' Becky answered vaguely. 'How old do you think he is, May?'

'Thirtyish, maybe more.' May shrugged.

'Oh don't say that.' Becky looked upset.

'What d' you care? You aren't going to settle down with him for life, you know. We're only going to the London Hippodrome with them.'

'How do you know where we're going?'

'Because Roger already has the tickets an' let me tell you those tickets are like gold–dust.' May paused to grin broadly. 'You may not know it yet but those men have got the money to buy whatever's going, and on Thursday we are going to be treated like real ladies.'

'Is it some special show?' Becky challenged.

'Of course it is,' May retorted as she pointed triumphantly to a poster on the wall. 'It's Jerome Kern's *Sunny* starring Jack Buchanan and Elsie Randolph. All London's fighting to see it and Roger said we're going on to have dinner after the show.'

They both giggled. 'You can be the one to tell Aunt Lil that we won't be home till the early hours of the morning,' Becky spluttered.

'Oh no I won't,' May protested, 'she'll eat me alive. She always thinks it's me that's leading you astray. One of these days I'm going to tell her that it's dainty little you that attracts men like flies. Let her know that they chase after you in droves.'

Becky lashed out at May, slapping her back with the flat of her hand. 'May Stevens, you do exaggerate.'

'That's as maybe, but you'll have to admit you do look so innocent half the time, with your baby face and those great brown eyes. Just for once, though, let me give you a word of warning. Gerald Palmer might be the best-looking man you've ever set eyes on but he's been around. I'd lay money on that.'

Becky was shocked by what May had said. Yet it only took a minute for her to realize that May was probably right. Suddenly in that moment she told herself to act a bit more cautiously.

Then in her mind's eye she pictured Gerald again. He really was so good-looking. She thought of his deep soft voice, his cheeky grin, the way he had looked at her, held her hand for so long. Somehow, through no fault of her own, he had come into her life and the urge to go out with him, to be near him, was more than she could control.

I'll be all right, she thought to herself, he's a lovely man.

May watched Becky's expression, saw the way she smiled. She was so gullible! That one thought made her all the more determined to keep an eye on Becky, and more so on Gerald Palmer.

Chapter Twenty

THE TIME WAS seven o'clock in the morning.

Robert Matthews stood on the opposite side of the road staring at the frontage of Coventry Street Corner House. He was well satisfied.

The white and gold façade looked splendid. And so it should for the appearance of the building was the public face that Lyons was presenting to the world. The paintwork was in good condition and the brass highly polished. It was not widely known that Joseph Lyons, a street trader at the time, who had in 1887 consented to his name being used for the new catering company, was in fact the great-grandfather of Robert Matthews.

Robert had been given a privileged upbringing and had known since he was in his teens that a position within the catering company was his for the asking. While still at school he had rebelled against the idea. It had been his mother who had changed his mind. Gentle, kind and very beautiful she had used no blackmailing pressure, simply took him for meals at different establishments owned by the company, at different times of both day and night.

Interest had come first and finally appreciation.

He would now be the first to admit that he was totally addicted to the art of bulk catering. His working life was as fulfilled as any man had the right to expect. In fact he would go as far as agreeing that he loved his work, although he asked for no favours from anyone.

There wasn't a part of the company with which he was not familiar, from the dozens of items of food for Lyons' very extensive menu which were cooked in large premises at the back of Cadby Hall during the night to the wholesalers who provided the fresh meat carcasses and the fine fish that was filleted by special chefs, right down to the cleaners who saw to the waitresses' dressing rooms and the ladies' lavatories.

Time for me to get myself some breakfast, he decided, crossing the road and letting himself in through the front door. Manageress and waitresses were now in the shop and the ground floor was open to customers.

Robert was of the opinion that Lyons owed the success of its teashops to a meticulous system of supervision. In every premises there were ladies similar to Mrs Nicholls and Miss Timson who at all times had the good of the company at heart. Besides beady-eyed head waiters such as Mr Gower there was another important group, the team of observers.

They acted as normal customers, paid their bills and left. Later they sent a report to head office, with comments on the standard of the service and the food, noting anything at all unseemly.

No ordinary member of staff ever knew who they were.

Having eaten well and signed for his meal the next two hours would be taken up with routine checks throughout the entire building. Robert knew full well that by midday almost every seat in each of the restaurants would be taken. There were often several business parties being held at the same time but the small intimate restaurants situated on the upper floors only functioned at night and the problems involved in coping with these parties simultaneously at lunchtime was very much on his mind this morning. At an extraordinary meeting of shareholders held three weeks ago it had been decided another branch of the company should be formed.

It was to be known as the Outside Catering Department, dealing with private functions, even those held on race-courses, besides banquets, garden parties and many other events.

Selective recruiting of girls considered suitable for special training had already begun. That was the main reason why he was here at Coventry Street this morning.

At three o'clock, the lunchtime rush was over. Becky and May didn't say anything to each other, but their thoughts were troubled. It wasn't a good sign when the manageress told them to report to the main office.

'I hate these lunchtime shifts,' May complained. 'Only good thing about them is we do get our evenings free.'

'Come in,' Florence Nicholls called in answer to the tap on the door. Oh my God! Both girls were astounded to see Robert Matthews, Mrs Nicholls and Miss Timson grouped behind the desk.

'Well, don't just stand there, come and sit yourselves down,' Florence Nicholls said, smiling as she always did.

'Yes, come and hear the new proposal.' Miss Timson, tall, self-assured and dressed today in a grey tailored costume, was a woman who knew what the girls were about to learn would be of great benefit to them and she saw no reason not to enjoy the telling. 'Don't keep them in suspense,' she urged Robert Matthews.

He looked taken aback. He stood there. Tall. Taller than Miss Timson. He murmured, 'Good afternoon.'

'Good afternoon, sir,' May and Becky answered in unison.

He smiled faintly. His light blue eyes were clear, his face thin and brown but Becky was silently smiling to herself because of the waistcoat he was wearing. May would describe it as dandified! Yet it wasn't. The material was a corded silk, the colour blue, darker than the blue of his eyes. Worn with his stiff-collared white shirt and black morning suit it relieved the sombre look no end.

Robert Matthews felt that Rebecca was appraising him and was instantly embarrassed. 'I imagine you are wondering why we have asked you here when obviously you'd much rather be on your way home.' He took out a sheaf of papers from a briefcase that lay on the table and unfolded them. 'The shareholders have decided to branch out, diversify so to speak.' He knew he sounded flustered, but that was because he was flustered. He took a deep breath, letting it out slowly.

Rebecca Russell had that effect on him. She had from the very first meeting. She was so slight. He felt she was vulnerable, and although from having observed her when working on many occasions he knew she was not, he still felt the urge to protect her.

Drawing himself up to his full height he proceeded to outline the programme the company was embarking on. 'Each of you has been selected because of the way you have adapted and performed since becoming employees of Lyons. You have achieved every standard asked of you and you may look upon this new employment as not only promotion but as an award for all your endeavours.'

May was the first to find her voice. 'Sir, do we have to decide now?' she asked, despising herself for sounding so wooden.

Robert Matthews turned to Florence Nicholls, and she, wondering why Robert didn't seem in complete charge of himself this afternoon, quickly got to her feet and took over.

'I know this proposition has been sprung on you,' she began, looking first at Rebecca and then at May. 'Naturally you will be given time to digest all that you have been told. If you decide that you do want to be part of this new enterprise you will be informed of the date the special training will commence and given a few days' leave prior to that date.'

Although Mrs Nicholls was still smiling her tone was dismissive, but May refused to be dismissed just like that.

'Please, ma'am, where would we be sent to do this training?' she asked.

Florence Nicholls' self-assurance flowed out. She considered herself a good judge of character and from the start had seen it as inevitable that these two girls, so totally different in looks and upbringing, would not only be good waitresses but go on to become an asset to the company.

She allowed herself another smile, and went on, 'Orchard House's premises are being enlarged, so more than likely it will take place in Clerkenwell.' Then, almost as an after-thought, she added, 'You will be provided with new uniforms and coronet caps.'

'Thank you,' both girls murmured and were on their feet and outside in the corridor before they realized it.

Becky leant against the wall and closed her eyes. 'What a brilliant oportunity,' she said softly.

May was grinning broadly. 'What a turn up for the book! Think of all the places we'll get t' go to. And all the big-nobs we'll meet.'

'There you go again, May. We shan't exactly be meeting big-nobs as you call them, we shall be waiting on them.'

'Same meat, different gravy,' May laughed loudly. 'Come on, wait till we tell Aunt Lil we'll be living it up. Rubbing shoulders with the upper crust, don't you know.'

Becky followed as May set off on a run. She too was laughing now. May could be a proper comic when she liked. 'Rubbing shoulders with the upper crust!' It was the way it came out. May could impersonate the upper classes to a tee when it suited her.

May and Becky's first visit to the Royal Ascot race meeting had them both gasping in surprised delight.

Without any hesitation, after a long discussion with Aunt Lil, they had both signed up to be employees of the newly-formed Lyons Outside Catering Department. They were due to start their training the first week in July. Since it was now almost a year since they had started to work as Nippies they were granted a whole week's holiday.

'Don't go home to your parents, not straight away,' Gerald Palmer had pleaded. 'Spend a few days with me. At least let me take you to the races. You haven't lived if you've never been on a racecourse.'

The men that frequented Lyons Corner Houses late at night were different. Older, richer and very often married men. Most wanted to shower the Nippies with presents, take them to interesting places on their days off and spend enormous amounts of money on them. What did they want in return? the sensible girls asked themselves. Becky reassured herself time and time again that Gerald was not like that. May, much to her regret, had come to the conclusion that she was wasting her time trying to tell Becky to be careful.

It was a gorgeous day, the sun high in the sky. Becky couldn't believe that she was actually here, at Royal Ascot, her spirits soaring by the minute as she stood on the bright green grass and looked around. The ladies were a picture in brightly-coloured dresses and fluffy hats, large and small. And the men were a sight to behold. Elegant! There was no other word for their grey morning suits and top hats.

Gerald had moved away to stand by the rail, looking sunburned and healthy. Gosh he was tall, Becky thought to herself as across the space their eyes met and held. He had removed his hat and the brilliant sun was showing up signs of grey in his dark hair. She had become accustomed to well-dressed men but she had never met one, or seen one, who looked so at ease no matter what he was wearing.

'Rebecca, there you are,' Roger Macclesfield exclaimed. 'May is getting worried about you. She wants you to come over to where the jockeys are and there are so many people that I would like you to meet.'

Becky looked towards where Gerald had been standing but he was no longer in sight. Disappointed, she turned and went with Roger.

'There you are,' May cried, looking very smart in a cream-coloured suit and a pale yellow hat, excitement making her cheeks looked flushed.

The jockeys came out and stood around the owners of the

horses in little groups. What bright colours the jockeys wore, Becky and May both noted.

Roger was intent on introducing Becky. She felt bewildered by it all: faces she had never seen before, names she would never remember. She felt lost without Gerald being there. Then suddenly his hand was on her shoulder and he turned her round to face him.

'Miss me?' he teased, bending his head and planting a soft lingering kiss on her lips.

He had kissed her! In front of all these people he had kissed her. Her heart was thumping, nineteen to the dozen. From that moment her whole world changed. She swallowed, steadying her breathing. It was love. It had to be. Why else would he kiss her in public for everyone to see? It was an open declaration. There would be no more dithering. She wanted to be with him, every minute of every day.

'Welcome to horse racing,' Gerald said cheerfully, handing Becky a glass of champagne.

The jockeys swung up on to the horses and moved away to go down to the starting gates. Most of the crowds went off to their reserved boxes, others to the stands.

'May, Becky, we're all going to watch from the grass, as near to the rails as we can get,' Roger said as he glanced apologetically at May.

'I don't mind in the least,' May answered quickly. Then in an aside to Becky she whispered, 'If we get half a chance we'll shoot off later, have a peep into some of the boxes cos that's where we'll be working before long.'

Among much laughter and a lot of chatter the four of them set to the studying of race cards. Gerald and Roger insisted that the girls accepted a pound note as their first stake money. With a feeling of foreboding Becky agreed to place a bet of just ten shillings. May, throwing caution to the wind, went the whole hog and staked the full pound.

'Beginner's luck,' Roger cried, waving his hat above his head, allowing his short dark hair to blow free in the wind.

'Ignorance must be bliss,' Gerald declared as he tore his betting slips into shreds.

Both girls were ecstatic. By sheer luck they had backed the winning horse at four to one.

It seemed they were spending countless hours waiting around Tote queues while Gerald and Roger backed their hunches, all the time encouraging them to have a flutter.

'We've both won a packet!' Roger announced, grinning broadly. 'Come on, time we stood you drinks at the bar.'

Gerald was the life and soul of the party and as Becky stood back watching him the thought crossed her mind that he was spending a great deal of money with more good nature than sense.

'Now's our chance,' May whispered, tugging at the sleeve of Becky's pretty floral dress, 'we can sneak off an' get a peep into some of the boxes.'

Gerald had his back to the bar, surrounded by men in grey morning suits and looking remarkably carefree. Becky caught his eye and mouthed, 'We're going to find the ladies.'

He raised his glass in acknowledgement, laughing roguishly, and winked at her. She laughed back and the moment was gone, but for Becky the declaration that he loved her had been made and that was enough for now. Full of contentment and wonder that such a lovely man as Gerald would have time for her she followed May out of the bar.

The boxes were about five yards by four, most of the space being filled with well-dressed men and women. The far end wall was sheer windows looking out over the lovely course, with a glass door opening on to a flight of steps which led down to the viewing balcony.

After they had peered into at least three of the boxes May suddenly murmured, 'I wonder what they'll look like with a dining table?'

'Wonderful I should think,' Becky thoughtfully answered. 'Set up with what, twelve places for lunch? Or do you think there's room for more?'

'I'd say twelve is about right. Just think, Becky, you and me coming to all the races being part an' parcel of all this and getting paid for it!' May was buzzing with enthusiasm.

'It will be great,' Becky said, and meant it, but she had to voice her thoughts, so she went on, 'we won't be coming dressed up as we are today, we shall be on duty, here to work and remember what Mr Matthews said? Some of the dos such as Masonic dinners will be seating as many as a hundred, maybe more. This new venture is all very well but it isn't going to be dead easy so don't kid yourself.'

'Oh, you!' May gave Becky a playful push. 'You can be a proper old wet blanket when you choose. Anyway let's live for today, don't know about you but I'm starving.'

Gerald and Roger did them proud. It was an excellent lunch. For the girls the best part was the fresh strawberries served with thick clotted cream. By the coffee-brandy-cigar stage the restaurant was thinning out as people went dashing out yet again to back their hopes on the next race. There was a good deal of speculation between Roger and Gerald about two horses that apparently they had been given the tip-off for this afternoon.

'Well,' Roger said calmly, 'it's not a bit of good us even thinking of backing the hot favourite, the odds are too short.'

'I agree,' Gerald declared, getting to his feet and taking a tightly rolled bundle of black and white five-pound notes from his pocket. 'Nothing ventured nothing gained.'

The girls followed at a slower pace, each having given Roger one pound to place on the same horse for them.

From where they stood they couldn't see much of the race, only a flashing view as the horses tore up to the winning post. They listened to the announcement of the winner's number. Becky took hold of May's arm and shook it. 'We won, I'm sure we've won.' She was laughing with pleasure, her big brown eyes wide with amazement.

The rest of the afternoon slid away fast.

Becky was both sad and sorry when it was time for the last race.

'No, May, I'm not risking my winnings,' Becky declared, having seen both Gerald and Roger lose on the previous race. Silently she totted up just how much the day had brought her. Forty-four pounds and ten shillings! It was a fortune!

Becky grinned at May. 'I've won quite a bit today. How about you?'

'Enough to frighten Aunt Lil into thinking I'm in danger of becoming a compulsive gambler.'

Becky laughed out loud. 'Your Aunt Lil,' she said, 'knows you a whole lot better than you give her credit for.'

May grinned back at Becky. 'Well, it hasn't been our own money we've been playing with, has it?'

'No, and I felt guilty about that at first. I offered my winnings to Gerald, but he laughed his head off.'

'My conscience doesn't trouble me as much as yours seems to, I only offered Roger his pound stake money back. He told me not to be so daft.'

'Getting to be a crafty pair, aren't we?' Becky whispered.

May nodded her agreement. 'Been a smashing day though, hasn't it? So here goes, last race,' she said, walking towards Roger, holding out two pound notes. 'I'll risk that amount on number five.'

'At least none of us have lost our shirts today,' Roger said as he tucked May's hand through the crook of his arm. Then pulling her close and grinning broadly he added, 'Come on you big spender, come with me, let's see if we can take the bookies for another few pounds.'

'Becky, would you like to go up to the bar for another drink?' Gerald asked as May and Roger left them.

'No, thank you, I've had so much to eat and drink today that I feel I shall burst if I have anything else. But you don't need to stay with me if you'd like a drink.'

'You think I don't want to stay with you?'

The colour rose in her cheeks and before she could form

an answer Gerald said quickly, 'I'd like to spend the rest of my life with you. You have enjoyed today, haven't you?'

'Oh, Gerald! More than I can tell you. It has been a truly lovely day.'

Gerald took one of her hands and held it between both of his. 'Becky,' he said very quietly, 'you are on holiday for the rest of the week. Why don't we make it a truly lovely week? Spend it together. What do you say?'

Becky sighed softly. 'Gerald, I can't. My parents know I have this time off and I must go to see them.'

'You could go for the day. I'll run you down.'

'No Gerald, you don't understand. I haven't been home since New Year, that's six months, they expect me. Besides it's my goddaughter's birthday and her mother, my best friend, is expecting another baby in a few weeks' time and I shan't get another chance to visit them.'

Gerald gave her a dry look. 'Are you a do-gooder?'

Becky looked startled. 'No, I'm not. What an odd thing to ask.'

He made an apologetic gesture. 'Putting everyone else before your own pleasure, I just thought you might be.'

She shook her head. 'My family and friends are very important to me but as to doing good, I wouldn't have the time, even if I had the urge.'

'But what about me? You haven't time for me, is that what you're saying?'

'Gerald, don't twist my words,' she protested as she freed her hand and let it rest on his arm.

He smiled, easing the situation, taking away any seriousness and said, 'When you return to London do you promise that every moment you are not working will be spent with me?'

'Yes, oh yes.' She nuzzled her head against him.

'That's that settled then.' He grinned now, and hugging her closer to him he bent his head and placed his lips on hers in a long lingering kiss that sent tingles right through to her very soul.

Chapter Twenty-one

'OH, SORRY, MAY I change that destination to Kingston?' Becky, having made a sudden decision, asked the young man in the railway ticket office.

The booking clerk raised his head and smiled. If it had been an ordinary housewife he would probably have told her briskly to make up her mind. But this young lady was a dream! So small and dainty that only her head and shoulders were visible above the counter. He leant forward. Her face was lovely, creamy skin and those dark eyes, a man could forget he was married when confronted by someone like her. She looks like she has a rainbow around her head, he thought, looking at the tiny close-fitting hat she had perched on her dark hair. It was all pale shades of pink and blue, pale mauve and cream, the cream matching the loose jacket she was wearing. He shook his head reluctantly.

'Going on further than Raynes Park, are you then?'

'Yes. I'm sorry to have troubled you, I wasn't thinking.'

Becky gave him the sweetest smile as he passed over her ticket and said, 'No trouble at all, platform eight, Miss.'

The train pulled away from the station and Becky leant back in her corner seat of the carriage and relaxed. It was only at the last minute that she had resolved to visit Ella before going home to her mum and dad. With time now to think she was feeling remorseful. She had written regularly to Ella but it wasn't the same as seeing her. If she was honest with herself she felt that she had become too wrapped up in her job, her new social life and indeed her new friends. She sighed. Yes, Gerald Palmer in particular!

If only there were more hours in the day. And what would you do with them if there were? she asked herself. Spend them with Gerald, she freely admitted.

Gerald didn't seem to work. No matter what time of the day or night she finished her shift he was there waiting for her. No one had ever paid her so much attention or tried to lavish so many pretty gifts on her.

As children Ella and she had been inseparable and she loved Ella dearly. Becky bit her lip. Why had her thoughts begun to run along these lines? There was no getting away from it. Where Ella was concerned there was always a small voice inside her head that troubled her. Ella and her problems disturbed her.

Yet it isn't my fault that things are not that rosy for Peter and Ella, she thought. They chose to do what they did. Now that is not strictly true, Becky quickly chided herself. One day they let their emotions get the better of them and they ended up getting married when the truth was they just didn't have enough money to set up a home together. The one good thing to come out of it all was baby Margaret. She was lovely: a real little poppet.

It didn't seem possible that she would be one year old before this month was out. Then there would be another baby! God above, they could have done without another one to feed and clothe.

Becky felt very warm as she walked up Mill Street. She looked around with faint amusement. If ever I doubted I had done the right thing in moving to London to work as a waitress for Lyons, the sight of these ragged kids playing out in the street while some of the mothers had nothing better to do than chat with their neighbours on the doorsteps would convince me, she reassured herself.

In the middle of the road, almost outside Ella's front door, the milkman on his second round of the morning had set down his cart and was surrounded by women, each carrying a jug, and each waiting to be served. Becky recognized Rosie Dawson, a big friendly woman who worked for Annie Smith in the Swan and was reputed to be well-off because she had three sons all working on the river barges.

'Gonna call in and see Ella, are you, luv?' She smiled at Becky, noting her smart dress and jacket, aware that she was employed by Lyons up in London. 'She'll be pleased to see yer. Needs all the friends she can get right now.'

Becky frowned, hesitating for a moment. 'Well, best hurry on in then, eh? I'll be real pleased to see her.'

Becky tapped twice on the door and when there was no reply edged it open, went down the narrow passage and quietly opened the door to the kitchen. And there was Ella . . . heavily pregnant, seated in a wooden armchair, a snow-white shawl wrapped round her shoulders, and her face turned to where Margaret was sitting on a blanket playing with building bricks. Ella's blue eyes were round and intense, staring at the baby with such love that it brought a lump to Becky's throat.

The room was clean and tidy; what furniture there was had been well-polished and there was a small vase of marigolds set down in the centre of the table. What did shock Becky was the pallor of Ella's face. With all the lovely June weather they had had recently surely there should have been some colour in her cheeks. There wasn't. Ella's face was grey, like a piece of dried-up parchment. The skin seemed to be stretched over her cheekbones and her lovely fine fair hair hung lifelessly over her thin shoulders. The very look of Ella frightened Becky so much that she gasped softly, causing Ella to turn around. Her eyes lit up and then filled with tears as she struggled to stand on her feet.

'Becky!' she said in a voice strangled with emotion. 'Oh, Becky, I've missed you so much.'

'And I've missed you.' Rushing into the room, Becky threw her two arms around that bulky figure and hugged her close. They clung to each other and laughed, and Ella cried, letting the tears run down her face on to Becky's shoulder until baby Margaret decided she wanted some of the attention her mother was getting and yelled out in protest.

'Thanks for all your lovely letters,' Ella said through her tears. 'I'm sorry I don't write to you all that often but I do read your letters over and over. Oh, Becky, I've been praying you'd come home soon.'

'Well, I'm here now,' she said warmly. Then, pushing herself up straight, Becky sniffled away her own tears and looked at Ella's face. 'Look at you,' she cried, brushing a limp lock of hair from her friend's forehead.

They gazed at each other quietly for a minute. Soon Ella said in a soft voice, 'I'll put the kettle on, make us some tea, before we settle down to tell each other all our news.'

Becky dropped to her knees, smiling now, her face lit up with pleasure as she took a good look at her goddaughter.

'Who's grown into such a big girl since I saw you last?' Becky crooned, lifting Margaret up into her arms and resting back on her heels. Baby Margaret merely gurgled at her. 'You are so bonny,' Becky went on as she nestled her face into the baby's neck, 'and you smell so sweet, all talcum powder and nice soap. I could bite lumps out of you, yes I could.' She tickled the little mite under her arms and again around her tummy which sent the baby off into peals of laughter and made her wriggle so much that Becky had difficulty in holding on to her.

'Put her into her highchair,' Ella said, coming back into the room carrying a tea tray on which she had set out a dish of homemade cakes, cups and saucers and small plates. Setting the tray down on the table she turned and Becky quickly asked, 'Where are you going now?'

'To fetch the teapot and the milk.'

It was painfully obvious to Becky that every move Ella made was an effort.

'Here, sit yourself down again, I'll go.' She bent low, picked up three brightly coloured bricks from the floor and set them down on the table of the highchair in which she had securely fastened the baby. 'There you are sweetheart, snug as a bug in a rug, Auntie won't be a moment.'

With the tea poured out and the two of them settled one each side of the table and the baby crunching on a Farley's rusk, there was much to talk about.

'You go first,' Becky instructed Ella. 'I told you most of what has happened to me in my letters so hurry up, bring me up to date.'

Ella drained her cup and turned to look Becky full in the face. 'Shall I start with the good news or the bad?'

Wisely Becky didn't comment on that statement. 'Wherever you like, take your time,' she told Ella.

'Well, I'll give you the good news first.' A faint smile came to her lips. 'Thanks to your dad at least Peter and I now know we are legally married.'

Becky's eyes lit up with surprise. 'Ella, that's marvellous. How come?' The thought of Ella being free of at least that worry made Becky cry out, 'Oh, it's wonderful news!'

'Yes,' Ella agreed, sounding very subdued. 'Must say we were relieved. It was bad enough for me, and though at first I didn't realize it for Peter it was ten times worse. Nobody will ever know what he's been through this last six months.'

Becky saw the pain in her eyes and her heart ached for her. 'Tell me what my dad found out,' she urged.

'After a lot of searching, different records – you wouldn't believe how your dad has been an absolute brick – he found out that Peter's wife has been dead for years. Soon after their wedding ceremony apparently. It seems she was killed up in Liverpool, her dad an' all, an Army truck caused the accident, failed brakes. Don't know the details. Accidental death, the records show. That's why she never answered any of Peter's letters. With the War being on and them having just moved up to Liverpool it seems no one down here was notified. Not at the time anyway.'

'Sad news,' Becky said, doing her best to express sympathy,

'but you must have felt as if a great burden had been lifted from your shoulders.'

'Not really,' Ella lied, and her cheeks flushed up.

'Well, how about Peter?'

'Sort of. Nice to know he wasn't a bigamist.'

'So the pair of you should be feeling on top of the world, waiting for the new baby an' all.'

Ella dropped her gaze to the floor and shifted uncomfortably in her chair. Becky was quiet then, sensing that something was wrong. Leaning across the table she stroked Ella's hair and said very softly, 'I'm sorry. You said you had bad news as well as good.' Then, in a lighter tone, 'Don't tell me if you don't want to, you were always telling me I was too nosy.'

'No. It's all right. You are the best friend anyone in this world could wish for and you're bound to find out sooner or later.' She paused, not certain it was fair to burden Becky with more of her troubles. 'Peter's lost his job, he's been out of work nearly two months,' she murmured.

'Two months!' Becky gaped at her in disbelief. 'Why has nobody told me? How the hell have you managed?'

Ella fidgeted, twisting her hands together. 'It isn't for want of trying. Honestly, Becky, Peter has walked miles. He would do anything. Take any job.' Her eyes were brimming with tears and her voice sounded strangely saddened. She sighed, and when she spoke again it was from the heart. 'Sometimes I think God is punishing me and sometimes I feel so ashamed because even though Margaret is such a beautiful child and I love her dearly I wish she had never been born. I can't help it, Becky, you and I made such plans when we were young and you're doing everything you said you would and there's me without a penny to my name.'

Becky had to swallow and take a deep breath before she was able to form an answer. She couldn't blame Ella one bit for feeling as she did. There couldn't be a more terrible time to be unemployed. With so many men in the same boat and things the way they were, thousands were tramping the streets looking for work. It might be ages before Peter got another job. What could she possibly say to Ella? Her normally quick-thinking mind had gone blank.

'Peter will find something soon.' Ella's quiet voice cut in on Becky's thoughts. 'There isn't a day he doesn't go out looking.'

'Where is Peter now?' Becky ventured to ask.

Ella lowered her head, covered her face with her hands and quietly wept. Becky thought it best to give her a minute or two. She lifted the baby from the highchair into her arms and went to stand and stare out of the kitchen window.

At that moment the door to the garden shed opened and Peter appeared, slouching along the garden path. His head was down, his shoulders rounded. One hand was rammed into his trouser pocket and from the other hand he dangled two pairs of old boots. All told he looked thoroughly dejected. Two months with no money coming in, it must seem like an eternity. Becky closed her eyes and prayed. Please God, let him find a job soon. Please! It is bad enough now – whatever will they do when the new baby arrives?

When she opened her eyes Peter was opening the back door, calling out to Ella as he came into the house. 'Ella, you there? I've managed to fix both Ted's boots and mine. Bit of a job though, the leather wasn't up to much. Still, they'll last us a bit longer now.'

As Peter turned to close the door behind him, Becky stepped forward.

'God, it's you, Becky!' he exclaimed as though he were unable to believe what he was seeing. 'You're a sight for sore eyes.'

'I've been here some time,' she said, and smiled. 'Didn't know you were hiding yourself away in that shed.'

'I didn't intend to be so long. I was going to take that little rascal for a walk.' He grinned, stooping to kiss Margaret's cheek. 'But I can see I haven't been missed, cuddling up in your auntie's arms eh?' he whispered to the baby. 'No sooner you're inside the door and you're spoiling my daughter,' he said as he smiled, teasing Becky.

'What were you doing in the shed?' Becky asked, thinking that she already knew the answer.

'Making good use of the skills my father taught me when we lived in Northampton.' He held both pairs of boots up in the air, letting them dangle by their laces. 'Trying to do the impossible really, make good out of bad.'

'Stop your chattering out there,' Ella called, her voice sounding a lot lighter now that Peter had put in an appearance. 'Come on in and I'll make a fresh pot of tea.'

Becky went through the motions, talking too much, playing with the baby, telling them snippets of what she did at work, yet all the time her mind was racing ahead. She asked herself the same question twice over. Will it work? Seeing Peter with those boots, an idea had popped into her mind without her realizing it. An idea she couldn't wait to put to her father.

Putting on her jacket, taking a fond farewell of both Ella and Peter, smothering the baby in kisses, she promised she would be back the very next day.

'You don't have to come traipsing all this way over here,' Ella whispered, giving the baby to Peter to hold. Then looping her hand through Becky's arm she said, 'I'll come to the door with you.'

On the doorstep Becky hugged her dear friend gently.

'Becky, you're to think on what I've said.' Ella was suddenly being very serious. 'You only have a few days so you must spend them with your family.'

'Who's being the bossy one now?' Becky asked, looking Ella straight in the eye. 'Don't tell me what I must do. I shall be back here some time tomorrow. All right?'

A smiling Ella nodded her head.

There was determination in her step as Becky walked towards the tram stop. She wondered whether her father would agree to help her. Someone had to help Peter and Ella and who better than herself? After all, fate had been kind to her, so far. Who knows what would have happened if she had gone along a similar road to that which Ella had taken? She shuddered at the thought.

She didn't ever want to be poor. Being poor was making an old woman out of Ella long before her time, sitting there feeling helpless with Peter out of work. It must be so humiliating for both of them not to be able to pay the rent or feed and clothe their baby properly.

Poor Peter! Walking miles in an old pair of boots that he had cobbled together with a cheap piece of leather. How long would they last, for Christ's sake?

Thank God the weather was good. What if Peter was still unemployed come the winter? If there was no money for food and clothing there certainly wouldn't be any for coal. Then what? With two babies, it didn't bear thinking about.

Ella, sitting deep in thought, worried out of her life. Peter slouching up the garden path, dangling those old boots he had worked on for hours when really all they were fit for was the dustbin. It would be a long time before she could get those pictures out of her mind.

The tram came along and Becky boarded it, still with the one thought uppermost in her mind. She couldn't live like Ella was having to. Scrimping and scraping for every penny. She just couldn't. Like most girls when she had first left school her aim had been to fall in love, get married, and have babies. Now she knew that life wasn't as simple as that.

Her mind was made up. The man she married would have to be in a position to provide her with some of the good things rich people took for granted. Maybe if she had not been lucky enough to land her job with Lyons, she might never have realized that there was a big world out there and it had so much to offer.

But she *had* got the job. She was a trained waitress working in the West End of London. And she was going further.

After more special training she was to be employed by the newly-formed Outside Catering Department and the events she would soon be attending would open up an even wider view of life.

Now she was used to eating really well, visits to the theatre, having money of her own, going places and doing things she had previously never even dreamt of. Not that her wonderful parents had ever kept their children short. But then her dad had been one of the lucky ones. He had always had a good job with a regular pay packet. On the other hand the life they led in Surrey was very limited. It suited them fine, and it had suited her until she had seen how the other half lived.

Becky was thinking hard by now, her eyes staring and her forehead creased in a deep frown. I've seen what it's like to be rich and now I know first-hand what it's like to be poor and one thing's for certain, I know which is best, she said to herself. But was that a selfish attitude to take? She couldn't, or perhaps wouldn't, give herself a truthful answer.

Her thoughts turned to Gerald Palmer. Could he give her the kind of life she now yearned for? I think I am in love with him but when I'm apart from him I'm not really sure what that kind of love really is. I only know that my family mean the world to me, I love each of them with all my heart, but that's a different kind of feeling to the one I have for Gerald. If 'love' meant being happy with someone, longing to see them again, thinking about them day and night, and your whole body tingling whenever that person touched you or even looked at you in that special way, then, yes, she was in love with Gerald.

Did her future lie with him? He was handsome, kind and good, he loved her, so he said, and he had money. Yet he had never mentioned marriage.

As May was always telling her, she would have to tread warily, because there were times when she was apart from Gerald that a warning bell would ring in her head and her instincts told her not to let her heart rule her head.

Suddenly she felt uneasy. It was Ella and her problems that she should be concerned with, not her own. Compared to Ella she didn't have a worry in the world. She was hoping against hope that her dad would go along with the proposition she was going to put to him. Her dad could make it possible. He had to be able to, because if Peter didn't find some way of earning a living soon God alone knew how he and Ella would manage.

'Well, I'll be blowed.' Joe Russell, having listened attentively to every word that his headstrong daughter had uttered, now leant back in his armchair and scratched his greying hair.

Their evening meal over, everything cleared away, there was just Becky, and her mother and father sitting cosily around the table that was now covered with Joyce's best red chenille tablecloth.

'You might not believe this, Becky lass, but I watched Peter getting further and further down in the dumps and I asked myself this question: "What can the lad do that he's been trained for?"' Joe's ruddy face was creased with anxiety. 'The only thing I could come up with was that he was trained to fight for his country.'

'Him and a few thousand more,' his wife scoffed, 'but that don't seem to count with the Government. Breaks yer heart to see the men that are tramping the streets these days.'

'You haven't answered my question, Dad,' Becky pleaded. 'Do you think if we clubbed together and got him all the tools Peter could set up a trade, mending boots in his garden shed?'

'After a while I came up with that same idea, luv, when I found out that his dad had practically taught him the trade. It wouldn't work though.'

'Dad! Just tell me why not?' Becky begged, her tone serious.

'Because the enquiries I made proved that it wasn't practicable. Peter would have to get the landlord's permission for a start.'

'Yeah, and he'd want a share of the profit for himself,' Joyce butted in again. 'He'd say Peter was using his property to run a business.'

'Exactly,' Joe said, 'and that would defeat the object. The repairs Peter would be doing would be for men in the same position as himself and what could they afford to pay? Precious little if you ask me. No, if we are going to set Peter up with a little business it has to be in the town on a busy street where there would be plenty of passing trade. He'd be much better off seeking the kind of person who can afford to pay to have their shoes repaired rather than doing favours for his mates.'

'Oh yes, Joe, and pigs would fly if they had wings,' Joyce mocked, dismissing the idea although like the rest of her family she would do anything to help Peter and Ella. She was almost afraid to go round to see Peggy these days. Peggy was worried sick knowing that each day things were getting worse for her Ella and Peter and with a second baby on the way she was at her wits' end, not knowing how she could help. After all she was on her own with no man behind her.

That woman has done well when you think about it, Joyce was musing to herself, and now her only daughter and her first grandchild are stuck out there in Kingston with Peter out of work and herself not in a position to help much. Joyce shook her head and looked at her own bonny daughter. My, she looked a picture, she'd done well for herself since she'd left home. There wasn't a day that passed that she didn't miss her but there again she thanked God for Lily Maynard. She looked after her niece, May, and Rebecca as if they were her own. Giving them both a damn good home is Lily. Yet Becky never forgot her family and where her real home was. Never a week passed that she didn't write a letter home.

It must break Peggy's heart when she compares the difference in the way our two girls have turned out. I bet she often wonders whether things might not have been different if her man hadn't been killed in the War. Heartbreaking really when you think about it. She sighed softly.

'I could put up a bit of money, about fifty pounds actually,' Becky told her parents, using a very quiet voice, knowing full well they would be surprised that she had such a sum of money.

Both heads spun round to stare at their daughter.

'Fifty pounds!' her mother cried.

'A lot of money that,' her father said drily. 'Care to tell us how you came by it, luv?'

Becky half-closed her eyes. A white lie in a good cause wouldn't hurt, she was saying to herself, aware that if she said she had won most of it at the races her parents would be horror-struck.

'Well it wasn't from gratuities,' she told them sweetly. 'You know we aren't allowed to accept tips. It was two bonus payments. One of twenty pounds six months ago and another twenty pounds when we agreed to join this new training scheme. The rest I've managed to save.'

'Well I never,' her mother said, her eyes wide with amazement. 'Your father's always telling me what a marvellous opening it was for you to go and work at Lyons. I believe him now an' all.'

Becky said a quick prayer. I know it's a lie, but please God, it really is in a good cause.

'Well,' her father said thoughtfully, 'if you're sure you want to part with your savings.' He waited and Becky eagerly nodded her head. 'There's a few of us that will put a little into the pot, one never knows when we ourselves might need a helping hand.'

'That's true,' Joyce said gratefully, 'And what goes round comes round, I always say.'

'I'll start in on it first thing in the morning,' Joe Russell declared. 'Don't worry lass, we'll get Peter sorted out. There must be suitable premises somewhere.'

'Oh, Dad! I knew you wouldn't let me down. If anyone can do it you can.' She jumped to her feet, came round behind his chair and threw both arms around her dad's broad shoulders, leant over and started planting kisses on his forehead.

'Get orf,' he yelled, 'get yerself up to bed. Me saying I'd try and fix Peter up don't make it so. Just you remember that. I'm no miracle worker.'

Becky looked across at her mother and they both burst out laughing. 'No, and you ain't no angel either,' his wife told him, still laughing fit to burst as she held the door open for Becky.

Becky hesitated in the doorway. 'Goodnight, Mum, Goodnight, Dad. You wanna know something? I love you both.'

Joe Russell didn't have to search far. It really was the case that truth is often stranger than fiction, he was telling himself as he strode home two days after listening to Becky plead for help for Peter.

'Where's Becky?' Joe asked his wife the minute he set foot inside the house.

'Round the corner, gone to see Peggy. She went out early this morning to buy little Margaret's birthday present and then went over to Ella's again. Came back in a right depressed state she did.'

'Well, go down the garden and give her a shout over the fence. Tell her to bring Peggy round here with her. What I've got to tell them will put a smile on their faces, I'll be bound.'

Joyce hurried to put her cleaning things back in the cupboard and to set the teacups out ready. Couldn't have a discussion without a cup of tea.

'I have found the ideal place for Peter to run his own business repairing boots and shoes. And best of all it is right in the centre of Tooting Broadway and you can't get a busier place than that.' Joe Russell drew himself up to his full height, puffed out his chest and let his amazing news sink in. He glanced at the three faces in turn, thrilled to bits to see that they were gazing at him as if he were a magician who had just pulled off a fantastic trick.

'You mean it, Dad?'

He nodded.

Joyce stubbornly wanted to know all the details. 'Start from the beginning,' she said briskly.

'I don't know how I'm ever going to be able to repay you,' Peggy James mumbled.

'Don't be so daft,' Joe Russell said quickly. His heart was so full that he had to take a deep breath before he could begin to tell them all his news. 'Almost the first bloke I spoke to yesterday morning put me onto Luke Wyneberg, he works in the railway ticket office at Worcester Park. Seems his uncle has had this cobbler's shop for years. It got too much for him, although he did employ one man, and he's been trying to flog off the lease for ages. He didn't have any luck and because he's over seventy and not in very good health he closed the shop down a month ago. Windows have been boarded up ever since.'

A hush settled over everyone as they gazed at Joe in amazement.

'Oh, Joe, you're a good man.' Joyce stared at her husband and pointing to Becky murmured, 'Look at her face, you've made her day.'

'Women!' Joe exclaimed, laughing loudly, 'you've all jumped to the conclusion that it's all cut an' dried. You might at least let me finish.'

'Go on then, Dad, have your moment of glory,' Becky said, her eyes twinkling with devilment.

'Well, just you listen to this, Miss Clever-Clogs.' Her father said as he grinned broadly. 'This morning I've been to Tooting with Luke. The place really is ideal. The position, as I've already said, couldn't be better and the living accommodation upstairs really surprised me. There's a big living room and a roomy kitchen, two bedrooms and believe it or not a bathroom. The ground floor is just the large front shop with another room at the back which has obviously been used as a workroom.

'With a jolly good clean and a bit of outlay for material Peter could be in business within a very short time.

'The setup is complete. It hasn't been touched. There's a high counter just inside the shop door, and a workbench runs the full length of the far wall and as far as I could tell there was a great many tools of the trade lying about. Out in the back room there was a Singer sewing machine which was worked by means of a foot treadle and another machine whose purpose Luke and I could only guess at. We came up with the idea between us that it might be a finishing machine.'

'Oh, Dad!' Becky couldn't put her feelings into words, so she smiled and squeezed his arm.

'Hang on, lass, I've got the gory details to tell you yet.'

Now comes the crunch, Becky was thinking; the fear that all this was going to cost far more than all Peter's friends could come up with was nagging away at her.

'Don't look like that,' Joe said, directing his voice at Peggy, 'I won't say it was easy cos it weren't but I think I've been able to swing it. It's all down to Luke. He's the only living relative that Mr Wyneberg has. We did quite a bit of bargaining and here's what Luke finally proposed. Fifty pounds key money, Peter can rent the premises at a very low rent for one year. By the end of the year the rent will be increased or, should Peter feel he is doing well, Luke has promised he will be given the option of buying the lease. I've told him I shall go over and lay all the facts before Peter this evening and if he's in agreement we'll contact the solicitor who is acting for Luke and on behalf of Mr Wyneberg tomorrow.' The room was charged with excitement and Joe held up his hand and added, 'Luke has agreed to pay for the premises to be cleaned and to distemper the walls of the shop.'

Joyce and Peggy hugged each other, both near to tears,

then Joyce stood back and looked at her daughter. 'You're a good girl, Becky. A couple of days ago yer dad said he wasn't a miracle-worker. Well, now he's proved he is, but it was you that set the ball rolling.'

Peggy came to stand in front of Becky. 'Thanks, luv,' she said gratefully, 'my Ella's got a damn good friend in you.'

'Sharing troubles is what friends are for,' Becky said kindly, wishing she could be around to see all these preparations get underway. Alas, she had to return to London. She had a new job waiting for her and who knew what else the future might hold?

Chapter Twenty-two

'CAREFUL,' LILY MAYNARD called out anxiously, 'the way you're slamming that iron about your uniform will be ruined.'

Becky stopped ironing and stared at Aunt Lil. 'It's these damn pearl buttons, they're driving me mad,' she replied, frowning.

'Well it's not like you to cuss, and it sounds vulgar and common which is definitely not like you and while I'm about it I might just as well 'ave my say. Something is wrong with both you and May.'

'What?' Becky snapped as she laid the flat iron down on its stand and turned to face Aunt Lil.

'I said things are not right with the pair of you.'

'How d' you make that out?'

Aunt Lil regarded her curiously. 'Becky, luv, I could be blind in one eye an' still see that neither of you two girls are acting normal. One minute you're both as nice as pie, the next you're biting my head off. And you've become so moody. Is there anything you'd like to tell me?'

'No. Nothing.'

'Sorry for asking,' Lil said and turned to walk away.

Becky's mood changed abruptly, and she thrust her arm out. 'I'm sorry, Aunt Lil, I didn't mean to snap at you.'

'That's all right, luv, leave that ironing. I'll finish it for you in a minute, but I've just made a fresh pot of tea so give May a call and we'll all sit down and have a cup together.'

I'm a nervous wreck, Becky thought to herself as she went out into the passage to call up the stairs to May. I just wish I could creep back up to bed, pull the covers right up over my head and stay there in the darkness until my head stops throbbing. But there's no chance of that. Not for hours to come.

Lil had laid out the big breakfast cups and saucers. She poured milk from the bottle into a china jug that had a pattern of roses on each side. She was brooding over what the future held for her two girls when May and Becky came into the room together.

'Here, one of you kneel down on the hearth rug and make the toast.' She held out the long-handled toasting fork, on which she had speared a thick slice of bread, and Becky took it. 'And you, May, can fetch the rashers of bacon from the oven and put them on the table. It'll be your own fault if they're dried up, lying in bed till this time of the day.'

With a full plate in front of each of them and their tea poured out Aunt Lil thought, well, it's now or never. Taking a deep breath she stated, 'It's been all of eight months since you two started this outside catering lark and I can't say that just lately it's been doing you a lot of good.'

May moved her toast around and pretended to study the pattern on her plate. Lil sensed both girls' reluctance to discuss the matter.

'Well, if you won't let on what's gone wrong I'll take a wild guess. You're both doing nicely, as regards funds. You've told me that much and very generous you are to me and I know you, Becky, send money home to yer mum, so it can't be that. A lot of your money comes from bonuses, am I right?'

Becky took a sip of her tea and placed the cup down on the saucer. 'Yes that's quite right, Aunt Lil. When the company or client pay the total bill to Lyons they apparently add a percentage for the staff, and it's given to us once a month as a bonus.'

'So, is the work too much? Is that what's getting you down?'

'Nothing's getting us down,' May snapped.

'Look here young lady,' Lil pointed a finger at her niece, 'you can't kid me, I know you too well. Sitting there looking all gormless. A jolly good night's sleep is what both of you could do with. A quarter to three it was this morning when you two crept up the stairs and don't bother to tell me that you were working t' that hour cos I wasn't born yesterday.'

May and Becky looked at each other and the realization that they were going to have to come up with some explanation was apparent to both of them.

'Oh, Aunt!' May couldn't hide the emotion in her voice as she caught hold of Lily's hand. 'We don't mean to snap at you. We both appreciate everything you do for us. It's just that some of these functions are damned hard work. We do earn nearly twice as much as we did at the Corner House but don't get much free time. Evening social gatherings aren't so bad but some of the daytime functions can carry on over into most of the evening and by then our feet are killing us.'

'That's typical of you, May. Skirt around the truth. Everything you've said about the job I'm sure is dead right. Being on your feet for hours on end can't be a picnic for either of you. But don't take me for a complete fool.'

The colour rose in May's cheeks as she stared at her aunt.

'No men friends, keeping you out all hours of the night?' Lil asked the question, looking at each girl in turn. 'You can't tell me you've got your noses to the grindstone morning, noon and night. What about all these new clothes? Where are you off to when you wear them, eh? All right, tell me I'm a nosy old bitch and what you two choose to do in your free time is none of my business but just remember this, fancy feathers don't make fine birds and the men you're going out with might just have the sense to see that. If they don't then they aren't worth bothering about.'

Lily Maynard sighed heavily and leant back in her chair. She'd had her say. As deeply as she cared for each of these girls there was not much else she could do short of meeting them daily when they finished work and forcibly dragging them home. They weren't children. They were grown-up young ladies and much as it pained her to stand by and watch they had to be allowed to make their own mistakes. She just hoped and prayed if the time came when they really needed her she would still be around to help them pick up the pieces.

Becky had never felt so guilty. May's Aunt Lil had taken her in, treating her as if she were her own daughter and this was how she was repaying her. She looked around the homely living room. Every surface was covered with photograph frames containing happy pictures of Lily and her husband, her sister and her family but no children of her own. Such a tiny grey-haired lady was Lil, yet energy and enthusiasm for life still burst from that small frame. She dressed in a very old-fashioned way, almost always with a shawl draped round her shoulders. She was like a relic from another age but of one thing Becky was certain, Aunt Lil had a big heart and she loved her dearly.

May stood up, eyes downcast, as she apologized to her aunt. 'We'll come straight home this evening, Aunt Lil, promise. All we have on is an afternoon do and as soon as we've cleared up we'll head straight home, nice cosy evening round the fire. How's that sound?'

Lil's eyes were wide and Becky thought she saw a glimmer of amusement in them. 'That go for you too, Becky?' Lil asked. 'Cos if it does I'll have a roast dinner ready.'

'Certainly does, can't wait,' Becky said, and smiled with relief. Aunt Lil was an absolute darling. Both she and May were causing her a lot of worry and when she came to think about it she hadn't played fair with her own family. Two months into 1927 and she hadn't been home since Christmas and then it had only been a flying visit just for the one day. She hadn't even seen Ella. She had left presents for both Ella and Peter with her parents and both girls had been remembered too but it wasn't the same as seeing them and giving the presents in person.

Both girls! It didn't seem possible but it was true. Ella had given birth to her second daughter in July last year. That made just thirteen months between Amy, the new baby, and Margaret. God alone knows how Ella manages, Becky was saying to herself, remembering that if it weren't for her dad she wouldn't get half as much news from home. Sometimes she met her dad on the railway station if their turns fitted in and sometimes he popped into Lil's house in South Lambeth Road. According to him, Peter was holding his own in his business venture. Only just, it seemed, but then again as Aunt Lil was fond of saying, a crust is better than no bread at all.

'You finished daydreaming?' May asked Becky with laughter in her voice, 'because we ought to be making a move.'

'I'll finish off your uniform and pack it in yer case,' Lil told Becky as she ushered them out of the kitchen. 'What about you, May, is your outfit all right?'

'My apron an' cap could do with an iron rubbed over them, please.'

'Hurry up then, fetch them and hand them down over the banisters.'

Lil shook her head as she took the padded iron holder down from where it hung on a hook to the side of the mantelshelf. 'Young girls!' she said aloud. Winding it round the handle she raised the hot iron from the range and spat on the clean surface.

If only she could iron out the girls' difficulties as easily as she could iron their dresses. The pair of them could protest till the cows came home, she hadn't any illusions about what they were getting up to. How could she expect either of them to find a working-class lad, marry him and settle down, after the life they'd become accustomed to? Out on the town with these young toffs. Did they really see their future with that type of man? If they did she was very much afraid that they were in for a rude awakening.

It was bitterly cold, with frost still sparkling on the rooftops, and the pavements were treacherous to walk on even though it was now almost eleven o'clock when May and Becky climbed aboard the tram. The atmosphere inside was damp and steamy. The passengers were mainly women, wrapped up well against the cold, scarves tied over their heads and knotted tightly beneath their chins, clutching empty baskets or shopping bags.

May and Becky each wore a small close-fitting hat, the only adornment being a bow of ribbon which had been chosen to tone in with the grey coat that Becky wore and the plum-coloured coat of May's respectively.

'They're making for Vauxhall Bridge market I suppose,' May remarked as she looked about her.

'Yeah, at least we don't have to wonder where our next meal is coming from, do we?' Becky replied.

'Got a lot t' be grateful for when you work it out,' May sighed.

The afternoon function they had been assigned to was being held on the third floor of the Coventry Street Corner House.

'Long time since we walked through these doors,' Becky stated as she let the big door swing to behind her.

'Good, I'm glad to see some of you are early, there is so much to do.' Miss Paige spoke in a clipped voice full of authority. She was in charge of all the female staff that worked on Outside Catering. She was small and plump and showed signs of having been very beautiful in her younger days. Her complexion was dark, her cheeks well-rouged. Her brown eyes were smiling as she approached May and Rebecca.

'I always know I may rely on you two,' she said, smoothing a hand over the crisp, white damask tablecloth. May had begun to lay out the fine china while Becky was sorting out the heavy silver cutlery.

More girls arrived and cries of greetings were called to May and to Becky. It was good to be back in Coventry Street, to be surrounded by well-remembered things and good friends.

Today's do was a small, intimate ladies' afternoon tea. It would feel different, easy.

'A piece of cake, this do,' May remarked as they unfurled yet another small tablecloth.

When they had to cope with large numbers some of the cloths used could measure as much as twenty-four feet in length and as most of the Nippies would agree, tablecloths of that size were a bugger to lay straight.

'They're all a bit posh like,' Becky remarked as the well-dressed ladies trooped in and took their places at the small round tables which were each set for six. 'Maybe, when we're older, we'll be going to afternoon dos such as this '

'Yeah, an' maybe we'll be like those women on the tram. Half a dozen kids at home an' us out looking for the cheapest cuts of meat,' came May's quick reply.

Becky shrugged and laughed. 'Not me! I'll make sure of that.'

'Suppose you're banking on Gerald Palmer offering to marry you so's you can live happy ever after.'

'Oh, May, don't tease. Not today, please.'

May straightened her starched apron and twisted the cuffs of her long sleeves. 'Stop lying to yourself, Becky. I know now I didn't pick a winner in Roger Macclesfield but then I never let things get out of hand. Gerald Palmer is . . .' May stopped abruptly, flicking her hand through the air in a gesture that was almost angry. 'For crying out loud, don't look at me like that, Becky. You don't need me to tell you what Gerald's intentions are. I'm beginning to wonder if you have all your marbles straight. You're inclined to believe everything he tells you, no matter how many times he lets you down you go back for more.'

'But . . .' Becky bit her lip. She didn't want to hear this. Not from her best friend. Tears were stinging the back of her eyelids. She blinked hard. Becky might have understood her friend's attitude better if May had told her more about why Roger Macclesfield had suddenly disappeared from sight.

All she really knew was that she had heard May sobbing in the early hours of the morning and had gone along to her bedroom. Just to see the state that May was in had made her heart ache. There hadn't been anything that she could do except climb in beneath the covers and hold her close.

Never ever will I forget the words that May uttered between her sobs. Even remembering them now makes me shudder, Becky was saying quietly to herself, the memory still vivid.

'It's not fair, Becky.' May had raised her tearstained face from the pillow, and whispered the words.

Becky had patted her affectionately. 'No one ever said life was fair.'

'I'm sorry I woke you up, Becky.'

'Don't be daft, May. We're friends, remember.'

May had sniffed hard before replying. 'Just tell me this, Becky. Why is it that both you and I had to attract rotters? Both Gerald and Roger acted like real gents to us at first. We told ourselves what we wanted to believe, that we'd found two good 'uns, but it turned out that I for one hadn't had that sort of luck.'

'It's not your fault, May. It's a shame that Roger went off without a word and I only wish you would tell me the real reason.'

Becky still tried to shut out the sad picture of May sitting up in bed, telling her, 'When it came down to rock bottom I hardly knew anything at all about Roger. Now I want to forget him. Just make sure that Gerald doesn't use you the same way!'

Those last words of May's had given Becky a few sleepless nights and they still rankled as she turned them over in her mind.

'Hark at them!' May had come alongside Becky and broken into her thoughts. 'You'd think to hear these women chattering away that the room was full of magpies.'

Becky laid her tray down on the dumbwaiter and laughed.

'I've just had a word with Miss Paige and she said we can take fifteen minutes, get ourselves a cuppa.'

'Thank God for that,' May said with a grin. 'I hate it when we have to stand around the wall while all the speeches and presentations are being made.'

'Hey, wait for me,' Becky protested as May made a beeline for the still room.

Shoes kicked off and a most welcome cup of tea in her hand, Becky let her mind wander back to Gerald. Here and now she would agree that she ought to heed May's warnings. Right from the start May had distrusted Gerald. Then again May hadn't been so wise when it came to Roger. Poor May, she had been let down badly.

That hadn't altered the way she felt. The moment she saw Gerald her heart would start thumping nineteen to the dozen. Becky sighed heavily. It was all right to be wary and suspicious when she was apart from Gerald, but a different matter when she was with him. His very nearness made her throw caution to the wind. It was his face, his smile, and those eyes! Looking into Gerald's eyes her whole world changed.

He liked her, maybe even loved her, look how he looked at her, the attention he paid her, the presents he offered. Was all that because of true feelings he had for her?

Sometimes she was sure it was. He often did say he loved her. I love him, she breathed. God help me I do. Totally and utterly. He's the man I would like to be with every day and every night for the rest of my life.

Be honest, she chided herself. There had been times when Gerald's desire had got the better of him and when she had put a stop to his wandering hands he had become very ill-tempered. Of one thing she was sure, she wouldn't be able to keep him dangling much longer. If she refused him again, it would be over. All of it. Not just the theatre trips, race meetings and days on the river but also her dreams of a wonderful secure future.

She thought of Ella. Peter was a nice enough fellow but

what had he given Ella? Two lovely daughters, but with hardly a breathing space between the two of them. No means of support until she and her dad had stepped in and even now, by all accounts, they lived a hand-to-mouth existence.

She didn't want to end up like Ella.

A sudden surge of guilt swept over her. Was she really in love with Gerald? Maybe she was in love with his way of life and the good times he provided. Did Gerald love her? May would assure her he didn't. Many's the time she had suspected that May was right.

Gerald wanted her. Oh yes! If she gave in to his demands would he propose marriage? She was tempted to find out. Marriage to Gerald Palmer would mean genuine security. Never having to scrimp and save. Gerald might be her only chance.

A roaring cheer came from the restaurant, and the sound of clapping. May sat up in her chair, reached over and patted Becky's knee. 'Wakey, wakey, luv, all the girls are making a move, so let's be having you. The quicker we see this lot off the quicker we'll be home eating Aunt Lil's roast.'

The prospect made Becky's mouth water. She shook her head to clear it. An evening indoors, sitting around a well banked-up fire with Aunt Lil and May for company, well, she couldn't imagine anything nicer.

Even Gerald Palmer couldn't top that. Not tonight he couldn't.

Chapter Twenty-three

PAUSING BEFORE THE full-length mirror set in the door of her wardrobe, Becky inspected herself from top to toe. She wore a calf-length, sleeveless black dress with a black long-sleeved chiffon jacket. The only adornment was a small silver brooch which she wore high on the left shoulder of the dress. Her hair had been set that afternoon and lay thick and silky in the new shorter style that still suited her so well. The sides curled forward covering her ears and framed her face beautifully.

She looked right, she decided.

Gerald Palmer was taking her for dinner and then on to a show. She reached for her white swagger coat; it wasn't exactly suitable for evening wear but it was the best she had. Being three-quarters in length and with a full swing to the back she could get away with draping it around her shoulders. Taking up her small black evening bag she hurried down the stairs and out into the front garden.

It had been a lovely bright day bringing a promise of spring and with Easter less than three weeks away, Aunt Lil was on her knees setting out a few bedding plants in sheltered spots.

'It's getting chilly out here, Aunt Lil. Shouldn't you pack up for today and go inside?'

'Oh, I've almost finished, dear. Another five minutes and I will go indoors,' she promised cheerfully. 'You have a lovely evening.'

Becky turned as a car drew into the kerb and Gerald called out, 'Good evening, Mrs Maynard.'

Lily just raised her hand in reply.

Becky leant down and kissed Aunt Lil. 'Don't stay out here till you catch a cold, will you?'

'No, truly, I'm almost done. Go on, enjoy yourself.'

Watching Becky walk down the path, get into the car and drive off with Gerald, Lily Maynard was recalling her brief encounter with Gerald Palmer when Becky had first taken up with him. She had disliked him on sight. She had sensed a kind of ruthlessness beneath that charming smile, and she wondered, as she had so many times since, why was it that men with money, men who dressed so well, seemed to have a special attraction for young women. Becky could daydream all she liked but if marriage was what Gerald Palmer had in mind then she'd eat her hat. Toffs like him didn't marry working girls. She had been wrong about Roger Macclesfield. Him she had believed to be a good one.

Oh, May hadn't said anything. Not one word. She hadn't needed to. Just one look at May's face and she could tell how she was suffering. Let down just as sure as Becky would be the way she was going on, but you couldn't tell them. They wouldn't thank you for it and they'd go their own way no matter what advice she dished out. Trouble with Becky was, she was such a trusting little soul.

One day both girls may be lucky and meet a decent man, she was wishing as she gathered up her gardening tools. The words were as much a prayer as a wish.

'Will you be working over Easter?' Gerald asked Becky when they were seated in the lounge bar of the restaurant having coffee and after-dinner liqueurs.

Becky wondered why Gerald had bothered to ask that question. Bank holidays were a time when Gerald disappeared, rarely if ever mentioning where he had been. Up to now she had never set eyes on him during any public holiday. She had always assumed that he spent the time with his parents, not that she knew anything about his mother and father. Gerald shied away from answering any personal questions.

A weary sigh escaped from Becky's lips before she answered. 'Afraid so. Three days on the trot. Huge luncheon with royalty in attendance at the Albert Hall on the Thursday before the holiday.'

'Oh! What's that in aid of?'

'Some charity. Not sure which one. Itinerary we've been given merely states that as soon as coffee is served we are to marshal a line of young children up on to the stage in single file. Apparently each child is presenting a purse of money which has been collected for good causes.'

'Where do the children come from? Are they sons and daughters of diplomats?'

'I wouldn't think so, more like from Guides' and Scouts' organizations would be my guess.'

'You will get a few days off following the holiday?'

Suddenly Becky was uncomfortably aware of Gerald's eyes on her.

'Why don't we go down to Brighton for the rest of the week?' he asked casually. 'I've got a pal who has a nice place the other side of Hove. Don't worry, Becky,' he teased, 'I'm sure he'll find you a single bedroom even if I have to muck in with another chap.'

Gerald noticed that she coloured up and hesitated for a moment before answering. 'I don't think I should expect to stay with your friend. He's never met me.'

'Oh come on, Rebecca,' he pleaded, sounding very formal with the full use of her name. 'My friends drop in on each other all the time. They will love you. Besides you say yourself you are always worn out after waiting on several large gatherings. There's nothing more restful than lying on a chaise-longue and gazing out over the sea. I'll pick you up in the car at ten on Thursday. Find a cosy pub on the way down to have lunch, arrive at John's place about four, stay at least over the weekend and you'll feel so fit and well you won't know yourself. I promise.'

Becky looked at his smiling face. He was as eager as a schoolboy for her to agree. She wavered. 'All right. But . . .' her lip trembled, which only endeared her to him all the more. 'What if your friend doesn't like me? Doesn't want me to stay in his house?'

'That won't happen. It won't be like that. How can I convince you? John Gadsdon and I were at university together. He will make you very welcome.'

The die was cast. There was no going back, not unless she wanted Gerald to walk out of her life forever. Gerald leant forward, took Becky's liqueur glass from her hand and set it down on the table. His eyes were wide and bright, his smile beaming as he took her hands between his own. 'Darling,' he whispered, 'however hard you try you'll never make me happier than you have at this moment. I can't wait to have you all to myself.'

'I'm glad you're pleased,' she told him, her head still buzzing with misgivings.

'Pleased? That's the understatement of the year.'

'What will you be doing over Easter?' she asked, more to dampen his enthusiasm than out of curiosity.

There was a moment of silence before he answered, during which Becky felt that she had asked the wrong thing. 'I have to go to Scotland,' he told Becky. 'My long-suffering parents have given me an ultimatum.'

Good job I'm working then, Becky thought to herself, but had the good sense not to utter the words aloud. A sudden thought struck her. Ultimatum? She'd give a lot to know the exact terms or better still to be a fly on the wall while Gerald was in Scotland. Even a crystal ball would be useful where Gerald was concerned.

'For goodness sake try and look happy,' Gerald rebuked her. 'It's time we were making a move if we are to get to the theatre in time.' Ever the gentleman, Gerald rose to his feet, took her hand and raised it to his lips. Becky couldn't help laughing. 'That's better, that's my darling girl,' he whispered, his lips now brushing softly against her ear.

Becky took a step backwards and smiled up at him at the same time reflecting to herself that it was a good job Gerald wasn't able to read her thoughts.

Brighton weather at this time of the year was glorious: too cold for swimming in the sea, but with the nice warm breezes of perfect spring days. What a beautiful, busy place! Becky was delighted as Gerald drove all along Brighton sea-front, revealing not one pier but two. The wide promenade was colourful with residents and day-trippers taking gentle exercise. Across the wide road lay the great squares with massive, tall, graceful houses on three sides and a centre patch of emerald grass surrounded by ornate railings. To her the whole area was fascinating.

Gerald headed towards Hove, with its even more select gardens and a better class of cafés and taverns. Soon he had left the seafront behind, climbing upwards with the Downs in the distance, taking a route along narrow leafy lanes.

From the road the house had been invisible, protected from nosy-parkers by tall hedges and a long rutted driveway. At first sight Becky had squealed with surprise. It was so old, looking as if it hadn't altered for centuries, gathering over the years a protective covering of ivy and moss. Tiny little windows set deep in the stone walls sparkled a welcome.

The moment of pleasure had gone as soon as Gerald had put the key in the door and with a great smile on his face bid her enter. One look around and she wanted to flee, run away, vanish. Go anywhere other than stay here. She felt trapped. She couldn't look at Gerald. She stood with her hand clenched over her mouth, somehow managing to control her panic.

'You knew no one else would be here,' Becky's accusation came out in a clear, clipped tone.

'Would you have come if I'd told you we would have the place to ourselves?'

'That's not the point,' Becky protested, but before she could say another word Gerald crossed the floor to stand directly in front of her, his face flushed, his eyes stern. Without haste he took hold of her arms and held them in a tight grip.

'You need to grow up, Rebecca. I think I have been very patient with you. You know exactly how I feel about you, you've known from the very beginning. I love you. You drive me wild at times the way you tease and then walk away. A man can only take so much.'

While he had been speaking his grip on her arms had tightened until he was hurting her. She lifted her head and looked at him. 'You really believe I set out to tease you?'

He read the expression on her face and smiled. 'Yes, I do believe it. You accept everything and give nothing in return.'

'What have I got to give you?' she asked cautiously.

'Don't put on your little girl act, Becky,' he said sternly. 'You know damn well I don't mean material things. A few days. A whole week, a lifetime, that's what I want to spend with you, but if the whole idea of being alone with me is so repulsive to you then get back in the car and I will drive you straight back to London.' He released his hold on her and turned to leave the room.

'Why didn't you tell me before?' Becky said at last.

He turned back to face her. 'I was saving it. The thought of us being together in this lovely house. It was something I'd dreamt of. Most of the time when I do get to see you, you're tired out from having been on your feet for hours. This was to be our time. Time for each other and time with each other. Do you not feel the same?'

Tears were stinging the back of her eyes. Oh, he could be such a lovely man at times, so gentle, how could she not love him?

'But . . . Gerald, if we stay here won't someone find out?'

Gerald laughed. 'You, my darling, are one of a kind! I promise we will be very discreet.'

She smiled.

'Does that smile mean I can bring our cases in?'

She nodded.

'Right, then I shall give you a grand tour of inspection. After that I shall feed you. See, I have thought of everything, right down to ham, bread, eggs and milk.'

'Gerald, you have been very clever.'

If he thought there was more than one way of taking that statement he had the sense to keep quiet.

Gerald gathered up the suitcases and bags and said, 'Follow me. Bathroom and lavatory facing us, top of the stairs.'

The bath was huge with brass taps and a copper water-heater fixed to the wall. The lavatory was boxed in with a wooden frame and also had a wooden seat. Its long chain had a china handle with a pattern of flowers on it. Further along the passage Gerald put down the things he was carrying and opened another door. The first impression Becky got was of bright sunshine streaming out from the room beyond.

'Go right in, take a look at the view,' he ordered with a grin.

'Unbelievable,' Becky cried, 'I can see the sea.'

'I wasn't lying when I said you could stretch out, rest and look at the sea. In the next room there are french windows which open out on to a balcony and that's where I pictured you.'

'Oh Gerald, everything is so old, these wooden floorboards don't even look safe an' yet everything is so beautiful. Really lovely.'

'Will you stay?' he very quietly asked. 'I do want you to be happy.'

Turning her head away from the window, she answered just as quietly. 'I think we shall both be very happy here.'

In three strides he was beside her. For a moment there was silence as they looked at each other. And then Gerald smiled and said, 'I do love you Rebecca, and I'm never going to let you go.' He opened his arms wide. It was all she needed.

'Oh, Gerald . . .'

Her feet began to slip on the polished wood as she moved. He caught her and swung her up into his arms, twirling her round and round, and their bags and cases lay unheeded out in the passage where Gerald had put them down. He carried her to the big bed, gently laid her down and then stretched himself alongside of her.

There was no one to disturb them. No necessity for them to leave that beautiful room.

Becky's thoughts had run along the lines that when Gerald finally made love to her it would be painful and very embarrassing. Happily, there was no embarrassment. At the first touch of his fingers on her bare flesh she felt Gerald was taking her away from reality. At one point she had cried out the pain was so sharp, like a jagged knife cutting into her. For the main part it was as if Gerald had transported her into a seventh heaven. He was tender, loving, concerned. She would never be able to put into words exactly how she felt.

She must have slept.

'Hello,' he said. He was standing beside the bed, holding a tray of tea, smiling down at her. He was bare-chested and she immediately thought how marvellous he looked. His body was tanned and his shoulders broad.

She struggled to sit up. 'Fancy me falling asleep.'

'They say there is a first time for everything, well let me tell you, young lady, this is the first time that I have brought tea to a lady in bed.' He laughed. 'Must be true that love does funny things to a person.'

Becky raised herself up on her elbows. 'Love?' she queried softly.

He laid the tea tray down on a side table and with one hand he tucked the sheet around her bare shoulders. It was a tender gesture. Then he placed his lips to her forehead. 'I love you very much,' he said huskily.

Becky's eyes lit up with joy. 'Shall I tell you something?'

'What?'

'I love you.'

His expression became serious. 'I hope you do. I'll pour us both out a cup of tea, shall I?'

With Gerald sitting on the side of the bed and Becky propped up by the pillows, they drank their tea in a companionable silence.

'Becky, would you mind if I suggested we didn't go out tonight? I can light a fire downstairs and we could make do with the food we've got here. I don't want to share you with a host of people in a restaurant, not tonight.'

'Oh, Gerald! That's a lovely idea. I don't want to share you either.'

First Gerald showed her the layout of downstairs. The kitchen had a stone-flagged floor, two huge larders and a cooking range the like of which she had never seen before. A door opened out to a neat garden at the end of which lay toolsheds and a wooden hut that was stacked to the rafters with cut logs. 'Hold your arms out,' Gerald insisted, 'we'll each carry an armful of these logs and then the fire will burn all the evening.'

A real log fire and just herself and Gerald. Becky couldn't wait. Surely she couldn't ask for a more romantic setting than that?

Back inside the house Becky marvelled at the splendour of the dining room which to her mind resembled a very posh antique shop.

'We won't bother to eat in here,' Gerald grinned. 'Come and see the sitting room, it's very cosy.'

Cosy was the right word, Becky decided. Warm and

welcoming with soft creamy wallpaper. Two settees covered
in a floral chintz and scattered with huge plump cushions were
drawn up on each side of the fireplace while smaller chairs and
oval side tables were set around the room. The lighting came
from two brass lamps, each with a pleated cream silk shade
with long fringe and tassels.

'Soon have the fire going,' Gerald told her. 'By the
time you've bathed and changed this room will be nice
and warm.'

Later, with the curtains drawn and the fire blazing in
the open hearth, they ate a simple meal and by the time
they both agreed it was time for bed, Becky was positive that it had been one of the nicest evenings she had
ever spent.

Next morning Becky made the bed, hung the clothes they
had worn the previous day in the wardrobe, put the suitcases
out of sight under the bed and went downstairs to find Gerald
was laying the table for breakfast.

Gerald looked totally different. He was wearing brown
corduroy trousers, a cream coloured polo-necked jumper,
and heavy brogue shoes. Casual clothes made him look even
more handsome, she concluded.

'You're an old lazybones,' he complained. 'I've been up
for ages.'

She threw her arms around his neck. 'Have I told you that
I love you?'

'Not today you haven't.'

'Well, I do.'

'And I love you, my darling.'

'Say it again,' she begged.

'I'll say it a hundred times if you want. I love you, Rebecca
Russell.'

'You haven't kissed me today.'

'Well, we can soon remedy that.' He kissed her. Many
times. Long lingering sweet kisses. Finally he broke the

embrace. 'I see I shall have to be more strict with you.' Playfully he slapped her bottom. 'Sit yourself up at the table. I need nourishment to keep up with you.'

Her eyes twinkled. 'Then you'd better eat a hearty breakfast.'

'I fully intend to,' he answered, grinning broadly.

Becky hummed quietly to herself as she washed the breakfast dishes. She had never felt happier. It was as if she and Gerald were already married. The future now looked bright for her. And the good thing about it was that Gerald would be able to provide all the things they would need. There would be no scrimping and hard times such as Ella and Peter had had to endure. Thank you, she prayed silently in her head. I am so lucky to have Gerald.

'Shall I get the car out or shall we walk and explore?' Gerald asked, rising from his chair.

'Let's walk.' Becky smiled in a satisfied way. 'It's such a lovely morning and I'd love to walk by the sea.'

Gerald laughed out loud. 'In that case I shall get the car. Just because you can see the sea from the bedroom window doesn't mean it's nearby. We are high up here, that's the reason for the lovely views.'

Later in the day Gerald parked the car and they scrambled down over a wooden jetty on to the beach. The tide was high and once out in the open the breeze caught Becky's hair and blew it about. 'I wish I had brought a scarf to wear,' she moaned.

Taking a clean white handkerchief from his pocket Gerald tied a knot in each of the four corners. 'Here, try this,' he said, drawing her to him and pulling the handkerchief tightly over her head. Suddenly he roared with laughter and Becky made to snatch the knotted cap from her head.

Gerald grasped her hand. 'No, leave it. Sorry I laughed but you remind me of the picture-postcards which always illustrate men day-trippers to the seaside with big fat bellies, rolled-up trouser legs, braces and a knotted handkerchief on their red balding heads.'

She looked at him in amazement. 'Oh, thanks a lot! You really know how to boost a girl's morale.'

Gerald decided he'd be better off out of Becky's reach. Still laughing fit to burst he sped off along the sand, his heavy shoes leaving deep footprints.

Becky watched. He was a different person tucked away down here in Sussex. More relaxed, easy-going – she was finding it very easy to love this man.

The day was turning out to be one of cloud and sunshine, with the sun popping in and out. She took a big breath and was surprised at the sharpness of the salt breeze. Together they walked, holding hands, until they found a grassy path that led up to a cobbled promenade. They sat on the stone wall and watched the sea come crashing in until the tide was so full that they were getting drenched from the spray.

When they felt hungry Gerald decided that they would return to the car and find themselves a local pub where they could have lunch.

The next two days passed all too quickly. Becky often wondered if she wouldn't wake up to find she was dreaming. They had no contact with the rest of the world. Gerald never even bought a newspaper when he went to the local shops for fruit, milk and bread. Neither of them saw the necessity for regular meals and they had only dined out one evening.

Becky woke on Sunday morning to the sad realization that it was to be their last day. Tomorrow, early in the morning, they would be returning to London. She did her best to close her mind to the prospect, refusing to think about it, and was glad when Gerald suggested they took a flask of coffee and go out for a walk.

Becky sighed softly as she looked around. She had to leave all this stillness behind. It was a lovely morning even though the wind was sharp. Each of them wore heavy sweaters and were sitting side by side high up on the Downs. Somewhere in the distance the grass was being mowed. Becky sniffed. The smell of the fresh-cut grass was wonderful. She leant back on her elbows and watched the wild flowers moving with the breeze, so small and pretty compared with the large floral arrangements that she often had to help display when waiting at functions. She ran her hands through the grass and found a long spiky piece. She pulled at it, tugging it out by the root. She held it up to the light and Gerald laughed. 'What are you going to do with it?' he asked.

'Smell it,' she ordered, pushing it towards his face.

'It's damp and dirty,' he cried, knocking it away and pulling her closer. He put his hand under her chin and lifted her oval face to his, kissed her small nose, marvelled at her big brown eyes and finally placed his lips on hers. Whenever Gerald kissed her, Becky was lost. She would have done anything for him, she decided, as her heart pounded and cheeks grew warm and flushed. Anything at all.

'I love you, Rebecca,' he said, pressing his lips against the top of her head, kissing her thick silky hair. 'I never want you to leave me.'

Suddenly an uneasy thought came to Becky. Gerald's mood had altered. He sounded very serious. She groped for an answer. 'Oh . . . Oh . . . Gerald, is this a proposal then?'

There was a long silence, then Gerald cleared his throat. 'I told you I never want you to leave me . . . but . . .' He hesitated and cleared his throat again, looked down, studied his shoes. When he looked up he fixed his eyes on Becky. 'I don't ever want to leave you but I can never marry you,' he announced, surprising himself and shocking her to the roots of her being. There, it's out at last, he thought. He had finally come out with the truth. Had found the courage to tell her what he should have told her months ago. Guilt surged through him as he sat gazing at Rebecca. Stupefied, totally at a loss for words, she stared back at him, distress and disbelief plainly showing on her face.

'Becky, my darling, believe me, please. We'd get married

tomorrow if it were up to me.' Gerald couldn't stop now, words began to tumble out of him breathlessly and in a great rush. 'My wedding is already arranged, and has been for ages. It is an agreement between our parents. It is not a matter of us loving each other, capital funds and land are the principal reasons.'

Becky's head was buzzing. She had felt the colour drain from her cheeks. She was praying for it not to be true, only hearing him as if from a long way off.

'Becky, say something, anything, just talk to me,' he begged her.

'Oh,' was about the only word she could mutter. She looked ghastly, her face had lost all of its colour, she was shaking and Gerald was truly alarmed as she gazed at him in disbelief.

'Becky, listen to me. I must make you understand.' He took hold of her shoulders and gently turned her face to him. 'As soon as funds are made available to me, real funds I assure you, we will find you a flat. Somewhere nice but discreet. You will be my wife in everything but name. Trust me, Becky. Please.'

There was a dumbfounded look still on Rebecca's face and she appeared to be incapable of moving. Yet in her mind's eye she was torturing herself. Gerald being married. Not to her but to some high society lady. She could actually feel the sense of glamour and excitement there would be at such a wedding.

The reception. Oh, she knew all about those. But only by waiting on the guests. She was good enough for that. In fact if you were to ask her superiors at Lyons they would probably express the opinion that she was excellent. There would be shimmering crystal chandeliers blazing from high up in the ceiling and masses and masses of flowers. Perhaps Nippies to run around with huge silver trays offering champagne from the very finest of glasses. Gerald would be seated at the top table side by side with his bride. Maybe he would request that she be on duty for that occasion. Maybe not. Maybe she should be waiting somewhere, a hotel room perhaps, in case his bride didn't suit his sexual demands. After all he knew now that she suited him just fine. After three days and three nights he could certainly boast that he had had her on approval.

What was it he had said? When 'his funds' were available it was his intention to set her up in a discreet flat, their very own love nest.

A weary sigh came from Gerald and Becky watched as he ran his hands through his hair distractedly. She was conscious of the fact that he was disappointed in her reaction. At this moment his charm and magnetism had deserted him. She still could not fully comprehend what his words had meant. She was however fully aware that she had been used. More than that, he had suggested that if and when he had the money he could go on using her for the rest of her life. Or at least until he tired of her.

Sadly her innermost bitter thought was that she had only herself to blame. She had believed only what she wanted to believe. She had spun her own dream. A dream that the good life and a good marriage could only come if a girl married a man that was well-off.

A peculiar feeling began to flow over her. She wanted to be sick. She was suffocating. She had the urge to get up and run. To run as fast as she could and not stop running until she had put a great distance between herself and Gerald Palmer.

As she struggled to her feet Gerald swung round, guessing what she had in mind. 'Wait, wait, don't be so silly,' he yelled at her.

Becky took no notice. She was up and running downhill as fast as her legs would carry her.

With a rush, Gerald went after her, confident that he could make her see sense if only she would stop and listen to him. With a flying tackle he caught her around the legs and she went down like a nine-pin. The trouble began as he went down on top of her. 'God Almighty,' he called out at the top of his voice, doing his damndest to dig his heels in, find some kind of a foothold. Nothing helped. He couldn't stop either of them from rolling and bouncing downhill. It was minutes before they came to a halt.

Gerald got to his feet and quickly bent to give Becky a hand. One glance and the look on his face was astonishment, which quickly changed to one of shock.

She looked a mess. She was lying on her side, not moving. Blood was trickling down one leg and there was a nasty graze on her forehead. This can't be happening, Gerald was telling himself. A marvellous three days couldn't possibly end like this. He tried to pick her up in his arms and then decided he might do more harm than good if he moved her.

He could see one solitary man not far away, probably the person who had been cutting the grass.

He pulled his sweater off, gently covered Becky's legs with it, straightened up and braced himself, then moving with speed and judgement he raced across the open ground.

Chapter Twenty-four

BECKY WANTED TO open her eyes, but she couldn't. The effort involved was too much. It felt as if her lashes were glued together.

She couldn't remember where she was. She didn't care much. When she tried to move every bone in her body ached and her head was splitting. She felt rather than saw someone lean over the bed in which she was lying and then a cool wet cloth was wiping her brow, her eyes and round her face. A dry cloth followed, doing exactly the same, being very gentle.

'Miss Russell, now you're awake would you like a cool drink?' It was a woman speaking, her voice calm and quiet.

Becky managed to open her eyes a fraction and saw whiteness everywhere; even the person bending over her was dressed in white.

'Don't struggle, Miss Russell. Have a few sips of water, I've got a feeding cup here for you, then if you still want to sit up I'll put the backrest up and fetch you some more pillows.'

'You're a nurse? I'm in hospital, aren't I?' Oh dear God, she swallowed, forcing herself to forget.

'Yes, you are. We've been taking good care of you, and the doctor was pleased that you had rested well during the night.'

Gerald! Tumbling, bumping, rolling over and over unable to stop or get away from him. No wonder she felt so sore. She had her wits about her now, fully aware of why she had been trying to get away from Gerald.

'Have a few more sips and then I'll leave you in peace

for a little while.' The kindly young nurse held the funny cup which had a spout to Rebecca's lips and very gratefully she drank.

'Thank you,' she said, then winced as she tried to move her arm out from under the bedsheet. She found she was wearing a cotton gown that had no fastenings and no sleeves. Her arm was badly grazed from the elbow down to her wrist.

'Can you lean forward a little, my dear?' the nurse asked. Becky tucked her head down and wriggled her bottom down the bed a little. It took a lot of effort. Nurse tugged at the metal backrest, and the jolt it gave sent sparks flying in Becky's head. Four pillows were plumped up, the door opened and another nurse appeared. 'Oh good,' said the first one that was seeing to the bed. 'You're just in time to help me raise Miss Russell up.'

Each nurse placed a hand under Becky's armpits and with no effort at all lifted her gently into position and she was able to rest her shoulders and head back against the mound of clean cool pillows.

'Does your head still hurt?' the second nurse asked with concern.

Becky forced a half-smile. This nurse was older but much prettier with ginger hair peeping out beneath her cap and a sprinkling of freckles across her nose. 'It feels as if there's a man inside banging away with a hammer,' Becky said in a voice that was little more than a whisper.

'I'll get the doctor to prescribe something for you that will help and then you can have a nice sleep, the doctor will be in to see you again later.'

The first nurse stayed in the room, tidying away what appeared to be washing things.

'How long have I been here?' Becky asked.

'Since midday yesterday,' the girl replied. 'Doctor was afraid you might be suffering from concussion. You were unconscious, that was why I was on duty here with you all night.'

Becky did not answer immediately and when she did it was only to murmur, 'Thank you.'

She made a supreme effort to sit up when the older nurse returned and gave her two tablets to swallow. She managed to drink some more water but was thankful when she felt soft hands pressing her back against the pillows and the blinds were drawn.

She wanted to sleep but her mind was taking her back to those sunny Sussex Downs. One minute she had been the happiest girl alive. Gerald had brought her away. To be on their own. To make love to her. To prove that he loved her, that he never wanted to be apart from her. They would be married, of that she had been certain. What other conclusion was there?

Oh, there had been another one! Another entirely different outcome, according to Gerald. He would make her his mistress. See her whenever he could spare the time away from his wife.

How silly she had been! Head in the clouds. Mrs Gerald Palmer – it had never been on the cards. Gerald Palmer came from a different world. She was Rebecca Russell from New Malden, working in a laundry until she had had the good fortune to get a job with Lyons. She had never been inside a London theatre until Gerald took her.

But she had been a virgin until Gerald took her.

Thinking back, Gerald had never seemed to take her seriously. There had always been that teasing look in his eye, sometimes even mocking. But he was so handsome that just looking at him took her breath away and he could be so charming.

Had been so charming!

She now knew that were she daft enough ever to see him again she could never hope to be anything more to him than just a kept woman. God, what was there for her to do now? She didn't feel as if she was any good to man nor beast. She felt guilty. She certainly felt used, in more ways than one.

She hadn't known a thing for the past twenty-four hours and now the tablets were working and she felt herself drifting back into nothingness. She fought it, but the medicine was too strong for her. Finally she yielded to it, and fell into a deep sleep once more.

The room seemed quite dark when Becky was woken by the door to her room being opened.

'Are you awake?' The redheaded nurse smiled warmly. 'Because you've got a visitor. I'll pull the curtains back while you sit yourself up.'

Oh no, Becky thought, horrified. What if it were Gerald? Relief flooded through her as May put her head around the door and the nurse grinned. 'Another redhead. She'll be able to cheer you up. I'll come back later, bring you both a cup of tea.'

'Hello, Becky, how are you?' May Stevens asked, forcing her tone to be bright and cheerful.

May was shocked. She couldn't miss the look of sadness on Rebecca's pale face and that awful bruise to the side of her forehead. She walked unsteadily across the room, where, with shaking hands, she made a great pretence of unbuttoning her coat before moving a chair up to the side of the bed. Leaning over the bed she softly kissed Becky's cheek, sat down on the chair and folded her hands in her lap. She stared down at them. Gerald Palmer had at least had the grace to come to the house and give her the news that Becky was in hospital. A Brighton hospital of all places. Those few minutes with that man would be fresh in her mind for a long while yet.

Thank God Aunt Lil hadn't been at home. The irony of the situation was that Aunt Lil was down at New Malden, spending a few days with Becky's parents. Both she and Becky had good reason to be grateful for that.

May Stevens smothered a sigh. This hospital room was deathly quiet. She wanted to mention Gerald Palmer, to ask Becky for her version of the events that had resulted in her admission to hospital, but before she could, Becky started to speak, as if it were a great relief to unburden herself. In words that almost choked her she gave May the bare bones of the weekend she had spent with Gerald.

A long silence followed and May felt she shouldn't be the one to break it. Much as her heart ached for Becky, and her hatred of Gerald Palmer festered like a sore within her, she stayed quiet.

A deep sigh escaped Becky's lips, and she said in a quiet sorrowful voice, 'I've been such a silly fool. I really did believe that Gerald loved me, that he wanted to marry me.' Becky's lips had begun to tremble and her eyes were wide and staring in her face that was white as chalk.

May took hold of her hand and peered deeply into her friend's eyes, and said in a tight voice, 'You're not the first to be deceived by a good-looking man and you won't be the last. I know full well that is no consolation to you right now but believe me, Becky, the pain will pass and you will see Gerald for the worthless man he really is.'

Becky was crying softly, the tears running unheeded down her cheeks. 'I'm lying when I say I believed Gerald would ask me to marry him. It was what I wanted, not what he wanted.'

May's green eyes were brimming with tears. 'We all make the same mistakes, Becky, luv,' she said calmly. 'Don't take all the blame on yourself.'

'I think I knew . . . all along . . . deep down inside. From the beginning I think I always knew Gerald had no intentions of marrying me,' she sobbed. 'I just kept hoping. Oh, May, the worst part is I do have to blame myself. You saw through Gerald and so did Aunt May and she only really met him the once.'

May took both of her hands in her own, doing her best to soothe her, to comfort her and the two girls gripped each other hard. But suddenly Becky pulled one hand away, rubbed at her eyes and cried out, 'Oh God, why did I do it? Why did I stay? Why didn't I walk away?'

May Stevens shook her head. Much as she loved Becky she had no answer for her. She had asked herself the same question dozens of times. She hadn't gone as far as letting Roger Macclesfield make love to her but she had believed with all her heart that his intention had been that one day he would propose to her. Everyone had liked Roger. Aunt Lil had gone so far as to say, 'He is a good man.' He had suddenly dropped her like a stone. The memory still hurt badly. They had met since, once in the street. Showing determination she had refused to sidestep. 'Why?' had been the only word she had uttered. How she wished she had never asked.

'Because, my dear, I came to realize that one cannot make a silk purse out of a sow's ear.'

That statement had hurt her more than a blow ever could have. She had never told a soul and it wouldn't help Becky to tell her now.

Becky's quiet sobbing slowly lessened, and finally it stopped. The two girls drew their hands free. May delved into her handbag, brought forth a clean handkerchief and wiped her friend's face.

Becky asked quietly, 'Does Aunt Lil know?'

'No, she doesn't, and neither she nor your parents need to be told. It would have been a different matter if you hadn't come round this morning. That is the way you want it to be, isn't it?'

'Oh May, I'm so lucky to have a friend like you. I couldn't bear it if they were to find out.'

For the first time since entering the room, May Stevens grinned broadly. 'I reckon we're damned lucky to 'ave each other. No other sod seems to want us.'

Becky looked startled and then realizing that what May had said was meant to make her laugh, she too attempted to smile. 'Tell me, how did you get here? How did you wangle the time off?'

'Aah! There yer 'ave a very different story,' May said, deliberately slipping back into her cockney form of speech. 'It were like this 'ere. Someone 'ad t' be told cos I ain't got any intentions of going back to the Smoke till I can take you with me. Miss Paige was my first thought. Then I sez t' meself, no, Mr Gower is a safer bet. Nice man is Mr Gower. Remember 'ow good 'ee were t' me when me mum died.'

Becky wiped her face with the handkerchief. For the moment tears were not needed and with little effort, even though the side of her face was very sore, she found she was laughing. 'Oh May,' she breathed.

Brushing a damp strand of hair back from Becky's forehead, May asked, 'Am I tiring you or shall I go on?'

'Please May, go on. You're the best tonic I could wish for.'

'Well, my luvverly. As usual Mr Gower came up trumps. He's a diamond is that man. Not only did he promise to cover for me and you with Miss Paige until such time as we reappeared, 'ee also found me a knight on a white charger.'

At this point, using her hip to push open the door, the youngest of the two nurses that had been attending to Rebecca came in bearing a wooden tray which held two cups and saucers, a pot of tea, a jug of milk, a plate of thinly cut bread and butter, and a dish on which was set out an assortment of small fancy cakes.

'Here we are then, young ladies, I'll put the tray on your locker, Miss Russell, and perhaps your friend will see to you. I'm sure you don't need me to stay.'

'No, we'll be fine thank you, Nurse.' It was May who answered the nurse, all the while thinking to herself that the only decent thing that Gerald Palmer had done was splash out some cash and make sure that Rebecca had been given a private single room. Not that Becky had queried it and she wasn't about to raise the matter. The toerag hadn't done it out of the goodness of his heart. Guilt was probably the only reason.

Becky run her fingers through her hair. It felt matted and greasy. She looked at her fingers and moaned; they were dirty.

'Don't tell me you're worried about your hair,' May exclaimed and began to laugh. 'We're a right pair, we are.'

Very gingerly Becky sipped at her tea, but she managed to eat two half slices of the thin bread and butter, although her lips felt sore and swollen.

'I've just remembered,' Becky said, 'before our tea arrived you were telling me that Mr Gower had found you a knight on a white charger. How come?'

'Bit of an exaggeration, that was,' May said, establishing a humorous tone for the telling of the remainder of the story. 'My knight was a Lyons van driver and 'is charger was one of the company's Leyland Tiger delivery vehicles. Very distinctive. Just as the name on the outside of all Lyons premises are emblazoned in pure gold leaf to make it too expensive for other firms to copy the same goes for all its vans now, don't yer know. You can see them coming for miles.'

'Really May! Don't tell me that this van driver was given permission by Mr Gower to drive you all the way down to Brighton,' Becky exclaimed, sounding doubtful. 'And I don't believe for one minute that Lyons vans have gold leaf advertisements on the sides.'

'Oh, there's nothing wrong with yer brain box, is there then?' May laughed. 'You're soon back on form. You're 'alf right, but only 'alf. This driver, who incidentally turned out t' be an old mate of mine, had a delivery to make in Horsham an' I was supposed to make me own way from there, but being the bloke that he is, he said what nobody don't know about won't 'urt 'em and we came sailing right through all along the sea-breezy front at Brighton an' on up the 'ill to this 'ospital.'

'That was very kind of your friend and very generous of Mr Gower in the first place.' Becky's eyes clouded and her lips trembled again. 'How much does Mr Gower know?'

'Not much, an' you don't need me to tell you that he is the soul of discretion. But there again Becky, he's not daft, he's known that you an' I 'ave been doing the town with some of the flash toffs so we can't blame 'im if 'ee puts two an' two together an' comes up with four. Can we?'

'No,' Becky sighed. 'Still, I will have to thank him.' Then looking at May carefully she asked, 'What about this old friend who's suddenly appeared on the scene? I didn't know you knew any of our van drivers.'

'Nor did I, until today. It was like being struck by lightning when Stan Riley climbed out of that cab. ''Adn't seen 'im for years. At one time Stan lived in the same tenement as me an' me mum. His dad 'ad a scrap yard in Bermondsey, 'is family were well known in the East End, in fact 'is brother was a right villain. I was scared stiff of Mick Riley when I was a kid, so was half the population of the streets where I grew up.'

'And this Stan Riley is a reformed character?'

'Stan didn't need reforming, he always was a good 'un. Like most of the fellas from the East End they call a spade a spade and live their lives accordingly.'

'Is that why I'm being treated to all this cockney language?' Becky said, doing her best to smother a yawn.

'No, in the first place I was trying to make you laugh, but I suppose talking like that came easy, me 'aving been with Stan. Must say it took me back, listening to him. Sort of reminded me of me roots.'

Becky did smile, but only for a moment. In her mind's eye she was picturing the tenement where May had been brought up. All those narrow streets, grimy walls, stone staircases and gaslight. Dear May, she had tried hard to better herself and she had done so well.

Becky couldn't help herself, she yawned again.

May was on her feet in an instant. 'Oh I'm sorry, Becky. I've tired you out, I didn't mean to stay so long. I'll go now and come back in the morning.'

'Please May, don't be sorry. Seeing you was just what I

needed.' She let her shoulders go back to rest against the pillows and smiled weakly. 'Having an East Ender for a friend doesn't mean you have to forget to speak nicely. Remember what Mr Gower always tells us. Think before we speak.'

May tucked the clothes in gently around Becky and pressed her lips to her forehead. 'Go to sleep again, you'll feel heaps better tomorrow and I'll be in to see you early in the morning.'

'Where are you going to spend the night?' Becky asked, her voice already sounding drowsy.

'Go to sleep and stop worrying, the hospital has already fixed me up with a bed and breakfast.'

Becky was two-thirds asleep as May quietly closed the door. Her mind was in a turmoil. She felt she could have battered Gerald Palmer to a pulp with her bare hands. Yet she was also turning over what Becky had said about Mr Gower. Think before we speak. How often he had said that! Damned pity he hadn't added another warning: think before you act.

Chapter Twenty-five

BECKY WAS STILL being plagued by thoughts of Gerald Palmer. It seemed that almost every time she closed her eyes she could see his handsome face. 'Try as I do I just can't put the thought of that weekend behind me,' she complained to May. 'I remember every thing we did together and every loving word he said.'

There has always been something hypnotic about him, May thought miserably, but she was saved from answering by a sharp rap on the front door. 'I'll go, stay where you are,' she ordered Becky. 'I won't be a moment.' Pleasure and relief showed on May's face as she opened the door to find Mr Gower standing on Aunt Lil's doorstep.

Her breath came out in a gasp. 'How kind of you to come, how did you know Rebecca was home? How did you know we would be here?'

'If you will allow me to come inside I will answer all your questions and put your mind at rest because I am the bearer of some very good news.'

'Come in, come in, believe me, Mr Gower, I have never been more pleased to see anyone in my whole life.'

'Look who's here,' May cried as she pushed open the door to the living room. But seeing the look of fear that came to Becky's face she added quickly, 'It's Mr Gower.'

'I hope I'm not intruding,' he said as he smiled and held out a neat bouquet of sweet-smelling freesias.

Becky stood up and took the flowers, pressing her face to the bright colours of the petals to sniff the heavy perfume. 'They are lovely, thank you, Mr Gower.'

'I am pleased to see you looking so much better than I had feared.' Good old Mr Gower, May muttered to herself, he's saying all the right things to Becky. 'I have brought a letter to show you, Rebecca, to show both of you actually,' Mr Gower said, reaching inside his top coat.

May quickly crossed the room. 'Here, let me take your coat and would you like a cup of tea or coffee?'

'Well, I did not intend to stay but how can I refuse the company of two such clever young ladies? I will have a coffee, May, if you're sure it's no trouble.'

'No trouble at all,' May assured him, 'I'll make some for all of us, but first, tell me please, what have we done that makes you refer to us as being clever?'

'Aah.' His smile was broad, his eyes twinkling. 'You run along and see to the coffee and then I will tell you.'

With only the two of them left in the room, Mr Gower pulled a chair up and sat down so that he was facing Becky, thinking all the while what a pleasant and nicely kept living room this was. He said, 'I bet you think I'm a bit of a crafty monkey getting May out of the room like that.'

Becky looked at him anxiously, wondering what was coming next.

'Rebecca, because I have your interest at heart and because I have known you for a very long time, learnt to respect you, and have a great regard for you in a fatherly way, I feel that gives me licence to speak my mind. To offer you advice and help, not only now but at any time in the future if you feel the need, even if it is only to talk. I shall always be there. That, my dear, is a promise.'

Becky began to cry silently. This was such a good man. Often in the past she had likened him to her father and she hadn't been wrong.

In the two days she had remained in the hospital after the arrival of May, she had made a decision. She had bravely decided that she wouldn't give up and go home to her family with her tail between her legs. No. She would put the past behind her and make a fresh start. It wouldn't be easy but she was certainly a lot wiser now than she had been in the past.

From the pocket of her cardigan she took a handkerchief, wiped her eyes, raised her head and ventured a smile.

'That's better, 'Mr Gower said brightly. 'Now the reason I wanted to talk to you on your own is because this is a matter between you and me only. You do trust me. Don't you?'

Becky nodded.

'I know most of what has happened to you and what I don't know I can surmise. I feel partly to blame. I could have given you more advice, but I wonder whether you would have heeded it. We all have to have our own experiences and very expensive some of them turn out to be. Most parts of London have young men living at the expense of older women, and then there are the greedy ones, waiting for their inheritance to materialize, knowing full well they must marry the partner chosen for them by their parents. They see lovely young girls and some of them try it on, knowing that nothing can come of such relationships.'

Becky said nothing. Her gaze had dropped, she was staring at the carpet.

'One last piece of information to divulge and then this matter need never be spoken of again,' Mr Gower quietly told her, leaning forward to give a reassuring pat to her arm. 'I have it from a friend of mine who is a reporter on one of those glossy society magazines that an announcement is to appear in next month's issue about the forthcoming wedding of Miss Amelia Claremont and Gerald Palmer.'

Becky looked at him, frowning. 'Thank you for telling me,' she said with resignation.

'Better you heard it from me,' Mr Gower began, and then stopped abruptly. Becky's cheeks had reddened. 'Are you all right?' he asked, his voice full of concern.

'I misjudged Gerald so much,' she whispered, feeling that she owed Mr Gower some sort of an explanation. 'I assumed he wanted the same things I did.'

Sympathy kept him from commenting; instead he reflected for a moment, before saying slowly, 'The gossip columnists love Amelia Claremont, although I fail to see the reason why. I suppose the main grounds are that the young lady has very wealthy parents.'

Becky couldn't form a reply. She gave a small smile of thanks, raised her eyebrows and clutched tightly at the hand that Mr Gower was holding out to her.

May, who had been biding her time, listening at the door, deliberately dropped two teaspoons.

Mr Gower grinned to himself and hurried to hold the door open, knowing full well that the clatter had been May's way of warning them she was ready to come back into the room.

'Coffee for everyone, and you can be a devil if you like an' have an enormous sugary jam doughnut,' May told them, her bright smile hiding her true feelings.

'I hope you bought the doughnuts from Lyons?' Mr Gower said, his face deadpan serious.

May put the tray down on to the table and turned to stare at him, not sure that she had heard right. Surprisingly, Becky giggled and then Mr Gower burst out laughing.

'You're 'aving me on, the pair of you are 'aving me on!' May cried, doing her best to stifle her own amusement.

'Took you a long time to realize that fact, Miss Stevens,' Mr Gower said as he grinned. 'And by the bye I think you dropped a couple of aitches on the way and that we cannot have, not from one of our top waitresses.'

May paused, coffeepot in hand ready to pour the hot drink into three of Aunt Lil's best cups. 'What's with the top waitress? First you call us clever and now we're bracketed with the best. Are you buttering us up because you want something?'

'Not at all,' he said quietly. 'Quite the reverse. First let me ask you both a question. Soon after you were transferred to the Outside Catering Unit do you remember being asked to take a written examination?'

'Don't I just!' May exclaimed loudly. 'Please, don't tell me we have to go through all that palaver again.'

Mr Gower shook his head, finding it difficult to hide his amusement. 'And you, Rebecca?'

'Only too well, Mr Gower. There were forty-eight questions, and at first sight I thought the papers set out in front of me had to be handed out along the row. Miss Paige soon put me right. Each participant had eleven pages to go through. Some of the girls hadn't finished when Miss Paige called time.'

'Daft questions most of them were,' May shot back at him, 'such as on which side of each guest do you stand when serving food, clearing dirty plates, placing clean plates and serving coffee. I wouldn't have minded but we'd been doing the job for weeks!'

'I know,' Mr Gower commiserated. 'Miss Paige was instrumental in getting the board to accept that fact and it was then decided that if more than seventy-five per cent of the set questions were answered correctly that was achievement enough.'

'Enough to keep our jobs, apparently,' May boldly stated.

'More than that,' Mr Gower replied. He got to his feet, and looking as pleased as punch walked to where May had laid his coat across the back of a chair, put his hand into one of the pockets and withdrew two small, square dark-blue boxes. Handing one box to each girl, he said, 'Congratulations.'

Becky just sat and stared at her brooch, which had four points. She knew what it was but couldn't get the words out of her mouth to express her delight. The four points of each brooch formed a star. The centre held a small raised disc. This gold disc had been engraved with their names and date of passing the examination.

'It's a gold star!' May cried, her voice full of surprise.

Mr Gower was beaming at both of them. 'The brooch is not the only reward, it has another benefit,' he told them, his tone sounding triumphant. 'A cash bonus goes with it.

To be incremented annually and paid to each person when their holiday leave becomes due. You will be permitted to wear your gold stars on your uniform if you should wish to do so.'

'We'd be proud to do so,' Becky told him, really smiling this time.

May was much more demonstrative. To Mr Gower's discomfort, but secretly to his amusement, May flung her arms around his neck. Softly she whispered, 'You're a brick. You know that, don't you? Coming here, doing what you've done, has worked wonders for Becky. Look at her. Look at her face.'

Mr Gower looked. And what he saw pleased him very much. Becky was sitting up straight in her chair, her eyes were bright and her fingers nimble as she pinned her gold star to the front of the cardigan she was wearing.

'I had better pour this coffee,' May declared, 'before it goes stone cold.'

They sipped their coffee and like three schoolkids they each had a doughnut, licking their fingers between mouthfuls and grinning widely as they wiped the last of the jam up from side plates that were also part of Aunt Lil's best tea service.

'You said you had a letter to show us,' May reminded Mr Gower.

He drained the last of his coffee, smiled at May and said, 'Can't remember when I last ate a doughnut, I'd forgotten how good they taste.' Replacing his cup on the table he took an envelope from his jacket pocket and withdrew a single sheet of headed notepaper.

His tone instantly became businesslike. 'You will be interested to know that the stars entitle you to be sent out to larger venues in future. This matter will be gone into at greater length by Miss Paige at the next staff meeting but tonight I thought I would steal the show and leak the information. After all you are my protegées, been under my wing from the beginning. I feel responsible for you and I am very proud of you both.'

The girls looked at each other. It was May that answered, 'For someone that's probably never seen Ireland you're full of blarney.' She raised her eyes, flashing with merriment, to meet his. You know, Mr Gower, I reckon if anyone ever kissed the Blarney Stone it was you. Still, we'll buy it, go on, tell us where some of these new locations are likely to be.'

Laughing at May's candid humour, he said, 'Olympia in Hammersmith for one and the Mansion House, no less, for another.'

'The Lord Mayor's residence? Opposite the Bank of England?' Becky asked.

'That's right,' Mr Gower confirmed.

'Crikey, we'll have to mind our p's and q's,' May laughed. 'The Mansion House is attached to the police court.'

Becky smiled, sat back in her chair and sipped the last of her coffee. Silently she was thanking God that she still had her job to look forward to. With the varied functions she was called upon to participate in and the variety of people she met surely she should have no bother in putting the episode of Gerald Palmer well out of her mind.

Mr Gower cast a glance in May's direction and having got a nod from her he picked up the coffeepot and poured himself another cup. They are both good girls, he thought. The best. So honest and straightforward. Trouble is they expect to be treated as kindly as they treat others. He looked again at Rebecca. She's such a delicate-looking little thing. There's not a devious bone in her body. Thankfully she now has her eyes open with regard to Gerald Palmer. That young man was heading for trouble and then some. Knowing full well that Rebecca had taken up with that layabout he had felt his hands were tied, utterly helpless. He wished he could have prevented her being hurt. He stifled a sigh, saying to himself, I suppose things could have been a whole lot worse.

His thoughts turned to May. She was a different kettle of

fish. A rough diamond some would say, but he had reason to know that she had a heart of gold. Many a youngster that had started work at Lyons with stars in their eyes would have packed up and left months ago if it hadn't been for May Stevens. He knew a lot more about May and the help she gave to new staff than he would ever let on.

They say that opposites did attract and it was certainly true of these two lasses. From what he knew of Rebecca she had led a sheltered life before coming to work in London. Born and bred in Surrey, the only daughter, three brothers and doting hard-working parents, while May had been born in the East End of London. An only child, her father dead, leaving just her and her mother to cope the best way they could. No wonder she had become a girl who had a bit of toughness in her. She'd learned how to take care of herself and had done remarkably well in smoothing out her own rough edges since gaining employment with Lyons.

Best of friends from the outset, these two, and it would take more than a caddish man such as Gerald Palmer to shatter the bond that now existed between them.

Mr Gower cleared his throat and ventured carefully, 'May I suggest you both pay a visit to Rebecca's parents? Wait until say Friday, have the weekend at home and come back to start work on the late shift Monday.'

May looked at Becky swiftly, then lifted her shoulders in a slight shrug. 'I'd really like that, if you don't think your parents would mind,' she said, adding in an undertone, 'your bruises will be gone by then.'

Becky was thoughtful for a few seconds, and then she murmured in a gentle loving tone, 'I would really love to go and see my mother and father but I wouldn't have gone unless you had agreed to come with me.'

'That's settled then,' Mr Gower said as he caught hold of Becky's arm reassuringly. 'You'll look after each other and your parents will be happy to see you. Now, I think that perhaps I should get off home, my wife will be thinking that I've left her.'

There was a pause, as Becky stared into the caring eyes of this kind man who had shown so much understanding, and the smile she gave him was winsome. 'I will never forget your kindness,' she said softly.

He glanced away, unable, suddenly, to find the words to express his feelings. He made for the door, then paused. 'Don't forget we expect our top waitresses to be punctual.'

He was relieved to hear Rebecca laugh as May accompanied him to the front door.

Chapter Twenty-six

'PENNY FOR YOUR thoughts,' Joyce Russell said as she watched her husband climb into bed beside her.

'You were a long time in the scullery tonight, doing the washing up, I'd give more than a penny to know what you and Becky were talking about behind my back,' Joe exclaimed, but there was a hint of teasing in his voice.

Joyce smiled at him. 'You're worried about our Becky, aren't you?'

'Oh, I don't want to be a wet blanket,' he sighed, 'but don't you think she's looking peaky? No one is more thrilled than I am that she's home for the weekend and more than pleased to have May with her an' all. It's just that . . . there's more t' this visit than meets the eye.'

Joyce was momentarily startled by this statement. She frowned. He was only voicing what she had feared all the evening and Lil Maynard was of the same opinion. Lil had said she felt something must have happened during the time she'd been staying down here in New Malden. She was blaming herself for having left the two girls on their own.

'Don't be so daft,' she had chided Lily. 'Neither of them are kids. You can't be expected t' be behind them all the time.'

The girls were amicable, sociable, and very well turned out. The dresses and coats they were wearing hadn't come from any street market. They were two very smart young ladies. So what were they all getting so upset about?

'You're right Joe,' Joyce said, doing her best not to show too much concern. 'I have to agree that Becky is not exactly bubbling over . . . too quiet, like. Normally when she gets home she doesn't stop talking for the first couple of hours. About the job, funny customers, awkward ones, where she an' May have been, who they've met. There's been none of that tonight.'

Joe leant across and placed his arm around his wife's shoulders, 'Do you think she's finding it hard to cope? She's ambitious, that little girl of ours, perhaps she's pushing herself too hard.'

Joyce gave him a playful dig in the ribs, 'Little girl! I suppose she will always be that to you. Nice as it was to have her as Daddy's girl you've got t' remember Joe, Rebecca is almost twenty-one years old, and we were having children by the time we'd reached that age.'

'I know, I know, but I also know that something is not right. I can't for the life of me put me finger on it, she played cards all right this evening yet I had the weird feeling that May wasn't taking her eyes off our Becky. Here! You don't think she's been extravagant, do yer? Got herself into some kind of a fix over money?'

Joyce smiled. 'If I'm sure of one thing I'm sure it's got nothing to do with money. She was telling me what she's going to buy for our little 'uns and for Ella's girls tomorrow. She'll be spending a pretty penny one way an' other, you'll see.'

Joe nodded, remained silent. He'd been longing to get Becky on his own ever since she had walked into the house. 'Ah well,' he muttered, 'at least she's home until Monday. Better get ourselves to sleep, see what the morning brings. Good night my love,' he said, planting a kiss on Joyce's cheek.

'Good night Joe, try not t' worry so much. If there's anything t' tell then it's to you that Becky will be doing the telling, that's for sure. Sleep well, my luv.'

A lot of heads turned as the five women made their way from stall to stall this Saturday morning in Kingston market. They certainly seemed to be enjoying themselves, haggling with the stallholders, laughing a lot. Besides Becky and her mother there was Ella's mum, Peggy James, Aunt Lil and May. Each one carried a rapidly filling shopping bag. Tomorrow, being Sunday, the Russells would be getting a visit from their two married sons. Jack and his wife Ada would be bringing their son Ronnie. Becky had found it hard to believe when her mum reminded her that Ronnie was coming up to seven years of age. Also there would be her brother Tom, his wife Joan, and Joey, who was almost five. The youngest of her three brothers was Fred. Twenty-five and still not married. He'd got a good job though. He'd been made manager of the Co-op Bakery where he had worked ever since he left school.

This Sunday there would also be Ella and Peter and their two daughters. At least Becky was hoping that they would come. She and May were going to Tooting this afternoon to pay a long overdue visit to Ella and Becky had been instructed to give them a special invitation.

'I think that's the lot,' Joyce Russell said with a sigh of relief as she placed a large piece of loin of pork onto the top of the bag that her friend Peggy was carrying.

'You bought Bramleys at the veg stall, were they for the apple sauce?' Peggy asked Joyce.

'Yes, why, don't you think I got enough?'

'Yes, 'course you did, but I'm just going to go back and buy some more. Thought if I make two big apple pies this afternoon that will help towards the pudding seeing as how there is going to be such a gang of us.'

'Great idea, that'll be a big help, thanks Peggy.'

'And I'll pop over and get some dried fruit,' Lily Maynard declared. 'If you'll let me have the run of your kitchen, Joyce, I'll knock up a load of cakes an' make a trifle for tea.'

'That's ever so kind of you, Lil, but you don't have to.'

'I know I don't have to any more than you have to have

me down here for a holiday. Please, let me do something to help.'

'All right then, but before we get on the tram with this load of shopping I suggest we have a cuppa in the market café.'

Becky looked at May and shook her head. Turning to her mother she said, 'Mum, May and I are going over to Bentalls. I told you I want to do a bit of shopping for the kids. If there's time we'll pop back home but if we don't put in an appearance you'll know we've gone straight to Tooting.'

'What about your dinner?' her mother protested.

Both girls laughed. 'Mum, we don't eat dinner midday. If we're hungry we might get a sandwich but with the breakfast you cooked us this morning it won't matter much if we don't eat anything else all day.'

'How about you, May?' Joyce asked. 'Don't think you've got to starve just because my daughter says you should.'

'Oh, Mrs Russell! Starve is the last thing that will happen to me while I'm staying with you. Just look at what you've bought for tomorrow.'

'You wait,' Joyce Russell laughed loudly, 'when my tribe get their feet under the table it does me a power of good to see them all eat heartily and tomorrow will be extra special because our Becky's home, you and your aunt are here and if Ella and Peter come and bring their girls that will make Peggy's day.'

Very soon after thrusting their way through the crowds of shoppers in the market, Becky and May were pushing through the big doors of Kingston's largest department store, and taking the stairs up to the children's department.

Rebecca was smiling to herself as she thought of Ella's two little girls. Shame really that she didn't see very much of them, or of Ella come to that. At least today she wouldn't visit them empty-handed; she had enough money to buy them some really pretty things. She still worried about Ella and Peter, despite the fact that her dad said they weren't doing too badly. Just about managing was how he put it, well, that could mean anything.

'Spoilt for choice here,' May exclaimed as she held up a pretty white dress trimmed with yellow ribbons. 'I think this would be lovely for the youngest one.'

Becky raised her eyebrows. 'I think it's very sweet but it's a party dress and I don't see Ella trotting her kids off to parties very often.'

Overhearing Becky's remark a saleslady came to her side. 'This area is solely for party dresses, mostly organdie and such like. Shall I show the everyday selection? We have a great choice for both girls and boys.'

'Yes please,' Becky said, grinning widely at May.

A moment later the young lady was taking skirts, blouses, small jumpers adorned with teddy bears and pretty calico dresses from the stands and fanning them out along the counter.

'How old is the child?' she enquired.

'I'm buying for two, both girls, one will be two in June and the other one is just a baby,' Becky explained.

'You make your choice, browse a bit, and then I will see that you have the right sizes.'

Half an hour later the girls were making their way to the toy department each carrying a large shopping bag. Becky had bought one skirt and two tops for each child. May had bought three tiny pairs of white ankle socks for each of Ella's girls because as she said they were so pretty she couldn't resist them and they didn't cost a fortune.

'Now, what do I get for my nephews? Clothes wouldn't interest them.'

'Your mum told me that one boy is seven and the other boy will soon be five, perhaps they would like books.'

They settled for a school satchel for Joey as he would soon be starting school and Becky felt it might make him feel right grown-up. May wasn't to be left out and she insisted on buying him a fire-engine that gave out sparks as you pushed it along.

For Ronnie, Becky purchased a leather football and May bought him a kite that had endless streamers for a tail.

Becky glanced up at the store clock; it was almost half past twelve. 'If we go back home we'll never get to Tooting,' she moaned to May. 'You know what my mum is, she'll want to see everything we've bought and she'll want us to have something to eat.'

May giggled. 'So what's the problem? We don't have to go back, you did say we might not.'

'Right then, we won't,' Becky shot back, grinning. 'Come on, don't dawdle, there's a coffee shop downstairs and we'll grab a snack there.'

As they made their way down the staircase, both girls were aware of the glances cast in their direction. At nearly twenty-one they were both attractive, full of health and vitality. Today May was wearing a dark green cloche hat from beneath which her reddish hair curled over her ears. The fur collar that Becky's mother had made was draped around the shoulders of her long coat. Mostly it was her red hair and green eyes that set her apart. Becky was shorter but just as smart. Her choice of hat was a wide-brimmed felt, sporting a colourful feather in the band. Around the collar of her dark grey coat she had draped a bright red scarf which set off her big brown eyes to a tee.

Arriving at the café, they managed to find an empty table and they both gratefully sat down. Suddenly May said, 'You should wear red more often, Becky. It does something for you, makes your skin glow.'

'Why thank you, May,' she answered, giving her a funny look. 'Can't think why you've suddenly noticed, I often do wear red.'

'Yeah, I know. Perhaps it's because today you seem . . .' She hesitated, not sure if she should speak her mind.

'Go on,' Becky urged, 'today I seem what?'

'Better. Yes, that's it. Today you seem to have pulled your shoulders back, put the past couple of weeks behind you and you're once more showing a smiling face to the world.'

Now it was Becky's turn to dither. Much as she loved May, counted herself fortunate to have her as a friend, she couldn't entirely open her heart to her. It had taken a great deal of effort on her part to be more like her old self today. Last evening she had been a wet blanket. She knew she had and she knew her behaviour had upset her mother and father. Envy was a funny word to use, but the truth was that was how she had felt. Envious.

Her parents had such a loving relationship; even after nearly thirty years they still adored each other. Her brothers had their wives and sons. Ella had Peter and two lovely little girls. Maybe none of them had a great deal of material things but they had each other. No one wanted her. Certainly not Gerald. Except of course as a bit on the side.

An awful expression that. It had kept her awake at night, only because no matter how Gerald had tried to wrap it up she knew it to be the truth. Then, waking up this morning to find her mum standing beside the bed holding out a cup of tea, she knew she was loved. Count your blessings, my girl, she had berated herself. There and then she had decided Gerald Palmer could ruin his own life by marrying someone he didn't love but from now on she wasn't going to let him ruin hers. He wasn't going to be any part of her life. Not even a small part.

She looked across at May, gave her a small smile. 'I'm glad you think I look better. I feel better because I have made a decision. I am not even going to think about Gerald Palmer ever again. At least I am going to try hard not to.'

May grinned at her, her expression one of genuine delight. 'Good on yer Becky, the bugger's not worth it.'

'May!'

May flashed her a lopsided grin. 'Sorry, but swear words are all I can think of to describe that stinker.'

Becky couldn't find words to answer that, so hiding her amusement she beckoned to the waitress who had been hovering a few feet away. 'Please may we have two coffees and two toasted teacakes, if that's all right with you, May?'

'Yes thank you.' May nodded at the waitress, then laughing at Becky she said, 'You an' me both need to mix with a few more normal people, we've been brushing too close to the gentility and they ain't what they're cracked up to be.'

Becky remembered Roger Macclesfield and how upset May had been when he left her high and dry. 'Seems like we've shared a common fate,' she said quietly to May, stretching out her hands and taking both of May's hands between her own. Suddenly they found themselves wrapped in the extraordinary warmth that only true friendship can bring.

Then Becky fell to wondering. Had May, like herself, gone through an agonizing period of sleepless nights, terrified that she might be pregnant? She wasn't even sure that May had slept with Roger.

She only knew that she, herself, had been so besotted with Gerald Palmer that she had been scatty enough to let herself believe her whole future would be entwined with his. How wrong she had been.

The relief of finding out that her ordeal was well and truly over was something she would never forget. When her period had started she had gone down on her knees, there and then in the bathroom, and thanked God. And at that moment she had vowed never again to be so trusting where men were concerned. One thing she was certain of, the experience had left her a whole lot wiser.

They stepped down from the tram at Tooting Broadway and had barely reached the pavement when Becky heard her name being called and turning quickly she saw Mary Marsden waving frantically from the island in the middle of the road. 'Becky, wait, wait a minute!' she yelled above the noise of the traffic.

'Who is that? May asked.

'Mary Marsden. I've told you about her. I went to her and Tom's wedding which reminds me, it's not Mary Marsden, it's Mary Ferguson now.'

Mary reached the pavement safely and threw her arms around Becky's neck. 'Cor, I'm ever so pleased t' see you, Becky. Look at you! Ain't you the lady. No wonder we don't get t' see yer these days, too busy working up in London I suppose.'

'Mary, I'm sorry. I don't get home nearly enough but with the summer coming I promise I'm going to try harder. We're off to see Ella now, why don't you come with us?'

Mary stepped back and took a good look at May and seeing the expression on her face Becky hastened to say, 'Oh I'm sorry Mary, this is my friend May. We met when I first went for an interview with Lyons and we've worked together ever since.'

''Allo May,' Mary beamed at her. 'Becky's always been my friend since I came home from service. I miss her these days.'

May gently touched Mary's arm. 'I'm going to see to it that both she and I visit more often so perhaps you'll be my friend also.'

'Yeah, I will,' Mary said as she smiled enthusiastically.

'Come on then, let's get going to see Ella,' Becky said, tucking her hand into the crook of Mary's arm.

'I can't come with you,' Mary said, and looked crestfallen. 'Me mum an' dad ain't been too well and they've 'ad t' give up their 'ouse an' move into a flat. They live 'ere now, in Tooting, Defoe Road, I'm on me way t' see them now.'

'Oh that is a shame.' Both Becky and May expressed their sympathy.

'Do you still live with Tom's mother?' Becky enquired.

'Yes, but Tommy's 'ad the whole 'ouse altered. Lovely it is. Two separate flats. When Tom's 'ome you must come round t' tea, Becky. You've never been.'

'Never been asked,' Becky said, grinning.

'Well, you're being asked now and you May, you're being asked an' all.'

'Right,' they both agreed. 'Next visit and that's a promise.'

'Bye then Becky, tell Ella I'll see 'er on Thursday.' She planted a kiss on Becky's cheek and then did the same to May. 'Don't work too 'ard, the pair of you.' And waving her hand she trotted off in the opposite direction, looking a bit frumpish in her tweed coat and woolly hat.

'She's got her feet well and truly on the ground,' May commented as they watched her go.

'She certainly has. Doesn't ask for much out of life. Proper down-to-earth is Mary. She and Tom were made for each other.'

'This is it,' Becky declared, staring up at the large plate glass window that bore a notice which stated, 'Heels repaired while you wait'. To the side a young man stood behind a workbench, wearing a leather apron, working away like fury. He made a fascinating sight and Becky and May were not the only two to stop and stare in amazement.

A shoemaker's last was secured to the bench and a boot placed over the foot of the last was being repaired. The young man's mouth was full of tiny rivets and with unvarying speed he spat out one rivet at a time, clasping it between his forefinger and thumb of his left hand. Using his right hand and a small hammer he rhythmically tapped each nail into the new leather sole making a good and speedy job of repairing the boot.

'Wonder he don't swallow one an' choke himself,' a woman remarked, causing a ripple of amusement to run through the watchers.

The shop door opened and Becky looked up to see Peter standing there. At first glance she thought how well he looked; certainly he had put on weight. He too was wearing a leather apron and as he came across the pavement, hand outstretched, she could see his fingers were stained much the same colour as her brothers' always were, caused by them working in the tanning factory.

'Becky, come on in. My God, it's good to see you.'

'It's good to see you too,' Becky told him. 'And this is May, May Stevens, I'm sure you've heard all about her.'

'Yes, I have,' Peter hastened to say. 'Ella tells me your letters are full of what you and May get up to. Come along inside, go upstairs, Ella will be thrilled to see both of you.'

They followed Peter through the shop that smelt strongly of good leather and boot polish out to the back staircase.

'Ella, Becky and her friend are here, take the gate away from the top of the stairs,' Peter called loudly and Ella responded, 'I'm coming, won't be a moment.'

On the top landing Becky fell into Ella's outstretched arms and May stood back silently as the two lifelong friends hugged each other tightly. Within minutes of meeting Ella, May decided she was a charming pleasant young woman. Furthermore she felt at ease with her immediately, not in the least as if she were intruding.

'Told you, didn't I,' Becky whispered to May, 'everyone likes Ella.' All the while she was studying her friend. Ella looked great. She hadn't known they were coming but even so she was neatly dressed in quite the latest fashion. Long hobble black skirt, a cream cotton blouse which had leg-o'-mutton sleeves and a row of pearl buttons leading three inches up from her wrist. A plain black velvet shawl was draped across her shoulders. Her long fair hair, she still hadn't had it cut, was coiled into a tight bun at the nape of her neck.

Sensing that Becky was eyeing her, Ella did a twirl. 'All my own work, takes you back to our rummaging at jumble sales and hours of needlework afterwards. Do you remember?'

'Oh Ella, how could I ever forget? You look fantastic, really you do, but where are the girls? I can't wait to see them.'

'Aah, we've so much room up here that Peter decided they could have a playroom. Gives Peter and me a bit of privacy now an' then,' she said softly, her cheeks flushing slightly.

Both Becky and May smiled.

'Yeah well, come and meet them, they'll probably knock you over before you get inside the door.'

What lovely little girls, was May's first thought, and Becky certainly wouldn't have contradicted her. Margaret was a young replica of Eleanor, with long fair hair, creamy skin and big blue eyes. Amy, the baby, obviously took after Peter. She had the same colour hair and eyes that danced with mischief and chubby cheeks that dimpled as she smiled.

'Amy's already proving to be a tomboy,' Ella laughed, 'she's long and lean and it won't surprise me if she grows taller than Margaret.'

Margaret was across the room in an instant. 'Auntie Becky,' she cried, 'are you going to stay to tea? You've got to, cos we haven't seen you for a long time.'

'Of course I am,' Becky told her, sweeping her up into her arms and holding her close.

'Can I sit next to you?' Margaret asked, her head on one side, looking appealing.

'Of course you may, if Mummy says so, and perhaps Amy might like to sit on my other side.'

Amy wasn't going to be outdone. She wrapped her arms around May's legs and demanded that she too be picked up.

In no time at all a cloth had been spread over the big round table that stood in the centre of the living room and Ella had soon prepared lots of nice things. 'Fruit and jelly,' Margaret cried as May set the two bowls down on the table. 'They're me favourite.'

'Haven't you got a nice mummy?' May smiled. 'She told me she made the jelly after you had gone to bed last night.'

'Yes, but she's Amy's mum too,' Margaret wisely said.

Becky looked at May and they both giggled. These kids were comical.

Margaret put her head on one side and pulled a funny face. 'Auntie Becky,' Margaret whispered, tugging at Becky's skirt, 'we haven't got enough chairs for us all to sit up at the table.'

'Oh ssh, pet,' Ella said, and she sounded embarrassed. 'Margaret, you can sit on my lap and Amy can go in her highchair.'

Amy loudly protested when they tried to put her in her chair and clung to her Auntie Becky.

Ella took a deep breath before murmuring, 'I'm so sorry but if you'll give me a minute . . . I think I can sort something out . . .'

'Can we do anything, luv?' Becky asked.

Ella didn't reply; she was tugging a long plank of wood across the floor. When she had it alongside the table she made a gesture for Becky to follow her. Once inside the little girls' bedroom, Ella said, 'If you clear off that bedside table I'll do the other one and then we can use them for the plank to rest on and so make a form to sit on.'

'Great idea,' Becky replied, lifting a small nightlight and several books and placing them on to the floor. Once she had lifted the cloth it became apparent that the bedside table was a tall wooden orange box upended and covered to serve a very good purpose.

'You're a genius,' Becky laughed.

'Don't know about that, it's more a case of needs must when the devil drives. We haven't any money to spare for more furniture yet. Don't get me wrong, Becky, I'm not complaining, Peter is doing his best, but for the moment any spare cash has to be ploughed back into buying more stock. He can't repair boots if he hasn't got the leather.'

'Oh, Ella, luv, nothing worth having comes easy, we both know that and I think you and Peter have done wonders. The girls are an out and out credit to you both.'

'Thanks, Becky. I hope I haven't offended your friend, May.'

'Don't give it another thought. There's nothing standoffish about May, give yourselves time and I bet you'll have this place well and truly furnished.'

Ella laughed. 'Well I'm glad you know how things are. You must have thought I was putting on airs when I said the girls had a playroom to themselves.' She laughed again, even louder. 'It's only until we can afford to furnish that room and then it will become the parlour, now what d' yer think of that?'

'I think, Mrs Tomson, that you are in danger of getting ideas above your station in life and that it would be a good idea if we took these two boxes back to the living room, set them up and you gave us this wonderful tea the girls have been going on about.'

There was a great deal of laughter as the makeshift form was set in place and everyone was finally settled around the table. When Ella was cutting the Victoria sponge she'd made that morning, Margaret asked if she might say something to her Auntie Becky.

'I'll have to let her, Becky,' said Ella, grinning. 'She'll say it, anyway.'

'Well I just want to tell Auntie that me an' Amy are ever so glad she brought her friend May with her cos we think she's ever so nice.'

'Why, thank you, Margaret, and I have to tell you I'm really glad your auntie did bring me here today because I think you are two very nice little girls.'

Amy giggled.

'You're a pair of little imps,' Ella told her daughters, while doing her best not to smile. 'And you, Margaret, have a smear of jam on the end of your nose.'

Margaret shrieked. Everyone one else roared with laughter. Undeterred by the lack of comfortable chairs to sit on this was proving to be a very happy teatime.

One hour became two and still the three girls sat at the table, talking non-stop. The children had taken themselves off to the playroom.

'Well,' Becky breathed out, 'between us I think May and myself have filled you in on every last detail of how Lyons manage their company. Do you fancy becoming a Nippy, Ella?'

'I've got a job,' Ella said, sounding really proud.

'Oh, good on you,' Becky cried, 'no wonder you look so perky, must be doing you the world of good. Why didn't you tell us before instead of letting us rabbit on about our work?'

'Because you'll probably say it's ridiculous. I don't get paid. Mary Ferguson helps there as well.'

'We won't say any such thing,' Becky hastened to assure her. 'Is it some charity that you work for?'

'You must enjoy doing whatever it is,' May butted in, 'and after all that's what counts the most. Tell us, where is it you work?'

Ella put her cup and saucer to one side and walked over to the big bay window that looked out over the busy Mitcham Road. 'Over there,' she said, pointing her finger. 'Don't have far to travel, do I?' Both girls rushed to stand by her side.

'But that's the Central Hall!' Becky exclaimed, looking at the great building with its mighty flight of stone steps leading up to the entrance and immediately thinking to herself, she hasn't gone all religious, has she? We all need God in our lives but to work for nothing was something that Ella could not afford to do.

May's thoughts were running along the same lines. Being practical she turned to Ella and said, 'Look luv, why don't you tell us all about this job?'

'I will,' Ella quietly said, 'if you don't think I will be boring you. It's a bit of a long story.'

'Well, let's sit down again,' Becky said as she squeezed Ella's hand and added, 'best if you start at the beginning.'

'I got this idea,' Ella began, 'because people round here

are so nice but they're poor. So many men are unemployed and most of the women have an awful job to make ends meet and as for clothing their kiddies, it would break your heart to see some of the poor little mites, especially when it's bitter cold. I thought, why not swap things? Children grow out of their clothes and nobody wants to buy them.' Ella paused and looked Becky straight in the eye, hoping for her approval. She got it.

'I think that was a great idea.'

'So do I,' May added, 'I'm dying to know how it worked.'

'Right from the word go it worked all right,' Ella went on as she smiled at them both. 'It was getting it off the ground that was the hard part. I didn't have any money to rent premises, couldn't even afford a stall in the market.' She paused again and laughed out loud. 'I tried to persuade Peter to let me use a room up here. He went mad. Said business was bad enough without a load of women and tribes of kids traipsing through the place all day long. So I found out who the vicar was at the Central Hall, paid him a visit and both he and his wife were enthusiastic about the idea.

'Big man is Alan Burdett, I was a bit scared of him at first, thought he looked more like a rugby player than a vicar, but he came up trumps. He lets us have the use of the church hall every other Thursday, twelve till four. Mrs Burdett even did some hand-bills for us and saw to it that they were given out to young mothers outside the schools. And to the older women at mothers' meetings, we've had a good response from them.'

'Ella, you say *we* have had good results. Are other women involved besides yourself?' Becky asked sensibly.

'Yeah, I was wondering that,' May chipped in.

'You'd be surprised. I got Mary interested from the start, but as time has gone on we sometimes have more helpers than we need.'

'That's marvellous, Ella, really great, you clever old thing,' Becky told her quickly.

'Tell us more about what you swapped, what kind of people came?' May's interest was genuine.

'The first week was a washout. Nobody came. Mrs Burdett, Mary and myself sat there like dummies. Margaret was disappointed because I had told her she would be able to play with all the kiddies I expected the mothers to bring. Amy slept in her pram the whole afternoon because she was only a baby then, but we've been going nearly a year now.'

'And you've never let on,' Becky cried.

'Sorry, you know I've never been a letter writer and when you did come home there never seemed time to talk about it.'

'Don't go off the subject,' May pleaded, 'I'm all ears.'

'The second Thursday was a day I will never forget,' Ella began, smiling to herself. 'By two o'clock there was such a commotion going on that Alan Burdett came flying up the stairs to see if I was all right. Women had turned out their cupboards and drawers, washed long-forgotten baby clothes, jumpers, school uniforms that were now too small for their sons or daughters, jackets with patches on the elbows, coats that had been given a new set of buttons, you name it, they brought it.

'Now we are far better organized. We have the hall for one hour on a Monday morning, staffed by volunteers. Goods are accepted in advance and a receipt given. Then we sort the goods and different ladies do various tasks. I'm in charge of the baby clothes. I thread new ribbons at the neck and cuffs of matinée coats, iron small dresses and romper suits and generally do any sewing repairs to the garments that may be needed. I look forward to these sessions now. Everyone has a good laugh.'

Ella paused for breath again. 'I don't know about you two but I've talked myself dry. I'll make a fresh pot of tea and then I must see about getting the dinner ready for Peter. Saturday is a long day for him – he started work downstairs before six this morning.'

'I'll make the tea,' Becky volunteered, 'then May an' I will have to be making a move or Mum will be going spare because we're not back in time for dinner.'

'Oh, I thought you would be staying for the evening.' Ella was unable to keep the disappointment out of her voice.

'No, sorry, luv.' But Becky grinned at her and quickly added, 'But we'll be seeing all of you again tomorrow. The whole family, your mum an' all, will be at our house for the day and my mum said if you and Peter don't come and bring the girls she'll be over here first thing Monday morning to know the reason why.'

'That's marvellous.' Ella sounded both delighted and excited as she grabbed hold of Becky and drew her close. 'Gosh Sunday dinner, all together round the one table! It's been so long I shan't sleep tonight, I know I won't. I can't wait. We'll be there. Bright and early. Oh, thank yer mum for me.'

'You can thank her yourself tomorrow, you daft girl.'

At that moment May came into the room with a newly laid tray. 'Actions speak louder than words,' she said grinning to Becky, 'I've made the tea while you two were still nattering nineteen to the dozen. We'll have a quick cup before we set off.'

Ella came downstairs to see them off, carrying Amy in her arms. Margaret, her legs wrapped around Becky's waist and her arms around her neck, was quite content to be made a last-minute fuss of.

The little group stood back, waiting to say goodbye to Peter. A woman with frizzy hair and a very loud voice was complaining to him that she wanted a different-shaped rubber heel put on her shoes. Peter glanced their way. Becky mouthed, 'See you tomorrow.' He raised his eyebrows in question. 'At my mum's for dinner,' she mouthed again. His eyes lit up and he nodded his head.

The tram they wanted was waiting. The driver was leaning against the side of the tram chatting to his conductor and smoking a cigarette. Becky and May climbed aboard, settled themselves on the slatted wooden seat and burst out laughing.

May was the first to recover. 'Talk about how the other half live!'

'No comparison, is there?' Becky asked.

'Not when you compare it with the wealth we see every day. The jewellery some of the women we wait on wear, when you think about it, the cost of one necklace would probably keep an ordinary family for a lifetime.'

'You enjoyed coming here to see Ella though, didn't you, May?'

'You bet yer life I did. I think she's smashing. No wonder you and her have been friends all these years. I mean it, she's great.'

'I'm thrilled to know she's working, even if it's only voluntary work. Really showed a bit of initiative, I'd say. When she was first married it was awful. She went downhill quicker than a sleigh on a slippery slope. She was nothing more than a skivvy. Peter had no money and no prospects. I'd take a bet that life isn't all roses even now for either of them but at least they seem happy and are getting by.'

'Yeah, and their little girls are a credit to them.'

'They are certainly that,' Becky agreed, wriggling her bottom to a more comfortable position as the tram rumbled on its way.

Sunday had been everything that anyone could wish for.

A nice dry day with just enough wind to allow more than half the family to take the children over into the field opposite the house. Watching from an upstairs window Joyce found it hard to decide who was enjoying themselves the most, her sons or her grandsons. The football that the girls had bought for Ronnie was certainly taking a bashing, while young Joey, with the help of his father, had taken charge of the kite, running his little legs off as the colourful toy flew high in the sky.

Now it was ten o'clock at night. The house seemed very quiet, even still, with all the young families having departed for their own homes. May came back down the stairs to where only Rebecca and her mother remained.

'You're ready for bed,' Becky remarked. May had washed and brushed her hair till it shone like burnished copper and she was wearing a pretty cotton housecoat.

Immediately she said, 'I couldn't go to sleep without telling you both how much my aunt and I have appreciated what you've done today.'

'I'm glad you both enjoyed yourselves,' Joyce answered.

'Mrs Russell . . .' May began, her tone very emotional. 'Enjoyed is not perhaps the right word, it's more than that. Our feelings are hard to describe. Aunt Lil has been regretting that she was never blessed with children and watching your close family has made me realize how much I missed when growing up as an only child. We want to thank you and Mr Russell for allowing us to be included.'

'Oh, May, come here an' give me a kiss,' Joyce replied as she got to her feet and held her arms open wide. May went into them and her own arms automatically went round this kindly mother.

'It works both ways, you know, May,' Joyce said gently. 'Your aunt has been a godsend to me, giving our Becky a home and watching over her like she does. Without Lily I would have spent many a sleepless night wondering how my daughter was faring in London. Anyway, time you were in bed, it's back to the grindstone for you both tomorrow. There's one more thing to be said though, May: I want you to regard this as your home, just as much as Becky does. You are welcome here whenever you feel like making the journey. You don't have to wait to be asked. Remember that, won't you?'

'Well, likely I shall take you up on that.' May's face was a picture to behold, she was smiling broadly but her eyes were glistening with tears and as a single tear escaped and rolled down her cheek, Becky gave her a playful push saying, 'Come on dafty, no waterworks, go on up and I'll follow you in just a minute.'

'Mum, you are the absolute tops,' Becky said, her voice no more than a small whisper.

For a moment her mother said nothing, but sat watching her as she drew off her stockings, then she said with resignation, 'Becky, I used to tell myself that I could read you like a book. But not anymore. You've brightened up a lot today, so seeing Eleanor yesterday and again today seems to have worked wonders for you but I am quite sure all hasn't been well with you lately. You could tell me, whatever it is. You know that?'

Becky rolled her stockings into a ball, then she crossed the room to the couch where her mother still sat and, bending low, said, 'Mum, there is nothing for you to worry about. I promise you. I love you and Dad more than I know how to tell you and if I were really in trouble I would come running to you like a shot.'

'If you're sure.' Joyce's voice was low.

Becky forced a smile. 'I'm very sure.' And with that her head came down and snuggled into her mother's breasts.

Joyce drew in a long tight breath. She still wasn't convinced. She closed her eyes tightly as she hugged this only daughter of hers and prayed hard that the Good Lord would watch over her.

Chapter Twenty-seven

IT WAS TWO-THIRDS of the way through 1928 when Becky received a letter from Peter Tomson. She read it through twice before deciding that she wouldn't hurt his pride. The matter had never been mentioned between them and she was pleased that her contribution had helped to open up new horizons. She would accept his offer of repayment and be grateful that things had turned out as well as they had. It was after all a very nice letter.

Dear Becky,

I have only recently found out from your father that you were the main contributor to the fund that set me up in business. I am finding it hard to express my feelings. Just to say thank you seems so inadequate.

I am in a position now to repay your kindness and I have put forward the suggestion that I pay the sum of ten pound each month for the next six months. The ten pound extra being in the way of interest.

Your father has accepted my proposal but not completely. He insists that you will only accept repayment of the original loan.

I have known for a long time that you are a good friend to Eleanor but was not aware of the depth of your kindness towards me.

Recently I allowed an older man to use one of the sheds we have in the back yard in order to repair bicycles. He had walked for miles day in day out searching for employment without success. Not only has he worked

up a nice little business he now has a contract with the
Post Office to repair the red bikes used by their telegram
boys. Now he pays me a weekly rent. So you see, my
dear Rebecca, your generosity to me has enabled me to
help another. I am truly grateful to you.

Eleanor and the girls send you their love as I do, come
home and see us soon, Peter.

Folding the letter and replacing it in the envelope, Becky
sighed. Another autumn would soon be upon them and
still the employment situation was no better. Educated men
were begging in the streets. So many young men had died
in the War and many of those who had survived were too
sick to work. The fit and able got no sympathy from the
Government; it was the same everywhere. So many men
chasing so few jobs.

Why? Becky asked herself yet again, as did so many other
young women who were fighting to get equal rights for
themselves. Why were there no jobs to be had? Had the
owners of the manufacturing businesses made their pile
during the War? All this poverty was causing a great deal
of social unrest.

While standing at the bus stop Becky was still mulling over
what Peter had said in his letter. 'There's such a gulf between
the working classes and the middle class,' she muttered, more
to herself than to May.

'What are you going on about?' The bus had come into
view and May grabbed Becky's arm. 'You want to be grateful
that we've got a job to go to, you can't take the worries of
the world on your shoulders. You should have learnt that
by now.'

Seated beside May on the lower deck of the bus, Becky
was quietly nodding to herself. She knew that what May was
saying made sense. But then these days May was a whole lot
more sensible. She and Stan Riley had been seeing quite a bit
of each other since he had driven her down to Brighton, over

a year ago now. Although very pleased that May had met up with a young man with whom she had grown up there were times now when Becky felt quite lonely.

During the summer months, with the long light evenings, the two of them had walked on Hampstead Heath, taken boat rides on the Serpentine in Hyde Park and generally enjoyed each other's company. Becky had been invited to go along, several times, but she felt she would have been the odd one out.

Aunt Lil thoroughly approved of this young man whose family she had been well acquainted with in her younger days. And why not? He was presentable, of average height, had a good head of brown hair, a nice clean healthy complexion and more to the point he had a good job driving a delivery van for Lyons. What Aunt Lil liked most about him was that Stan Riley didn't talk fancy, his head wasn't full of big ideas.

'I'll tell you this much,' Aunt Lil had called out when watching May get herself ready to go out one evening. 'There's some that would tell you that the Rileys were a family of villains and that the flat they lived in was little more than a mucky-dump. Seventy per cent true, I'd say. Though even in a barrel of rotten apples you can nearly always find one good one and I'd say that you, May, have been lucky enough to come across a good one in Stan.

'D'you know he disappeared from the tenements soon after his father died, cleared off and got himself lodgings? Soon after that the police were around that family so often you'd 'ave thought they were taking up residence. Dolly Riley, Stan's mother, ups sticks an' goes t' live with her sister in Clacton. Can't say as 'ow I blamed her. But it says a lot for Stan the way he's got on with his life.'

'You with us?' May asked grimly, shaking Becky out of her daydreaming. 'You know, before long we'll have the big firms giving their annual dinners, most firms like to get them well out of the way before Christmas.' Without waiting for an answer, May got to her feet and signalled to the conductor that they wanted to get off the bus at the next stop.

Once inside the building the girls quickly changed into their uniform and Becky, ready first, was reading the notices that were pinned up on the notice board.

'Here, come and look at this, May. Funny, it's just what you were remarking on as we got off the bus.'

'Well I never,' May exclaimed as she ran her eye down the printed page.

'Move over or else read it out loud,' said someone. Two or three more waitresses had gathered to see and hear what was going on.

May cleared her throat and began to read from the top of the page. 'The 1928 annual dinner for the construction company Bovis will be held the first week in November. Date and place as yet undecided. In keeping with the spirit of the occasion, the menus will be printed on wood veneer and laid out in the form of a building specification.'

'Good morning, ladies.' All heads turned as the clipped tones of Robert Matthews made them jump. Not one girl had heard him approaching. 'Winter cometh,' he continued, smiling, 'and indoor festivities begin.'

'Company's going to town on that one,' Joyce Johnson, one of the Nippies who had been with Becky and May right from the start, ventured, nodding her head towards the notice board.

'That's right,' Mr Matthews agreed. 'It isn't just the small details that make Lyons such a popular firm and it makes no difference whether we are catering for king or commoner, Lyons will always go to great lengths to make each event special for that particular client. The personal touch always counts.'

'Yes it does,' the merry voice of Florence Nicholls broke in. 'And Mr Matthews, may I remind you that our waitresses are needed on several floors if lunch is ever going to be served today?'

Robert Matthews laughed heartily. 'Don't make out that you're such a dragon, Florence. The girls and myself have good reason to know that you are a soft touch and only grumble now and again to prove that your voice is one of authority.'

Most of the girls giggled but at the same time they moved swiftly to put the finishing touches to their caps and aprons and were soon on their way.

'All right for them to jest among themselves, them being the bosses, but we mere mortals still jump when they're around,' May declared.

Becky looked at her swiftly but made no comment. She was still glancing at Robert Matthews, thinking how wonderful he looked. He had a marvellous tan, his bright blue eyes were brilliant and his hair, always so fair, was now almost white, bleached by the sun. His apparel wasn't dull either. Beneath his black jacket he was wearing a waistcoat, grey silk brocade, no less. 'He looks like a Greek god,' Becky murmured to herself.

May heard and was flabbergasted. Amazement swept across her face as she stared at Becky in disbelief. 'He looks like what?'

A huge smile spread over Becky's face. 'Well, I think he looks great.'

'Are you saying you fancy him?'

Becky stared at her, speechless.

'Well whether you do or not is neither here nor there cos if we don't get a move on we'll both be out of a job and then you will never set eyes on the gorgeous Mr Matthews ever again.'

'Now you're being real daft,' Becky protested. 'Can't I admire a man without you going on?'

'You can if you like but it won't get you anywhere.' With that May sprinted across the floor, held the door open wide and yelled, 'Come on, last one in the still room gets to polish all the cutlery.'

Becky was after her in a flash but she was still wondering where Mr Matthews had been to acquire such a tan and whether or not he had taken a companion with him.

During the week before the Bovis annual dinner, the activity and excitement had grown to such an extent that all the waitresses were affected.

It was a bright but cold day, and both May and Becky had worn not only hats but scarves as well to keep themselves warm on the way to work. Arriving at the back door of the building where the dinner was to take place, May smiled at Becky and said, 'Here we go.' Then she pushed the door open and said, 'Well, it's lovely an' warm in here, so that's one blessing.'

They passed through the great kitchen, walking slowly, taking it all in for this was the first time they had worked in these premises. There were so many white-coated staff and men wearing tall chef's hats that it was difficult to imagine how they could work in such harmony.

'Look,' May said, pointing to the far end of the kitchen, 'there's Mrs Nicholls, she'll tell us where we're to go.'

They dodged passed the hot range that had an amazing number of cast-iron pans arrayed along the top and Mrs Nicholls greeted them cheerfully, saying, 'Trust you two to use the wrong entrance. But never mind, come through here, go up those stairs and the first room facing you at the top has been set up as a changing room.'

They followed her directions and halfway up the staircase May remarked, 'Mrs Nicholls doesn't alter, does she?'

'No, except her hair is turning grey, but I know what you mean. She's a very nice lady, very friendly,' Becky replied.

'She is, there's no side to her. We've always got on well with her, haven't we?'

'They say listeners never hear any good of themselves but I don't seem to be doing so badly.'

Both girls turned their heads sharply at the sound of Florence Nicholls' voice.

May was the first to recover. 'You shouldn't wear those soft-soled shoes, though I suppose they're good if you want to creep up behind us girls without being heard.'

'I'll have a little less sauce from you tonight, May Stevens, you should have learned by now I don't need to creep up on you. I have eyes in the back of my head and two sets of ears. There's not much goes on in this company that I don't get to hear about in one form or another.'

Each girl placed a hand to her mouth in order to hide a grin.

They had reached the top of the stairs and Becky held the door open for Mrs Nicholls to enter the staff room first. She did so, laughing loudly as she passed, and Mrs Nicholls' laughter was to set the tone for the whole evening. There were only about sixty waitresses on duty tonight, for compared to some functions this dinner was a small affair.

The sight of the menu was the first item that had the girls giggling. The company had fulfilled its promise. Printed on wood veneer the choice of food was set out exactly in the manner of a builder's specification.

The main course – Brickwork. This consists of roast beef laid in vegetable mortar. Dessert – Joinery. Mort ice anystyle, with a choice of black or white for the finishing.

'Look at the bottom, look at it!' several voices yelled in unison.

'Cor, if that don't take the biscuit I don't know what does,' May laughed sharply.

A request at the bottom of the menu read:

NB: Please don't tip the exca-vaiters.

However the impeccably dressed Nippies were more than pleased when, having taken up their allotted places before serving the first course, the entire ensemble rose to its feet, cheered and waved their serviettes.

*   *   *

It was one o'clock in the morning when two tired but happy girls dragged themselves over the step and into the hall to be confronted by Aunt Lil, pink dressing gown tied tightly around her waist, pink furry slippers on her feet and curlers in her hair. She made a welcoming sight.

'Dead beat, are you? Fancy a cuppa or a bowl of broth before you climb the stairs?' she enquired, grinning as she added, 'It ain't all honey is it, being top waitresses in the West End of London?'

May was already seated on the bottom tread of the staircase. 'Oh, my poor feet,' she moaned as she gently eased her black shoes off and began rubbing her toes.

'Aunt Lil, I've said it before and I'll say it again, you are a diamond!' Becky murmured as she wriggled her bottom on to the step next to May. 'I could kill for a cup of tea but I wouldn't have had the strength to make it for myself.'

'Glad to know this old body is still of use to you fair ladies,' was Aunt Lil's comment as she turned to go. Then she changed her mind and threw back over her shoulder, 'Five minutes an' it will be on the table, so if you can't walk you'd better crawl cos I've never yet served tea in me hall and I've no intention of starting now.'

Becky looked at May and merely smiled. May smiled back at her. Turning their heads they could see into the kitchen through the open door. Aunt Lil had already set out cups, plates and food on the table. She had probably spent half the day baking and these last hours of the day sitting in her big wooden armchair set to the side of the fire, resting her feet on the brass fender.

Of course she would never admit it but even if she did go up to her bed they knew she never slept until she heard both of them were safely indoors.

'We're both very lucky,' Becky murmured softly. 'She's like a mother hen where we're concerned.'

'Yes.' May nodded. 'She's a brick, isn't she?' She paused

and sighed, then went on, 'Makes you wonder what will happen if and when we decide to get married.'

Alarm bells went off in Becky's head. We get married? Did May mean herself and Stan Riley? Or did she mean us, herself and me?

She couldn't let her thoughts form an answer because Aunt Lil was standing in the open doorway insisting, 'Come and get this cup of tea right now, I'm not 'aving you fall asleep sitting out there in the cold.'

Becky stared at this tiny woman who was like a second mother to her and thought just how much she had come to love her. Then she got to her feet, pulled May up and said aloud, 'We're keeping our guardian angel from her bed. Let's have our tea and then we'll all go up together.'

Chapter Twenty-eight

BECKY WALKED ALONG the Embankment deep in thought, her hands thrust into the pockets of her coat.

It was a cold, clear night with lots of stars in the sky and there was a bright moon. The wind was blowing up from the Thames and she snuggled her chin deep into her fur collar.

She was very much preoccupied with thoughts that had been troubling her for some time. Somehow she knew that things between May and Stan Riley were a whole lot more serious than May painted them to be.

Not that she blamed May. Oh no. It was May's own business and she would confide in her when the time was right. After all, both she and May were almost twenty-three and that would be a good time to get married. At least for May it would be. Stan was a nice bloke. She liked him a lot. He didn't have any pretensions of grandeur, his feet were firmly planted on the ground and they struck her as being ideally suited to one another. The question was, where would they live when they did decide to tie the knot?

May would never leave her aunt and to be fair-minded there was more than enough room in Aunt Lil's house for them all to live without ever intruding on one another's privacy. What about me? was the woeful thought that seemed to be forever in her mind. I'm sure both Aunt Lil and May would insist that I stay on and have a room as always. I couldn't do that. I would feel I was trespassing. Besides, I would hate to spoil such a friendship as May and I have. I've been so lucky, Becky said to herself. Ever since I came to London I have never been lonely. Never been on my own.

Of course I have missed my family, at times very much so, but what a godsend it was when May and I met on that very first day. Then May's mother died and Aunt Lil stepped in and she's taken care of us both ever since, filling in all those gaps that would have been left. Bless her.

What now? What options do I have? I'm not hard up. I earn good money. I suppose I could rent a flat somewhere but it would have to be on the other side of the river. My income won't stretch to West End prices. Alternatively I could go into lodgings. But do I want to live in a strange house with people I've never set eyes on before?

The very thought made her shudder. She stopped walking, turned and leant her elbows on the parapet, staring down into the deep waters of the Thames. As she stood still she felt rather than saw a tall man leaning over the wall also staring at the water. Since it was too cold to linger she turned away at the same time as the man did and they came face to face.

The man's eyes widened and he leant forward to look into Becky's face then said, 'Rebecca?'

Becky had been frightened for a moment; she seemed unable to speak except to mutter, 'Mr Matthews.'

He was unable to take his eyes off her. She looked entirely different out of uniform. Her long heavy coat emphasized her narrow waist and that close-fitting hat framed a face that in the moonlight looked to be that of a small child.

'What on earth are you doing walking the Embankment on your own at this time of night?' He bellowed the question at her and she drew away, taking two steps backward. 'Oh, I'm sorry. I didn't mean to shout. Are you on your way somewhere?'

Becky recovered, took a deep breath and answered him with a smile. 'No, I didn't want to go home just yet and it isn't much after seven o'clock. The river fascinates me, it's never still. When I first came to London I used to come here quite often.'

'That's as maybe, but I am not leaving you out here on

your own,' he said gently. 'I'd be wondering and worrying about you all night.'

'It's all right,' she quickly replied, 'I am quite grown-up.'

'Well you don't look it,' he said, giving her a quirky grin, 'and I'm now going to take charge of you.' He took a grip on her arm and tucked it through his, and with determination he made sure that they set off at a brisk pace, leaving the Embankment behind them and making their way up the Strand. 'Keep your eyes peeled for a cab,' he ordered.

They reached Trafalgar Square without having spotted one that was for hire. Robert glanced down at Becky. 'Would you like a hot drink? I know I could use one.'

'Yes, please,' she agreed. Then with a wide grin she said, 'Which Lyons would you suggest?'

He laughed back at her, 'Oh no. We're not having a busman's holiday.' Still laughing, he added, 'Instead, Miss Russell, I shall take you slumming.'

Minutes later and Becky couldn't believe it! They were only a short distance from Nelson's Column and here they were, standing in the road, by the side of a brilliantly lit coffee-stall, munching on bread rolls that held a long hot sausage generously smeared with Colman's mustard. And that wasn't all. Perched on the high counter in front of them were two enormous china mugs filled with boiling coffee which the big, fat stallholder had made from a bottle of Camp liquid.

She was a Nippy for Lyons and the man with her, well, she didn't quite know how to describe him even to herself, except to say that he had a top job with the same firm. It would take some believing if she related this to Aunt Lil or even to May. Bringing May to mind brought a smile to Becky's lips. That was one person who certainly wouldn't swallow this story.

Robert Matthews chewed on his roll, all the while looking at Rebecca. She was a dainty person. She had an oval face that was adorable, high cheekbones, a small nose and thick dark hair that he had often admired as it lay against her face when flattened by her waitress cap. Her eyes were large and deep dark brown with thick lashes that curled without any help from that mascara colouring that had become so fashionable.

He picked up his mug and took a sip of his coffee, suddenly wishing it were something stronger. Rebecca Russell unnerved him. She always had from the first moment he had set eyes on her. She also intrigued him, and he longed to know whether some of the stories he'd heard about her were true or just jealous rumours.

He had been an only child; now both his parents were dead and all he had were distant elderly relatives. He had known a few young ladies since he had lived on his own, but he had not experienced the kind of feelings that Rebecca roused in him. There was something about her that tugged at his heartstrings, made him want to watch out for her. He knew that Mr Gower thought the world of her and he was nobody's fool.

'I'm sorry it's only bottled coffee,' Robert said, making an apologetic face. 'Leave it if you don't like it, Rebecca.'

She shook her head. 'It's fine, Mr Matthews, nice and hot and the sausage roll is going down a treat.'

He lowered his head and smiled at her. 'Do you not think we could dispense with the Mr Matthews? My name is Robert.'

'I know full well what your Christian name is but it wouldn't do for me to use it. All you bosses use the girls' Christian names, which is nice, but it would be disrespectful if we did the same.'

'Is that how you see me? One of the bosses?'

'Well, that's exactly what you are, aren't you?'

'That's clever,' he laughed.

'What is?' she challenged.

'Answering a question with a question. I work for my living just the same as you do.'

Oh dear. Becky suddenly wished she was anywhere else but here. Had she upset him? Gone too far, been too cheeky?

Although Becky had no way of knowing it, Robert Matthews was kicking himself for having responded so abruptly. He instantly regretted it. What he really wanted to do was take her in his arms and if they stood here, so close to each other, for much longer he wouldn't be able to resist the urge to kiss her.

So, reluctantly, he placed his coffee mug back on to the counter, and took a deep breath of the cold air, endeavouring to speak calmly. 'It's cold standing here, and it's getting late, I'd better get you home. You stay where you are and I'll go and find a cab.'

'It's all right,' she told him, touching his arm. 'I can get a bus from Trafalgar Square and I'll be home in no time.'

'Miss Russell!' He sounded quite shocked. 'A gentleman doesn't meet a young lady, wine and dine her and then leave her to make her own way home. Whatever can you be thinking of?'

Becky realized that he was teasing her and she chuckled as he hurried away towards the bright lights of the square.

In no time at all he must have found a cab because he was back and as the cab drew into the kerb Robert jumped out, helped Rebecca to get in, telling her to give the address to the cabbie, jumped inside after her, and slammed the door. They sat close to each other, saying nothing as the cab rumbled on its way to South Lambeth Road.

When the cab reached her destination Robert once again jumped out and helped her down on to the pavement. Becky groaned to herself as the front door was thrown open and Aunt Lil stood in the shaft of light that was pouring out of the hallway. At least she is dressed, Becky breathed thankfully, looking really neat and tidy, but did she have to open the door at that very moment?

'Where have you been?' Aunt Lil called out, sounding really worried.

Oh no! Becky gasped in horror. Robert Matthews was asking the cab driver to wait and now, not giving her time to protest, he had gripped her arm and was leading her up the garden path toward the house.

'Are you all right, Becky? I knew May wasn't coming home until late but I was expecting you home about half past six. I haven't known what to do.' By the time Aunt Lil had finished speaking they had reached the foot of the stone steps. Leaning forwards, peering into the darkness Aunt Lil said, 'Thank you for bringing her home, young man. Are you sure she isn't hurt or anything? Don't just stand there the pair of you, come in, come on in.'

Robert turned his gaze away from the tiny lady and looked at Becky. She shrugged her shoulders and they both smiled. 'You'd better do as she says or I shall never hear the end of it. Do you mind coming in for a moment?'

With his voice full of merriment he said, 'Not at all,' and then taking hold of Becky's hand, he climbed the steps with her. Like a couple of naughty schoolchildren, they faced Aunt Lil.

Becky made the introductions and Aunt Lil had to tilt her head back in order to look Robert over from top to toe. 'My, he's a tall one,' she said, ushering him into the living room where a good fire was roaring up the chimney and a pot of bronze chrysanthemums, standing in a copper bowl, had been placed in the centre of the table.

'This is cosy,' Robert exclaimed.

Aunt Lil immediately asked him to take off his overcoat, sit down and have something to eat and drink.

Thankfully Becky listened as he declined. 'The cabbie won't be in the best of moods if I keep him hanging about,' he quickly explained. 'He'll be wanting to get back to the West End, that's where the money is made at this time of night. But you mustn't blame Rebecca for being late home, it was entirely my fault. Will you forgive me?'

Becky couldn't believe it. Aunt Lil was looking all coy. It just went to show what a charmer Robert Matthews could be. Becky went to the front door with him and thanked him for bringing her home. They shook hands and she told herself that she had only imagined that he had held on to her hand for a lot longer than was necessary. All the same she gave a little sigh of relief as she closed the front door and went back to face the questioning she knew was bound to come from Aunt Lil.

Three weeks had gone by and Becky hadn't set eyes on Robert Matthews. Jolly good job too, she repeatedly said to herself, but it was only a half-truth. She had constantly found herself hoping that she would see him again. Only during the course of the day's work, she would chide herself, but again that wasn't entirely true. She often wondered what it would be like to actually be taken out by Robert Matthews.

Sometimes her thoughts were more sensible. At those times she would assure herself the meeting with Robert Matthews was best forgotten. Deep down he was probably no different to Gerald Palmer. Except he did work for his living. That was another thing that preyed on her mind. Robert Matthews seemed to pick and choose what he would do. His job with Lyons seemed to be very flexible. There would be days when he always seemed to be around; she had often felt his eyes watching her as she carried out her duties. Then he would disappear, like now, and nobody would set eyes on him for weeks.

These days when May caught her daydreaming she would give her a good old dressing-down. Having heard from Aunt Lil a very colourful version of the evening Mr Matthews had brought 'our Rebecca' home, May had been like a dog with a bone.

'Keep your head on your shoulders,' was one of May's favourite terms, 'have sense. See through him. Realize he's not one of our kind.'

All a bit daft, Becky wanted to yell back, but she didn't because she knew so well that May only had her good at heart and didn't want her to be hurt again.

Becky was just making up her mind to go to the ladies and make herself tidy before going back on duty when she saw him coming across the floor towards her. She gave a gasp of surprise. She had spent her entire tea break thinking about him and here he was in the flesh.

She hastily got to her feet, almost toppling the chair over, and he quickly straightened it, saying, 'I'm sorry. Did I startle you?'

Becky shook her head in protest; she felt as if she were dreaming.

Robert Matthews stepped away from her and very quietly asked, 'How are you? You look tired. Not working too hard, are you?'

'I'm fine, really. Saturday is always a busy day. I'm just going to change my shoes – pity we aren't able to have a spare pair of feet.'

He did not laugh as she had expected he would. Instead he enquired, 'Are you off tomorrow?'

She didn't answer him immediately, but she had her head tilted back and was looking straight at him when she said, 'Yes, I am.'

'Would you allow me to take you for a drive? I thought we might go as far as Richmond.' She stiffened slightly and Robert Matthews had noticed the reaction. He inclined his head towards Becky. 'If you'd rather not.'

The staff room had gone quiet, the rest of the girls having bustled off to do the remainder of their shift. There would be plenty of people about this afternoon, having done their shopping and in need of afternoon tea. What should she do now? Half of her wanted to yell that she'd love to go with him. The cautious part of her was warning her not to start something she would regret. Remember Gerald! But he was in the past. Was she going to let him ruin her life for ever? Surely she was entitled to one mistake. Blow Gerald and everything about him. She was being given an opportunity to find out if this tall blond man was sincere or not. She made her mind up, she was going to take it. And to hell with the consequences.

'Thank you for extending the invitation.'

He laughed, quite loudly, and Becky, thinking to herself that it was a happy laugh, smiled at him.

'This conversation,' he said, 'is getting very stilted. It's not as if we are complete strangers. Don't forget you have allowed me to buy you dinner before now. Oh yes, and take you home in a cab. So will you or won't you come out with me tomorrow?'

She knew he was teasing her again but she didn't mind one bit. 'I would like to, very much.' Becky's voice was quiet.

'Good,' he grinned, 'that's settled. I know where you live, I'll pick you up at eleven o'clock in the morning. Oh, and you might persuade your aunt that my intentions are honourable.' He turned away, came back and with a mischievous look in his eye, added, 'On second thoughts, don't bother. I shall reassure her myself. Till tomorrow then, Rebecca.'

The last four words were soft and full of feeling. But Becky did not reply to them. She just stood and watched him walking away, every inch a gentleman in a fine grey suit, and his usual waistcoat beneath the jacket. Not until she could no longer see him did she make a move towards the washroom.

Having washed her hands and splashed her face with cold water she now studied herself in the full-length mirror. She looked very smart in her Nippy uniform; she wouldn't be allowed on the restaurant floor if she didn't. Daily inspection of every waitress employed by Lyons wasn't just a matter of routine. It was thorough, never altering in all the time that she had been employed by them. Now, as she had countless times, she renewed her thanks to God Almighty for having been given the privilege of being trained, finally, to become a tip-top London waitress.

All the same, she sighed deeply to herself, life's not easy. Not by any means. She had mistakenly thought that mixing with the well–off toffs would provide the opportunity for her to find a suitable husband. She had seen how the other half lived and she didn't want to be poor.

'You've been very lucky, so far,' she said aloud to her reflection in the mirror, 'you could have fared a lot worse. A whole lot worse! Let's hope you've learnt your lesson.'

She hastened back to the restaurant, for she was late, and the waitress who was sharing her station this afternoon glared at her. She didn't mind. For the next three hours she was run off her feet, while all the time her imagination was running wild. Tomorrow she was being taken out by Robert Matthews.

Chapter Twenty-nine

BECKY WAS READY well in time, standing in the front room looking out of the window ready to make a dash for it as soon as Robert arrived. She was wearing her long grey coat over a navy-blue two-piece suit, a black velvet hat and black kid gloves.

'About what time shall I expect you back?' Aunt Lil asked as she poked her head round the door.

'I really don't know, shouldn't think it will be late, but please, Aunt Lil, don't start worrying about me.'

Aunt Lil came closer and walked around Becky, inspecting her from head to toe. 'I'm glad you've put on your big coat. It's a lovely bright day but not very warm, there's quite a wind blowing.'

Before Becky had a chance to answer her, there was a loud rat-a-tat-tat on the front door.

'I'll go,' Aunt Lil said, leaving the room like a shot.

Becky groaned. The only thing she was thankful for was that she was ready to set off, so there was no reason why they should hang about and give Aunt Lil the chance to question him.

The sight of Aunt Lil re-entering the room caused Becky to smile. She was carrying a bunch of flowers and looking very pleased with herself. Beaming, she said, 'Your Mr Matthews brought these for me. Aren't they nice? And they smell really lovely.'

Becky agreed that they were indeed lovely and turned to face Robert. But he wasn't looking at her, he was smiling at Aunt Lil, saying, 'How are you, Mrs Maynard? I hope you have forgiven me for keeping Rebecca out so late last time we met.'

Becky didn't know quite what to say or do. She was looking at this wonderful man whom she had regarded as her boss for going on four years now, and trying not to take any notice of the look on Aunt Lil's face. She had to press her lips tightly together to stop herself from grinning. Aunt Lil was loving the attention. And Robert Matthews was being an absolute gentleman.

'Thank you again for the flowers,' Aunt Lil was saying.

'Not at all. Not at all. And I promise I shall have Rebecca home here no later than seven o'clock.'

Seven o'clock! She had thought they were only going for a run out, perhaps home in time for tea. Becky warned herself to stay calm. She walked over to her aunt and kissed her on the cheek. They stared at each other for a moment then Becky patted her arm and whispered, 'Don't worry about me, I'll be fine.'

'See that you are, and have a nice time, bless you.'

Becky walked towards the door, while Robert took Lil's hand between his own and said quietly, 'I'll take care of her. We won't be back late. I promise.'

'Thank you,' Aunt Lil answered in a conspiratorial whisper. They were outside the house now and he had his hand on Rebecca's elbow leading her towards a smart Austin motorcar that stood at the kerb. She felt very important as Robert opened the nearside door and handed her into the passenger seat. 'Comfortable?' he asked before closing the door and going round to get into the driver's seat.

The car itself was black but the interior upholstery had Becky gasping in surprise. It was all leather, tan in colour, and the rich smell that comes only from good leather had her sniffing with delight.

'Sunday markets are causing all this traffic,' Robert said. 'But don't worry, we'll soon be out of it.'

'Oh, it doesn't worry me,' she replied with a grin, looking

along Wandsworth High Street that was thick with traders of all sorts. Costermongers had their stalls set out, young lads were pushing barrows and handcarts, and on the pavement at intervals were the shellfish stalls.

'Every Londoner's favourite Sunday tea, cockles, whelks, winkles and shrimps plus the odd stick of celery,' Robert told her with a change in his accent, making the statement into a kind of sing-song.

'Not much different from Kingston market, which is quite near to where I was born and brought up,' Becky laughingly told him. 'And I still regard it as home.'

'And so you should. I think you are extremely lucky not only to have Mrs Maynard to take care of you but still have your parents and brothers back in New Malden.'

Becky turned her head to stare at him. 'You've made it your business to know a lot about me!'

'Please.' He took a hand off of the steering wheel and laid it lightly on her knee just for a second before saying, 'I wasn't prying. I admit I did want to know more about you, though I have known you since the time you first applied for a job with Lyons. Sometimes, such as when you were given promotion, we do update our records. Shall I tell you something, Rebecca? I envy you. I have admired you from the moment I first set eyes on you but when I became aware of the fact that you had a loving family as well as May Stevens for a friend and her aunt as a second mother, I truly did envy you.'

Becky was utterly bewildered. She remained silent, lost in thought. What had Robert Matthews got to be envious about? He had everything. Good job, plenty of money or so it seemed or he wouldn't own such a motorcar as this one she was riding in. There was something else that was niggling away at her. Difficult to pin it down. He had said 'we' update the records. Not the firm. Not the company. But 'we'. Oh, well, she wasn't going to let anything spoil today. This was a rare chance to have a nice day out.

'We're driving through Putney now,' Robert told her, wisely doing his best to change the subject. 'Now the scenery will get better.'

Soon they had left the rows of terraced houses behind and Becky noticed that most properties were now detached with nicely cared-for gardens. She was about to say that they couldn't be too far from her home but decided to let that pass. The signs placed on the walls stated that Richmond was in the county of Surrey. Indeed she was remembering how, as a young girl, she, Ella and all of their brothers had often walked along the towpath and sometimes even been taken on outings as far as Richmond Hill. Not that she could recall such imposing surroundings as those that Robert was driving through at this moment.

The houses were so large! They boasted great big double gates with a smaller gate set in the end of a high solid wall that held a board which stated 'Tradesmen' in large painted letters.

Passing all these obvious signs of wealth Robert suddenly said, 'Here we are. Richmond Park.'

'Oh, Mr Matthews, it is lovely.'

He switched off the engine, turned and smacked her hand gently. 'We are going to spend a lovely day together, have lunch soon and most probably tea before I take you home, so will you please start calling me Robert?'

'I'll try to remember,' she said, her cheeks reddening. 'It just doesn't seem right.'

'Nothing would please me more. Say it now, go on, just say Robert.'

'Robert,' she said quietly.

'There you are, it isn't difficult, is it?'

'No,' she agreed, smiling.

'Shall we walk?' Robert asked, coming round to her side and opening the door.

She stood on the gravel drive looking at the great trees, the shrubs and the wonderful green grass that seemed to stretch for miles. When he took her hand she didn't feel shy or awkward, just happy.

They walked on and on, nodding at parents out for a Sunday stroll with their kiddies, and young men proudly parading their fiancées.

'We'd better turn back or we shall be late for lunch,' Robert remarked.

They hadn't gone very far when three small boys came tearing up to them, 'Mister, would you please help us get our kite down?' the tallest of the three boys asked politely.

'We can't reach it,' the smallest of the three echoed, which made both Becky and Robert laugh because this little mite was very tiny.

'I'll help if I can,' Robert agreed. 'Show me where it has got caught.'

The kite could be seen quite clearly once all three lads had pointed a finger in the right direction. The body of the kite was white, the tail flapping in the wind was bright orange, mauve, blue, green and yellow and for a moment Becky felt quite homesick as her mind flew back to the weekend that she and May had spent in New Malden. Hadn't they bought such a kite for her nephew and hadn't the whole family gone over to the field opposite the house in order to fly the kite while her mum, Ella's mum, and Aunt Lil had prepared the midday Sunday dinner? It was at times like this that she missed her family.

'Hold my coat will you please, Rebecca?'

Robert's request brought her back to the present with a start. They had walked a few yards without her noticing and were now standing beneath a big oak tree, the branches of which had tangled the young lads' kite.

As he removed his jacket Becky wanted to do more than laugh. Robert wasn't wearing one of his usual smart waistcoats; instead he had on a knitted pullover of an intricate pattern and she found herself wondering who loved him enough and also had enough patience to knit him such a garment. It had to be an older woman, she decided, at the same time coming to the conclusion that the pullover suited Robert. It made him look more carefree, and younger. Up until now she would have set his age at thirty-two or thirty-three, but looking at him now she was sure he wasn't a day over thirty, maybe only twenty-eight.

Robert looked up, then around, and shook his head. 'There isn't anything lying about that is long enough to reach it,' he muttered. 'Oh well, here goes,' and laughing loudly he reached up to grab hold of two thick branches, found himself a foothold on the trunk of the tree and began to climb. The kite wasn't that high and within minutes Robert was untangling the strings that were caught between twigs.

'Oh, that's great!'

'You're super, Mister.'

'Yes, well done, thanks ever so much.'

The cries from the lads, as Robert freed their kite and held it out wide enabling it to float down to the ground, had both Robert and Becky laughing fit to burst.

'Thanks again,' the eldest boy called as the trio raced across the grass, the colourful toy streaming out behind them.

'Come on,' Robert urged, grabbing Becky's hand and starting to run, 'see if we can keep up with them as far as the car.'

Breathing heavily they reached the car and between gasps they were both still laughing as Robert used a handkerchief to brush away at the knees of his trousers. Straightening up he said, 'Does you good to mix with youngsters now and again.'

'I agree,' Becky laughingly replied, 'even if they do leave you feeling your age.'

'Oh, you poor old soul,' Robert taunted her, 'you are out of condition. I see I shall have to take you in hand, bring you out here more often, see that you get more fresh air in your lungs. Meanwhile, young lady, our lunch will be ready and waiting.'

As they got in to the car, Becky was again confused. She had wanted to agree wholeheartedly to his suggestion that they came out together more often but then he had added that their lunch was waiting and she had no idea where or why they were expected for lunch.

'Where are we going?' Becky asked after he had been driving for a few minutes.

'We're almost there,' he replied and seconds later he turned the car into a lane, drove over a hump-backed bridge which straddled a rippling stream and only a few yards further on left the road, turning in between two iron gates that were open as if they were expected, drove a short distance and stopped the car in front of a small but very pretty house.

Becky gazed at the thick covering of ivy that had a hold over most of the wall, it wasn't just green ivy but had shades of deep red entwined. She hadn't time to take in any more details because the front door had opened and a stout woman, in her mid-fifties Becky guessed, with iron grey hair in a knot on top of her head, was smiling them both a welcome.

Becky thought the woman's hairdo was the shape of a cottage loaf but she kept her thoughts to herself.

'Come on, come on,' Robert urged taking Becky's hand and ushering her towards the porch.

'Hello, Caroline,' he called. 'Have we kept you waiting?'

'No, not at all. Bring the young lady in and let's get the introductions over and done with.'

Robert laughed loudly and when they drew near he said, 'This is the young lady I told you about, Caroline. Her name is Rebecca Russell. Rebecca, this is Caroline Louise James.'

The woman took Becky's hand, smiling broadly. 'Oh we are formal this morning, I cannot remember when Robert last called me Caroline. I've been Carrie to him since he learnt to say his first words. Anyway don't you struggle with Caroline, you just call me Carrie and may I say how pleased I was when he told me he was bringing you to lunch. We don't see half as many visitors as we should and sometimes none for weeks on end.'

Becky decided this woman was nice. Very nice. She could easily take to her though at the moment she hadn't any idea who she was or how she fitted into Robert's life, despite the fact that she seemed to have been forewarned that Robert was bringing her here for lunch today.

And that wasn't the only surprise.

Having been led down a narrow passage that led out to a surprisingly spacious hall she was amazed to see a large, portly, white-haired gentleman standing in the doorway of what seemed to be a sitting room. Behind him Becky could see the flames from a log fire lighting up an open fireplace.

'Welcome my dear,' he said, his hand outstretched, his voice loud. Becky took his hand and had to suck in her breath, his grasp was so firm. 'Sit you down young lady, I'm too old to stand,' he added as he sank heavily on to the chair which Robert had pushed forward.

'Rebecca, this is my Uncle Maurice, though now that I am a grown man I'm allowed to drop the "uncle" and use his Christian name.' Robert turned from Rebecca to face his uncle saying, 'Uncle, this is—'

'I know who she is,' Uncle Maurice hastily interrupted. 'You've talked of her often enough. How'd you do, Rebecca. Come and sit beside me, we'll have a glass of Madeira and get to know each other, shall we?'

Robert looked embarrassed as he shrugged his shoulders and pulled a chair closer to the fire for Rebecca.

'Shall I put the finishing touches to the lunch?' Caroline asked practically. 'The table is all set in the dining room and I can be ready to serve in about fifteen minutes.'

'Perfect, Carrie,' Robert said, flashing her a smile that thanked her for saving the day.

Her coat and hat off, a glass of wine in her hand, Becky sat gazing about her. It was a small room, a lot smaller than the front room in Aunt Lil's house and even smaller than the main family room at home in New Malden, but it was cosy and beautifully furnished. Everything from the beams in the ceiling to the pictures on the walls and the actual furniture was old and lovingly cared for. The carpet, lampshades and the draped curtains at the small windows were a maze of autumn colours.

'Lunch is all ready, if you'd like to come through.' Carrie's voice was jolly. 'Sit yourself down, Rebecca, anywhere you like since there are only the four of us, it doesn't really matter.'

Robert held a chair out for Becky and when she was seated he took the chair opposite for himself.

At first glance this dining room had made Becky catch her breath. It was a much larger room than the cosy sitting room they had just left. It had to be the most beautiful room she had ever seen. Again the room was heated by a bright log fire and to each side of the open fireplace a settee had been drawn up. The walls were wood-panelled, the furniture again old, still shining from years of polishing.

Although Carrie sat down to eat with them she seemed to be forever jumping to her feet to see to the next course.

'Is that it now? Have we reached the main course?' Uncle Maurice's voice came from deep down in his throat. 'You've been like a cat on hot bricks ever since you set foot in that kitchen this morning, one would think we were entertaining royalty. Been cooking since the crack of dawn she has,' he finished on a laugh.

Carrie was now placing a heavily-laden tray on a side table, and in a cheery voice said, 'I'd rather prepare a meal for Rebecca any day. Royalty would frighten me to death whereas Rebecca is friendly, she would put anyone at ease.'

A smile spread over Robert's face as he jumped to his feet, saying, 'Let me bring that lot nearer to the table, Carrie, and then we can all help ourselves to the vegetables.'

'Good idea, Robert, perhaps now you'll do as you're told,

Carrie. Come on, sit down and enjoy your own cooking,' Maurice ordered.

'Bossy pair, aren't they?' Carrie grinned as she retook her seat next to Becky.

Becky agreed with Carrie. She felt she had known that she could be friends with this stout cheery lady from the moment they had shook hands. Yet this house and the three people in it were a puzzle. So the men were uncle and nephew, but she had heard Maurice thanking Robert and telling him how much he was enjoying staying here with Carrie to take care of him. Where did he live? And to whom did this cottage belong? And even more to the point, where did Carrie fit in? She wasn't a maid or even the cook. She was a lot more than that. Hadn't she admitted that she had known Robert from the day he was born?

Feeling thoroughly confused Becky decided that she would wait until such time as Robert thought fit to enlighten her. Meanwhile she was going to enjoy this plate of lovely roast lamb that Carrie had set down in front of her.

Throughout the whole of the meal Becky felt at ease. It was almost as if they were family. She hadn't reckoned on having lunch with folk that she didn't know but it had turned out so well. Happy and relaxed she set her spoon down into her sweet-dish and sat back with a satisfied sigh.

'Would you like some more trifle, Rebecca?'

'Oh no, thank you Carrie. I've had a wonderful lunch.'

'Then I'll fetch the cheese and the coffee.'

'Stay where you are,' came the order from Robert. 'Talk to Rebecca, I'll fetch the coffee.'

'I don't suppose you are acquainted with the family history?' Carrie spoke softly to Rebecca as Robert left the room and Maurice moved from the dinner table to seat himself in a corner of a settee by the fire.

Becky made no reply; she merely smiled.

'The whole framework I'll leave out, that's Robert's business. I'll just put you in the picture as to where I fit in. You must be wondering by now, hired help sitting down to eat with the family and guests.'

Becky found the last statement tricky. Of course she had been wondering but she surely couldn't admit as much. She was saved from forming an answer by Carrie throwing back her head and laughing out loud. 'It was naughty of Robert to bring you here without explaining. For want of a better word I used to be nanny to Robert. He grew up, his father died and his mother never had much interest in him after that, or anyone else for that matter. She saw Robert safely settled, persuaded him to join the family business and after that, well, the truth is she never wanted to live. She and her husband were everything to one another, never known two people so in love as those two were. With her husband gone she willed herself to go too. No matter what the doctors had to say at the time that is the simple truth.'

Becky felt it was such a sad story yet she couldn't resist asking one question. 'Have you looked after Robert ever since?'

She got no answer.

'Poor Rebecca.' Robert had entered the room and having set down the tray he was carrying he looked sheepishly at Rebecca. 'If I had told you I intended to bring you to lunch with Caroline and my Uncle Maurice I was afraid you might have shied away, so instead I have let Carrie bear the brunt of my cowardliness. What are you thinking now?' he asked, handing her a cup of coffee.

Becky looked into his eyes. They were full of sadness and she felt unable to hide her own feelings. 'I was thinking that this is a beautiful house and that I have been very privileged to be invited here for lunch today. I shouldn't have asked questions of Carrie, I'm sorry.'

The sadness in his eyes intensified. 'I've done this all wrong,' he muttered, more to himself than to her. 'Rebecca, when you've had your coffee I would like to show you the grounds and tell you the history of this house. Will you come with me?'

Rebecca nodded her head and Robert smiled at her. It was a gentle smile as if he were trying to thank her for something.

Their coffee finished, he now got to his feet and, standing in front of Rebecca, he said, 'We'll go into the garden now while it's still light. It won't take long, there's not a great deal to see.'

At the end of the hall he pushed open a heavy door and they were in the kitchen. It was a large square room, the main feature being the huge kitchen range which had an open grate and an oven to each side of it. Most of the floor space was taken up by a white wood-topped table.

'This way.' Robert pointed to the large window that had a white painted door to the side. 'This door leads out to the herb garden and on through to the main lawn. It shouldn't be muddy today but there are boots in the shed if you would like to change your shoes.'

'No, it's all right,' Becky assured him, thankful that she wasn't wearing high heels.

As he had said, there wasn't too much garden but what there was was well-planned. 'Easy to set out and easy to maintain,' Robert explained. 'Carrie can't do too much.' He paused and laughed and Becky knew that he meant she was too fat. 'A gardener comes once a week now and twice a week during the summer months. I love this house, I come here as often as I can, it's a place to unwind in peaceful surroundings.'

Questions were still nagging away inside Becky's brain. If only he would get round to telling her what she was doing here.

'We won't go down beyond the lawn, as least not today, but there is a pond and a marshy piece of land which has become a sanctuary for countless birds and wildfowl. Lovely sight when the weather is warmer. Come, we'll sit in the summerhouse for a while and then we'll go back into the house.'

The summerhouse was quaint, almost like a doll's house. It had a white wrought-iron table and chairs with red padded cushions. Three sides of the house were all windows, giving a complete view of the garden and also of the house.

Becky sat down and laid her head back against the top of the chair. She was silent for once. When Robert had held open the door of this summerhouse she had squeezed past him, her hand had accidentally brushed against his and she had almost jumped out of her skin. Touching his fingers had been like an electric shock and she had pulled her hand away quickly. That hadn't been what she wanted to do. Grab hold of him and hold on tightly was what she had really felt like doing.

'I expect you are wondering about Carrie,' Robert said, startling her.

She took a deep breath and admitted, 'Yes, to be honest I am. Does she live here on her own?'

'Mostly she does. It suits her fine, she does have friends in the village and she always knows where I am and how she can get in touch with me. Carrie has been part of my life from the day I was born.'

'I gathered that much from what she told me.'

'Did she tell you this was my grandmother's house when she was alive?'

'Oh no, nothing about your family, only that both your parents are dead.'

'Didn't you want to ask her?' Robert had the grace to smile. 'I thought all females were blessed with a deal of curiosity.'

'That's as maybe,' Becky answered him quietly. 'You don't ask questions when you first meet someone.'

Robert Matthews was having a funny effect on her, making her aware of emotions that were sending her off-balance. There wasn't much room in this summerhouse and he was sitting so close to her. Their knees were almost touching. As if reading her thoughts, Robert said, 'You arouse the curiosity in me.' His voice was low and husky.

'But you know everything there is to know about me,'

she said, sounding quite indignant. 'You've only to check the records.'

Robert moved his chair slightly, sat back, draped one arm over it, and gave her a long, very meaningful look. 'Well then, perhaps it is about time I evened up the score. I won't start at the beginning, not yet, we'll settle the matter of Carrie first. As a young woman she was employed by my parents to be nanny to me. I was an only child and when my father died and my mother became ill Carrie was always there even though my grandmother came to live in our house. It was, and still is, a family-owned house in Hampstead and that is where Uncle Maurice, my father's elder brother, lives at present. When my mother also died matters continued much as they had been for a long time with Carrie and my grandmother being there for me.'

All the while Robert had been talking he had not taken his eyes away from Becky and under his close scrutiny she felt the colour rise in her cheeks. As if to reassure her, Robert took hold of her hand and held it as he continued, 'This small house belonged to my grandmother and when she died she left it to me. It has always seemed right that Carrie should live here for as long as she wished to. She has never married.'

In the silence that followed Becky closed her eyes. Piecing together the half that Carrie had told her and now what Robert had added, it was in some ways a very sad story. For Carrie a happy ending? Maybe. For Robert a lonely life? She had no way of telling, but it did explain why he had said he was envious of her having parents and three brothers.

Robert touched her arm lightly. 'I feel I should go the whole hog and tell you about my position with Lyons. That's if I am not boring you.'

'No, no,' she cut in, giving him a small, almost shy smile, 'I would like you to tell me. I would have to be very dim-witted not to have realized that you are more than just an employee of the company.'

'I never lied to you,' he hastened to say. 'You assumed

what you wanted to from the first, and given that you only saw part of my duties, no one could blame you. The truth is my great-grandfather was one of the founders of Lyons. Truly Rebecca, I have never tried to hide that fact from you.'

She was unconvinced, but she tried to smile.

She had already been led up the garden path by Gerald Palmer. Was Robert of the same mind? Did he see her as just one of the waitresses employed in the family firm? He must be as well-off financially as Gerald, probably a great deal more so. That being the case, then why was he bothering with her? As well as this beautiful house he had admitted there was a house in Hampstead and apart from that God knows what else. He could have any young lady he chose, one from a wealthy background such as his own, she thought bitterly. Again she asked herself, why is he bothering with me? She bit her lip, blinking rapidly to keep the angry tears back. Casual affairs were probably part of his life since he never seemed to be in the same place for any length of time but if he thought he was going to add her to his list then he was greatly mistaken. Once bitten was enough.

She got to her feet and made to push by him, seething inside because she had let herself believe that this time she had found a decent young man who worked for his living. She couldn't deny that she was attracted to him, what girl wouldn't be? He had boyish good looks and a kind of mesmerizing charm. Of course she had known that he was well up in his job with Lyons, had been aware of that from the beginning, but to find out that he owned part of that great company! Well, it puts me well out of his league, she muttered under her breath.

Her problem now was how to get home. She didn't have much choice; she would just have to keep quiet during the journey and let Robert drive and in order to do that she knew she would have to keep a grip on her feelings.

Robert was wondering how things could so suddenly have gone wrong between them. He placed a restraining hand on her arm. 'Don't go, Rebecca, not like this, please, sit down again and let's talk.'

Becky slumped down onto the chair again, instinctively feeling she should at least give him a chance.

Robert remained standing. 'Rebecca.' He tried to put a hand on her shoulder but she wriggled away. 'I wish to God I had made my position clear to you when we first met. It is unfortunate that I didn't because even then I was attracted to you. You had such charming appeal, not in the least worldly, you not only looked different, you acted differently to most of the young girls I had come into contact with. Even then I wanted to ask you out but you seemed so young and I was away out of London so often I thought I would wait. See if you liked the work, if you were going to stay with the company. Maybe I was wrong to bide my time, but I don't think so.'

Even feeling as angry as she did Rebecca still could not ignore the note of sincerity there was in his voice. 'But why? Just answer me that one question. Why would you, a man who owns part of a vast company, be interested in a girl who worked for him as a waitress?'

'If you want to put it like that what causes any man from any walk of life to be attracted to a particular female? And vice versa, come to that. I don't know the answer, do you?'

Becky was finding that just sitting here looking at him was tormenting her and she mumbled, 'I come from a working-class family.'

'Oh!' Robert laughed loudly, and Becky felt she could have hit him, but as she raised her hand to do so he caught it and said, 'Now you will listen to me. The man who consented to his name being used when the company was being formed was a Joseph Lyons. He earned his living as street trader but he also had some exhibition know-how. He spoke well, was of a presentable appearance and like me he had a persuasive manner. His style appealed to the men who were putting up the money, an agreement was drawn up on a single sheet of paper and as I have always been given to understand signed by all the men concerned on a train journey between London and Manchester. That Joseph Lyons was my great-grandfather. Now you tell me, does that make me a better person than you?'

'You still only work from choice,' Becky mumbled defiantly.

'You are wrong. Totally wrong. I have to work as does every male member of the board. We carry no dead wood. We need to work, it would be soul-destroying not to. Besides which it is mainly the involvement of the directors, at every level, that has helped make Lyons the great company it is today.' Robert took a deep breath and leant towards her. 'You can be very maddening, do you know that?'

Even Becky had to grin as he said those words.

The sight of her grinning prompted him to keep going, and he took another deep breath and plunged in. 'It was always expected that I would join the company. I never wanted to. My father, whom I hero-worshipped, and my mother simply adored, had died so suddenly of a heart attack and I was supposed to take his place. My mother, a wonderful loving lady whom no one could ever replace, was very persuasive and I have lived to be thankful that she was. There is hardly a job within the company that I haven't been taught to tackle. From waiter to van driver I have done it all with the exception of training to be a chef.'

He sat back, looked across the small table at Rebecca. She had a face that was positively lovely but at the same time she looked so innocent. He had heard rumours that she had been out and about with what were to him the wrong kind of men. Even news of one in particular, Gerald Palmer, had reached his ears but he didn't care. He understood that coming to London and seeing how the other half lived, she naturally wanted as much out of life as possible. It was bad luck that she had been attracted to an unreliable man.

He had sown a few wild oats of his own in the past

but this was serious. Rebecca Russell was to him without equal.

'I would like to get to know you really well, Rebecca,' he said, 'and I want you to know me, too, but that will never happen if you insist that I come from a different class of people from your own. I don't care what your background is and you shouldn't care about mine. We both work for our living. I have thought about you often, from the first day that we met, and as I've already said I would like to get to know you better, and, as far as I am concerned, that is all that matters.'

'Robert,' Becky began sheepishly, 'I have to tell you, recently I was mixed up with a young man . . . I went away with him . . . for the weekend.'

There was a slight pause as he levelled his eyes to hers. Then, speaking very slowly, he asked, 'Is it over and done with?'

'Yes,' she answered at once, giving him a direct straightforward look. 'But . . .'

'No buts, you have said it is over and that is good enough for me. Promise me you won't dwell on it, or let it come between us, put it from your mind and we shall never mention it again. Will you promise?'

'All right, if you say so.'

He stared hard at her, reached out and took her hand. She was trembling. He was so overcome by his feelings for her that he could not speak; he didn't want to frighten her off. For the moment things between them were very much up in the air, although he did feel he had made a little headway against her preconceived notion that all bosses were beyond the reach of their employees.

Eventually he said, 'My turn to tell you that there have been women in my life, I won't deny that, but I can say, hand on heart, there has never been anyone special.'

How badly he wanted to add, none that could compare with you. Should he use this opportunity and tell her exactly how he felt about her? How when he was miles away from her he wasn't able to concentrate on any business matters because his mind was full of her? Even sleeping the picture of her lovely gentle face and those big brown eyes crept into his dreams.

He made a sudden decision and threw caution to the wind. 'I love you, Rebecca. I think I have from the moment I first set eyes on you. Please, don't back away from me,' he pleaded. 'I will never ask you to be anything but what you are. I don't want to change even the smallest thing about you. I love you, I love *you*.'

Her face told him nothing. She didn't look pleased, she didn't smile, but she did hold out her hand which he quickly took hold of and raising it to his lips he kissed each finger in turn.

'Don't fret Rebecca, I won't hurry you in any way. We shall take things slowly, become firm friends. Please, just say you'll agree to that for the time being.'

This time she did smile, though her thoughts were in a turmoil. Her heart never told her the same thing two days running. He is sincere, it said most times they met, then when she didn't see him it became uncertain. No matter what he said his life was very different from hers. He lives in another world. I don't hanker after what he has, I only want him to be the lovely man that I am halfway sure he is.

Robert put a stop to her daydreaming. He pulled her close, hugged her tight before saying, 'Carrie will be wondering why I've kept you out in the cold for so long, shall we call a truce for now and go and have some tea?'

Becky closed the door of the summerhouse firmly behind her and took the hand that Robert was holding out to her, sighing softly under her breath as she did so. Me, Rebecca Russell, meaning that much to Robert Matthews! Whichever way she looked at it he was still a major shareholder of a great company such as Lyons.

Could there be any future for the two of them together? Only time would tell.

It was almost six o'clock when Robert finally said he had better see about getting her home.

'I hope we get to see you again soon,' Carrie said, hugging Rebecca goodbye.

'Keep in touch, a bit more often,' Maurice bellowed at Robert.

Becky got into the passenger seat and Robert closed the door. She leant out of the window. 'Thank you, Carrie, for everything,' she called, and Robert drove off with her still waving her arm.

'Have you ever regretted your decision to become a Nippy?' Robert half-laughed, breaking the silence.

'No, never. Not for one moment,' she replied.

'Achieved all your ambitions then, have you?'

Becky thought for a moment before saying, 'Not quite. I still have one.'

'And that is?'

Without hesitation she said, 'To serve at a function in the Mansion House.'

'Really?'

'Yes, really.'

'What in heaven's name is so special about the Mansion House?'

'Icing on top of the cake,' she laughed. 'The official residence of the Lord Mayor of London.'

They had driven quite a distance in complete silence and Robert was feeling pleased with himself for having broken the ice. 'You sound like Dick Whittington,' he said with a grin.

'Well then, all I need is a fairy godmother to grant my wish.'

'How about a demon-king?' They looked at each other and burst out laughing.

Then, looking very thoughtful, Robert said, 'It is not beyond the realms of possibility. In 1925, which is the year I think you joined the company, we did one of our biggest functions ever.'

'What, at the Mansion House?'

'No. The event was much larger than that. It was a banquet for the Freemasons, held at Olympia. As I remember, about eight thousand guests sat down and were served by more than a thousand waitresses, probably nearer thirteen hundred.'

Becky frowned. 'But surely that was before the Outside Catering Unit was formed.'

'Officially, yes. But as far back as 1921 the company was taking on such functions. Waitresses were drawn from Lyons tearooms up and down the country. Then demand became so great that it was decided to make outside catering a special entity. Young ladies were chosen.' He paused, took his eyes off the road for a second and smiled at Rebecca. 'You and your friend May Stevens were among the first to be given special training and from then on that branch of Lyons has existed independently.'

'Well I never! Kind of pioneers in the field of catering, would you say?'

'Yes, Miss Big Head! That is exactly what I would say.'

'Why, thank you Mr Matthews.'

When they had both stopped laughing, Robert was about to bring up the subject of when they would meet again but they had run into a patch of fog and he had to give his full attention to the main road.

'This is rather sudden,' he said gloomily.

Becky sat back in her seat and remained silent. The traffic was only crawling along and their headlamps, unable to pierce the fog, merely lighting up the blanket so that seeing through it was even more impossible.

Crossing Wandsworth Bridge was a bit dicey. The fog was worse, rising thickly and swirling up and around from the

Thames. When finally Robert drew the car in to the kerb in South Lambeth Road he breathed a sigh of relief.

'Are you coming in?' Becky asked quietly.

'No, I won't, thank you. I don't like this peasouper, I think it will get even worse before the night is out. I have to be in Manchester early tomorrow and I'm just wondering if it wouldn't be better if I got a train up tonight.'

Ever the gentleman, he got out of the car, came round and held the door open for Becky. She hesitated for just a moment and when he made no move she very quietly said, 'Thank you for a lovely day. I enjoyed it very much and I learnt a lot.' Giving him no time to answer she turned on her heel, opened the gate and walked up the path towards the house.

'Take care!' he called and before she had her key in the lock she heard the car drive off.

So that was it. It was over before it had even got started. Slowly she took off her hat and coat, walked down the long hallway and into the kitchen. The light was on, the fire well banked up and a note from Aunt Lil lay on the table. May was out for the evening with Stan Riley and Aunt Lil had gone along the road to play cards in a neighbour's house. She felt lonely. With only herself in the house, everything seemed terribly quiet.

Chapter Thirty

IT WAS WEDNESDAY, Becky's day off. Having decided that she would spend the day with her parents she had been up since seven o'clock. After a night of heavy rain the early part of the morning had been dull and dark, but now the sun had finally struggled through the murky clouds.

Becky stood at the window. The passing traffic was heavy and she couldn't decide whether to set off for the railway station now or to wait until the peak hour had passed. You've only got the one day, so there is no time to waste, she sensibly said to herself as she went back upstairs to put on her hat and coat.

Preoccupied with all that she was going to tell her family she hurried down the front path. She was surprised by the unexpected brightness of the sunshine reflected in the still-wet pavements, the glittering colours of the few leaves that were left on the trees in the street, and the funny damp smell. It was kind of a wet woolly smell, such as when Aunt Lil was drying jumpers indoors. It's coming on winter she reminded herself, thinking that autumn had soon come and gone.

Buttoning up the top button on her coat and pulling on her gloves, she drew herself up straight and was about to stepout for Victoria Station when a familiar black car drew slowly into the kerb alongside her.

'Would the lady like a lift?' Robert Matthews had wound down the window and was smiling broadly at her.

Becky's heart gave a lurch. She was thrilled to see him. It was seventeen days since he had driven off in the fog, she knew because she had kept count, and never a word had she heard from him in all that time.

By the time she had calmed herself enough to at least say, 'Good morning,' he was out of the car and standing on the pavement in front of her.

'Rebecca, how are you?' He was wearing cord trousers, a thick Arran jersey and a three-quarter length car coat, and when he put out a hand and touched her cheek she could scarcely believe it. She even wondered whether she was dreaming.

He drew back from her. He still felt she was very special. Her sweet face, glowing with health, her eyes, such big dark brown eyes. 'You're looking very smart, are you going somewhere important?'

'I'm on my way to the station because I'm going to spend the day with my parents, but what are you doing here this time in the morning?'

He took her by the elbow, steered her towards the car and opened the passenger door, before saying, 'Get in, I'll run you to the station.' Given no time to protest she sank down into the leather seat and within seconds Robert was seated beside her and the car was moving.

She glanced at him. He looked tired, his blond hair wasn't as neat as usual, in fact it looked if he needed to visit a barber's shop and there was a night's stubble on his chin. All the same, just looking at him had her glowing inside. She had thought never to see him again, except at work and that would have been terrible, so near and yet so far. Not now. Here she was in his car, she could put out a hand and actually touch him. Instead she reminded him, 'You never answered my question.'

'And what question was that?'

'How come you were in South Lambeth Road at this time in the morning?'

'I wanted to see you.'

'Oh,' was all she muttered and he laughed loudly.

'Don't sound so surprised. I only got back to London early this morning and I have to confess I looked up the rota for today and discovered you were not on duty. So I came to find you.'

'But why so early?'

'I had a feeling you wouldn't waste a day, that you would be off out and about, so I took a chance hoping to catch you before you left. Good job I learnt early in life that the early bird catches the worm.'

Becky grinned. 'Oh, so I'm a worm am I?' Then before he had time to answer she called out sharply, 'We're at Stockwell, you've come the wrong way.'

'I know what I'm doing,' Robert told her, sounding just a little ill-at-ease. 'I couldn't let you get on the train, I would have only seen you for about a quarter of an hour.'

'But . . .' she protested strongly. 'I must go home, I sent a postcard to my mum, she'll be expecting me. Please Robert, take me back to the station.'

He turned his head and beamed at her with a grin as wide as the Cheshire Cat's. 'How long do you think it will take me to get you to New Malden?'

'You mean you're coming with me?' Becky twisted her hands, mentally hugging herself with anticipation. A whole day with him! Then almost immediately her thoughts changed. What would she do with him? Could she take him home? Would he want to spend a day with her family?

As if he had read her thoughts he said, 'I don't have to come to the house if you'd rather I didn't. I know I'm showing signs of travel weariness so I could go off somewhere, get myself a shave and a bite to eat and pick you up this evening when you're ready to leave.'

Becky felt awful! He had taken her to visit his lovely house in Richmond, she had eaten with Carrie and his Uncle Maurice and now she was acting as if she was ashamed to let him see where she lived, ashamed for him to meet her parents.

'I'm sorry,' she said quietly. 'You took me by surprise. You most certainly won't go off somewhere. My parents would love to meet you and I'm sure they will make you most welcome.'

Through Balham and Tooting down into South Wimbledon, Robert was whistling as he drove. On through Merton Park, up over Carter's Bridge and suddenly he said, 'From here on in I'm lost.'

Becky laughed. ''Course you are, you're a townie.' Then as if the thought had just come to her she exclaimed, 'D'you know I haven't any idea where you do live. Proper deep dark horse, aren't you?'

'Most of the time it seems as if I live in hotel rooms. I do have a flat in Chelsea, just off Cheyne Walk, very near the river. Lovely spot in the summer.'

It wasn't a nice life, she decided, pretty lonely being all over the place never having relatives to visit and chew over everyday happenings with. But there again he took part in all the glamour. Had this lovely car, ate the best food, stayed in the best hotels. Which side of the coin was best? Hard question to answer!

'Turn right up there,' Becky said, pointing to Burlington Road. 'We are now in New Malden and Albert Road is the first turning on the left.'

'I hope your parents won't mind me coming,' Robert said, not feeling so sure of himself now. 'Will your mother like me?'

'My mother likes everybody.'

Robert turned to face her and gave her a smile that was rather woeful. 'I hope so.'

With Robert by her side Becky looked at Albert Road through different eyes. Just the line of twelve terraced houses, with her home the last of the row. Each had its own little front garden with a short path that led up to the porch. Suddenly she smiled to herself, wondering what Robert would make of the fact that the house had no electricity. Wondered if he

had ever had to put a match to a gas mantle when entering a
room in the dark. What if he should ask to use the bathroom?
She knew what her father would say: 'Sorry mate, we ain't
got one.' They were the proud owners of a flush toilet, her
mother's pride and joy, but it was positioned just outside the
kitchen door.

Living here in New Malden did have its compensations
and if Robert couldn't see them then he was a fool. There
was no traffic rushing up and down Albert Road. Not even
fumes from buses in Burlington Road. Only trams that ran
on tracks. Facing their upstairs bedroom windows were
green fields golden with gorse most of the year and at
the end of the road there was Harry Horsecroft's farm
with fresh eggs and plump chickens for the asking. The
thought of Harry had Becky giggling as she wondered if
he still liked to drink down at the Fountain pub. Did the
locals still lift him up into his flat cart? And more to the
point did his old horse still manage the short journey to bring
him home?

Here in the country, not that far from London, everyday
life was entirely different to the life that Robert apparently
led. And that's a fact! Becky grinned to herself as Robert
turned the car into the road where she had been born and
brought up. It was as if it had all been planned.

Her father was walking down the street, wearing his
railwayman's uniform, swinging his empty lunch box, his
morning paper sticking out from his jacket pocket, just
coming home from having done an early shift. Becky watched
him; he was still a big, thickset man. She saw he still took
long strides. Her mother was waiting at the gate, looking as
always a quiet, respectable lady dressed in dark colours, her
dress covered by a floral apron.

Becky had to swallow hard to get rid of the sudden lump
in her throat as she watched her parents kiss and her father
pat her mother's back as if to say everything is all right, I'm
home safe and sound.

Becky was out of the car almost before the wheels had stopped turning. 'Hello, Mum, Dad.'

Her dad's arms were round her tight. 'Gosh I've missed you,' he crooned, lowering his head, kissing her.

'Rebecca,' her mother said, tears shining in her eyes as she pulled her daughter close to her chest.

The three of them were so absorbed in each other that Robert just stood quietly by and watched. Then Joyce Russell quite suddenly became aware of Robert standing there. She nodded her head towards him and raised her eyebrows to her husband. Robert was only a few yards away. But at once, realizing that this young man was with his daughter, he covered the short distance, held out his hand and said, 'I'm Rebecca's father, Joe Russell, pleased t' meet you, son.'

'I'm Robert Matthews, a workmate of your daughter's and I'm very pleased to meet you, sir.'

'Robert, this is my mother,' Becky said, wishing that her voice sounded more firm.

He held out his hand to Joyce. 'Now I know where Rebecca gets her colouring and good looks from.'

'Starting off with flattery, are we?' Becky whispered to him as her mother led the way into the house. 'And don't call my father sir.'

He nearly smiled at that but he was still feeling nervous. 'Well, don't you dare start on about me being one of your bosses,' he warned, stern-faced.

'I don't think either of us want to pursue that line of questioning,' she grinned.

'Take off yer coat, lad,' Joe Russell ordered, 'I'll not be long getting out of me uniform. I'll bet you a tanner mother has the kettle on an' the tea will be nicely brewed by the time I come downstairs again.'

Joyce was feeling slightly intimidated by this tall blond young man but she was determined not to show it. Becky followed her through to the scullery and as her mother bent over to lift the kettle, she whispered, 'You didn't mind me bringing Robert home, did you, Mum?'

'Of course not, luv. For my money you could bring who you like with you just so long as you come home yourself.' But to herself she was thinking what a nice solid, dignified young man this Robert Matthews seemed. Wide-shouldered and long-legged. Only one thing was worrying her. If he worked for Lyons teashops, he must have a very good position. That car that was standing outside their house hadn't come cheap. She just hoped that Rebecca knew what she was doing!

'Mum, the day will never dawn when I stay away too long. Shall I take the tray through?'

They drank their tea out of Joyce's large everyday cups. Had she known that Becky was bringing a young man with her she would have got the best china out of the cupboard and washed it. Through the kitchen window could be seen two lines of washing flapping high in the brisk morning breeze. And further down in the garden that backed on to theirs, Peggy James had also taken advantage of the weather and hung out snowy white sheets and pillowcases.

There was a tap on the kitchen door and it opened at the same time. 'You there Mrs Rus . . .' Tommy Ferguson, his head halfway round the door, looked stunned. ''Allo Becky,' he said, a smile full of pleasure lighting up his rugged features. 'I didn't know you was going t' be 'ome.'

'We didn't know ourselves, till yesterday,' Joyce hastened to tell him.

Becky got to her feet. She couldn't believe the difference in this old friend of hers. He always used to look so shabby, his clothes old, even threadbare. Today he was wearing a smart tweed coat and he had a scrubbed, clean look about him. Marriage clearly suited him. 'Hello, Tom,' she said, tilting her face up for him to kiss her. 'How are you an' how's Mary?'

'Mary's the reason I'm 'ere,' he said, turning to look at Joyce. 'She's into this bring and swap thing with Ella, you know, over at the Central 'all in Tooting an' she said you'd got a parcel of things for 'er an' would I pick it up this morning seeing as 'ow I don't start me shift till two o'clock.'

Joyce gave him a big smile as he stopped talking and caught his breath. 'I'll pop upstairs and get the parcel for you, it's all ready. Pour Tom a cup of tea, Becky, I won't be a moment.'

Becky and her father both remembered their manners and each started to speak at the same time.

'Sit yerself down, Tom. This is . . .'

'Tom, I would like you to meet Robert Matthews, he's a friend of mine.'

Robert smiled at Tom, stood up and held out his hand. 'Nice to meet you, Tom.'

Tom shook Robert's hand, his eyes never leaving Robert's face. 'Becky an' I 'ave known each other since when we were kids,' he declared, sounding as if he were jealous of her new-found friend.

'Here, take your tea,' Becky said to Tom as he seated himself down next to her father, 'I'll see if Mum's got any biscuits in the barrel.'

'No, 'onest Becky, I don't want anything to eat, this tea is fine. Mary will 'ave me dinner ready and I'll 'ave t' be going cos I clock on at two.'

Joyce came back into the room, watched as Tom drained his cup and then held out a large brown paper carrier bag. 'It's only a few bits and pieces I made, thought some little kiddy might be glad of them, but there are some things in there that Ella's mother has run up. She got the material given to her so she said will you tell Ella they didn't cost her anything.'

'Will do, Mrs Russell, thanks, 'ope t' see yer soon. You too, Mr Russell. 'Bye Becky, luv.'

Tom was halfway to the door, carrier bag clutched under one arm, when he stopped in his tracks, turned and looked at Robert. 'You're a lucky bloke, mate. I 'ope you realize that.'

I do. Very much so, Robert said quietly to himself.

Robert's protests fell on deaf ears.

'There is more than enough to go round,' Joyce assured him as she spread a red-and-white checked tablecloth over the big table and placed a bowl of apples and bananas to one side. There were no more interruptions as the four of them sat down to what seemed to Robert an enormous shepherd's pie flanked by three dishes of vegetables. When he thought he had eaten his fill Joyce came back with a deep apple pie and a jug of custard. When they had finished, Becky made coffee and bringing in the tray she was happy to hear her father and Robert discussing the rights and wrongs of the railways. Presently Becky asked, 'Would you like to go for a walk, Robert? I'll show you the school I went to.'

It was her mother that answered, 'Good idea, and I'll have tea ready by the time you get back.'

Becky looked at Robert and they both groaned. 'Mother, we have to leave soon. Robert didn't get much sleep last night, he was working late and I have a six o'clock start in the morning.'

'But you must have some tea before you set off.'

Even Becky's dad laughed at that. 'Joyce, do you think they starve these young people up in London?'

''Course not.'

'Mum, we've eaten enough to last us at least until suppertime. We'll have a short walk and then we'll come back and have just a cup of tea before we set off. All right?'

When Robert and Becky had left them, Joe leant his elbows on the table and asked, 'Well what d'yer think, Mother?'

'He talks as if he went to a posh school, but really I couldn't help liking him. What d'you think?'

'Young days yet,' her husband warned her. 'Must say our Becky looks a darn sight better than she did a while back. Never did make head nor tail of that visit. Very nice having her and May here for nearly a week but I still say t' this day there was more went on afore they came down than either of them ever let on.'

'When will you be back?' her mother asked Becky as they stood in a group on the doorstep.

'Just as soon as I can manage it.'

'We'll be here,' her father told her, unnecessarily.

'You'd better be,' Becky laughed.

'I wish you didn't have to go,' her mother said feebly. 'A day isn't long enough.'

'Goodbye, Mr Russell, thanks for making me so welcome.'

''Bye Robert. Anytime. Be glad t' see you.'

'Thank you for my lunch, Mrs Russell, it was delicious. Just the job.'

'I'm glad you enjoyed it, Robert.' Joyce smiled broadly, reaching up her hand to pat his arm. 'Thank you for driving our daughter down; we appreciate it.'

Both her father and mother stayed on the doorstep watching the car drive away, until the taillight went out of sight as it turned the corner. They went back into the house, closed the door, and both were hoping for the same thing.

'If it's t' be, Mother, it will be,' Joe said optimistically. 'Things have a way of turning out for the best if left alone.'

Chapter Thirty-one

CHRISTMAS WASN'T VERY far off. Another two weeks and it would be here. Robert had offered to take Rebecca down to Richmond for both Christmas Day and Boxing Day. She wasn't clear as to whether that meant she was invited to spend a night there but in any case she wouldn't be able to accept the invitation. Her own family saw little enough of her as it was and she knew darn well that for her mother and her father Christmas wouldn't be Christmas unless they had their complete family with them.

All three sons and Becky herself knew that anyone they cared to bring along with them would be welcome to join in the festivities. There would be a few spare presents laid beneath the tree solely for that purpose.

Ella's last letter had been bursting with news of Margaret and baby Amy and what they were hoping for from Father Christmas. Peter was closing the shop at five o'clock on Christmas Eve and travelling down to Ella's mum. As a family they were staying with Peggy in George Road for the four days of the holiday. Shame really that Peggy's two sons, both married, had moved up to the Midlands and their mother only saw them once or twice during the summer months. Must be true what they say: a daughter's a daughter all your life, a son's a son till he takes a wife.

But that wasn't so with Joyce and Joe Russell. With Christmas dinner over everybody would gather for their tea and the giving and opening of presents in Albert Road. And that included Peggy James, Ella, Peter and their two little girls. Becky grinned to herself. What a crowd. Once again her mother would be in her glory. Both Jack and Tom, with their wives and their small sons, would be there. Their lives wouldn't be worth living if they refused to come. Even Fred, Becky's youngest brother, was bringing a young lady to tea with them this year. According to Ella's letter she had seen Fred in Tooting with a girl she knew by sight.

'Her name is Molly Cousins and she is a cashier in Tooting Co-op,' wrote Ella. 'Peter said that's probably how they met, seeing as how your Fred is manager of the Co-op Bakery, not that the bakery is actually in Tooting. Your Fred did introduce me to her and she seemed ever so nice, friendly like, wonder if they'll be getting married? Be lovely, wouldn't it? We haven't had a wedding since Tom and Mary's.'

Becky sighed. They were so busy at Lyons with functions right up to the Christmas and beyond. She would miss Robert, of course she would. Everybody gathered in my parents' house will have a partner except me, she thought dolefully.

This year not only were Aunt Lil and May coming down for Christmas, Stan Riley would be coming with them. Still, Christmas was a time for families, and Aunt Lil and May had become as much a part of the Russell family as had Ella and her mum over the years.

Her own mother seemed to have taken it for granted that she and Robert were going steady, as she put it, when she urged her daughter to invite him to join them. That wasn't exactly true. It wasn't like that at all. There would be days on end when she wouldn't see hide nor hair of Robert. Oh, he was very attentive when he was in London, Becky reminded herself hastily, but there were times when she was sure he was only offering her his friendship. There was never any question of romance. Robert did pay her compliments, bought her chocolates and flowers, had even taken her to see *Broadway Melody*, which was the first-ever musical film to have a sound track. It had been an amazing experience.

Yet he had never taken her dancing. And he certainly

never kissed her. Mostly when he appeared out of the blue she got an exciting, bubbly kind of feeling and more often than not she was tempted to make the first move. Throw caution to the wind and sling her arms around his neck and cry out loud, Robert, I've missed you. But she never did.

'You're mad, you know that, Becky. He's probably just as much afraid of making the first approach as you are and if you keep it up much longer we'll be pushing you down the aisle in a Bath chair,' May had laughingly warned her, when Becky had told her how she felt about Robert.

Becky felt it had been a lovely Christmas, as always. A truly family affair. Church early on Christmas morning with just her mum and dad for company and then home to sweat and slave helping her mum in the kitchen, preparing enough food to last an army for a week.

Christmas Day teatime!

'Leave the front door open till everyone has arrived,' Joe Russell had yelled up the passage. 'I'm sick an' tired of getting up to open it.' Then came the real chaos. Nothing short of bedlam.

'This is for you, Grandma.'

'No it isn't, that's Grandad's present.'

'Cor, look what I've got!'

'No need to look. Just cover your ears,' Becky said to May as young Joey began to beat the life out of his new drum and Ella's two girls were having a competition to see who could blow the longest blast on their tin whistles.

The floor was covered in wrapping paper, amidst screams crackers were being pulled and there were tears from Amy because her balloon had gone off bang. Fred and his girlfriend Molly Cousins, a slim, very pretty friendly girl with bouncing dark hair that reached to her shoulders, had made the day by announcing that come Whitsun they were getting wed.

'Told you so!' Ella laughed at Becky, as they huddled together with a hot mince pie and a glass of sherry in the far corner of the room. 'Get your needlework box out and start sewing, I expect Molly will want my two as her bridesmaids and we'll be expected to make the dresses.'

'Hasn't she got any family of her own?' Becky found herself asking.

'Only an elderly aunt she lives with.'

Becky looked hard at Ella. 'How come you know so much about her when me an' most of the family have only met her for the first time today?'

'Running a swap shop in Tooting you get all sorts coming along. Young mums with kids. Old people looking for a warm coat, even men who are out of work are glad to swap a garden tool or such-like for a thick pullover or a stout pair of boots. I don't need to buy the *Wandsworth Borough Herald* no more, I get all the news, good and bad, first-hand.'

Becky chuckled several times as she relived that Christmas teatime. That had been five days ago though. As for Robert, she hadn't seen him since the first week in December, he hadn't been in London once in all that time. Well, not to her knowledge anyway. Robert was, however, on duty for the New Year's Eve gathering that Becky and May had been allocated to. In comparison to some such functions this New Year's party was small. It was held on a private estate in Banstead, which wasn't far from Epsom; the house was old and very grand, standing alone within acres of parkland. The catering and service ordered from Lyons was for three hundred.

'Surprised to see your Robert Matthews in attendance for a do on such a small scale,' May whispered out the corner of her mouth to Becky as they prepared to serve the first course in what to ordinary people was still a vast dining hall.

'He is not my Robert Matthews,' Becky muttered under her breath.

'Oh no? Well you could have fooled me. My guess is he wangled himself in here tonight simply because he knew you would be waiting table.'

Becky half-believed her. Maybe that is what you want to believe, she chided herself many times during the course of the evening as she and the other Nippies served delicious hot food, including thick slices from whole sirloins of beef and great roast turkeys, not to mention the mouth-watering sweets that had all been prepared by Lyons chefs in the customer's own kitchens on the actual premises. As the evening wore on it was more wine than food that the waitresses were offering the guests.

It was quite late when the sound of a band playing could be heard coming from another part of the house and the host rose to his feet to suggest that his guests might like to adjourn to the ballroom, promising them that drinks would still be available and that champagne would be served five minutes before midnight in order that they might toast in the coming New Year of 1929.

May and Rebecca were just folding the last of the table-cloths when Robert Matthews walked in on them. 'All silverware is checked and packed,' he told them, 'glassware also with the exception of the crystal champagne glasses which half a dozen of the girls are now setting out. I think it's time you two got yourselves something to eat. Come along, Miss Timson or Miss Paige will show you where to go, leave that, our drivers will come in to carry the linen out to our vans.'

May smiled her thanks and moved off and Becky would instantly have followed but for the restraining hand that Robert put on her arm. 'Come hell or high water, Rebecca, I want to be near you when twelve o'clock strikes. I am going to make a New Year's resolution, one that I intend to keep, and I very much want you to hear it.'

Becky was finding it difficult to match the soft caring voice Robert had just used to the loud voice that had barked firm orders to all and sundry during the course of the evening.

The New Year was at least half an hour old before Becky caught sight of Robert again. She had been kept busy serving her share of the champagne and right now she felt she would have sold her soul just to be able to drop down on a bed and sleep for days on end.

'You look tired,' Robert said softly as at last he had her to himself. 'And no wonder. It was a very busy evening, and every one of you girls sailed through it with flying colours.'

'Shall I tell you something in return, Robert? I'm not the only one; you look deadbeat yourself.'

'I know,' he sighed, 'I haven't been to sleep for thirty-six hours and it is just beginning to hit me. But I was determined to be wherever you were this evening. Getting to see you is getting harder for me than performing a miracle.'

Becky found herself smiling in spite of the sadness in his tone.

He took her by the shoulders. 'Listen carefully: I, Robert Matthews, am determined to travel to far-flung stations no more. I have served my time and served it well. In future I shall be London-based and my free time will coincide with yours or I will know the reason why.' Then, for the first time ever, he kissed her. Gently, full on the lips.

As she gasped, half from surprise and half from sheer delight, he drew back and looked deep into her eyes. With great tenderness, he took her in his arms, lowered his head and placed his lips on hers and kissed her again. Very firmly this time.

Her first reaction, as he loosened his hold, was to shout out his name at the top of her voice but she didn't give way to that pleasure.

'Happy New Year, Rebecca.' Even his voice sounded like a gentle caress.

With her heart thumping against her ribs she smiled. 'I'm glad you're going to ease up a little,' she told him. 'Have time to do some of the things you enjoy.'

'Some of the things we both enjoy,' he said, returning her smile. 'Now hurry up, the coach will be waiting for you and,' he paused and his smile changed to a wide grin, 'if I'm not mistaken I can see Miss May Stevens peering out

from behind that pillar. I wish you both a very, very happy
New Year. Good night, Rebecca.'

'Good night, Robert, I wish you all the best for the New
Year.' Then because her heart was still thumping away like
mad and she couldn't think of anything else to say she walked
away from him to where an excited May was eagerly waiting
for her.

'Now tell me he is not your Robert Matthews,' May
whispered, and as Becky laughed May added, 'You're not
the only one who has seen the New Year in with a kiss, I
didn't even know Stan was one of the van drivers tonight
until he crept up behind me.'

'Oh May, isn't that lovely. I am pleased for you.'

'And me for you,' May assured her as she held out Becky's
winter coat for her to put on.

Then with their arms linked they went out to get on one of
the coaches that would drop each and every Nippy off within
yards of her own front door. Lyons were very particular when
it came to providing transport for their special waitresses who
had been out on late-night assignments.

Chapter Thirty-two

FOUR MONTHS OF 1929 had gone by before Becky's ultimate ambition was to become a reality. Even then she couldn't quite believe it.

'There couldn't be much more of a palaver if this do was taking place at Buckingham Palace instead of at the Mansion House,' May grumbled to Becky as they listened to yet another set of instructions.

'Have to say I agree with you,' Becky whispered. 'If it were an Army officer planning a military operation he couldn't do so with more precision than this lot.'

'A system of signals has been designed to instruct not only the kitchen staff but also you girls who are part of the waiting staff.' Efficient was how Miss Paige sounded this morning, and she also looked the part.

'Been on a diet I shouldn't wonder,' May muttered as they wrote in their notebooks.

'No, I don't think so, it's more the suit she's wearing, a straight skirt makes all the difference. It not only slims her hips down, it makes her look a bit taller.'

'If your conversation is so interesting perhaps one of you should come to the front of the room and let us all hear what it is you have to say.' Both May and Becky found themselves feeling flustered as they raised their heads to see Miss Paige standing within a few feet of where they were sitting.

'Sorry, Miss Paige,' they uttered in unison.

'Very well, with your permission I shall continue.' Silence hung heavy over the entire room. There wasn't a girl that would have dared to even smile. Small Miss Paige might be, friendly and kind, but when she was in charge of any business matter she let it be known she would brook no interference. 'On this occasion,' Miss Paige began, her voice loud and clear, 'the banquet area will be set out in seven sections, each one to be designated by a different colour. You girls coming originally from Coventry Street Corner House will be banded within the yellow section.'

Pencils could be heard scratching the pages as the colour yellow was recorded. God help the girl who forgot on the day.

'Very well, ladies, that will be all for this morning. I shall pin a notice on the board when I have further information, giving you the time and date of our next meeting.'

In the noise of chairs being scraped back and everyone talking at once, May grinned at Becky. 'On the warpath today, wasn't she? And it was our scalps that we nearly lost.'

'It's not too late to lose them yet, you shouldn't be so cocksure, Miss Stevens, even walls have ears at times.'

May turned her head quickly and let out a gasp of relief. 'Oh, it's you Mr Gower, where did you spring from?'

'Never you mind, I suppose it's not your fault if your tongue runs away with you at times. What I am here for is to offer both of you an invitation, though the Lord above knows whether you deserve it or not.'

Becky turned her most beguiling smile on and softly said, 'Get on with you, Mr Gower, you know full well we're your two favourite waitresses in all of London.'

'Well!' Mr Gower's look was stern, but only for a second, then he smiled broadly. 'There's not much to choose between either of you, is there? What I've come to tell you is that in three days' time I shall be going to the Mansion House to iron out the last few details. As a special favour, not that I think you deserve it,' he paused and smiled, 'you may both come with me and if we're lucky we shall be taken on a tour of the Mansion House. At worst you will be able to have a thoroughly good look at the Egyptian Hall which is where the banquet is to be held.'

May and Becky looked at each other in disbelief.

'D'you really mean it or are you having us on?' May asked.

Becky in her usual quiet way merely mumbled her thanks.

'You don't have to thank me, it's Mr Matthews who has done the arranging. He said the Lord Mayor's residence had always held an attraction for you, so here's your chance. I would appreciate it if you didn't make our visit widely known although we really shall be going on official business.'

'You will, don't know about us,' May answered cheekily.

'Yes, well. Best bib an' tucker and all that and best behaviour especially you, May. No telling the footmen or whatever that you like his knickerbockers.'

All three of them showed signs of amusement as they went their separate ways.

Rebecca saw him before he saw her.

He stood with his back to her, but then he moved his head slightly and she caught a glimpse of his face and her heart missed a beat. Oh Robert, she sighed to herself. He looked so at home in these regal surroundings of the Mansion House, so well turned out and yes, so handsome. Even more amazing was the fact that he was actually talking to the Lord Mayor of London.

Mr Gower hovered a few feet away. She and May were standing next to an enormous potted palm, one of the many exotic plants used to enhance the entrance hall of this beautiful building. Becky stepped back further behind the plant so that she was partially hidden from view herself but able to observe the two men quite clearly. She felt afraid. Out of her depth. She could never hope to meet Robert's standards. His life belonged in an entirely different league to her own. Becky, May and Mr Gower had arrived at the Mansion House about three-quarters of an hour ago, and,

after having been greeted by a female member of staff, Mr
Gower had left them to be taken on a tour of the premises
while he climbed the main staircase to the first-floor office
in order to settle the business that was the reason for him
being here.

Much to the amusement of Miss Jackson, their prim,
neatly-dressed, very businesslike guide, Becky and May were
gasping in surprise at almost regular intervals as they made
their way through the building.

'Underground cells!' May exclaimed in sheer amazement.

'Oh yes,' Miss Jackson quickly assured her. 'The Lord
Mayor is also the chief magistrate of the City, and at times
the Mansion House serves as a police court, though as you
can see the comfort of the cells is dubious.'

'How many cells are there?' Becky enquired, her eyes
roving over the heavy wire grid that covered the door of
each cell.

'Eleven in all, ten for men and one for women,' Miss
Jackson told them.

That statement had both Becky and May giggling, and
when May laughingly stated, 'Well, we all know men are
the worse villains,' even Miss Jackson tittered.

It was, however, the great tapestries and the enormous
Waterford glass chandelier that hung in the Egyptian Hall
that brought forth the biggest gasp of admiration from each
of the girls.

'When your company has set up this room in readiness
for the coming banquet it will take on an entirely different
atmosphere,' Miss Jackson guaranteed as she shook hands with
them each in turn before taking her leave.

'Fancy spending your working life in a building such as
this,' Becky mumbled more to herself than to May as she
watched the trim young lady walk between the magnificent
tall gold pillars which rose to the domed ceiling of the
Egyptian Room.

'Yeah,' May said cheekily to Becky, 'especially if she lives in a tenement block in the East End and has to go home to that every night!'

The two girls had to quickly smother their mirth as Mr Gower appeared to escort them back to Coventry Street and the reality of working for their living.

Becky hadn't seen Robert leaving and apparently he wasn't going to put in an appearance on the night of the Mansion House banquet. Ah well. So much for his New Year's resolution! On average she had seen him once a month this year and there had been nothing exciting about any of those meetings. Robert had, at all times, seemed preoccupied though Becky had felt a little disappointed to see him looking so fit and pleased with himself. At least he had given her an explanation of sorts.

'Arrangements take time,' he had said, 'especially if they are to have a lasting effect. Believe me, Rebecca, I am getting the situation sorted out.' With that she had to be content. Even more frustrating was the fact that when she did see him all he greeted her with was an affectionate kiss on the cheek. I get more from my brothers, she reminded herself ruefully, at least they give me a hug as well.

The night of the actual banquet had finally arrived, and Miss Jackson was proved right! The Mansion House was a blaze of light and the Egyptian Room had been truly transformed. The whole setting was inspiring, the guests elegant.

The men wore evening dress, their ties black. The women were clothed in glamorous gowns, their jewels sparkling beyond description. It was an extremely dignified gathering with the cream of London society.

There was no time for reflecting on who or what was what. Even with one Nippy placed behind every other chair the waitresses had their work cut out to serve each and every varied course that was on the menu.

The colour coding of the staff worked well. Each area of

the great dining hall was served by its own chefs, superinten-
dents and other staff all the way down the line.

It was an experience not to be missed, was the unanimous
verdict of every waitress on duty that night as they prepared
to serve the final champagne for the Loyal Toast.

What a contrast! Becky thought as she read her mother's
letter for the third time. What a funny affair this coming
wedding of her brother Fred and Molly Cousins was turning
out to be. Perhaps funny wasn't the right word, she chided
herself. It wasn't Fred's fault any more than it was Molly's
fault that it kept being put off because they just didn't have
the money to buy furniture, bedding and whatever else it took
to set up home together. Never mind paying for a wedding
reception.

Upper-class folk never gave a thought to such details.
They called in a catering firm and the strain was taken from
them. All they had to do was pay the account at the end of
the day.

There was two ways of looking at the problem, Becky kept
telling herself. On the one hand you had all this hunger and
poverty with thousands of unemployed up and down the
country and on the other hand perhaps she ought to be a
whole lot more grateful. If it weren't for the upper classes
Lyons wouldn't be so successful. The ordinary Lyons teashops
which could be found in every high street from one end of
the country to the other did bring catering to the masses, so
to speak. Even the poor lashed out now and again and had a
cup of tea and perhaps a toasted bun.

But it was the rich that held the private parties. And the
great thriving businesses, of which there were far too few, that
held banquets and suchlike purely for professional reasons.
Entertaining clients was a way of selling their merchandise
and without their custom you'd soon be out of a job. Becky
nodded her head, knowing her thoughts were all too true,
but that didn't help Fred and Molly with their plans.

Neither did King George or Queen Mary and the way they rode around London in their open carriage! Becky threw back her head and laughed loudly as that reflection came to mind. It had been last week; she and May had been trying to cross the main road into Hyde Park when the police had held pedestrians back. As the carriage passed they'd had a clear sighting of the King dressed in full ceremonial uniform, the Queen in her fur-collared coat, laid open to reveal all her jewellery and as always wearing an elegant veiled hat. They certainly were a regal couple but the sight of them was a sharp contrast to the demonstrations and the hunger marches which were being organized up and down the country.

Molly and Fred's wedding was to have been at Whitsun but as that was now only three weeks away and no plans had been settled it seemed unlikely. In any case the weather during April and on into the first few days of May had been ghastly. Day after day the rain lashed down. It was supposed to be spring yet both May and Becky, and a good many more people, hurried to work bunched up in macintoshes and scarves and their hats pulled well down over their ears.

Aunt Lil was forever yelling for them to hurry up and close that front door because when it was open gusts of cold air swept down the passage causing smoke to billow out from the kitchen range.

Both May and Becky were longing for a cup of hot tea as they got off the bus feeling grateful that at least, for the moment, it had stopped raining. Becky stretched her arms above her head and yawned as May put her key in the door and let them into the house. Straight away they heard voices and May automatically looked at her watch. 'It's just on half past six, sounds as if Aunt Lil has visitors. Any ideas?' May asked as she hung her outdoor clothes on the hall stand.

'Only one way to find out,' Becky replied, leading the way down to the kitchen.

'Good God!' She couldn't have been more taken aback if

there had been a trio of angels sitting there. 'What on earth are you doing here?' she asked, looking first at her father and then at her mother, hoping for good news but fearing she'd hear bad.

'London isn't that far away from New Malden,' her father chided as he rose to his feet. 'We don't exactly live in the back of beyond.'

Becky allowed herself to be kissed, all the while looking over her father's shoulder at her mother's smiling face and the rather amused look on Robert Matthews' countenance.

'I felt I wanted to see you,' Robert said by way of explanation as he too got to his feet. 'I thought I'd miss you if I came to the Corner House, so I came straight here. Your aunt kindly invited me in.'

Rebecca was touched. 'I'm glad she did,' she said, doing her best to reassure him. 'Were you already here, Mum?'

'Yes love. We wanted to discuss your brother's wedding with you, and with Lily and May. We've had a family pow-wow an' yer dad thought it best if we found out what you think of the outcome.'

'An' it being me day off . . .' her father added.

'I'll leave you all to it.' Robert placed the cup and saucer he had been holding back on to the table and took a step towards the door.

'Robert, you'll do no such thing,' Joe Russell declared.

Robert stopped and looked back. 'Sit down, lad,' Aunt Lil said encouragingly. 'If you're gonna get an invitation t' this wedding I'd say it concerns you almost as much as the rest of us.'

May spluttered, pulling her handkerchief down from her sleeve and covering her mouth. Oh, it was so funny to hear Robert Matthews being told to sit down in her aunt's kitchen.

Becky's heart leapt with gratitude. She could have hugged Aunt Lil. Robert had done exactly as he was told, whereas he could have been out of the front door and halfway up the street by now and God knows when she would get to see him again. Oh God bless you, Aunt Lil. Though what the hell her father was thinking of she couldn't fathom! Robert invited to her brother's wedding! Well she'd lay ten to one he'd shy away from that.

Robert was watching the different reactions flick across Rebecca's face and as their eyes met he grinned and he mouthed the words, 'I've missed you.'

'Any tea in that pot?' May asked.

'I'm just about to make a fresh pot an' get us all something to eat. You can come and help me,' Aunt Lil replied, nodding her head in the direction of the scullery.

I get the message, good luck, said the silent wink May gave Becky as she slid by her.

Becky went to sit down next to Robert before she eyed her parents. 'So, you came up to London in order to tell me what you've all decided to do about our Fred getting married. Is that right?'

Joe Russell made an exasperated face. 'Give me an' yer mother a chance to set the facts out before you get uppity, young lady.'

Robert smiled at them all, took Becky's hand in his. 'Your parents are going to do the wedding from their house, the catering as well, seems as if everyone has agreed to pitch in and help, even me,' Robert told her, as though it were the most natural thing in the world for him to be involved in their family plans for her brother's wedding.

Becky was dumbfounded. She couldn't find words to say. She leant back in her chair, closed her eyes, counted to ten and then opened them again. Her parents and Robert were waiting for her to comment.

'We wanted to tell you before we went ahead so you an' May can make sure you put in for the time off. What d'you think?' her mother asked.

'I think,' she told them, 'that you are all being very kind, acting with the best of motives, but have you given the idea enough thought?'

'Enough thought?' Joe Russell exclaimed crossly. 'Here we've all been, trying to work out ways an' means ever since Christmas. It's bad enough for yer brother but it's even worse for his lass. We all feel right sorry for Molly, don't we, Mother?'

'Yes we do,' Joyce agreed. 'I went t' see that aunt of hers, didn't get me anywhere.'

Becky felt duly chastized. 'Why, what's wrong with Molly?'

'There's not a thing wrong with Molly,' her mother said quickly. 'It's that selfish old aunt of hers. She took Molly in when she were a child but that girl has repaid her ten times over an' now because she wants to get married the aunt is playing up something rotten.'

'Leave it out, Joyce,' Joe Russell pleaded. 'I said I'd get it sorted out and I have.' Turning full face to Becky he said, 'They live in Derrington Road, Tooting and by rights the council could put the aunt into a one-bedroom flat once Molly leaves home. Instead they're going to let a friend move in with her, a lady about the same age as herself, so that solves that problem though she still refuses to have anything at all to do with the wedding, won't even come to the church, so she says.'

Becky smiled to herself, a little bit grateful that she hadn't been living at home while all this wrangling had been going on. Robert saw her smile and decided it was time to be practical. 'Why don't you tell Rebecca what you have in mind for the reception?'

That was right up Joyce's street. She was going to relish having the whole family come to her house for this wedding.

'Well, if they set the date for the second Saturday in June, hopefully the weather will have settled down and we can have the wedding breakfast in the garden.'

'And if it rains?'

'Yer dad has been promised a loan of two very big tents an' all the neighbours have come in with the offer of chairs an' tables. Ella's mum, Ada an' Joan, that's me two daughters-in-law,' she said by way of explanation to Robert, 'and meself will manage the food very well. It won't be the first time we've had a gathering in Albert Road.'

'But Mum . . .'

Becky was allowed to get no further with her protest; her dad thought it was about time he was allowed a say. 'I've already knocked part of the fence down between Peggy's garden and ours, been meaning to do it for years an' never got round to it.'

Robert was laughing outright but Becky was astonished. 'How the hell does knocking the fence down come into all this?'

'A gate, if you'll listen an' let me finish,' her dad said, undoing the buttons of his jacket and loosening his tie. 'Peggy has come up trumps, as usual, not only going t' help with the food but agreed that your brothers can set up a bar in her garden an' she's promised t' sleep some of the guests. Can't see many of you going home on the night of the wedding, though there'll be a few that will have to kip down on the floor.'

Becky had begun to give up hope that she would ever be able to make head or tail of her family's plans. They'll be telling me next that Robert is going to sleep in one of the tents alongside all me brothers!

Aunt Lil saved the day by coming back into the room bearing a tray set out with teacups and two piled-up plates of bread and butter. 'Do you like fish an' chips?' she asked Robert and when he grinned and nodded his head, she said, 'Thank God for that. I've got the plates in the oven and May's gone up the road to fetch some for all of us. Joyce, give us a hand to clear and lay this table, will you?'

Becky didn't know where to look. This was a nightmare.

First off her parents had invited Robert Matthews to Fred's wedding. A wedding that was going to be done on a shoestring because nobody could really afford a big splash. He had admitted he was going to be involved, in what way she didn't yet know and was too scared to ask. Now, to top the lot, Aunt Lil had calmly asked if he liked fish and chips! Not would you like to stay and eat with us, which would at least have given him the opportunity to excuse himself, but put in a way that took it for granted that he would. The way things are going, she muttered beneath her breath, you shouldn't be surprised if May comes back with six individual parcels and Aunt Lil hands them round still wrapped in newspaper!

It wasn't like that at all. In fact as Becky looked round the smiling faces of those seated around this big kitchen table and watched as May passed the vinegar bottle to Robert the contents of which he vigorously shook over his meal, she felt relaxed and happy.

Aunt Lil had done them proud. Cod and chips, crisp and golden, served on her best dinner plates with the red and gold band round the edge. Bread and butter on side plates that were part of the same dinner service, hot strong tea in cups that also matched and fish knives and forks that only saw the light of day on high days and holidays. It was a meal good enough for a king and by the look on Robert's face as he tucked into his plateful he was really enjoying it.

The only pleasure that was denied Becky that night was saying good night to Robert while on their own. She had felt frustrated when he had insisted that he drive her parents to the railway station, adding that it wasn't out of his way at all.

The three women stood in the lighted doorway and watched as Robert settled Becky's mum and dad into the car. Then with a final wave from him the car was quickly out of sight.

'Well, well, well!' May couldn't resist the teasing. 'Staff room memo tomorrow I think. Mr Matthews, top executive, dines with waitress in South London on fish an' chips.'

'I'll kill you if you so much as breathe a word,' Becky cried, doing her best to sound serious but not quite succeeding.

'You just let me know if she opens her mouth even a crack and I'll do the job for you,' Aunt Lil declared as the three of them set to to do the washing-up.

Nevertheless it was two happy girls, arms around each other's shoulders, who later went thoughtfully up the stairs to bed.

Straightening her cap, checking her stocking seams, Rebecca was heading for the morning inspection, her mind full of last night, Robert and fish and chips, when standing in the corridor she noticed Mr Gower, beckoning to her in a manner that could only be described as secretive.

'You are early,' he told her in a low whisper, 'come into my office, it won't take a minute.' Ushering her before him, he quietly closed the door and when she raised her eyebrows in question, he smiled at her. 'Rebecca, last night I was given a piece of news that I think will be of great interest to you.'

Oh yeah. An awful lot seemed to have taken place yesterday, she was saying to herself as she sat down in the chair he offered her.

'Mr Gerald Palmer now lives in Delhi! How's that for good news?'

'Delhi?' Her mind was a blank.

'Delhi as in India. Headquarters of the Indian Government.'

'Oh!' Becky suddenly realized what he was talking about.

'Yes, he's out of the country. Out of your hair. I just thought I would let you know.'

'Thanks, Mr Gower, you really are a guardian angel of mine, and I do appreciate it. Do you have any details?'

'Yes, if you're sure you want to hear them.'

'Make it more positive if I know he has really gone.'

'Oh, he's really gone all right. Got a job in the Embassy out there. Don't suppose the fact that Amelia Claremont, now Gerald's wife, and her parents can boast friendship with people in high places has anything to do with the appointment,' Mr Gower told her, not even trying to keep the sarcasm from his voice.

'I don't care if the devil himself got him the job,' Rebecca laughed. 'Do you know, Mr Gower, it has been my one dread that Gerald would turn up some time, mainly late at night, pleading his cause and still wanting me for his bit on the side.'

Mr Gower looked shocked. He hadn't realized that Rebecca could sound so bitter. 'You shouldn't talk about yourself like that, young lady. It isn't nice and what happened was not your fault.'

She smiled, a lovely gentle smile that showed the real affection she felt for this older man who had, over the years, become her friend.

'In many ways it was my own fault, Mr Gower. I have a friend, we've known each other since we were children, she got pregnant and married in haste. Love soon departs when poverty comes in the door. Both she and her husband found that out. I didn't want that to happen to me. I was going to marry a rich man. Gerald Palmer singled me out, and I was daft enough to think I loved him and that he was the answer to all my prayers. I couldn't have been more wrong, could I?'

'Never mind all that now. It's in the past and I just had to tell you that the man was no longer around for you to worry about.'

'Thank you again, Mr Gower, I'd better get a move on, mustn't be late.'

'I'll come with you, my presence will ward off any questions but, Rebecca, as we walk, please, tell me what happened to your friend?'

'Her name's Eleanor, she is still very much my friend. Her husband's name is Peter. They have weathered most of their storms and he now works for himself repairing boots and shoes. They have two lovely little daughters, Margaret and Amy, and I am godmother to both of them.'

'What a lovely happy ending to your story,' Mr Gower said, putting out his hand and laying it on her shoulder. 'And just you remember, the future is what counts and it is going to turn out just as good for you as it has for your friend Eleanor.'

'Yes, I'll remember,' she answered him, a smile lighting up her lovely big brown eyes.

Chapter Thirty-three

'WE DON'T WANT to go to school,' Ronnie, the eldest of Becky's two nephews, declared. 'If Uncle Fred is getting married tomorrow an' you all say you've so much to do why can't Joey an' me stay off and help?'

Ada Russell looked at her mother-in-law and moaned. 'Joan and I were going to wait and take them to school before coming here but we thought it best to get an early start.'

'You did right, and they've been good boys,' their grandmother told them placidly, 'but you do have to go to school. Now, finish up your toast and get yourselves ready.'

Ronnie gave up, lapsing into silence. Joey drank the last of his milk. It was nice here in his grandmother's house with so many aunts all getting lots of food ready for this wedding. Much better than going to school. He decided he might as well have a try. 'Grandma, it's Friday and we don't do much at school on a Friday. I could carry things for you, I'm six now, and Ronnie could help Grandad put up the other tent cos he's only got one up so far.'

Joyce reached across the table and rumpled his curly hair. 'Yes, I know you would both be a big help, but you have to go to school. And anyway your Grandad will meet you both this afternoon and bring you back here. There will still be plenty of jobs for each of you to do.'

Both little boys sighed deeply.

Becky looked at her mother and then at the faces of her brothers' wives, then turning her gaze on to her two nephews she smiled at them lovingly. Her thoughts were confused. While in London she was happy enough in her job. She counted herself lucky to be part of the everyday hurly-burly of London. Now, though, she watched enviously as Ada and Joan rubbed a flannel around their sons' faces and ran a comb through their hair. She saw the expression in Ada's eyes as she said, 'Auntie Joan is going to take you but I'll be here when Grandad brings you back this afternoon.'

Ronnie held up his face for his mother to kiss him, then came to where Becky was standing. ''Bye Auntie Becky, I can't wait for t'morrow t' come, can you?'

Becky squeezed his hand, kissed his cheek. 'It will be a grand day, well worth waiting for, you'll see.'

It was late in the afternoon and all the women were beginning to feel it was time that they stopped, made a pot of tea and put their feet up if only for half an hour. The front door was propped open. What with the kitchen range banked high because the oven was in constant use and the oven and all burners on the gas stove in the scullery going full pelt, the house was hot and airless. June was living up to its name, flaming June, and while that was great for eating outside and probably for those who would end up sleeping in the tents tomorrow night it didn't go far towards helping today.

'Good God!' Joyce Russell lifted the corner of her apron and wiped the sweat from her forehead. 'There's a Lyons delivery van drawn up outside the house,' she called to the cluster of women, who having taken chairs outside were sitting near the back door escaping from the heat of the kitchen.

May looked across to where Becky sat. 'Are you expecting a van?'

'There's a black car drawn up behind it now,' Becky's mother called before Becky had time to answer May. 'You two better come an' see what's going on.'

Raising her eyebrows in question Becky got to her feet, wishing that she had time to take off the apron her mother had insisted she wore, followed by May, who had on an

enormous wraparound flowered overall. They went through
the house and out into the street.

Stan Riley was busy taking boxes from the back of the van
and stacking them on to the pavement. Robert Matthews was
having a hard job trying to manoeuvre out from the back seat
of his car a large square white box. Both men saw the girls,
stopped what they were doing, looked at each other and burst
out laughing.

'Oh, very funny,' May said, looking directly at Stan. 'So
we look a sight and so would you if you'd been slaving away
all day as we have.'

Robert did say, over the top of the white box he had
managed to extract from his car, 'Hello girls, glad to see
you've been making yourselves useful,' but he said it in an
absent sort of way as he crossed the pavement and walked
straight up the garden path towards the house. Becky watched
as Stan kissed and hugged May. Not knowing what else to do
she turned and followed Robert.

The big kitchen table had been pushed right back against
the wall and was already more than half-covered with meat
platters, plates, dishes and bowls of every shape and size. Joyce
rushed to clear a space so that Robert could dump his box.

'That's just the bottom tier,' he told Joyce. 'There is
another smaller one and I have a silver stand and the knife
in the car. I'll fetch them.'

Robert left the room and Becky stared at her mother. 'You
didn't tell me he was bringing the wedding cake!'

'He asked me not to.'

'Did he?' was all she could think of to say. 'I'll give him a
hand to carry the rest in.'

'Stan will probably need some help.' Joyce flung wide a
white tablecloth, spreading it out to cover more than half of
the dishes on the table.

'Mother!' Becky was obviously exasperated. 'I didn't think
they were coming down until tomorrow but you aren't a bit
surprised to see them, are you?'

'No.' Joyce pushed a strand of hair off her face, and heard both of her daughters-in-law laugh. But it was Peggy James who came to the rescue, by saying, 'Calm down, Becky, what you didn't know you couldn't worry about and they're here now so let's be grateful. From what your mum tells me that Robert of yours has been very generous.'

'Oh.' Becky was lost for words. She was beginning to get flustered, and no wonder. Not only was her boss coming to her brother's wedding, it seemed he was providing the wedding cake and God alone knows what else. A Lyons van outside their front door, would you believe, and Stan Riley delivering goods! She breathed a sigh of relief as Robert came back into the room accompanied by her father.

'Finished now till Tuesday afternoon,' Joe Russell said cheerfully as he greeted the room full of women. 'Seems I'm just in time. I found these two townies outside and Jack and Tom aren't far behind. They've stopped at the paper shop for some cigarettes.'

Joyce bent over the kitchen range and lifted the lid of a huge black saucepan, picked a long-handled spoon from the hook where it hung beside the fireplace and stirred the contents. 'Good job I got up early and put this pot of braising beef on, with a load of vegetables and some dumplings it should be enough to feed us all. So busy seeing about things for tomorrow we nearly forgot you'd all be coming in starving.'

Becky watched her mother with admiration. She saw her as a small warm-hearted lady who asked nothing more out of life than to have her family around her and to know that each and every one of them was healthy and happy. She would go to great lengths to see that they were.

Robert had come to stand beside Becky. She still felt self-conscious about him being here. 'I'm sorry it's like this, all the chaos, we seemed to be doing all right and then somehow it's got disorganized, but it will all turn out all right in the end.'

'You bet yer life it will,' her father broke in. 'While your mother is getting the veg ready, you girls see about setting the table up in the front room and me and the lads will get that other tent up. First one went up with no bother last night.'

The men trooped out making for Peggy's back garden. 'I've still a few things to fetch from the car,' Robert whispered to Becky. 'Come and help me, please.'

'What do you think of that?' Robert asked her, stepping away from his car and holding out a reel of wide white satin ribbon. 'It's to decorate the two cars your brothers have hired for tomorrow and for my own because your father has said I may have the honour of driving him and the bride to the church. It's nice that he's giving the bride away, isn't it?'

'You seem to have become very much involved in all this.' Inwardly Becky was furious, especially so with her father. Now he'd got Robert acting as chauffeur! 'I haven't been told anything, you turn up with the wedding cake and all plans set out nicely, how do you think it makes me feel? The fact that my father has been using you.'

'Oh no.' Robert sounded shocked. 'I offered, I very much wanted to help, believe me, Rebecca, to be caught up in all this excitement is a real pleasure for me. I think I must have led a very dull life before I met you and your family.'

'But my father never said a word to me.'

'That wasn't his fault. I asked him not to.'

'And Stan Riley? How does he come into it? What on earth is he doing with a delivery van?'

'Rebecca, it is no great deal. Stan isn't staying the night, he's just dropping off a few items of food and some trestle tables. He'll be getting an early train down in the morning.'

'Are you staying the night?' Becky steeled herself for his answer.

'Well, the wedding is at ten o'clock, have to be up early, lots to be done at the last minute and your friend's mother, Peggy, has offered me a room for the night. Be childish to refuse, don't you think?'

Becky nodded. It was wonderful to have him here, but suddenly she felt a little shy. 'I'm sure we're all very grateful to you and I'm flattered that you even accepted my parents' invitation. The only thing is . . . well . . .'

'You're going to tell me that the sleeping arrangements won't be what I'm used to?'

'Now you're reading my mind. But, yes, that is what I'm doing my best to point out.'

'Rebecca, have you ever stayed in a hotel bedroom on your own? It can be the loneliest place on earth. Soulless. Occupied only by strangers. A room that no one leaves a mark on. No one speaks to you, except to pass the time of day. I know what goes on in that head of yours. You think I am wealthy. Far better-off than you are and when you're with me you act as if you are treading on eggs. Afraid to say what you really feel.'

The dejected look in Robert's eyes was too much for Becky. She wanted to throw herself at him, comfort him, but he wasn't finished with her yet. 'It is you that are so much better-off than I. Both parents still alive, loving you, protecting you. A great big family of relations and friends. Somewhere to go when you have time off. Birthdays and events to look forward to. Let me tell you now, when your father shakes my hand and in parting says to me, "Take care now, son, come and see us soon," I feel part and parcel of his family and I go away believing that he cares, that he would be pleased to see me again. And that, Rebecca, is a feeling that no amount of money on earth can buy.'

'Oh Robert, I'd no idea.'

Robert smiled. 'Confession time over, come on, I'd better go and give your brothers a hand.'

By eight o'clock everybody had been fed, Stan Riley had taken his leave and everything else had come to a stop. Because it was such a lovely warm evening everybody had gathered in the garden. Jack had hung a dartboard onto the wall of the shed and amidst much ragging and suggestions that Fred should get to bed early because he'd need all his strength tomorrow when he became a married man, a serious game was in progress.

Joe Russell was partnering Robert against his two sons; the game now on was the decider in a match of three games. It was a very close call with Jack and Tom having won the first set and Robert and Joe taking the second.

'Sixteen you need for the game, Robert,' Fred, who was doing the marking, called out.

'G'on my son, show them what you're made of,' Joe Russell cheered him on.

Robert poised his dart, double eight he needed, he aimed, missed by a whisker scoring only eight. He flexed his muscles, took a deep breath and his second dart found its mark. Double four. 'Yes,' Joe Russell yelled and his sons patted Robert on the back.

'That's only for starters,' Tom told him, 'we'll show you what's what tomorrow.'

Robert's eyes lighted on Rebecca. Although she was smiling she looked bewildered. If he could have read her thoughts at that moment he would have laughed. Once again he had her confused. Darts were very much a public-house game. She wouldn't have put Robert down as a darts player. She was learning more about this man with every minute that passed.

May Stevens' thoughts were running along the same lines. She'd bet a week's wages that there wasn't one person at Cadby Hall who had ever seen Robert Matthews throw a dart. God, but he was a dark horse! Out of the top drawer, no mistake about that. She hoped to God he wasn't dilly-dallying with Becky, seeing how the other half lived, so to speak. She didn't think so. The look in his eyes as he watched Becky move about had to be seen to be believed. Either he adored her or he was a damn good actor.

'I thought I might go for a short walk before going

to bed.' Robert was standing in front of her, his eyes twinkling.

Becky brightened. 'Oh, do you want company?'

'I hadn't counted on going on my own.'

Five minutes previously she had been thinking if she didn't get to bed soon she would fall down. Now she couldn't wait to get out of the house.

It was a lovely evening, very still and warm. They went out the front way and crossed over the road to the fields that lay beyond. They had walked quite a distance without any conversation.

'Are you all right?' were the first words that Robert spoke.

'Yes.'

'You are a ninny. You worry over the slightest thing. You never wanted me to come to your brother's wedding, did you?'

'No.' She felt she had to tell him the truth. 'Somehow I just couldn't see you fitting in. Please, don't get me wrong, I love my family but all three of my brothers are rough diamonds.'

'Oh Becky! There are times when I feel like giving you a good shaking. I wouldn't be here if I didn't want to be. I was really pleased when your parents invited me.' He sighed and shook his head. 'How many times must I spell it out for you? I think you have a wonderful family. I envy you. And more to the point I love you.'

Suddenly she was in his arms, his mouth gently covering hers and she had such a feeling of pleasure as his tender kisses gradually became more long and lingering. Robert was here. She was in his arms and once more he had declared that he loved her.

Her feelings had changed. All her fears and doubts had been swept away. Robert wanted her and she wanted him. It no longer mattered that they had been born into different backgrounds, they were a young man and a young woman who loved each other. This feeling of wellbeing had happened so suddenly, so naturally, that she kept her eyes closed wanting it to last for ever.

All too soon he took his arms from around her and stood back. Rebecca shook her head slowly from side to side as though disbelieving what had actually happened.

'Now tell me you don't want me here,' he said in a voice that was little more than a whisper.

'Oh Robert,' she gently sighed, 'I want you here, of course I do.'

'Rebecca, will you tell me you love me?'

She took a step forward, standing on tiptoe to kiss him. Robert pressed his face to hers. 'Say it Rebecca, please, go on, say it out loud.'

'I love you. I love you, you know full well I do.'

'That'll do for me,' he laughed. 'Now we had better turn back before I forget myself and let my feelings run away with me.'

Hand in hand they walked, not saying a word, but neither of them could hide the smile that was on their lips nor mask the sparkle that shone from their eyes.

Chapter Thirty-four

'MORNING, MAY.' BECKY raised herself up on her elbows, screwing her eyes up against the sunshine that was pouring in through the open curtain. 'Doesn't seem as if we've been in this bed for more than a couple of hours.'

'I know what you mean,' May mumbled. 'Yesterday was a long day.'

'I was going down to make us some tea but I changed my mind.'

'Why?'

'Just lift your head off that pillow an' you'll know why.'

May half sat up. 'What on earth is all the fuss and commotion about?'

'I can't imagine and I'm not yet in a fit enough state to go and find out.' Becky reached for the glass of water that had stood by the bed all night and had a little drink. She set down her glass and shook May's shoulder. 'You'd better move yourself. I'm sure I heard Stan's voice coming from downstairs.'

'Oh blast,' May grumbled, 'that's all I need for him to see me before I'm properly awake. But Becky, I would like you to know that I'm ever so grateful to your mum an' dad for inviting Stan to your Fred's wedding.'

'Hoping it will give him ideas, are you?'

'Well, I could ask the same question of you, Becky. You really like Robert, don't you?'

Becky grinned. 'He seems so different when he's away from London, not dealing with the company.'

'He looks different, if that's what you mean, not such a

stuffed shirt. Real handsome I thought when he arrived yesterday, grey flannels, no jacket, short-sleeved shirt open at the neck showing golden hairs on his chest. I'll tell you what, if he was to walk about like that in the Corner House you'd have to fight the girls off. They'd be forming a queue to get at him.'

Becky looked amazed. 'I've never thought of him like that, he always seems kind of shy.'

'Maybe with him it's a case of once bitten, twice shy. It isn't only us girls that get taken for a ride, you know. Men like him are considered a jolly good catch, and you never know, someone might have put out the bait. But what are we going on about? As you said, we'd better move ourselves and you, Becky Russell, ought to be thanking your lucky stars that whatever befell Robert before you met him he had the sense to wriggle free.'

Deep in thought Becky crossed the room to the marble-topped washstand, poured water out of the enormous jug into the bowl, took off her nightdress and began to wash herself. When she had finished she wrung out her facecloth, placed a dry towel ready for May and said, 'Now you get out of bed and come and wash. There's a hell of a lot still to do before we set off for the church.'

Already the front room had been stripped of furniture and against the two main walls long trestle tables had been set up and were already spread with appetizing joints of meat and ham, savoury pies, bowls of salad and delicious-looking sweet flans and trifles. Away in one corner of the room a square table had been covered with a white linen cloth the drapes of which reached to the floor. Dead centre stood one of Lyons' silver bases, such as were used in very highbrow functions, and on it had been placed the two-tiered wedding cake. To one side lay the long silver-handled knife.

'Thank goodness we don't have a wedding in the family every day of the week,' Joyce Russell said to her daughter as she hurried into the room, her arms full of serviettes. She set half of the pile down at one end of the long table and then the other half at the other end.

'Mum, I'm sorry we're so late coming down, I meant to wake up early.'

'Never mind, lass, take May and the pair of you go an' get some breakfast. It's all laid out on the kitchen table, sorry there's nothing hot but you can make yourselves some toast an' boil eggs if you like.'

'But Aunt Joyce, you've all done so much already,' May protested. 'You're making us feel guilty.'

'Don't worry,' said Joyce. 'Go on, do as I say and then you can see to the flowers and buttonholes and perhaps you can go through to Peggy an' see if she needs a hand with the beds or whatever. Or perhaps yer brothers need a hand setting out the drinks. By the way May, your aunt is in the scullery, she's baking fresh rolls, so don't go banging any doors.'

May and Becky looked at each other and together they scurried to the door. Once out of her mother's sight Becky burst out laughing and May did the same. Becky was the first to quieten down. 'What did my mother say when the question of Fred an' Molly getting married was first discussed? "Seeing as how they haven't got much money we'll put on a bit of a do for them." Makes you wonder what would have happened if they had decided to give them a posh wedding, don't it?'

'Oh, Becky, I know we can't help laughing but they're all doing their best, working like slaves if you ask me. Time they come back from the church everyone will be so worn out they won't want to eat or drink.'

'Don't you believe it, May, if the world were coming to an end and there was still food about my brothers would stay behind to see it off. What makes me laugh is the difference between getting this reception ready and when we're doing one for Joey Lyons.'

'Yeah, all order an' precision and we get paid for doing it.'

*   *   *

Peter and Ella arrived with their two little girls just as Becky and May were on their way upstairs to change. They came in a small van that belonged to a man who had a greengrocery stall in Tooting market. Margaret and Amy, together with cases that held the dresses, petticoats, shoes and bonnets they would later wear to the wedding, plus cloth-covered dishes of food that were Ella's contribution to the feast and pretty posies of flowers for the girls to carry as they were to be bridesmaids, were packed in so tightly at the back that it took some time to get them out.

When that had been achieved safely, Becky led them through to the garden and told them to play in one of the tents until it was time for them to get ready. Their grandmother James, seeing them from her kitchen window, flew out to greet them.

'Come upstairs with us,' May said to Ella. We haven't got that long, it's turned half past eight already. We can all get dressed in your room, can't we Becky?'

'Of course we can,' Becky agreed.

May sat at the dressing table, wrapped in an old dressing gown that belonged to Becky's mum, and brushed her copper-coloured hair. What to wear had been no problem for her: she had bought her outfit. Unlike Becky, Ella and both of their mothers, neither she nor her Aunt Lil were clever with their needle. When she had finished doing her hair, and applied a little make-up, she squirted herself with the toilet water that Becky had bought for her birthday. Then she stepped into the long silk skirt that had all the colours of a peacock's fan in it, put on the plain blouse that picked up the predominant shade and added a wide belt.

'I love it,' Ella declared.

'Yes, that was a good buy,' Becky agreed. 'It makes you look so tall and slim.'

'You both look good too,' May said, settling herself on the edge of the bed and gratefully accepting one of the glasses of sherry that Ella had poured out for each of them. 'You two work wonders with a length of material.'

'Old habits die hard,' Ella told her, 'it was a case of needs must when we were young, weren't it, Becky?'

'Certainly was, luv,' Becky quickly agreed, 'but I've never regretted those days, stood us in good stead. By the way, when I popped downstairs for that bottle both your mum an mine were almost in tears.'

'What?'

'Oh don't worry, nothing has gone wrong. It's just that all the kids are dressed in their finery and the sight of them, even the boys, looking like little angels was all too much for their emotions.'

'What did you think of Margaret and Amy's dresses?' Ella asked.

Becky took a sip of her sherry and laughed. 'Fishing for compliments, are we?'

'Well, you had seen the dresses half-finished but the bonnets you made for each of them did the trick. Even Peter was bowled over when they had a dress rehearsal. I'd swear he had tears in his eyes. They did look so sweet, it was enough to choke you. You'll know what I mean when you have kids of your own.'

Becky looked at May. 'Best get on downstairs,' she said practically.

Everyone was waiting nervously, the women in the front room, the men lining the passage. Fred put his head round the door. 'Mum, how long since Dad left?'

'Oh do stop worrying, son. Yer dad went down to Mrs Dywer's before eight o'clock just t' make sure that Molly was all right, and it's only about ten minutes since he left ready to go.'

'Nice of your neighbour to let Molly stay the night in her house,' Aunt Lil commented.

'The cars are ready,' Ada called, making a grab for her Ronnie.

'The first car is for you, Ella, and the bridesmaids,' Joan shouted, making sure she had hold of her Joey's hand.

'Come on Mum, you can get in the back with us, we'l put the girls on our laps and Peter can sit up front with Jack. Ella was issuing instructions left right and centre.

'For goodness sake get in the car,' Tom pleaded, 'I'n driving the second car so I'll bring me mum and Aunt Lil. May and Becky can ride in the back.'

'What about me?' Fred sounded right doleful and everyone burst out laughing.

'No one's likely to forget the groom, yer silly sod. Let's just get all this lot settled in the pews and then I'll come back for you seeing as how I'm your best man. The bride won't be on time, I'll stake me life on that.'

The room had emptied when Tom came running back into the house. 'Hey little brother,' he yelled, 'I haven't got a buttonhole and Gawd Almighty neither have you. I'll take mine with me, get yours fixed on quick an' by the way you're entitled to one drink t' steady yer nerves but don't go hitting the bottle hard while you're waiting, remember you've got vows to make.'

'Jesus, is it worth it!' Fred sighed as he made for the sideboard and reached for the bottle of whisky.

'What's keeping the bride I wonder?' May said, turning her head to look back to the open door of the church.

People were rustling in their seats; the church was very full. Becky had her eyes to the front. Her two brothers, Tom and Fred, were moving about nervously, each with his hands clasped behind his back.

There was a commotion in the porch and organ music filled the church, then Molly came slowly up the aisle on Joe Russell's arm. She looked absolutely lovely. Just as a bride should look. A floating figure draped in pure white, with Margaret and Amy in the palest of pink, their bonnets trimmed with the same fresh summer blooms as those in the posies they carried, treading carefully behind.

Becky glanced to where Ella and Peter sat. They were

holding hands, their eyes were fixed on their two daughters and anyone would have to be blind not to see how proud they were. Those two had endured some hard times yet over the years they had found the meaning of true love.

How could she ever have thought that what she had felt for Gerald Palmer had been love? It had been an obsession. Nothing more.

As the bride drew level with her, Becky smiled at what was to be her new sister-in-law and Molly smiled back. A smile full of joy, Becky thought enviously. And then Molly looked ahead to where her husband-to-be stood and her eyes lit up. Fred, looking so much like a younger edition of his father, though not so tall, his dark hair slicked down, his new grey suit immaculate, his eyes seeing no one but Molly.

The moment the bride reached the altar rail, Robert slid into the pew alongside Becky, took her hand in his and squeezed it. While they waited for the sound of the organ to die away Becky looked at Robert. 'Doesn't Molly look happy? You can feel she and Fred are right for each other.'

Robert nodded. He felt pretty happy himself, right now. This family he had come to know had a kind of permanency about them. You could feel the happiness the minute you walked through their front door. There was a companionship about them that he had never known in his life.

Fred's voice was loud and clear. 'To have and to hold from this day forth, in sickness and in health, till death us do part.' He gave the words their full meaning and more.

Becky glanced up at Robert, catching him unawares. He was looking down at her with such an expression in his eyes that it was all she could do to sit still. She knew, at that moment, if you loved a person it didn't matter whether he were king or commoner. There were no rights or wrongs to loving someone. You just did. She knew it now. Full well. She wanted to belong to Robert, to spend her whole lifetime with him, to make him happy.

The ceremony was over. The organ swelled its music out

again as the newly-weds came down the aisle. Molly's face was wreathed in smiles. Becky leant forward, looking to where May and Stan were sitting. May was wiping tears from her eyes but even so Stan had his arm around her shoulders. The tears May was shedding were tears of joy.

Outside the church the sun shone down from a cloudless blue sky and chaos had returned again to the Russell family. The mood of the wedding guests was now bent on enjoyment. The air was filled with laughter and excited screams from the children as the folk with Brownie cameras endeavoured to get them to stand still long enough to have their photographs taken. On the grass and pathways friends and neighbours were milling about but there were two couples who were oblivious to all that was going on around them.

Robert drew back, then changed his mind and placed his lips against Rebecca's once more. It was a kiss that needed no explaining. It said all that was in his heart. Every ounce of feeling that he could drag up from his body was there to be passed from his lips to hers.

'From today, no more buts, no more long partings, you are my sweetheart, my love for the rest of my life.'

The words were said in little more than a whisper but Rebecca heard every word. Her only answer was to breathe, 'I love you, Robert.'

Robert gently took her hand between both of his and then lifting her fingers to his lips he held them there for a long moment before saying, 'Rebecca, will you marry me?'

Only yards away Stan Riley was making the same request to May Stevens.

Ella, her own mother, Becky's mother and May's Aunt Lil stood in a group and the same happy smile was on each of their faces.

'If I 'adn't seen it with me own eyes I never would have believed it. Look at them, happy as two pairs of larks,' Aunt

Lil declared. 'When it all boils down it's feelings what count in the end. Just goes to show, don't it?'

Ella laughed out loud as arm in arm, across the grass, came Rebecca and Robert, followed closely by May and Stan.

Turning back to face the three women, a broad grin still on her face, Ella said, 'I'm going to predict that before this year is out Lyons are going to lose two Nippies and Robert and Stan are each going to gain a wife.'

Thank God the sun was shining, Becky was thinking to herself. They never would have got this host of friends and relatives inside the house.

'Went off extremely well I thought,' Robert said. 'I have to tell you yet again, Rebecca, you are so lucky, you have a truly wonderful family.' Side by side they gazed down the garden to where Becky's mum and dad were surrounded by grandchildren, each looking as pleased as punch.

Suddenly Dolly Ferguson's voice rang out. 'Would yer look at that!' she yelled, her big bosom heaving as she pointed her finger to where young Joey was feeding Amy with pieces of chocolate. 'Talk about starting young!'

'Going to take after all the Russell men, eh Dad,' Tom, Joey's father, commented. 'We've all had an eye for the ladies.'

The whole garden echoed with laughter.

Mary and Tom came to where Rebecca and Robert were standing. 'Me mum's still got a mouth on her, ain't she, Becky?' said Tom.

Before Becky had a chance to form a reply, Mary said, 'Yeah but I've lived t' know she's got a heart of gold to go with it.'

'How about that,' Becky exclaimed. 'I think it's wonderful the way things have turned out for you two. You both get on well with Dolly now, don't you?'

'Yeah, you get t' learn in this life it takes all sorts,' Mary wisely answered. 'Smashing day though, great t' all be together like this. Come on Tommy, you can get me a drink.'

Becky turned to Robert. 'If ever there were two youngsters who started out with everything set against them it was Tommy Ferguson and Mary Marsden and look at them today. They live for each other.'

Becky felt Robert's arm go round her shoulders, and placing his lips close to her ear he whispered, 'The sooner you set a date for us to be married the sooner we'll be able to give your parents another grandchild.'

Becky's heart missed a beat as she pictured herself holding their own baby. Again she looked across at her parents. Years ago they had found the formula for happiness and contentment. She turned her eyes to look up at Robert and she knew she, too, had found the man who could give her just that.

Within six months the forecast Eleanor had made outside the church had come true.